THE HOMEWOOD BOOKS

the HOMEWOOD books

John Edgar Wideman

University of Pittsburgh Press

Pittsburgh and London

Published by the University of Pittsburgh Press, Pittsburgh, Pa. 15260
Copyright © 1981, 1983, 1992, by John Edgar Wideman
All rights reserved
Eurospan, London
Manufactured in the United States of America

Damballah copyright © 1981 by John Edgar Wideman
Originally published, in paperback, by Avon Books, 1981.

Hiding Place copyright © 1981 by John Edgar Wideman
Originally published, in paperback, by Avon Books, 1981.

Sent for You Yesterday copyright © 1983 by John Edgar Wideman
Originally published, in paperback, by Avon Books, 1983.

Library of Congress Cataloging-in-Publication Data

Wideman, John Edgar.
    The homewood books / John Edgar Wideman.
        p.   cm.
    Reprint (1st work). Originally published: New York : Avon Books, 1981.
    Reprint (2nd work). Originally published: New York : Avon Books, 1981.
    Reprint (3rd work). Originally published: New York : Avon Books, 1983.
    Contents: Damballah — Hiding place — Sent for you yesterday.
    ISBN 0-8229-3831-6
    1. Afro-Americans — Pennsylvania — Pittsburgh — Fiction.   2. Pittsburgh (Pa.) —
Fiction.   I. Wideman, John Edgar. Damballah. 1992.   II. Wideman, John Edgar.
Hiding place. 1992.   III. Wideman, John Edgar. Sent for you yesterday. 1992.
IV. Title.
PS3573.I26H6   1992
813'.54 — dc20   91-18997
                                                                                              CIP

A CIP catalogue record for this book is available from the British Library.

CONTENTS

PREFACE

THE publication of *The Homewood Books* by the University of Pittsburgh Press is a special event for me. For various reasons, including the lack of enthusiastic offers from major hardback publishers and my rather naive hope that lower prices and softcovers might entice a larger black readership, *Hiding Place* (1981), *Damballah* (1981), and *Sent for You Yesterday* (1983) were originally issued in paperback. This strategy failed to produce the explosion in sales I'd wished for, yet some pleasant surprises did occur. *Hiding Place* and *Damballah* broke ground for new fiction in paperback by being reviewed in the *New York Times Book Review*. *Sent for You Yesterday* won the PEN-Faulkner Prize, surprising, even embarrassing Avon Books, since they hadn't bothered to submit my novel for the competition. Avon's attempt to cash in and catch up with the sudden notoriety of novel and novelist resulted in publication of the *Homewood Trilogy*, a fat paperback containing all three Homewood books. Editions in various formats have followed here and abroad, but none in this country in hardback.

Hard covers lend an air of permanence, as does university press publication. I welcome that illusion but appreciate much more a kind of symmetry, a sense of coming home. On elementary school trips to the natural history museum, or Shadyside Boys Club knothole gang excursions to Forbes Field to watch the Pirates lose, or just trundling through the Oakland section by trolley or bus on the way to "dahn tahn" Pittsburgh, I'd be struck by the looming silhouette of Pitt's Cathedral of Learning. Though I had passed it countless times, this gray eminence, visible on a clear day even from the heights of Brushton Hill in Homewood, remained as mysterious, unreachable, and irrelevant to my life as the fabled churches and monuments of Europe I'd encountered only in pictures.

So it feels right that the University of Pittsburgh is now undertaking the job of presenting and preserving my fiction. We've been neighbors a long time. And it's about time to acknowledge we share a city. Whatever else that city is, it is also a project of communal imagination, a vision we are responsible for dreaming and redreaming, a project we will understand better as we stretch it and reshape it to embrace the views from Homewood.

Expediency was the main reason the three Homewood books were first issued in a single volume, but there are other grounds for publishing them together. The books are linked by shared characters, events, and, of course, locales. The fictionalized black community Homewood that grows resolutely under the uneasy eyes of its white neighbors is an embodiment of the deeds, words, ancestors, and offspring of John French. Deeper patterns of structure, theme, and language also serve as unifying devices. Music, for instance, is a dominant, organic metaphor. Albert Wilkes, of *Sent for You Yesterday*, is a piano player, and Doot, the narrator of that novel, discovers truths about himself and his history by learning to dance. Lives of individual singers such as Reba Love Jackson, song as a magical mode of storytelling, storytelling as a means by which values can be transmitted and sustained are explored in the tales of *Damballah*. Tommy's music and the music of Bess, the songs they sing, hum, whistle, remember, and yearn for, the contrasting rhythms of their voices render the counterpoint of *Hiding Place*.

The three books offer a continuous investigation, from many angles, not so much of a physical location, Homewood, the actual African-American community in Pittsburgh where I was raised, but of a culture, a way of seeing and being seen. *Homewood* is an idea, a reflection of how its inhabitants act and think. The books, if successful, should mirror the characters' inner lives, their sense of themselves as spiritual beings in a world where boundaries are not defined by racial stereotypes or socioeconomic statistics.

The value of black life in America is judged, as life generally in this country is judged, by external, material signs of success. Urban ghettoes are dangerous, broken-down, economically marginal pockets of real estate infected with drugs, poverty, violence, crime, and since black life is seen as rooted in the ghetto, black people are identified with the ugliness, danger, and deterioration surrounding them. This logic is simple-minded and devastating, its hold on the American imagination as old as slavery; in fact, it recycles the classic justification for slavery, blaming the cause and consequences of oppression on the oppressed. Instead of launching a preemptive strike at the flawed assumptions that perpetuate racist thinking, blacks and whites are doomed to battle endlessly with the symptoms of racism.

In these three books again bound as one I have set myself to the task of making concrete those invisible planes of existence that bear witness to the fact that black life, for all its material impoverishment, continues to thrive, to generate alternative styles, redemptive strategies, people who hope and cope. But more than attempting to prove a "humanity," which should be self-evident anyway to those not blinded by racism, my goal is to celebrate and affirm. *Where did I come from? Who am I? Where am I going?* These unanswerable questions — the mysteries of identity and fate they address — are what I wish to investigate.

The gathering and rounding this volume represents may be clarified with a few remarks about the way these works were composed. Parts of *Damballah*, a collection of related stories, were written first. As I drafted and redrafted individual stories, I found myself not really finishing them so much as stopping work on one so I could get on with another. No matter how I tinkered and crafted the material, more needed to be said. The short story form felt too exclusive. Good stories need to stand on their own feet, and mine seemed to require their neighbors. Part of the problem was coming to terms with the vastness, the intimidating nature of the project I'd undertaken.

By 1973 I'd published three novels. It was hard to admit to myself that I'd just begun learning how to write — that whole regions of my experience, the core of African-American language and culture that nurtured me, had been barely touched by my writing up to that point. If a writer's lucky, the learning process never stops, and writing continues to be a tool for discovery. The early versions of the stories which eventually engendered *Damballah* were my way of returning to basics, my attempt to forge a new language for talking about the places I'd been, the people important to me.

My grandmother Freeda French died in 1973. I'd just begun teaching at the University of Wyoming, and the news of her death both emphasized and collapsed the two thousand miles separating Laramie from Pittsburgh. The trip home with my wife and children for my grandmother's funeral was the beginning of these three books. As family and friends sat late into the night, fueled by drink, food, talk, by sadness and bitter loss, by the healing presence of others who shared our grief and our history, the stories of Homewood's beginnings were told, stories I'd been hearing all my life without understanding, until those charged moments, their resonance, their possibilities for written literature. I've been building upon those tales ever since — not only the striking, mysterious, outrageous particulars, but the imperative suffered and passed on — that such rituals, such tellings must survive if we as a people are to survive.

It became clear to me on those nights in Pittsburgh in 1973 that I needn't look any further than the place I was born and the people who'd loved me to find what was significant and lasting in literature. My university training had both thwarted and prepared this understanding, and the tension of multiple traditions, European and African-American, the Academy and the Street, animates these texts.

That the books be read in the sequence arranged here is a suggestion, not an order. Tales in *Damballah*, "The Watermelon Story" for example, were written at the same time as late drafts of *Sent for You Yesterday*. *Hiding Place* in its first compressed essence found its way into the story collection. Sections of *Sent for You Yesterday* evolved during the period the earliest Homewood stories were being put on paper. The simple fact is that I wrote three books simultaneously. They jostled, bumped, merged, and teased each other into existence. As writer, part of the artistic problem was untangling the strands, cutting the cords so individual stories could be separated without killing the vast, unruly organism pulsing in my imagination.

I intend motion and resonance of various kinds, from the small scale of the shortest stories to the longest sustained narrative. Do not look for straightforward, linear steps from book to book. Think, rather, of circles within circles within circles, a stone dropped into a still pool, ripples and wave motion. Or imagine the Great Time of our African ancestors, a nonlinear, atemporal medium in which all things that ever *have been*, *are*, or *will be* mingle freely, the space that allows us to bump into relatives long dead or absent friends or children unborn as easily, as significantly, as we encounter the people in our daily lives. By the time I had published the first two books in this sequence, I had discovered and refined the narrative voice that creates the third. I believe I came to know that voice better, that I could be both more sure-handed and daring with it. So the careful reader can watch/listen for those kinds of stylistic progression.

Another species of movement which I hope results in a resolution of sorts is the gradual unfolding of the narrator's character, the Doot who finally essays his dance at the conclusion of the trilogy. If the books achieve unity, Doot's presence in all of them should become apparent. While he's been humming the music, writing the stories, they've been making him. His/my voice is inseparable from the Homewood voices I've been hearing since my ears and eyes opened. As the Swan Silvertones chant in their version of "Blessed Assurance," *This is my story, this is my song.*

DAMBALLAH

TO ROBBY

Stories are letters. Letters sent to anybody or everybody. But the best kind are meant to be read by a specific somebody. When you read that kind you know you are eavesdropping. You know a real person somewhere will read the same words you are reading and the story is that person's business and you are a ghost listening in.

Remember. I think it was Geral I first heard call a watermelon a letter from home. After all these years I understand a little better what she meant. She was saying the melon is a letter addressed to us. A story for us from down home. Down Home being everywhere we've never been, the rural South, the old days, slavery, Africa. That juicy, striped message with red meat and seeds, which always looked like roaches to me, was blackness as cross and celebration, a history we could taste and chew. And it was meant for us. Addressed to us. We were meant to slit it open and take care of business.

Consider all these stories as letters from home. I never liked watermelon as a kid. I think I remember you did. You weren't afraid of becoming instant nigger, of sitting barefoot and goggle-eyed and Day-Glo black and drippy-lipped on massa's fence if you took one bit of the forbidden fruit. I was too scared to enjoy watermelon. Too self-conscious. I let people rob me of a simple pleasure. Watermelon's still tainted for me. But I know better now. I can play with the idea even if I can't get down and have a natural ball eating a real one.

Anyway . . . these stories are letters. Long overdue letters from me to you. I wish they could tear down the walls. I wish they could snatch you away from where you are.

DAMBALLAH
good serpent of the sky

"Damballah Wedo is the ancient, the venerable father; so ancient, so venerable, as of a world before the troubles began; and his children would keep him so; image of the benevolent, paternal innocence, the great father of whom one asks nothing save his blessing. . . . There is almost no precise communication with him, as if his wisdom were of such major cosmic scope and of such grand innocence that it could not perceive the minor anxieties of his human progeny, nor be transmuted to the petty precision of human speech.

"Yet it is this very detachment which comforts, and which is evidence, once more, of some original and primal vigor that has somehow remained inaccessible to whatever history, whatever immediacy might diminish it. Damballah's very presence, like the simple, even absent-minded caress of a father's hand, brings peace. . . . Damballah is himself unchanged by life, and so is at once the ancient past and the assurance of the future. . . .

"Associated with Damballah as members of the Sky Pantheon, are Badessy, the wind, Sobo and Agarou Tonerre, the thunder. . . . They seem to belong to another period of history. Yet precisely because these divinities are, to a certain extent, vestigial, they give, like Damballah's detachment, a sense of historical extension, of the ancient origin of the race. To invoke them today is to stretch one's hand back to that time and to gather up all history into a solid, contemporary ground beneath one's feet."

One song invoking Damballah requests that he "Gather up the Family."

Quotation and citation from Maya Deren's
Divine Horsemen: The Voodoo Gods of Haiti

Contents

Family Tree

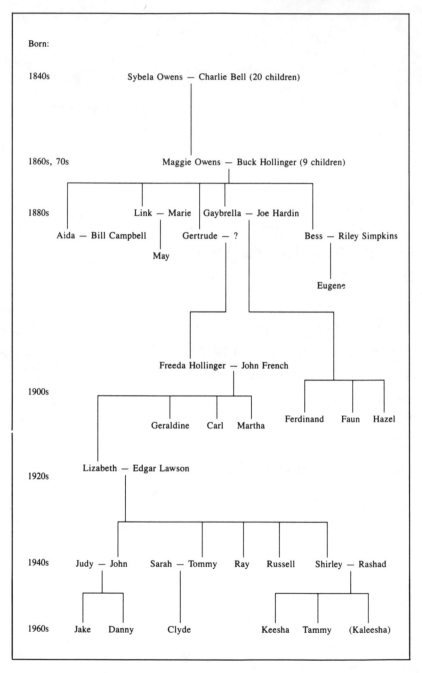

Born:

1840s   Sybela Owens — Charlie Bell (20 children)

1860s, 70s   Maggie Owens — Buck Hollinger (9 children)

1880s   Link — Marie   Gaybrella — Joe Hardin

Aida — Bill Campbell   Gertrude — ?   Bess — Riley Simpkins

May

Eugene

Freeda Hollinger — John French

1900s

Geraldine   Carl   Martha   Ferdinand   Faun   Hazel

Lizabeth — Edgar Lawson

1920s

1940s   Judy — John   Sarah — Tommy   Ray   Russell   Shirley — Rashad

1960s   Jake   Danny   Clyde   Keesha   Tammy   (Kaleesha)

A Begat Chart

1860s Sybela and Charlie arrive in Pittsburgh; bring two children with them; eighteen more born in next twenty-five years.

1880s Maggie Owens, oldest daughter of Sybela and Charlie, marries Buck Hollinger; bears nine children among whom are four girls — Aida, Gertrude, Gaybrella, Bess.

1900s Hollinger girls marry — Aida to Bill Campbell; Gaybrella to Joe Hardn (three children: Fauntleroy, Ferdinand, Hazel); Bess to Riley Simpkins (one son: Eugene) — except Gert, who bears her children out of wedlock. Aida and Bill Campbell raise Gert's daughter, Freeda.

1920s Freeda Hollinger marries John French; bears four children who survive: Lizabeth, Geraldine, Carl and Martha.

1940s Lizabeth French marries Edgar Lawson; bears five children among whom are John, Shirley and Thomas.

1960s Lizabeth's children begin to marry, propagate — not always in that order. John marries Judy and produces two sons (Jake and Dan); Shirley marries Rashad and bears three daughters (Keesha, Tammy, and Kaleesha); Tommy marries Sarah and produces one son (Clyde); etc. . . .

Damballah

ORION let the dead, gray cloth slide down his legs and stepped
into the river. He picked his way over slippery stones till he stood
calf deep. Dropping to one knee he splashed his groin, then scooped
river to his chest, both hands scrubbing with quick, kneading spi-
rals. When he stood again, he stared at the distant gray clouds.
A hint of rain in the chill morning air, a faint, clean presence rising from the far side of the hills. The promise of rain coming to
him as all things seemed to come these past few months, not through
eyes or ears or nose but entering his black skin as if each pore had
learned to feel and speak.

He watched the clear water race and ripple and pucker. Where
the sun cut through the pine trees and slanted into the water he
could see the bottom, see black stones, speckled stones, shining
stones whose light came from within. Above a stump at the far
edge of the river, clouds of insects hovered. The water was darker
there, slower, appeared to stand in deep pools where tangles of
root, bush and weed hung over the bank. Orion thought of the
eldest priest chalking a design on the floor of the sacred obi. Drawing the watery door no living hands could push open, the crossroads where the spirits passed between worlds. His skin was becoming like that in-between place the priest scratched in the dust.
When he walked the cane rows and dirt paths of the plantation
he could feel the air of this strange land wearing out his skin, rubbing it thinner and thinner until one day his skin would not be
thick enough to separate what was inside from everything outside.
Some days his skin whispered he was dying. But he was not afraid.
The voices and faces of his fathers bursting through would not

drown him. They would sweep him away, carry him home again.

In his village across the sea were men who hunted and fished with their voices. Men who could talk the fish up from their shadowy dwellings and into the woven baskets slung over the fishermen's shoulders. Orion knew the fish in this cold river had forgotten him, that they were darting in and out of his legs. If the whites had not stolen him, he would have learned the fishing magic. The proper words, the proper tones to please the fish. But here in this blood-soaked land everything was different. Though he felt their slick bodies and saw the sudden dimples in the water where they were feeding, he understood that he would never speak the language of these fish. No more than he would ever speak again the words of the white people who had decided to kill him.

The boy was there again hiding behind the trees. He could be the one. This boy born so far from home. This boy who knew nothing but what the whites told him. This boy could learn the story and tell it again. Time was short but he could be the one.

"That Ryan, he a crazy nigger. One them wild African niggers act like he fresh off the boat. Kind you stay away from less you lookin for trouble." Aunt Lissy had stopped popping string beans and frowned into the boy's face. The pause in the steady drumming of beans into the iron pot, the way she scrunched up her face to look mean like one of the Master's pit bulls told him she had finished speaking on the subject and wished to hear no more about it from him. When the long green pods began to shuttle through her fingers again, it sounded like she was cracking her knuckles, and he expected something black to drop into the huge pot.

"Fixin to rain good. Heard them frogs last night just a singing at the clouds. Frog and all his brothers calling down the thunder. Don't rain soon them fields dry up and blow away." The boy thought of the men trudging each morning to the fields. Some were brown, some yellow, some had red in their skins and some white as the Master. Ryan black, but Aunt Lissy blacker. Fat, shiny blue-black like a crow's wing.

"Sure nuff crazy." Old woman always talking. Talking and telling silly stories. The boy wanted to hear something besides an old woman's mouth. He had heard about frogs and bears and rabbits too many times. He was almost grown now, almost ready to leave in the mornings with the men. What would they talk about? Would Orion's voice be like the hollers the boy heard early in the mornings when the men still sleepy and the sky still dark and you couldn't really see nobody but knew they were there when them cries and hollers came rising through the mist.

Pine needles crackled with each step he took, and the boy knew old Ryan knew somebody spying on him. Old nigger guess who it was, too. But if Ryan knew, Ryan didn't care. Just waded out in that water like he the only man in the world. Like maybe wasn't no world. Just him and that quiet place in the middle of the river. Must be fishing out there, some funny old African kind of fishing. Nobody never saw him touch victuals Master set out and he had to be eating something, even if he was half crazy, so the nigger must be fishing for his breakfast. Standing there like a stick in the water till the fish forgot him and he could snatch one from the water with his beaky fingers.

A skinny-legged, black waterbird in the purring river. The boy stopped chewing his stick of cane, let the sweet juice blend with his spit, a warm syrup then whose taste he prolonged by not swallowing, but letting it coat his tongue and the insides of his mouth, waiting patiently like the figure in the water waited, as the sweet taste seeped away. All the cane juice had trickled down his throat before he saw Orion move. After the stillness, the illusion that the man was a tree rooted in the rocks at the riverbed, when motion came, it was too swift to follow. Not so much a matter of seeing Orion move as it was feeling the man's eyes inside him, hooking him before he could crouch lower in the weeds. Orion's eyes on him and through him boring a hole in his chest and thrusting into that space one word *Damballah*. Then the hooded eyes were gone.

On a spoon you see the shape of a face is an egg. Or two eggs because you can change the shape from long oval to moons pinched together at the middle seam or any shape egg if you tilt and push the spoon closer or farther away. Nothing to think about. You go with Mistress to the chest in the root cellar. She guides you with a candle and you make a pouch of soft cloth and carefully lay in each spoon and careful it don't jangle as up and out of the darkness following her rustling dresses and petticoats up the earthen steps each one topped by a plank which squirms as you mount it. You are following the taper she holds and the strange smell she trails and leaves in rooms. Then shut up in a room all day with nothing to think about. With rags and pieces of silver. Slowly you rub away the tarnished spots; it is like finding something which surprises you though you knew all the time it was there. Spoons lying on the strip of indigo: perfect, gleaming fish you have coaxed from the black water.

Damballah was the word. Said it to Aunt Lissy and she went upside his head, harder than she had ever slapped him. Felt like crumpling right there in the dust of the yard it hurt so bad but he bit his lip and didn't cry out, held his ground and said the word again and again silently to himself, pretending nothing but a bug on his burning cheek and twitched and sent it flying. Damballah. Be strong as he needed to be. Nothing touch him if he don't want. Before long they'd cut him from the herd of pickaninnies. No more chasing flies from the table, no more silver spoons to get shiny, no fat, old woman telling him what to do. He'd go to the fields each morning with the men. Holler like they did before the sun rose to burn off the mist. Work like they did from can to caint. From first crack of light to dusk when the puddles of shadow deepened and spread so you couldn't see your hands or feet or the sharp tools hacking at the cane.

He was already taller than the others, a stork among the chicks scurrying behind Aunt Lissy. Soon he'd rise with the conch horn and do a man's share so he had let the fire rage on half his face and thought of the nothing always there to think of. In the spoon, his face long and thin as a finger. He looked for the print of Lissy's black hand on his cheek, but the image would not stay still. Dancing like his face reflected in the river. Damballah. "Don't you ever, you hear me, ever let me hear that heathen talk no more. You hear me, boy? You talk Merican, boy." Lissy's voice like chicken cackle. And his head a barn packed with animal noise and animal smell. His own head but he had to sneak round in it. Too many others crowded in there with him. His head so crowded and noisy lots of time don't hear his own voice with all them braying and cackling.

Orion squatted the way the boy had seen the other old men collapse on their haunches and go still as a stump. Their bony knees poking up and their backsides resting on their ankles. Looked like they could sit that way all day, legs folded under them like wings. Orion drew a cross in the dust. Damballah. When Orion passed his hands over the cross the air seemed to shimmer like it does above a flame or like it does when the sun so hot you can see waves of heat rising off the fields. Orion talked to the emptiness he shaped with his long black fingers. His eyes were closed. Orion wasn't speaking but sounds came from inside him the boy had never heard before, strange words, clicks, whistles and grunts. A singsong moan that rose and fell and floated like the old man's busy hands above the cross. Damballah like a drum beat in the chant. Damballah a place the boy could enter, a familiar sound he began to anticipate, a sound outside of him which slowly forced its way inside, a sound measuring his heartbeat then one with the pumping surge of his blood.

The boy heard part of what Lissy saying to Primus in the cooking shed: "Ryan he yell that heathen word right in the middle of Jim talking bout Sweet Jesus the Son of God. Jump up like he snake bit and scream that word so everybody hushed, even the white folks what came to hear Jim preach. Simple Ryan standing there at the back of the chapel like a knot poked out on somebody's forehead. Lookin like a nigger caught wid his hand in the chicken coop. Screeching like some crazy hoot owl while Preacher Jim praying the word of the Lord. They gon kill that simple nigger one day."

Dear Sir:
The nigger Orion which I purchased of you in good faith sight unseen on your promise that he was of sound constitution "a full grown and able-bodied house servant who can read, write, do sums and cipher" to recite the exact words of your letter dated April 17, 1852, has proved to be a burden, a deficit to the economy of my plantation rather than the asset I fully believed I was receiving when I agreed to pay the price you asked. Of the vaunted intelligence so rare in his kind, I have seen nothing. Not an English word has passed

through his mouth since he arrived. Of his docility and tractability I have seen only the willingness with which he bares his leatherish back to receive the stripes constant misconduct earn him. He is a creature whose brutish habits would shame me were he quartered in my kennels. I find it odd that I should write at such length about any nigger, but seldom have I been so struck by the disparity between promise and performance. As I have accrued nothing but expense and inconvenience as a result of his presence, I think it only just that you return the full amount I paid for this flawed *piece of the Indies.*

You know me as an honest and fair man and my regard for those same qualities in you prompts me to write this letter. I am not a harsh master, I concern myself with the spiritual as well as the temporal needs of my slaves. My nigger Jim is renowned in this county as a preacher. Many say I am foolish, that the words of scripture are wasted on these savage blacks. I fear you have sent me a living argument to support the critics of my Christianizing project. Among other absences of truly human qualities I have observed in this Orion is the utter lack of a soul.

She said it time for Orion to die. Broke half the overseer's bones knocking him off his horse this morning and everybody thought Ryan done run away sure but Mistress come upon the crazy nigger at suppertime on the big house porch naked as the day he born and he just sat there staring into her eyes till Mistress screamed and run away. Aunt Lissy said Ryan ain't studying no women, ain't gone near to woman since he been here and she say his ain't the first black butt Mistress done seen all them nearly grown boys walkin round summer in the onliest shirt Master give em barely come down to they knees and niggers man nor woman don't get drawers the first. Mistress and Master both seen plenty. Wasn't what she saw scared her less she see the ghost leaving out Ryan's body.

The ghost wouldn't steam out the top of Orion's head. The boy remembered the sweaty men come in from the fields at dusk when the nights start to cool early, remembered them with the drinking gourds in they hands scooping up water from the wooden barrel he filled, how they throw they heads back and the water trickles from the sides of they mouth and down they chin and they let it roll on down they chests, and the smoky steam curling off they shoulders. Orion's spirit would not rise up like that but wiggle out his skin and swim off up the river.

The boy knew many kinds of ghosts and learned the ways you get round their tricks. Some spirits almost good company and he filled the nothing with jingles and whistles and took roundabout paths and sang to them when he walked up on a crossroads and yoohooed at doors. No way you fool the haunts if a spell conjured strong on you, no way to miss a beating if it your day to get beat, but the ghosts had everything in they hands, even the white folks in they hands. You know they there, you know they floating up in the air watching and counting and remembering them strokes Ole Master laying cross your back.

They dragged Orion across the yard. He didn't buck or kick but it seemed as if the four men carrying him were struggling with a giant stone rather than a black bag of bones. His ashy nigger weight swung between the two pairs of white men like a lazy hammock but the faces of the men all red and twisted. They huffed and puffed and sweated through they clothes carrying Ryan's bones to the barn. The dry spell had layered the yard with a coat of dust. Little squalls of yellow spurted from under the men's boots. Trudging steps heavy as if each man carried seven Orions on his shoulders. Four grown men struggling with one string of black flesh. The boy had never seen so many white folks dealing with one nigger. Aunt Lissy had said it time to die and the boy wondered what Ryan's ghost would think dropping onto the dust surrounded by the scowling faces of the Master and his overseers.

One scream that night. Like a bull when they cut off his maleness. Couldn't tell who it was. A bull screaming once that night and torches burning in the barn and Master and the men coming out and no Ryan.

Mistress crying behind a locked door and Master messing with Patty down the quarters.

In the morning light the barn swelling and rising and teetering in the yellow dust, moving the way you could catch the ghost of something in a spoon and play with it, bending it, twisting it. That goldish ash on everybody's bare shins. Nobody talking. No cries nor hollers from the fields. The boy watched till his eyes hurt, waiting for a moment when he could slip unseen into the shivering barn. On his hands and knees hiding under a wagon, then edging sideways through the loose boards and wedge of space where the weathered door hung crooked on its hinge.

The interior of the barn lay in shadows. Once beyond the sliver of light coming in at the cracked door the boy stood still till his eyes adjusted to the darkness. First he could pick out the stacks of hay, the rough partitions dividing the animals. The smells, the choking heat there like always, but rising above these familiar sensations the buzz of flies, unnaturally loud, as if the barn breathing and each breath shook the wooden walls. Then the boy's eyes followed the sound to an open space at the center of the far wall. A black shape there. Orion there, floating in his own blood. The boy ran at the blanket of flies. When he stomped, some of the flies buzzed up from the carcass. Others too drunk on the shimmering blood ignored him except to join the ones hovering above the body in a sudden droning peal of annoyance. He could keep the flies stirring but they always returned from the recesses of the high ceiling, the dark corners of the building, to gather in a cloud above the body. The boy looked for something to throw. Heard his breath, heavy and threatening like the sound of the flies. He sank to the dirt floor, sitting cross-legged where he had stood. He moved only once, ten slow paces away from Orion and back again, near enough to be sure, to see again how the head had been cleaved from the rest of the body, to see how the ax and tongs, branding iron and other tools were scattered around the corpse, to see how one man's hat and another's shirt, a letter that must have come from someone's pocket lay about in a helter-skelter way as if the men had suddenly bolted before they had finished with Orion.

Forgive him, Father. I tried to the end of my patience to restore his lost soul. I made a mighty effort to bring him to the Ark of Salvation but he had walked in darkness too long. He mocked

Your Grace. He denied Your Word. Have mercy on him and forgive his heathen ways as you forgive the soulless beasts of the fields and birds of the air.

She say Master still down slave row. She say everybody fraid to go down and get him. Everybody fraid to open the barn door. Overseer half dead and the Mistress still crying in her locked room and that barn starting to stink already with crazy Ryan and nobody gon get him.

And the boy knew his legs were moving and he knew they would carry him where they needed to go and he knew the legs belonged to him but he could not feel them, he had been sitting too long thinking on nothing for too long and he felt the sweat running on his body but his mind off somewhere cool and quiet and hard and he knew the space between his body and mind could not be crossed by anything, knew you mize well try to stick the head back on Ryan as try to cross that space. So he took what he needed out of the barn, unfolding, getting his gangly crane's legs together under him and shouldered open the creaking double doors and walked through the flame in the center where he had to go.

Damballah said it be a long way a ghost be going and Jordan chilly and wide and a new ghost take his time getting his wings together. Long way to go so you can sit and listen till the ghost ready to go on home. The boy wiped his wet hands on his knees and drew the cross and said the word and settled down and listened to Orion tell the stories again. Orion talked and he listened and couldn't stop listening till he saw Orion's eyes rise up through the back of the severed skull and lips rise up through the skull and the wings of the ghost measure out the rhythm of one last word.

Late afternoon and the river slept dark at its edges like it did in the mornings. The boy threw the head as far as he could and he knew the fish would hear it and swim to it and welcome it. He knew they had been waiting. He knew the ripples would touch him when he entered.

Daddy Garbage

"Be not dismayed
What ere betides . . ."

DADDY Garbage was a dog. Lemuel Strayhorn whose iceball cart is always right around the corner on Hamilton just down from Homewood Avenue is the one who named the dog and since he named him, claimed him, and Daddy Garbage must have agreed because he sat on the sidewalk beside Lemuel Strayhorn or slept in the shade under the two-wheeled cart or when it got too cold for iceballs, followed Strayhorn through the alleys on whatever errands and hustles the man found during the winter to keep food on the stove and smoke in the chimney of the little shack behind Dunfermline. The dog was long dead but Lemuel Strayhorn still peddled the paper cups of crushed ice topped with sweet syrup, and he laughed and said, "Course I remember that crazy animal. Sure I do. And named him Daddy Garbage alright, but can't say now why I did. Must have had a reason though. Must been a good reason at the time. And you a French, ain't you? One of John French's girls. See him plain as day in your face, gal. Which one is you? Lemme see now. There was Lizabeth, the oldest, and Geraldine and one more . . ."

She answers: "Geraldine, Mr. Strayhorn."

"Sure you are. That's right. And you done brought all these beautiful babies for some ices."

"You still make the best."

"Course I do. Been on this corner before you was born. Knew your daddy when he first come to Homewood."

20

"This is his grandson, Lizabeth's oldest, John. And those two boys are his children. The girls belong to Lizabeth's daughter, Shirley."

"You got fine sons there, and them pretty little girls, too. Can hear John French now, braggin bout his children. He should be here today. You all want ices? You want big or small?"

"Small for the kids and I want a little one, please, and he'll take a big one, I know."

"You babies step up and tell me what kind you want. Cherry, lemon, grape, orange and tutti-frutti. Got them all."

"You remember Mr. Strayhorn. Don't you, John?"

"Uh huh. I think I remember Daddy Garbage too."

"You might of seen a dog around, son, but wasn't no Daddy Garbage. Naw, you way too young."

"Mr. Strayhorn had Daddy Garbage when I was a little girl. A big, rangy, brown dog. Looked like a wolf. Scare you half to death if you didn't know he was tame and never bothered anybody."

"Didn't bother nobody long as they didn't bother him. But that was one fighting dog once he got started. Dogs got so they wouldn't even bark when Daddy Garbage went by. Tore up some behinds in his day, yes, he did."

"Wish you could remember how he got that name."

"Wish I could tell you, too. But it's a long time ago. Some things I members plain as day, but you mize well be talking to a light post you ask me bout others. Shucks, Miss French. Been on this corner making iceballs, seem like four hundred years if it's a day."

"You don't get any older. And I bet you still remember what you want to remember. You look fine to me, Mr. Strayhorn. Look like you might be here another four hundred at least."

"Maybe I will. Yes mam, just might. You children eat them ices up now and don't get none on them nice clothes and God bless you all."

"I'm going to ask you about that name again."

"Just might remember next time. You ask me again."

"I surely will. . . ."

Snow fell all night and in the morning Homewood seemed smaller. Whiteness softened the edges of things, smoothed out the spaces between near and far. Trees drooped, the ground rose up a little higher, the snow glare in your eyes discouraged a long view, made you attentive to what was close at hand, what was familiar, yet altered and harmonized by the blanket of whiteness. The world seemed smaller till you got out in it and understood that the glaze which made the snow so lustrous had been frozen there by the wind, and sudden gusts would sprinkle your face with freezing particles from the drifts as you leaned forward to get a little closer to the place you wanted to go, the place which from your window as you surveyed the new morning and the untouched snow seemed closer than it usually was.

The only way to make it up the alley behind Dunfermline was to stomp right into the drifted snow as if the worn shoes on your feet and the pants legs pegged and tucked into the tops of your socks really kept out the snow. Strayhorn looked behind him at the holes he had punched in the snow. Didn't seem like he had been zigzagging that much. Looked like the tracks of somebody been pulling on a jug of Dago Red already this morning. The dog's trail wandered even more than his, a nervous tributary crossing and recrossing its source. Dog didn't seem to mind the snow or the cold, sometimes even seemed fool enough to like it, rolling on his side and kicking up his paws or bounding to a full head of steam then leaping and belly flopping splay-legged in a shower of white spray. Still a lot of pup in the big animal. Some dogs never lost those ways. With this one, this garbage-can-raiding champion he called Daddy Garbage, Strayhorn knew it was less holding on to puppy ways than it was stone craziness, craziness age nor nothing else ever going to change.

Strayhorn lifts his foot and smacks off the snow. Balances a second on one leg but can't figure anything better to do with his clean foot so plunges it again into the snow. Waste of time brushing them off. Going to be a cold, nasty day and nothing for it. Feet get numb and gone soon anyway. Gone till he can toast them in front of a fire. He steps through the crust again and the crunch of his foot breaks a stillness older than the man, the alley, the city growing on steep hills.

Somebody had set a lid of peeling wood atop a tin can. Daddy Garbage was up on his hind legs, pushing with his paws and nose against the snow-capped cover. The perfect symmetry of the crown of snow was the first to go, gouged by the dog's long, worrying snout. Next went the can. Then the lean-backed mongrel sprawled over the metal drum, mounting it and getting away from it simultaneously so he looked like a clumsy seal trying to balance on a ball. Nothing new to Strayhorn. The usual ungodly crash was muffled by the snow but the dog's nails scraped as loudly as they always did against garbage cans. The spill looked clean and bright against the snow, catching Strayhorn's eye for a moment, but a glance was all he would spare because he knew the trifling people living in those shacks behind Dunfermline didn't throw nothing away unless it really was good for nothing but garbage. Slim pickins sure enough, and he grunted over his shoulder at the dog to quit fooling and catch up.

When he looked back again, back at his solitary track, at the snow swirls whipped up by the wind, at the thick rug of snow between the row houses, at the whiteness clinging to window ledges and doorsills and ragtag pieces of fence, back at the overturned barrel and the mess spread over the snow, he saw the dog had ignored him and stood stiff-legged, whining at a box disgorged from the can.

He cursed the dog and whistled him away from whatever foolishness he was prying into. Nigger garbage ain't worth shit, Strayhorn muttered, half to the dog, half to the bleakness and the squalor of the shanties disguised this bright morning by snowfall. What's he whining about and why am I going back to see. Mize well ask a fool why he's a fool as do half the things I do.

To go back down the alley meant walking into the wind. Wind cutting steady in his face and the cross drafts snapping between the row houses. He would snatch that dog's eyeballs loose. He would teach it to come when he called whether or not some dead rat or dead cat stuffed up in a box got his nose open.

"Daddy Garbage, I'm gonna have a piece of your skull." But the dog was too quick and Strayhorn's swipe disturbed nothing but the frigid air where the scruff of the dog's neck had been. Strayhorn tried to kick away the box. If he hadn't been smacking at the dog and the snow hadn't tricked his legs, he would have sent it flying, but his foot only rolled the box over.

At first Strayhorn thought it was a doll. A little dark brown doll knocked from the box. A worn out babydoll like he'd find sometimes in people's garbage too broken up to play with anymore. A little, battered, brown-skinned doll. But when he looked closer and stepped away, and then shuffled nearer again, whining, stiff-legged like the dog, he knew it was something dead.

"Aw shit, aw shit, Daddy Garbage." When he knelt, he could hear the dog panting beside him, see the hot, rank steam, and smell the wet fur. The body lay face down in the snow, only its head and shoulders free of the newspapers stuffed in the box. Some of the wadded paper had blown free and the wind sent it scudding across the frozen crust of snow.

The child was dead and the man couldn't touch it and he couldn't leave it alone. Daddy Garbage had sidled closer. This time the swift, vicious blow caught him across the skull. The dog retreated, kicking up a flurry of snow, snarling, clicking his teeth once before he began whimpering from a distance. Under his army great-coat Strayhorn wore the gray wool hunting vest John French had given him after John French won all that money and bought himself a new leather one with brass snaps. Strayhorn draped his overcoat across the upright can the dog had ignored, unpinned the buttonless vest from his chest and spread it on the snow. A chill was inside him. Nothing in the weather could touch him now. Strayhorn inched forward on his knees till his shadow fell across the box. He was telling his hands what they ought to do, but they were sassing. He cursed his raggedy gloves, the numb fingers inside them that would not do his bidding.

The box was too big, too square shouldered to wrap in the sweater vest. Strayhorn wanted to touch only newspaper as he extricated the frozen body, so when he finally got it placed in the center of the sweater and folded over the tattered gray edges, the package he made contained half newspaper which tustled like dry leaves when he pressed it against his chest. Once he had it in his arms he couldn't put it down, so he struggled with his coat like a one-armed man, pulling and shrugging, till it shrouded him again. Not on really, but attached, so it dragged and flopped with a life of its own, animation that excited Daddy Garbage and gave him something to play with as he minced after Strayhorn and Strayhorn retraced his own footsteps, clutching the dead child to the warmth of his chest, moaning and blinking and tearing as the wind lashed his face.

An hour later Strayhorn was on Cassina Way hollering for John French. Lizabeth shooed him away with all the imperiousness of a little girl who had heard her mama say, "Send that fool away from here. Tell him your Daddy's out working." When the girl was gone and the door slammed behind her, Strayhorn thought of the little wooden birds who pop out of a clock, chirp their message and disappear. He knew Freeda French didn't like him. Not anything personal, not anything she could change or he could change, just the part of him which was part of what drew John French down to the corner with the other men to talk and gamble and drink wine. He understood why she would never do more than nod at him or say *Good day, Mr. Strayhorn* if he forced the issue by tipping his hat or taking up so much sidewalk when she passed him that she couldn't pretend he wasn't there. *Mr. Strayhorn,* and he been knowing her, Freeda Hollinger before she was Freeda French, for as long as she was big enough to walk the streets of Homewood. But he understood and hadn't ever minded till just this morning standing in the ankle-deep snow drifted up against the three back steps of John French's house next to the vacant lot on Cassina Way, till just this moment when for the first time in his life he thought this woman might have something to give him, to tell him. Since she was a mother she would know what to do with the dead baby. He could unburden himself and she could touch him with one of her slim, white-woman's hands, and even if she still called him *Mr. Strayhorn,* it would be alright. A little woman like that. Little hands like that doing what his hands couldn't do. His scavenging, hard hands that had been everywhere, touched everything. He wished Freeda French had come to the door. Wished he was not still standing tongue-tied and ignorant as the dog raising his hind leg and yellowing the snow under somebody's window across the way.

"Man supposed to pick me up first thing this morning. Want me to paper his whole downstairs. Seven, eight rooms and hallways and bathrooms. Big old house up on Thomas Boulevard cross from the park. Packed my tools and dragged my behind through all this snow and don't you know that white bastard ain't never showed. Strayhorn, I'm evil this morning."

Strayhorn had found John French in the Bucket of Blood drinking a glass of red wine. Eleven o'clock already and Strayhorn hadn't wanted to be away so long. Leaving the baby alone in that empty icebox of a shack was almost as bad as stuffing it in a garbage can. Didn't matter whose it was, or how dead it was, it was something besides a dead thing now that he had found it and rescued it and laid it wrapped in the sweater on the stack of mattresses where he slept. The baby sleeping there now. Waiting for the right thing to be done. It was owed something and Strayhorn knew he had to see to it that the debt was paid. Except he couldn't do it alone. Couldn't return through the snow and shove open that door, and do what had to be done by himself.

"Be making me some good money soon's I catch up with that peckerwood. And I'm gon spend me some of it today. Won't be no better day for spending it. Cold and nasty as it be outside, don't reckon I be straying too far from this stool till bedtime. McKinley, give this whatchamacallit a taste. And don't you be rolling your bubble eyes at me. Tolt you I got me a big money job soon's I catch that white man."

"Seems like you do more chasing than catching."

"Seems like you do more talking than pouring, nigger. Get your pop-eyed self on over here and fill us some glasses."

"Been looking for you all morning, man."

"Guess you found me. But you ain't found no money if that's what you looking for."

"Naw. It ain't that, man. It's something else."

"Somebody after you again? You been messing with somebody's woman? If you been stealin again or Oliver Edwards is after you again . . ."

"Naw, naw . . . nothing like that."

"Then it must be the Hell Hound hisself on your tail cause you look like death warmed over."

"French, I found a dead baby this morning."

"What you say?"

"Shhh. Don't be shouting. This ain't none McKinley's nor nobody else's business. Listen to what I'm telling you and don't make no fuss. Found a baby. All wrapped up in newspaper and froze stiff as a board. Somebody put it in a box and threw the box in the trash back of Dunfermline."

"Ain't nobody could do that. Ain't nobody done nothing like that."

"It's the God awful truth. Me and Daddy Garbage on our way this morning up the alley. The dog, he found it. Turned over a can and the box fell out. I almost kicked it, John French. Almost kicked the pitiful thing."

"And it was dead when you found it?"

"Dead as this glass."

"What you do?"

"Didn't know what to do so I took it on back to my place."

"Froze dead."

"Laid in the garbage like wasn't nothing but spoilt meat."

"Goddamn . . ."

"Give me a hand, French."

"Goddamn. Goddamn, man. You seen it, sure nuff. I know you did. See it all over your face. God bless America . . . Mc-Kinley . . . Bring us a bottle. You got my tools to hold so just get a bottle on over here and don't say a mumbling word."

Lizabeth is singing to the snowman she has constructed on the vacant lot next door to her home. The wind is still and the big flakes are falling again straight down and she interrupts her slow song to catch snow on her tongue. Other kids had been out earlier, spoiling the perfect whiteness of the lot. They had left a mound of snow she used to start her snowman. The mound might have been a snowman before. A tall one, taller than any she could build because there had been yelling and squealing since early in the morning which meant a whole bunch of kids out on the vacant lot and meant they had probably worked together making a giant snowman till somebody got crazy or evil and smacked the snowman and then the others would join in and snow flying everywhere and the snowman plowed down as they scuffled on top of him and threw lumps of him at each other. Till he was gone and then they'd start again. She could see bare furrows where they must have been rolling big snowballs for heads and bodies. Her mother had said: "Wait till some of those roughnecks go on about their business. Probably nothing but boys out there anyway." So she had rid up the table and scrubbed her Daddy's eggy plate and sat in his soft chair dreaming of the kind of clean, perfect snow she knew she wouldn't see by the time she was allowed out; dreaming of a ride on her Daddy's shoulders to Bruston Hill and he would carry her and the sled to a quiet place not too high up on the slope and she would wait till he was at the bottom again and clapping his hands and shouting up at her: "Go, go little gal."

"If you go to the police they find some reason put you in jail. Hospital got no room for the sick let alone the dead. Undertaker, he's gon want money from somebody before he touch it. The church. Them church peoples got troubles enough of they own to cry about. And they be asking as many questions as the police. It can't stay here and we can't take it back."

"That's what I know, John French. That's what I told you." Between them the flame of the kerosene lamp shivers as if the cold has penetrated deep into its blue heart. Strayhorn's windowless shack is always dark except where light seeps through cracks between the boards, cracks which now moan or squeeze the wind into shrill whistles. The two men sit on wooden crates whose slats have been reinforced by stone blocks placed under them. Another crate, shortside down, supports the kerosene lamp. John French peers over Strayhorn's shoulder into the dark corner where Strayhorn has his bed of stacked mattresses.

"We got to bury it, man. We got to go out in this goddamn weather and bury it. Not in nobody's backyard neither. Got to go on up to the burying ground where the rest of the dead niggers is." As soon as he finished speaking John French realized he didn't know if the corpse was black or white. Being in Homewood, back of Dunfermline wouldn't be anything but a black baby, he had assumed. Yet who in Homewood would have thrown it there? Not even those down home, country Negroes behind Dunfermline in that alley that didn't even have a name would do something like that. Nobody he knew. Nobody he had ever heard of. Except maybe crackers who could do anything to niggers, man, woman or child don't make no difference.

Daddy Garbage, snoring, farting ever so often, lay next to the dead fireplace. Beyond him in deep shadow was the child. John French thought about going to look at it. Thought about standing up and crossing the dirt floor and laying open the sweater Strayhorn said he wrapped it in. His sweater. His goddamn hunting sweater come to this. He thought about taking the lamp into the dark corner and undoing newspapers and placing the light over the body. But more wine than he could remember and half a bottle of gin hadn't made him ready for that. What did it matter? Black or white. Boy or girl. A mongrel made by niggers tipping in white folks' beds or white folks paying visits to black. Everybody knew it was happening every night. Homewood people every color in the rainbow and they talking about white people and black people like there's a brick wall tween them and nobody don't know how to get over.

"You looked at it, Strayhorn?"

"Just a little bitty thing. Wasn't no need to look hard to know it was dead."

"Can't figure how somebody could do it. Times is hard and all that, but how somebody gon be so cold?"

"Times is surely hard. I'm out there every day scuffling and I can tell you how hard they is."

"Don't care how hard they get. Some things people just ain't supposed to do. If that hound of yours take up and die all the sudden, I know you'd find a way to put him in the ground."

"You're right about that. Simple and ungrateful as he is, I won't be throwing him in nobody's trash."

"Well, you see what I mean then. Something is happening to people. I mean times was bad down home, too. Didn't get cold like this, but the cracker could just about break your neck with his foot always on it. I mean I remember my daddy come home with half a pail of guts one Christmas Eve after he work all day killing hogs for the white man. Half a pail of guts is all he had and six of us pickaninnies and my mama and grandmama to feed.

Crackers was mean as spit, but they didn't drive people to do what they do here in this city. Down home you knew people. And you knew your enemies. Getting so you can't trust a soul you see out here in the streets. White, black, don't make no difference. Homewood changing . . . people changing."

"I ain't got nothing. Never will. But I lives good in the summertime and always finds a way to get through winter. Gets me a woman when I needs one."

"You crazy alright, but you ain't evil crazy like people getting. You got your cart and that dog and this place to sleep. And you ain't going to hurt nobody to get more. That's what I mean. People do anything to get more than they got."

"Niggers been fighting and fussing since they been on earth."

"Everybody gon fight. I done fought half the niggers in Homewood, myself. Fighting is different. Long as two men stand up and beat on each other ain't nobody else's business. Fighting ain't gon hurt nobody. Even if it kill a nigger every now and then."

"John French, you don't make no sense."

"If I make no sense out no sense, I be making sense."

"Here you go talking crazy. Gin talk."

"Ain't no gin talking. It's me talking and I'm talking true."

"What we gon do?"

"You got a shovel round here?"

"Got a broken-handled piece of one."

"Well get it, and let's go on and do what we have to do."

"It ain't dark enough yet."

"Dark as the Pit in here."

"Ain't dark outside yet. Got to wait till dark."

John French reaches down to the bottle beside his leg. The small movement is enough to warn him how difficult it will be to rise from the box. Nearly as cold inside as out and the chill is under his clothes, has packed his bones in ice and the stiffness always in the small of his back from bending then reaching high to hang wallpaper is a little hard ball he will have to stretch out inch by painful inch when he stands. His fist closes on the neck of the bottle. Raises it to his lips and drinks deeply and passes it to Strayhorn. Gin is hot in John French's mouth. He holds it there, numbing his lips and gums, inhaling the fumes. For a moment he feels as if his head is a balloon and someone is pumping it full of gas and there is a moment when the balloon is either going to bust or float off his shoulders.

"Gone, nigger. Didn't leave a good swallow." Strayhorn is talking with his mouth half covered by coatsleeve.

"Be two, three hours before it's good and dark. Sure ain't sitting here that long. Ain't you got no wood for that fire?"

"Saving it."

"Let's go then."

"I got to stay. Somebody got to be here."

"Somebody got to get another taste."

"Ain't leaving no more."

"Stay then. I be back. Goddamn. You sure did find it, didn't you?"

When John French wrestles open the door, the gray light enters like a hand and grasps everything within the shack, shaking it, choking it before the door slams and severs the gray hand at the wrist.

It is the hottest time of a July day. Daddy Garbage is curled beneath the big wheeled cart, snug, regal in the only spot of shade on the street at one o'clock in the afternoon. Every once in a while his ropy tail slaps at the pavement. Too old for most of his puppy tricks but still a puppy when he sleeps, Strayhorn thinks, watching the tail rise up and flop down as if it measures some irregular but persistent pulse running beneath the streets of Homewood.

"Mr. Strayhorn." The young woman speaking to him has John French's long, pale face. She is big and rawboned like him and has his straight, good hair. Or the straight, good hair John French used to have. Hers almost to her shoulders but his long gone, a narrow fringe above his ears like somebody had roughed in a line for a saw cut.

"Have you seen my daddy, Mr. Strayhorn?"

"Come by here yesterday, Miss French."

"Today, have you seen him today?"

"Hmmm . . ."

"Mr. Strayhorn, he has to come home. He's needed at home right away."

"Well now . . . let me see . . ."

"Is he gambling? Are they gambling up there beside the tracks? You know if they're up there."

"Seems like I might have seen him with a few of the fellows . . ."

"Dammit, Mr. Strayhorn. Lizabeth's having her baby. Do you understand? It's time, and we need him home."

"Don't fret, little gal. Bet he's up there. You go on home. Me and Daddy Garbage get him. You go on home."

"Nigger gal, nigger gal. Daddy's sure nuff fine sweet little nigger gal." Lizabeth hears the singing coming closer and closer. Yes, it's him. Who else but him? She is crying. Pain and happiness. They brought the baby in for her to see. A beautiful, beautiful little boy. Now Lizabeth is alone again. Weak and pained. She feels she's in the wrong place. She was so big and now she can barely find herself in the immense whiteness of the bed. Only the pain assures her she has not disappeared altogether. The perfect white pain.

She is sweating and wishing for a comb even though she knows she should not try to sit up and untangle the mess of her hair. Her long, straight hair. Like her mama's. Her Daddy's. The hair raveled on the pillow beside her face. She is sweating and crying and they've taken away her baby. She listens for footsteps, for sounds from the other beds in the ward. So many swollen bellies, so many white sheets and names she forgets and is too shy to ask again, and where have they taken her son? Why is no one around to tell her what she needs to know? She listens to the silence and listens and then there is his singing. *Nigger gal. Sweet, sweet little nigger gal.* Her Daddy's drunk singing floating toward her and a nurse's voice saying *no*, saying *you can't go in there* but her Daddy never missing a note and she can see the nurse in her perfect white and her Daddy never even looking at her just weaving past the uniform and strutting past the other beds and getting closer and singing, singing an ignorant darky song that embarrasses her so and singing that nasty word which makes her want to hide under the sheets. But it's him and he'll be beside her and he'll reach down out of the song and touch her wet forehead and his hand will be cool and she'll smell the sweet wine on his breath and she is singing silently to herself what she has always called him, always will,

Daddy John, Daddy John, in time to the nigger song he chants loud enough for the world to hear.

  "Got to say something. You the one likes to talk. You the one good with words." John French and Lemuel Strayhorn have been working for hours. Behind them, below them, the streets of Homewood are deserted, empty and still as if black people in the South hadn't yet heard of mills and mines and freedom, hadn't heard the rumors and the tall tales, hadn't wrapped packages and stuffed cardboard suitcases with everything they could move and boarded trains North. Empty and still as if every living thing had fled from the blizzard, the snow which will never stop, which will bury Dunfermline, Tioga, Hamilton, Kelley, Cassina, Allequippa, all the Homewood streets disappearing silently, swiftly as the footprints of the two men climbing Bruston Hill. John French first, leaning on the busted shovel like it's a cane, stabbing the metal blade into the snow so it clangs against the pavement like a drum to pace their march. Strayhorn next, tottering unsteadily because he holds the bundle of rags and paper with both hands against his middle, thinking, when the wind gives him peace enough, of what he will say if someone stops him and asks him what he is carrying. Finally the dog, Daddy Garbage, trotting in a line straighter than usual, a line he doesn't waver from even though a cat, unseen, hisses once as the procession mounts higher toward the burying ground.
  In spite of wind and snow and bitter cold, the men are flushed and hot inside their clothes. If you were more than a few feet away, you couldn't see them digging. Too much blowing snow, the night too black. But a block away you'd have heard them fighting the frozen earth, cursing and huffing and groaning as they take turns with the short-handled shovel. They had decided before they began that the hole had to be deep, six feet deep at least. If you had been close enough and watched them the whole time, you would have seen how it finally got deep enough so that one man disappeared with the tool while the other sat exhausted in the snow at the edge of the pit waiting his turn. You'd have seen the dark green bottle emptied and shoved neck first like a miniature headstone in the snow. You would have seen how one pecked at the stone hard

ground while the other weaved around the growing mound of snow and dirt, blowing on his fingers and stomping his feet, making tracks as random as those of Daddy Garbage in the untouched snow of the cemetery. . . .

"Don't have no stone to mark this place. And don't know your name, child. Don't know who brought you on this earth. But none that matters now. You your own self now. Buried my twins in this very place. This crying place. Can't think of nothing to say now except they was born and they died so fast too. But we loved them. No time to name one before she was gone. The other named Margaret, after her aunt, my little sister who died young too.

"Like the preacher say, May your soul rest in peace. Sleep in peace, child."

Strayhorn stands mute with the bundle in his arms. John French blinks the heavy snowflakes from his lashes. He hears Strayhorn grunt *amen* then Strayhorn sways like a figure seen underwater. The outline of his shape wiggles, dissolves, the hard lines of him swell and divide.

"How we gonna put it down there? Can't just pitch it down on that hard ground."

John French pulls the big, red plaid snot rag from his coat pocket. He had forgotten about it all this time. He wipes his eyes and blows his nose. Stares up into the sky. The snowflakes all seem to be slanting from one spot high over his head. If he could get his thumb up there or jam in the handkerchief, he could stop it. The sky would clear, they would be able to see the stars.

He kneels at the edge of the hole and pushes clean snow into the blackness. Pushes till the bottom of the pit is lined with soft, glowing fur.

"Best we can do. Drop her easy now. Lean over far as you can and drop her easy. . . ."

Lizabeth: The Caterpillar Story

DID you know I tried to save him once myself. When somebody was dumping ashes on the lot beside the house on Cassina Way. Remember how mad Daddy got. He sat downstairs in the dark with his shotgun and swore he was going to shoot whoever it was dumping ashes on his lot. I tried to save Daddy from that.

It's funny sitting here listening at you talk about your father that way because I never thought about nobody else needing to save him but me. Then I hear you talking and think about John French and know there ain't no way he could have lived long as he did unless a whole lotta people working real hard at saving that crazy man. He needed at least as many trying to save him as were trying to kill him.

Knew all my life about what you did, Mama. Knew you punched through a window with your bare hand to save him. You showed me the scar and showed me the window. In the house we used to live in over on Cassina Way. So I always knew you had saved him. Maybe that's why I thought I could save him too.

I remember telling you the story.

And showing me the scar.

Got the scar, that's for sure. And you got the story.

Thought I was saving Daddy, too, but if you hadn't put your fist through that window I wouldn't have had a Daddy to try and save.

Had you in my lap and we were sitting at the window in the house on Cassina Way. You must have been five or six at the time. Old enough to be telling stories to. Course when I had one of you children on my lap, there was some times I talked just to hear myself talking. Some things couldn't wait even though you all didn't understand word the first. But you was five or six and I was telling you about the time your Daddy ate a caterpillar.

The one I ate first.

The very one you nibbled a little corner off.

Then he ate the rest.

The whole hairy-legged, fuzzy, orange and yellow striped, nasty rest.

Because he thought I might die.

As if my babygirl dead wouldn't be enough. Huh uh. He swallowed all the rest of that nasty bug so if you died, he'd die too and then there I'd be with both you gone.

So he was into the saving business, too.

Had a funny way of showing it but I guess you could say he was. Guess he was, alright. Had to be when I look round and see all you children grown up and me getting old as sin.

Nineteen years older than me is all.

That's enough.

I remember you telling me the caterpillar story and then I remember that man trying to shoot Daddy and then I remember Albert Wilkes's pistol you pulled out from under the icebox.

That's a whole lot of remembering. You was a little thing, a lap baby when that mess in Cassina happened.

Five or six.

Yes, you were. That's what you was. Had to be because we'd been on Cassina two, three years. Like a kennel back there on Cassina Way in those days. Every one of them shacks full of niggers. And they let their children run the street half-naked and those burr heads ain't never seen a comb. Let them children out in the morning and called em in at night like they was goats or something. You was five or six but I kept you on my lap plenty. Didn't want you growing up too fast. Never did want it. With all you children I tried to keep that growing up business going slow as I could. What you need to hurry for? Where you going? Wasn't in no hurry to get you out my lap and set you down in those streets.

I remember. I'm sure I remember. The man, a skinny man, came running down the alley after Daddy. He had a big pistol just like Albert Wilkes. And you smashed your fist through the glass to warn

Daddy. If I shut my eyes I can hear glass falling and hear the shots.

Never knew John French could run so fast. Thought for a moment one of them bullets knocked him down but he outran em all. Had to or I'd be telling a different story.

It's mixed up with other things in my mind but I do remember. You told me the story and showed me the scar later but I was there and I remember too.

You was there, alright. The two of us sitting at the front window staring at nothing. Staring at the quiet cause it was never quiet in Cassina Way except early in the morning and then again that time of day people in they houses fixing to eat supper. Time of day when the men come home and the children come in off the streets and it's quiet for the first time since dawn. You can hear nothing for the first time and hear yourself think for the first time all day so there we was in that front window and I was half sleep and daydreaming and just about forgot I had you on my lap. Even though you were getting to be a big thing. A five- or six-year-old thing but I wasn't in no hurry to set you down so there we was. You was there alright but I wasn't paying you no mind. I was just studying them houses across the way and staring at my ownself in the glass and wondering where John French was and wondering how long it would stay quiet before your sister Geraldine woke up and started to fuss and wondering who that woman was with a baby in her lap staring back at me.

And you told the caterpillar story.

Yes, I probably did. If that's what you remember, I probably did. I liked to tell it when things was quiet. Ain't much of a story if there's lots of noise around. Ain't the kind you tell to no bunch of folks been drinking and telling lies all night. Sitting at the window with you at the quiet end of the afternoon was the right time for that story and I probably told it to wake myself up.

John French is cradling Lizabeth in one arm pressed against his chest. She is muttering or cooing or getting ready to throw up.

"What did she eat? What you saying she ate? You supposed to be watching this child, woman."

"Don't raise your voice at me. Bad enough without you frightening her."

"Give it here, woman."

His wife opens her fist and drops the fuzzy curled remnant of caterpillar in his hand. It lies there striped orange and yellow, dead or alive, and he stares like it is a sudden eruption of the skin of the palm of his hand, stares like he will stare at the sloppy pyramids of ash desecrating his garden-to-be. He spreads the fingers of the hand of the arm supporting the baby's back; still one minute, Lizabeth will pitch and buck the next. He measures the spiraled length of caterpillar in his free hand, sniffs it, strokes its fur with his middle finger, seems to be listening or speaking to it as he passes it close to his face. His jaws work the plug of tobacco; he spits and the juice sizzles against the pavement.

"You sure this the most of it? You sure she only ate a little piece?"

Freeda French is still shaking her head yes, not because she knows the answer but because anything else would be unthinkable. How could she let this man's daughter chew up more than a little piece of caterpillar. Freeda is crying inside. Tears glaze her eyes, shiny and thick as the sugar frosting on her Aunt Aida's cakes and there is too much to hold back, the weight of the tears will crack the glaze and big drops will steal down her cheeks. While she is still nodding yes, nodding gingerly so the tears won't leak, but knowing they are coming anyway, he spits again and pops the gaudy ringlet of bug into his mouth.

"I got the most of it then. And if I don't die, she ain't gonna die neither, so stop that sniffling." He chews two or three times and his eyes are expressionless, vacant as he runs his tongue around his teeth getting it all out and down. . . .

Someone had been dumping ashes on the vacant lot at the end of Cassina Way. The empty lot had been part of the neighborhood for as long as anybody could remember and no one had ever claimed it until John French moved his family into the rear end of the narrow row house adjoining the lot and then his claim went no farther than a patch beside the end wall of the row houses, a patch he intended to plant with tomatoes, peppers and beans but never got around to except to say he'd be damned if he couldn't make something grow there even though the ground was more rock and roots than it was soil because back home in Culpepper, Virginia, where the soil so good you could almost eat it in handfuls scooped raw from the earth, down there he learned about growing and he was going to make a garden on that lot when he got around to it and fix it to look nearly as good as the one he had loved to listen to when he was a boy sitting on his back porch with his feet up on a chair and nobody he had to bother with from his toes to the Blue Ridge Mountains floating on the horizon.

Ashes would appear in gray, sloppy heaps one or two mornings a week. The shape of the mounds told John French they had been spilled from a wheelbarrow, that somebody was sneaking a wheelbarrow down the dark, cobbled length of Cassina Way while other people slept, smothering his dream of a garden under loads of scraggly ash. One afternoon when Lizabeth came home crying with ash in her hair, hair her mother had just oiled and braided that morning, John French decided to put a stop to the ash dumping. He said so to his wife, Freeda, while Lizabeth wept, raising his voice as Lizabeth bawled louder. Finally goddamned somebody's soul and somebody's ancestors and threatened to lay somebody's sorry soul to rest, till Freeda hollering to be heard over Lizabeth's crying and John French's cussing told him such language wasn't fit for a child's ears, wasn't fit for no place or nobody but the Bucket of Blood and his beer drinking, wine drinking, nasty talking cronies always hanging round there.

So for weeks Lizabeth did not sleep. She lay in her bed on the edge of sleep in the tiny room with her snoring sister, afraid like a child is afraid to poke a foot in bath water of an uncertain temperature, but she was frozen in that hesitation not for an instant but for weeks as she learned everything she could from the night sounds of Cassina Way, and then lay awake learning there was nothing else to learn, that having the nightmare happen would be the only way of learning, that after predictable grunts and alley clamors, the cobblestones went to sleep for the night and she still hadn't picked up a clue about what she needed to know, how she would recognize the sound of a wheelbarrow and find some unfrightened, traitorous breath in herself with which to cry out and warn the man who pushed the barrow of ashes that her father, John French, with his double-barreled shotgun taller than she was, sat in ambush in the downstairs front room.

Even before she heard him promise to shoot whoever was dumping ashes she had listened for her Daddy to come home at night. He'd rummage a few minutes in the kitchen then she'd listen for the scrape of a match and count his heavy steps as he climbed to the landing; at *twelve* he would be just a few feet away and the candlelight would lurch on the wall and her father would step first to the girls' room, and though her eyes were squeezed as tightly shut as walnuts, she could feel him peering in as the heat of the candle leaned closer, feel him counting his daughters the way she counted the stairs, checking on his girls before he ventured the long stride across the deep well of the landing to the other side of the steps, the left turning to the room where her mother would be sleeping. Once in a while partying all by himself downstairs, he would sing. Rocking back and forth on a rickety kitchen chair his foot tapping a bass line on the linoleum floor, he'd sing, *Froggy went a courtin and he did ride, uh huh, uh huh.* Or the songs she knew came from the Bucket of Blood. His husky voice cracking at the tenor notes and half laughing, half swallowing the words in those songs not fit for any place but the Bucket of Blood.

Most times he was happy but even if she heard the icebox door slammed hard enough to pop the lock, heard his chair topple over and crash to the floor, heard the steps groan like he was trying to put his heel through the boards, like he was trying to crush the humpback of some steel-shelled roach with each stride, hearing even this she knew his feet would get quieter as she neared the end of her count, that no matter how long it took between steps when she could hear him snoring or shuffling back and forth along the length of a step like he had forgotten *up* and decided to try *sideways*, finally he would reach the landing and the staggering light from the candle her mother always set out for him on its dish beside the front door would lean in once then die with the bump of her parents' door closing across the landing.

Lizabeth could breathe easier then, after she had counted him safely to his bed, after the rasp of door across the landing and the final bump which locked him safely away. But for weeks she'd lain awake long after the house was silent, waiting for the unknown sound of the wheelbarrow against the cobblestones, the sound she must learn, the sound she must save him from.

"It got to be that bowlegged Walter Johnson cause who else be cleaning people's fireplaces round here. But I'll give him the benefit of the doubt. Every man deserves the benefit of the doubt so I ain't going to accuse Walter Johnson to his face. What I'm gon do is fill the next nigger's butt with buckshot I catch coming down Cassina Way dumping ash."

She knew her father would shoot. She had heard about Albert Wilkes so she knew that shooting meant men dead and men running away and never coming back. She could not let it happen. She imagined the terrible sound of the gun a hundred times each night. If she slept at all, she did not remember or could not admit a lapse because then the hours awake would mean nothing. Her vigilance must be total. If she would save her father from himself, from the tumbling cart and the gray, ashy faced intruder who would die and carry her father away with him in the night, she must be constant, must listen and learn the darkness better than it knew itself.

"Daddy." She is sitting on his knee. Her eyes scale her father's chest, one by one she climbs the black buttons of his flannel shirt until she counts them all and reaches the grayish neck of his long johns. Their one cracked pearl button showing below his stubbled chin.

"Daddy. I want to stay in your hat."

"What you talking about, little sugar?"

"I want to live in your hat. Your big brown hat. I want to live in there always."

"Sure you can. Yes indeed. Make you a table and some chairs and catch a little squirrel too, let him live in there with you. Now that sounds like a fine idea, don't it? Stay under there till you get too big for your Daddy's hat. Till you get to be a fine big gal."

Lizabeth lowers her eyes from his long jaw, from the spot he plumped out with his tongue. He shifted the Five Brothers tobacco from one cheek to the other, getting it good and juicy and the last she saw of his face before her eyes fell to the brass pot beside his chair was how his jaws worked the tobacco, grinding the wad so it came out bloody and sizzling when he spit.

She was already big enough for chores and hours beside her

41

mother in the kitchen where there was always something to be done. But hours too on the three steps her Daddy had built from the crooked door to the cobbled edge of Cassina Way. Best in the summer when she could sit and get stupid as a fly in the hot sun after it rose high enough to crest the row houses across the alley. If you got up before everybody else summer mornings were quiet in Cassina, nothing moving until the quiet was broken by the cry of the scissors-and-knife man, a jingling ring of keys at his waist, and strapped across his back the flintstone wheel which he would set down on its three legs and crank so the sparks flew up if you had a dull blade for him to sharpen, or by the iceman who would always come first, behind the tired clomp of his horse's hooves striking Cassina's stones. The iceman's wagon was covered with gray canvas that got darker like a bandage on a wound as the ice bled through. *Ice. Ice. Any ice today, lady?* The iceman sang the words darkly so Lizabeth never understood exactly what he cried till she asked her mother.

"He's saying *Any ice today, lady*, least that's what he thinks he's saying. Least that's what I think he thinks he's saying," her mother said as she listened stock-still by the sink to make sure. For years the iceman was Fred Willis and Fred Willis still owned the horse which slept some people said in the same room with him, but now a scowling somebody whose name Lizabeth didn't know, who wore a long rubber apron the color of soaked canvas was the one talking the old gray horse down the alley, moaning *Ice, ice, any ice today, lady* or whatever it was she heard first thing behind the hollow clomp of the hooves.

Stupid as a fly. She had heard her Daddy say that and it fit just how she felt, sun-dazed, forgetting even the itchy places on her neck, the cries of the vendors which after a while like everything blended with the silence.

Stupid as a fly during her nightlong vigils when she couldn't learn what she needed to know but she did begin to understand how she could separate into two pieces and one would listen for the wheelbarrow and the other part would watch her listening. One part had a Daddy and loved him more than anything but the other part could see him dead or dying or run away forever and see Lizabeth alone and heartbroken or see Lizabeth lying awake all night foolish enough to think she might save her Daddy. The watching part older and wiser and more evil than she knew Lizabeth could ever be. A worrisome part which strangely at times produced in her the most profound peace because she was that part and nothing else when she sat sun-drugged, stupid as a fly on the steps over Cassina Way.

Bracelets of gray soapsuds circled her mother's wrists as she lifted a china cup from the sink, rinsed it with a spurt of cold water and set it gleaming on the drainboard to dry. The same froth clinging to her mother's arms floated above the rim of the sink, screening the dishes that filled the bowl. Each time the slim hands disappeared into the water there was an ominous clatter and rattle, but her mother's fingers had eyes, sorted out the delicate pieces first, retrieved exactly what they wanted from the load of dishes. If Lizabeth plunged her own hands into the soapy water, everything would begin to totter and slide, broken glass and chipped plates would gnaw her clumsy fingers. Some larger pieces were handed to her to dry and put away which she did automatically, never taking her eyes from her mother's swift, efficient movements at the sink.

"Lizabeth, you go catch the iceman. Tell him five pounds."

Lizabeth shouted, *Five pound, we want five pound.* She knew better, her mother had told her a hundred times: pounds and miles, *s* when you talking bout more than one, but her Daddy said *two pound a salt pork* and *a thousand mile tween here and home* so when the wagon was abreast of the last row houses and the echo of the hooves and the echo of the blues line the iceman made of his call faded down the narrow funnel of Cassina Way she shouted loud as she could, *Five pound, five pound, Mister.*

The horse snorted. She thought it would be happy to stop but it sounded mad. The driver's eyes went from the little girl on the steps to the empty place in the window where there should be a sign if anybody in the house wanted ice. When his eyes stared at her again, they said you better not be fooling with me, girl, and with a grunt much like the horse's snort he swung himself down off the wagon seat, jerked up an edge of the canvas from the ice and snapped away a five pound chunk in rusty pincers. The block of ice quivered as the iron hooks pierced its sides. Lizabeth could see splintered crystal planes, the cloudy heart of the ice when the man passed her on the steps. Under the high-bibbed rubber apron, the man's skin was black and glistening. He hollered once *Iceman* and pushed through the door.

If she had a horse, she would keep it in the vacant lot next door. It would never look nappy and sick like this one. The iceman's horse had bare patches in his coat, sore, raw-looking spots like the heads of kids who had ringworm. Their mothers would tie a stocking cap over the shaved heads of the boys so they could come to school and you weren't supposed to touch them because you could get it that way but Lizabeth didn't even like to be in the same room. Thinking about the shadowy nastiness veiled under the stockings was enough to make her start scratching even though her mother washed and oiled and braided her thick hair five times a week.

She waited till the wagon had creaked past the vacant lot before she went back inside. If her pinto pony were there in the lot, nibbling at the green grass her Daddy would plant, it would whinny at the sad ice wagon horse. She wondered how old the gray horse might be, why it always slunk by with its head bowed and its great backside swaying slowly as the dark heads of the saints in Homewood A.M.E. Zion when they hummed the verses of a hymn.

"That man dripping water in here like he don't have good sense. Some people just never had nothing and never will." Her mother was on her hands and knees mopping the faded linoleum with a rag.

"Here girl, take this till I get the pan." She extended her arm backward without turning her head. "Pan overflowed again and him slopping water, too." She was on her knees and the cotton housedress climbed up the backs of her bare thighs. Her mama's backside poked up in the air and its roundness, its splitness made her think of the horse's huge buttocks, then of her own narrow hips. Her mama drew the brimful drain pan from under the icebox, sliding it aside without spilling a drop. "Here," her arm extended again behind her, her fingers making the shape of the balled rag. She had to say *Here girl* again before Lizabeth raised her eyes from the black scarifications in the linoleum and pushed the rag she had wrung into her mother's fingers.

"I don't know why I'm down here punishing these bones of mine and you just standing there looking. Next time . . ."

Her mother stopped abruptly. She had been leaning on one elbow, the other arm stretched under the icebox to sop up the inevitable drips missed by the drain pan. Now she bowed her head even lower, one cheek almost touching the floor so she could see under the icebox. When her hand jerked from the darkness it was full of something blue-black and metal.

"Oh, God. Oh, my God."

She held it the way she held a trap that had snared a rat, and for a moment Lizabeth believed that must be what it was, some new rat-killing steel trap. Her mama set the wooden kind in dark corners all over the house but when one caught something her mother hated to touch it, she would try to sweep the trap and the squeezed rat body out the door together, leave it for John French to open the spring and shake the dead rodent into the garbage can so the trap could be used again. Her mama held a trap delicately if she had to touch it at all, in two fingers, as far from her body as she could reach, looking away from it till she dropped it in a place from which it could be broomed easily out the door. This time the object was heavier than a trap and her mama's eyes were not half-closed and her mouth was not twisted like somebody swallowing cod liver oil. She was staring, wide-eyed, frightened.

"Watch out . . . stand back."

On the drainboard the gun gleamed with a dull, blue-black light which came from inside, a dead glistening Lizabeth knew would be cold and quick to the touch, like the bloody, glass-eyed fish the gun lay next to.

"You've seen nothing. Do you understand, child? You've seen nothing and don't you ever breathe a word of this to a soul. Do you understand me?"

Lizabeth nodded. But she was remembering the man in the alley. Must remember. But that afternoon in the kitchen it was like seeing it all for the first time. Like she had paid her dime to the man at the Bellmawr Show and sat huddled in the darkness, squirming, waiting for pictures to start flashing across the screen. It had to begin with the caterpillar story.

"I got the most of it then. And if I don't die, she ain't gonna die neither, so stop that sniffling."

Lizabeth has heard the story so many times she can tell it almost as well as her mother. Not with words yet, not out loud yet, but she can set the people — her father, her mother, herself as a baby — on the stage and see them moving and understand when they are saying the right words and she would know if somebody told it wrong. She is nearly six years old and sitting on her mother's lap as she hears the caterpillar story this time. Sitting so they both can look out the downstairs window into Cassina Way.

Both look at the gray covering everything, a late afternoon gray gathered through a fall day that has not once been graced by the sun. Palpable as soot the gray is in the seams between the cobblestones, seals the doors and windows of the row houses across the alley. Lights will yellow the windows soon but at this in-between hour nothing lives behind the gray boards of the shanties across the way. Lizabeth has learned the number *Seventy-Four-Fifteen* Cassina Way and knows to tell it to a policeman if she is lost. But if she is Lizabeth French, she cannot be lost because she will be here, in this house certain beyond a number, absolutely itself among the look-alikes crowding Cassina Way. She will not be lost because there is a lot next door where her Daddy will grow vegetables, and her mother will put them in jars and they will eat all winter the sunshine and growing stored in those jars and there are three wooden steps her Daddy made for sitting and doing nothing till she gets stupid as a fly in that same sun, and sleeping rooms upstairs, her sister snoring and the candle poked in before her Daddy closes the door across the deep well.

The end house coming just before the empty corner lot is Lizabeth and Lizabeth nothing more nor less than the thinnest cobweb stretched in a dusty corner where the sounds, smells and sights of the house come together.

Lizabeth watches her mother's eyes lose their green. She sits as still as she can. She is not the worm now like her mama always calls her because she's so squirmy, she is nothing now because if she sits still enough her mother forgets her and Lizabeth who is nothing at all, who is not a worm and not getting too big to be sitting on people's laps all day, can watch the shadows deepen and her mama's green eyes turn gray like the houses across Cassina Way.

"There was a time Cassina Way nothing but dirt. Crab apple trees and pear trees grew where you see all them shacks. Then the war came and they had a parade on Homewood Avenue and you should have seen them boys strut. They been cross the ocean and they knew they looked good in their uniforms and they sure was gon let everybody know it. People lined up on both sides the street to see those colored troops marching home from the war. The 505 Engineers. Everybody proud of them and them strutting to beat the band. Mize well been dancing down Homewood Avenue. In a manner of speaking they were dancing and you couldn't keep your feet still when they go high stepping past. That big drum get up inside your chest and when Elmer Hollinger hits it your skin feels about to bust. All of Homewood out that day. People I ain't never seen before. All the ones they built these shacks for back here on Cassina Way. Ones ain't never been nowhere but the country and put they children out in the morning, don't call them in till feeding time. Let them run wild. Let them make dirt and talk nasty and hair ain't never seen a comb.

"That's why I'ma hold on to you, girl. That's why your mama got to be mean sometimes and keep you in sometime you want to be running round outdoors.

Lizabeth loves the quiet time of day when she can just sit, when she has her mama all to herself and her mama talks to her and at her and talks to herself but loud enough so Lizabeth can hear it all. Lizabeth needs her mother's voice to make things real. (Years later when she will have grandchildren of her own and her mother and father both long dead Lizabeth will still be trying to understand why sometimes it takes someone's voice to make things real. She will be sitting in a room and the room full of her children and grandchildren and everybody eating and talking and laughing but she will be staring down a dark tunnel and that dark, empty tunnel is her life, a life in which nothing has happened, and she'll feel like screaming at the darkness and emptiness and wringing her hands because nothing will seem real, and she will be alone in a roomful of strangers. She will need to tell someone how it had happened. But anybody who'd care would be long dead. Anybody who'd know what she was talking about would be long gone but she needs to tell someone so she will begin telling herself. Patting her foot on the floor to keep time. Then she will be speaking out loud. The others will listen and pay attention. She'll see down the tunnel and it won't be a tunnel at all, but a door opening on something clear and bright. Something simple which makes so much sense it will flash sudden and bright as the sky in a summer storm. Telling the story right will make it real.)

"Look at that man. You know where he been at. You know what he's been doing. Look at him with his big hat self. You know he been down on his knees at Rosemary's shooting crap with them trifling niggers. Don't you pay me no mind, child. He's your Daddy and a good man so don't pay me no mind if I say I wish I could sneak out there and get behind him and boot his butt all the way home. Should have been home an hour ago. Should have been here so he could keep an eye on you while I start fixing dinner. Look at him just sauntering down Cassina Way like he owns it and got all the time in the world. Your sister be up in a minute and yelling soon as her eyes open and him just taking his own sweet time.

"He won too. Got a little change in his pocket. Tell by the way he walks. Walking like he got a load in his pants, like other people's nickels and dimes weigh him down. If he lost he'd be smiling and busting in here talking fast and playing with youall and keep me up half the night with his foolishness. Never saw a man get happy when he gambles away his family's dinner. Never saw a man get sour-faced and down in the mouth when he wins."

Lizabeth doesn't need to look anymore. Her Daddy will get closer and closer and then he'll come through the door. Their life together will begin again. He is coming home from Rosemary's, down Cassina Way. He is there if you look and there if you don't look. He is like the reflection, the image of mother and daughter floating in the grayness of Cassina Way. There if she looks, there if she doesn't.

She stares at the pane of glass and realizes how far away she has been, how long she has been daydreaming but he is only a few steps closer, taking his own good time, the weight of somebody else's money in his pockets, the crown of his hat taller than the shadowed roofs of Cassina Way.

Her mama's arms are a second skin, a warm snuggling fur that keeps out the grayness, the slight, late-afternoon chill of an October day. She hums to herself, a song about the caterpillar story her mama has just told. Her baby sister is sleeping so Lizabeth has her mother to herself. Whenever they are alone, together, is the best time of the day, even if it comes now when the day is nearly over, sitting at the window in her mama's lap and her mama, after one telling of the caterpillar story, quiet and gray as Cassina Way. Because Lizabeth has a baby sister Geraldine she must love even though the baby makes the house smaller and shrinks the taken-for-granted time Lizabeth was used to spending with her mama. Lizabeth not quite six that early evening, late afternoon she is recalling, that she has not remembered or relived for five years till it flashes back like a movie on a screen that afternoon her mother pulls the revolver from under the icebox.

Her mother screams and smashes her fist through the windowpane. A gunshot pops in the alley. Her Daddy dashes past the jagged space where the windowpane had been, glass falling around his head as he bounds past faster than she has ever seen him move, past the empty, collapsing frame toward the vacant lot. A gun clatters against the cobbles and a man runs off down the corridor of Cassina Way.

My God. Oh, my God.

Her mama's fist looks like someone has tied bright red strings across her knuckles. The chair tumbles backward as her mother snatches her away from the jagged hole. Baby Geraldine is yelping upstairs like a wounded animal. Lizabeth had been daydreaming, and the window had been there between her daydream and her Daddy, there had been separation, a safe space between, but the glass was shattered now and the outside air in her face and her mama's hand bleeding and her mama's arms squeezing her too tightly, crushing her as if her small body could stop the trembling of the big one wrapped around it.

"Lizabeth . . . Lizabeth."

When her mama had screamed her warning, the man's eyes

leaped from her Daddy's back to the window. Lizabeth saw the gun but didn't believe the gun until her mama screamed again and flung her fist through the glass. That made it real and made her hear her own screams and made her Daddy a man about to be shot dead in the alley.

If a fist hadn't smashed through the window perhaps she would not have remembered the screaming, the broken glass, the shots when she watched her mama drag a pistol from under the icebox and set it on the bloody drainboard.

But Lizabeth did remember and see and she knew that Albert Wilkes had shot a policeman and run away and knew Albert Wilkes had come to the house in the dead of night and given her father his pistol to hide, and knew that Albert Wilkes would never come back, that if he did return to Homewood he would be a dead man.

"You're a fool, John French, and no better than the rest of those wine-drinking rowdies down at the Bucket of Blood and God knows you must not have a brain in your head to have a gun in a house with children and who in the name of sense would do such a thing whether it's loaded or not and take it out of here, man, I don't care where you take it, but take it out of here." Her mother shouting as loud as she ever shouts like the time he teased her with the bloody rat hanging off the end of the trap, her Daddy waving it at her mama and her mama talking tough first, then shouting and in tears and finally her Daddy knew he had gone too far and carried it out the house. . . .

Lizabeth remembered when the gun was dragged from under the icebox so there was nothing to do but lie awake all night and save her Daddy from himself, save him from the trespassing cart and smoking ashes and the blast of a shotgun and dead men and men running away forever. She'd save him like her mama had saved him. At least till he got that garden planted and things started growing and he put up a little fence and then nobody fool enough to dump ashes on something belonged to John French.

You ought to paint some yellow stripes and orange stripes on that scar, Mama.

Don't be making fun of my scar. This scar saved your father's life.

I know it did. I'm just jealous, that's all. Because I'll never know if I saved him. I'd sure like to know. Anyway an orange and yellow caterpillar running across the back of your hand would be pretty, Mama. Like a tattoo. I'd wear it like a badge, if I knew.

Don't know what you're talking about now. You're just talking now. But I do know if you hadn't been sitting in my lap, I'da put my whole body through that window and bled to death on those cobblestones in Cassina Way so just by being there you saved me and that's enough saving for one day and enough talk too, cause I can see John French coming down that alley from Rosemary's now and I'm getting sad now and I'm too old to be sitting here crying when ain't nothing wrong with me.

Hazel

"Don't worry bout what hates you. What loves you's what you got to worry bout." — Bess

THE day it happened Hazel dreamed of steps. The black steps her brother Faun had pushed her down. The white steps clinging to the side of the house she would not leave till she died. Down the steep black stairwell you always fell faster and faster. In the first few moments of the dream you could count the steps as parts of your body cracked on each sharp, wooden edge. But soon you were falling so fast your body trailed behind you, a broken, rattling noise like tin cans tied to a wedding car. The white steps were up. You mounted them patiently at first. The sun made them gleam and printed their shadow black against the blank, clapboard wall. If you looked up you could see a pattern repeated endlessly to the sky. A narrow, slanted ladder of nine steps, a landing, another bank of bare, bone white railings and steps leaning toward the next landing. Patiently at first, step by step, but then each landing only leads you to another flight of steps and you have been climbing forever and the ground is too far away to see but you are not getting any closer to the top of the building. The sun dazzles you when you stop to catch your breath. You are dizzy, exposed. You must hurry on to the next landing. You realize you cannot stop. You understand suddenly that you are falling up and this dream is worse than your brother's hands flinging you down into the black pit.

"Eat your peas now, honey." Her mother was busy halving peas into neat green hemispheres so Hazel wiggled her tongue at the ones prepared for her, the ones her mother had shoved with the edge of her knife into a mound in one compartment of her plate. They're good and juicy her mother said as she speared another pea. Can hardly catch them, she said as she sliced the pea and its two halves disappeared in the gray soup covering the bottom of the plate's largest section. Her mother boiled everything and always splashed water from pan to plate when she portioned Hazel's meals into the thick, trisected platter. If my food had those little wings like fish it could swim to me, Hazel thought. I'd put my lips on my plate and open my mouth wide like the whale swallowing Jonah and my food just swim to me like that.

"Here's the rest now. You eat up now." The knife squeaked through the flood, driving split peas before it, tumbling them over the divider so the section nearest Hazel was as green as she remembered spring.

"Have a nice breast of lamb cooking. By the time you finish these, it'll be ready, darling."

So green she wanted to cry. Hazel wished she knew why her tears came so easily, so suddenly over nothing. She hated peas. Her mother boiled them till the skins were loose and wrinkled. Pure mush when you bit into them. And who ever heard of cutting peas in half. *So you don't choke, darling. Mama doesn't want to lose her baby. Can't be too careful.* She had screwed up her face and stuck out her tongue at the peas just a moment before when her mother wasn't looking but now she felt like crying. Mushy and wrinkled and wet didn't matter at all. She didn't want to disturb the carpet of green. Didn't want to stick her fork in it. It was too beautiful, too green. A corner of spring in the drab room she would never leave.

Her mother never gets any older. She's slim, dainty, perfect as she rises and crosses to the stove, a young girl from the back, her trim hips betraying no sign of the three children they've borne. The long, straight hair they say she inherited from her mother Maggie is twisted and pinned into a bun on top of her head. A picture of Maggie they say when she lets it down and gathers it in her hands and pulls it forward and lets it fall over one shoulder the way Maggie always wore hers. Grandmother Maggie in the oval photograph on the mantelpiece. That's your grandmother, Hazel. Looks like a white lady, don't she? She could sit on her hair. Black and straight as any white woman's. Liked to let it hang like it is in the picture. She'd sit and play with it. Curl the end round her fingers. *That's your grandmother. It's a shame she didn't live long enough for you to see her. But she was too delicate, too beautiful. God didn't make her for living long in this world.*

Not one gray hair in the black mass when her mother swept it over her shoulder, two handfuls thick when her mother Gaybrella pulled and smoothed the dark river of hair down across her breast. Like a river or the wide, proud tail of a horse.

If her mother was not getting older, then she must be getting younger, Hazel thought, because nobody stood still. Hazel knew no one could stand still, not even a person who lives in a chair, a person who is helpless as a little baby, a person who never leaves the house. Even if you become Hazel, a person like that, you can't stand still. Some days took a week to pass. Some nights she'd awaken from her dreams and the darkness would stun her, would strike her across her mouth like a blow from a man's fist and she'd sink down into a stupor, not awake and not asleep for dull years at a time. She knew it hurt to have children, that women sweated and shrieked to wring life out of their bodies. That's why they called that hard, killing work *labor*, called it a woman's bed of pain. She knew it hurt to have a child dragged from your loins but it couldn't be any worse than those nights which were years and years ripped away from the numb cave of nothingness which began at her waist.

You couldn't stand still. You got older and more like a stone each day you sat in that chair, the chair which had been waiting at the foot of the stairs your brother pushed you down. So her mother was growing younger, was a girl again in her grace, in her slim body crossing to the stove and raising the lid to check the boiling breast of lamb.

"It's getting good and tender. It's almost done." Lamb smell filled the room, the shriveled pea halves were already cold to the touch. Hazel mashed one under her finger. As she wiped the mush on the napkin beside her plate she wondered what God used to clean his hands. How He got her off his thumb after he had squashed her in the darkness at the bottom of the steps.

The day it happened she dreamed of steps and thought of

swallowing peas and chewing the lamb her mother Gaybrella had boiled to tastelessness. Until the day it roared beside her Hazel had never seen death. Death to her was that special look in her mother's eyes, a sneaky, frightened look which was not really something in the eyes but something missing, the eyes themselves missing from her mother's face. Death was her mother's eyes hiding, hiding for a whole morning, a whole afternoon, avoiding any encounter with Hazel's. Someone had knocked at the door early and Hazel had heard voices in her sleep. Her mother had shushed whoever it was and by the time Hazel was awake enough to listen the whispering on the other side of the door had stopped. Then the outside door was shut and bolted, a woman's footsteps had clattered down the three flights of outside steps and a strange something had emptied her mother's eyes. Hazel hadn't asked who had arrived at dawn, or asked what news the visitor had carried. She hadn't asked because there was no one to ask. Sometimes their three rooms at the top floor of Mr. Gray's house seemed smaller than a dress mother and daughter were struggling to wear at the same time. But the day of the empty eyes her mother found a million places in the tiny rooms to hide. Hazel had hummed all the songs she knew to keep herself company. By two o'clock her nervousness, the constant alert she forced herself to maintain had drained her. She was ready to cry or scream and did both when her mother had appeared from the bedroom in her long black coat. Her mother never left the house alone. Once or twice a year on Ferd's arm she might venture down into the Homewood streets but never alone. With her head tied in a scarf and her body wrapped from ankles to chin in the column of black she had faced Hazel for the first time that day. Her mother Gaybrella had looked like a child bundled up for an outing on a winter day. A child whose wide eyes were full of good-bye.

She's leaving me. She's going away. The words were too terrible to say. They were unthinkable but Hazel couldn't think anything else as she had stared at the pale girl woman who had once been her mother, who was too young now to be her mother, at the child who was going away forever.

"It's John French, sugar." Her mother's eyes had gone again. There was no one to ask why, or how long, no one but her own pitiful, crippled self in the room she would never leave. John French was a big, loud, gentle man who brought her candy and fruit. Her mother smiled at him in a way Hazel had never seen her smile before. Those kisses he planted on Hazel's forehead each time he left smelled of wine and tobacco. Coming and going he'd rattle the three flights of stairs which climbed the outside of Mr. Gray's clapboard house.

"You don't come on down outa here like you got good sense, Gay, I'ma come up and get you one day. Drag you if I have to. Fine woman like you cooped up here don't even see the light of day. I'ma come up here and grab you sure enough."

John French who was an uncle or an in-law or whatever you were to somebody when he married your mother's niece. Cousin Freeda who was Gert's girl. Aunt Gert and Aunt Aida and Aunt Bess your mother's sisters. John French had daughters who would be relatives too. Nice girls he said. *I'ma get those hussies come to see you some time.* How many years had it been since he said that. How many years before Lizabeth knocked on Sunday morning. She said it was Sunday and said she was just stopping by on her way home from church. And said her Daddy said hello. And said he's not doing so well. Heart and all and won't listen to the doctor. My Daddy's hardheaded, stubborn as a mule, she said. How many years ago and Lizabeth still coming, still dropping by on Sundays to say hello. That's how you know it's a Sunday. Lizabeth knocking in her Sunday clothes and, Hi, how you all doing? That's how you know Sunday still comes and comes in winter when she wears a big coat and in summer when she's sweating under her Sunday clothes. She'll take off the little hats she wears and set them on the table. In spring they look like Easter baskets. Girl, it's hot out there. Phew, she'll say and stretch out her legs. Ain't fit for a dog out there. Aunt Gay, she'll say. You should have heard Miss Lewis this morning. She can still sing, Aunt Gay. Old as she is she can still get that whole church shouting. You ought to come the next time she's singing. She always does a solo with the Gospel Chorus and they're on every third Sunday. You ought to come and I'll stay here with Hazel. Or Hazel could come too. We could get somebody to help her down the steps. We could get a wheelchair and somebody would give us a ride. Why don't both you'all come next third Sunday?

John French in Lizabeth's face. His high cheekbones and long jaw. White like her Daddy and his French eyes and the good French hair he used to have and she still does. Lizabeth is like John French always worrying them to come down into the world. A girl then a woman. The years pretty on her. Lizabeth can get up when she's finished with her tea in winter or her lemonade in summer, get up and walk away on two strong legs so the years do not pile up on her. She does not lose them by the fistful in the middle of the night and wake up years older in the morning. Lizabeth is not a thousand years old, she is not a stone heavy with too many years to count.

It's John French, sugar. Her mother had never said more than that. Just stood there in her long black coat, in the body of that child she was becoming again. Stood there a moment to see if her silence, her lost eyes might do what she knew words couldn't. But silence and eyes staring through her, around her, hadn't checked Hazel's sobs so Gaybrella left and tiptoed down the three flights of steps and returned in two hours, tiptoeing again, easing the door open and shut again, saying nothing as she shed the black coat and washed her hands and started water boiling for dinner.

Death was that something missing in her mother Gaybrella's eyes. Death was her mother leaving to go to John French, leaving without a word, without any explanation but Hazel knowing exactly where she was going, and why and knowing if her mother ever leaves that way again it will be death again. It will be Aunt Aida or Aunt Bess if she leaves again, if there is anyone else who can make her tip down the steps, make her lose her eyes the way John French did.

The day it happened (the *it* still unthinkable, unsayable as it was when her mother stood draped in black on the threshold) began with Bess *yoo-hooing* from the yard behind Mr. Gray's house.

"Yoo-hoo. Yoo-hoo, Gay." Little Aunt Bess yodeling up from the yard. That made it Tuesday because that's when Aunt Bess came to do the wash. First the dream of steps, of black steps and white steps, then the day beginning with Aunt Bess hollering "*Yoo-*

hoo. What you got today? it's Tuesday. What you got for me?"

Her mother hated to drop the bundle of laundry into the yard but short-legged Bess hated all those steps and since she was the one doing the favor she'd yoo-hoo till she got her sister's attention and got her on the landing and got the bundle sailing down to her feet.

"Oww. Look at that dust. Look at that dust lapping at my things. If they weren't dirty before, they're dirty now.

"You wouldn't be dropping them down here if they wasn't dirty in the first place. I know you're the cleaningest woman in the world sister Gaybrella, but you still get things dirty."

"Let's not have a conversation about my laundry out here in public."

"Ain't no public to it. Ain't nobody here but us chickens. This all you got for me, Gay?"

"I can do the rest."

"Just throw it all down here. Don't make no sense for you to be doing no rest."

"You know I can't do that. You know I don't let anybody touch the rest."

"You can be downright insultin sometimes. Holding on to them few little things like you don't trust your own sister or something. And me bending over your wash every week."

"If it's too much trouble, I'll do it all myself. Just bring it back up here and I'll do it all myself."

"Shut up, woman. I've been doing it all these years. What makes you think I'ma stop today?"

"Then you know I can't give you everything. You know I have to do our private things myself."

"Suit yourself. Mize well run my head against a brick wall as try to change your ways. If you got sheets in here I'll have to hang them on this line. Won't have room on mine today."

"Go ahead. You know I dry the little business I have right up here."

"Say hello to that sweet angel, Hazel. Yoo-hoo, Hazel. You hear me girl?"

"She hears you, Bess. The whole neighborhood hears you."

"What I care about some neighborhood, I'm saying hello to my angel and anybody don't like it can kiss my behind."

"Please Bess."

"Don't be pleasing me. Just throw the rest of your dirty clothes down here so I can go on my way. Don't you be washing today. Don't do it today."

"I'm going inside now. Thank you."

"And don't you be thanking me. Just listen to me for once and don't be washing youall's underwear and hanging it over that stove."

"Good-bye."

And the door slams over Bess's head. She yells again. *Don't wash today,* but not loud enough to carry up the three flights of steps. She is bending over and pulling the drawstrings of the laundry bundle tighter so there is enough cord to sling the sack over her back. She is a short, sturdy-legged, reddish-yellow woman. Her skin is pocked with freckles. No one would guess she is the sister of the ivory woman who dropped the bundle from the landing. Bess hefts the sack over her shoulder and cuts catty-corner through the backyards toward the intersection of Albion and Tioga and her washing machine.

It happened on a Tuesday because her mother slammed the door and came in muttering about that Bess, that uncouth Bess. Her tongue's going to be the death of that woman. She married below her color but that's where her mouth always wanted to be anyway. Out in the street with those roughnecks and field-hands and their country nigger ways. Her mother Gaybrella just fussing and scolding and not knowing what to do with her hands till she opened the wicker basket in the bathroom where she stored their soiled private things and ran the sink full of water and started to wash them out. That calmed her. In a few moments Hazel could hear her humming to herself. Hear the gentle lapping of the water and the silk plunged in again and again. Smell the perfumed soap and hear the rasp of her mother's knuckles as she scrubbed their under-things against the washboard.

A warm breeze had entered the room while her mother stood outside on the landing talking to Bess. A spring, summer breeze green as peas. It spread like the sunlight into every corner of the room. Hazel could see it touching the curtains, feel it stirring the hair at the nape of her neck. In the chair she never left except when her mother lifted her into bed each night Hazel tried to remember the wind. If she shut her eyes and held her palms over her ears she could hear it. Pulled close to the window she could watch it bend trees, or scatter leaves or see snowflakes whirl sideways and up in the wind's grasp. But hearing it or watching it play were not enough. She wanted to remember how the wind felt when you ran into it, or it ran into you and pasted your clothes to your skin, and tangled your hair into a mad streaming wake and took your breath away. Once she held her cupped hands very close to her face and blew into them, blew with all her might till her jaws ached and tears came. But it wasn't wind. Couldn't bring back the sensation she wanted to remember.

"Mama." Her mother is stringing a line above the stove. Their underthings have been cleaned and wrung into tight cylinders which are stacked in the basin her mother set on the sideboard.

"Bess never did listen to Mama. She was always the wild one. A hard head. She did her share of digging Mama an early grave. Mama never could do anything with her. Had a mind of her own while she was still in the cradle. I don't know how many times I've explained to her. There are certain things you wear close to your body you just can't let anybody touch. She knows that. And knows better than to be putting people's business in the street."

"Mama."

"What's that honey?"

"Could you set me on the landing for a while?"

"Honey I don't trust those stairs. I never did trust them. As long as we've been here I've been begging Mister Gray to shore them up. They sway and creak so bad. Think you're walking on a ship sometimes. I just don't trust them. The last time I went down with Ferdinand I just knew they wouldn't hold us both. I made him go first and held on to his coattail so we both wouldn't have to be on the same step at the same time. Still was scared to death the whole way down. Creaking and groaning like they do. Wouldn't trust my baby out there a minute."

"Is it warm?"

"In the sun, baby."

"I won't fall."

"Don't be worrying your mama now. You see I got these things to hang. And this place to clean. And I want to clean myself up and wash my hair this morning. Don't want to be looking like an old witch when Bess comes back this afternoon with the laundry. We can't slip, darling. We have to keep ourselves neat and clean no matter what. Doesn't matter what people see or don't see. What they never see are the places we have to be most careful of. But you know that. You're my good girl and you know that."

"If the sun's still out when you finish, maybe . . ."

"Don't worry me. I have enough to do without you picking at me. You just keep me company awhile. Or nap if you're tired."

Hazel watched as piece by piece her mother unrolled and pinned their underclothes on the line stretched above the stove. The back burners were lit. Steam rose off the lace-frilled step-ins and combinations.

"I have a feeling Ferdinand will come by today. He said last time he was here he was being fitted for a new suit and if I know my son it won't be long before he has to come up here to his mama and show off what he's bought. He's a good son. Never lost a night's sleep worrying over Ferdinand. If all mothers' sons were sweet as that boy, bearing children wouldn't be the burden it surely is. It's a trial. I can tell you it's a trial. When I look at you sitting in that chair and think of the terrible guilt on your other brother's shoulders, I can't tell you what a trial it is. Then I think sometimes, there's my little girl and she's going to miss a lot but then again she's blessed too because there's a whole lot she'll never have to suffer. The filth and dirt of this world. The lies of men, their nasty hands. What they put in you and what they turn you into. Having their way, having their babies. And worst of all expecting you to like it. Expecting you to say *thank you* and bow down like they're kings of the world. So I cry for you, precious. But you're blessed too. And it makes my heart feel good to know you'll always be neat and clean and pure."

It was always "your other brother" when her mother spoke of Faun. She had named him and then just as carefully unnamed him after he pushed his sister down the stairs. Her mother was the one who blamed him, who couldn't forgive, who hadn't said his name in fifteen years. There was Ferdinand and "your other brother." Hazel had always shortened her brother's names. To her they had been Ferd and Faun from the time she could speak. Her mother said every syllable distinctly and cut her eyes at people who didn't say *Fauntleroy* and *Ferdinand*. I gave my sons names. Real names. All niggers have nick-names. They get them everywhere and anywhere. White folks. Children. Hoodlums and ignorant darkies. All of them will baptize you in a minute. But I chose real names for my boys. Good, strong names. Names from their mother and that's who they'll be in my mouth as long as I live. But she was wrong. Fauntleroy became "your other brother." Faun had forced his mother to break her promise to herself.

Ferd was a timid, little man, a man almost dandified in his dress and mannerisms. He was nearly as picky as their mother. He couldn't stand dust on his shoes. His watch chain and the gold eagle head of his cane always shone as if freshly polished. A neat, slit-eyed man who pursed his lips to smile. When he sat with them he never looked his sister in the eye. He'd cross his leg and gossip with his mother and drink his tea from the special porcelain cups, never set out for anyone but him. Hazel knew he didn't like their mother. Never adored her the way she and Faun always did. To him Gaybrella was never a fairy princess. As a child he made fun of her strange ways. Once he had pursed his lips and asked them: If she's so good, if she's so perfect, why did Daddy leave her? But daddies had nothing to do with fairy princesses and they giggled at the silliness of his question. Then, like their father, Faun had run away or been run away, and ever since in Ferd's voice as he sat sipping tea and bringing news of the world, Hazel could hear the sneer, the taunt, the same mocking question he had asked about their father, asked about the absent brother. Hazel knew her mother also heard the question and that her mother saw the dislike in Ferd's distant eyes but instead of ordering him from the room, instead of punishing him the way she punished Faun for the least offense, she doted on Ferdinand. His was the only arm she'd accept, the only arm she'd allow to lead her down into the streets of Homewood.

Faun was like the wind. There were days when Hazel said his name over and over to herself. Never Fauntleroy but *Faun*. Faun. She'd close her eyes and try to picture him. The sound of his name

was warm; it could lull her to sleep, to daydreaming of the times
they ran together and talked together and shared a thousand secrets. He was her brother and the only man she had ever loved.
Even as a girl she had understood that any other man who came
into her life would be measured against Faun. Six days a week
he killed animals. He always changed his clothes at work but Hazel
believed she could smell the slaughterhouse blood, could feel the
killing strength in his hands when he pinched her cheek and teased
her about getting prettier every day. Her big brother who was like
the wind. Changeable as the wind. But his mood didn't matter;
just staying close to him mattered. That's why they fought. Why
they raged at each other and stood inseparable against the world.
So when he was twenty and full of himself and full of his power
over other women and she was seventeen and learning what parts
of him she must let go and learning her own woman powers as
he rejected them in her and sought them in others, when they
rubbed and chafed daily, growing too close and too far apart at
once, the fight in the kitchen was no different than a hundred others, except his slaughterhouse hands on her shoulders pushed harder
than he meant to, and her stumbling, lurching recoil from a blow
she really didn't feel much at all, was carried too far and she lost
her balance and tumbled through the kitchen door someone had
left unlocked and pitched down the dark steep stairwell to Mr.
Gray's second floor where the chair was waiting from which she
would never rise.

"I expect him up those stairs anytime." Her mother had let her
hair down. It dangled to her waist, flouncing like the broad, proud
tail of a horse as she swept the kitchen floor.

Then it happened. So fast Hazel could not say what came first
or second or third. Just that it happened. The unspeakable, the
unsayable acted out before her eyes.

A smell of something burning. Almost like lamb. Flames
crackling above the stove. Curling ash dropping down. Her mother
shouting something. Words or a name. A panicked look back over
her shoulders at the chair. Hazel forever in the chair. Then flames
like wings shooting up her mother's back. Her mother wheeling,
twisting slim and graceful as a girl. Her mother Gaybrella grabbing the river of her hair and whipping it forward over her shoul-

ders, and the river on fire, blazing in her fists. Did her mother scream then or had she been screaming all along? Was it really hair in her hands or the burning housecoat she was trying to tear from her back? And as she rushed past Hazel like a roaring, hot wind, what was she saying, who was she begging for help? When her mother burst through the door and crashed through the railing into thin air who was she going to meet, who was making her leave without a word, without an explanation.

Fifteen years after the day it happened, fourteen years after Hazel too, had died, Lizabeth rode in the ambulance which was rushing with sirens blaring to Allegheny County Hospital. She was there because Faun was Gaybrella's son and Hazel's brother and she had stopped by all those Sundays and was one of the few who remembered the whole story. She had heard Faun had returned to Homewood but hadn't seen him till one of the church sisters who also possessed a long memory asked her if she knew her cousin was sick. So Lizabeth had visited him in the old people's home. And held his hand. And watched the torment of his slow dying, watched his silent agony because the disease had struck him dumb. She didn't know if he recognized her but she visited him as often as she could. A nurse called the ambulance when his eyes rolled to the top of his head and his mouth began to foam. Lizabeth rode with Faun in the screaming ambulance so she was there when he bolted upright and spoke for the first time in the two months she had been visiting him. "I'm sorry . . . I'm so sorry," was what he said. She heard that plainly and then he began to fail for the last time, tottering, exhausting the last bit of his strength to resist the hands of the attendants who were trying to push him back down on the stretcher. She thought he said, *Forgive me*, she thought those were Faun's last words but they sputtered through the bubbling froth of his lips and were uttered with the last of his fading strength so she couldn't be sure.

The Chinaman

*The toasts — long, bawdy, rhymed narratives invented by
black street bards — contain much new slang but also
preserve older words and ways of speaking. In the toasts
the Chinaman appears as a symbol of decay and death.
— See* Toasts *— Wm. Labov* et al.

OUTSIDE her window the last snow of the season is white only
until it touches the pavement. Frceda's thoughts are her thoughts
only until they reach the cloudy pane of glass where they expire
silently, damp as tears, like snow against asphalt.

To believe who she is Freeda must go backward, must retreat,
her voice slowly unwinding, slowly dismantling itself, her voice
going backward with her, alone with her as the inevitable silence
envelops. Talking to herself. Telling stories. Telling herself.

Once . . . once . . . her first baby born premature and breathless. The snow falling and her cousin May snatches away the child
from the others who have shrieked, keened, moaned and are already beginning to mouth prayers for the dead. The door slams,
shaking the wooden row house on Cassina Way, shattering the calm
the women's folded hands and bowed heads are seeking. They
realize the still, blue baby is gone. And that May is out there in
the snow like a crazy woman with the dead child in her arms and
ain't took time for coat or nothing she'll catch her death too in
the blizzard that has its hand inside the house now and flings the
door again and again crashing against its frame.

Once . . . how many years ago . . . Freeda was a baby then,
she was forgiving then, burying her head in the wet pillow, hiding

her eyes from theirs because she does not want to read the death of her firstborn in the women's faces. She wants to forgive. Forgive John French for the nights he loved her. Forgive the eyes of the women who smiled knowingly when she complained, who showed her their scars and wrinkled flesh, who said *Jesus* and smiled, and winced when she did and said *Everything's gon be all right, child* and *Thank Jesus* and *Ain't she beautiful she carries high like her mama, Gert* and *Her skin's so pretty*, and *Eat, honey-child, eat everything you want you eating for two now.* Who held her hand and rubbed her back and trudged through the snow to boil water and boil rags and stand on tired feet when it was time for her baby to come.

But their eyes are not the eyes of children. She cannot believe they knew everything else and didn't know the baby was twisted wrong side down in her belly. Freeda passes her gaze from one face to the other. They were ready to pray. They had been praying all along so they knew all along and she couldn't forgive. If someone would press her face down into the pillow she would turn blue like her baby was blue. The women's sorrowing, helpless faces would go away. She could forgive them. Her aunts, her neighbors, her cousin May, a girl like she is still a girl. Freeda knows their faces better than she knows her own. She hates what hovers sorrowing in their eyes.

Freeda hears the women rush away. The ragged, noisy lift of a flock of pigeons scared from the sidewalk. They are abandoning her. They were mountains rimming the valley of her pain. They were statues, stiff as the mourning women huddling over the broken body of Jesus in the picture in the Sunday school corner of Homewood A.M.E. Zion Church. Now they are fleeing and she is alone. Not even her baby beside her, if there was a baby borne to her by that sea of pain.

May . . . May . . . They are shouting through the open door.

May is kneeling in the snow across Cassina Way where it has drifted waist deep. She hunches forward shielding the baby from the wind, while she plunges its naked body into the snow. She must turn her face into the wind to see the others. Her hair, her eyebrows and cheeks are caked with white. She is a snow witch and nobody moves a step closer. She hollers something at them which the wind voids.

Then May struggles to her feet, and stomps back through the gaping door with the baby in her arms. She is praising Jesus and Hallelujahing and prancing the floor before anybody can grab the door and get it shut behind her.

"Wouldn't be for that I be telling a different story altogether. Yes indeed. She so tiny could fit in a shoebox. Naw, I ain't lying. If I'm lying, I'm flying. It's the God's truth, sure enough. Didn't weigh but a pound and a half. Weeniest little thing you ever did see. Called her mite. You know like little mighty mite. Course there was something else in that name too. Couldn't help but think that little girl child *might* make it and she *might* not. And everybody scared to call her anything but *mite*. Such a tiny little thing. Feed her with one of them eye droppers. Didn't sleep or nap less it be on somebody's bosom so she stay warm. Little thing curl up just like an eensy-beensy monkey, curl up right on your chest with that thumb in her mouth. The cutest thing. She got that little thumb and gone. Couldn't hardly see the nails on her fingers they so tiny."

The firstborn, Lizabeth, our mother, saved by May in the snow. May's told the story a hundred times but each time it's new and necessary. If she didn't tell the story right, there would be no baby shuddering to life in her arms when she runs through the crashing door. There would be no Lizabeth, none of us would be gathered in my grandmother's house on Finance Street listening to May tell how Geraldine came next. And then the boy, Carl, birthed by my grandmother. Making it all seem so easy. Spring born. Bright and cleansing like the new rain sluicing along the curb. A boybaby in Freeda's arms, plump and crying. Peace. As if his coming was a promise to her of how it would always be. How it should be easy. So when the twins came and died, one at birth, the other named Margaret after Daddy John's sister, holding on a week, whatever peace brought by the first son was shattered, broken and strewn in Freeda's path like bits of glass, like the dry, splintered bones in the Valley of the Shadow she must cross in her bare feet as her body swells again and again life and death share her belly. Finally

Martha. Four then. The seasons passing. The children real then. As real as his weight on her body. John French pressing her down into the starched sheets, her body a leaf between the pages of a book. Sometimes, straightening the bed, when she pulls back the homemade quilt she sees her form etched in the whiteness. She touches her edges, her hollows, smooths the wrinkles, pats the indentations, laying her hands where his have been, finding herself as she leans over the sprawled figure his bulk has pressed into the sheets.

Because she knows one day she will roll back the patchwork, velvet-edged, storytelling quilt and there will be nothing. Because her body's outline not deepened by his weight is only a pale shadow, a presence no more substantial than what might be left by a chill wind passing over the sheet.

Freeda watches the snow beat noiselessly against the window. Watches it disappear like the traces of her body when she pounds the white sheet. The faces of the women gather around her again, but they are older now, wrinkle old, gray old, like her own face last time she saw it in the oval mirror of the oak dresser at the foot of their bed. She calls it their bed even though she knows the faces, crowded and stomped down as the sooty hills on which Homewood is dying, have come to tell her John French is gone. If you are just a child and marry a man, one day you will grow up and the man will be gone. He can't wait and you can't hurry. Even though trying hard to hurry and to wait are the best part of your love, what makes your love better than what passes for love around you. One day he'll be gone and that will be that. Twice your age when he stole you. Twice your age when he sat with his elbows on his knees and his shoulder's hunkered and his eyes downcast, sprawled all arms and legs on the stool in your Aunt Aida's front room while you said to her in the back room where she and Uncle Bill slept, I'm married now and she said, Yes you are now. I can tell just looking at you. John French married you good. Married you real good, didn't he? Saying the words so they hurt so you felt brazen like the ungrateful wench and hussy she didn't say you were. Not calling any names. Not fussing but saying the words so *married* was a door slammed, so *married* was the ashes of all those years Aunt Aida and Uncle Bill had sacrificed to raise her. John French is quiet as she's ever seen him in her life till Aunt Aida leaves her in the dark little bedroom and whispers something to her man Bill and Uncle Bill goes to the closet and gets not the shotgun he had loaded and set inside there but his jug of whiskey and two glasses and pours and hands one to John French.

Yes, she wants to scream. Of course he's dead. What else is he supposed to be with me lying up here an old woman. He was too big to move wedged between the seat of the toilet and the edge of the bathtub. She had heard him fall all the way from the kitchen and flew up the steps two and three at a time getting to him. Ain't no room to put my knees, he'd grumble. Shame when a man can't even squat right in his own house. She crashed open the door with both hands. She had heard him groan once while she rushed up the steps but he lay still now and her heart leaping in her chest was the only sound in the bathroom. But when she clambered on her knees under the sink so she could touch him and raise his face from the pool of vomit spreading on the linoleum she could hear the pipes gurgle and the leaky guts of the toilet hissing. She did as much as she could before she ran to the door and screamed into Cassina Way for help.

It was Fred Clark who came first. Who helped her drag John French from between the toilet and the tub that was always bumping his knees. He must have died while she was at the door because he was dead weight when they lifted him and dead when they laid him across *their* bed.

Someone always comes . . . Homewood people are good about coming. And they're best about coming around when there's nothing they can do. When someone's dead and the faces hovering around you are like flowers cut for a funeral. Fred Clark came and then Vernetta sent that useless pigeon-toed man of hers and they got John French laid across *their* bed. And Vernetta Jones down at the bottom of the steps moaning, *Have mercy, Have mercy.* Moaning it like you know she's gon moan it everytime she tells the story she can't wait to tell about John French dying in the bathroom and *I heard Freeda screaming for help and sent Ronald over there and I was so shocked you know how much I done prayed for John French to do right I was so shocked I couldn't even get up the steps I just stood at the bottom praying God have mercy, God have mercy cause I knowed he was dead.*

Freeda counts the faces. There are three. But then there are three more and three more and more threes than she can count above her. Then there is one face hiding behind the others. A face the others cannot see because they stare down at her, stare with their eyes full of tears and their mouths full of prayers so they never see the yellow face grinning behind them, the man who is the only man in the room, the Chinaman with his shriveled yellow walnut of a face. He laughs at her, he is the only one who knows she knows John French is long dead.

The curled edge of the clawfoot tub and the bottom of the sink are cold as she crawls to him. Her feet sneak away and run naked into the snow. Once she had dreamed it would happen this way. A cold, white dream which made her shiver long after she awakened. In the dream the Chinaman sat on a fence. He flashed teeth like gold daggers and laughed and laughed at his ownself trying to make a dollar out of fifteen cents. Chinky, chinky, Chinaman and she was laughing too but then he started to melt, started to run down out of the funny pajama-looking suit he was wearing. Then his face blew up like a watermelon. The skin got fatter and fatter so it swoll up and closed his eyes and closed his mouth and all the rest of him just yellow water running down the fence. And she knew she shouldn't be laughing. Knew that he wasn't laughing at himself but at what was going to happen to her when he finished melting and all the insides of him exploded through that big moon face. She began to shiver when she realized the face was filled with something cold. Like snow only it would be the color of the stuff leaking down out of his pant legs, that pee color and oily like that stuff only cold, colder than anything she had ever touched, cold so the icy pieces of jelly when they flew against her body would turn her to stone.

Three months had passed since my grandmother's death. I had flown to Pittsburgh alone to her funeral. When I returned home I hadn't said much about her. The weather in Pittsburgh had been cold and damp. On the day of the funeral it rained. There wasn't much to say about all of that, about the gray streets and somber gray hills crowded with ramshackle houses and the gray people shrouded in raingear or huddling under umbrellas. I couldn't talk about that because it was too depressing, and I couldn't talk about the storytelling and whiskey all night after we buried my grandmother either. You had to be part of the whole thing to understand why we could laugh and get high while Aunt May, tucked back into an overstuffed chair so her stockinged feet barely touched the rug, told us the stories of Homewood. Our laughter wouldn't seem appropriate unless you had been there through everything and heard how she was saying what she was saying. So I didn't talk much when I got home. I let the trip slowly seep inside me. Sipped it without really tasting it the way I sipped Jim Beam that night May told stories.

Our family had begun its annual migration East. Five hundred miles the first day and another three hundred next day before a flat. There had been a sickening swerve and I hit the brake too hard and lost control but luckily just for an instant and then the Custom Cruiser let me guide it onto the shoulder of the highway. As I began the process of changing the tire, which meant first unpacking a summer's worth of luggage to get at the spare in the back of the station wagon and finding one piece of the jack missing, and cursing the American way of leaving little things out, the sky over my shoulder had divided itself neatly into a layer of dense gray and one of luminous, spooky whiteness. The dark half above squeezing light out of the sky; all the energy in the band of white squirming and heating up as it is compressed into a smaller and smaller space. Then drum rolls of thunder and jagged seams of light splitting the darkness.

We were in Iowa. One of those featureless stretches of Interstate 80 which are a way of getting nowhere fast. Judy yelled at me to get inside the car. She has a morbid fear of lightning so I feel it's my duty to cure her, to treat thunderstorms with disdain and nonchalance and survive. So I take my good time stuffing in the last few boxes and suitcases I had unloaded. The highway would buckle each time a semi passed. I winced every time, stepping backward, swaying in the blast of hot air as the trucks exploded just a few feet away. That sudden caving in of the earth scared me more than the threat of thunderbolts delivered from the sky.

The first rain drops were as big as eggs. Not falling but flung in handfuls so they struck inside the station wagon spattering the bags before I could get the tailgate shut. Behind the wheel again I dried my hands, face and the back of my neck. I felt like I had been running a long time, running fast and strong and the exhilaration of my body had made me slightly breathless, a little giddy.

"Why are you so foolish? Why did you stay out there till the last minute?"

"You wouldn't believe me if I told you."

"It's not funny. Look at the boys. You've managed to terrify them acting like a fool." In the faces of the children strapped in their carseats behind us I could see the echo of their mother's fear, an immense silence welling behind their eyes.

But it was good in a way. The steady drumming on the roof, the windows steamed shut, the windblown sheets of rain suddenly splashing against the metal skin. All hell breaking loose outside, but we were inside, cocooned, safe, together. I liked the isolation, the sudden detour. "Hey, you guys. It's like being in a space ship. Let's pretend we're on our way to Mars. Prepare for blast-off."

And there was the business of assigning roles, the squabbles over rank, the exact determination of a noise level for our rocket motors which would not encourage the migraine Judy felt coming on.

But we were launched successfully from that Iowa plain. Though we were knee deep in water, some of our controls smoking and sputtering, our ark rose, shuddering in the girdle of rain but quickly through it, gathering speed and thrusting pure and swift wherever. . . .

So I could relinquish the controls and shut off the intercom and plead the weariness of six days exploring a virgin planet, battling the Dictosaurs, the Todals, the men whose heads grow beneath their shoulders. The ship was safe in other hands so I could shut my eyes and listen to the rockets purr calmly through the Intergalactic night.

That's when I saw her. When my grandmother, Freeda, came to me. She is wearing a thin, gray cardigan, buttonless, perhaps another color once, mauve perhaps as I look more closely or perhaps the purplish blue of the housedress beneath the worn threads gives the wool its suggestion of color. The sleeves of the sweater are pushed back from her wrists. One long hand rests in her lap. The skin on the back of her hand seems dry and loose. If she tried to lift anything heavier than the hand to which it was attached, her fragile wrist protruding from the cuffed and frayed sweater sleeve would snap. She sits in her wooden rocker in front of the fireplace which has been covered over with simulated-brick Contact paper. Just over her head is the mantelpiece crowded with all of our pictures. The television set is muttering a few feet away. Bursts of laughter and applause. Dull flickers of light as the image twitches and rolls. She reaches inside the front of her dress and fumbles with a safety pin which secures the handkerchief cached there against her underclothes. Lilies hidden beneath her dress. Lilies spreading in her lap as she unties the knotted corners of the flowered handkerchief. In the center of the handkerchief a few coins and two or three bills folded into neat squares, one of which she opens as slowly as she had opened the silk. When she learned to talk again after her second stroke, she could only manage a minimal movement of her lips. Her head moves from side to side with the effort of producing the strange, nasal, tonal language of rhythms and grunts. If you listened closely, you could detect the risings and fallings of familiar sentence patterns. The words blurted and elided but you could get the message if you listened.

Take it. Take it. Take it, Spanky. I am leaving home. The first one in the family to go off to college. She thrusts the money in my hand. Take it. Go on, boy. A five-dollar bill as wrinkled and criss-crossed as the skin at the corners of her eyes.

Over the wind and rain and rockets and the cars driven by madmen still careening past on the invisible highway I hear her offering the money . . . the strange, haunted whine I would write if I could.

Three months after her death and finally it was time. I needed to talk about her. The storm deserted us. We limped to a gas station and they fixed the flat and promised they'd have a whole jack for us next morning. We decided to stop for the night just down the road a ways in the place the mechanic had recommended, a Holiday Inn overlooking the Mississippi River. After the kids were asleep I began to talk about my grandmother. I wished for May's voice and the voices of my people in a circle amening and laughing and filling in what I didn't know or couldn't remember, but it was just me whispering in the dark motel room, afraid to wake my sons.

For sixteen years they took care of her. My Aunt Geraldine and Uncle Carl, the only son. The other girls, my mother and her sister Martha, had married. Within a week after her husband's death Freeda had a stroke, almost dying, and though her body recovered, her will did not. Wanting only to follow her dead husband everybody said. To be with John French they all said. Yet she was still their mother. And they still lived under her roof, so for sixteen years Geraldine and Carl nursed the shell she had become. The last year of her life she spent mainly in the hospital. She had stopped moving and seldom talked. Her blood thickened so there was always the threat of pneumonia or a clot that needed watching. Endless shots and medicines which might achieve three or four lucid hours a week. During her last month at home before the final confinement in Allegheny Hospital she became deeply agitated. Like a light bulb which glows unnaturally bright just before it pops, she seemed to improve. Her eyes were animated again, she struggled to speak and be listened to. My Aunt Geraldine and Uncle Carl were excited. Talked of miraculous remissions, reprieves, God changing his mind in the eleventh hour. Even though it was terror filling her eyes, even though her gestures and nasal keening described a phantom who had begun to prey on her.

Carl understood the word first, the sound Freeda had begun to repeat constantly. For weeks it had remained a mystery, part of her improved condition, part of her terror. Then, with the certainty of something known all along, Carl matched a word to the sound. A word not discovered but remembered. He couldn't believe the word had escaped him so long once he matched it to the sound she had been shaping. *Chinaman.* When he repeated it back to her the first time aloud, her chin dropped to her chest. A gagging sound came from her throat. As if the word summoned a Chinaman, diabolical and menacing beside the rocker. *Chinaman. Chinky, chinky Chinaman, sitting on a fence. Trying to make a dollar out of fifteen cents.* Hiding in corners. Hovering over her bed at night. Pulling her clothes awry. Raking his nails across her face and hands, inflicting the red wounds she showed them in the morning.

Of course he followed her to the hospital. Every member of the family knew him. The Chinaman's vigil as faithful as the shifts of relatives who tended my grandmother as she lay dying. She slept most of the time. Drugged. Too fatigued to lift her eyelids. I began disbelieving in her. I was glad I was far away and didn't have to trek to the hospital. But the others were faithful. They did the bathing, the touching, the holding on till nothing else remained. It was to them she complained of the Chinaman. But against the background of her slow, painful dying, the Chinaman became for the family a figure of fun. Mama's Chinaman. They talked about him like a dog. Transformed him into an aged suitor courting her with flowers, candy and teenage awkwardness. Made fun of him. Told stories about his appearances and disappearances, his clothes, his hiding places, how he whistled at the nurses and pinched their behinds. The Chinaman became a sort of Kilroy for the family. His signature turning up in unexpected places. His name implicated in any odd or obscene occurrence in the hospital.

One day they moved an Asian man into a room down from my grandmother's ward. The people in my family became acquainted with his people, sharing cigarettes and gossip in the visitors' lounge. Since both patients slept most of the day, the social gatherings in the lounge offered an opportunity to exchange commiserations, but also a chance to return to the world of health and well-being without totally deserting the realm of the sick. . . .

But the story was stiff, incomplete. I said I'd tell the rest when Judy felt better. She fell asleep quickly but I heard paddle-wheeled steamers packed with cotton and slaves ply the river all night long.

Two more days on the road. Then we are in my mother's kitchen. The house is quiet. Relatives and friends in and out all day as always during our summer visits. It's good to see everybody but the days are long, and hot and busy so it's also good when the last person leaves. My mother, Lizabeth, and my wife and I are in the kitchen. It's after twelve and the house is quiet. *Five things*, my mother says. *Five things in my life I'll never forget.* One was Faun asking forgiveness in the ambulance. She doesn't tell us what the other three are, but she does tell us about the Chinaman.

"Carl and I were sitting with Mama at the hospital. It must have been around six because I heard them collecting the dinner trays. She had had a bad day. I still don't know how she lasted as long as she did. Her arms weren't any bigger around than this . . . there just wasn't anything left . . . how she held on I'll never know. She had been coughing all day and they were always worried about it getting in her lungs. Anyway we were kinda down and just sitting listening to the awful rattling in her sleep when he walked in leaning on the arm of his daughter. She was a nice girl. We always talked in the lounge. She was steady about coming to see her father. You could tell she was really worried about him and really cared. A pretty girl, too. Well, she only brought him as far as the door. I guess she heard Mama sleeping and how quiet we were so she just waved from there and sort of whispered her father was going home in the morning and good luck. And the old Chinaman peeked around into the room. I guess he was curious about Mama so he poked his head in and looked at her and then they were gone. That's all. Stopped to say good-bye just like we would have said good-bye to them if we could have taken Mama home out of that place.

"Mama never woke up again. She died early the next morning and when I walked down the hall with the nurse I looked in that Chinese man's room and it was empty.

"That's just the way it happened. I was there, I know. He peeked in and Mama never woke up again. I can't tell you how many times I've asked myself how she knew. Because Mama did know. She knew that Chinaman was coming for her. That he'd tip in her door one day and take her away. Things like that happen in people's lives. I know they do. Things you just can't explain. Things that stay with you. Not to the day I die will I understand how Mama knew, but I do know things like that don't just happen. Five times in my life I've been a witness and I don't understand but I'm sure there's a plan, some kind of plan."

I am sleepy but the story gets to me the way it did the first time I heard it. My mother has told it, finished it like I never can. And the shape of the story is the shape of my mother's voice. In the quiet house her voice sounds more and more like May's. My mother doesn't wave her arms like May or rise and preacher-strut like May when May gets the spirit. My mother's hands drum the table edge, or slowly the fingertips of one hand stroke and pull and knead those of the other. For her the story of the Chinaman is a glimpse of her God who has a plan and who moves in mysterious ways. For me the mystery of the Chinaman is silence, the silence of death and the past and lives other than mine.

I watch my mother's pale fingers shuttle in and out of one another. I watch my wife slip into her own quietness, distant and private. The silence is an amen.

The Watermelon Story

THE first time he saw somebody get their arm chopped off was in front of the A&P on Homewood Avenue. They used to pile watermelons outside at the alley corner of the store. A big plate glass window where they stuck Sale signs and Specials This Week signs and propped church posters and advertisements for this and that on the bottom inside ledge was at that end of the store too. A window starting almost on the sidewalk and running up twice as tall as a man so they needed long ladders to wash it when they used to try and keep things clean in Homewood. Watermelons would be there piled three and four high, the green ones shiny, the striped ones cool as if the sunshine couldn't ever melt those pale veins of ice shooting through their rinds. Mostly the winos would stay over in the trees, below the tracks in the Bums' Forest during the heat of the day but sometimes you'd get one straying off, too high or too dry to care, and then he'd wander up where people doing their shopping, wander through there stumbling or singing or trying to get his hands on somebody's change till he got tired of people looking through him and at him and church ladies snorting and kids laughing like the circus was in town or staring like he was some kind of creature from Planet X and then he'd just settle hisself in a piece of shade where the settling looked good and nobody'd mind him no more than they would a cat or dog sleeping under the porch. But the one he saw with his arm hanging by bloody threads, dangling so loose the man in the white apron had to hold the weight of it so it wouldn't just roll on down between the watermelons, that wino had decided for some reason to sit on the stack of melons in front of the A&P.

Must have nudged one of the front ones, the bottom ones holding the stack together and when they all started to rolling like big fat marbles under him he must have leaned back to catch hisself and they pitched him through that plate glass window. Like trying to walk on marbles. Must have been like that. His legs going out from under him all the sudden and him full of Dago Red and dozing in that July sun so he was probably dreaming something and the dream got snoring good to him and Homewood Avenue a thousand miles away. Like having the rug jerked out from under your feet and you know you're falling, know you're going to hit the ground so you throw your arm back to catch yourself and ain't the ground you catch but a whole A&P windowful of glass slicing down on your shoulder.

Must have been easy at first. I mean your fist punches through real quick and busts a clean hole and your arm just passes right on through too. Ain't bleeding, ain't even scratched, it's through that tunnel real easy and quick and nothing hurts, you don't even know you're in trouble, specially with all that sweet wine and sun and you're just waiting for the goddamn watermelons to stop acting a fool so your feet and your behind can find the pavement but then that glass comes down like a freight train, snaps shut like a gator's jaws and you know, you know without looking, without feeling the pain yet either, you know it got you and that screaming behind your ear is not falling, crashing glass anymore, it's you waking up and saying hello and saying good-bye to your arm.

Must have been like that even though he didn't see it happen and he wasn't the man. He dreamed it like that many years later and the dream was his, the throne of watermelons belonged to him, green and striped and holding the heat of the sun. And when it topples and topples him with it into the bath of cool glass, the shattering glass is there ringing like a cymbal in his ear even after he opens his eyes. He dreamed it that way and often without warning when he was walking down the street his shoulder muscle would twitch, would tremble and jerk away from the ax in its dream. Like his arm was living on borrowed time and knew it. The shock of seeing a severed arm in the white aproned lap of the man who had run from inside the store meant that arms didn't have to stay where they were born. Nothing had to stay the way it was. He

79

had wondered if all that blood soaking the apron was wino blood or if the bald white man kneeling beside the hurt wino had brought pig blood and cow blood and blood from lambs and wall-eyed fish from inside the store. Was the man surrounded by the green sea of melons a butcher, a butcher who was used to bloody parts and blood spattered clothes, a butcher cradling the wino's arm so the last few threads won't break. Is he whispering to the wino, trying to help him stay still and calm or is the wino dreaming again, moaning a song to the lost arm in his dream.

The A&P is gone now. They scrubbed the blood from the pavement and stopped stacking watermelons on the sidewalk. One of the grown-ups told him later the wino's life had been saved by a tourniquet. Somebody in the crowd had enough sense to say Forget about that thing. Forget about trying to stick that arm back on and had ripped the apron into strips and made a tourniquet and tied it around the stump to stop the bleeding. That saved him. And he had wanted to ask, Did anybody save the arm, but that sounded like a silly question, even a smart-alecky question, even when he said it to himself so instead he imagined how the only black man who worked in the A&P, Mr. Norris who always sat two rows down toward the front of Homewood A.M.E. Zion Church, pushed his iron bucket that was on wheels through the wide double doors of the A&P. The melons had skittered and rolled everywhere. People trying to get closer to the blood had kicked holes in some, some had plopped over the curb and lay split in the gutter of Homewood Avenue. A few of the biggest melons had walked away when folks crowded around. But it wasn't Mr. Norris's job to count them and it wasn't, he told the produce manager, his job to scrabble around Homewood Avenue picking watermelons, wasn't no part of his job, Mr. Norris told him again as he hummed Farther Along and slopped soapy water on the dark splotches of blood. Mr. Norris had made a neat, rectangular fence of watermelons in front of the broken window to keep fools away. Nobody but a fool would get close to those long teeth of glass, jagged-edged teeth hanging by a thread, teeth subject to come chomping down if you breathe on them too hard. Mr. Norris had kept his distance and gingerly swept most of the glass into a corner of his watermelon yard. Then the bucket and mop. When the pavement dried he'd sprinkle some sawdust like they have behind the fish counter. There were smears of blood and smears of watermelon and he'd dust them all. He slooshed the heavy mop up and back, up and back, digging at the worst places with soapy water.

Rather than ask a question nobody would answer and nobody would like, he imagined Mr. Norris taking his own good time cleaning the mess off the sidewalk. Though ninety-nine percent of the shoppers were black, Mr. Norris was the only black man working for the A&P, and that made him special, made him somebody people watched. Mr. Norris had rules. Everybody knew what they were and understood his slowness, his peculiar ways were part of his rules. Watching his hands or his face or the poses he struck, you'd think he was leading an orchestra. The way he carried himself had nothing to do with wiping shelves or scrubbing floors or carting out garbage unless you understood the rules and if you understood the rules, and understood they came from him, then everything he did made sense and watching him you'd learn more than you would from asking dumb questions and getting no answers.

They wouldn't have left the arm for Mr. Norris to broom up. They'd know better so of course they'd take it with them, wherever they took the wino, wherever they took the tourniquet, the stump, the bloody strips of apron.

Don't try to stick it back on. Leave that damn thing be and stop the bleeding.

He hadn't been there when the one man with good sense had shouted out those words. He didn't see how you wrapped a stump, how you put on a handle so you could turn off the blood like you turn off a faucet. Turn and quit. He thought that's what she said at first. Those words made sense at first till she explained a little bit more and told him not *turn and quit*, it's *tourniquet*, like you learn in first aid or learn in the army or learn wherever they teach one another such things. Then she said, Uggh. I couldn't do it. I couldn't get down there with my hands in all that mess. They'd have to carry me away if I got too close to it. Me, I wouldn't be no more good. But thank God somebody with good sense was there, somebody with a strong stomach to do what have to be did.

As he listened he heard May saying the words and remembered

it was her then. May who told the story of the accident and then told him later, No, he didn't die. He lost that arm but he's still living, he's still back up in the Bum's Forest drinking just as much wine with one arm as he did with two.

And May's story of the lost arm reminded her of another story about watermelons. About once there was a very old man Isaac married to an old woman Rebecca. Was in slavery days. Way, way back. Don't nobody care nothing about those times. Don't nobody remember them but old fools like me cause I was there when Grandpa told it and I ain't never been able to forget much, least much of what I wanted to forget. Well I was there and he told me how it was way back then. There was this Isaac and Rebecca and they was old when it started. Old before those olden days way back, way, way back. It was Africa you see. Or Georgy or someplace back there it don't make no difference no way. Niggers be niggers anyplace they be. If you get my meaning. But this old man and old woman they be living together ninety-nine years and they's tired and they ain't got child the first to hold they old heads, they's childless you see. Old lady dry as a dry well and always was and looks like she's fixin to stay the very same till Judgment Day. So they was some old, sad people. Had some good times together, everybody got good times once in a while, and they was good to each other, better to each other than most people be these days. He'd still pat them nappy knots up under her head rag. She'd rub that shoulder of his been sore for fifty years when he come in from the fields at night. They was good to each other. Better than most. They did what they could. But you ain't never too young nor too old to be hurt. And a hurt lived with them all the days of their lives, lived every day from can to caint in that itty bitty cabin in the woods. They loved God and wasn't scared of dying. Naw, they wasn't feared of that like some sinners I know. And they wasn't ungrateful niggers neither. And I could name you some them, but I ain't preaching this morning. I'm telling youall a story bout two old people didn't never have no babies and that's what hurt them, that's what put that sadness on they hearts.

Youall heard bout Faith? Said I wasn't preaching this morning but youall heard that word, ain't you? Ain't asking if you understand the word. I'ma give you the understanding to go with it.

Just tell me if you heard the word. That's Faith! Faith what I'm talking bout. And if you don't know what I'm talking bout just you listen. Just you think on them old, old people in that itty bitty shack in the woods, them people getting too old to grunt. Them people down in Egypt with the Pharaohs and bitter bread and burdens all the days of they lives. Well, they had Faith. Youall heard bout the mustard seed? That's another story, that's another day. But think on it. Old as they was they ain't never stopped praying and hoping one day a child be born unto them. Yes they did, now. This old Isaac and old Rebecca kept the faith. Asked the Lord for a child to crown they days together and kept the Faith in they hearts one day He would.

Well old Isaac had a master grow watermelons on his farm. And old Isaac he have the best knuckle for miles around for thumping them melons and telling you when they just perfect for the table. He thump and Melon, Mr. Melon, he talk back. Tell his whole life story to that crusty knuckle, Uncle Isaac knock at the door. Yoo-hoo, How you do? Melon say, You a day early, man. Ain't ready yet, Isaac. Got twenty-four hours to go. You traipse on down the patch and find somebody else today. Come back tomorrow I be just right, Brother Isaac.

That was in Africa. Way, way back like I said. Where people talk to animals just like I'm sitting here talking to youall. Don't you go smiling neither. Don't you go signifying and sucking your teeth and raisin your eyebrows and talking bout something you don't know. This old lady got sense just good as any you. Like they say. You got to *Go there to Know there*. And ain't I been sitting on Grandpa's knee hearing him tell bout slavery days and niggers talking to trees and stones and niggers flying like birds. And he was there. He knows. So in a manner of speaking I was there too. He took me back. Heard old Isaac. Rap, rap, rapping. Out there all by hisself in that melon patch and Ole Massa say, Fetch me a good, big one. Got company coming, Isaac. My sister and her no good husband, Isaac, so fetch one the biggest, juiciest. Wouldn't give him the satisfaction of saying he ever got less than the best at my table. So old bent Isaac he down there thumpin and listenin and runnin his fingers long the rind. It's low mo hot too. Even for them old time Georgy niggers it's hot. Isaac so old and dry and tough he don't sweat much anymore but that day down in the patch, water runnin off his hide like it's rainin. He hear Rebecca up in the kitchen. Isaac, Isaac, don't you stay away too long. And he singing back. Got sweaty leg, Got sweaty eye, But this here nigger too old to die. And he picks one with his eye. A long, lean one. Kinda like these people going round here you call em loaf-of-bread head. Long like that. He go over and squat down in the vines and thump it once good with that talking knuckle of his.

Now don't you know that melon crack clean open. Split right dead down the middle just like somebody cleave it with a cane knife. And don't you know there's a baby boy inside. A little chubby-legged, dimple-kneed, brown-eyed boy stuck up in there perfect as two peas in a pod. Yes it was now. A living breathing baby boy hid up in there smiling back at Isaac, grabbing that crusty knuckle and holding on like it was a titty.

Well, old Isaac he sing him a new song now. He's cradling that baby boy and running through the field and singing so fine all the critters got out his way. Rattlesnakes and bears and gators. Nothing was going to mess with Old Isaac on that day. They heard his song and seen the spirit in his eyes, and everything moved on out the way.

And here come old Rebecca, skirts flying, apron flapping in the breeze. Took off fifty years in them twenty-five steps tween the back of that itty bitty cabin and her man's arms. Then they both holding the baby. Both holding and neither one got a hand on him. He just floating in the air between them two old, happy people. Thank the lord. Thank Jesus. Praise his name. They got so happy you coulda built a church right over top them. One of them big, fancy white folks' churches like youall go to nowadays and they so happy they'd of rocked it all by theyselves. Rocked that church and filled it with the spirit for days, just them two old happy people and that baby they loved so much didn't even have to hold it. He just floated on a pillow of air while they praised God.

That's just the way it happened. Isaac found that baby boy in a watermelon and him and Rebecca had that child they been praying for every day. It was Faith that bring them that child. Faith and God's will. Now He couldn't do nothing nice like that these days. Youall niggers ain't ready. Youall don't believe in nothing. Old man bring home a baby first thing you do is call the police or start wagging your tongues and looking for some young girl under the bed. Youall don't believe nothing. But the spirit works in mysterious ways his wonders to perform. Yes He does now. In them old slavery Africa times there was more miracles in a day than youall gon see in a lifetime. Youall jumping up and down and ooing and ahhing cause white men is on the moon and you got shirts you don't have to iron. Shucks. Some them things Grandpa saw daily scare the spit out you. And that's just everyday things. Talking to flowers and rocks and having them answer back. Youall don't believe in none that. Youall too smarty panted and grown for that. But old Isaac and Rebecca waited. They kept the faith and that fine son come to light they last days in this Valley of the Shadows.

Now I could say that's all, I could end it right here. Say Bread is bread and wine is wine, If anybody asks, this story's mine. End it happy like that, with a rhyme like the old folks ended their stories. But there's more. There's the rest goes with it so I'ma tell it all.

He heard the rest, and it was how the spirit took back the boy. The rest was the weeping and wailing of old Isaac and Rebecca. The rest was the broken-hearted despair, the yawning emptiness of their lives, a hole in their lives even bigger than the wound they had suffered before the child came. He listened. He'd never heard such a cruel story before. He was scared. He was a boy. For all he knew they had found him in a watermelon. For all he knew he might be snatched back tomorrow. Would the grown-ups cry for him, would they take to their beds like old Isaac and Rebecca and wait for death.

May looked round the room catching nobody's eye but everybody's ear as she finished the rest of her story.

Where was all that praying? Where was all that hallelujah and praise the Lord in that little bitty cabin deep in the woods? I'll tell you where. It was used up. That's where it was. Used up so when trouble came, when night fell wasn't even a match in the house. Nary a pot nor a window. Just two crinkly old people on a shuck mattress shivering under they quilt.

He wanted to forget the rest so he asked if the wino could grow another arm.

May smiled and said God already give him more'n he could use. Arms in his ears, on his toes, arms all over. He just got to figure out how to use what's left.

The Songs of Reba Love Jackson

The First Song is for Mama

THE first song I'm going to sing is for my mama. My first song always been dedicated to Mama and always will be long as I'm drawing breath. Been wearing the white rose in memory of Mama twenty-five years now. Some of you know what I'm talking about. Some of you wore mourning white the first time last Mother's Day Sunday and some been pinning red to they breast gon be pinning white next time round so my first number always been for Mama and always will be long as God give me strength to raise my voice in His praise. Cause that's what Gospel is. Singing praise to God's name. So I'ma sing a praise song and dedicate it to the one loved me best on this earth. The one I loved best and still do. What a Friend. Yes, Lawd. What a Friend We Have.

One for Brother Harris in Cleveland

When the phone rang so much talking and one another thing going on didn't nobody stop to answer it you know how you be busy and everybody think the other person gon get it but it just keep ringing and might be ringing still if there ain't been a napkin close to me that don't look used so I wiped the grease off my fingers and my mouth and picked up the phone.

Hello, hello, I said this the residence of Miss Reba Love Jackson saying the whole name I don't know why but I said it all into the phone and didn't get no answer except for some buzzing at the other end.

Hello, hello again and again I say this Miss Reba Love Jackson's residence.

Then this voice sorta scratchy and faraway sounding like it do when it's long distance. I could tell something wrong. Hear it plain as day in the voice. Poor man talking like he can hardly keep from crying and what I'm supposed to say? Nobody but me still ain't paid no tention to the phone. What with folks eating and talking and somebody at the piano striking off chords, nobody but me still ain't bothered bout no phone, so I'm standing there by myself and poor man must of thought I was Reba Love cause he say his name and commence to telling me his trouble and I felt so bad standing there I didn't want to cut the poor man off and I didn't want to hear what ain't my business to hear but what you going to do?

Finally I had to say wait a minute hold on a minute Sir and I laid down the receiver and got Reba Love to come. I stood beside her while she listened. Seems like I could understand better. Watching how Reba Love listened. How the face of that saint got sad-eyed while she shook her head from side to side. I'm hearing the man and understanding him better than when I was holding the phone my own self. Reba Love nodding like she do when she sings sometimes but she don't say a word.

Then she sighs and talks in the phone, "Yes yes yes. Surely I can do that little thing for you. *I Stood on the Bank of Jordan.* Yes, yes."

And she put her hand over the phone and ask me tell everybody be quiet please. And after some shushing and having to go around and bodily shut some people up, Reba Love's apartment quiet as church on Monday. She still have her hand over the mouthpiece and say, "This is my old friend Brother Harris from Cleveland and he just lost his mama and he needs for me to sing."

And didn't one more chicken wing crack or ice cube bump round in nobody's Coca-Cola. She raised the receiver like it was a microphone and child I ain't never heard no singing like it. Not Mahalia, not Bessie Griffin, not Sallie Martin. None of them, and I done heard them all, not one coulda touched Reba Love Jackson that evening.

She did it alone at first. The first verse all by herself and the chorus too, just her solo. Then the second verse and she stops and looked around and whispered into the phone, "I got some good folks here with me and they gon help me sing," whispered it and didn't lose a note, made it all seem like part of what she was singing and believe me when it was time for the rest of us to join in we were *there*, Sister, yes we were now, we were *there*, and Hattie Simpson sat her big self down at the piano too and you better believe Cleveland ain't never heard nothing like it.

For Blind Willie Who Taught Me to Sing

The blind man lay drunk and funky, his feet stretched out on the sidewalk so you had to be careful not to trip over them. Precious Pearl Jackson almost shouted, Look child, look and see the kind of man your daddy is, because she knew somewhere in some city her daughter's no good father would be sleeping off a drunk, probably outdoors like this tramp now that it was summer, snoring like him and like him barefaced and past shame. She didn't say a word but clutched her daughter's hand tighter, tugging her over and past the blind man's filthy lap-tongued brogans.

"Mama, you hurting me."

"You ain't been hurt yet, girl. Just come on here and don't be lagging."

Precious Jackson dreams of different streets. Streets lined with gold and glittering jewels. Streets pure as drifted snow where she can promenade clothed in a milk-white garment whose hem touches the pavements but receives no corruption there. If she had the strength, she would run from her door to the door of the church. People could think she was crazy if they wanted to, but if God granted her the power she would run as fast as the wind down Decatour and across Idlewild and over Frankstown and up the final long block of Homewood, sprinting so her long feet barely touch the ground, clutching her girl to her breast, not breathing till they were safe inside The Sanctified Kingdom of Christ's Holiness Temple. If she could, she would run every step. And it would be like flying. They would not taste of this evil city the Devil had tricked her to, not one swallow of the tainted air. She wondered how it would feel to fly closer to the sun. To have it burn the tacky clothes from her back, and then the skin gone too, all the flesh dropping away like old clothes till the soul rises naked to the Father's side.

Precious Jackson looks down at the gray pavement. She is tall and black and rail thin. Her cropped hair is plastered to her skull by a black net cap. Her round, pop eyes are full and hungry; they burn like the eyes of the saints who never sleep. A sudden breeze drives litter along the high curb and swirls newspapers against the steel gates barricading the shopfronts. Cardboard cartons overflowing with garbage line the curb. Broken glass sparkles in the sunlight. Somebody's crusty, green sock inches down the sidewalk. She knows the blind man. He was a blues singer. Sang the Devil's music in the bars here along the strip. One Saturday night they found him in the Temple. On his knees, they said. Praying in tongues, they said. She remembered him at the mourners' bench. Hunched over on his knees like a man taking a beating. When he arose she expected to see torn and bloody clothing, stripes from the whip. And when he testified it was like reading a book she had sworn to God she would never open. The blind man told it all. She thought the Temple's whitewashed walls would smoke before he finished. So many toils and snares. Listening to the blind man confess his sins, she realized how good her God had been to her. How merciful the straight, hard path He had led her to. Then that mouth of the Devil raised his voice in praise of the Lord. The saints amened his testimony. There was shouting and falling out. The saints offered the hand of Fellowship. The blind man swore by God's grace never to sing blues. Promised to use his voice only to praise God's goodness.

Now he was back in the street again, singing nastiness again. That was him stretched out on the pavement, drunk as sin. She hoped God would snatch his voice as He had snatched his eyes.

The Temple would be visible when they turned the next corner. With its red door as a beacon her eyes would not stray to the fallen city. Precious Pearl envied the people who went to tall churches, churches whose spires could be seen from afar. To be meek and humble, to ask no more than God saw fit to give, to praise affliction because it was a sign of His glorious will, all of this she understood and lived. But she would have liked to wor-

ship Him in a cathedral with a mighty organ, and a roof halfway
to heaven.

"Come on, gal. Why you lagging this morning?"

Precious Jackson's long feet in flat-heeled shoes slapped the sidewalk. Her daughter was a pitty-pat, pitty-pat keeping up.

"Do you love Jesus?"

"Yes, Mama."

"Do you love Him better than yourself?"

"Yes, Mama."

The words breathless as mother and daughter rushed through
the empty, Sunday morning streets. One Sunday in the Temple
the blind man sang *Nearer My God to Thee*. Precious Jackson had
wept. She had put her arm around her child's stiff, thin shoulders
and wept till the song was over.

The sky was a seamless vault of blue. Would it be a sin to paint
the ceiling of her church that color. The door, like the door of The
Sanctified Kingdom of Christ's Holiness Temple, would be the red
of his martyred blood.

A train hooted down by the tracks. Hooted again and Precious
Jackson could hear the rattling cars jerked behind it, the sound
putting her teeth on edge, then fading, getting soft and white as
lamb's wool just before it disappeared. She stopped suddenly and
her daughter bumped into her legs. Precious Pearl Jackson felt
herself nearly topple. She smacked down where she knew the girl's
head would be, her hard head plaited over with cornrows no thicker
than scars. Perhaps the world was over. Perhaps everybody was
gone. Only the blind blues singer, the girl, and herself, Precious
Pearl Jackson, forgotten, left behind. God sweeping the city clean
and taking the saints to His bosom in shining silver trains. Perhaps
what she had heard was the last load of the blessed taking off for
the sun in a beautiful metal bird.

For Old Time Preachin

In those days you could hear real preachin. Not the prancin and
fancy robes and sashayin and jump around like wanta be Retha
Franklin, James Brown or some other kinda rock and roll super-
star with lectronics and guitars and pianos and horns and ain't

never saying a mumblin word what touch the soul. Real preachin is what I'm talkin about. The man what been there hisself and when he shout for a witness, witness be fallin from they seats and runnin down the aisle. Those old time preachers could tear up a meetin. Tear it up, you hear. And you talk about talkin. Mmmm. They could do that. Yes indeed. *E*pistemology and *Co*smology and *On*tology and *Deu*teronomy. They was scholars and men and knew the words. Used to be meetins, what you call revivals today, over in Legion Field where the white boys played baseball. Peoples drive they trucks and wagons up here full of chairs just so they can sit in the outfield cause the bleachers packed every day to hear them preachers. Real preachin. What you call testimony. Cause the old timers they knew the world. They knew the world and they knew the Word and that's why it was real.

I could name you some. I can see them now just as plain as day. Now I ain't sayin they didn't use showmanship. Had to do that. Had to draw the people in fore they could whip a message on em, so they had their ways, yes indeed, a sho nuff show sometimes. But that be just to get people's tention. You know what I mean. They had this way of drawin people but there was more to em than that. Once those brothers got hold to you they twist and toss and wrestle you like you seen them little hard-jawed dogs get hold to a rat. And you come out feelin like you sure enough took some beatin, like somebody whipped all the black off you and turned you inside out and ain't nothin ever goin to be the same.

There was one. Prophet Thompson from Talledega. They had this kinda stage set up at one end the ballpark. Well, you could see the preachers and the singers comin and goin. Takin their turns. Now Prophet Thompson he ain't about to walk up to the platform. Nothing easy like that for him. When his turn come he rides up on this big, gray, country mule. Yes, he did. And you ought to heard the shoutin. Prophet ain't said a word yet and they carryin people out the stands. You woulda thought they screamin for the Prophet but all us from the country know those brothers and sisters done got happy behind that lap-eared mule. Mmmp. And the Prophet he knows how to sit a mule. And how to get off one and tie him down so he stays. You woulda believed the place on fire and people burnin up if you heard the tumult and the shoutin from far off. The air be bucklin and them wooden seats rattlin where they stomp they feet and people up off those foldin chairs in the outfield, standin up beatin them funeral parlor chairs like they was tambourines. And the Prophet ain't said nary a word. Just rode in on a mule.

Shoot. That man coulda just rode on out again and left everybody happy. But they was preachers. Real preachers. He knew what to do. That country mule ain't nothin but a trick to get folks' tention. Yes. They knows mules and knows country and the Prophet he just let them have they fun with all that. But when he's on the platform, he knows what to say.

"He brought me up here all the way from the red clay of Talledega, Alabama. So I knows he could get me this little distance to the altar."

And he had to just stand there while the people jump up and down and they clothes fallin like it be raining clothes. Stand there till he ready to say some more, then it's like thunder through the microphone and if he had said *Ground open up and let the spirits of the dead shout too*, nobody been surprised to hear voices comin out that green grass. What he said was, "Some of you all know what I'm talkin about. Some of you know who brought me out of the wilderness and onto this stage in the middle of a darkling plain. Yes Lord. Some of you know the God I speak of, but some of you still thinkin bout old Martin, my mule, and he's good, he's good and faithful, but he ain't nothin but a mule."

You see how he got em. Got em hooked. They don't know whether to run away or stand still. Whether he's talkin to em or about em. Then he commence to preach.

Real preachin. And Prophet Thompson not the onliest one. I could name a many. Seen women throw down mink coats for a preacher to walk on. Seen the aisles lined with furs. First man I ever saw play piano with his feets, it was right here. Back when they used to meet in Legion Field. Preachin and singin like nobody these days knows how to do. I remember seein Reba Love Jackson and her mama, Precious Pearl Jackson, right here every year till her Mama took her away up North. I remember Reba Love in a little baby gown sittin barebottomed in the grass while all that singin goin on, her and the rest of them barebottomed babies and now I see some of them around here gettin bare on top they heads. They say Reba Love's comin back next spring. Won't that be somethin? Won't it though? I heard her Mama dead now. They say Precious Pearl left the Devil down here and died a fine, Christian woman. I knew her well. Let me tell you what I think. Reba Love Jackson be lookin for her Mama when she come back. And you know somethin, God willin she will find her cause this her home. This where it all began. Yes she will. Find her right here and when she does she's gon sing. Sing it. And by The Grace of the Lord I'll live long enough for to see it. To hear that old time singin one more time before I die.

For Somebody Else

Through the windows of the bus Reba Love tries to imagine what it would feel like to be another person. She had heard one of the singers say just a few minutes before, *New Jersey,* and the name of somebody's hometown in the state, so it is night and they are crossing New Jersey and she knows they will stay in a hotel in Newark because the manager knows somebody there who will let them crowd four or five in a room and pay a special rate. She knows many of the gospel groups stay there. She has heard the hotel's name lots of times on the circuit. But nothing out the window is helping her to be someone else. Everything she thinks of, all of the words or voices coming to her will speak only to Reba Love Jackson, speak to her and who she is or will not speak at all. She tries to picture a person she doesn't know. One of the men she can't help seeing when she sings. A man at a concert or in a church who she has never laid eyes on before and probably will not again. The kind of man she is drawn to in spite of herself. A brown man with soft eyes. A man with meat on his bones. Who could laugh with her and grin at the big meals she loves to cook. But this stranger, this unknown, easy man who is not too beautiful, not too young, who does not seem to belong to some hawk-eyed, jealous body else, this stranger who is not really a stranger because she has seen him everywhere and knows she'll see him again, cannot draw her out of herself. This man she has never met, or only met long enough to hear his name before her mother steers him away and returns with some wrinkled, monkey-faced deacon, can not move her from who she is.

She is a Bride of Christ. Sanctified in His service. But there is no mystery here either. What once seemed immense beyond words is as commonplace as cooking and cleaning for a flesh and blood man. Moments of passion surely, surely come, but they are pinpricks of light in the vast darkness which has settled upon her, distant stars which dazzle but do not warm the night sky.

She is not a Bride of Christ. Not since the summer she was thirteen and her mother took her south to visit their People. Seven years away from them and she had just about forgotten her country cousins. Half the people down there seemed to have her last name. Even Tommy Jackson. Little, lightskinned, fast talking T.J. She can't hear him running anymore through the weeds but she can hear T.J.'s holler and the greetings of the others as they bay like bloodhounds over where the picnic cloth is spread under the trees. She is picking up her drawers from the ground. Funny how she was more shamed of her drawers than her bare butt and came out of them so fast she almost scared T.J. away. Once he got his hand up in there she just wanted her underwear gone no matter if she was going to let him do it to her or not. Didn't really seem so important after all. If he did or not. Even after a million warnings and a million threats that this, that or the other thing will happen sure as night follows day or damnation sin, the same old silly stories even after her mother ought to know she knows better. The country girls tell the stories to each other and laugh at them together and mock their mothers telling them. She could never laugh at her mother. Or hurt her any other way. Her mother was a place to stand, a place to lean. Her mama had patched the old underwear so it covered her backside decently. The patches were a secret, a secret between mother and daughter. And though she could open her legs to T.J., she could not share such secrets.

The grass prickly on her skin when she sat down to pull on her drawers. Sitting because she needed to sit. So the pain and the sweet, warm wetness could run out of her body slowly, on her time, according to her mood instead of the way T.J. had rushed it in. Like he was being chased. Sitting with the Sunday dress still like a wreath around her narrow hips. Suddenly she worried about the wrinkles.

Would they fall out? Then she thought about the others girls. Sitting on blankets all day. And the careless ones on grass or even dirt and how all the Sunday dresses will need to be scrubbed and scrubbed. She puts her hand there. The springy hair, the wet and sticky. Her hand. Her fingers like his fingers but his didn't learn anything, didn't stay in one place long enough to let her answer them. Like his fingers only hers are dark like the darkness down there. Her skin night skin like the skin over the windows of the bus. Forever, you could be a thing forever. Or once, one time could change it forever.

She couldn't say no. Couldn't say why she had not said no. So she lied once to her mother and perhaps to God and wore the saints' white dress, the Bridal Dress sanctified and holy in His name.

These things she could not speak of. Like she could not speak of the dead man they found that same day stuck in the roots along the riverbank. The dead man who had been lynched, the grown-ups whispered. When they got him up on shore they sent the children away. Away to play. And she couldn't say no. Couldn't speak about some things. She could only sing them. Put her stories in the songs she had heard all her life so the songs became her stories.

Is there ever any other way she asked herself? Am I to be Reba Love Jackson all the days of my life? Her thoughts are lost in the rumble of the bus. Lights wink and blink and climb the night sky. She is racing across New Jersey in a Greyhound. Could her mother follow the swiftness of her flight? Would her mother be watching all night? Did saints need to sleep? Want to sleep?

She would always be Reba Love Jackson. Till He touched her and brought her on home.

For All Her Fans in Radio Land

       . . . just for voice level could you please say your full name

Reba Love Jackson

that's fine, just fine. Now lemme do a little lead-in: It is my privilege this morning to be talking to Miss Reba Love Jackson, a great lady who many call the Queen Mother of Gospel. She is here in our studio on behalf of Watson Productions who right

now at the Uptown Theatre, Sixtieth and Market, are presenting
Miss Reba Love Jackson along with a host of other stars in the spec-
tacular once-a-year Super Gospel Caravan. Yes indeed. The Gospel train is stopping here for three days starting this evening at
7:00 P.M. It's the really big one youall been waiting for so get down
to the Uptown and pick up on what these soul-stirring folks is all
about . . . that's enough . . . I can fill in later . . . Gotta get some
other promo stuff in . . . hmmph . . . but now a Miss a Jackson . . . why don't we start at the beginning . . . Could you tell
our audience Miss Reba Love Jackson, Gospel Queen, where you
were born

outside Atlanta Georgia in a little place called
Bucolia. Wasn't much to it then and ain't much to it now. Little
country town where everybody one big family and God the head
of the house

I know what you mean. We all know what she means
don't we soul brothers and sisters? Yes siree. Down home country.
We knows all about it, don't we? Fried chicken and biscuits and
grits and the preacher coming over on Sunday wolfing down half
the platter . . . Lawd . . . Lawd . . . Lawd . . . but you go on
Miss Reba Love Jackson. Tell it like it was.

we didn't have much. But there was only my
mama and me and we got along. Mama Precious was a saint.
Didn't nobody work harder than my mama worked. Only heard
stories about my father. He died when I was a baby. Worked on
the railroad my mama said and got killed in an accident. Didn't
nobody in Bucolia have much. We children left school about the
age of ten, eleven, and worked in the field with the grown-ups.
Mighty little childhood then. Folks just didn't have the time they
do nowadays to play and get education. What I learned I learned
from Sunday school and from my mama. But that's the learning
stays with you. Cause it's God's truth. Some educated folks . . .

yes. Yes. Educated fools. We all know some like that.
But let's go on Miss Reba Love Jackson . . . unlike so many enter-
tainers especially your fellow gospel singers, you've been known
for a militant stance in the area of civil rights. Could you tell our
audience a little about your involvement in the Movement.

I never did understand no movement, nor no

97

politics, nor nothing like that. People just use my name and put me in that stuff. It's the songs I sing. If you listen those songs tell stories. They got words. And I've always believed in those words. That's why I sing them. And won't sing nothing else. God gave me a little strength and I ain't going to squander it on no Devil's work. We's all God's creatures and it ain't in the Bible to sit in the back of no buses or bow down to any man what ain't nothing but breath and britches. White or black ain't meant to rule God's children. He's the only Master.

right on. Right on, Sister.

Trouble is people don't listen to Gospel music. They pat they feet awhile then they go back on out in them mean streets. They Sunday Christians, so somebody can see them say, Look at Miss Jones in her new hat and new coat. Ain't she something. Go to church to be seen, don't go to hear the Word. That's what keeps the world the crying shame it is. There's a song says, This old world can't last much longer, Reeling and rocking so early in the morning. Another one says, They'll be Peace in the Valley someday. Sure enough, it's gonna come. But it's God trumpet say when. Ain't gon be them white folks telling nobody nothing. Not with their Atom bombs and Hydrogen bombs and naked women and selling people dope and liquor and blowing up little girls in church and dogs and hoses they keep just to hurt people with and every one of them from the President on down full of lies. No. We got to stop bleeding for white people and start leading ourselves in the path of righteousness. He gave His only begotten Son to show the way.

well you sure do tell it like it is . . . now could you say a little about how you got into show business . . . I mean how you rose up to become a household word to millions of your fans.

wasn't more'n five or six years ago outside of Memphis and we still going around in a raggedy old station wagon. Seven of us singers and no little people in the group. I remember cause Claretta, bless her soul, was sick and we have to stop every half hour or so and that road was hot and dusty and we had three hundred miles to go before we stop for good and had to sing when we got there and Claretta getting worse cause the car had to keep moving. These two cracker state patrols stop us and everybody out they say. And all us womens standing on that highway in the hot sun and these crackers laughing behind they dark glasses and talking about body searches. And talking nastier and nastier. Only thing save us Claretta she ain't said nothing she too scared like the rest of us to say a thing to these nasty patrol but I see her getting all pale like she did when we have to stop the car. Poor child can't hold it no longer and when she start to going right there standing up beside the road and moaning cause she's so ashamed, well that broke it all up and . . .

       yes, mam. I'm sure there are plenty of stories you could tell about the hardships of living in the South

          wasn't only South. You find some of your meanest crackers right here walking the streets of Philadelphia and New York. I been coming this way many a year and let me tell you

       our audience shares your indignation. We know the crosses you had to bear but I bet folks would like to hear how you rose from your humble beginnings to be a star

         God didn't gift me with no fine voice. But he did lay burdens on me and gave me strength to bear them. When I sing people know this. They hear their stories in my songs, that's all

        you're too modest. Miss Reba Love Jackson is an inspiring Christian lady. But they don't call her the Queen of Gospel for nothing. You've got to hear her to believe her. Get on down to the Uptown. Better be there bright and early for a good seat

         I ain't never had the voice of no Mahalia or Willie Mae Ford or none of them . . . but I listened to the best . . . I was raised on the best holy singing ever was. I remember them all coming to Bucolia . . . Kings of Harmony, Selah Jubilee Singers, the Heavenly Gospel Singers from Spartanburg, South Carolina, the Golden Gates, The Hummingbirds and Nightingales and the Mighty Mighty Clouds of Joy . . . and me sitting with my mama listening and thinking if I ever get to Heaven some day please, please, Jesus, let it be like this. Me at my mama's side and angels shaking the roots of the firmament with their voices. The old time people could sing and preach so good it was like they put their hands inside you and just rooted around till they found where you needed to be touched . . . they . . .

I'm sorry to cut you off but our time is running out and our audience wants to hear a little more about what to expect when they catch you at the Uptown . . . I have a piece in my hand written about one of your performances all the way across the pond in Gay Paree. Listen up, youall: "Reba Love Jackson galvanizes the audience . . . No lady on the stage but a roaring black pantheress, leaping, bounding, dancing her songs . . . she embodies what is primitive and powerful in the African soul."

that must be pretty old. Ain't been to Paris, France but once and that was long ago. They tell me I used to get pretty lively when I sang. Kicking up my heels and what not. To tell the truth I never thought much about it. I just sang the old songs and let them take me where they wanted to go. Now I been out here singing a long, long time. Can't hardly remember a time I ain't been out here singing and I'm getting like the fish when the water gets cold. They stop jitterbugging around and sink down to the bottom and lie real still and they be there on the bottom muck alright but you got to go down deep with something special to get them to move.

we'll go on believing what the French soul brother said about you Miss Reba Love Jackson. Our audience can judge for themselves . . . get a taste of that good old time religion when the Super Gospel Caravan pulls into the Uptown tonight. This is one fan who knows he won't be disappointed. I got a feeling Reba Love Jackson, Queen Mother of Gospel, you'll make these clippings seem tame . . . cut.

One for Her Birthday

It is June 19, her birthday, and she is sixty-five years old and celebrating by going to the ocean beach for the first time in her life. Atlantic City is like nothing she's ever seen. She is almost giddy in her new slacks suit (her mother never wore pants, not even to work in the fields) sitting it seems a mile above the Boardwalk in a cart driven by a black boy. The intermittently overcast day does not dissipate her spirits. Sheets of fine mist blown up from the water refresh when they daintily sprinkle her face. She had worried at first about her voice. The coarse salt air lodging in her throat and the horror of a cold when she faces the crowd in Convention Hall. But she felt fine. Her voice was a brawny animal still secure at the end of its leash. When she tugged it would be there, and she would turn it loose to do its work at the proper time. She tasted the salt on her tongue. The snapping flags, the striped umbrellas, the bright clothes of the passersby, the giant Ferris wheel blazing with light even in the middle of the afternoon, the calliope disembodied within the roar of the surf, everything she could see, smell, hear, and touch celebrated her birthday.

When the cart arrived at a section of beach littered with dark bodies, she commanded the boy to stop. She hadn't noticed colored bathers elsewhere on the white sand. The boy called back ". . . this Chickenbone Beach, mam," and she understood immediately. This was the place she'd been looking for all along even though she hadn't known it until that moment.

"Wait here please, young man." She was paying him by the hour so she knew he would. She was pleased by his obedience, by the extravagance of it all: a suite in the hotel, a taxi to the boardwalk, a new suit just because she wanted it. People knew her name. Strangers would come up to her on the street and say, You Reba Love, ain't you? Pleased to meet you Miss Reba Love. Leaning against the tubular railing which divided the boardwalk from the beach she rubbed her shoes then the nylon Peds from her feet, exposing wrinkled toes and battered, yellowing toenails. Bad feet. Looked like her mother's long toes splayed down there in the hot sand. Her orange bell-bottoms flap in the stiff breeze. As she marches toward the ocean the soles of her feet squeak with each step. The sand whispers, swishing like the sumptuous robes they wear on stage. Black bodies and ivory bodies and every shade between, halfnaked on the sand.

She thinks of her voice again when the first swirl of icy ocean water laps her toes. Backing away quickly she gasps and hikes up the razor creases of her slacks. Behind her the thumping of bongos and conga drums. In front the restless beard of her Father, a million shades of gray and frothy white. The ocean is too large, too restless. All the dead are out there. Rich and poor, black and white, saints and sinners. And plenty room for the living. Room for those bodies stretched like logs drying in the sun. The wind is furrowing the stiff bristles of her Father's beard, tangling them, caking them with dried spittle and foam as He roars His anger, His loneliness. Depths out there the living will never fill. In the thunder of the surf she can hear newborn babies crying.

The motion of the sea becalms the spinning earth. The breakers unraveling from the horizon freeze to a green shimmer. She wishes she could see His eyes. Eyes which never close and never open. His eyes wherever they are. She wants to see what He sees looking down on her bare head.

A gull shrieks. Then cold shackles draw tighter around her ankles. Holes are opening up in the earth, slowly, subtly, drawing her down. She knows if she does not muster her strength and flee, screaming horses will drag her with them under the waves.

One More Time for Blind Willie

Hate to talk about your mommy she's a good ole soul
She got a buck skin belly and a rubber asshole
Oh Shine, Shine, save poor me
I'll give you more white pussy than you ever did see

Blues verses and toasts and nasty rhymes keep the blind man awake with their spinning and signifying. Voices and voices within voices and half the laughter with him and half at him. The bouncer pitched Blind Willie down the steep, narrow stairs of the speakeasy. Old Willie tumbles out of control. "Told you not to come begging around here bothering the customers." Pitching down so many steps Willie can hear the parts of his body cracking as he falls helpless. So many knife-edged steps Blind Willie has time to fear the horrible impact at the bottom, how his body will be curled into the shape of an egg when he reaches the bottom and the last collision will crack him and scatter him.

Stagolee begged Billy,
"Oh please don't take my life.
I got three hungry children
And a very sickly wife."

First he had believed he was in hell when he awoke to all the moaning and groaning around him. A smell of chemicals in the air. Little teasing voices tormenting him. Then he knew he was still alive because he wasn't burning. He was cold, freezing cold. Colder than he'd ever been. He wished for newspapers to stuff under his clothes. He dreamed of the overcoat he lost in a coon-can game down by the railroad tracks. Heard himself singing about cold hearts and cold women. He was too cold to be dead. He was someplace where white people were talking and laughing.

White hands were peeling away his skin. White eyes lay on him like a blanket of snow. White feet stomped on his chest.

Shine, Shine . . .

The bouncer and the fall were black. Black hands had pushed him down the endless steps. But the crash, the dying into a thousand pieces are white.

Lord . . . Help me . . . Help me to hold out

If he could sing now it would be a saint's song. He is on his knees in the Amen Corner of the Temple. He is slamming his fists against the door which even in the darkness throbs red and hot as blood. He smells perfume. Hears a woman's hips, black hips swishing, rubbing against something trying to hold them in. He remembers undressing Carrie May. Pulling down her girdle. The texture of her goosebumpy skin and the rubbery panels. Then how silky she was, how soft with nothing on.

Nearer . . .

The perfume is a cloud over his head. He is swooning, he is trying to catch his breath, and hold his heart in his chest, and will his belly back down where it belongs so his lungs can fill with air. He is trying to remember the words to a song that gal, Reba Love Jackson sings. She is humming it to help him remember. She is smiling and saying *Come on . . . Come on in . . .* to his sweet tenor. They will sing together. One more time.

This Last Song's for Homewood

Whenever I cross these United States of America it does my heart good to stop here and see youall again. Some of you know I got roots here. Deep roots go way back. Lived here in Pittsburgh for a time. Mama worked for some white folks on Winebiddle Street. We lived in Homewood. Many a day I sat waiting for that trolley to bring my mama home. Stopped at Penn and Douglas Avenue and Mama had to walk five blocks to get home. And some of you knows how long five blocks can be after you been scuffling all day in the white people's kitchen. Yes Lawd. Doing all day for them then you got to ride a trolley and foot slog it five blocks and start to cooking and cleaning all over again for your own. It's a long mile. My mama walked it. Yes she did. We all been walking that long mile many a day. You know what I'm talking about. Yes you do, now. Reba Love Jackson ain't always been standing on stage singing praises to the Lawd. I sang His praises down on my knees, youall. *This is my story, This is my song.* Yes. *Praising my Savior. All the day long.* Sang with a scrub brush in my hand. Sometimes I think I ain't never sung no better than I did all by myself on my knees doing daywork in the white folks' kitchen. But I know something about Homewood. In the summertime I'd walk to meet Mama. I'd take her shopping bag and her hand and walk home beside her. I remember every step. Every tree and crack in the pavement from the trolley stop to our little rooms behind Mr. Macks's Grocery. Wasn't a happier little girl in the world than me when I was walking Mama home. Could tell you plenty about Homewood in those days but youall come to hear singing not talking and that's what I'm going to do now. Sing this last one for Homewood. . . .

Across the Wide Missouri

THE images are confused now. By time, by necessity. One is Clark Gable brushing his teeth with Scotch, smiling in the mirror because he knows he's doing something cute, grinning because he knows fifty million fans are watching him and also a beautiful lady in whose bathroom and bedroom the plot has him awakening is watching over his shoulder. He is loud and brisk and perfectly at ease cleaning his teeth before such an audience. Like he's been doing that number all his life. And when he turns to face the woman, to greet her, the squeaky clean teeth are part of the smile she devours. This image, the grinning, self-assured man at the sink, the slightly shocked, absolutely charmed woman whose few stray hairs betray the passion of her night with him, a night which was both endless and brief as the time between one camera shot fading and another bursting on the screen, may have been in *Gone With the Wind*, but then again just as likely not. I've forgotten. The image is confused, not clear in itself, nor clearly related to other images, other Rhett Butlers and Scarlett O'Hara's and movies flashing on and off with brief flurries of theme song.

It is spring here in the mountains. The spring which never really arrives at this altitude. Just threatens. Just squats for a day or a few hours then disappears and makes you suicidal. The teasing, ultimately withheld spring that is a special season here and should have its own name. Like Shit. Or Disaster. Or something of that order. The weather however has nothing to do with the images. Not the wind or the weather or anything I can understand forces this handsome man grinning at a mirror into my consciousness. Nor do geography or climate account for the inevitable suc-

cession—the river, the coins, the song, the sadness, the recollection—of other images toppling him and toppling me because it
happens no matter where I am, no matter what the season. In the
recollection there is a kind of unmasking. The white man at the
mirror is my father. Then I know why I am so sad, why the song
makes me cry, why the coins sit where they do, where the river
leads.

I am meeting my father. I have written the story before. He
is a waiter in the dining room on the twelfth floor of Kaufman's
Department Store. Not the cafeteria. Be sure you don't get lost
in there. He's in the nicer place where you get served at a table.
The dining room. A red carpet. Ask for him up there if you get
lost. Or ask for Oscar. Mr. Parker. You know Oscar. He's the head-
waiter up there. Oscar who later fell on hard times or rather hard
times fell on him so hard he can't work anywhere anymore. *Wasn't
sickness or nothing else. Just that whiskey. That's whiskey you see
in that corner can't even lift his head up off the table.* Ask for your
daddy, Mr. Lawson, or ask for Mr. Parker when you get to the
twelfth floor. I have written it before because I hear my mother
now, like a person in a book or a story instructing me. I wrote
it that way but it didn't happen that way because she went with
me to Kaufman's. As far as the twelfth floor anyway but she had
to pay an overdue gas bill at the gas company office and ride the
trolley back to Homewood and she had to see Dr. Barnhart and
wanted to be home when I got there. The whole idea of meeting
my father for lunch and a movie was hers and part of her idea
was just the two of us, Daddy and me, alone. So my mother pointed
to the large, red-carpeted room and I remember wanting to kiss
her, to wait with her at the elevators after she pushed the button
and the green arrow pointed down. If I had written it that way
the first time I would be kissing her again and smelling her perfume and hearing the bells and steel pulleys of the elevators and
staring again apprehensively through the back of my head at the
cavernous room full of white people and the black men in white
coats moving silently as ghosts but none of them my father.

The entrance way to the restaurant must have been wide. The
way overpriced restaurants are with the cash register off to one
side and aisles made by the sides of high-backed booths. Wide but

cordoned by a rope, a gold-braided, perhaps tasseled rope, stretched between brass, waist-high poles whose round, fluted bases could slide easily anywhere along the red carpet. A large white woman in a silky, floral patterned dress is standing like she always does beside the pole, and the gold rope swallows its own tail when she loops both ends into a hook at the top of one of the poles.

I must have said then to myself *I am meeting my father*. Said that to myself and to the woman's eyes which seemed both not to see me and to stare so deeply inside me I cringed in shame. In my shyness and nervousness and downright fear I must have talked a lot to myself. Outside the judge's chambers in the marble halls of the courthouse, years later waiting to plead for my brother, I felt the same intimidation, the same need to remind myself that I had a right to be where I was. That the messages coded into the walls and doors and ceilings and floors, into the substances of which they were made, could be confronted, that I could talk and breathe in the storm of words flung at me by the invisible architects who had disciplined the space in which I found myself.

Daddy. Daddy. I am outside his door in the morning. His snores fill the tiny room. More a storage closet than room, separated from the rest of the house so the furnace doesn't heat it. The bed is small but it touches three walls. His *door* is actually a curtain hanging from a string. We live on the second floor so I am out in the hall, on a landing above the icy stairwell calling to him. *Your father worked late last night. Youall better be quiet this morning so he can get some sleep*, but I am there, on the cold linoleum listening to him snore, smelling his sleep, the man smell I wonder now if I've inherited so it trails me, and stamps my things mine when my kids are messing around where they shouldn't be. I am talking to myself when he stirs in that darkness behind the curtain. He groans and the mattress groans under him and the green metal cot squeaks as he shifts to another place in his dreaming.

I say to myself, *Where is he?* I stare at all the black faces. They won't stay still. Bobbing and bowing into the white faces or gliding toward the far swinging doors, the closely cropped heads poised and impenetrable above mandarin collars. Toomer called the white faces petals of dusk and I think now of the waiters insinuating themselves like birds into clusters of petals, dipping silently, si-

lently depositing pollen or whatever makes flowers grow and white
people be nice to black people. And tips bloom. I am seeing it in
slow motion now, the courtship, the petals, the starched white coats
elegant as sails plying the red sea. In my story it is noise and a
blur of images. Dark faces never still long enough to be my father.

"Hey, Eddie, look who's here."

There is a white cloth on the table that nearly hangs to the
floor. My knees are lost beneath it, it's heavy as a blanket, but
Oscar has another white cloth draped over his arm and unfurls
it so it pops like a flag or a shoeshine rag and spreads it on top
of the other so the table is covered twice. When Oscar sat me down,
two cups and saucers were on the table. He went to get my father
and told me he'd be right back and fix me up and wasn't I getting
big and looked just like my daddy. He had scraped a few crumbs
from the edge of the table into his hand and grinned across the
miles of white cloth at me and the cups and saucers. While he was
gone I had nudged the saucer to see if it was as heavy as it looked.
Under the edge closest to me were three dimes. Two shiny ones
and one yellow as a bad tooth. I pushed some more and found
other coins, two fat quarters neither new nor worn. So there I was
at that huge table and all that money in front of me but too scared
to touch it so I slid the ten-pound cup and saucer back over the
coins and tried to figure out what to do. Knew I better not touch
the table cloth. Knew I couldn't help spotting it or smudging it
if my hand actually touched the whiteness. So I tried to shove the
money with the base of the saucer, work it over to the end of the
table so it'd drop in my hand, but I couldn't see what I was doing
and the cup rattled and I could just see that little bit of coffee in
the bottom come jumping up out the cup and me worried that
whoever had forgotten the quarters and dimes would remember
and surely come back for them, then what would I say would I
lie and they'd know a little nigger at a big snow white table like
this had to be lying, what else I'm gonna do but lie and everybody in the place know the thief had to be me and I was thinking
and worrying and wondering what my father would do if all those
people came after me and by that time I just went on and snatched
that money and catch me if you can.

"Look who's here, Eddie." And under my breath I said shut up

Mr. Oscar Parker, keep quiet man you must want everybody in here listening to those coins rattling in my pocket. Rattling loud as a rattlesnake and about to bite my leg through my new pants. Go on about your business, man. Look who ain't here. Ain't nobody here so why don't you go on away.

Then my father picked up the saucers and balled up the old top cloth in one hand, his long fingers gobbling it and tucking it under his arm. Oscar popped the new one like a shoeshine rag and spread it down over the table. Laid it down quiet and soft as new snow.

"Busboy'll git you a place setting. Eddie, you want one?"

"No. I'll just sit with him."

"Sure looks like his daddy."

"Guess he ought to."

"Guess he better."

I don't remember what I ate. I don't recall anything my father said to me. When I wrote this before there was dialogue. A lot of conversation broken by stage directions and the intrusions of restaurant business and restaurant noise. Father and son an island in the midst of a red-carpeted chaos of white people and black waiters and the city lurking in the wings to swallow them both when they take the elevator to the ground floor and pass through Kaufman's green glass revolving doors. But it didn't happen that way. We did talk. As much as we ever did. Both of us awkward and constrained as we still are when we try to talk. I forget all the words. Words were unimportant because what counted was his presence, talking or silent didn't matter. Point was he was with me and would stay with me the whole afternoon. One thing he must have asked me about was the movies. I believe I knew what was playing at every theater downtown and knew the address of every one and could have reeled off for him the names of the stars and what the ads said about each one. The images are not clear but I still can see the way the movie page was laid out. I had it all memorized but when he asked me I didn't recite what I knew, didn't even state a preference because I didn't care. Going with him was what mattered. Going together, wherever, was enough. So I waited for him at the table. Wondering what I had eaten, running my tongue around in my mouth to see if I could get a clue. Because the food had been served and I had wolfed it down but he was all I tasted. His presence my feast.

He came back without the white coat. He brought a newspaper with him and read to himself a minute then read me bits and pieces of what I knew was there. Him reading changed it all. He knew things I had never even guessed at when I read the movie page the night before. Why one show was jive, why another would be a waste of money, how long it would take to walk to some, how others were too far away. I wanted to tell him it didn't matter, that one was just as good as another, but I didn't open my mouth till I heard in his voice the one he wanted to see.

He is six foot tall. His skin is deep brown with Indian red in it. My mother has a strip of pictures taken in a five and dime, taken probably by the machine that was still in Murphy's 5&10 when Murphy's was still on Homewood Avenue when I was little. Or maybe in one of the booths at Kennywood Amusement Park which are still there. They are teenagers in the picture, grinning at the automatic camera they've fed a quarter. Mom looks pale, washed out, all the color stolen from her face by the popping flashbulbs. His face in the black and white snapshots is darker than it really is. Black as Sambo if you want to get him mad you can say that. Black as Little Black Sambo. Four black-as-coal spots on the strip. But if you look closely you see how handsome he was then. Smiling his way through four successive poses. Each time a little closer to my mother's face, tilting her way and probably busy with his hands off camera because by picture three that solemn grandmother look is breaking up and by the final shot she too is grinning. You see his big, heavy-lidded, long-lashed, theatrical eyes. You see the teeth flashing in his wide mouth and the consciousness, lacking all self-consciousness and vanity, of how good he looks. Black, or rather purple now that the photos have faded, but if you get past the lie of the color he is clearly one of those *brown-eyed, handsome men* people like Chuck Berry sing about and other people lynch.

"Here's a good one. Meant to look at the paper before now, but we been real busy. Wanted to be sure there was a good one but it's alright, got a Western at the Stanley and it's just down a couple blocks past Gimbels. Clark Gable's in it. *Across the Wide Missouri.*

The song goes something like this: *A white man loved an Indian Maiden* and la de da-/-la de da. And: *A-way, you've gone away . . . Across the wide Mis-sour-i.* Or at least those words are in it, I think. I think I don't know the words on purpose. For the same reason I don't have it on a record. Maybe fifteen or twenty times in the thirty years since I saw the movie I've heard the song or pieces of the song again. Each time I want to cry. Or do cry silently to myself. A flood of tears the iron color of the wide Missouri I remember from the movie. *A-way, we're gone a-way . . . Across the wide Missouri.* It's enough to have it in pieces. It's enough to have heard it once and then never again all the way through but just in fragments. Like a spring which never comes. But you see a few flowers burst open. And a black cloud move down a grassy slope. A robin. Long, fine legs in a pair of shorts. The sun hot on your face if you lie down out of the wind. The fits and starts and rhythms and phrases from the spring-not-coming which is the source of all springs that do come.

The last time I heard the song my son called it *Shenandoah.* Maybe that's what it should be called. Again I don't know. It's something a very strong instinct has told me to leave alone. To take what comes but don't try to make anything more out of it than is there. In the fragments. The bits and pieces. The coincidences like hearing my son hum the song and asking him about it and finding out his class learned it in school and will sing it on Song Night when the second grade of Slade School performs for their parents. He knew the words of a few verses and I asked him to sing them. He seemed pleased that I asked and chirped away in a slightly cracked, slightly breathless, sweet, second grade boy's voice.

Now I realize I missed the concert. Had a choice between Song Night and entertaining a visiting poet who had won a Pulitzer Prize. I chose — without even remembering *Across the Wide Missouri* — the night of too many drinks at dinner and too much wine and too much fretting within skins of words and too much, too much until the bar closed and identities had been defrocked and we were all cliches, as cliche as the syrupy Shenandoah, stumbling through the swinging doors out into Laramie's cold and wind.

I will ask my son to sing it again. I hope he remembers the words. Perhaps I'll cheat and learn a verse myself so I can say the lyrics rather than mumble along with the tune when it comes into my head. Perhaps I'll find a way to talk to my father. About things like his presence. Like taking me to the movies once, alone, just the two of us in a downtown theater and seeing him for the whole ninety minutes doing good and being brave and handsome and thundering like a god across the screen. Or brushing his teeth loudly in the morning at the sink. Because I understand a little better now why it happened so seldom. (Once?) It couldn't have been only once in all those years. The once is symbolic. It's an image. It's a blurring of reality the way certain shots in a film blur or distort in order to focus. I understand better now the river, the coins, the song, the sadness, the recollection. I have sons now. I've been with them often to the movies. Because the nature of my work is different from my father's. I am freer. I have more time and money. He must have been doing some things right or I wouldn't have made it. Couldn't have. He laughed when I told him years later about "finding money" on the table. I had been a waiter by then. In Atlantic City during summer vacations from school at the Morton Hotel on the Boardwalk. I knew about tips. About some people's manners and propriety. Why some people treat their money like feces and have a compulsion to conceal it, hide it in all sorts of strange places. Like under the edge of saucers. Like they're ashamed or like they get off playing hide and seek. Or maybe just have picked up a habit from their fathers. Anyway he laughed when I told him and said Oscar probably damned a couple of poor little old white ladies to hell for not leaving him a tip. Laughed and said, *They're probably burning in hell behind you "finding" that money.*

I understand a little more now. Not much. I have sons of my own and my father has grandsons and is still a handsome man. But I don't see him often. And sometimes the grandson who has his name as a middle name, the one who can say *Shenandoah* if he wants to call it that, doesn't even remember who his grandfather is. *Oh yeah,* he'll say. *Edgar in Pittsburgh, he'll say. Your father. Yeah. Yeah I remember now.*

But he forgets lots of things. He's the kind of kid who forgets lots of things but who remembers everything. He has the gift of feeling. Things don't touch him, they imprint. You can see it some-times. And it hurts. He already knows he will suffer for whatever he knows. Maybe that's why he forgets so much.

Rashad

*Rashad's home again. Nigger's clean and lean and driving
a mean machine. They say he's dealing now, dealing big in
the Big D, Deetroit. Rashad's into something, sure nuff.
The cat's pushing a silver Regal and got silver theads to
match. Yea, he's home again. Clean as he wants to be.
That suit ain't off nobody's rack. One of a kind. New as a
baby's behind. Driving a customized Regal with RASHAD
on the plate.*

IT was time for it to go, all of it. Nail and banner both. Time she
said as she eased out the nail on which it hung. Past time she thought
as she wiggled the nail and plaster trickled behind the banner, spattering the wall, sprinkling the bare floorboards in back of the chair
where the rug didn't reach. Like cheese, she thought. All these
old walls like rotten cheese. That's why she kept everybody's pictures on the mantelpiece. Crowded as it was now with photos of
children and grandchildren and nephews and nieces and the brown
oval-framed portraits of people already old when she was just a
child, crowded as it was there was no place else to put the pictures
of the people she loved because the rotten plaster wouldn't take
a nail.

The banner was dry and crinkly. Like a veil as she rolled it in
her hands, the black veils on the little black hats her mother had
worn to church. The women of Homewood A.M.E. Zion used to
keep their heads covered in church. Some like her Grandmother
Gert and Aunt Aida even hid their faces behind crinkly, black veils.
She rolled the banner tighter. Its backside was dusty, an arc of

mildew like whitish ash stained the dark cylinder she gripped in both hands. How long had the banner been hanging in the corner. How long had she been in this house on Finance street? How long had the Homewood streets been filling with snow in the winter and leaves in fall and the cries of her children playing in the sunshine? How long since she'd driven in the nail and slipped the gold-tasseled cord over it so the banner hung straight? No way to make the banner stand up on the mantelpiece with the photos so she'd pounded a nail into the wall behind the overstuffed chair cursing as she had heard the insides of the rotten wall crumbling, praying with each blow of the hammer the nail would catch something solid and hold. Because embroidered in the black silk banner was the likeness of her granddaughter Keesha, her daughter's first baby, and the snapshot from which the likeness on the banner had been made, the only photo anybody had of the baby, was six thousand miles away in her daddy's wallet.

Rashad had taken the picture with him to Vietnam. She had given it up grudgingly. Just before he left, Rashad had come to her wanting to make peace. He looked better than he had in months. I'm clean, Mom. I'm OK now, he'd said. He called her mom and sometimes she liked it and sometimes it made her blood boil. Just because he'd married her daughter, just because there'd been nobody when he was growing up he could call mom, just because he thought he was cute and thought she was such a melon head he could get on her good side by sweet talking and batting his droopy eyelashes and calling her mom, just because of all that, and six thousand miles and a jungle where black boys were dying like flies, just because of all that, if he thought she was going to put the only picture of her granddaughter in his hot, grabby, long-fingered hand, he better think again. But he had knocked at her door wanting to talk peace. Peace was in him the way he'd sat and crossed one leg over his knee, the way he'd cut down that wild bush growing out the top of his head, and trimmed his moustache and shaved the scraggly goat beard, peace was in his hands clasped atop his knees and in the way he leaned toward her and talked soft. I know I been wrong, Mom. Nobody knows better than me how wrong I been. That stuff makes you sick. It's like you ain't yourself. That monkey gets you and you don't care nothing about nobody. But

I'm OK now. I ain't sick now. I'm clean. I love my wife and love my baby and I'ma do right now, Mom.

So when he asked she had made peace too. Like a fool she almost cried when she went to the mantelpiece and pulled out the snapshot from the corner of the cardboard frame of Shirley's prom picture. She had had plans for the photo of her granddaughter. A silver frame from the window of the jewelry shop she passed every morning on her way to work. But she freed it from the top corner of the cardboard border where she had tucked it, where it didn't cover anything but the fronds of the fake palm tree behind Shirley and her tuxedoed beau, where it could stay and be seen till she got the money together for the silver frame, freed the snapshot and handed it to her granddaughter's daddy, Rashad, to seal the peace.

Then one day the package came in the mail. The postman rang and she was late as usual for work and missed her bus standing there signing for it and he was mad too because she had kept him waiting while she pulled a housecoat over her slip and buttoned it and tied a scarf around her head.

Sign right there. Right there where it says received by. Right there, lady. And she cut her eyes at him as if to say I don't care how much mail you got in that sack don't be rushing me you already made me miss my bus and I ain't hardly answering my door half naked.

I can read, thank you. And signs her name letter by letter as if maybe she can read but maybe she had forgotten how to write. Taking her own good time because his pounding on the door again after she hollered out, Just a minute, didn't hurry her but slowed her down like maybe she didn't quite know how to button a housecoat or wrap her uncombed hair in a scarf and she took her time remembering.

Thank you when she snatched the package and shut the door louder than she needed to. Not slamming it in the mailman's face but loud enough to let him know he wasn't the only one with business in the morning.

Inside, wrapped in pounds of tissue paper, was the banner. At first she didn't know what it was. She stared again at the rows of brightly colored stamps on the outside of the brown paper.

Rashad's name and number were in one corner, "Shirley and Mom" printed with the same little-boy purple crayon letters across the middle of the wrapping paper. Handfuls of white tissue inside a grayish box. Then the black silk banner with colored threads weaving a design into the material. She didn't know what it was at first. She held it in her fingertips at arm's length, righting it, letting it unfurl. It couldn't be a little fancy China doll dress Rashad had sent from overseas for Keesha, she knew that, but that's what she thought of first, letting it dangle there in her outstretched arms, turning it, thinking of how she'll have to iron out the wrinkles and be careful not to let her evil iron get too hot.

Then she recognized a child's face. Puffy-cheeked, smiling, with curly black hair and slightly slanting black eyes, the face of a baby like they have over there in the jungle where Rashad's fighting. A pretty picture with a tiny snowcapped mountain and blue lake worked into the background with the same luminous threads which raise the child's face above the sea of black silk. Though the baby's mouth is curled into a smile and the little mountain scene floating in the background is prettier than anyplace she has ever been, the banner is sad. It's not the deep creases she will have to iron out or the wrinkles it picked up lying in its bed of tissue paper. It's the face, something sad and familiar in the face. She saw her daughter's eyes, Shirley's eyes dripping sadness the way they were in the middle of the night that first time she ran home from Rashad. Pounding at the door. Shirley standing there shaking on the dark porch. Like she might run away again into the night or collapse there in the doorway where she stood trembling in her tracks. He hit me. He hit me, Mama. Shirley in her arms, little girl shudders. You can't fight him. He's a man, baby. You can't fight him like you're another man.

Shirley's eyes in the baby's face. They used to tease her, call Shirley *Chink* because she had that pale yellowish skin and big eyes that seemed turned up at the corners. Then she remembered the picture she had sent away with Rashad. She read the word in the bottom corner of the banner which had been staring at her all this time, the strip of green letters she had taken for part of the design till she saw her daughter's eyes in the baby face and looked closer and read *Keesha.*

How many years now had they been teasing Keesha about that picture hanging in the corner of the living room?

Take it down, Grammy. Please take that ugly thing down.

Can't do that, baby. It's you, baby. It's something special your daddy had made for you.

It's ugly. Don't look nothing like me.

Your daddy paid lots of money for that picture. Someday you'll appreciate it.

Won't never like nothing that ugly. I ain't no chinky-chinky Chinaman. That's what they always be teasing me about. I ain't no chinky baby.

How many years had the banner been there behind the big spaghetti gut chair in the dark corner of her living room? The war was over now. Rashad and the rest of the boys back home again. How long ago had a little yellow man in those black pajamas like they all wear over there held her granddaughter's picture in his little monkey hand and grinned at it and grinned at Rashad and taken the money and started weaving the face in the cloth. He's probably dead now. Probably long gone like so many of them over there they bombed and shot and burned with that gasoline they shot from airplanes. A sad, little old man. Maybe they killed his granddaughter. Maybe he took Rashad's money and put his own little girl's face on the silk. Maybe it's the dead girl he was seeing even with Keesha's picture right there beside him while he's sewing. Maybe that's the sadness she saw when she opened the package and saw again and again till she learned never to look in that corner above the mush springed chair.

Keesha had to be eleven now, with her long colty legs and high, round, muscley butt. Boys calling her on the phone already. Already getting blood in her cheeks if you say the right little boy's name. Keesha getting grown now and her sister Tammy right behind her. Growing up even faster cause she's afraid her big sister got a head start and she ain't never gonna catch up. That's right. That's how it's always gon be. You'll have to watch that child like a hawk. You think Keesha was fast? Lemme tell you something. You'll be wishing it was still Keesha you chasing when that Tammy goes flying by.

They get to that certain age and you can't tell them nothing.

No indeed. You can talk till you're blue in the face and they ain't heard a word. That's the way you were, Miss Ann. Don't be cutting your big China eyes at me because that's just the way you were. Talked myself blue in the face but it was Rashad this and Rashad that and I mize well be talking to myself because you were gonna have him if it killed you.

She unrolls the banner to make sure she didn't pull it too tight. It's still there, the bright threads still intact, the sad, dead child smiling up at her. The dead child across the ocean, her dead grand-daughter Kaleesha, her own stillborn son. When you looked at it closely you could see how thicker, colored threads were fastened to the silk with hundreds of barely visible black stitches. Thinner than spider's web the strands of black looped around the cords of gold and bronze and silver which gave the baby's face its mottled, luminous sheen. From a distance the colors and textures of the portrait blended but up close the child's face was a patchwork of glowing scars, as ugly as Keesha said it was. Rashad had paid good money for it sure enough but if the old man had wept when he made it, there must have been times when he laughed too. A slick old yellow man, a sly old dog taking all that good money and laughing cause it didn't matter whose face he stuck on that rag.

She had heard Rashad talk about the war. One of those nights when Shirley had run back home to Mama he had followed her and climbed through a basement window and fallen asleep down-stairs in the living room. She heard him before she saw him stretched out on her couch, his stingy brim tipped down over his eyes, his long, knobby-toed shoes propped up on the arm of the couch. His snores filled the room. She had paused on the steps, frightened by the strange rumbling noise till she figured out what it had to be. Standing above him in the darkness she'd wanted to smack his long shoes, knock the hat off his nose. He's the one. This is the nigger messing over my little girl. This the so-called man whipping on my baby. She thought of her sons, how she had to beg, how she just about had to get down on her knees and plead with them not to go to their sister's house and break this scrawny nigger's neck.

He's sick, Mama. He can't help it. He loves me and loves the baby. He came back sick from that filthy war. They made him sick again over there.

She looked down at Rashad sleeping on her couch. Even with the trench coat draped over his body she could see how thin he was. Skin and bones. Junkie thin because they just eat sugar, don't want nothing but sugar, it's all they crave when that poison gets hold to them. Her sons wanted to kill him and would have if she hadn't begged them on her knees.

She has to fight her own battles. Your sister's a grown woman. Stay away from there, please.

She had felt the darkness that night, heavy as wind swirling around her. She had come downstairs for a glass of wine, the sweet Mogen David in the refrigerator which once or twice a month would put her to sleep when nothing else would. She had a headache and her heart had been pounding ever since she opened the door and saw Shirley with Keesha in her arms standing on the porch. There had been calls earlier in the evening, and Keesha howling in the background and Shirley sobbing the second time and then it was midnight and what was she going to do, what could she say this time when the baby was finally asleep and the coffee cups were empty and there were just the two of them, two women alone in the middle of the night in that bright kitchen. Finally Shirley asleep too but then her stomach and her pounding heart turned her out of bed and she checked Shirley and the baby again and tipped down the steps needing that glass of wine to do the trick and there he was, the sound of his snoring before she saw him and then the night swirling like a wind so she was driven a thousand miles away from him, from his frail, dope-smelling bones under that raggedy trench coat, a thousand miles from him and anyone, anything alive.

It was his screaming which broke her sleep again, the last time that night or morning because one had bled into the other and she heard him yell like a man on fire and heard Shirley flying down the stairs and by the time she got herself together and into her robe and downstairs into the living room, Shirley was with him under the trench coat and both were quiet as if no scream had clawed sleep from her eyes and no terror had nearly ripped his skinny body apart.

Sunday morning then, too late and too tired to go to church then so it was the three of them at the table drinking coffee and nodding with that burden of no sleep from the night before, Shirley, Rashad, her own weary self at the table when he talked about the war.

I was a cook. Had me a good job. You know. Something keeps your butt away from the killing. A good job cause you could do a little business. Like, you know. A little hustle on the side. Like be dealing something besides beans to them crazy niggers. Little weed, little smack. You get it from the same gooks sold you the salt and pepper. Had me a nice little hustle going. Been alright too cept some brothers always got to be greedy. Always got to have it all. Motherfucker gon gorilla me and take my little piece of action. Say he's the man and I'm cutting in on his business. Well one thing led to another. Went down on the dude. Showed him he wasn't messing with no punk. Eyes like to pop out his head when I put my iron in his belly. You know like I thought that was that and the nigger was gon leave me alone but he set me up. Him and some of them jive MPs he's paying off they set me up good and I got busted and sent home. Still be in jail if I hadn't copped a plea on possession and took my dishonorable.

Yeah, they be killing and burning and fragging and all that mess but I only heard stories about it, I had me a good job, I was feeding niggers and getting niggers high. Getting them fat for the jungle. And getting my ownself as messed up as you see me now, sitting here at this table not worth a good goddamn to nobody.

She knew there was more to tell. She knew he had been in bad fighting once because her daughter was always reading the newspapers and calling her on the phone and crying and saying, He's dead, Mama. I know he's dead and my poor little girl won't never know her daddy. That was before his good job, before the dope he said was as easy to get as turning on a faucet. But he wouldn't talk about the fighting. He'd dream about the fighting and wake up screaming in the night but he wouldn't talk.

Now she had it down, rolled in her hands, and had to put the banner someplace. It was time to take it down, she knew that but didn't know where to put it now it was off her wall. Where the nail had been, a dug-out, crumbly looking hole gaped in the plaster. If she touched it, the rotten wall might crack from floor to ceiling, the whole house come tumbling down around her heels. A knuckle-sized chunk of wall gone but she could fix it with patch-ing plaster and in the dark corner nobody would hardly notice. The paint had sweated badly over the chair and a stain spread across the ceiling over the corner so one more little spot a different color than the rest wouldn't matter because the rest wasn't one color, the rest was leaks and patches and coming apart and faded and as tired of standing as she was tired of holding it up.

One day she'd like to tear the walls down. Go round with a hammer and knock them all down. She knew how the hammer would feel in her fist, she knew how good each blow would feel and she could hear herself shouting hallelujah getting it done.

But she needed someplace to put the banner. She was late as usual and Shirley and the girls would be by soon to go to church. Shirley might be driving Rashad's new car. On Sunday morning he sure wouldn't be needing it. Be dinnertime before he was up and around so he might give Shirley the keys so she could drive the girls to church in style. The girls loved their daddy and he loved them. When he came to town it was always a holiday for the girls. Presents and rides and money and a pretty daddy to brag on for months till he appeared again. She wondered how long it would be this time. How long he'd be flying high before somebody shot him or the police caught up with him and then he'd be dead or in jail again and he'd fall in love again with "Shirley and Mom."

Here she was with the banner still in her hand and the kitchen clock saying late, you're late woman and she's still in her robe, hasn't even filled the tub yet but she just had to stop what she was supposed to be doing and take it down. Well, when the girls come knocking at the door, calling and giggling and signifying and Shirley sits behind the wheel honking to rush her, she'll fling open the door and stuff it in their hands. It will be gone then. Someplace else then, because she never really wanted that sad thing in the first place. She didn't understand why she'd left it hanging this long, why she let it move in and take over that dark corner behind the chair. Because it was a sad thing. A picture of somebody wasn't ever in the family. More of Rashad's foolishness. Spending money when he has it like money's going out of style. Rashad living like a king and throwing a handful of money at the old yellow man when the banner is finished. Rashad living fast because he knows he's gonna die fast and the old chink grinning up at the black fool, raking in the dollars Rashad just threw on the floor like he got barrels of money, stacks of money and don't know how to give it away fast enough.

She loves him too. That handful of money he throws over his shoulder would feel like the hammer in her hand. She'll pray for Rashad today. And Tommy. So much alike. A long hard prayer and it will be like hoisting the red bricks of Homewood A.M.E. Zion on her shoulders and trying to lift the whole building or trying to lift all of Homewood. The trees and houses and sidewalks and all the shiny cars parked at the curb. It will be that hard to pray them home, to make them safe.

She starts up the stairs with the rolled banner still in her hand. She'll soak a little in the tub even if it makes her later. They can wait awhile. Won't hurt them to wait a little while. She's been waiting for them all the days of her life and they can just sit tight awhile because she needs to pray for them too. Pray for all of them and needs all her strength so she'll soak in the tub awhile.

At the top of the steps, at the place they turn and her sons have to stoop to get by without bumping their heads on the low ceiling, at that turning where she always stoops too, not because her head would hit if she didn't but because the slight bend forward of her body brings them back, returns her sons to this house where they all grew tall, taller than the ceiling so they had to stoop to get past the turning, at that place near the top of the stairs when she stoops and they are inside her again, babies again, she thinks of the old man sewing in his hut no bigger than a doghouse.

Rashad would lean in and hand him the photo. The peace offering she sent with him all those miles across the ocean. The old man would take the snapshot and look at it and nod when Rashad pointed to the banners and faces hanging in the hut. A little wrinkled old man. A bent old man whose fingers pained him like hers did in the morning. Swollen fingers and crooked joints. Hands like somebody been beating them with a hammer. She had kept it hanging this long because he had sewn it with those crippled fingers. She took it down because the old man was tired, because it was time to rest, because Keesha was almost grown now and her face was with the others decorating the mantel.

She saw him clearly at that turning of the stairs and understood the sadness in the eyes. The lost child she would pray for too.

Tommy

HE checks out the Velvet Slipper. Can't see shit for a minute in the darkness. Just the jukebox and beer smell and the stink from the men's room door always hanging open. Carl ain't there yet. Must be his methadone day. Carl with his bad feet like he's in slow motion wants to lay them dogs down easy as he can on the hot sidewalk. Little sissy walking on eggs steps pussyfooting up Frankstown to the clinic. Uncle Carl ain't treating to no beer to start the day so he backs out into the brightness of the Avenue, to the early afternoon street quiet after the blast of nigger music and nigger talk.

Ain't nothing to it. Nothing. If he goes left under the trestle and up the stone steps or ducks up the bare path worn through the weeds on the hillside he can walk along the tracks to the park. Early for the park. The sun everywhere now giving the grass a yellow sheen. If he goes right it's down the Avenue to where the supermarkets and the 5&10 used to be. Man, they sure did fuck with this place. What he thinks each time he stares at what was once the heart of Homewood. Nothing. A parking lot and empty parking stalls with busted meters. Only a fool leave his car next to one of the bent meter poles. Places to park so you can shop in stores that ain't there no more. Remembers his little Saturday morning wagon hustle when him and all the other kids would lay outside the A&P to haul groceries. Still some white ladies in those days come down from Thomas Boulevard to shop and if you're lucky get one of them and get tipped a quarter. Some of them fat black bitches be in church every Sunday have you pulling ten tons of rice and beans all the way to West Hell and be smiling and yakking all the way and saying what a nice boy you are and I knowed your mama when she was little and please sonny just set them inside on the table and still be smiling at you with some warm glass of water and a dime after you done hauled their shit halfway round the world.

Hot in the street but nobody didn't like you just coming in and sitting in their air conditioning unless you gonna buy a drink and set it in front of you. The poolroom hot. And too early to be messing with those fools on the corner. Always somebody trying to hustle. Man, when you gonna give me my money, Man, I been waiting too long for my money, Man, lemme hold this quarter till tonight, Man. I'm getting over tonight, Man. And the buses climbing the hill and turning the corner by the state store and fools parked in the middle of the street and niggers getting hot honking to get by and niggers paying them no mind like they got important business and just gonna sit there blocking traffic as long as they please and the buses growling and farting those fumes when they struggle around the corner.

Look to the right and to the left but ain't nothing to it, nothing saying move one way or the other. Homewood Avenue a darker gray stripe between the gray sidewalks. Tar patches in the asphalt. Looks like somebody's bad head with the ringworm. Along the curb ground glass sparkles below the broken neck of a Tokay bottle. Just the long neck and shoulders of the bottle intact and a piece of label hanging. Somebody should make a deep ditch out of Homewood Avenue and just go on and push the row houses and boarded storefronts into the hole. Bury it all, like in a movie he had seen a dam burst and the flood waters ripping through the dry bed of a river till the roaring water overflowed the banks and swept away trees and houses, uprooting everything in its path like a cleansing wind.

He sees Homewood Avenue dipping and twisting at Hamilton. Where Homewood crests at Frankstown the heat is a shimmering curtain above the trolley tracks. No trolleys anymore. But the slippery tracks still embedded in the asphalt streets. Somebody forgot to tear out the tracks and pull down the cables. So when it rains or snows some fool always gets caught and the slick tracks flip a car into a telephone pole or upside a hydrant and the cars just lay there with crumpled fenders and windshields shattered, laying there for no reason just like the tracks and wires are there for no reason now that buses run where the 88 and the 82 Lincoln trolleys used to go.

He remembers running down Lemington Hill because trolleys come only once an hour after midnight and he had heard the clatter of the 82 starting its long glide down Lincoln Avenue. The Dells still working out on *Why Do You Have to Go* and the tip of his dick wet and his balls aching and his finger sticky but he had forgotten all that and forgot the half hour in Sylvia's hallway because he was flying, all long strides and pumping arms and his fists opening and closing on the night air as he grappled for balance in a headlong rush down the steep hill. He had heard the trolley coming and wished he was a bird soaring through the black night, a bird with shiny chrome fenders and fishtails and a Continental kit. He tried to watch his feet, avoid the cracks and gulleys in the sidewalk. He heard the trolley's bell and crash of its steel wheels against the tracks. He had been all in Sylvia's drawers and she was wet as a dishrag and moaning her hot breath into his ear and the record player inside the door hiccuping for the thousandth time caught in the groove of gray noise at the end of the disc.

He remembers that night and curses again the empty trolley screaming past him as he had pulled up short half a block from the corner. Honky driver half sleep in his yellow bubble. As the trolley careened away red sparks had popped above its gimpy antenna. Chick had his nose open and his dick hard but he should have cooled it and split, been out her drawers and down the hill on time. He had fooled around too long. He had missed the trolley and mize well walk. He had to walk and in the darkness over his head the cables had swayed and sung long after the trolley disappeared.

He had to walk cause that's all there was to it. And still no ride of his own so he's still walking. Nothing to it. Either right or left, either up Homewood or down Homewood, walking his hip walk, making something out of the way he is walking since there is nothing else to do, no place to go so he makes something of the going, lets them see him moving in his own down way, his stylized walk which nobody could walk better even if they had some place to go.

Thinking of a chump shot on the nine ball which he blew and cost him a quarter for the game and his last dollar on a side bet. Of pulling on his checkered bells that morning and the black tank top. How the creases were dead and cherry pop or something on the front and a million wrinkles behind the knees and where his thighs came together. Junkie, wino-looking pants he would have rather died than wear just a few years before when he was one of the cleanest cats in Westinghouse High School. Sharp and leading the Commodores. Doo Wah Diddy, Wah Diddy Bop. Thirty-five-dollar pants when most the cats in the House couldn't spend that much for a suit. It was a bitch in the world. Stone bitch. Feeling like Mister Tooth Decay crawling all sweaty out of the gray sheets. Mom could wash them every day, they still be gray. Like his underclothes. Like every motherfucking thing they had and would ever have. Doo Wah Diddy. The rake jerked three or four times through his bush. Left there as decoration and weapon. You could fuck up a cat with those steel teeth. You could get the points sharp as needles. And draw it swift as Billy the Kid.

Thinking it be a bitch out here. Niggers write all over everything don't even know how to spell. Drawing power fists that look like a loaf of bread.

Thinking this whole Avenue is like somebody's mouth they let some jive dentist fuck with. All these old houses nothing but rotten teeth and these raggedy pits is where some been dug out or knocked out and ain't nothing left but stumps and snaggleteeth just waiting to go. Thinking, that's right. That's just what it is. Why it stinks around here and why ain't nothing but filth and germs and rot. And what that make me? What it make all these niggers? Thinking yes, yes, that's all it is.

Mr. Strayhorn where he always is down from the corner of Hamilton and Homewood sitting on a folding chair beside his ice-ball cart. A sweating canvas draped over the front of the cart to keep off the sun. Somebody said the old man a hundred years old, somebody said he was a bad dude in his day. A gambler like his own Granddaddy John French had been. They say Strayhorn whipped three cats half to death try to cheat him in the alley behind Dunfermline. Took a knife off one and whipped all three with his bare hands. Just sits there all summer selling iceballs. Old and can hardly see. But nobody don't bother him even though he got his pockets full of change every evening.

Shit. One of the young boys will off him one night. Those kids was stone crazy. Kill you for a dime and think nothing of it. Shit. Rep don't mean a thing. They come at you in packs, like wild dogs. Couldn't tell those young boys nothing. He thought he had come up mean. Thought his running buddies be some terrible dudes. Shit. These kids coming up been into more stuff before they twelve than most grown men do they whole lives.

Hard out here. He stares into the dead storefronts. Sometimes they get in one of them. Take it over till they get run out or set it on fire or it gets so filled with shit and nigger piss don't nobody want to use it no more except for winos and junkies come in at night and could be sleeping on a bed of nails wouldn't make no nevermind to those cats. He peeks without stopping between the wooden slats where the glass used to be. Like he is reading the posters, like there might be something he needed to know on these rain-soaked, sun-faded pieces of cardboard talking about stuff that happened a long time ago.

Self-defense demonstration . . . Ahmed Jamal. Rummage Sale. Omega Boat Ride. The Dells. Madame Walker's Beauty Products.

A dead bird crushed dry and paper-thin in the alley between Albion and Tioga. Like somebody had smeared it with tar and mashed it between the pages of a giant book. If you hadn't seen it in the first place, still plump and bird colored, you'd never recognize it now. Looked now like the lost sole of somebody's shoe. He had watched it happen. Four or five days was all it took. On the third day he thought a cat had dragged it off. But when he passed the corner next afternoon he found the dark shape in the grass at the edge of the cobblestones. The head was gone and the yellow smear of beak but he recognized the rest. By then already looking like the raggedy sole somebody had walked off their shoe.

He was afraid of anything dead. He could look at something dead but no way was he going to touch it. Didn't matter, big or small, he wasn't about to put his hands near nothing dead. His daddy had whipped him when his mother said he sassed her and wouldn't take the dead rat out of the trap. He could whip him again but no way he was gon touch that thing. The dudes come back from Nam talking about puddles of guts and scraping parts of people into plastic bags. They talk about carrying their own bags so they could get stuffed in if they got wasted. Have to court-martial his ass. No way he be carrying no body bag. Felt funny now carrying out the big green bags you put your garbage in. Any kind of plastic sack and he's thinking of machine guns and dudes screaming and grabbing their bellies and rolling around like they do when they're hit on Iwo Jima and Tarawa or the Dirty Dozen or the Magnificent Seven or the High Plains Drifter, but the scream-ing is not in the darkness on a screen it is bright, green afternoon and Willie Thompson and them are on patrol. It is a street like Homewood. Quiet like Homewood this time of day and bombed out like Homewood is. Just pieces of buildings standing here and there and fire scars and places ripped and kicked down and cars stripped and dead at the curb. They are moving along in single file and their uniforms are hip and their walks are hip and they are kind of smiling and rubbing their weapons and cats passing a joint fat as a cigar down the line. You can almost hear music from where Porgy's Record Shop used to be, like the music so fine it's still there clinging to the boards, the broken glass on the floor, the shelves covered with roach shit and rat shit, a ghost of the music rifting sweet and mellow like the smell of home cooking as the pa-trol slips on past where Porgy's used to be. Then . . .

Rat Tat Tat . . . Rat Tat Tat . . . Ra Ta Ta Ta Ta Ta Ta . . .

Sudden but almost on the beat. Close enough to the beat so it seems the point man can't take it any longer, can't play this soldier game no longer and he gets happy and the smoke is gone clear to his head so he jumps out almost on the beat, wiggling his hips and throwing up his arms so he can get it all, go on and get down. Like he is exploding to the music. To the beat which pushes him out there all alone, doing it, and it is Rat Tat Tat and we all want to fingerpop behind his twitching hips and his arms flung out but he is screaming and down in the dirty street and the street is ex-ploding all round him in little volcanoes of dust. And some of the others in the front of the patrol go down with him. No semblance of rhythm now, just stumbling, or airborne like their feet jerked out from under them. The whole hip procession buckling, shattered as lines of deadly force stitch up and down the Avenue.

Hey man, what's to it? Ain't nothing to it man you got it baby hey now where's it at you got it you got it ain't nothing to it something to it I wouldn't be out here in all this sun you looking good you into something go on man you got it all you know you the Man hey now that was a stone fox you know what I'm talking about you don't be creeping past me yeah nice going you got it all save some for me Mister Clean you seen Ruchell and them yeah you know how that shit is the cat walked right on by like he ain't seen nobody but you know how he is get a little something don't know nobody shit like I tried to tell the cat get straight nigger be yourself before you be by yourself you got a hard head man hard as stone but he ain't gon listen to me shit no can't nobody do nothing for the cat less he's ready to do for hisself Ruchell yeah man Ruchell and them come by here little while ago yeah baby you got it yeah lemme hold this little something I know you got it you the Man you got to have it lemme hold a little something till this evening I'll put you straight tonight man you know your man do you right I unnerstand yeah that's all that's to it nothing to it I'ma see you straight man yeah you fall on by the crib yeah we be into something tonight you fall on by.

Back to the left now. Up Hamilton, past the old man who seems to sleep beside his cart until you get close and then his yellow eyes under the straw hat brim follow you. Cut through the alley past the old grade school. Halfway up the hill the game has already started. You have been hearing the basketball patted against the concrete, the hollow thump of the ball glancing off the metal backboards. The ball players half naked out there under that hot sun, working harder than niggers ever did picking cotton. They shine. They glide and leap and fly at each other like their dark bodies are at the ends of invisible strings. This time of day the court is hot as fire. Burn through your shoes. Maybe that's why the niggers play like they do, running and jumping so much cause the ground's too hot to stand on. His brother used to play here all day. Up and down all day in the hot sun with the rest of the crazy ball players. Old dudes and young dudes and when people on the side waiting

for winners they'd get to arguing and you could hear them bad-
mouthing all the way up the hill and cross the tracks in the park.
Wolfing like they ready to kill each other.

His oldest brother John came back here to play when he brought
his family through in the summer. Here and Mellon and the courts
beside the Projects in East Liberty. His brother one of the old dudes
now. Still crazy about the game. He sees a dude lose his man and
fire a jumper from the side. A double pump, a lean, and the ball
arched so it kisses the board and drops through the iron. He could
have played the game. Tall and loose. Hands bigger than his
brother's. Could palm a ball when he was eleven. Looks at his long
fingers. His long feet in raggedy ass sneakers that show the crusty
knuckle of his little toe. The sidewalk sloped and split. Little plots
of gravel and weeds where whole paving blocks torn away. Past
the dry swimming pool. Just a big concrete hole now where people
piss and throw bottles like you got two points for shooting them
in. Drooping like a rusty spiderweb from tall metal poles, what's
left of a backstop, and beyond the flaking mesh of the screen the
dusty field and beyond that a jungle of sooty trees below the railroad tracks. They called it the Bums' Forest when they were kids
and bombed the winos sleeping down there in the shade of the
trees. If they walked alongside the track all the way to the park
they'd have to cross the bridge over Homewood Avenue. Hardly
room for trains on the bridge so they always ran and some fool
always yelling, *Train's coming* and everybody else yelling and then
it's your chest all full and your heart pumping to keep up with
the rest. Because the train couldn't kill everybody. It might get
the last one, the slow one but it wouldn't run down all the crazy
niggers screaming and hauling ass over Homewood Avenue. From
the tracks you could look down on the winos curled up under a
tree or sitting in a circle sipping from bottles wrapped in brown
paper bags. At night they would have fires, hot as it was some summer nights you'd still see their fires from the bleachers while you
watched the Legion baseball team kick butt.

From high up on the tracks you could bomb the forest. Stones
hissed through the thick leaves. Once in a while a lucky shot shattered a bottle. Some gray, sorry-assed wino motherfucker waking
up and shaking his fist and cussing at you and some fool shouts

He's coming, he's coming. And not taking the low path for a week because you think he was looking dead in your eyes, spitting blood and pointing at you and you will never go alone the low way along the path because he is behind every bush, gray and bloody-mouthed. The raggedy, gray clothes flapping like a bird and a bird's feathery, smothering funk covering you as he drags you into the bushes.

He had heard stories about the old days when the men used to hang out in the woods below the tracks. Gambling and drinking wine and telling lies and singing those old time, down home songs. Hang out there in the summer and when it got cold they'd loaf in the Bucket of Blood on the corner of Frankstown and Tioga. His granddaddy was in the stories. Old John French one of the baddest dudes ever walked these Homewood streets. Old, big-hat John French. They said his granddaddy could sing up a storm and now his jitterbug father up in the choir of Homewood A.M.E. Zion next to Mrs. Washington who hits those high notes. He was his father's son, people said. Singing all the time and running the streets like his daddy did till his daddy got too old and got saved. Tenor lead of the Commodores. Everybody saying the Commodores was the baddest group. If that cat hadn't fucked us over with the record we might have made the big time. Achmet backing us on the conga. Tito on the bongos. Tear up the park. Stone tear it up. Little kids and old folks all gone home and ain't nobody in the park but who supposed to be and you got your old lady on the side listening or maybe you singing pretty to pull some new fly bitch catch your eye in the crowd. It all comes down, comes together mellow and fine sometimes. The drums, the smoke, the sun going down and you out there flying and the Commodores steady taking care of business behind your lead.

"You got to go to church. I'm not asking I'm telling. Now you get those shoes shined and I don't want to hear another word out of you, young man." She is ironing his Sunday shirt hot and stiff. She hums along with the gospel songs on the radio. "Don't make me send you to your father." Who is in the bathroom for the half hour he takes doing whatever to get hisself together. Making everybody else late. Singing in there while he shaves. You don't want to be the next one after him. "You got five minutes, boy. Five minutes and your teeth better be clean and your hands and face shining." Gagging in the funky bathroom, not wanting to take a breath. How you supposed to brush your teeth, the cat just shit in there? "You're going to church this week and every week. This is my time and don't you try to spoil it, boy. Don't you get no attitude and try to spoil church for me." He is in the park now, sweating in the heat, a man now, but he can hear his mother's voice plain as day, filling up all the empty space around him just as it did in the house on Finance Street. She'd talk them all to church every Sunday. Use her voice like a club to beat everybody out the house.

His last time in church was a Thursday. They had up the scaffolding to clean the ceiling and Deacon Barclay's truck was parked outside. Barclay's Hauling, Cleaning and General Repairing. Young People's Gospel Chorus had practice on Thursday and he knew Adelaide would be there. That chick looked good even in them baggy choir robes. He had seen her on Sunday because his Mom cried and asked him to go to church. Because she knew he stole the money out her purse but he had lied and said he didn't and she knew he was lying and feeling guilty and knew he'd go to church to make up to her. Adelaide up there with the Young People's Gospel Chorus rocking church. Rocking church and he'd go right on up there, the lead of the Commodores, and sing gospel with them if he could get next to that fine Adelaide. So Thursday he left the poolroom, *Where you tipping off to, Man? None of your motherfucking business, motherfucker*, about seven when she had choir practice and look here, Adelaide, I been digging you for a long time. Longer and deeper than you'll ever know. Let me tell you something. I know what you're thinking, but don't say it, don't break my heart by saying you heard I was a jive cat and nothing to me and stay away from him he ain't no good and stuff like that I know I got a rep that way but you grown enough now to know how people talk and how you got to find things out for yourself. Don't be putting me down till you let me have a little chance to speak for myself. I ain't gon lie now. I been out here in the world and into some jive tips. Yeah, I did my time diddy bopping and trying my wheels out here in the street. I was a devil. Got into everything I was big and bad enough to try. Look here. I could write the book. Pimptime and partytime and jive to stay alive, but I been through all that and that ain't what I want. I want something special, something solid. A woman, not no fingerpopping young girl got her nose open and her behind wagging all the time. That's right. That's right, I ain't talking nasty, I'm talking what I know. I'm talking truth tonight and listen here I been digging you all these years and waiting for you because all that Doo Wah Diddy ain't nothing, you hear, nothing to it. You grown now and I need just what you got. . . .

Thursday rapping in the vestibule with Adelaide was the last time in Homewood A.M.E. Zion Church. Had to be swift and clean. Swoop down like a hawk and get to her mind. Tuesday she still crying and gripping the elastic of her drawers and saying No. Next Thursday the only singing she doing is behind some bushes in the park. *Oh, Baby. Oh, Baby, it's so good.* Tore that pussy up.

Don't make no difference. No big thing. She's giving it to somebody else now. All that good stuff still shaking under her robe every second Sunday when the Young People's Gospel Chorus in the loft beside the pulpit. Old man Barclay like he guarding the church door asking me did I come around to help clean. "Mr. Barclay, I wish I could help but I'm working nights. Matter of fact I'm a little late now. I'm gon be here on my night off, though."

He knew I was lying. Old bald head dude standing there in his coveralls and holding a bucket of Lysol and a scrub brush. Worked all his life and got a piece of truck and a piece of house and still running around yes sirring and no mamming the white folks and cleaning their toilets. And he's doing better than most of these chumps. Knew I was lying but smiled his little smile cause he knows my mama and knows she's a good woman and knows Adelaide's grandmother and knows if I ain't here to clean he better guard the door with his soap and rags till I go on about my business.

Ruchell and them over on a bench. Niggers high already. They ain't hardly out there in the sun barbecuing their brains less they been into something already. Niggers be hugging the shade till evening less they been into something.

"Hey now."

"What's to it, Tom?"

"You cats been into something."

"You ain't just talking."

"Ruchell man, we got that business to take care of."

"Stone business, Bruh. I'm ready to T.C.B. my man."

"You ain't ready for nothing, nigger."

"Hey man, we're gon get it together. I'm ready, man. Ain't never been so ready. We gon score big, Brother Man . . ."

They have been walking an hour. The night is cooling. A strong wind has risen and a few pale stars are visible above the yellow pall of the city's lights. Ruchell is talking:

"The reason it's gon work is the white boy is greedy. He's so greedy he can't stand for the nigger to have something. Did you see Indovina's eyes when we told him we had copped a truckload of color tee vees. Shit man. I could hear his mind working. Calculating like. These niggers is dumb. I can rob these niggers. Click. Click. Clickedy. Rob the shit out of these dumb spooks. They been robbing us so long they think that's the way things supposed to be. They so greedy their hands get sweaty they see a nigger with something worth stealing.

"So he said he'd meet us at the car lot?"

"That's the deal. I told him we had two vans full."

"And Ricky said he'd let you use his van?"

"I already got the keys, man. I told you we were straight with Ricky. He ain't even in town till the weekend."

"I drive up then and you hide in the back?"

"Yeah dude. Just like we done said a hundred times. You go in the office to make the deal and you know how Indovina is. He gon send out his nigger Chubby to check the goods."

"And you jump Chubby?"

"Be on him like white on rice. Freeze that nigger till you get the money from Indovina."

"You sure Indovina ain't gon try and follow us?"

"Shit, man. He be happy to see us split . . ."

" With his money?

"Indovina do whatever you say. Just wave your piece in his face a couple times. That fat ofay motherfucker ain't got no heart. Chubby his heart and Ruchell stone take care of Chubby."

"I still think Indovina might go to the cops."

"And say what? Say he trying to buy some hot tee vees and got ripped off? He ain't hardly saying that. He might just say he got robbed and try to collect insurance. He's slick like that. But if he goes to the cops you can believe he won't be describing us. Naw. The pigs know that greasy dago is a crook. Everybody knows it and won't be no problems. Just score and blow. Leave this mother-fucking sorry ass town. Score and blow."

"When you ain't got nothing you get desperate. You don't care. I mean what you got to be worried about? Your life ain't shit. All you got is a high. Getting high and spending all your time hustling some money so you can get high again. You do anything. Nothing don't matter. You just take, take, take whatever you can get your hands on. Pretty soon nothing don't matter, John. You just got to get that high. And everybody around you the same way. Don't make no difference. You steal a little something. If you get away with it, you try it again. Then something bigger. You get holt to a piece. Other dudes carry a piece. Lots of dudes out there hold-ing something. So you get it and start to carrying it. What's it mat-ter? You ain't nowhere anyway. Ain't got nothing. Nothing to look forward to but a high. A man needs something. A little money in his pocket. I mean you see people around you and on TV and shit. Man, they got everything. Cars and clothes. They can do something for a woman. They got something. And you look at yourself in the mirror you're going nowhere. Not a penny in your pocket. Your own people disgusted with you. Begging around your family like a little kid or something. And jail and stealing money from your own mama. You get desperate. You do what you have to do."

The wind is up again that night. At the stoplight Tommy stares at the big sign on the Boulevard. A smiling Duquesne Pilsner Duke with his glass of beer. The time and temperature flash beneath the nobleman's uniformed chest. Ricky had installed a tape deck into the dash. A tangle of wires drooped from its guts, but the sound was good. One speaker for the cab, another for the back where Ruchell was sitting on the rolls of carpet Ricky had stacked there. Al Green singing *Call Me*. Ricky could do things. Made his own

tapes; customizing the delivery van. Next summer Ricky driving
to California. Fixing up the van so he could live in it. The dude
was good with his hands. A mechanic in the war. Government
paid for the wasted knee. Ricky said, Got me a new knee now.
Got a four-wheeled knee that's gonna ride me away from all this
mess. The disability money paid for the van and the customizing
and the stereo tape deck. Ricky always have that limp but the cat
getting hisself together.

Flags were strung across the entrance to the used car lot. The
wind made them pop and dance. Rows and rows of cars looking
clean and new under the lights. Tommy parked on the street, in
the deep shadow at the far end of Indovina's glowing corner. He
sees them through the office window. Indovina and his nigger.

"Hey, Chubby."

"What's happening now?" Chubby's shoulders wide as the door.
Indovina's nigger all the way. Had his head laid back so far on
his neck it's like he's looking at you through his noseholes instead
of his eyes.

"You got the merchandise?" Indovina's fingers drum the desk.

"You got the money?"

"Ain't your money yet. I thought you said two vans full."

"Can't drive but one at a time. My partner's at a phone booth
right now. Got the number here. You show me the bread and he'll
bring the rest."

"I want to see them all before I give you a penny."

"Look, Mr. Indovina. This ain't no bullshit tip. We got the stuff,
alright. Good stuff like I said. Sony portables. All the same . . . still
in the boxes."

"Let's go look."

"I want to see some bread first."

"Give Chubby your keys. Chubby, check it out. Count em. Make
sure the cartons ain't broke open."

"I want to see some bread."

"Bread. Bread. My cousin DeLuca runs a bakery. I don't deal
with bread. I got money. See. That's money in my hand. Got plenty
money buy your television sets buy your van buy you."

"Just trying to do square business, Mr. Indovina."

"Don't forget to check the cartons. Make sure they're sealed."

Somebody must be down. Ruchell or Chubby down. Tommy had heard two shots. He sees himself in the plate glass window. In a fishbowl and patches of light gliding past. Except where the floodlights are trained, the darkness outside is impenetrable. He cannot see past his image in the glass, past the rushes of light slicing through his body.

"Turn out the goddamn light."

"You kill me you be sorry . . . kill me you be real sorry . . . if one of them dead out there it's just one nigger kill another nigger . . . you kill me you be sorry . . . you killing a white man . . ."

Tommy's knee skids on the desk and he slams the gun across the man's fat, sweating face with all the force of his lunge. He is scrambling over the desk, scattering paper and junk, looking down on Indovina's white shirt, his hairy arms folded over his head. He is thinking of the shots. Thinking that everything is wrong. The shots, the white man cringing on the floor behind the steel desk. Him atop the desk, his back exposed to anybody coming through the glass door.

Then he is running. Flying into the darkness. He is crouching so low he loses his balance and trips onto all fours. The gun leaps from his hand and skitters toward a wall of tires. He hears the pennants crackling. Hears a motor starting and Ruchell calling his name.

"What you mean you didn't get the money? I done wasted Chubby and you ain't got the money? Aw shit. Shit. Shit."

He had nearly tripped again over the man's body. Without knowing how he knew, he knew Chubby was dead. Dead as the sole of his shoe. He should stop; he should try to help. But the body was lifeless. He couldn't touch . . .

Ruchell is shuddering and crying. Tears glazing his eyes and he wonders if Ruchell can see where he's going, if Ruchell knows he is driving like a wild man on both sides of the street and weaving in and out the lines of traffic. Horns blare after them. Then it's Al Green up again. He didn't know how, when or who pushed the button but it was Al Green blasting in the cab. *Help me Help me Help me . . .*

Jesus is waiting . . . He snatches at the tape deck with both hands to turn it down or off or rip the goddamn cassette from the machine.

"Slow down, man. Slow down. You gonna get us stopped." Rolling down his window. The night air sharp in this face. The whir of tape dying then a hum of silence. The traffic sounds and city sounds pressing again into the cab.

"Nothing. Not a goddamn penny. Wasted the dude and we still ain't got nothing."

"They traced the car to Ricky. Ricky said he was out of town. Told them his van stolen when he was out of town. Claimed he didn't even know it gone till they came to his house. Ricky's cool. I know the cat's mad, but he's cool. Indovina trying to hang us. He saying it was a stickup. Saying Chubby tried to run for help and Ruchell shot him down. His story don't make no sense when you get down to it, but ain't nobody gon to listen to us."

"Then you're going to keep running?"

"Ain't no other way. Try to get to the coast. Ruchell knows a guy there can get us IDs. We was going there anyway. With our stake. We was gon get jobs and try to get it together. Make a real try. We just needed a little bread to get us started. I don't know why it had to happen the way it did. Ruchell said Chubby tried to go for bad. Said Chubby had a piece down in his pants and Ruchell told him to cool it told the cat don't be no hero and had his gun on him and everything but Chubby had to be a hard head, had to be John Wayne or some goddamned body. Just called Ruchell a punk and said no punk had the heart to pull the trigger on him. And Ruchell, Ruchell don't play, brother John. Ruchell blew him away when Chubby reached for his piece."

"You don't think you can prove your story?"

"I don't know, man. What Indovina is saying don't make no sense, but I heard the cops ain't found Chubby's gun. If they could just find that gun. But Indovina, he a slick old honky. That gun's at the bottom of the Allegheny River if he found it. They found mine. With my prints all over it. Naw. Can't take the chance. It's Murder One even though I didn't shoot nobody. That's long, hard time if they believe Indovina. I can't take the chance. . . ."

"Be careful, Tommy. You're a fugitive. Cops out here think they're Wyatt Earp and Marshall Dillon. They shoot first and maybe ask questions later. They still play wild, wild West out here."

"I hear you. But I'd rather take my chance that way. Rather they carry me back in a box than go back to prison. It's hard out there, Brother. Real hard. I'm happy you got out. One of us got out anyway."

"Think about it. Take your time. You can stay here as long as you need to. There's plenty of room."

"We gotta go. See Ruchell's cousin in Denver. Get us a little stake then make our run."

"I'll give you what I can if that's what you have to do. But sleep on it. Let's talk again in the morning."

"It's good to see you, man. And the kids and your old lady. At least we had this one evening. Being on the run can drive you crazy."

"Everybody was happy to see you. I knew you'd come. You've been heavy on my mind since yesterday. I wrote a kind of letter to you then. I knew you'd come. But get some sleep now . . . we'll talk in the morning."

"Listen, man. I'm sorry, man. I'm really sorry I had to come here like this. You sure Judy ain't mad?"

"I'm telling you it's OK. She's as glad to see you as am. . . . And you can stay . . . both of us want you to stay.

"Running can drive you crazy. From the time I wake in the morning till I go to bed at night, all I can think about is getting away. My head ain't been right since it happened."

"When's the last time you talked to anybody at home?"

"It's been a couple weeks. They probably watching people back there. Might even be watching you. That's why I can't stay. Got to keep moving till we get to the coast. I'm sorry, man. I mean nobody was supposed to die. It was easy. We thought we had a perfect plan. Thieves robbing thieves. Just score and blow like Ruchell said. It was our chance and we had to take it. But nobody was supposed to get hurt. I'd be dead now if it was me Chubby pulled on. I couldna just looked in his face and blown him away. But Ruchell don't play. And everybody at home. I know how they must feel. It was all over TV and the papers. Had our names and where we lived and everything. Goddamn mug shots in the Post Gazette. Looking like two gorillas. I know it's hurting people. In a way I wish it had been me. Maybe it would have been better.

I don't really care what happens to me now. Just wish there be some way to get the burden off Mama and everybody. Be easier if I was dead."

"Nobody wants you dead. . . . That's what Mom's most afraid of. Afraid of you coming home in a box."

"I ain't going back to prison. They have to kill me before I go back in prison. Hey. man. Ain't nothing to my crazy talk. You don't want to hear this jive. I'm tired, man. I ain't never been so tired. . . . I'ma sleep . . . talk in the morning, Big Brother."

He feels his brother squeeze then relax the grip on his shoulder. He has seen his brother cry once before. Doesn't want to see it again. Too many faces in his brother's face. Starting with their mother and going back and going sideways and all of Homewood there if he looked long enough. Not just faces but streets and stories and rooms and songs.

Tommy listens to the steps. He can hear faintly the squeak of a bed upstairs. Then nothing. Ruchell asleep in another part of the house. Ruchell spent the evening with the kids, playing with their toys. The cat won't ever grow up. Still into the Durango Kid, and Whip Wilson and Audie Murphy wasting Japs and shit. Still Saturday afternoon at the Bellmawr Show and he is lining up the plastic cowboys against the plastic Indians and boom-booming them down with the kids on the playroom floor. And dressing up the Lone Ranger doll with the mask and guns and cinching the saddle on Silver. Toys like they didn't make when we were coming up. And Christmas morning and so much stuff piled up they'd be crying with exhaustion and bad nerves before half the stuff unwrapped. Christmas morning and they never really went to sleep. Looking out the black windows all night for reindeer and shit. Cheating. Worried that all the gifts will turn to ashes if they get caught cheating, but needing to know, to see if reindeer really can fly.

Solitary

TO reach the other world you changed buses twice. The first bus took you downtown and there you caught another to the Northside. Through the Golden Triangle, across the Sixth Street Bridge, the second bus shuttled you to Reed Street on the Northside where you waited for one of the infrequent expresses running out Allegheny River Boulevard to the prison. With perfect connections the trip might take an hour and three quarters each way but usually a whole day was consumed getting there and getting back with the visit to her son sandwiched between eternities of waiting. Because the prison was in another world. She hadn't understood that at first. She had carried with her into the prison her everyday expectations of people, her sense of right and wrong and fairness. But none of that fit. The prison mocked her beliefs. Her trips to see her son were not so much a matter of covering a certain distance as they were of learning the hostile nature of the space separating her from him, learning how close and how far away he would always be. In the time it took to blink, the time it took for a steel gate to slam shut behind her, he would be gone again, a million miles away again and the other world, gray and concrete, would spring up around her, locking him away as abruptly as the prison walls.

One Sunday, walking the mile from the prison gate to the unsheltered concrete island which served as a bus stop and shivering there for over an hour in freezing November rain she had realized the hardships connected with the visits to her son were not accidental. The trips were supposed to speak to her plainly. Somebody had arranged it that way. An evil somebody who didn't miss a trick.

They said to reach him you must suffer, you must fight the heat and cold, you must sit alone and be beaten by your thoughts, you must forget who you are and be prepared to surrender your dignity just as you surrender your purse to the guard caged outside the waiting room entrance. In the prison world, the world you must die a little to enter, the man you've traveled so far to see is not your son but a number. He is P3694 and you must sit on a hard, wooden bench in a filthy waiting room until that number is called. Then it's through steel doors and iron bars and buzzing machines which peek under your clothes. Up stairs and down stairs and across a cobbled corridor dark and chill even in summer and you are inside then and nothing you have brought from the outside counts. Not your name, your pain, your love. To enter you must be prepared to leave everything behind and be prepared when you begin the journey home to lose everything again.

That is the trip she must take to see him. Not hours and buses but a brutal unraveling of herself. On the way back she must put herself together again, compose herself, pretend the place she has been doesn't exist, that what surrounds her as the bus lumbers along the Boulevard is familiar and real, that the shopping center and factories and warehouses crowding the flanks of Allegheny River Boulevard served some useful, sane purpose and weren't just set out to taunt her, to mock her helplessness. Slowly she'd talk herself into believing again. This bus will take me to Reed. Another will cross the bridge into town. I'll catch the 88 and it will shudder over the Parkway and drop me five blocks from home. And when I am home again I will be able to sit down in the brown chair and drink a cup of coffee and nod at some foolishness on TV, and nothing I do, none of these little lies which help me home again will hurt him or deny him. Because he is in another world, a world behind stone walls higher than God's mercy.

Sometimes she says that to herself, says the prison is a place her God has forsaken. But if He is not there, if His Grace does not touch her son then she too is dwelling in the shadow of unlove. If she can make the journey to the Valley of the Shadow, surely He could penetrate the stone walls and make His presence known. She needs weeks sometimes to marshall her strength for the trip. She knows what it costs her: the sleepless nights, the rage and helplessness, the utter trembling exhaustion bracketing the journey. How she must fight back tears when she sees his face, hears his voice. How guilt and anger alternate as she avoids people's faces and shrinks into a corner of a bus. She prays the strangers won't see her secrets, won't laugh at her shame, won't shatter in the icy waves of hatred pouring from her frozen heart. She knows her blood pressure will soar sky high and the spasms of dizziness, of nausea will nearly knock her off her feet. She needed weeks to prepare for all of that and weeks of recovering before she gathered strength enough to begin planning another trip, but she rode the buses and walked the miles and waited the eternities. Surely the walls weren't too tall, too thick for Him. He could come as a cloud, as a cleansing wind.

The prison was built close to the river. She wondered if the men could see it from their cells. She had meant to ask Tommy. And if her son could see it, would the river flowing past make him feel better or feel worse. In spring the sloping bank beyond the iron fence of the visitors' parking lot turned green. The green wasn't fair, didn't make sense when she noticed it for the first time as she stopped in the asphalt and gravel margin between the prison's outer wall and the ten-foot-tall iron fence along the river. A border of green edging the brown river which didn't make sense either as she stopped to blow her nose. For a moment as she paused and stared across the water everything was absolutely still. A wad of tissue was balled in her fist, the river glided brownly, silently past but nothing else was real. Everything so still and quiet she believed that she had fallen out of time, that she had slipped into an empty place between worlds, a place unknown, undreamed of till that moment, a tiny crack between two worlds that was somehow in its emptiness and stillness vaster than both.

The green was sectioned by the iron spears of the fence. Between the sharp points of the spears clusters of spikes riveted to the top railing of the fence glittered in the sun. The sky was blue, the river brown, the grass green. The breeze off the water whispered spring and promised summer but God let his sunshine play in the crowns of needle-pointed spikes. Near the top of the wall she could make out a row of windows deeply recessed, darker than the soot-grimed stones. If Tommy was standing at one of the screened windows could he see the river, the green, the gray pit into which she had slipped?

A coal barge hooted. She stuffed her tissue back in her purse. She thought she could hear the men's voices echoing from behind the walls, voices far away in a cave, or deep inside a tunnel, a jumbled, indistinct murmur out of which one voice would eerily rise and seem to mutter inches from her ear. If she could, she would have run from the yard. The voices hated her. They screamed obscenities and made fun of everything about her. She didn't have the strength to run but wouldn't have run if she could because that would only give them more to laugh at, would bring them howling and nipping at her heels as she fled to the bus stop.

From the visitors' entrance to the bus stop was a walk of nearly a mile. A nameless street paralleled one black prison wall, then crossed a flat, barren stretch of nothing before it intersected Allegheny River Boulevard. From the bus stop she looked back at the emptiness surrounding the prison. The dark walls loomed abrupt and stark. Like the green river bank the walls had no reason to be there, nothing connected them to the dusty plain of concrete. The walls were just there, like the lid of a roasting pan some giant hand had clamped down. It made no sense but it was there and no one could move it, no one was trying to disturb the squat black shape even though her son was dying beneath it.

This is the church and this is the steeple. Open the doors and out come the people. She let her hands form what she was thinking. Her wiggling fingers were ants scrambling for a wedge of daylight.

Her God had razed the proud walls of Jericho with nothing more than screaming horns. She let her hands fall to her sides and closed her eyes, but the walls were still there when she looked again.

On the first of the buses back to Homewood she tried to think of what she'd say to the others. What she would tell them when they asked, How is he? Should she say he's a million miles away? That his name is different in the other world? That he is heavier, thicker in the shoulders, but the baggy prison clothes hang loosely on his body so he seems like a little boy? Should she say his bitterness toward her is mellowing? Or does his anger hurt her less now only because she has listened so many times to his accusations? He says he has relived every single moment of his life. He turns the days over and over, asking questions, reconstructing incidents, deciding what he should have done, analyzing what he did do and what others did to him. In the story of his life which he dreams over and over again, she comes up a villain. Her love, her fears are to blame. She held the reins too tightly or she let him run loose; she drowned him in guilt with her constant questions, her tears at his slightest trespass or she didn't ever really pay enough attention to him. His hurting words would tear her down. She'd stop trying to defend herself, grow numb. His voice would fade from her consciousness and her mind would wander to a quieter, safer place. She'd daydream and free herself from the choking web of his bitterness. She'd want to ask him why he thought she made these wearying journeys. Did he think she came to be whipped? Did he think he had a right to take out his frustrations on her just because she was the only one who'd listen, who'd travel the million miles to where he was caged? But she wouldn't ask those questions. She'd listen till she drifted to that leaden, numb place where nothing could touch her. If someone to scream at was what he needed, she'd be that someone.

She wouldn't tell them anything like that when they asked, How is he? At the bus stop on Reed Street she rehearsed what she would say, what she always said, *Better. He's doing better. It's a hateful place but he's doing better.* Corrugated tin sheeting and transparent plastic panels formed a back and slanting half-roof partially enclosing the platform. Like standing in a seashell when the roar of traffic buffeted her. This morning only an occasional car rumbled by. All over town they were ripping up the old trolley tracks and asphalting their cobblestone beds but at this end of Reed Street anything that moved rattled against the cobbles like it was coming apart. She was alone till a boy crossing from the far side of the street joined her on the platform. His transistor radio was big as a suitcase and his music vibrated the shelter's tin roof. He was skinny like Tommy had been. A string bean, bean pole like her son Tommy and like him this one pranced when he walked and danced to the music while he was standing still.

Tommy was *Salim* now. She had told them his new name but she had no words for what had happened to his eyes, his cheekbones, the deepening shadows in his face. To herself she'd say his eyes burned, that his flesh was on fire, that the bones of his face were not hard and white, but something kindling beneath his skin, that the fire burned with sharp knife edges and his skin hung on the points of flame and the dark hollows of his face were where the fire shone blackly through his brown skin. His eyes screamed at her. It hurt him to be what he was, where he was, but he had no words for it either. Only the constant smoldering of his flesh, the screaming of his eyes.

"He's stronger much stronger. The Muslim business and the new name scare me but it's something for him to hold on to. They have their own little group. It gives him a chance to be somebody. He has his bad days of course. Especially now that the weather's getting nice. He has his bad days but he's made up his mind that he's going to stay on top of it. He's going to survive."

She'd say that. She'd answer with those words each time one of them asked about him. She'd say the words again and again till she was certain she believed them, till she was certain the words were real.

He'd been in the Behavior Modification Unit six weeks now. Six weeks out of the six months of solitary confinement they'd slapped on him. They called it the B.M.U., the Hole. To her it was a prison within a prison. Something worse happening after she thought she'd faced the worst. Twenty-three hours a day locked in his cell. Forty-five minutes of exercise in the yard if a guard was free to supervise him. If not, tough. Twenty-four hours alone in a ten by eight box. One meal at eleven, the other at two. *If you could call them meals, Mom.* Nothing till the next eleven o'clock meal except coffee and a hunk of bread when he was awakened. Two meals in three hours and no food for the next twenty-one. A prison within a prison. A way of telling him and telling her never to relax, never to complain because things could always get worse.

Instead of staying on the last bus till it reached her stop she got off at Frankstown and Homewood. They had both stood when the visiting room guard called his number. Tommy had wrapped his arms around her and hugged her, drawn her as close as he could to the fires alive inside him. Then he had turned from her quickly, striding across the scarred floor toward the steel gate from which he had entered. He hadn't turned back to look at her. The smell of him, the warmth, the strength of his arms circling her so suddenly had taken her breath away. She had wanted to see his face again, had almost cried out at those shoulders which were a man's now, which sloped to his arms and long, dangling hands and tight round butt and gangly legs with his bare ankles hanging down out of the high water prison pants. She had believed nothing could hurt more than the bottled-up anger he spewed at her but she had been wrong. The hug hurt more. His arms loving her hurt more. And when he turned like a soldier on his heel and marched away from her, eyes front, punishing the floor in stiff, arm rigid strides she was more alone than she had ever been while he raged.

So she stepped off the bus at Frankstown and Homewood because she didn't want to be alone, didn't want to close her front door behind her and hear the bolts and chains clicking home in the stillness, and didn't want to greet the emptiness which would rush at her face, pelt it like the dusty, littered wind when it raced across the barren plain outside the prison walls.

This was his street, Tommy's stomping ground. One hot summer night they'd burned it. Looted and burned Homewood Avenue so the block between Hamilton and Kelley was a wasteland of vacant lots and blackened stone foundations and ramshackle wooden barricades guarding the craters where stores and shops had once done business. This was the same Homewood Avenue her Daddy had walked. Taller than the buildings in his high-crowned, limp-brimmed hat. Big-hat John French strutting like he owned Homewood and on his good nights he probably did, yes, if all the stories she had heard about him were true, he probably did own it. Her father, her sons, the man she married, all of them had walked up and down Homewood Avenue so she got off before her stop because she didn't want to be alone. They'd walk beside her. She could windowshop in Murphy's 5&10, listen to the music pouring from the open door of the Brass Rail and Porgy's Record Shop, look at the technicolored pictures advertising coming attractions at the Bellmawr Show. She could hear it and see it all, and walk in the company of her men even though the storefronts were boarded or demolished altogether or transformed to unfamiliar, dirty-looking shops and her men were gone, gone, gone.

148

On the far corner of Homewood and Kelley the brick and stone Homewood A.M.E. Zion church stood sturdy and solid as a rock. She almost crossed over to it. Almost climbed the cement steps and pushed through the red door. She knew she'd find silence there and knew at the foot of the purple-carpeted aisle she could drop to her knees in a familiar place and her God would listen. That if she left her pride in the ravaged street and abandoned her hate and put off her questions He would take her to His bosom. He would bathe her in the fount of His Grace and understand and say well done. She almost stepped off the broken curb and ran to His embrace but the stolid church they had purchased when white people started running away from Homewood didn't belong on the Avenue this afternoon. She stared at it like she'd stared at the prison and the green river bank. He had to have a plan. For her life or anybody's life to make sense He had to have a plan. She believed that and believed the plan would reveal His goodness but this long day she could only see gaps and holes, the way things didn't connect or make sense.

Now she knows she is walking to the park. Homewood Avenue with its ghosts and memories was not what had drawn her off the bus early. Homewood Avenue was just a way to get somewhere and clearly now she understood she was walking toward the park.

She turned left at Hamilton, the street where the trolleys used to run. Then past the library where the name of her great uncle Elmer Hollinger was stamped on the blackened bronze plaque with the rest of the Homewood veterans of World War I. The family went back that far. And farther when you listened to May and Gert tell about the days when bears and wildcats lived in Homewood and Great-great-grandfather Charley Bell was the one first chopped down a tree here. Past the library then across Hamilton and up the hill alongside old Homewood school. The building in which she had started first grade was still standing. Tinny looking outcroppings and temporary sheds hid most of the old walls but her grade school was still standing. Somewhere she had a picture of her third grade class posed on the front steps, between the thick columns which supported the porch of old Homewood school. More white faces than black in those days, and long aproned dresses, and stiff collars and she is a pale spot at the end of one row, couldn't tell she was colored unless you looked real close and maybe not even then. No one was smiling but she remembered those days as happy, as easy, days she quickly forgot so each morning was like starting life all over again, new and fresh. Past the school yard where they're always playing basketball, past the pool the city stopped filling years ago so now it's just a huge garbage can you can smell from blocks away in the summer. At the top of the hill a footbridge to the park crosses the railroad tracks. They say the little house below the bridge on a platform built out from the park side of the tracks was where the trains stopped for George Westinghouse. His private station, and any train his people signaled knew it better stop for him. He was like a king they said. Owned half of Pittsburgh. The park belonged to him. The two white buildings where the maintenance men keep their tools and tractor were once a stable and a cottage for his servants. It was Westinghouse Park because the great man had donated it to the city. Kids had broken all the windows in the little house. For as long as she could remember it had been an empty shell, blind and gutted, a dead thing beside the tracks.

From the footbridge she could look down on the shape of the park, the gravel paths dividing it into sections, the deep hollow running along Albion Street, the swings and slides in a patch of brown over near the tracks, the stone benches, the whitewashed buildings at the far end. In spite of huge trees blocking her view she saw the park in detail. She had been coming to Westinghouse Park since she was a baby so she could see it with her eyes closed.

From the bridge the grass seemed a uniform green, a soft unbroken carpet the way it is in her dreams when she comes with her mother and her sisters and brother to sit on the steep sides of the hollow. On summer Sundays they'd wear white and spread blankets on the grass and watch the kids whooping like wild Indians up and down the slope, across the brown floor of the hollow their feet had rubbed bare. She had wondered why her mother dressed them in white then dared them to come home with one spot of dirt on their clothes. She had envied the other children romping and rolling down the sides of the hollow. Sunday is the day of rest her mother would say. God's peace day so she'd dress them in white and they'd trudge up Tioga Street to the park with rolled blankets tucked under their arms. Her mother would read the magazines from the Sunday paper, watch the grown-ups promenade along the paths, and keep track of every breath her children drew. *Mama got eyes like a hawk,* her brother would whisper. *Eyes in the back of her head.* Sooner or later he'd escape just long enough to get grass stains on his knee or backside, just long enough for his sisters to see a white streak flashing in the whirl of dark bodies down in the hollow. Then she'd get mad at her brother Carl and join her voice with her mother's summoning him back. *Running with that pack of heathens like he ain't got good sense.* Sometimes her bones ached to tumble and somersault down the green slope, but there were moments, moments afloat with her sisters on the calm, white clouds of their dresses, when she knew nothing could be better than the quiet they shared far away from anyone, each in her own private corner of the bluest sky.

She calls her brother from the open door of the Brass Rail. *Carl, Carl.* Her voice is lost in the swirl of music and talk animating the darkness. The stale odor of beer and pee and disinfectant blocks the entrance. Her brother Carl is at the far end of the bar talking to the barmaid. He is hunched forward, elbows on the chrome rail, his long legs rooted in the darkness at the base of his stool. He doesn't hear her when she calls again. The stink rolling in waves from the open door of the men's room works on her stomach, she remembers she's eaten nothing since coffee in the morning. She starts when a voice just inside the door shouts her brother's name.

"Carl. Hey Carl. Look here, man."

Her brother turns toward the door and frowns and recognizes her and smiles and begins to dismount his stool all at once.

"Hey Babe. I'm coming." He looks more like their daddy every day. Tall like him, and bald on top like John French, even moving like their father. A big man's gentle, rolling shuffle. A man who walked softly because most things had sense enough to get out of his way. A large man gliding surely but slowly, like John French once did through the streets of Homewood because he wanted to give the benefit of the doubt to those things that couldn't move quite so quickly as others out of his path.

"Could you walk with me a minute? Walk with me up to the park?"

"Sure, Babe. Sure I'll walk with you."

Did he sound like John French? Was his voice getting closer to their father's? She remembers words John French had said. She could hear him laugh or hear his terrible coughing from the living room that year he sat dying in his favorite chair. Those noises were part of her, always would be, but somehow she'd lost the sound of her father's speaking voice. If Carl was getting more like him every day maybe she'd learn her father's voice again.

"I've just been to see Tommy."

"No need to tell me that. All I had to do was look at your eyes and I knew where you'd been."

"It's too much. Sometime I just can't take it. I feel like I'd rather die than make that trip."

"You try and relax now. We'll just walk a little bit now. Tommy knows how to take care of hisself in there and you got to learn how to take care of yourself out here. Did you take your medicine today?"

"Yes. I swallowed those hateful pills with my coffee this morning for all the good they do."

"You know how sick you get when you don't take em. Those pills are keeping you alive."

"What kind of life is it? What's it worth? I was almost to the park. I got as far as the bridge and had to turn around and come back. I wanted to walk over there and sit down and get my nerves together but I stopped halfway across the bridge and couldn't take another step. What's happening to me, Carl? I just stood there trembling and couldn't take another step."

"It's hard. It's hard out here in the world. I know that and you know that, it's hard and cold out here."

"I'm no child. I'm not supposed to break down and go to pieces like I did. I'm a grown woman with grown children. I walked all the way from Frankstown just to go to the park and get myself together but I couldn't get across that silly bridge. I need to know what's happening to me. I need to know why."

"Let's just walk. It's nice in the park this time of day. We can find us a bench and sit down. You know it'll be better in the park.

Mama'll keep her hawk eyes on us once we get to the park."

"I think I'm losing Him."

"Something happen in there today? What'd they do to Tommy?"

"Not Tommy. Not Tommy this time. It's God I'm losing. It's Him in me that's slipping away. It happened in the middle of the bridge. I was looking down and looking over into the park. I was thinking about all those times I'd been to Westinghouse Park before. So much on my mind it wasn't really like thinking. More like being on fire all over your body and rushing around trying to beat down the flames in a hundred places at once and doing nothing but making it worse. Then I couldn't take another step. I saw Mama the way she got after her stroke, the way she was when she stopped talking and walking after Daddy died. You remember the evil look she turned on anybody when they mentioned church or praying. I saw her crippled the way she was in that chair and I couldn't take another step. I knew why she cursed Him and put God out of her life when she started talking again. I knew if I took another step I'd be like her."

She feels Carl's arm go around her shoulder. He is patting her. His big hips get in the way and bump her and she wants to cry out. She could feel the crack begin at the top of her forehead, hear it splitting and zigzagging down the middle of her body. Not his hard hip bone that hurt. She was a sheet of ice splintering at the first touch.

"I'd lose Him if I took another step. I understood Mama for the first time. Knew why she stopped walking and talking."

"Well, I'm here now. And we're gon cross now to the park. You and me gon sit down under those big pretty trees. The oldest trees in Homewood they say. You musta heard May tell the story about the tree and the bear and Great-great-granddaddy Bell killing him with a pocket knife. That woman can lie. You get her riding a bottle of Wild Turkey and she can lie all night. Keep you rolling till your insides hurt."

"Mama was right. She was right, Carl."

"Course she was. Mama was always right."

"But I don't want to be alone like she was at the end."

"Mama wasn't never alone. Me and Gerry were there under the same roof every morning she woke up. And you and Sissy visited all the time. Mama always had somebody to do for her and somebody she could fuss at."

She hears her brother's words but can't make sense of them. She wonders if words ever make sense. She wonders how she learned to use them, trust them. Far down the tracks, just beyond the point where the steel rails disintegrated into a bright, shimmering cloud on the horizon line she sees the dark shape of a train. Just a speck at this distance. A speck and a faint roar rising above the constant murmur of the city. She had never liked standing on the skimpy bridge with a train thundering under her feet. Caught like that on the bridge she wouldn't know whether to run across or leap under the churning wheels.

Her God rode thunder and lightning. He could be in that speck the size of a bullet hurtling down the tracks. If you laid your ear on the track the way Carl had taught her you could hear trains long before you'd ever see them. In a funny way the trains were always there, always coming or going in the trembling rails so it was really a matter of waiting, of testing then waiting for what would always come. The black bullet would slam into her. Would tear her apart. He could strike you dead in the twinkling of an eye. He killed with thunder and lightning.

She stopped again. Made Carl stop with her in the middle of the bridge, at the place she had halted before. She'd wait this time, hold her ground this time. She'd watch it grow larger and larger and not look away, not shut her ears or stop her heart. She'd wait there on the shuddering bridge and see.

The Beginning of Homewood

I have just finished reading a story which began as a letter to you. A letter I began writing on a Greek island two years ago, but never finished, never sent, a letter which became part of the story I haven't finished either. Rereading makes it very clear that something is wrong with the story. I understand now that part of what's wrong is the fact that I never finished the letter to you. The letter remains inside the story, buried, bleeding through when I read. What's wrong is the fact that I never finished the letter, never sent it and it is buried now in a place only I can see. Because the letter was meant for you. I began by trying to say some things to you, but they never got sent, never reached you so there is something wrong about the story nothing can fix.

In a way the story came before the letter. The story concerned the beginning of Homewood and a woman, a black woman who in 1859 was approximately eighteen years old. She was the property of a prosperous farmer who employed slave labor to cultivate the land he owned near Cumberland, Maryland. I wanted to tell the story of the woman's escape, her five-hundred-mile flight through hostile, dangerous territory and her final resettlement in Homewood, a happy ending or beginning from our point of view since this woman turns out to be Great-great-great-grandmother Sybela Owens. The idea of the story had been on my mind for years, ever since I'd heard Aunt May tell it the night of Grandpa's funeral. For some reason being in Europe again sharpened the need to get it down on paper. Maybe the trip to the concentration camp at Dachau, maybe the legend I'd heard about Delos, an island sacred to Apollo where no one was allowed to be born or to die,

155

maybe the meals alone in restaurants where no one else was speaking English, maybe the Greek word *helidone* which means swallows and sounds like a perfect poem about birds, maybe all of that had something to do with sharpening the need. Anyway I was sitting in a cafe scribbling messages on postcards. Halfway through the stack I got tired of trying to be cute and funny and realized the only person I needed to write was you. So I started a letter in my notebook. And that's when the first words of Sybela Owens's story said themselves. Five or six sentences addressed to you and then the story took over.

Aunt May's voice got me started on the story. Sitting in a cafe, staring out at the gray sky and gray sea, and mad because it was my last morning on the island and I'd been hoping for blue skies and sunshine, sitting there trying to figure out why I was on a Greek island and why you were six thousand miles away in prison and what all that meant and what I could say to you about it, I heard Aunt May's voice. She was singing Lord reach down and touch me. I heard the old church rocking through the cries of sea birds. *Lord, reach down and touch me*, the Gospel Chorus of Homewood African Methodist Episcopal Zion Church singing, *Touch me with Thy holy grace* because *Lord if you would touch me, Thy touch would save me from sin*. And Aunt May was right there singing with them. You know how she is. Trying to outsing everybody when the congregation harmonizes with the Gospel Chorus. She had on one of those funny square little hats like she wears with all the flowers and a veil. I could hear her singing and I could feel her getting ready to shout. In a minute she'd be up and out in the aisle shaking everything on her old bones she could shake, carrying on till the ushers came and steadied her and helped her back to her seat. I could see the little hat she keeps centered just right on top of her head no matter how hard the spirit shakes her. And see her eyes rolling to the ceiling, that yellow ceiling sanctified by the sweat of Deacon Barclay and the Men's Auxiliary when they put up the scaffolds and climb with buckets of Lysol and water and hearts pumping each year a little less strongly up there in the thin air to scrub the grit from the plaster so it shines like a window to let God's light in and let the prayers of the Saints out.

That's when the story, or meditation I had wanted to decorate with the trappings of a story began. At least the simple part of it. The part concerning the runaway and her dash for freedom, the story I had been trying to tell for years. Its theme was to be the urge for freedom, the resolve of the runaway to live free or die. An old, simple story, but because the heroine was Great-great-great-grandmother Sybela Owens, I felt the need to tell it again.

What was not simple was the crime of this female runaway set against your crime. What was not simple was my need to tell Sybela's story so it connected with yours. One was root and the other branch but I was too close to you and she was too far away and there was the matter of guilt, of responsibility. I couldn't tell either story without implicating myself.

This woman, this Sybela Owens our ancestor, bore the surname of her first owner and the Christian name, Sybela, which was probably a corruption of Sybil, a priestess pledged to Apollo. The Sybil of Greek myth could see the future but her power was also a curse because like the black woman tagged with her name centuries later, Sybil was a prisoner. A jealous magician had transformed the Greek Sybil into a bird, caged her and robbed her of speech. She possessed only a song and became a bauble, a plaything in a gilded cage set out to entertain dinner guests in the wizard's palace. This was to be her role for eternity, except that once, addressed by a seer who heard a hauntingly human expressiveness in her song, she managed to reply, "My name is Sybil and I wish to die."

On the plantation Sybela Owens was called Belle. Called that by some because it was customary for slaves to disregard the cumbersome, ironic names bestowed by whites, and rechristen one another in a secret, second language, a language whose forms and words gave substance to the captives' need to see themselves as human beings. Called Belle by others because it was convenient and the woman answered to it. Called Belle by a few because these older slaves remembered another black woman, an African who had lived with a cage on her shoulders for twenty years and the cage had a little tinkling bell attached to it so you knew when she was coming and naturally they had started calling her Bell, in derision at first, mocking her pride, her futile stubbornness on a point most of the women had conceded long before, a point which peopled the plantation with babies as various in hue as the many colors of Joseph's coat, then Belle because she had not broken, Mother Belle finally because she was martyr and saint, walking among them with the horrible contraption on her shoulders but unwavering, straight and tall as the day the iron cage had been fitted to her body; her pride their pride, her resistance a reminder not of the other women's fall, but of the shame of those who had undone them. Called Belle because they saw in this beautiful Sybela a striking resemblance, a reincarnation almost of the queenly, untouchable one who had been sent to suffer with them.

Every morning the slaves were awakened by the blast of a conch shell. Blowing the conch horn would have been a black man's job. To be up before everybody else while the sky was still dark and the grass chilly with dew. A black man would have to do it. And do it to the others who hated to hear him as much as he hated the cold walk in his bare feet to the little rise where he was expected to be every morning and every morning like he was some kind of goddamn rooster stand there and blast away on the conch till other feet started shuffling in the rows of dark huts.

Sybela would have heard the conch shell a thousand mornings. Strangely, the first morning of her freedom when she heard nothing but bird cries and the rasp of crickets, she missed the horn. The three or four dresses in which she had cocooned herself unfurl as she rolls away from Charlie Bell's hard back. She shivers as a draft runs up between her clothes and her skin, breaking the seal of heat. She stares at the horizon while the sky drifts grayly across the mirror of her eyes. In the rifts between the dark hills, mist smolders dense and white as drifted snow; the absolute stillness is stiller and more absolute because of the ground noise of birds and insects. She rises to a sitting position and lifts her arm from the rags beneath which her children sleep and hugs the mantle of her entire wardrobe closer to her body. In the quiet moments of that first morning of freedom she misses the moaning horn and hates the white man, her lover, her liberator, her children's father sleeping beside her.

Charlie Bell had stolen her, her and the two children, stolen them from his own father when he learned the old man intended to include them in a lot of slaves sold to a speculator. She had no warning. Just his knock, impatient, preemptive as it always was

when he decided to take her from her sleep. Using no more words
than he did when he demanded her body, he made it clear what
he wanted. In a few minutes all that was useful and portable was
gleaned from the hut, the children roused, every piece of clothing
layered on their backs and then all of them rushing into the night,
into the woods bordering the northern end of the plantation. He
pushed them without words, a rage in his grunts, in his hands,
rage she felt aimed at her and the frightened children though it
was the forest he tore at and cursed. The dark woods responded
to his attack with one of their own: branches whipped at the runaways' faces, roots snarled their feet, dry wood snapped loud enough
to wake the dead.

It began, like most things between them, in silence, at night.
After an hour or so they had to carry the children. Charlie Bell
lifted Maggie who was older and heavier than her brother, and
Sybela draped Thomas in the sling across her chest not because
she conceded anything to the man's strength but because when she
bowed into the darkness she reached for the sobs of fear and exhaustion she knew the man could not quiet. Maggie would cling
to Charlie Bell, the plunge through the forest would become a game
as she burrowed her head into his shoulder. She would be riding
a horse and the jostling gallop, the fury of the man's heartbeat
would lull her to sleep. But the boy was frightened more by the
white man than the crashing forest. Thomas was not much more
than a baby but he would scramble along on his thin, bowlegs till
he dropped. Never complaining, Thomas would pick himself up
a hundred times and not even notice the shrieks of invisible animals, but he could not abide the man's presence, the man's anger,
and he whined until Sybela pressed him to sleep against her body.

The first morning of her freedom she looked quickly away from
the white man, forgetting the knife-thrust of hatred as she listened
to the complaints of her body and surveyed the place where exhaustion had forced them to drop. Charlie Bell must know where
they are going. She had heard stories of runaways traveling for
weeks in a great circle that brought them back to the very spot
where they had begun their escape. The man must know. All white
men seemed to know the magic that connected the plantation to
the rest of the world, a world which for her was no more than a

handful of words she had heard others use. The words *New Or-leans, Canada, Philadelphia, Cumberland* were impossible for her to say. Except silently to herself, sifting them through her mind the way old heathen Orion was always fingering the filthy string of beads he wore around his neck. She did not hear the conch shell and realized for the first time in her life she was alone. In spite of the children still tied to her with strings that twisted deep inside her belly, in spite of the man, she knew she could just walk away from all of them, walk away even if the price was heavy drops of her blood dripping at every step because she was nowhere and no one was watching and the earth could swallow her or the gray sky press down like a gigantic pillow and snuff out her life, her breath, the way Charlie Bell had tried once, and it would be no-body but her dead, nobody knowing her death just like nobody heard in the silence of this morning her thoughts; and that was the thing she would not walk away from, the drone of her voice speaking to itself, monotonous and everlasting as cricket hum. She could not leave it, or bury it and cry over it; she was nothing but that sound, and the sound was alone.

I wanted to dwell on Sybela's first free morning but the chant of the Gospel Chorus wouldn't let me sit still. *Lord, reach down and touch me.* The chorus wailing and then Reba Love Jackson soloing. I heard May singing and heard Mother Bess telling what she remembers and what she had heard about Sybela Owens. I was thinking the way Aunt May talks. I heard her laughter, her amens, and *can I get a witness,* her digressions within digressions, the webs she spins and brushes away with her hands. Her stories exist because of their parts and each part is a story worth telling, worth examining to find the stories it contains. What seems to ramble begins to cohere when the listener understands the pro-cess, understands that the voice seeks to recover everything, that the voice proclaims *nothing is lost,* that the listener is not passive but lives like everything else within the story. Somebody shouts *Tell the truth.* You shout too. May is preaching and dances out between the shiny, butt-rubbed, wooden pews doing what she's been doing since the first morning somebody said *Freedom.* Freedom.

One of the last times I saw you, you were in chains. Not like

Isaac Hayes when he mounts the stage for a concert or poses for an album cover, not those flaunted, ironic, who's-shucking-who gold chains draped over his ten-thousand-dollar-a-night brown body but the real thing, old-time leg irons and wrist shackles and twenty pounds of iron dragged through the marbled corridors of the county courthouse in Fort Collins, the Colorado town where they'd finally caught up with you and your cut buddy Ruchell. I waited outside the courtroom for a glimpse of you, for a chance to catch your eye and raise my clenched fist high enough for you and everybody else to see. I heard a detective say: "These are a couple of mean ones. Spades from back East. Bad dudes. Wanted in Pennsylvania for Murder One."

You and Ruchell were shackled together. In your striped prison issue coveralls you were the stars everyone had been awaiting. People murmured and pointed and stared and the sea of faces parted for your passage. In the eyes of the other greencoveralled prisoners waiting to be arraigned there was a particular attentiveness and awe, a humility almost as they came face to face with you — the Big Time. Your hair was nappy and shot straight out of the tops of your heads. Made you look a foot taller. Leg irons forced you to shuffle; your upper bodies swayed to make up for the drag of the iron. Neither of you had shaved. Neither looked down at the gaggle of deputies shooing back the crowd. The two of you could have been a million miles away discussing Coltrane or pussy. Everything about your faces disclaimed the accident that was happening to your bodies. The slept-in, too small coveralls, the steel bracelets, the rattling pimp-strut shuffle through the marbled hallway some other black prisoner had freshly mopped. You were intent on one another, smiling, nodding, whispering inside a glass cage. I thought of your ambition to be an entertainer. Admired the performance you were giving them.

Bad dudes. Mean nigger men. Killers.

If they had captured Great-great-great-grandmother Sybela Owens, they would have made a spectacle of her return to the plantation, just as they paraded you, costumed, fettered through the halls. Because they had not allowed you soap or combs or mirrors or razors, you looked as if you had been hiding for days in the bush, bringing some of its wildness with you into the clean halls of justice. She too, if they had caught her, would have returned part wild thing. Her long hair matted, her nails ragged and caked with mud, her skirts in tatters, the raw smell of the woods soaked into her clothes and skin. She would have struggled to walk unbowed behind the horses, at the end of the rope depending from her wrists to saddle horn. Her eyes would have been fixed in the middle distance, beyond the slumped backs of the sleepy riders, above the broken line of slave row cabins the hunting party finally reached. Her shoes would he gone, her wrists bloody. There would be dark splotches across her back where the coarse homespun cloth has fused with her flesh. The shame she will never speak of, more bearable now than it will ever be because now it is a fiery pain in her groin blotting out the humiliation she will remember and have to deal with once the pain has subsided. A funky, dirty black woman, caught and humbled, marched through the slave quarters like the prize of war she is, like the pawn she is in the grand scheme of the knights on horseback. But her eyes are on the moon. Like yours. I ask myself again *why not me*, why is it the two of you skewered and displayed like she would have been if she hadn't kept running. Ask myself if I would have committed the crime of running away or if I would have stayed and tried to make the best of a hopeless situation. Ask if you really had any choice, if anything had changed in the years between her crime and yours. Could you have run away without committing a crime? Were there names other than "outlaw" to call you, were there words other than "crime" to define your choice?

Mother Bess is down off Bruston Hill now. She talks about you and asks about you and says God give her strength she's crossing that river and coming over to see you. She talks about Sybela Owens. May saw Sybela Owens too. May was staring at the tall, straight trees behind the house when she felt eyes on her, eyes which had burrowed right down into the place where she was daydreaming. May let her own eyes slowly find the ones watching her. Cautiously she lowered her gaze down past the tall trees, the slant of the roof, the rhythmed silhouette of gray shingles and boards, down past the scarred post supporting the porch roof, the knobby uprights of the rocking chair's back, stopping finally at the old woman who sat dark and closed as a fist. Sybela Owens's ancient eyes blinked in the bright sunlight but did not waver; they had waited patiently as if they had all the time in the world for May to reach them. Then it was May's turn to wait. She quieted everything inside herself as the old eyes shushed her and patted her and said her name in a way she had never heard it said before. *May.* The eyes never left her, but after an instant which seemed forever, May was released. Sybela Owens's eyes never left her but they had fallen asleep again. Among the million brown wrinkles and folds in the old woman's face were two invisible shutters which slid down over her eyes. They were in place again and though May could not see through them, she understood that Grandmother Owens could still look out.

"And let me tell you all something. That's right. You all listen up because I'm gon tell you what you ain't never heard. That's right. And you heard it from May and May be long gone but you all remember where you heard it. Yes indeed. About Grandmother Owens now. She had power. A freeing kind of power. I heard them say it and you might hear somebody say it and think that's just old people talking or them old time down home tales don't nobody believe no more but you listen to me and hear me tell it like it was because I was there, me, May, and I wasn't nothing but a child in knickers but I had sense enough to know it when I felt it, sense enough to let the power touch me, yes Lawd, reach down and touch me, and I felt it from my nappy head down to my dirty toes, felt it even though I was a child, felt it raising me up from scratching at my backside and playing in dirt. Grandmother Owens touched me and I felt it. Felt all the life running out me and something new filling me up at the same time. Just as clear as a bell I heard her say my name. And say so many other things there ain't no words for but they all rushing in so fast felt my whole self moving out the way to make room. Thought her power gon bust me wide open. Bust me clean open and I be running down off that hill like melting snow."

And Mother Bess said, Tell the truth. Said, Yes. Yes. And May kept on telling.

"That's all. Ain't no more. Old as she was and young as I was, she let me feel the power. And I'm a witness. That's what I am now. Your Aunt May's a witness. I'm telling you it happened and

I don't know much else about Grandmother Owens except what I been told cause that's the only time I seen her. Just before they brought her down off Bruston Hill. Didn't last a month they say. Took her down off that hill and she was dead in a month, a month after they carried her down. Strong enough to fight when they came for her. But she let them take her. Know she let them cause if she set her mind on not moving, nobody on God's green earth could budge that woman a inch. Because she had the power. I'm a witness. Had it still as sure as she sitting in that rocking chair in petticoats and a black cape and a long black dress. Sun hot as fire and she never sweat one bit. Had it and touched me with it. And changed my life. Yes she did. Told me to live free all this time and be a witness all this time. And told me come a day her generations fill this city and need to know the truth.

"Yes, Lawd. Everybody talking about heaven ain't going there. Hmmph. And everybody talking about freedom ain't been free and never gon be. If the Lord set a burden on you so heavy you can't move nothing but one thumb, you better believe what I'm telling you, the wiggling of that one thumb make you the freest thing in the world. Grandmother Owens now. She suffered in Egypt. She suffered under them cruel pharaohs. Told her when to jump and when to spit and beat her unmerciful she didn't jump or spit fast enough to suit em. That's what it was all about. Evil pharaohs and Hebrews who was God's chosen people, chosen to suffer and get hard like iron in a fire. Now youall see people just like I do, see them every day strutting round here in them fancy clothes or riding them big cars and they don't know they's still jumping and spitting when they told. They don't know it. Too ignorant to know it. Hmmph. And tell you *g'wan out my face, nigger*, you try and tell them something. But it be the same. Pharaohs and Hebrew children. Cept some few like Grandmother Owens get up one morning and gone. Run a hundred miles a day with little children on her back, her and that white man Charlie Bell and them babies run by night and sleep by day, crisscrossing rivers and forests full of alligators and wolves. Now that's something, ain't it? Grandmother Owens wasn't hardly no more than a child. Hardly old as Shirley sitting there but she got up one bright morning and heard the freedom trumpet and lit out not knowing a thing but she was gon keep running till she free. . . ."

On the first night of her first day of freedom after the children had finally fallen asleep under her arm and Charlie Bell's restless tossing had quieted to the grunting and twitching of a hound dog dreaming of a hunt, and the stars and insects reigned absolute in the darkness, Sybela thought she saw a star fall and remembered the old story about a night when all of heaven had seemed to come unstuck and hundreds of stars plummeted from the sky and you couldn't hear the rooster or the conch horn next morning for the prayers rising from the cabins. Niggers took the fiery night for a sign of Judgment Day coming. And the story said didn't nobody go to work that morning and didn't none the white folks come round and say a mumbling word neither. She believed she saw the star go, let go like a leaf does a tree, then tumble not like a leaf but with a stone's dead heaviness through water. But the dark waters of the sky closed up without a ripple so she couldn't be sure whether she saw a star fall or not. The swift turning of her eye loosed one of the tears brimming there and it slanted coolly and hotly down her cheek and she didn't know its source any more than she understood why one star tumbled and the other didn't and after she dug the back of her hand into both eyepits and her eyes were bone dry again she couldn't be sure if there had been a tear any more than she could be sure the flicker of motion crossing a corner of her eye had been an actual star's dying.

"They some the first settle here in Homewood. On Hamilton Avenue where Albion comes in. Trolley cars used to be on Hamilton but Charlie and Sybela Owens come here long before that. Most the city still be what you call North Side now. Old Allegheny then. Wasn't but a few families this side the river and hardly none at all out this way when Grandmother Owens come. Brought two children from slavery and had eighteen more that lived after they got here. Most born up on Bruston Hill after the other white men let Charlie know they didn't want one of their kind living with no black woman so Charlie he up and moved. Way up on Bruston Hill where nobody round trying to mind his business. Stead of killing them busybodies he took Grandmother Owens up there and that's the start of Homewood. Children and grandchildren coming down off that hill and settling. Then other Negroes and every other kind of people moving here because the life was good and everybody welcome. They say the land Charlie owned on Hamilton was fixed. After he left, nothing grow or prosper there. They say Grandmother Owens cursed it and Charlie warned all them white folks not to touch his land. He said he would go to keep peace but nobody better not set a foot on the land he left behind. That spiteful piece of property been the downfall of so many I done forgot half the troubles come to people try to live there. You all remember where that crazy woman lived what strangled her babies and slit her own throat and where they built that fancy Jehovah Witness church over on Hamilton that burnt to the ground. That's the land. Lot's still empty cept for ashes and black stones and that's where Grandmother Owens first lived. What goes round comes round, yes it does, now."

And Mother Bess said Preach. Said Tell the truth.

Sybela's story could end here but it doesn't. I still hear May's voice:

"It hurts me. Hurts me to my heart. I remembers the babies. How beautiful they were. Then somebody tells me this one's dead, or that one's dying or Rashad going to court today or they gave Tommy life. And I remembers the babies. Holding them. Seeing them once or twice a year at somebody's wedding, somebody's funeral or maybe at the Westinghouse picnic. Sitting on a bench at Kennywood Park watching the merry-go-round and listening to the music and a brown-skinned boy walk by with his arm around a little gal's shoulder and he grin at me all sheepish or turn his head real quick like he don't know the funny looking old lady on the bench, and I know he's one of the babies and remember the last time I saw him and how I patted his nappy head and said *My, my, you sure are getting big* or *My, my, you're grown now, a big man now*, and remember him peeking at me with the same sheepish grin and don't you know that's what I remembers when I hear he's robbed a store or been sent to prison or run off from some girl he's left with a baby, or comes around on Westinghouse picnic day at Kennywood Park to ask me for some ride money or to show me his family, his babies and let me hold them a minute."

My story could end here, now. Sybela Owens is long dead, rocking on the porch in her black cape like the sea taxis on their anchors when the water is too mean for the journey to Delos. Great-great-great-grandmother Owens is meeting May's eyes, gazing through the child to the shadowy generations, to storms which will tilt the earth on its axis. The old woman watches her children fall like stars from the night sky, each one perfect, each one a billion years in the making, each one dug from her womb so the black heavens are crisscrossed infinitely by the filaments of her bright pain which no matter how thinly stretched are unbreakable and connect her with her progeny and each point of light to every other. The vision blinds her. She sighs and crosses her wrists under the ruins of her bosom.

It could end here or there but I have one more thing to tell you. The Supreme Court has decided to hear a case in which a group of inmates are arguing that they had a right to attempt an escape from prison because conditions in the prison constituted cruel and unusual punishment and thereby violated the prisoners' human rights. It's a bitch, ain't it? The Court has a chance to say yes, a chance to author its version of the Emancipation Proclamation. The Court could set your crime against Sybela's, the price of our freedom against yours. The Court could ask why you are where you are, and why the rest of us are here.

So the struggle doesn't ever end. Her story, your story, the connections. But now the story, or pieces of story are inside this letter and it's addressed to you and I'll send it and that seems better than the way it was before. For now. Hold on.

HIDING PLACE

FOR MORT, ELISE, AND TAKAJO

Special spirits . . . special place.

Went to the Rock to hide my face
Rock cried out, No hiding place

Afro-American Spiritual

Family Tree

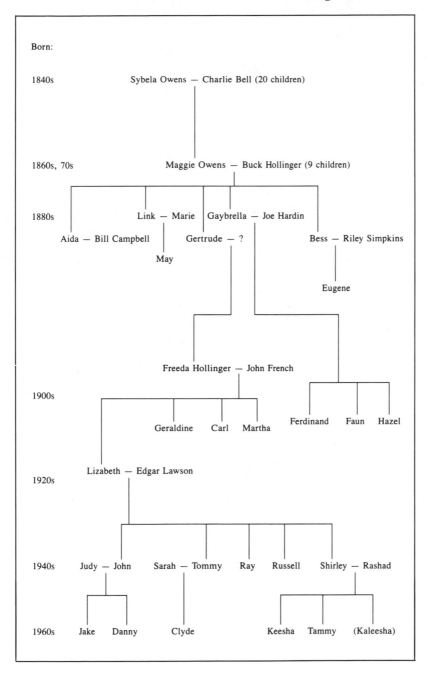

Born:

1840s   Sybela Owens — Charlie Bell (20 children)

1860s, 70s   Maggie Owens — Buck Hollinger (9 children)

1880s   Link — Marie   Gaybrella — Joe Hardin

Aida — Bill Campbell   Gertrude — ?   Bess — Riley Simpkins

May

Eugene

Freeda Hollinger — John French

1900s

Geraldine   Carl   Martha   Ferdinand   Faun   Hazel

Lizabeth — Edgar Lawson

1920s

1940s   Judy — John   Sarah — Tommy   Ray   Russell   Shirley — Rashad

1960s   Jake   Danny   Clyde   Keesha   Tammy   (Kaleesha)

Clement

CLEMENT listened to them talk. Two men dead. Niggers caught, and niggers running away. He snorted some of that nasty stuff down out his head. Tasted like blood in his raw throat but he swallowed because ain't no place to spit. Full this morning. Head felt like a bucket of soggy grits. Couldn't keep his eyes dry for blinking and the snot rag balled in his back pocket had been folded and refolded so many times he didn't want to touch it anymore.

He knew that if he waited long enough somebody would want something. So he listened to the men tell each other lies. Morning lies that were slow and lazy as worms. Everybody still too evil to laugh and joke so somebody would mutter something under his breath like he was just talking to hisself but if you listened you'd know he was lying and wanted somebody to hear it. So there they were, those lazy morning lies all over the floor of the barbershop, spotting the marbled green squares of linoleum like the hair balls later on in the day.

Clement sees the floor covered with kinky, matted hair. Then he is a broom whisking it into a pile in the corner away from the door. You get it just about up and some fool come swinging in the door and jiving back over his shoulder and you got to begin all over again, the wind catch that hair and start it to flying and rolling.

He listens to Al who says the Hi Hat was jumping last night. He listens to Lloyd describe the size of the knot he put upside his old lady's head when she told him there wasn't no coffee in the house to be made and that's why she was laying up in bed like the Queen of Sheba or Miss Ann or some gawdamn body like she ain't got good sense. Clement listens and watches the lies squirm and wiggle across the floor. That spit-stained, foot-scuffed, ciga-rette-butt-burned, hair-growing floor he knows every inch of.

Big Bob's hands in the mirror behind his back, tying the green smock. If hands had eyes they would watch themselves pull the string tight and make a bow above Big Bob's fat ass. But hands needed eyes to do something behind your back when you're not looking so Clement tried to catch them looking at themselves in the mirror. Winking maybe at theyself cause they got the bow so nice and even. In the mirror you could see the back of Bob's sign. The dusty backside of the sign and see it backwards too. BIG BOB that would light up red except the last big "B" so it was BO when it was red, BIG BO like Little Bo Peep and her sheep.

And see black wool all over the floor if you stood up close to the mirror and looked down into it, dreaming down into it, past the spots and dull, cracked edges, past the clots of curling Bo Peep black sheep wool, dreaming while the broom goes on about its business and the voices of the men are coming at you from far away like there is something like a mirror and the voices sink into it then leak out again far away so when you hear them it's not the men you hear now but the men talking yesterday or a week ago some-where inside something like a mirror.

Hey, Clement. Get your butt up off that chair, boy. Them chairs for my customers, you know that. If you gon sleep, go on in the back.

Aw leave em lone, Bob. He ain't doing nothing but dreaming up on a little pussy.

Nothing is what that lazy nigger be doing all the time.

You too hard on the boy.

I keep a roof over his head and food in his mouth. Now if that's hard I sure would appreciate somebody being hard on me. Wouldn't be out here at dawn dealing with all you nappyhead niggers.

Ain't no way to talk to the public.

Yeah, Bob. You talk nasty we gon take our business elsewhere. Sure nuff.

Why don't you do just that. Why don't youall go over to Mr. Tivoli's. Go on over there so he can run you out with that shot-gun he keeps for parting colored folks' hair.

You know we love you, Big Bob. Ain't gon leave you for no dago.

Even though you can't cut hair a lick.

Even though you talk about folks like a dog.

Even though I ain't had a hit since I been playing my figure here.

Just cause your number is trifling as you is Burgess, ain't no reason to blame me. Big Bob always pays. You play, I pay.

Clement. Simple as you is, boy, you ought to be lucky. Gimme a number to play, Clement.

Play your mama.

What you say, boy?

You heard em. You heard em good and plain just like everybody else did.

Sure nuff told you what to play.

Don't care if you's feebleminded you little scrufty pickaninny. I'll go upside your burr head you start playing the Dozens at me.

You asked him what to play . . .

And he told you.

Yes he did.

What's your mama's name, Burgess? Big Bob, look up his mama's name in the book.

Which book you talking about?

Ow, wheee.

You see that. You niggers always signifying.

You the one said *what book*. You the one playing Dozens and putting people's mamas' names in little black books people carry round in their hip pockets.

You all just getting deeper and deeper.

Go on and look it up in the Dream Book.

Just leave it alone now. It's too early in the morning for this mess.

Simpleminded or not, that boy better watch his mouth.

Clement don't mean no harm. Here boy. Tell Claudine to send me over some warm milk. These niggers is on my nerves already this morning and I gots to take my medicine.

Big Bob's hand is studded with eyes. They are hidden in the folds of his dumpling-colored palm. If he opened his hand wide Clement knew they'd be there staring up at him. No Sale sits in the long window of the cash register. Big Bob slams it shut with his other hand as Clement takes the quarter from his plump fingers.

It was too early in the morning to talk about people's mamas. Since Clement never had a mama he could remember it was never too early or too late or any time at all to talk about his. Clement wondered if she was alive or dead. If he ever passed her in the Homewood streets and didn't even know it was his own mama who was smiling or cut her eyes at him or flounced past him, through him, dressed to kill on somebody's arm like her son wasn't even on the pavement. He believed his mama wore perfume. But when he tried to understand its smell all he could think of was the pomade-and-lather-thick air of Big Bob's. He knew she would smell good. Not good like the men thought they smelled when Big Bob splashed his hands with lotion from the tall, colored bottles and slapped his hands together and patted it on their bumpy necks. A different good. A real good. Like some women Clement passed on the street. Or some of the women who came in Bob's to play their numbers.

He knew she'd smell good and speak softly. There be nothing bout her to make the men laugh or talk nasty so he would never hear them mention his mama's name in the barbershop. Anyway his mama had no name except the secret one he carried in his heart, the name he would never say, except to himself quietly in the middle of the night when he was almost asleep in Big Bob's backroom. Never say it to anyone even if somebody held a .357 magnum to his head and said *Say it or die, nigger* he wouldn't say her secret name because then somebody else could say it and touch her and he'd have to snatch one of Big Bob's straight razors and slit the nigger's throat.

If he had a razor long enough and needle-thin enough Clement would poke it up his nose hole and puncture the swollen bag of stuff clogging his head. It hurt to think on mornings like this when his head so full it would roll down off his shoulders and he'd need both hands to pick it up and press it back where it belonged.

Wouldn't smell his mama if she be sitting on his face. Not this morning. Her perfume, whatever it was like, be wasted on him this miserable sinus-thick morning. Clement thought of blind noses and blind hands, how they couldn't see any better than Mr. Raymond sitting there behind his big green shades on the corner rattling his cup and selling those yellow pencils with the gum band round them nobody takes when they drop in a penny. Clement had heard the men say Old Mr. Raymond bring you luck you drop a big piece of money in his coffee can after you have a good night and the bones been talking for you. Say it pleases your luck when you spread it around, say your luck will come back double you treat it right so some days you might see a hundred-dollar bill in that can. But anything can be blind as Mr. Raymond. Noses and hands and feet and ears. Even your mouth could be blind when your talk is heavy and your behind light. Or when you can't talk at all. Just sit and listen at the men's voices coming from far away while you sweep and the mirrors catch on fire and everybody in Big Bob's burning up but you can't say nothing cause your mouth is blind and you be burning up too.

Miss Claudine, Big Bob want his warm milk.

Good morning, Clement.

Good morning, Miss Claudine. I forgot again, Miss Claudine.

Nice folks don't put their *Gimmes* before their *Good mornings*. Now how many times have I told you that.

I'm sorry, Miss Claudine.

Least you remember the *Miss*. Which is a lot better than plenty of these supposed-to-be-grown-ups running around here who should know better. A little etiquette don't cost a cent. A little respect for people don't cost a thin dime and it can make a person feel like a million dollars. That's what I try to tell these gimme this and gimme that negroes always busting in here in such a hurry. Don't I be telling them all day, Mr. Lavender?

She sure does.

And you'd think since it's *free*, people'd be free in passing out a little respect. But here they come. Mouthful of gimme and hardly a much obliged passing they lips.

I'ma remember that *Good morning* next time, Miss Claudine.

You a good boy, Clement. You kinda forgetful but you a good boy. You better than you should be, growing up mongst that low-life riffraff hanging round the barbershop. You got the worst element in the community right there. Somebody needs to throw a bomb in there one Saturday afternoon about four o'clock. Rid the neighborhood of ninety-nine percent of its pimps and hustlers and dope peddlers and no-goods. I'd buy the bomb. Yessir, you find me a person got the heart to throw it and poor as I am I'll buy the bomb. Wonder is you ain't worse than you is, living the kind of life you do. It ain't your fault. You's a good boy and you seems to try hard even if you ain't got much sense to try with. Milk'll be a minute heating up. Tell that evil Big Bob what I said, too. Wish his overweight doughnut-butt self was right here now and I'd tell him to his face.

Mr. Lavender. Give this child one of them pastries. With the jelly on top like he likes. Look at you grinning from ear to ear. Wish I had room to take you in. But I done had all the children I'm gon have. Got grandchildren staying with me now. Got my hands full with my own babies or else I'd take you out of that hellhole.

Thank you, Mr. Lavender, and ain't he cute saying *thank you* just like I taught him. That's the kind you like ain't it, sugar. Go on and enjoy it, but take a napkin and keep your chin clean and wipe your hands when you done.

Here now. You tell Bob Henderson I didn't put no arsenic in it this morning. But you tell that blubberbutt, pigeon-toed excuse for a man I'm gon fix him good one day. Got a jar full of poison with his name on it. And tell him I'd buy the bomb.

Clement watches her fit the lid on the styrofoam cup. Her purple finger circles three times, twice softly pressing on the lid and once more spiraling in the air just above the sealed lips of the cup. He won't repeat to Big Bob anything Miss Claudine has said. He doesn't need to because Big Bob hears every word. She still loves me don't she, boy. She's still talking trash ain't she. That old Biddy would cut my heart out if she could. Cut it out and put it on a platter and just sit there and die happy looking at my heart on her platter on her table in her kitchen. We go back a long way. Thirty years if it's a day and she ain't never forgived or forgot Big Bob. But you don't know what I'm talking bout, do you, boy. Just words to you, ain't it, boy. Love just a word to you.

It's hot now. Be careful how you hold it. Don't spill it on yourself.

Thank you, Miss Claudine.

Don't you forget to tell him what I said.

But Clement knows he won't tell, knows he doesn't have to. He giggles to himself as his feet hit Homewood Avenue again. Giggles because he is carrying Big Bob in a little white cup. He can feel him splashing around inside. Big Bob laughing because he's heard every word Miss Claudine said.

Most mornings Miss Claudine takes the quarter but sometimes she says you put that back in your pocket. I know that skinflinty Negro don't never give you no spending change. She took it this morning when she handed him the cup full of Big Bob so Clement does not detour to the Brass Rail where anybody who can reach the counter can buy a glass of sweet wine they got a quarter to pay for it. He goes straight down Homewood a block and a half and pushes through the door of Big Bob's. The bell jingles to greet him just as it had jingled when he left. Good-bye and hello, the same thing if it's the bell talking.

Big Bob takes the cup and winks at Clement. The wink is good-bye and hello, no difference, just like the bell.

Old biddy still loves me, don't she. Milk's nice and warm as toasted titty.

He unlocks the cabinet below the cash register and hauls out the J&B by its skinny green neck. Two inches of warm milk splash into the sink and then the cup is brimful again as scotch rides the milk. Big Bob blows on the mixture, brews it with his little finger. He drains the cup slowly, steadily, never lowering it from his lips. His eyes are closed and his head tilted back on his shoulders so the rolls at the back of his neck swallow the collar of his polka-dot shirt.

Hmmmmmm. A man needs some strong medicine fortify his nerves in the morning. Specially if he got to deal all day with black folks.

Clement wishes he was the empty cup. Somebody needs to open the top of his head and pour out all the nasty stuff up there. It would be so thick and greasy in the sink bowl you'd have to wash it away with a blast from the spigot.

Not so bad now that he had been up awhile and walked to Miss Claudine's and back. Cold walks opened him up faster, but it would be a long time before he'd be taking cold walks. Just the middle of May but the weather had turned and already Clement had forgotten that the streets ever had been or ever again would be so bone-cracking cold he'd just want to curl up and die. Can't remember winter when it's summer and can't remember summer when it's winter. Ain't never been no winter and never be such a thing again when he trudges with his ears sweating and the hot ground coming up through his sneakers to the top of Bruston Hill to the old woman's house.

Clement would listen to the men talk a while longer. Wait and see if anybody wanted anything else. He'd run their errands and take whatever they'd tip him, and check out the Brass Rail, but then he'd go up Bruston Hill. Walk to the very top where she lived. He hears Miss Bess listening for his feet hit her raggedy porch. Miss Bess waiting on the top of Bruston Hill. Everything in him blind except the part hearing her silent call.

Bess

IT was spring and she was a girl again. A beautiful long-haired young girl again. She could watch and listen because somebody was telling a story about her. Maybe it was Aida talking. Little Aida whose feet never touched the floor when she sat in a chair. Aida would tell it wrong. She'd get days mixed up, and people's names all funny and sometimes you'd have to stop her and ask What'd you say girl because Aida could take a word and turn it inside out so Jesus hisself wouldn't know what that child be talking about. Aida thought it was cute. Talked baby talk longer than she should have, and what she used to do because she thought it was cute got to be a habit and now she's an old woman and you got to stop her just like you would a child and say What's that you said, say Stop a minute, Aida, I don't know what in the world you're talking about and Aida just smile her ain't-I-cute smile and wiggle her feet that still don't touch the floor and keep on telling her story like she ain't old as I am and should know better.

Could be somebody else telling it so she does not interrupt, does not try to pick out the voice, just watches and listens. Because in the story she is young and beautiful and the sky is like a pretty picture above her and green, green grass is under the blanket on which she's sitting in her white Sunday dress. She is not seeing any of that at the moment because her eyes are closed and her arms are stretched behind her and her throat and forehead are bare to the sun and the sun is a warm kiss putting her to sleep. What she saw last before her eyes shut were birds flying high above the trees. Birds so high they were black specks wheeling in formation, a handful of dark seeds scattered by an invisible hand.

187

Then the singing, just as she'd heard it the night before, in the terrible, floating space before sleep mercifully severed her head from her body.

Farther along . . . Farther along.

That old preacher, dead these many years, singing her man's song. Black Frank Felder, his big head like a bowling ball above the white collar, his tiny eyes squeezed shut, his mouth pained, busy at the corners like he's trying to talk to hisself while he's singing the words of the hymn.

Farther along we'll know more about you.

Ain't no doubt about it. He can sing. Yes he can now. Ain't no better than none them other chicken-stealing holy rollers but that man can chirp, Bess.

Her man would sit on the back step of Homewood A.M.E. Zion Church. He'd sit all Sunday morning back there in the alley with the cats and garbage cans to catch Frank Felder singing.

Farther along.

The song in the story just like it'd been in the dream, which wasn't a dream but the edge of a stormy sea, tossing, wailing, shaking her soul like a leaf till she drowned in sleep. The singing calm and peaceful as she leaned back on her hands and the weight of her body rested in her shoulders, and the weight was no burden, but was knowledge that she was strong and young and beautiful under her clothes under a picture-perfect sky. Her fingertips tickled the nappy grass where it escaped the edge of the blanket spread out beneath her to preserve her long, white Sunday dress.

He'll understand why.

The singing is part of the story she is watching and hearing as somebody tells it, somebody not her because she doesn't believe anything anymore. Not even enough to make stories. Especially stories where she can be young, can be anything but what she is at the top of this hill where everything began and she is nothing. Nothing now in the morning, nothing in the storms before sleep but somebody waiting to die. Yes. Yes.

Once upon a time her man whispered in her ear that she was silk and honey. Whispered and touched her so she turned to just what he said she was. Half wake under the blankets she could be anything, could be silk and honey and satin in his arms, in his hands when it wasn't morning yet, but not night either. A young once upon a time woman in his brown sleep-thick eyes. He was twenty years older than she was and always would be he said when he asked her to run away with him, asked her to marry him forever. But he never said forever. He said Baby I'm twenty years older than you and always will be. It don't seem much now, but it will later. Won't get no better, that's for sure. So if you take me now, you'll be taking those twenty years and those twenty years won't never go away. And she thought, One day. She thought, One morning, one night, one day is all that matters. And she was right. And he was right. The morning was magic and she was everything, anything he needed her to be. Though his eyes were puffy, and the stubble on his cheeks and chin would redden her skin, her silk and honey where he nuzzled her in the morning. Twenty years nothing at all. Twenty years everything whenever her man was gone and she asked herself, couldn't help asking herself, if he'd ever return.

Farther . . . Farther.

She used to hear: *Father. Father Along.* Like it was a name. A name for God or Jesus or whoever they thought they were singing to. And the man they sung to had a face, a walk, a way of making her feel when she pictured him, sang about him herself. Then she saw the song written in one of the hymnals stamped A.M.E.Z. in gold on the spine. It wasn't until they moved to the new church. She was grown by then but still thought everybody sang *Father. Father Along.* All the songs she'd learned, she'd learned by hearing the others sing. But in the new church they bought when the white people started running away from Homewood there were benches and metal racks on the slanting backs of the benches and in these racks were hymnals and prayer books and fans decorated with Bible verses and pictures from Sunday School books and the names of funeral parlors. In the stiff-backed black book with pages like tissue paper it was *Farther, Farther Along.* She had to read it twice to make sure. She thought it might be a different song, believed it had to be different from the one she'd been hearing and singing all her life, but it wasn't so she lost her Father Along, lost his smile, his infinite forgiveness, his dance, strut, glide, stomp, gentle walk, his brown eyes and the tender sweep of his garment. She lost her God.

Then it was her man. Her man's song, her man in the song, her man's voice blended with all the other singers when she heard it. She was afraid at first. Afraid of thunderbolts and crackling lightning because she thought about her man's hands, her man's breath whenever the others sang. She took what was holy and tucked it in bed beside her and loved it and let it love her and she was afraid for a long time. Perhaps always was, always will be. Perhaps she had been struck down just as part of her believed she should be, would be. Down couldn't be any further, any farther along than the top of this lonely hill where it all had begun and where she was dying.

But she was young again and it was spring and she'd listen till whoever was telling the story got tired of telling it.

Her fingers played in the coarse grass. Over her shoulder, up the slope and to the left toward the train tracks and the foot bridge, she could hear the chains of the swings creaking. Somebody would be flying, gulping the blue air and trying to swallow it, keep it down before the next rush, the next mouthful when the swing soared to the end of its tether and you thought it just might pitch you into the middle of the steel rails.

Bess . . . Bess.

It was her man calling. But he was long dead. He couldn't be telling the story. No one was telling the story because the sky was falling and the music dying and her man's voice was far away now, far and high away as the birds. Her man was a speck. A raisin, a seed, then a tiny hole in the sky like a stone makes just for a second when it hits the water.

Bess . . . Bess.

She is saying her own name alone in the light that is not morning yet or night still but in between somewhere so she's not sure either one has happened or will happen again. *Bess.* Saying her name so it's like *the end* and chases the story away.

Bess, why don't you come down off that Godforsaken hillside and stay with us. You know we'd love to have you.

It gets so bad up there in winter. Some days nobody could get up there to help you, don't care how hard they tried.

Winter is gone. Is someplace else. Not winter hands she is lifting to her face. Winter hands are cold and stiff. They sleep under a pile of rocks and the bruising rocks are packed in snow. You are barely able to light the stove with winter fingers. If you held them in the fire they would weep and crackle, but you wouldn't feel a thing, can't feel a thing for half the morning sometimes, then it's just the pain of thawing, of having them crippled and sore again at the ends of your arms.

That is how you begin feeling sorry for yourself. When you pity a hand, or a finger, or a foot that's so pitiful anybody would be sorry for it whether it was theirs or somebody else's. When part of you gets so pitiful it's just pitiful and nothing to do with you, just a pitiful thing laying there beside a coffee cup, too swollen and crippled up to raise the cup, then you know somebody's in trouble and you know it's you and you can't help but feel sorry.

Some mornings I got no feeling at all in my hands or my feet.

Sounds like poor circulation to me. Your heart's just not pumping blood the way it used to. Takes the blood a little longer to get everywhere it's supposed to be.

Some mornings it ain't just hands and feet. Seems like I got a rubber band or something too tight on my arms and legs. Some mornings them bands creep up farther and farther and it's like I'm turning to stone. Like they might just keep sliding up and won't be nothing left with feeling.

You need to come down off that hill. I bet half those aches and pains would go away if you come down off that hill.

As if those lights, those streets, that noise . . .

She can feel her hands under the quilt. Feel enough to know they are twisted and sore but not frozen winter hands. She wiggles her toes and counts all ten little piggies down there. Only one man ever touched her toes. Only one man counted them and took each one between his teeth and nibbled it, wiggled it and tried to chant the nursery rhyme with his mouth full of foot. But she says *Bess* again. And Bess is what she is now. Alone now at the top of Bruston Hill. Her veins draw the chill, carry the deadness from her limbs to the center of her body, to the place she never knew she had until her son borning took it away with him. There the flow converges, stops there in a lake or a pool that is blacker and deeper than night. There she feels nothing but the guttering in and the depth of the hole into which the icy waters spill.

At least get a phone up here, Mother Bess. Then if you get in trouble you can call one of us. And we could call you up every once in a while to check in.

Telephone in my bosom is what she thinks but does not say to her great-niece or granddaughter-in-law or whatever she is . . . This flimsy thing in pants and a blouse with too many colors like a African or some other old country fool be wearing. Drive up Bruston Hill like a man and got a man's pants hugging her narrow hips, showing her butt and skimpy drawers. Telephone in my bosom she started to say. And I can ring him up any time. But this little chocolate thing wouldn't know what I be talking about. And if she did know, think I still got religion. But it's just a song. Just something come to mind. And I ain't got no business saying it out loud. Ain't no Christian or nothing. Like she ain't got no business saying *trouble*. Nobody drive up Bruston Hill and wear pants like a man knows what trouble is. Trouble on the seat beside her but she don't know trouble.

Get on out here, girl. Cousin whoever you is. Your skimpy underwear's showing. Now go on and tell all them folks down there about trouble. About that crazy old bad-mouthed lady don't appreciate nothing.

She can smell the stink of spring. How everything the ice and snow kept covered all winter is outside again rotting, getting soft underfoot. The mud will stick to her shoes. Rising from the streets below, the sour smell of garbage the trash men spill, the mess people toss out their windows and back doors. People sneak up on Bruston Hill with truckloads of God knows what and dump it wherever they please. Soon the rains will come and begin to wash the mess back down where it came from, where it belongs. The gutters will overflow and milk cartons and cans and bones and cigarette butts and every kind of filth get stuck in the broken cobblestones stinking till more rain carries it away. And brings more.

Soon she won't have to light the stove in the morning. The wooden walls will get dark with sweat. Get loose and runny like everything does in spring. Then the dog days will turn her house into an oven. She'll sit from early morning till night on what's left of the porch, in what's left of her rocker, in what's left of her body. The house is a piece of clothing she has been wearing all these years. Like her wool sweater with holes in the elbows and patches and worn places thin and see-through as cellophane. The house like a sweater somebody painted on her body so she can't take it off. Not to patch or wash or give it a vacation. The house is painted on, stitched to her skin, wool threads and flesh threads all woven together now and she could no more take off the raggedy sweater than she could grab the black handle of a steam iron and press out the million wrinkles in her face.

The seeds Clement brought her still lie where he dropped them on the table. Packets with bright pictures of perfect vegetables she's never seen anywhere but on packages of seeds. She'd be afraid to eat something looks like them painted tomatoes. Look more like the heart torn out some live animal, something that bleeds and breathes and would still be thumping in your hand when you tried to eat it. She couldn't make up her mind about the garden. Not so much a question of planting it or not planting it this year, but never remembering the seeds until she sees them and then forgetting them till they flash up at her again. Even with the pile of packets right there on the table she sits at every day she might not see them for a week. Sometimes she hears them. Rattling like they did when Clement dumped them from the grocery sack.

Here they is, Miss Bess. She could hear them scratching to get out.

Late now for putting seeds in the ground. There was a time they turned the ground from the back porch all the way to the trees at the edge of the hill. Long straight furrows combed in the earth and they'd grow enough to can and get through the winter. Beans and peas and tomatoes and cucumbers and lettuce and turnips and mustard greens. Sticks marching in regular rows and strings stretched for the vines to climb. Corn and grapes and parsley. Once her brothers had shown her where sausage grew and the hole where she should lay the hambone and cover it with ash to grow a new ham. You see anything yet? Ought to be sprouting up pretty soon now. You sure you spread them ashes careful? You sure you been watering it every day? Maybe you put your ear to the ground you hear it oinking. A fence then to keep out stray dogs and cats. Raccoons still around too. Her daddy kept a shotgun in the cupboard but never got a shot at one. They thought they might catch one in their pigeon trap and baited it with bacon instead of bread but nobody was allowed to sit up all night and hold the string which was attached to the stick which held the box up in the air. None of the children could stay up all night at the window to pull the string when the raccoon went after the bacon under the box, so we never catched one either.

Spring smelled different then. So many things growing that nobody had planted. Sunflowers and goldenrods and pale little flowers she didn't know the names of. Trees and weeds and bushes. Like being in the country up on Bruston Hill. If somebody had asked her she might have claimed she lived on a farm.

In the daytime now a brownish cloud hovered over the purple-grey city below. The sprawl of city had its own distant sky, more roof than sky clamped over the wobbly hills. At night the city slept with its lights on. When you stood beneath the trees at the edge of the hill which marked the end of their garden, one star-sprinkled sky arched above you and another sky crowded by blinking stars lay at your feet. If you crushed something green and growing and rubbed the juice over your hands spring used to smell like that. A little sweet, a little sour, itchy almost and clinging like garlic because it's still there hours later if you pass your finger under your nose.

She had loved to dig in the ground then. On her hands and knees or flopped down flat on her belly if nobody was watching. Loved to dig in those days and loved to bury things. Hambones or any other foolishness. For a long time she believed anything she planted would grow. She was patient, in no hurry at all. She'd forget most of the things she had dug a home for and covered over, but forgetting them didn't mean she believed they'd never appear again. It just meant she'd be surprised. Surprised at how busy she'd been. How much she had cradled in the black earth.

Look at that child. Get up out that dirt, girl.

She gon dig a hole to China with her busy self.

Don't you get a inch closer to them beans, girl. Your father'll fix you good you dig up any of his beans.

She was the youngest so everybody had the job of watching over her. She was the youngest and always would be even though most the others dead now, buried now like they'd watched her bury tin cans and rusty spoons and leaves and just about anything she could get her hands on if somebody didn't keep an eye on her. And somebody always did. Even Mother Owens who everybody said couldn't see a thing no more, even her rocking on the porch, draped in the black cape she wore summer spring winter and fall, even Mother Sybela Owens's blind eyes following her as she tunnelled to China or wherever you get by digging all the time.

Tricked me into burying a hambone. Tricked me into trying to grow pigs' feet and roast pork and hog maws and hog jaws and chitterlings and snout and ears and tail and side meat and crackling gravy.

How long has it been, how many years ago was it her Grandmother Sybela Owens rocking on the porch and her down in the dirt digging like a groundhog. Now it was Mother Owens in the ground, and spring stinking, and I'll be in that rocker all day wearing this old house like Mother Owens wore that black cape. Up and back, up and back a million times till it's cool enough to go on inside. Maybe seeing what Mother Owens saw behind her blind eyes because when you rock long enough you start to look inside stead of outside and you listen to the chair and listen to things scratching and rattling like them seeds to get out. But you forget. You don't pay them no mind though they sitting right there in front your face. Gets too late then. Gets past the season for planting and then you're seeing Bess and Bess is all you see behind your eyes and all you want to see cause Bess is a stone, a dead something setting here with the rest of this mess tore out the earth and waiting for the rain to wash it away.

They talked like she was dead already. Or like she was a child, or like she just wasn't there in the room with ears and breath like the rest of them.

Mother Bess we can't let you do that.

There's nothing left up on that hill but a shack. She knows that.

She knows the old place has just rotted away. She's just being unreasonable and ornery. Trying to make people feel sorry for her. I'm willing to take her in or help out any of the rest of you who do. It's our responsibility and no sense in everybody getting upset. Let's just decide what to do without a lot of fussing and tears.

She doesn't really mean she wants to stay up there. I think she wants to visit. It was her home, after all. Some of us were born there too.

Have you been up there lately?

I drive past sometimes.

Have you looked? Have you stopped and really taken a good look?

More like a doghouse than someplace for a human being to live.

That's what I mean. Everything is caved in or torn down or falling apart. Just the shell of the main part of the house is left. Niggers carted away the pipes and the fixtures and shingles and boards and anything else worth a dime.

Nobody's lived there for ten years.

Ought to take better care of the place. That property might be worth something someday.

I don't think it's even in the family anymore. There were taxes owed when Granddaddy died and I don't think anybody ever paid them. Letters used to come to the house ever so often. I was barely making my own car note and mortgage so I didn't pay them no mind. Been years since I even seen one of those bills. City probably owns it now.

That's a shame. To just let it go like that. After all these years in the family.

Yes indeed. This family started up there. Really beautiful once up there. Member going up there when I was little. Saw Grandmother Sybela Owens in that black cape rocking on the porch. Looked just like she does in the photograph Geraldine has. Mother Owens the one run off with the white man and he stole her from his own daddy and they run off from slavery up here to Pittsburgh in the old days.

We all know the story. And now's not the time to tell it. But it's a crying shame to let go someplace been in the family so long.

Ought to thought about that twenty years ago.

Who had the money twenty years ago to do anything?

Who got it now?

Well, it doesn't matter now. It's either ours or not ours and that's water over the dam, but whether it's still in the family or not it's definitely not an old folks' home. So she's not going up there and she might as well stop thinking about that possibility. We have to decide who has room and who wants to keep her. Then she can take her pick.

Don't talk so hard, son. You're not as hard a man as you're trying to seem. Don't you see Mother Bess sitting there? We're not talking about a piece of furniture.

I'm sorry, Mama. I just don't want this to turn into one of those fussing and crying and somebody stomping around and slamming doors things.

That's the way this family does business.

And that's what's wrong. We don't take care of business. We fuss and argue and somebody wins out because they got more mouth or tears. Here we sit don't even know if the property up on Bruston Hill belongs to one of us or to the city of Pittsburgh. Now that's not what I call taking care of business.

Belongs to all of us. And always will.

Sure. Sure it does. Till the city decides one day to make it a parking lot then you'll find out real fast who it belongs to.

Not enough people up there to make no parking lot.

Oh Aunt Aida. That's not the point. The point is . . .

Point is I'm tired of youall talking all this mess. Somebody call me a cab. If none you want to take me up there I still got a little change and I can pay my own way. Walk if I have to.

Mother Bess.

Here we go.

Don't be Mother Bessing me. I ain't got to ask none of youall for nothing. I been grown a long time before most of youall was even thought about. Which one of you is gon *tell* me what I can do and what I can't do? Been out here in the world long enough to make up my own mind. You can either help me or let me alone. Don't make no nevermind to me but I'm gon up there. That's what crazy old Mother Bess gon do and you can help or get out the way.

Didn't go that day but the next morning old long-head Horton was up on the top of Bruston Hill starting to fix up that doghouse. And got some of them wild boys, them nephews, to chop the weeds. Run lectricity up there and Lawyer Lawson who ain't better than nobody just because he been to college who ain't a lawyer or God Almighty to nobody but hisself he start to calling round and finding out how much was owed and if that patch of ground still in the family. They all decided to help rather than stand in the way. Gave em all something to do awhile. Something to talk about. Teached them they better talk *to* people rather than *at* people.

Sometimes I sit here and count them. I got them on chairs like in Benson's Funeral Parlor, them folding chairs the church used to borrow on Sunday before they moved up to Homewood Avenue where the white folks used to be. I sit them down and get them quiet like they never is except at church or funerals. Get them with they mouths shut while they thinking or listening and ain't got nothing to say for a blessed minute. Then I can look at their faces. Count them while they're sitting still. Like I got an envelope of pictures and I can kind of just sort through them slow like, taking my good time cause I got all day in the rocker. Like that envelope of pictures Geraldine down on Finance Street has. Only I don't believe in no photographs. Too much like being dead when you got somebody stamped on a little piece of paper and they can't move, can't talk back, can't change, you got them trapped there and that's where they always be. Don't believe in photographs. Wouldn't have them in the house. Not even one of my man. Because that wouldn't be him. Not him nailed to no wall or pressed up in some book. His picture around here just remind me he's gone. Remind me he's dead because it wouldn't be him somebody had trapped on no scrap of paper.

But I like to count them. Count all the faces and look at them a long time so I can remember where they came from, whose eyes they got and whose nose and whose chin and whose color. I can get way back. Count those faces and count all the faces who been carrying the French eyes since somebody invented those French eyes by marrying a Hollinger. I like to take my time and do that. Go way back and come up slowly through those faces I catch sitting still and run my eyes over. Sometimes I even touch them. Touch them while I got them all arranged sitting quiet in they chairs.

The sweet babies. And some almost as old as me. Takes all kinds to make my people. You pass by a couple years ago you think that old lady's crazy as a loon rocking up on that porch and grinning like a Chessy cat at herself and rocking and smacking her thigh and talking and ain't a soul up there but her. But that's my people up there and I'm coming and going and sometimes it's enough to make me laugh out loud.

Used to do a lot of that. But I been up here too long now. Too many new faces and I can't see nothing in them. No names, no places. Just faces and I think on them and all I see is Bess, myself behind my eyes and I mize well be blind as Mother Owens cause I been up here on this hill too long. They all thought I'd get tired of it or get sick or die and they could bring me down again before too long. But some's dead who said I couldn't go up on Bruston Hill and I'm still here and they don't even try anymore to talk me down. Except they say *Come down off that Hill* because that's all they got to say to me. Say those words but don't mean em. Jump ten feet in the air if I said *OK I'm coming down.* They always say Come on down because there ain't nothing else to say and I cut my eyes at them or say something ignorant and nasty back cause that's all I got to say. Ain't no *come down* or *stay put* to it no more. I wear this house like Sybela Owens always wore her black cape like they always gon be saying *come down* and I'm always gon be Bess and nothing else and Bess is what's up here in this chair rocking and that's all there is to it.

Clement

CLEMENT heard her saying, No. He stopped in his tracks and listened at the door till he heard *No* again. Nothing strange about being miles away in Big Bob's and hearing her call him but to hear her voice on the other side of the door saying *No* or saying any damn thing, that made him freeze up in his tracks. Sound like she talking to somebody. It wasn't a crazy sound or mumbling like she sometimes does but she's saying *No* to somebody. And that didn't make sense because he'd been coming to her house for years it seemed and never in all that time had he known her to open her door to a visitor. They *just up here to neb around. They just want to prise into my business. They can come in when I'm dead. When I ain't got strength to answer the door, they can come in and bury me.* So he hesitated and waited for her to speak again or for whatever it was in there with her to answer.

That boy be coming here soon.

Who?

That boy Clement who runs to the store for me.

Don't let him in.

He got to come in.

Well, I'll go out back till he leaves.

You go out the back and stay out the back. You keep going wherever you got to go. Don't want you round here. Ain't no place for you here.

I ain't got no other place to go. Don't you understand? I tried to tell you they're after me. They probably watching every place down there by now. I got to lay low. Need some time. Need a place to hide for a little while.

No. This not gon be it. Don't want you here. Can't have you here. You done made the mess you in. Now you go on about your business and straighten it out. Go back where you came from and leave me be.

Mother Bess, I can't be walking up and down these streets in broad daylight. Don't you know what I'm talking about? Ain't you heard?

No, I ain't heard. And don't want to hear. But soon as it's dark your feets better hit the pavement. I want you out of here, boy. Do you hear me?

Till dark.

If that don't suit you, go now. Either way I want you out of here.

I'm a dead man if they catch me.

You can leave out that back door now or you can wait till it's dark. Whatever you did got the police on your tail ain't none my business. You the one they after and you the one got to answer for it. Dead is dead. You was born to die. Ain't nothing I done put the police on you. So don't be acting like I'm the one supposed to save you. It's no and that's all there is to it.

They said you was evil and crazy. That's what they always said.

No.

Aw, Mother Bess . . .

Listen at you. A grown man starting to snivel.

Clement is on his tiptoes backing away from the door. He feels like he's been standing on the crooked porch for hours, poised at the door, bobbing like a bird in slow motion up and back, his ear closer to the door then withdrawn, needing to hear and not to hear. Now he remembers for the first time how each board of the crooked porch has a mouth. How the boards squabble and squeak when he hops up to Miss Bess's door. They are as loud as Big Bob's door that rings hello and rings good-bye when you open it. For the first time he is aware of what he knew all the time because now he must ease off the porch without making a sound because it is quiet inside now, the talking has stopped and if Miss Bess wants to, she can look through the wooden walls and see him sneaking around.

Then he realizes it would be better to take one loud step forward, one loud bounce onto one of the loudest boards and call out *Miss Bess* like he always does. Then they'll know he's on the porch, at the door, instead of hearing him try to tiptoe with bells on his ankles back down the steps.

Miss Bess.

Clement can hear the man inside being suddenly more quiet than he's been since the talking stopped. He can feel the man shouting at him, *I'm not here, goddamnit*. It's OK, Clement thinks. You ain't there and I ain't gon bother you. Just gon stand here a minute and then I'm not here either.

Clement.

Yes, Mam. He can feel the man shouting. The stillness on the other side is so big you could lose all of Homewood in it. For all the sweet wine in the Brass Rail Clement wouldn't touch that doorknob, wouldn't push across the threshold and enter the shouting stillness where the old woman's eyes and the man's eyes are screaming at each other. Then she is shooing the man out the back door. Before Clement hears the familiar shuffle of her slippers there is one heavier, creaking lurch, the movement of someone who needs to pretend he is a ghost but whose first silent step nearly crashes through the floor and brings the whole raggedy house down on his shoulders.

When she opens the door Clement can't speak. He feels his face light up red as the sign in Big Bob's window. The letters flashing across his forehead tell Miss Bess everything. How he was sneaking around on the porch and listened to them talking and heard the man slip out the back. He couldn't speak and watched her read the confession burning in his cheeks and forehead.

You ready to go to the store?

Yes, Mam.

Well I ain't ready for you yet. Got to look round here and see what I need. You come by tomorrow afternoon.

Yes, Mam.

You hungry?

No, Mam.

You sick?

No, Mam.

Then what you standing there for?

Got a rock in my shoe.

Then you better sit down and take it out when you git to the bottom of the hill.

She slams the door not exactly in his face but halfway through the *mam* which he isn't saying exactly to her face but halfway over his shoulder as he turns on his heel after the yes and starts down Bruston Hill at exactly twice the speed her words suggested.

Tommy

DOWN there they wanted to kill him. In the city streets he was dead already. Dead as Chubby in the parking lot. Dead as Ruchell running and hiding like there was someplace, anyplace safe. He remembers these same tall trees from a dream or once upon a time when he was a kid and it was night and he had wondered how far it was to the glowing heart of the city. In the blackness the distant lights had been white and cold. But his hand had been warm, wrapped in somebody else's and both of them stood staring out over the edge of the world. Somebody had his hand and would protect him from the howling, winged creatures who swooped through the black skies. And he had believed he could rise on the wind and fly away, far away where the city sparkled. Only a matter of time. Only a matter of letting go the hand holding him under the tall trees at the back of his cousins' house on Bruston Hill.

He could see it all now from where he stood. The stretch of the city, how the hills flattened gradually towards the river and climbed again to the horizon. The North Side. The South Side. And he must be East. Because it was East End and East Liberty and East Hills if you rode the Parkway from downtown towards Homewood. But the city was not a map. It spread every way at once. The city was a circle and East Liberty niggers and Homewood niggers and West Hell niggers all the same, all dead and dying down there on the same jive-ass merry-go-round. All of them lost as him.

The morning haze had not lifted, would never lift. An iron-colored cloud covered everything. Domes, steeples, spires, the windowed towers, none of them broke through. A dirty, wet cloud smelling like wino pee. He shivered. The chill night mist blanketing the city had seeped inside his skin. He needed to tell someone how tired he was, how cold, how scared. If he could say it to somebody maybe it would end. Ruchell man, it was a bitch, man. Hiding up in the Bellmawr. Creeping through all the alleys in Homewood. I'ma go back one day and strangle every one of them fucking dogs barked at me. He could see Ruchell's crooked smile. Nigger, when you gon get some teeth in your mouth. He'd tell everything to Ruchell and there'd be a wall between them and all the motherfuckers trying to kill them.

His hands were shaking, trying to get away. Told them he didn't want to be on this goddamn hill neither. Didn't want the money swirling like dead leaves around Chubby's body. If he could stop shivering, if he could tell somebody, it would all go away. Even Indovina's face. That nasty, slobbery face a speck one second and giant the next, that nightmare face he had dreamed for years and never knew its name till right here, right now on this empty hill.

He could make no sense of the city. Even in the stillness of morning, in this quiet at the top of Bruston Hill. No streets down there, nowhere to put his feet, no air to breathe. They wanted him dead down there. A slab in the morgue with his name on it. Next to Chubby, next to all the rest in neat rows in that icy room under sheets with tags on their toes. He knew about that room. Knew it was waiting. Just two blocks down from the jail. Old timers said there were secret tunnels. You could travel under the sidewalks, get there from the jail without ever leaving the underground passages.

The city was far away. Then closer than his skin. Like the face in his nightmares it shrank to a tiny spot then ballooned big enough to swallow him. The city was a stack of dishes in a sinkful of greasy water. He could stir it with his hand. Then he could hear a radio click on. Night music splitting the day wide open. He is an ear or a piece of dust or the blot of light trapped in the cup of coffee his mother carves with her spoon in the empty house. She is too hurt, too weary, too scared to cry for him anymore. A thousand of him would fit on the handle of the spoon she scrapes along the bottom of her first cup of coffee of the day. Coffee's my company she told him once. If she didn't know crazy people talked to coffee, she'd talk to hers. Her first word in that empty, falling apart kitchen be thunder and storm. Blow him away.

From where he stood at the top of Bruston Hill the only sign of life was purplish smoke drifting from the mills along the river, the river he couldn't see below the wedge of skyscrapers crammed in the Golden Triangle. Once the city lights had been mysterious, a puzzle which excited him, a design which would stay unfinished until he made something from the scattered pinpoints of fire. But he had been there and back; the city dust coated his skin. It was morning again and he'd been running and hiding all night. People were waking up. Toilets flushing, window blinds rattling down there. Somebody barely got they eyes open and turning on WAMO, half dead but got the Doo Wah Diddy blasting already and lighting a match. Sonny down there. And Sarah. They'd both know by now. They'd both have heard the news. Somebody holier than Jesus with that I-told-you-so look about to bust open his gums would have got to them: Nigger ain't never been worth nothing and now he's a killer. Now they gon kill him too.

This the top of Bruston Hill. This the place in the stories all my people come from. He wondered how the tall trees held on to the edge of the hill. The drop was steep, nearly perpendicular. If you jumped you would tumble forever, leave a trail of meat from the trees to the invisible river. His knees and elbows skinned raw already. A dream had scared him awake in the middle of the night and he had ripped open the scab where his knee had oozed into his pantsleg. Did he scream or was the scream in the dream too? He didn't know. Just knew he had to get out of there. Buildings on Homewood Avenue a poor place to hide anyway. Cops search them when they're in the mood to beat on the winos and junkies. Scream could have brought cops running. So when he bolted from sleep, from the few minutes rest he had copped on the bare floor of the old Bellmawr Show, he gritted his teeth, swallowed another yell and crawled back down in the alley. Then alley by alley all the way up Bruston Hill till he found the trees and ruins and shanty.

But if he couldn't change her mind ain't found nothing. Everybody said she was evil and crazy. He leaned-back against one of the trees. He had been here before, maybe even touched this same tree before but nothing was familiar. Running and hiding all night

for what? To get here? To wind up nowhere? If he had reasons
for picking this jive place he surely didn't know what they might
be. Didn't know why or when his feet decided to climb Bruston
Hill. Couldn't think of any reason now. Made it to the top but
nothing said it's better now, you're OK now.

Nothing to it. Just the wooden shack she lived in and the blackened shell of the rest of the house where it had burned or collapsed
or been smashed down by a giant fist. Aunt Aida said the main
part of the house had burned right after the war. But she was always getting things mixed up. Talked to him one day for five minutes before he realized she thought she was talking to his sister,
Shirley. He wasn't even sure which war she meant. Aunt Aida had
lived through just about all the ones America ever fought. It was
in World War II they said that Mother Bess had lost her son. They
said she started getting funny way back then. Only had one child
and that one late, like Abraham and Sarah in the Bible they said.
She was near forty some when the son was born and her husband
way over fifty. Nobody believed it Aunt Aida said and to top it
all it was a big, healthy boy. But he died on Guam. Two days
after V-J Day is the way he's heard them tell it. The Pacific war
over and this Eugene, who was the only child Mother Bess had,
was shot by a sniper. Said he was looking for souvenirs. Something
special to bring home to his mama and this crazy jap didn't know
the war was over shot him dead on a beach six thousand miles
from home.

Unless you knew there had been a big house here, you wouldn't
have guessed it. Looked like somebody just patched together a shack
from all the piles of junk lying around. No straight lines or even
edges. Like you'd slap together a doghouse. Wall leaned one way.
Little overhang of porch another. Looked like somebody had ham-
mered together a door two sizes too small for the frame. Getting
out the back when that boy came to the door he had almost
stumbled over the rags she used to stuff the gap at the bottom.
One back window cracked but intact, the other boarded with a
tin Coca-Cola sign. Her house looked like the huts he had seen
in pictures of the West Indies or South America where black people
were still wild and don't live no better than animals. Shame they
let her live like this. But they said she was crazy and nobody could

talk her down off Bruston Hill so let her be if that's the way she
wants to live, if that's how she wants to die up there by herself.

The only other thing standing in the ruins of the old place was
the three-walled shed where he'd been trying to sleep. At least that
was all he could see from where he stood. If he didn't know better
he'd have said nobody lived here. No light coming out the house.
Nothing but the smokey city below and the wild hillside plunging
to meet it. Nobody else had tried to build this high on Bruston.
The few houses farther down on the other side of the cobblestone
street had been deserted for years. On this sloping crown of hill
where the cobbles died to hard packed earth and the dirt road itself disappeared a hundred yards down the far wooded flank, nobody but his people had raised a home.

Near the shack the weeds had been chopped and the withered
stubble of a garden enclosed by sticks. He didn't know how old
she was but knew she was long past the age when people can dig
in the ground and crawl around trying to grow things. The weeds
were already thick and green. They leaned over the clear space
before the sticks, shading the tangled edges of the garden. He could
see where somebody had dug rows and pushed in sticks, but the
garden plot looked untended, deserted like everything else.

He would go back in the shed if she wouldn't let him stay anywhere else. He was so tired he could sleep anyplace. Even standing up against these trees. If ever there had been a time in his life
when he had slept long enough and untroubled enough to want
to open his eyes in the morning, he had forgotten when. Sleep was
a black pit and he stood with his toes on the edge and somebody
kept shoving him, shoving between his shoulders so he toppled down
and fell and fell and fell deeper into the darkness till his own screaming jerked him awake. Sleep had been a trap, death by falling.
Yet he yearned for it. He needed to shut his eyes and forget. Then
maybe it would all go away. Nobody stretched out dead on Indovina's lot. Nobody chasing him down. But all the old woman could
say was *No*.

In the alleys the dogs go crazy. They come snarling at you and
the big ones rear up beating their paws on the fence and barking
loud enough to wake the dead. He had wanted to stop and punch
one in the face, blast it and send it sniveling back under the steps

where it was supposed to be asleep. Or grab one by its chain and whirl it around and around till it choked on its own spit. He had always wanted a dog. Loved dogs as a kid. But there had never been room, he never had the chance to raise one, to feed it and clean it and teach it not to shit all over the house so now dogs were just a pain in the ass. Their crap littering the streets and parks. Running at you and trying to raise the neighborhood when you're sneaking past at night. Dogs to run you off the streets, dogs to sniff out your stash, dogs eating better than niggers, dogs to bite your dick off you get too close to them old white ladies taking their Dobermans to shit in the park.

The skinned places on his elbows and knees hurt if he moved. Couldn't see a soul in any direction and he just wanted to slip down to the ground right there with his back against a tree trunk but he'd catch hell if he bent his knees. In his shirt pocket were matches and the stub of a reefer Ruchell stuck in his hand after they ditched the van. That's all, man. We still ain't got shit, man. You take care, brother. Later, man. A toke had eased him into that little bit of sleep in the Bellmawr. Didn't care now who was hounding his ass. Too tired to care. He was going to light up. He fished out the roach. A match flared in his cupped hands and he bent to it, enjoying the sulphur stink, the fire flickering an instant against his cheek. Pulled hard on the stub till hot ash singed his lips.

My Lord, what a morning. He could hear the lead tenor of the Swan Silvertones begin the song. A husky voice but crystal clear when it hit the notes. A voice going places sweet tenor ain't supposed to be able to go. Reaching high, reaching low so *My Lord* was a king and a friend and your own jive self walking cross that Valley of the Shadow. Song bitter and sweet as the smoke, not rushing through him but marching stately as a Gospel Chorus anthem. A kind of eyes front, chest out, shake your tail-feathers, spit-and-polish clean, march-strut like they teach you drilling with the Elks Saturday in Westinghouse Park. Yes, Lawd. Ain't they fine this morning. Don't they sound good. And nobody in the Homewood A.M.E. Zion Gospel Chorus is the Reverend Claude Jeter, lead singer of the Swan Silvertones, but when some old sister shouts it out, shouts *My Lord, what a morning* from the Amen Corner don't you know the voices rise up and if Reverend Jeter ain't here he should be cause we got his song and gone. Yes, Lawd.

They want him dead. They want to kill him but he made it through the night. A thousand years of night. Haze was lifting, the sun rising behind him. Standing under the trees behind the shack of Mother Bess, a crazy, half-dead, mean old lady and he ain't got a dime in his pocket and the city a percolating vat of lye below him and every cop in Pittsburgh on his tail and he's twenty-five years old and nothing, no good just like they been telling him all the days of his life, but he is smiling, smiling maybe for the first time in his life at his own silly smile, at the top of Bruston Hill, at the silly morning being a morning here, being morning here like it's always morning someplace in the world for no good reason. Just morning, yes. Just morning. And I'm here. One more time. Yes.

Bess

SHE sees his long feet poking from the corner of the shed. Long feet and fat nobby-toed shoes with heels high as a woman's. She can see that far and see that good and would thank Jesus for good eyes if she was still a Christian, but thanks nobody and praises no one's name, just stares with her good eyes at the feet protruding from the dark guts of the shed. In Highland Park Zoo she'd seen a snake once with its scaly head swoll up and the legs of a frog dangling out its jaws. Those legs were still kicking. Legs like a tiny, naked man's still kicking while that snake working at swallowing the rest. Long feet in the stub-toed shoes look like those things Minnie Mouse be wearing in the funny papers. Old-timey bubbly balloon shoes with them stick legs coming out. She can see his black socks and they make his ankles skinny black twigs. Birds all the sudden cheeping and leaping out the trees like something after them when she splashes the contents of the slop jar into the weeds. Ought to dumped it on his head. Ought to let him know just how I feel about somebody coming up here to worry me and get in my way.

The birds are settling into another tree. Like newspapers rustling. She can hear good too. Hear and see what she wants to even if there's precious little nowdays she wants to hear and see. Mize well be stone deaf and blind as a bat, mize well put her head in a bag as pay attention to what she's seen a million times before. Ought to emptied the slop jar on that fool's head. Who he think he is anyway stretched out in my woodshed like he own it?

Her long-dead sister's great-grandson's long feet in those silly shoes she can see weren't made for walking, which she can see from where she stands swinging the slop jar back and forth to air it out good, ain't made for walking and split where the sole should join the toe. If he's her sister's great-grandson he would be a . . . to her. He would be something she wouldn't want to claim walking around in raggedy funny-paper shoes. She knew his name and knew just exactly who he was but wasn't about to say his name to herself or to him when she kicked him on the bottom of those silly shoes and told him *Get on up from there. Go on away from here.* Wouldn't tell him nothing about what she knew. Just send him on his way. Back down to his mama's house on Finance Street if that's where the Lawsons still stayed. His brother the one thinks he knows everything. His brother the one talk like he's part God and part lawyer. Let him go on back down the hill and sleep in his brother's backyard.

She wouldn't have no milk for her coffee because of him. Needed Clement to buy milk today and needed some rolled oats and low on bread. No milk in her coffee all day and none in the first cup tomorrow morning either just because he decided to drop in on her like some long foot gorilla jump out one of these trees. If she could fly she'd do like the birds. Be gone soon's she saw him. Sit in the top of a tree till he stops hopping around and goes on about his business. But she ain't gone nowhere. She's at the top of Bruston Hill till it rots away or she rots away and you know I'm leaving here before it does. This hill been here long before Sybela Owens brought that white man from slavery. Been here longer than the city been here and longer than these trees.

She wonders what she'll be wearing on her feet when they find her and bring her down. In her trunk a pair of high topped, buttondown, hourglass-heeled ankle boots. They pushed her up four inches so she came to a different place on her man's shoulder when they were promenading arm-in-arm in Westinghouse Park and she leaned against him even though her mother would have died if she saw her daughter in public hanging like a hussy on a man's arm even if he is your husband. Those shoes, their leather yellow and soft as butter, hiked her up a good four inches and it was good to walk beside her man and have the world that little bit of distance farther away. Those yellow ankle boots were a killer. Yes they were now. Knew they looked good because she had the kind of feet to wear them. Slim, high-arched feet and trim ankles.

Only one man had touched her toes. Her man nibbled them and said what she already knew but what sounded best coming from his lips. You a fine woman. A silk and honey woman. Starting here, starting right here with these little fine toes and these fine ankle bones. Yes, a killer. And she was never one to be more humble than she should. No indeed. Not with the handsomest man in Homewood right next to your ear reminding you you the finest thing walk these streets in them fancy lemon butter buttondown boots.

The boots would be in the trunk with her other things. By now the rats had probably gnawed their own doorway into the trunk and chewed up everything taste good to them. Even if rats and mice had left the trunk alone those shoes would be stiff as boards. No color left and creased and wrinkled as her face even if the rats hadn't got at them. New they was the kind of thing she'd like to be wearing on her feet when they came to take her away. Laid up in the bed fine as a fairy tale princess and the first thing they see be those tall-heeled, yellow as bananas boots. She wanted them to be surprised. That she was dead and starting to stink worse than spring wouldn't surprise nobody. But to see her in one of her fancy dresses she had cached in the trunk, fancy gown and fancy ankle boots and hair done up all nice like she's waiting for her man to take her to the Elks Ball, well, that would stop them, that would make them think a little bit before they called up the undertaker and loaded her in like a sack of potatoes. How else they think she gon meet him. He been waiting a long time and deserved the best. The first time her man sees her after all these years she wants him smiling, she wants him saying *Um umm, ain't you something, girl.*

The birds screech again and scatter again, wheeling above the tall trees clinging to the edge of Bruston Hill. She hears children squawking and squealing, the voices of her brothers and sisters and cousins, her own voice right in the middle of the bird-like cries as they rush from one devilment to another free as the wind. It was the sound she had heard before Eugene came. While she was growing up the house had been full of children and some of them always laughing or crying or just plain making noise. So while she prayed for a child to bless the love she shared with her man, she heard ringing in her ears, echoes of that houseful of children romping and squabbling. And while she waited for her son Eugene to return from the war, the same bittersweet echoes played in that emptiness only he could fill by coming home again. When the war was over, when the news of V-J Day jiggled in a storm of static from the radio and her man grabbed her by the waist and spun her till they were both so dizzy he couldn't stand up any longer and she collapsed giddily on the floor beside him, the whole world was laughing, was grinning ear to ear and giggling like all the kids on Bruston Hill did when they thought they had gotten away with something, when they believed they were the smartest, slickest, prettiest things alive. But Eugene didn't come back, and she waited for word of him and the weeks after V-J Day turned into months and she did get word but didn't believe the telegram from the War Office her man had carried up the hill from the post office because that's the only way mail got to the top of Bruston Hill, and the months became years and she walked down the hill each morning to meet the mailman as he made his rounds. On those walks down the steep hill, rain or shine or snow or ice so bad you could hardly stand up, on the walks to get a letter which would tell her the telegram had been a mistake, that somebody had counted wrong, she'd hear the noise of a houseful of children chirping and flying and crashing into each other.

Always so many kids around it seemed like they came no matter what, landing on the top of Bruston Hill like rain and snow, like the change of seasons. To not have any when you wanted one so bad and then to squeeze out only one and then to lose that one on a beach six thousand miles from home when there wasn't even a war anymore, none of that seemed right, seemed possible. But that was her story. She was Bess and her story had happened to her. You could ask anyone. Even shortlegged, moon-faced Aida could get that one right. One baby. One boy child given and one taken away leaves none. No one. Leaves Bess where she is on top of Bruston Hill where children came thick and regular as flies or mosquitoes and grew like weeds and made so much noise nobody could ever forget they were around, could ever doubt the future since it would be lifted and carried on all those brown shoulders in all those brown bellies, on all those dirty brown feet scurrying around busy all the time, knock you down if you not careful.

She heard them now. Wheeling above the trees. Swooping and

spiraling and dipping as if wings were no big thing, as if anybody could grow them, as if darting through the empty air were a trick as easy to learn as learning to wait for death.

Inside the house she tucked the slop jar back in its corner. She brushed away a cobweb from her brow as she rose. Her hair was getting like that. Thin and wispy as what spiders spin in the corners of the house, dry as the skins of dust which floated everywhere when she got tired and didn't clean for a week. Once there had been more than enough hair to sit on. Long, thick hair all the way down her back. Of course he loved to brush it. And she'd let him. Fool loved to brush it best when he was drunk. Said it straightened out his head to stroke her long, soft hair and count the strokes and listen to it crackle in the winter. That man could put her to sleep brushing her hair. And more than once he'd passed out with the oak-backed brush clutched in his fist.

They all had that long, good hair. All her sisters. And they all breathed in whatever there was about Bruston Hill that made having babies easy as dancing. All of them but her. All but Bess who only got up on the ballroom floor once and did her number once and tripped and fell on her face before she could get back to her seat. Perhaps not always as easy as dancing. Some of the babies had come too early, some had been sickly and doomed, sometimes a spell of dryness, a winter of waiting and tears for this sister or that. Yet the hard times were never too hard. Of course you died a little but you couldn't stay dead because there was always that noisy mob to be fed and changed and yelled at when they knocked you off your feet or started tearing the house apart board by board. With that sound like the sea always in the background you couldn't stay dead long and your feet started to move in the rhythm of that sea song again so yes it had been as easy as dancing for all of them but her.

He would be Freeda's daughter Lizabeth's son. Freeda the quiet one raised by my sister Aida and Bill Campbell above the Fox Bar and Grill on Hamilton Avenue. Quiet as she was didn't stop her from running away with that gambling man John French. Quiet Freeda marrying a loud man twice as old as she was. Nineteen years between her and her man. Funny how things turn out. Gert had Freeda but Aida more like Freeda's mama. Aida raising Freeda while Gert gallivanting around. Then Lizabeth born dead. Freeda's first lying there blue as a piece of sky but May saved her. Little. twist this way or that none them be here. They catch Mother Owens keep her down in slavery wouldn't be no Bruston Hill. Now Lizabeth's son out in my shed and he's too long, his feet stick out like they waiting for somebody to come chop them off so he'll fit. Laying there dead to the world as that wood stacked for winter. Just about all gone now. Had enough to get me through and now it's just scraps for the cooking stove and no more trips through the snow to keep the fire going. Now the ground soft under foot. Spring stink and summer stink worse to come.

Long straight hair she could sit on and he'd comb and comb, whistling sometimes the way he did, the blues he said, not the low down dirty or the lost my woman and gone or the good morning or good night blues but hair brushing blues he said when I asked him what he was whistling because I thought it sounded sad and maybe he was brushing my hair and thinking he had no son and wondering if it was me or if it was him or both of us together wrong when love don't bring nothing but those sighs and that sweat and everything getting weak and good but nothing else, nothing afterward inside me growing but love and love ain't a small thing but it ain't a son neither nor a little girl with long hair her mama can comb or her daddy when she hops on his knee and she's like a doll in his big hands combing and that's what I thought might be the sad part in what he was thinking when he whistled but he just said hair brushing blues and smiled at me and I let it be.

That's another thing she hear around here sometimes getting crazy as a coot on this hill she hear him whistling the blues the way he did a thousand years ago or whenever it was they lived together. Aida's man Bill Campbell could play that guitar named Corrinne he brought from down home, said it was full of letters from home and he would read them when he played and you'd listen and know just what he was talking about even though you never been South yourself, never down there where Bill Campbell and John French born but you'd understand the messages when Bill Campbell played them and then your man would pick them up and whistle them to nobody but you and that was how you got a home you never been to or never saw except in that music they made. Sometimes she'd hear him whistling and stop what she was doing and try to get closer. But if the sound came from outside by the trees it'd be gone before she could get there and if she was outside he'd always whistle those blues in the house and be gone before she could get the door open. Not the kind of sound that got louder when you got closer. The kind you have to stand still to hear. Still so nothing is moving inside, not your heart, your wind or your blood. You had to stop it all and stand in your tracks and you could hear it plain as day. But when the music got too good and you had to move something and started toward where it seemed to be coming from that movement killed it, chased it away. You never got closer. It just got farther away. But when it got so good you had to move, you had to move. Even though you chased it away every time. Even though you know you crazy in the first place to hear it and even crazier to believe you could get closer to wherever it is. Because he is dead and gone. Her man and all the blues he ever had are gone, gone, gone.

My sister Gert's great-grandson out in my yard. Running from somebody, running from what he don't want to hear, from what has taken his eyes away and put two scared animals in his face.

It was his sister lost the baby. So many names, so many *great-grand* this and *in-law* that and cousins and names changing and changing again because getting married didn't mean a thing nowadays, getting married was just a way of confusing people and changing names like they was somebody new or somebody different and in a couple weeks the nigger out in the street chasing women again and all these silly girls got is a new name and babies and he's still having his fun. Then you hear about this one done broke up from that one and so and so is back together with whichamacallit and he's staying at his mama's now and her mama keeping the children. Don't none of it mean a thing. Ain't worth bothering about so she don't keep the names in her head. When she slows them down and looks into the faces like she's looking at snapshots then she puts it all together, follows the bloodlines which flow through her blood. The boy sleeping in her shed was a Lawson and his sister was Shirley, Lizabeth's middle child. She had seen the boy at the funeral when they buried Shirley's baby.

She said the words again to herself *buried Shirley's baby* and the words were what she had been avoiding all along since she saw the boy's face. But she couldn't help herself. Even if the words rocked the flimsy shack, rocked her soul as it plummeted with the crashing walls down toward the center of the earth. Sooner or later she'd put the faces together and say something like *buried Shirley's baby* and saying the words would be like hearing her man whistling the blues and knowing her first step toward him would crack the earth and knowing the crack was too high to get over and too wide to get around and too low to get under but knowing she can't help herself and moving anyway toward that sound, toward the emptiness which is all there is which is what she knows she will find after she has stepped toward him and the earth has swallowed him again, swallowed his hair brushing blues and all there is of him left to touch. Those words she said to herself, couldn't help saying to herself *buried Shirley's baby* moved her off of Bruston Hill and down again into the Homewood streets where people were singing and crying and making love and losing children and changing names like names could make a difference, like any of it made a difference.

She stood back from the sink so the spigot's first sloppy burst wouldn't wet her housedress. The water coughed on like it always did, like somebody was trying to pour a whole bucketful at once through the fingertip-size hole, and the hole choked and spit water everywhere and after the bucketful exploded, just a trickle, red with rust at first, staining the chipped place next to the drain, then the blood color washed away as a steady slow trickle cleansed the pipes. She waited till the water cleared and she washed her hands. Water smelled like iron. Hands smelled like iron when she held them to her face and sniffed. Old iron a long time underground. Only thing good about the water was its meanness, its nastiness which cut the nastiness of Henry Bow's moonshine. Regular water just curdle up and die you pour in Bow's whiskey. If she had still been a Christian she would have thanked Jesus for the little bit of warm life in her hands this morning. She dried them on the dishtowel hanging beside the sink. Yes she would have thanked Jesus for the little bit of live juice in her joints this morning and thanked him for mean water that tames mean whiskey and thanked

him for minding his own business and letting her mind hers without always having to be thanking Jesus.

Buried Shirley's baby,

She knew why she hated his long feet poking out of her shed.
That boy's feet belonged down the hill down in the Homewood
streets and that's where they should have stayed because now she
couldn't help herself, couldn't stop making the connections she knew
she'd have to make. The last time she had seen him was down below
in Homewood. She could hear his long feet shuffling up the aisle,
hear them pause beside the casket in the silence of the chapel and
then shuffle off again carrying the silence like dust so wherever he
goes you can look down at his feet and know he's been standing
beside death. She can hear his shuffle above the organ moan. He
walks like a boy who had never heard music, who has never danced.
His body ignores what the organ is playing, his body shies away
from the funeral march the way the children shy away from her
lips when their mothers bring them to kiss Mother Bess for good
luck. She has a moustache now and her bottom lip is creased like
the rim of a canyon. His skinny body hanging from his shoulders,
wide shoulders like a clothesline with him hanging down thin as
a sheet.

The child's dead. Everybody sad. But nobody wants to be here.
Why they here then? Why they crying and paying Benson? Why
all these big people sitting on these skimpy little chairs paying rent
to Benson? Why that boy pretending he a man in a man's suit too
big for him? Why he trying so hard to look like he ain't hearing
nothing, seeing nothing, ain't never danced nor heard no music
before?

Evil old woman thoughts. A crazy woman who watched an angel
pick apart a cobweb stuck to the roof of the chapel. So intent on
watching the angel she didn't hear the person next to her crying,
didn't answer the question somebody asked her till whoever it was
nudged her shoulder and said *Mother Bess, Mother Bess.* Perhaps
she dreamed the little finicky angel. Only a cellophane-winged angel
in a blue-eyed gown would have the patience to pick those dust
threads apart one by one and wind each one up into a ball and
tuck the balls into her blueeyed gown without snapping one thread.

Angels don't hurt things. Don't tear apart what other creatures have spent their precious time doing. Wasn't no point in ripping apart those little suncatching webs.

The dead child was . . . to her. Her sister's great-great-grand-daughter was what to her. Lizabeth's girl Shirley had lost the baby laid out on the satin quilt. Was that why a crazy old woman from off the top of Bruston Hill sitting in Benson's Funeral Parlor? Because they came and got her. Because she let them. And if she snored while the others wept, if someone had to snap her out of her dreams *Mother Bess, Mother Bess* and chase away her angel, why did they want her, why did she let them bring her?

The boy would not let the music do anything to him. He ig-nored it as he shuffled up the aisle, weightless between his stiff shoulders and shoes. He was not in its gloom, his heart did not take its message and pump his blood in slow, weepy surges. He said it was not music. His hips, his hands refused it. Didn't even know what it was supposed to be. Up the aisle and pausing and looking up at the ceiling and nodding once quickly into the dark box. Did he shut his eyes or was it just the droop of his long lashes made his eyes look closed?

Then it was her turn and somebody mumbling *Mother Bess* and somebody taking her arm like she was a china cup and lead-ing her from behind with pressure on her elbow like she was blind, like she couldn't see where she was going and needed somebody's busy fingers worrying her elbow like she was a baby taking its first steps and might fall and break into pieces all over Benson's chapel floor.

What she saw was white pillows and white fluff and a hole plung-ing through it all, a hole not stopping till it reached China or what-ever there was if you dug as far as you could dig into the black earth. The baby's dark face like a hole in the white satin, a dark eye staring from the bottomless depths of the hole. The eye was the hole, the hole was a way of seeing the dark shaft. This child, this daughter of her sister's great-granddaughter stared into a place an old woman could only glimpse as she rocked and rocked with both eyes pinched shut on the porch of the shack on Bruston Hill. This child staring forever, never blinking, beholding the darkness an old woman cannot bear for more than an instant before she turns away to lies.

Then she is being nudged again, steered again by whoever took that duty. You could trip over the thick music. The organ made the passage back to her seat treacherous because it moaned and dripped pain in slick pools over the floor. Nobody playing that music. It came from the mesh-faced box suspended in one corner of the ceiling. Nobody could play misery that long. If somebody felt bad as that organ sounded for as long as it groaned out its grief wouldn't nothing be left but a puddle of tears. Like the boy, she promised herself, she would never give in.

Back in her seat she swore she would never come down off Bruston Hill again. While the preacher spoke, she searched the ceiling for her angel. The angel was gone, but the cobweb she had picked apart had been made whole again closer to the chapel's three lean windows. Now it was not a veil but a beaded net to catch the light swimming through the colored glass.

She noticed for the first time the banks of flowers surrounding the casket, not because she saw them but because they stank of spring. Preacher didn't talk very long. Couldn't be much to say about a child. And this preacher didn't know how to preach. Spoke like a white man. Nothing in him of old Frank Felder. Reverend Felder be singing by now, have those glasses pushed up on his bald head and mopping tears with that white handkerchief big as a towel. His mouth be working like he's trying to talk to somebody while he's singing, two conversations at once and everybody singing from their seats, singing softer and slower as the verses of the hymn unravel, softer and slower till the last verse is a whisper like they're trying to hear what the old preacher is saying under his breath, hear what's being said to him. She wished for rockers on the bottom of the folding, funeral parlor chair. Old time music, old time preaching, the word not spoken but chanted. Loud in her, a tumult and shout and tambourine rattle so full in her breast she wanted to lay her head back and rock, rock, rock. Rock on home in the dip and squeak of her comfortable chair. *Father along. Father along.* She would take the baby on her lap and they'd rock together because what else could you say what else could you do

221

when a life ain't even got started good yet and that life gets taken away. They'd rock in the sunlight on the creaking boards of that old porch and when the sun dropped out the sky she'd hum the songs around the two of them like a blanket to keep off the cold.

She refused to go to the cemetery. She remembered that, remembered three or four of them with their bushy heads together, talking like they did when they pretended like she wasn't there. How every once in a while one of them would look up quick from the busy huddle of talk and check to see if she was still standing there and frown kind of disappointed she was. She refused so one of the lean young men in a bright colored suit had no business being worn to no funeral drove her back up Bruston Hill. The last thing she remembered from that day was the boy walking down Kelley Street. She saw him from the window of the car and he was halfway down the block but she could see he was still shuffling and see the pole jammed across the shoulders of that man's suit too big for him to be wearing. He was alone, moving away from the others as fast as those stiff shoulders and man's suit and grave dust all over his shoes would let him.

Tommy

IT is happening again. He is watching it happen again. That killing day. Sees himself check out the Brass Rail. Can't see shit for a minute in the darkness. Just the juke box and beer smell and the stink from the men's room door always hanging open. Uncle Carl ain't there yet. Must be his methadone day. Carl with his bad feet like he's in slow motion wants to lay them dogs down easy as he can on the hot sidewalk. Little sissy walking on eggs steps pussyfooting up Frankstown to the clinic. Uncle Carl ain't treating to no beer to start the day so he backs out into the brightness of the Avenue, to the early afternoon street quiet after the blast of nigger music and nigger talk.

Ain't nothing to it. Nothing. If he goes left under the trestle and up the stone steps or ducks up the bare path worn through the weeds on the hillside he can walk along the tracks to the park. Early for the park. The sun everywhere now giving the grass a yellow sheen. If he goes right it's down the Avenue to where the supermarkets and Murphy's 5&10 used to be. Man, they sure did fuck with this place. What he thinks each time he stares at what was once the heart of Homewood. Nothing. A parking lot and empty parking stalls with busted meters. Only a fool leave his car next to one of the bent meter poles. Places to park so you can shop in stores that ain't there no more. Remembers his little Saturday morning wagon hustle when him and all the other kids would lay outside the A&P to haul groceries. Still some white ladies in those days come down from Thomas Boulevard to shop and if you're lucky get one of them and get tipped a quarter. Some of them fat black bitches be in church every Sunday have you pulling ten tons

223

of rice and beans all the way to West Hell and be smiling and yakking all the way and saying What a nice boy you are and I knowed your mama when she was little and please sonny just set them inside on the table and still be smiling at you with some warm glass of water and a dime after you done hauled their shit halfway round the world.

Hot in the street but nobody didn't like you just coming in and sitting in their air conditioning unless you buy a drink and set it in front of you. The pool room hot. And too early to be messing with those fools on the corner. Always somebody trying to hustle. Man, when you gonna give me my money, man, I been waiting too long for my money, man, lemme hold this quarter till tonight, man. I'm getting over tonight, man. And the buses climbing the hill and turning the corner by the state store and fools parked in the middle of the street and niggers getting hot honking to get by and niggers paying them no mind like they got important business and just gon sit there blocking traffic as long as they please and the buses growling and farting those fumes when they struggle around the corner.

Look to the right and to the left but ain't nothing to it, nothing saying move one way or the other. Homewood Avenue a darker grey channel between the grey sidewalks. Tar patches in the asphalt. Looks like somebody's bad head with the ringworm. Along the curb ground glass sparkles below the broken neck of a Tokay bottle. Just the long neck and shoulders of the bottle and a piece of label hanging. Somebody should make a deep ditch out of Homewood Avenue and just go on and push the row houses and boarded storefronts into the hole. Bury it all, like in a movie he had seen a dam burst and the flood waters ripping through the dry bed of a river till the roaring water overflowed the banks and swept away trees and houses, uprooting everything in its path like a cleansing wind.

He sees Homewood Avenue dipping and twisting at Hamilton. Where Homewood crests at Frankstown the heat is a shimmering curtain above the trolley tracks. No trolleys anymore. But somebody forgot to take up the tracks and pull down the cables. So when it rains or snows some fool always gets caught and the slick tracks flip a car into a telephone pole or upside a hydrant and the cars just lay there with crumpled fenders and windshields shattered, laying there for no reason just like the tracks and wires are there for no reason now that buses run where the 88 and the 82 Lincoln trolleys used to go.

He remembers running down Lemington Hill because the trolleys only came once an hour after midnight and if he misses an 82 it will mean an hour on the windy corner. He thinks he can hear the clatter of the trolley starting its long glide down Lincoln Avenue. The Dells still working out on *Why Do You Have To Go* and the tip of his dick wet and his balls aching and his finger sticky but he forgets all that and forgets the half hour in Sylvia's hallway because he is flying now, all long strides and pumping arms and his fists opening and closing on the night air as he grapples for balance in a headlong rush down the steep hill. He can hear the trolley coming and wishes he was a bird soaring through the black night, a bird with shiny chrome fenders and fishtails and a Continental kit. He tries to watch his feet, avoid the cracks and gulleys in the sidewalk. He can hear the trolley's bell and crash of its steel wheels against the tracks. He was all in Sylvia's drawers and she was wet as a dishrag and moaning her hot breath into his ears and the record player inside the door hiccupped for the thousandth time caught in the groove of grey noise at the end of the disc.

He remembers and curses again the empty trolley screaming past him as he froze half a block from the corner. Honky driver half sleep in his yellow bubble. As the trolley lurched past the bottom of the hill, a red spark popped above its gimpy antenna. Chick had his nose open and his dick hard but he should have been cool, been out of there and down the hill because it was too late now. Nothing for it now but to walk. He had to walk that night and in the darkness over his head the cables swayed and sang long after the trolley had disappeared. He had to walk cause that's all there was to it. And still no ride of his own so he's still walking. Nothing to it. Either right or left, either up Homewood or down Homewood, walking his hip walk, making something out of the way he is walking since there is nothing else to do, no place to go so he makes something of the going, lets them see him moving in his own down way, his stylized walk which nobody could walk better if they had some place to go.

Thinking of a chump shot on the nine ball which he blew and cost him a quarter for the game and his last dollar on a side bet. Of pulling on his checkered bells that morning and the black tank top. How the creases were dead and grape pop or something on the front and a million wrinkles behind the knees and where his thighs came together. Junkie, wino-looking pants he would have rather died than wear just a few years ago when he was one of the cleanest cats in Westinghouse High School. Sharp and leading the Commodores. Doo Wah Diddy, Wah Diddy Bop. Thirty-five dollar pants when most the cats in the House couldn't spend that much for a suit. It was a bitch in the world. Stone bitch. Feeling like Mister Tooth Decay crawling all sweaty out of the grey sheets. Mama could wash them everyday, they still be grey. Like his underclothes. Like every motherfucking thing they had and would ever have. Doo Wah Daddy. The rake jerked three or four times through his bush. Left there as decoration and weapon. You could fuck up a cat with those steel teeth. You could get the points sharp as needles. And draw it swift as Billy the Kid.

Thinking it be a bitch out here. Niggers write all over everything don't even know how to spell. Drawing power fists look like a loaf of bread.

Thinking this whole Avenue is like somebody's mouth they let some jive dentist fuck with. All these old houses nothing but rotten teeth and these raggedy pits is where some been dug out or knocked out and ain't nothing left but stumps and snaggle-teeth just waiting to go. Thinking, that's right. That's just what it is. Why it stinks around here and why ain't nothing but filth and germs and rot. And what that make me? What it make all these niggers? Thinking yes, yes, that's all it is.

Mr. Strayhorn where he always is down from the corner of Hamilton and Homewood sitting on a folding chair beside his ice-ball cart. A sweating canvas draped over the front of the cart to keep off the sun. Somebody said the old man a hundred years old, somebody said he was a bad dude in his day. A gambler like his own Granddaddy John French had been. They say Strayhorn whipped three cats half to death try to cheat him in the alley behind Dun-fermline. Took a knife off one and whipped all three with his bare hands. Just sits there all summer selling ice balls. Old and can hardly see. But nobody don't bother him even though he got this pockets full of change every evening.

Shit. One of the young boys will off him one night. Those kids was stone crazy. Kill you for a dime and think nothing of it. Shit. Rep don't mean a thing. They come at you in packs. Like wild dogs. Couldn't tell those young bloods nothing. He thought he had come up mean. Thought his running buddies be some terrible dudes. Shit. These kids coming up been into more stuff before they twelve than most grown men do they whole lives.

Hard out here. He stares into the dead storefronts. Sometimes they get in one of them. Take it over till they get run out or set it on fire or it get so filled with shit and nigger piss don't nobody want to use it no more except for winos and junkies come in at night and could be sleeping on a bed of nails wouldn't make no nevermind to those cats. He peeks without stopping between the wooden slats where the glass used to be. Like he is reading the posters, like there might be something he needed to know on these faded pieces of cardboard. Like he might find out why he's twenty-five years old and never had nothing and never will. Like they might be selling a pill bring Sonny back and Sarah back and everything happy ever after.

Self-defense demonstration. Ahmed Jamal at the Syria Mosque. Rummage Sale. Omega Boat Ride in August. The Dells coming to the Diamond Roller Rink. Madame Walker's Beauty Products.

A dead bird crushed dry and paper thin in the alley between Albion and Tioga. Like somebody had smeared it with tar and mashed it between the pages of a giant book. If you hadn't seen it in the first place, still plump and bird colored, you'd never recognize it now. Looked like the lost sole of somebody's shoe. He had watched it happen. Four or five days was all it took. On the third day he thought a cat had dragged it off. But when he passed the corner next afternoon he found the dark shape in the grass at the edge of the cobblestones. The head was gone and the yellow smear of beak but he recognized the rest. By then already looking like the raggedy sole somebody had walked off their shoe.

He was afraid of anything dead. He could look at something dead but no way was he going to touch it. Didn't matter, big or small, he wasn't about to put his hands near nothing dead. His daddy had whipped him when his mother said he sassed her and wouldn't take the dead rat out of the trap. He could whip him again but no way he was gon touch nothing dead. The dudes come back from Nam talk about puddles of guts and scraping parts of people into plastic bags. They talk about carrying their own bag so they could get stuffed in if they got wasted. Have to court-martial his ass. No way he be carrying no body bag. Felt funny now carrying out the big green bags you put your garbage in. Any kind of plastic sack and he's thinking of machine guns and dudes screaming and grabbing their bellies and rolling around like they do when they're hit in Iwo Jima and Tarawa or The Dirty Dozen or The Magnificent Seven or The High Plains Drifter, but the screaming is not in the darkness on a screen it is bright, green afternoon and Willie Thompson and them are on patrol. It is a street like Homewood. Quiet like Homewood this time of day and bombed out like Homewood is. Just pieces of buildings standing here and there and fire scars and places ripped and kicked down and cars stripped and dead at the curb. They are moving along in single file and their uniforms are hip and their walks are hip and they are kind of smiling and rubbing their weapons and cats passing a joint fat as a cigar down the line. You can almost hear music from where Porgy's Record Shop used to be, like the music so fine it's still there clinging to the boards, the broken glass on the floor, the shelves covered with roach shit and rat shit, a ghost of the music rifting sweet and mellow like the smell of home cooking as the patrol slips on past where Porgy's used to be. Then . . .

Rat Tat Tat . . . Rat Tat Tat . . . Ra Ta Ta Ta Ta Ta Ta . . .

Sudden but almost on the beat. Close enough to the beat so it seems the point man can't take it any longer, can't play this soldier game no longer and he gets happy and the smoke is gone clear to his head so he jumps out almost on the beat, wiggling his hips and throwing up his arms so he can get it all, go on and get down. Like he is exploding to the music. To the beat which pushes him out there all alone, doing it, and it is Rat Tat Tat and we all want to fingerpop behind his twitching hips and his arms flung out but he is screaming and down in the dirty street and the street is exploding all around him in little volcanoes of dust. And some of the others in the front of the patrol go down with him. No rhythm now, just stumbling, or airborne like their feet jerked out from under them. The whole hip procession buckling, shattered as lines of deadly force stitch up and down the Avenue.

Hey man, what's to it? Ain't nothing to it man you got it baby hey now where's it at you got it you got it ain't nothing to it something to it I wouldn't be out here in all this sun you looking good you into something go on man you got it all you know you the Man hey now that was a stone fox you know what I'm talking about you don't be creeping past me yeah nice going you got it all save some for me Mister Clean you seen Ruchell and them yeah you know how that shit is the cat walked right on by like he ain't seen nobody but you know how he is get a little something don't know nobody shit like I tried to tell the cat get straight nigger be yourself before you be by yourself you got a hard head man hard as stone but he ain't gon listen to me shit no can't nobody do nothing for the cat less he's ready to do for hisself Ruchell yeah man Ruchell and then come by here little while ago yeah baby you got it yeah lemme hold this little something I know you got it you the Man you got to have it lemme hold a little something till this evening man I'll put you straight tonight man you know your man do you right I unnerstand yeah that's all that's to it nothing to it I'ma see you straight man yeah you fall on by the crib yeah we be into something tonight you fall on by.

Back to the left now. Up Hamilton, past the old man who seems to sleep beside his cart until you get close and then his yellow eyes under the straw hat brim follow you. Cut through the alley past the old grade school. Halfway up the hill the game has already started. You, have been hearing the basketball patted against the concrete, the hollow thump of the ball glancing off the metal backboards. Ball players half-naked out there under that hot sun, working harder than niggers ever did picking cotton. They shine. They glide and leap and fly at each other like their dark bodies are at the ends of invisible strings. This time of day the court is hot as fire. Burn through your shoes. Maybe that's why the niggers play like they do, running and jumping so much because the ground's too hot to stand on. His brother used to play here all day. Up and down all day in the hot sun with the rest of the crazy ball players. Old dudes and young dudes and when people on the side waiting for winners they'd get to arguing and you could hear them bad-mouthing all the way up the hill and cross the tracks in the park. Wolfing like they ready to kill each other.

His brother one of the old dudes now. Still crazy about the game. He sees a dude lose his man and fire a jumper from the side. A double pump, a lean, and the ball arched so it kisses the board and drops through the iron. He could have played the game. Tall and loose. Hands bigger than his brother's. Could palm a ball when he was eleven. Looks at his long fingers. His long feet in raggedy-ass shoes. The sidewalk sloped and split. Little plots of gravel and weeds where whole paving blocks torn away. Past the dry swimming pool. Just a big concrete hole now where people piss and throw bottles like you got two points for shooting them in. What's left of a backstop drooping like a rusty spiderweb from tall metal poles, and beyond the flaking mesh of the screen the dusty field and beyond that a jungle of sooty trees below the railroad tracks. They called it the Bums' Forest when they were kids and bombed the winos sleeping down there in the shade of the trees. If they walked the tracks all the way to the park they'd have to cross the bridge over Homewood Avenue. Hardly room for the trains on the bridge so they always ran and some fool always yelling *Train's coming* and everybody else yells and then it's your chest all full and your heart pumping to keep up with the rest. Because the train couldn't kill everybody. It might get the last one, the slow one, but it wouldn't run down all the crazy niggers screaming and hauling ass over Homewood Avenue.

From the track, you could look down on the winos curled up under a tree or sitting in a circle sipping from bottles wrapped in brown paper bags. At night they would have fires, hot as it was some nights you'd still see their fires when you sat in the bleachers watching the Legion team kick butt. From high up on the tracks you could bomb the Bums' Forest. Stones hissed through the thick leaves. Once in a while a lucky shot shattered a bottle. Some grey, sorry-assed wino motherfucker waking up and shaking his fist and cussing at you and some fool yells *He's coming, he's coming*.

He had heard stories about the old days when all the men used to hang out in the woods below the tracks. Gambling and drinking wine and telling lies and singing those old time, down home songs. Hang out there in the summer and when it got cold they'd loaf in the Bucket of Blood on the corner of Frankstown and Tioga. His granddaddy was in the stories, old John French one of the baddest dudes ever walked these Homewood streets. Old, big-hat John French. They said his granddaddy could sing up a storm and now his jitterbug father up in the choir of Homewood A.M.E. Zion, next to Mrs. So and So who hit those high notes. Sound almost like Reba Love Jackson. He was his daddy's son, people said. When he was singing regular, when he was tenor lead of the Commodores and they'd git round a bench and get down. Everybody knew the Commodores was the baddest group. If that cat hadn't fucked us over with the record we might have made the big time. Achmet backing us on the conga. Tito on bongos. Tear up the park. Commodores used to stone tear it up. Under the trees and the little kids and old folks all gone home and ain't nobody in the park but who supposed to be and you got your old lady on the side listening or maybe you singing pretty, trying to pull some fine bitch catch your eye in the crowd. Those were good days, real good days when everything got swift and mellow and fine. The drums, the smoke, the sun like fire in those big trees and you out there flying and the Commodores steady taking care of business behind your tenor lead.

You got to go to church. I'm not asking I'm telling. Now you get those shoes shined and I don't want to hear another word out you, young man. She is ironing his Sunday shirt hot and stiff. She hums along with the gospel songs on the radio. *Don't make me send you to your father.* Who is in the bathroom for the half hour he takes doing whatever to get hisself together. Making everybody else late. Singing in there while he shaves. You don't want to be the next one after him. *You got five minutes, boy. Five minutes and your teeth better be clean and your hands and face shining.* Gagging in the funky bathroom, not wanting to take a breath. How you supposed to brush your teeth, the cat just shit in there. *You're going to church this week and every week. This is my time and don't you try and spoil it, boy. Don't you get no attitude and try to spoil church for me.* He is in the park now, sweating in the heat, a man now, a father himself now but he can hear his mother's voice plain as day, filling up all the empty space around him just as it did in the house on Finance Street. She'd talk them all to church every Sunday. Use her voice like a club to beat everybody out the house.

His last time in church was a Thursday. They had up the scaffolding to clean the ceiling and Deacon Barclay's truck was parked outside. Barclay's Hauling, Cleaning and General Repairing. Young People's Gospel Chorus had practice on Thursdays and he knew Adelaide would be there. That chick looked good even in them baggy choir robes. He had seen her on Sunday because his mama cried and asked him to go to church. Because she knew he stole the money out her purse but he had lied and said he didn't and she knew he was feeling guilty and knew he'd go to church to make up to her. Adelaide up there with the Young People's Gospel Chorus rocking church. Rocking church and he'd go right on up there, the lead of the Commodores, and sing gospel with them if he could get next to that fine Adelaide. So Thursday he left the poolroom, *Where you tipping off to, Man? None of your motherfucking business, motherfucker,* about seven when she had choir practice and look here Adelaide I been digging you for a long time. I been knowing you for years girl, since your mama brought you in here and you wasn't nothing but a little thing in pigtails. Yeah I been digging on you a long time. Longer and deeper than you'll ever know. Let me tell you something. I know what you're thinking, but don't say it, don't break my heart by saying you heard I was a jive cat and nothing to me and stay away from him he's married and got a baby and he ain't no good and stuff like that I know I got a rep that way but you grown enough now to know how people talk and how you got to find things out for yourself. Don't be putting me down till you let me have a little chance to speak for myself. I ain't gon lie now. I been out here in the world and into some jive tips. Yeah, I did my time diddy boppin and trying my wheels out here in the street. I was a devil. I got into everything I was big and bad enough to try. Look here. I could write the book. Pimptime and partytime and jive to stay alive, but I been through all that and that ain't what I want. I want something special, something solid. A woman, not no fingerpopping young girl got her nose open and her behind wagging all the time. That's right. That's right, I ain't talking nasty, I'm talking what I know. I'm talking truth tonight and listen here I been digging you all these years and waiting for you because all that Doo Wah Diddy ain't nothing, you hear, nothing to it. You grown now and I need just what you got . . .

Thursday rapping in the vestibule with Adelaide was the last time in Homewood A.M.E. Zion Church. Had to be swift and clean. Swoop down like a hawk and get to her mind. Tuesday she still crying and gripping the elastic of her drawers and saying no. Next Thursday the only singing she doing is behind some bushes in the park. *Oh, Baby. Oh, Baby, it's so good.* Tore that pussy up.

Don't make no difference. No big thing. She giving it to somebody else now. All that good stuff still shaking under her robe every second Sunday when the Young People's Gospel Chorus in the loft beside the pulpit. Old man Barclay like he guarding the church door asked me did I come around to help clean.

Mr. Barclay, I wish I could help but I'm working nights. Matter of fact I'm a little late now. I'm gon be here on my night off, though.

He knew I was lying. Old bald dude standing there in his coveralls and holding a bucket of Lysol and a scrub brush. Worked all his life and got a piece of truck and a piece of house and still running around yes sirring and no mamming the white folks and cleaning their toilets. And he's doing better than most of these chumps. Knew I was lying but smiled his little smile cause he knows my mama and knows she's a good woman and knows Adelaide's grandmother and knows if I ain't here to clean he better guard the door with his soap and rags till I go on about my business.

Ruchell and them over on the bench. Niggers is high already. They ain't hardly out there in the sun bar-b-queing their brains less they been into something already. Niggers be hugging the shade till evening less they been into something.

Hey now.

What's to it, Tom?

You cats been into something.

You ain't just talking.

Ruchell man, we got that business to take care of.

Stone business, man. I'm stone ready to T.C.B.

You ain't ready for nothing, nigger.

Hey man, we gon get it together. I'm ready, man I ain't never been so ready. We gon score big, Brother Man.

The reason it's gon work is the white boy is greedy. He's so greedy he can't stand for the nigger to have nothing. Did you see Indovina's eyes when we told him we had copped a truckload of color TVs? Shit man. I could hear his mind working. Calculating like. These niggers is dumb. I can rob these niggers. Click. Click. Clickedy. Rob the shit out of these dumb spooks. They been robbing us so long they think that's the way things supposed to be. They so greedy their hands get sweaty they see a nigger with something worth stealing.

So he said he'd meet us at the car lot.

That's the deal. I told him we had two vans full.

And Ricky said he'd let you use his van.

I already got the keys, man. I told you we were straight with Ricky. He ain't even in town till the weekend.

I drive up then and you hide in the back.

Yeah dude. Just like we done said a hundred times. You go in the office to make the deal and you know how Indovina is. He's gon send out his nigger Chubby to check the goods.

And you jump Chubby.

Be on him like white on rice. Freeze that nigger till you get the money from Indovina.

You sure Indovina ain't gon try and follow us?

Shit, man. He be happy to see us split . . .

With his money.

Indovina gon do whatever you say. Just wave your piece in his face a couple of times. That fat ofay motherfucker ain't got no heart. Chubby is his heart and Ruchell stone take care of Chubby.

I still think Indovina might go to the cops. And I ain't gon back to no slammer. One year in the motherfucker like to drove me crazy, man and I ain't takin no chances. Have to kill me to get me in a cage again.

234

Ain't nobody gon no jail. What Indovina be tellin some cops? What he gon say? He was trying to buy some hot tee vees and got ripped off? He ain't hardly saying that. He might say he got robbed and try to collect insurance. He's slick like that. But if he goes to the cops you can believe he won't be describing us. Naw. The pigs know that greasy dago is a crook. Everybody knows it and won't be no problem. Just score and blow. Score and blow. Leave this motherfucking sorry ass town. Score and blow.

At the stoplight he stares at the big sign hanging over the Boulevard. A smiling Duquesne Pilsner Duke with his glass of beer. The time and temperature flash beneath the Duke's uniformed chest. Ricky had installed a tape deck in the dash. A tangle of wires drooped from its guts, but the sound was good. One speaker for the cab, another for the back where Ruchell was sitting on the roll of carpet Ricky had back there. Al Green: *Call Me.* Ricky could do things. He made his own tapes; he was customizing the delivery van. Next summer Ricky driving to California. Fixing up the van so he could live in it. The dude was good with his hands. He had been a mechanic in the war. Government paid him for the shattered knee. Ricky said, Got me a new knee now. Got a four-wheeled knee that's gonna ride me away from all this mess. Disability money paid for the van, the customizing, the stereo tape deck. Ricky would always have that limp, but the cat was getting hisself together.

Flags were strung across the entrance to the used car lot. Wind got them popping and dancing. Rows and rows of cars all looking clean and new under the lights. He parked on the street, in the deep shadow at the far end of Indovina's glowing corner. He sees them through the office window. Indovina and his nigger.

Hey, Chubby.

What's happening now? Chubby had shoulders wide as the door. He was Indovina's nigger all the way. Had his head laid back so far on his neck it's like he's looking at you through his noseholes instead of his eyes.

You got the merchandise?

You got my money?

Ain't your money yet. I thought you said two vans full.

Can't drive but one at a time. My partner's at a phone booth right now. Got the number here. You show me the bread and he bring the rest.

I want to see them all before I give you a penny. Indovina drums the desk top. His fingers are hairy. Look like they itch him.

Look, Mr. Indovina. This ain't no bullshit tip. We got the stuff, alright. Good stuff like I said. Sony portables. All the same . . . still in the boxes.

Let's go look.

I want to see some bread first.

Give Chubby your key. Chubby, check it out. Count them. Make sure the cartons ain't broke open.

I want to see some bread.

Bread. Bread. My cousin DeLuca runs a bakery. I don't deal with *bread*. I got money. See. That's money in my hand. I got plenty cash money buy your television sets buy your van buy you.

Just trying to do square business, Mr. Indovina.

Don't forget to check the cartons. Make sure they're sealed.

Somebody must be down. Ruchell or Chubby down. He had heard two shots. He sees himself in the plate glass window. In a fishbowl and patches of light gliding past. Except where the floodlights are trained the darkness outside is impenetrable. He cannot see past his image in the glass.

Turn out the goddamn lights.

You kill me you be sorry . . . kill me you be real sorry . . . if one of them dead out there it's just one nigger kill another nigger . . . you kill me you be sorry . . . you killing a white man.

Tommy's knee skids on the desk and he slams the gun across the man's fat, sweating face with all the force of his lunge. He is stumbling over the desk, scattering paper and junk, looking down at Indovina's white shirt, his hairy arms folded over his head. He is thinking of the shots. Thinking that everything is wrong, the lights, the shots, the white man cringing on the floor behind the steel desk. Him atop the desk, his back exposed to anybody coming through the glass door.

Then he is running. Flying into the darkness. He is crouching so low he loses his balance and trips onto all fours. The gun leaps from his hand and skitters towards a wall of tires. He hears the pennants crackling. Hears a motor starting and Ruchell calling his name.

What you mean you didn't get the money? Shit, man. I done wasted Chubby and you didn't even get the money. Aw, shit. Shit. Shit.

He had nearly tripped again over the man's body. Without knowing how he knew, he knew Chubby was dead. Dead as the sole of his shoe. He should stop; he should try to help. But the body was lifeless. He couldn't touch . . .

Ruchell is shuddering and crying. Tears glazing his eyes and he wonders if Ruchell can see where he's going, if Ruchell knows he is driving like a wild man on both sides of the street and weaving in and out the line of traffic. Horns blare after them. Then it's Al Green up again. He didn't know how, when or who pushed the button but it was Al Green blasting in the cab. *Help me Help me Help me . . .*

Jesus is waiting

And Ruchell crying like a baby and shaking all over Ruchell is clutching the wheel the way Sonny would hang on to the edge of his crib, when he woke up in the middle of the night soaking wet and wailing for somebody to come get him. *Help me Help me.* He snatches at the tape deck with both hands to turn it down or off or rip the goddamn cartridge from the machine.

Slow down, man. Slow down. You gon get us stopped.

Rolling down his window. The night air sharp in his face. The whirr of tape dying then a hum of silence. The traffic sounds and city sounds pressing again into the cab.

Clement

CLEMENT thinks about roller skates. Skates make his job easier. Be skating up and down Homewood Avenue. Be up and out Big Bob's and the Brass Rail and Miss Claudine's and the cleaners and the drugstore so fast nobody see him coming and going. Like lightning. Captain Lightning on his red skates with silver wheels and silver wings so fast he be back before they know he gone. Speedo. Zip. Zap. Won't see nothing but a blur. Captain Blur. Captain Flash when he come streaking down off Bruston Hill. Look out. Here he come. Zoooom. Them skates be tearing up that hill. Them skates be breaking his ass with all them holes in the streets. Homewood ain't no place for nothing got wheels. Bust up your ride. Bust you up you fool nough come rolling flown Bruston Hill. Captain Broke Butt. Captain Band-Aid Ass. You want see Clement you got to go to the hospital. Clement ain't doing his job. Laid up in bed. Big Bob go for his own warm milk and Miss Claudine don't speak. Act like she ain't never seen him before and he drink all that poison and she say, Carry him out please, Mister Lavender. Take his blubber butt on out here.

No. Clement ain't been round. Big Bob's got hair to the ceiling. Can't get the door open no more. Bell don't ring. Nothing. Like a jungle full of Brillo in there.

Miss Bess said come tomorrow afternoon. He can hear her plain as day. Her voice calling down off that mountain and it be like she standing right there talking in his ear. Some oleo. Some milk. Three pound potatoes. Yellow onions. Don't even have to go up and ask. Know just what she want sometimes and carry it up there. But she's calling and ain't nothing he can do. Captain Bandage strapped down in that hospital bed and he hears her but he stone out of business. Them skates still flying down Bruston but he ain't on top. His riding days done.

You hold on, Miss Bess.

Maybe she send down the ghost. Maybe she give the ghost one those shopping bags send him down here. Big Bob say he better not stop. Better keep running and never look back. Big Bob say they gon make him example. Say two dead niggers in one day embarrassing. Maybe they leave him alone till he get them groceries for Miss Bess. Maybe they see he ain't looking for no trouble. Maybe they see he a ghost already.

Big Bob turns on the TV for six o'clock news. Just news and ball games on Big Bob's TV. None the rest of that mess worth a good goddamn he say. Insultin to his intelligence he say. He turns on the news then opens his evening paper. Can't tell if he's watching or reading. Both he say if you fool enough to ask. *Both* and mind your own damned business cain't you see I'm busy minding mine.

Clement's business running errands. Clement's business keep this place clean. And listening for Mother Bess. He listens. But she said tomorrow afternoon. She call tomorrow. If that ghost don't take his job.

Tommy

SOMEONE pulling on his foot. Have him by the foot and dragging him out the cave where he's been hiding. A deep, dark, warm
cave. A cave as black and secret as his blood. Yes. He is hiding
deep in the rivers of his blood, in a subterranean chamber where
his own blood is gathered in a still, quiet pool. But they have him
by the foot dragging him out. He feels himself sliding, slipping,
and he tries to hold on with both his hands but the walls are slick
as ice cream, raw as meat. He can't get a handhold. He struggles
but he can't hold on. His arms are flailing but he doesn't know
how to swim so he is just flapping and flailing and beating his own
blood as they drag him out. He wants to scream but he doesn't
want to wake anybody up. If he wakes anyone up they'll just help
the others pull. So he shouts no no no as loud as he can but inside
so no one can hear. Splashing his own blood against the walls of
the tunnel. Then the no's are please are please please please like
James Brown in the song as light cracks the ceiling and floods in
a cresting wave, choking, surging, putting out his eyes if he opens
them, welding them shut forever if he doesn't.

Wake up. Wake up now. She is tapping his foot with a stick.
That evil old woman. He is lying in shadow and she is above him
staring down on him, the sunlight aflame on her shoulder. He looks
past her burning flesh into the tops of the trees which filter the
shafts of sunlight. Blinking in the sudden glare he can see through
her, past her, she is a ghost quivering without meat or bone and
he can see through her to the dark tree trunks, to the tip of the
hill to the burnished haze hanging over the city.

Come on you. Wake up, you. It's getting close to dark and I

240

want you away from here. The sun going down and I want your feet beating a path away from my door.

She steps closer to his face. She taps the stick harder now, not against the sole of his shoe now but harder now, a rat tat tat drumming against a log he had rolled from the shed to make room for himself. She was solid again, black and grey and brown, the lines of her face, the shape of her body sharply etched against the sky. Behind her, below her the city flamed.

Wake up, you. Sun's setting and least I can do is give you a cup of soup. You my sister's great-grandson and that's the best I can do before I send you on your way.

The drumming is inside his head. Her stick tapping against the log as loud as the *no*'s he had been screaming. Had she been pulling his foot? In the dream the grip on his ankle had been as tight, as heavy as a leg iron. This frail old woman didn't have that kind of strength left in her hands, nowhere in her body. But the stick chopped at the log like an ax. If she hit his foot the way she hit the wood she'd shatter his bones.

Hey, Mother Bess. Just gimme a minute to get myself together. That's what he wanted to say but he knew his words were jumbled, were just noise and all she'd hear were grunts and groans.

He sits up and bumps his head on something. A shelf, a two by four, a beam, something solid and wooden cracks him as he tries to straighten up into a sitting position. He rolls away from the blow and the scabs on his elbows and knee split but he keeps moving till he scrambles to his feet. Feet somebody had chained. Feet somebody had hold of dragging him down to hell.

You a sight. You sure are a sight.

He brushes at dirt and wood shavings and sawdust and leaves. The ground had been damp and his body was stiff.

Look at you. Ain't you a sight. Like something the cat drag in.

I'm in trouble, Mother Bess.

Any fool see that. But I don't want to hear about your trouble. I'ma feed you cause you my sister Gert's great-grandson. Cause I seen your mama, Lizabeth, the minute after she born. Prayed for you and your brothers and sister each time I heard Lizabeth had a baby on the way. Prayed if I was still praying at the time and if I wasn't praying I was hoping for the best for all youall because your mama Lizabeth was my sister's grandchild. So I'ma feed you and get you out of here as soon as it's dark but I don't want to hear none your troubles.

He watched her walk to the shack. She used the knobby stick like a cane to pick her way over the rutted ground. But the stick wasn't a cane because she didn't lean on it. The stick was more like those rods witches use to find water, or like those poles soldiers stick in the ground to find their way through a mine field. Because that's how she used it. Poking it slowly into the ground, picking, sorting, testing the broken earth as if parts of it were unfit, unsafe, as if she could take nothing for granted so she had to piece together slowly, cautiously, a path from the shed to the shack. He remembered being little and squatting down to watch ants cross the handfuls of dirt he'd throw in their way. Sometimes they darted over the barricade but sometimes they measured each step, rearing up on their back legs, probing with their antennas, pawing and peering side to side. That's how she crossed the yard. And the bowlegged stick wasn't a cane but like those long feelers jutting from the ants' faces.

Soon as he got to his feet he knew he was going to puke. He forced himself step by step till he stood where he had been standing that morning or a hundred mornings ago, whenever it was because once sleep came it had been like dying and now he had no way of telling whether hours had passed or days or a lifetime. Was the sun sinking over there beyond the invisible rivers the same sun he had watched rising on Bruston Hill just that morning? Did this fall go with that rise, or had there been a million years separating them, a million years and the sun bouncing like a basketball up and down, up and down so many times nobody cared or could tell the difference? And the thought of the sun rising and falling faster than his heartbeat, the thought of years rushing by too fast to count them, the thought of all the days of his life gone faster than even that, lost to him, gone gone gone and leaving nothing behind but the sour taste in his mouth and the swelling emptiness in his belly, all those thoughts brought the nastiness rushing to his throat and he puked down over the edge of the world, down into the molten sprawl of the city.

The last strength went out of him and he dropped to his knees so he wouldn't topple over the sheer edge of Bruston Hill, topple and fall forever, fall and bounce and split and tumble and unravel till he splashed in the rivers at the city's heart. Not much in his stomach to bring up but the shudders kept coming. Whole body wanted to turn itself inside out and jump through his throat. His spit was thick with mucus when he wiped the drool from his chin and tongued out the inside of his mouth. He stared at the little glistening puddle under the trees. Hardly a cupful. Felt like a herd of elephants stampeding in his stomach and now it just sat there mocking him. He wondered if the old woman had been watching. If she had seen him double over and fall to his knees, shaking and whining like a sick puppy. This was her place, her yard, she was the caretaker of these ruins at the top of Bruston Hill. He wanted to bury the vomit, scrub the carpet of grassy stubble. On his feet again he looked toward the house but the slanting overhang of the back porch darkened the window and he couldn't see through it, couldn't catch any sign of life, couldn't find her face and say he was sorry. Wouldn't say that anyway. So he damned his weakness and damned his sickness and damned the blind shack and the evil old woman inside spying on him.

Better come if you coming.

The golden light had begun to deepen, to redden behind him. Sky dying from fire red to dull grey like a cooling ash. He slouched toward the shack, skirting the remains of the garden, keeping his eyes fixed just ahead of his feet on the smouldering earth. He felt he was being led, felt as he had that night many years before when he stood under the tall trees at the back of his cousins' house, his hand clasped firmly within someone else's, someone who understood his fear, his sudden surges of daring, someone who stood silent and watchful but would not meddle. He believed he was being led, yet he wasn't in tow, wasn't being dragged by the feet.

He passed under the precarious roof of the porch, into its arch of shadow, stepping lightly on the ancient boards which buckled under his feet. The posts supporting the overhang were gaunt as bones, crooked as her cane as they stretched half in crimson light, half in grey shadow from the swaybacked floorboards to the roof. If he huffed and puffed he could blow the whole house down. A pile of old, shrieking wood, a cloud of dust at his feet.

Takes your time, don't you? You moves when you good and ready to move, don't you? You messes in people's wood and sleeps in their sheds like you owns em, don't you, Mister Man? Well you take your time over this bowl of soup. You got from now till dark to finish it and then you're getting on my time. And when you're on my time you got to go.

A shelf is built into the wall beside the thick iron woodstove. Her soup and her elbow rest on the waist-high slab.

Take my food standing up. You sit down there at the table. You see that bowl don't you?

Yes, Mam.

Then get to it. Ain't nobody issuing no invitations around here. And what you see in that bowl is what you get. So go on and eat.

Yes, Mam.

Takes mine standing up right by the stove. Don't need to be hauling stuff all round the room and fussing with this and that to get the table ready. Get my food hot right off the stove and standing's better for you anyway. Food can go straight down don't have to be climbing and turning corners and spilling in the wrong places. Just goes straight down where it's supposed to go and your belly ain't all twisted like it is sitting in a chair.

He blows on the steaming bowl of soup and blows on the spoon he dips then raises to his lips. Garlic and pepper and a rich meat tang float up in the cloud rising off the soup. He had forgotten the smell of food, forgotten that food could be hot and rich smelling and full of flavors. The aroma fed him. The smell of the soup seemed enough.

Don't need to study it. Don't need to talk to it. It's good soup. It's clean if that's what you looking for.

He wants to say something back to her, but the spoon is too close to his mouth and his hand is shaking so he leans down and swallows instead. Everything is in the taste of the soup. The failing light hovering in the bottom of the rear window and leaking under the splayed back door, the purple silhouette of the hills on the horizon, the smoke smell inside the shack, the hiss of wood in the stove's belly, the old woman's voice talking to the vegetables she had peeled and sliced and dropped into bubbling, seasoned stock.

All in the first taste of soup and he wants to tell her that but he doesn't know how, doesn't know how he can tell her about all that, about the simple coming together of things unless he tells her how things can fall apart, but the falling apart is the story of his trouble and she doesn't want to hear his trouble so he savors the taste and everything in it a few moments longer and says:

This sure is good soup, and says, Thank you Mother Bess.

Take your time. Enjoy yourself. Then I want you gone from here.

Light floats in the room, hangs in the darkness like oil twisting in vinegar. The soup burps and the wood hisses in the pit of the stove. Light gathered on her face makes it look greasy. But the light is floating, alive, it draws his eyes away from her lined, old woman's face and plays in the corners, the shadows of the room, focusing on objects, explaining the shape of the space. Light fixes the room's dimensions, uncovers its contents and he thinks of himself as a camera taking the room's picture. But the room won't stay still. He hadn't believed it would be easy. Everybody always said she was mean and half crazy. But he hadn't expected her to be so cold, so far away. He could talk to people. If he had any gift that was it. He could talk to people and they'd like him, they'd talk back and warm up when he smiled. He could get people talking and laughing with him even when they caught him red-handed in something he shouldn't be doing. He could make up something to say that would get a laugh. But Mother Bess just stood there slurping her soup. He mize well be on the moon or some damn place because she paid him no mind, she had shut a door between them and even though he could see through it and hear through it the door was miles thick and strong as iron.

The light that had pointed into the corners of the room, that had glided with a will of its own so his eyes surrendered to it, not knowing why they settled on this patch of crocheted quilt or that silvered edge of bent spoon, the light lost its curiosity, its restlessness and crouched under the dark wings of her hair, her hair parted in the center and framing her forehead like a hood. He knows his skin would sting if she turned her eyes on him. He knows she can feel him staring at her face, greasy and luminous as the light recedes, as the light reddens and deepens and grows too heavy to float. She looks like an old squaw. An old squaw or an old chief because in the movies the only difference is the flowing crown of feathers and that's the only way you can tell whether the old face, cracked and beat up as a mountain, is a man or woman. She has straight hair like an Indian, like all the old people on his mother's side of the family. He has his daddy's hair. Nappy and dirt brown. Combed so it's a cloud over his head, a bushy cloud making him taller than his brothers. He wonders what his hair looks like now. After the floor of the Bellmawr, the leaves and sawdust of the shed. Like a wild man probably. He can't remember the last time he combed it. The rake was gone, lost somewhere between Indovina's and Bruston Hill. Maybe the cops had it. Maybe Indovina, slick as he is, stabbed the needle-toothed comb into Chubby's heart. He rests the spoon against the inside of the bowl. Both hands dig into the tangled mass, the jungle atop his head.

Sounds like sandpaper. Grit collects beneath his nails, he dislodges a scab. He hunts for bugs scurrying at the roots. Then his face is stinging. She has him lined up over the spoon which she holds to her lips, not drinking, not lowering it but letting it pause against her pursed mouth so she can stare at him like Kilroy peeping over a wall. She is the color of mud now, clay red mud, redder than a comic book Indian, older than anything in Pittsburgh.

If he could think of something to say he'd say it but he can't, even though talk is his gift, so he lowers his hands from his hair, rubs them together beneath the edge of the table and retrieves the spoon from his soup. Which still tastes good. Almost too rich to hold down after so much nothing but still good. He dips in deep for the chunks of vegetables. Watches the freckled skin of the broth break apart like a spider web. Then there is the sound of her, the loud slurping sound of somebody who eats alone. If he made noises like that at the table his mother would yell or slap him if she was close enough. When you're old and alone all the time you get crazy, nasty habits. You get mean and evil. People wouldn't be saying those things all the time if wasn't no truth to it.

If she has a TV or radio or clock he can't find them. Mize well be in the old days when people lived in caves and what not because nothing in the room but a bed and table and chairs look like somebody made out of logs. That's all there is besides the stove and shelves around the walls she mize well be in some wild, old-

timey place where niggers still live like Africans or slaves. He looks
for a light bulb or a lamp, any sign of electricity, any object which
would bring him back to the world, to the time in which he belonged. Could be one of those huts in slave row, one of those nig-
gertown shacks clustered around Massa's big white house. All she
needs is a kerchief round her head. All he needs is a watermelon
and some chains. If the city is still there boogeying at the foot of
Bruston Hill somebody has turned the volume down, way down
so you can hear the blood behind your ears and the soup sloshing
around in the emptiness of your belly and the uncouth old woman
slurping her soup spoonful by spoonful without ever blowing on
it though it's hot as fire.

Once upon a time. Once upon a time, he thought, if them stories
I been hearing all my life are true, once upon a time they said
God's green earth was peaceful and quiet. Seems like people bigger then. They had time to listen, time to talk and room to move
round in. Aunt Aida talking bout people like they giants. That world
was bigger, slower and he'd get jumpy, get lost in it. Like now
in this stillness and quiet each sound seems too loud, seems strange
because the roar of the city isn't here to drown the noises of his
body, the noises of insects and trees and somebody else's breathing. But once upon a time him and Sarah alone in the middle of
the night. Just the two of them and the world sleeping and you
get mixed up. Can't tell whose stomach growls, who moans, whose
warm juice running down your thigh. Because it's late and the city's
asleep outside the window, outside the walls. You're in a story.
There's room enough to do what you need to do, what you have
to do. Sarah rolls closer and you can *hear* your fingers stroking
her skin, you can hear the line you trace up her back and over
her shoulder and down her breast. She is big as the sky. You can
hear her nipple stiffening, growing to meet the palm of your hand.
And when you hold your hand lightly above her breast so it just
touches, just barely rubs the hard tip of her softness you can hear
how it feels as your palm circles like coming in for a landing but
no hurry, no rush, just gliding in slow circles in the air while you
listen.

The stillness unbroken. Sarah rolls closer to him and rises slightly
on her elbow so the ring of darker brown around her nipples is

visible an instant as the covers fall away from her brown shoulders and he swallows hard because those soft eyes on her chest have a way of seeing through him and around him and taking his breath away. No matter how many times he stares at them or fondles them or mashes them with his chest when he's inside her. He swallows hard in the stillness because he is seeing another life, a life long gone. Then he is nothing. Smaller than nothing and alone. Stories are lies and Mother Bess pigging down her soup brings him back. Her loud slurping on the soup drowns the noise of his blood, the noise of his heart.

You make some dynamite soup, Mother Bess. It's not him talking. It's some jive, jack-leg preacher grinning and wiping grease from his liver lips and rolling his eyeballs at the platter of fried chicken he's already eaten half of. Yes, Mam, and I surely wouldn't mind helping myself to another piece. Rolling his eyes and showing his teeth and wiping his greasy chin on his handkerchief. Yes, Mam. Umm Ummm Mammy Bess. And he listens to the voice and it's not his but he can't remember what his should sound like so the voice keeps talking and he is ashamed, but talk is his gift, if he has a gift, so the voice continues its shuffling, its buck and wing, its step and fetchit grinning.

Till she cuts him off. Till she speaks from her post beside the stove, her elbow still leaning on the shelf where her empty bowl rests.

When you finish you bring that bowl up here. That's all there is and ain't nothing else. Just set it here by mine. We ain't got no waitress service here. I don't like to cook. Never did and never will. Don't like people talking about my cooking, neither. If people like what I fix they can eat. If they don't they can leave it setting. Don't like all that Mother Bess stuff neither. Wish I knew who started that Mother Bess mess. I ain't nobody's mama. Was once but that was a million pitiful years ago and ain't nobody on this earth got the right going around calling me mother now. I told them that. Don't know how many times I told them. But it's Mother Bess this and Mother Bess that like I ain't got sense enough to know my own name and they ain't got sense to listen when I tell them I ain't nobody's mama.

Hey, didn't mean no harm. Just trying to be sociable. You know, didn't mean to call you out your name. Like that's what I been hearing since I was a little kid. Mother Bess. All I ever heard.

Well, you heard wrong.

Sorry then. Didn't know you had a thing about your name.

Ain't had a name since those fools down there started with that Mother Bess stuff.

What you want me to call you then?

Don't need be calling me nothing cause I want you gone from here in a few short minutes. Be dark in a few minutes. Already getting dark in here.

Turn on some light, then.

Don't need lights. When it's dark people supposed to sleep.

Bet you ain't got no electricity.

They run a wire up here and it's still here far as I know but I sleeps when it's night the way decent people supposed to. Don't like no lectricity.

Sure a lot of things you don't like.

I suppose that's my business.

Tell me something you do like. Tell me something good before you run me away from here. I ain't heard nothing good for days. Tell me something you like.

What I like is what I got. I like peace and quiet and being left alone.

Must get lonely up here all by yourself.

And I like minding my own business. And other people minding theirs.

Hey, I'm just trying to be sociable.

You got a busy mouth.

Yeah. That's what I got alright. A busy mouth and a world of trouble. You got that right. But ain't nothing wrong with needing to talk. Told you I'm in real trouble. If you had a TV or a radio up here, you'd know. You probably the only one in Pittsburgh don't know by now. There's a man dead down there and the police after me because they think I did it. I'm running for my life and I'm scared.

I think running make more sense than talking.

I am running, I'm running so hard I feel like I'm coming apart. Everything I got's running. Hands, heart, eyeballs. Everything you see and don't see is running so hard I can't think straight. You see a man sitting at this table but that sitting man is moving faster than you ever seen anybody move. But ain't no place to run. Running fast as I can but I'm standing still cause ain't no place to run.

I see you sitting there. And I know who you are. Just exactly who you are.

Tell me about it.

You Lizabeth's son, Thomas. Your grandmother was my sister's girl. You wasn't even close to born when my sister Gert died. Freeda was her oldest. And some say the prettiest in her quiet way. John French your granddaddy. Strutting around in that big brown hat like he owned Homewood. Hmmph. Tell me I don't know. Know you coming and going. You a Lawson now. You and your three brothers and your sister in the middle. Don't know if she's Lawson now or not. Girls these days always marrying, always changing names like it makes a difference. Don't know what name she goes by but I know her too. I was there when your mama Lizabeth first seen the light of day. Snow was seven feet deep. You couldn't see people walking in the ditches they plowed. Snowing so hard and the wind blowing like to tore down that shack on Cassina Way. Lizabeth was Freeda's first. Came out blue as that shirt you're wearing. Yes indeed. Know all about it. I was there when that simple-minded May grabbed her up and run out in the snow. She did it so fast nobody raised a hand to stop her. Just grabbed up that tiny little sky blue baby and runned out the front door before anybody got their mouth open to say stop. Stuck that poor little naked thing down in a pile of snow and don't you know that blue child started to breathe. She started to breathe outside in all that snow and cold and freezing wind and been breathing ever since. That's your mama. And I know just who you are too.

I heard that story before. Heard Aunt Aida tell something like that. Didn't believe it. She's always talking some off the wall, old time mess like that.

Well, I ain't just talking. I'm a witness and couldn't care less what you believe. Your believes is your business. But I say what I know, not what I heard.

Sure ain't gon sit here and argue with you. If you was there you was there. All that old time stuff don't make me no nevermind. Wasn't even born yet.

You wasn't thought of. I'm talking about your mama. About the first time your mama seen the light of day and screamed to tell the world she was here.

Put her in the snow.

That's right. Stuck her in a snowdrift like you'd duck a dough-nut in your coffee.

Damn. In a pile of snow.

With the wind howling and beating on the boards of that shack on Cassina. Like to blowed it down. Front door just about tore off its hinges when May run through and had your mama dipped down in that snow before anybody could holler, Stop fool. Wasn't for that crazy May wouldn't be no Lizabeth and you wouldn't be sitting here neither.

Wouldn't be running neither.

Now don't put that on May nor your mama nor nobody else. You the one done whatever devilment you done. You the one got to pay now.

Need me a few days. Few days to catch up on sleep and get my head together. Won't be asking nothing else from you. I know how take care myself. Just need a few days.

Dark in here. And dark is my bedtime.

You a hard woman.

Life's hard. Didn't nobody never tell you? Didn't nobody never hold you up and look in your eyes and tell you you got to die one day little boy and they be plenty days you wish it be sooner stead of later? Didn't nobody never tell you that? Feel sorry for you if you a grown man and nobody ain't told you that.

Been told lots of things. But nobody got to tell me it's hard. Out here in the streets my whole life. I know it's mean out here.

You still a baby.

Well there's cops out there looking to kill this baby. And no-body ain't gon save me by sticking my ass in no snow pile. Old people always talking like they the only ones ever know trouble. Talking like the only hurt is the hurt put on them. Been hearing that jive all my life. About suffering and waiting. Like I ain't been suffering and waiting myself. Like I got all the time in the world. Like I got to suffer a little more and wait a little longer and . . . and what . . . what's supposed to happen after I suffer some more and wait some more? Tired of that bullshit.

Watch your mouth. You ain't in no barn.

I'm tired. Tired of it.

I'm tired too. And you crowding my bedtime.

You do all that talking about knowing who I am. You tell those stories and you still gon put me out in the street. You a hard woman. Don't understand you.

Hard and evil and crazy. Just like they say.

Well shit. I ain't begging.

This ain't no barn.

You got a glass for some water? If you can spare the water.

Rinse the bowl. Ain't no waitress service.

Damn.

Get your water. And don't be wasting your breath damning nothing in my house. Git your water and git.

He stands at the sink which gurgles like somebody has the pipe in a stranglehold, then as if the death grip is suddenly released, the spigot spatters him, the gagged, pent-up water splashes his pants and wets his arm and then trickles into the bowl, a trickle he mops around to rinse its insides. The water is nasty. He chugalugs, trying not to taste it but he can smell it and his mouth is full of old pennies. He spits into the sink and wants to wash out his mouth but there is only the nasty water dribbling from the faucet.

Her back is towards him. She is broad and short, squat like a beetle reared up on its hind legs. Her back hard as a beetle's back in the darkness across the room. He has the urge to stride across the room and hit her once, slam his fist into the dark shell. The blow would clang, like hitting one of those oldtimey knights in their iron suits. Just once to let her know what he could do if he wanted to. The world was hard, sure nuff. He knew all about that. Harder even than the shell wrapped around her old, thick back. World could bust her up. His fist could smash her dark shell into a thousand pieces. If not his fist then something harder, like the long handled steam iron the light had picked out on one of the shelves. It would be easy to knock her down. Nobody would miss her. She lived up here all alone. Evil and crazy. Could take what she wouldn't give. World was that hard. This Mother Bess who didn't want to be called Mother Bess, who was she anyway? What was she to him? Except somebody in his way. Somebody mean and crazy whose stubborn ways were pushing him towards his enemies.

That's how hard the world was. He could knock down this old bitch and take what she wouldn't give. Just cause she was there when his mother was born, just cause she told crazy stories and knew his name and the names of his brothers and sisters. What did any of that mean? What did it weigh? There were people out to kill him and some Mother Bess who was nobody's mama, who was nothing, who was old enough to be dead, who was she to stand in his way?

He coughed. The gritty water was stuck in his throat. In the silence, the stillness, he thought the cough would startle her, as it startled him. Make her turn around and face him and see how close he was to splitting that old beetle back, how easy it would be. But nothing moved. As crazy as she was she just might sleep standing up like a horse. All night the dark mass of her hulking beside the bed like a ghost haunting somebody asleep under the covers. Instead of a clang, instead of the brittle armor of an insect, his fist would pass through her. It would be like pounding at a door which suddenly opens. And the force of his blow, the lunge of his body into the punch would pull him into empty space, through her and falling forever.

He trips again over the rags beside the back door, slams the door behind him, and sinks again into the swaying boards before he stumbles off the lip of porch into the night.

Clement

CLEMENT is counting like that Count Dracula puppet they got on Sesame Street who's always counting everything. This time it's the balls of black wool he sweeps from the floor of Big Bob's barbershop. He is counting them as he stuffs them into a gigantic pillowcase. When he's done the pillow will be big enough to sleep on. A soft, cushioning bed in the back of Big Bob's and he'll throw away the skinny mattress spotted with bed bug blood and his blood. The balls are fuzzy soft and clean. Not like the wire and Brillo shit he usually brooms from the mottled green tiles. By late afternoon the balls of hair are dusty, matted with filth, but these are perfect. They even smell good. Not the smell of pomade and hair tonic and grease but popcorn, popcorn fresh from the glass tank at the movies. His bed will be white and soft. Like Violet's titties when she leans on the bar and squeezes her blouse between her arms so they sit there like a pillow. Clement feels himself sinking. Into the softness. Into the velvet blackness which lives inside the mirror. Lives inside her white blouse. A million Clements like the million shiny glasses stacked on the counter behind the bar and each one asleep, each one peaceful and dreaming like the glasses inside the mirror.

Bess

SHE does not dress or undress. Her man's eyes are not watching from the bed. He's not lying there with his hands ready to run up under her flannel gown, ready to undress her again when she's warm under the covers, so she doesn't undress because she never dresses she just puts something on and one day she remembers to take it off again. At night it's the buttons of a housecoat undone one by one by her clumsy fingers. She can get lost between buttons. A thought will come to her and fill her and when it leaves and she remembers again to unfasten the next button it will seem like years since she's undone the one before. Some of the rags missing half their buttons. Sometimes she's mad she'll just rip one open, split the front and shrug it off her shoulders and it'll be lying there in the morning like a skin she's shed and good for nothing no more. Sometimes her fingers so swoll up and ain't been warm all day she'll pull a flannel gown over top of what she's got on and sleep like that and pretend she doesn't care. She would have offered the pitiful thing some whiskey. She almost did when he asked for water and almost did again when she heard the faucet burst on and heard him drinking like water was going out of style. Some of Henry Bow's moonshine fix him up good. Burn his nasty mouth. Chase them scared rabbits out his eyes. But then he'd be sitting again and staying longer and if you offer one drink you probably got to offer him another. Next thing you know he's pouring his own and you got company for the night so she had just listened to him finish and set down the bowl and slam the door like some ungrateful pup. And that was that and now she got these buttons to fool with and Clement in the morning and that dry space before she dies into sleep, that space all the whiskey Henry Bow got won't fill.

Tommy

HE knew it was up there. That giant swollen frog of a water tower perched on its stilt legs. In the moonlight it looked even more like a frog. A frog somebody had made out of stuff from a junkyard. A giant soldered together frog made by somebody afraid of frogs. He knew it was up there but hadn't seen it all day till just this moment when its long shadow stretched down the hillside and he looked up from the black reflection into the sky which harbored its black silhouette. He had heard stories about kids climbing the tower. Long time ago when there was still a big house and still lots of his people on top of Bruston Hill. It could look like a frog or look like a teapot. A skinny ladder twisted up one side. Have to be crazy to go up that thing. The first time he'd seen it he'd asked what it was but nobody could tell him exactly or tell him how they filled it or why it was there growing in the middle of trees and bushes. Like a spaceship or some damn thing crash-landed and got stranded up there in the middle of those crazy people lived like hermits up on Bruston Hill. The water tower was grey and rusty. Nobody could tell him how much it held, or why it was there. Even now, even grown he hesitated at the edge of its shadow. A black shape which would soon be swallowed in the deeper blackness falling on Bruston Hill. That's all it was, etched there momentarily in the failing light. But he retreated, he stared and then backed off. If anything could have started him up that curling ladder it would be those questions he asked a long time ago. Nobody had answered them then. Nobody since. You'd have to get up there and see for yourself. You'd have to get up high enough to lift the lid and peek over the edge. The tower was the only thing taller than the trees at the back of her yard, the trees he used for guiding his steps back where he'd come from.

Bess

DON'T you think I knew you was out there? Don't you think I saw those long feet sticking out my shed? How you gon hide those long feet, those long legs? I knew you was out there. Where else you gon be?

She said it to herself a dozen times before she said it to him. And didn't say it to him when she shook him awake. No, she was quiet then, quiet as the morning which wasn't even morning yet, quiet as dawn, as the dew and darkness still hanging on when she wrapped her sweater around the nightgown and pulled on her coat over both and shuffled outside in her slippers to shake him awake. She was as quiet as the half sleep world when she took hold to the stick leaning against her bed and dragged it and dragged herself out to the shed where she knew he'd be sleeping. That quiet when she grabbed his shoulders like she grabbed the stick laid beside her bed in case him or some other nigger was crazy enough to try and take her house, grabbed the knob of bone in his shoulder which felt like the knob of her walking stick and shook him awake without saying what she'd said a dozen times to herself beginning when she dreamed the feet and again when she looked through the walls, through the black night and saw them poking out her shed and again when she made herself awake, made herself struggle with the sweater and pull on the coat saying it a dozen times at least before she crossed to the shed and shook him awake. And didn't say it out loud till he was sitting at the table again like something the cat drug in and she was starting a fire in the stove because he sat there shivering, his eyes closed, a shadow hardly more real than the shapes moving on the ceiling as the stove flared to life and she got the kettle and got that water going.

Then she spoke to the shadow as if speaking to it might stop its shivering, make it real.

Don't you think I knew you was out there? Don't you think I saw those long feet sticking out my shed? How you gon hide those long feet, those long legs? I knew you was out there. Where else you gon be?

His eyes are sleep-dulled. His flesh is puffy like it'd come off in dirty hunks if you pulled it. Pimply where the beard starts on his cheeks. She has good eyes but she lights the lamp for him and the yellow light claws one side of his face, stripping the skin, baring the scars, the pimples, the craters, the splinters of hair growing every which way.

What'd you do that for old woman? Why'd you wake me up and bring me in here for? I was dreaming. I was having a good dream and now you got me up and got me in here so you can tell me Git out again.

Hush, you. I knowed all along you was out there and knowed you ain't got the blood for it. Blood's too thin for sleeping outdoors. Look at you shaking like a leaf. Ain't no warmth in the ground yet. Ground's warm in the day after the sun been on it awhile but ain't no warmth seeped down deep yet. That ice still close under there. You can't see it but you can feel it at night. Look at you.

If you know so much why'd you put me out in the first place? Just hush.

Ain't much better in here. Like a damned icebox in here.

Pull you off one of them blankets off the bed. You got that thin blood. That's the problem.

Problem is you sent me out in the cold in the first place.

Stove gon heat up the place real quick.

Shit. Tell that to my teeth. Maybe they stop clicking. Maybe I won't freeze to death before it gets hot in here.

You sitting there like some Indin chief wrapped up in *my* blanket, at *my* table in *my* house and I got *my* weary old bones scampering around starting up *my* stove and fixing *my* coffee so's you can get something warm in *your* belly and you got the nerve to be signifying like the ungrateful pup you are.

What kind of game you playing, old woman? First you kick my butt out in the cold. Kick me out and tell me I was born to die and all that mess now you tell me you fixing me coffee and fussing over my thin blood. Don't know where you coming from. What kind of a game you playing?

Course I knew you was out there. Had to be there if there wasn't no place else to go. So just hush now and don't worry me while I'm fixing this coffee.

She lifts the cloth tacked like a curtain between two corner shelves and extracts a big jar of instant coffee and one of Henry Bow's jugs. The soup bowls are coffee mugs now and she sticks a spoon in each.

You got to cut this nasty water. Ain't nothing in it to hurt you. Minerals in it probably good for you, they taste so bad. Can't drink it less I cut it.

So it's whiskey first gurgling from the jug. Then she pours from the kettle and then the coffee is last, sprinkled straight from the jar. The spoons are for stirring and for tasting which she does without even blowing on the brew steaming in the spoon.

Can still taste the water.

And it's whiskey again, a good splash for her, a gurgle more for him and it's done.

Hey you. Don't be falling to sleep at my table. You so pitiful this morning. Here. Take this coffee. This'll thicken up your blood if you got any blood to thicken.

Then you gon let me stay here awhile?

You got my blanket wrapped around you. You sitting at my table drinking my coffee. I guess you might say you done moved in real comfortable.

I need to stay a few days. A few days till I get my head together.

You mean till hell freezes over. You mean till I'm dead and in my grave. Don't know nothing about that getting your head together mess. Head could use a combing if that's what you mean.

You know what I'm talking about.

Yes I do. Course I do. Know more about it than you. Lived too long and seen too much to believe a couple days on top of this hill gon change anything.

All I need's a little time. Little peace so I can stop running.

Listen at you. Listen at this poor child. The day you die is the day you stop running. And not one second sooner. You mize well go on back to that shed and start to dreaming again. You said it was a good dream didn't you. Cause that's as close as you gon get to standing still in this life. Mize well go on back there and start dreaming again.

You call this coffee, old woman?

Don't call it nothing. I drinks it. And if you don't like it don't say nothing, don't give it no name, just set it down.

I ain't complaining. Just saying it's strong, is all. And strong ain't hardly the word. This coffee got four feet and all of em kicking.

Water ain't good less you cut it. Coffee taste like rusty nails you don't cut it.

Well, you sure did slice this up right. You done carved it up in silver bullets and they gon make me happy if they don't kill me first.

Like two days on this hill gon make a difference. Like running ain't what every soul on God's green earth set here to do all the days of his life. Mize well go back to dreaming.

Leave my dreams alone, now. Don't need nobody getting in my dreams.

I know all bout you.

Well you sure in hell don't know nothing bout my dreams. Unless you a witch or some damn thing.

Watch your mouth.

Then leave my dreams alone. Don't be telling me you know what nobody in the world knows but me. How you know what's in my head? Got a son down there you don't know nothing about. Clyde. Be five in February. Aquarius, the water sign. His mama into astrology. She used to read all the books. Spooky how that stuff come true sometimes. She the one into it but she be talking all the time. Aquarius and it's funny cause I was dreaming bout the ocean and the beach and Clyde with me. Wasn't no beach like Chicken Bone in Atlantic City where niggers laid out side by side like they so used to the ghetto they get to all that open space they got to crowd up under one another to feel at home. Nothing like that. This was like those tropical paradises you see in magazines and what not. Like they got in ads telling you to fly here and fly there and you ain't even got bus fare in your pocket. A beach like that. All golden sand and palm trees and not a soul in sight. Not even that fine chick in a bikini they got in all the ads. Golden beach and blue waves and blue sky and just me and Clyde walking in wet sand with our shoes off and shirts off. He be smiling up at me and be listening to myself telling a story. You know how you in two places at once in a dream. Like that. Yeah. Me telling him a story and me listening too. Like really three people there and one like God or somebody so he can be on the beach and somewhere else too. Telling a story make Clyde happy. No fairy tale or nonsense like that. Telling him bout life. Real life. When life was good. When life full of good things and safe. And the story ain't just words. More like it is in them old songs. What made the story so good was that other me listening too. Watching over me and my son. The other me like some kind of god floating in the air so I could listen and make everything true. So I could make it happen.

Don't want to hear your troubles.

That ain't trouble. That's what I was dreaming till you come pulling on my foot. And you don't know nothing about it.

That's your trouble too. You just don't know it. You just don't understand yet what trouble is. That dreaming. That dreaming's where trouble start.

Already told you they after me. Them trigger-happy cops is what I call trouble.

You one comes and goes as you pleases, ain't you? Saw that from the first. Been knowing that since I first laid eyes on you. Come and go in your own good time.

I ain't begging no more. And I wish to hell I did have someplace else to go besides this godforsaken hilltop and that freezing barn like some slave or some wild animal sleeping outside.

Look you. Don't be telling me about your rather this and your rather that and your dreaming and where you'd rather be if you had all your rathers. I came up on this hill to die. Brought everything I needed with me. And this place up here is a graveyard full up with rathers. Brought everything I need. Not everything I want. Didn't say that. Said everything I need. What I want is buried in the cold ground. That's where my rathers is and that's where they gon stay till I get down there with them. Then I have all my rathers. So don't be telling me what you *would* if you *could*. Knew you was out there in the shed. Where else you gon be? Ain't no other way it could be. So here you is and here I is and that's that. So hush about rathers and drink your coffee.

Clement

IN the Brass Rail Clement hears the train less than a block away rattling across the tracks over Homewood Avenue, hears it coming behind a whistle and diesel shriek. No music, no traffic outside on Homewood Avenue. Noise of the train snatches the walls off the Brass Rail and you believe this the way the world ends, this how Big Foot Death come after you and jerk you away. After the train passes there are wavy lines and dots and buzzing like when the TV fucks up. So he waits for everything to get fixed. Waits for Carl's finger to start playing in the mouth of his Iron City bottle again, waits for Carl to finish what he was saying to his feet, waits for big-tittied Violet, doubled in the mirror, the front of her real, the back of her glowing in the dark glass, he waits for her to finish wiping the shot glass she has in her hand, wipe it and set it with the others she been polishing, set it with the million others in the mirror holding her white back. Clement's holding his breath too and might die unless somebody put a key in the lock and turn it so he can go on about his business. But things start up again. Carl mutters to his foot again and Clement sees the hand of the wall clock fall from one minute to the next so it's three minutes after eleven. It's almost afternoon and soon he better be climbing up that hill. Soon Miss Bess be calling cause she said tomorrow afternoon.

May day getting hot as June and Violet say she can't turn on the fan cause L.T. said Don't care if niggers be melting into puddles of grease. L.T. own the Brass Rail and he didn't care how hot it got the air conditioning wasn't coming on till the day it always came on and that won't be for two more weeks she said. Shoot, she said, if it was up to me I'd have it on. I'm here all day and I'd have it on. She said I don't know if it's better to have the door open or shut. It's shut now keeping out the white morning light. Carl still talking to his feet but loud enough for Clement or anybody else to listen if they want to. Then to Violet. Babe, bring me over another one of them Rocks. It was the third Rolling Rock nip to go with the double McNaughton's he ordered when Clement came in at three minutes to ten. Counting was one thing to do in the Brass Rail. Easy to keep up when just a few people like now. But Violet had sent Clement to Footer's with her pants suit. Footer's was where they footerized your clothes which meant you could get them back that same night clean as new. She sent him so he couldn't say for sure. Might be three Rocks. Might be four and maybe Carl had another double McNaughton's cause don't take him but a second to chugalug the double shot glass. Carl let it sit there for a long time, not touching it or looking at it. Like maybe he don't like it, or forgot it, or maybe Violet put the whiskey down front the wrong person. He let it sit there long as a hour sometimes then he snatch it up and drain it in a breath and she pour him another so he can pay it no mind. Clement keeps score and listens. Violet let him have a Seven-up from out the case in the back. Peedy warm but sweet. Got his thumb down in the bottle now. Like to make the poop sound. Like to make the sound of the train whistle coming through a tunnel with his top lip over the bottle mouth and blowing down in it.

Hey, Carl, you hear anything about Chester?

They got that Negro under the jail, babe. Bondsman won't touch him. Not even that bloodsucker Alphonse.

Why'd Chester go and do something like that?

All of us out here a little crazy but you got to be more than a little crazy to shoot your partner and call the police and tell them to come and get you.

Ain't the way I heard it. According to what I heard the cops made a mistake. Raided the wrong place and busted in shooting and killed Dupree and half-killed Chester and now they trying to blame it on Chester.

Well Dupree's dead and who's gon believe Chester? You got the cops story and that's the way it will go down.

   Clement had seen the spinning red lights two days before, the black and whites parked back to back and on the sidewalks and catty-corner blocking streets and alleys. He'd heard the guns popping like firecrackers and the sirens and the big voice in a bullhorn like on TV. In the doorway of the apartment building on Bennett and Kelley, stuffed in a doorway on the stone steps with a bunch of people because it was close enough to see the blood and you could stick your head out of the doorway till the cops shooed you back. Standing next to a funky old man got wine all down his T-shirt. Guns popping and the old dude grabbing at this purple belly and giggling. They got me, ooh, they got me.

   Yeah, babe. It's summertime sure enough. When colored folks start to killing each other two a day you know summertime's here. Too cold for all that mess till summertime. Ain't no robins come to Homewood for years but you know when summer comes. Niggers start dying like flies. Two a day.

   Nobody heard from your Tommy yet?

   Not yet, Lord help him. He still out there in the street. Those dirty dogs still hunting him down and I know Tommy ain't killed nobody.

   It's a shame.

   Worse than that. Worse than the worse you could imagine, girl. It's a damn crying shame. Ain't been over to my sister's yet today. Know I should go over there but she's just coming apart. She was pitiful last night. We all sat up with her after the police left. My heart ain't hard enough today. Can't watch what this mess doing to her.

   Always falls hardest on the mama. On the family.

   Well, Tommy ain't too happy neither. Wherever he is. Don't know what I want. If they catch him they gon put him under the jail. No little wrist slap nine months like he got last time. But if they don't catch him and put him away he's just a walking target. One them pigs shoot Tommy down and get a medal and nobody gon ask no questions. Just a matter of time.

   The ghost he heard yesterday morning has a name. Same name they talking bout in Big Bob's. Clement doesn't tell Carl that Tommy is dead already, a ghost already up on Bruston Hill in Miss Bess's house. Ain't nobody's business. Because when you do train noise deep in the bottle you could make the train fall from the sky and land on the bridge over Homewood Avenue like it does dropping like a cat with all four feet spinning before it hits the ground.

Clement watches Carl watch a man come in the door. Tall man in a suit ducked in the door and looked around real careful like maybe he in the wrong place, like maybe he subject to turn around and split somebody yell *Boo* real loud. But he lets the door swing shut behind him and tips in and sits beside Carl.

Violet. This my nephew, John. This Tommy's brother from out of town.

And the tall dude how-do-you-dos and pleased-to-meet-you or some such off the wall do like that and Violet plays it back perfect like she been saying such stuff all her life.

Man don't even order a drink. He just gets in Carl's ear and Carl twisting his big butt this way and that like the stool getting hot up under his buns.

Then Carl start to working his knees. Big thighs flapping like butterfly wings. Getting faster and faster like they pumping something to his mouth. Like he got to be working real hard down there under the bar so his mouth can make that lazy kind of Carl talk. You ain't never sure another word coming. They take they own good time. Don't know if Carl finished talking or just resting he take so long between words. And the man mize well stop whispering cause Carl tells everybody everything anyway. Tell his feet if nobody else listen. That loud slow Carl talk you be hearing even if you ain't listening. You be in the back peeing you still hear Carl preaching and that tall dude draws back like he don't know nobody talk that loud.

Your mama told you right. This just where I be most the time. Got my little throne here. You know what I mean?

Tall dude act like he ain't with Carl now. Sitting up straightbacked. Peeling at that label. *Budweiser, please* is what he ordered. And Violet bringing him a beer and a glass just as nice. He don't say Rock or Bud or Iron like somebody got good sense. He have to go and say *Budweiser, please* like Violet supposed to set something different on the bar nobody else ain't drinking.

Clement sees the Tommy face behind Miss Bess's wall now. The Tommy they all talking about. Miss Bess said come tomorrow afternoon and the ghost be gone.

Oh yeah. Yeah. Yeah. You know something, babe. I'm getting absentminded and pickle-brained as them old folks used to crack me up. Guess I'm one now. Old like Aunt Aida and the rest. You know how Aunt Aida was. And there was her sister Aunt Gert. She was your great-grandmother, but you wouldn't remember Aunt Gert, bless her soul. Aida and Bess and Gert and Gaybrella. All them Hollinger sisters a little nutty. Never knew what they'd say next. You got that science fiction mess these days but let me tell you Aunt Aida the original time traveler. She was a sure nuff trip. Aida be standing there looking you in the face having a conversation with somebody been dead thirty years. She always loved Tommy special. Bet she was wild like him in her day. Always asking after Tommy that first time he was in the slammer. She got so much in her head, can't keep it straight. It's funny too. Tommy used to visit Aunt Aida regular. No time for nobody else in the family but he'd take that baby of his over there see Aunt Aida. Never could understand that one. Running wild but always found time to see Aunt Aida. Half the time the poor old thing wouldna knowed whether the devil or Abraham Lincoln be knocking at her door.

The man beside Carl is listening with his head down. Stripping the label from his bottle of beer. His is Budweiser. *Budweiser, please.*

Violet babe, why don't you get up off some of those quarters?

L.T. don't like me using bar change in the jukebox till there's plenty customers.

You know I'm the best customer L.T. got. And my nephew here lives out with the white folks in Colorado. He don't get much soul music where he's at. He's the only colored out there and I know they don't allow no nigger music on the radio.

Colorado.

Yeah. Out west with the rich white folks.

You like it out there?

Course he does. No garbage in the streets, no junkies going through your mailbox. Wish I lived someplace they run all the trifling niggers away at sundown.

Violet says Hush Carl and tells the man she's sorry his brother in trouble. She whispers. Everything is whisper after Carl's big mouth. She don't smile, don't flirt at the stranger. When Violet smiles you see gaps and a broken tooth. But she don't care. She's good at flirting. Nobody counts her teeth. Don't like her smile she'll say *kiss my ass* in a minute. She's serious now. No flirt. No smile. When she leans over the bar like she's doing now looks like a pillow sitting there. White blouse with purple flowers. Titties like a pillow when she leans with her elbows on the bar and listens up close in the man's face.

Thank you. I appreciate your concern. And it's Wyoming, not Colorado.

Bet it's nice out there. Bet it's clean.

It's a good place to raise children.

Ain't that nice.

Her elbows are on the bar and her titties squeezed between them, glowing like her back glows in the dark mirror. She smiles now and wants to hear more. She is batting her eyelashes and as close to the man as the bar she keeps polished and shining will let her get. He sit straight on his stool. He don't lean away but he don't get down neither. If a train came now and hooted loud like they do, bet he'd jump ten feet in the air cause he can't get closer and he better not lean back so there ain't no room for him. Stool mize well be a pin head.

He's a nice man, Carl. Then her eyes in the mirror, winking at Carl. Carl's eyes in there following her. In the dark mirror with those shiny rows of glasses and the soft white pillow.

Mind's getting limpy as my feet. How many times you told me Wyoming? Know damned well youall live in Wyoming. You been out there what . . . two, three years now. Moved out West when Tommy had his first trouble. Yeah. And I still go and say Colorado. You know what it is, babe? All them places sound alike. That's what it is. I think Wild West and white folks, and one place sound just as good as the other.

Three years.

Brain getting bad as my feet. Got shots for a while but they still swell up soon as it's hot. Feet ain't worth a damn. It's all I can do to get myself to work. Old man Strayhorn told me once the worse kind of pain was foot pain cause a poor man always got to use his feet. Seems like since my feet been bad I got to do more walking than I ever did in my life. Walk to work. Walk to the clinic for my methadone. Be sitting at home wanting a Rock so bad I can taste it. But I just sit there thinking and smacking my lips a half hour before these feet decide to walk cross the floor.

Terrible how they do you. They just stick you in jail and let you rot. Wasn't nothing wrong with my feet till I went to jail. Went through the war and everything. In the jungle and the ocean and done every kind of nasty work a poor man has to do to stay alive. Went through all that and my feet fine till they rotted in the goddamn jail. Jail's a killer. Jail eats you up. Hope Tommy's a thousand miles away. Hope he's halfway to Timbuktu and ain't looking back.

I guess it's good that Tommy knows his way around. That should help.

Oh yeah. Your brother ain't no baby. He been in the joint before. He know his way around, alright. Trouble is he know too much. Know what it's like behind them bars.

But he'd be safer there than where he is right now. Wherever that is. While he's running he's in danger of getting gunned down by a cop.

Hope he's a thousand miles away from here.

They don't always ask questions first.

You got that right. These Wyatt Earp Marshall Dillon motherfuckers don't like nothing better than blowing away a nigger if he look at them cross-eyed. We got plenty niggers dead resisting arrest. Hope that boy's long gone from here.

Then you don't know anything? Haven't heard anything?

Wish I knew. Wish I got a post card from Hawaii or some damn place ten thousand miles away.

Mom worries that they'll bring him home dead. She says she can't sleep because every time she closes her eyes she sees him in a box, dead in a box.

Your mama always was the worrying kind. Your mama always did feel things more than other folks. She bleeds for people. My big sister's a worrier like her mama and always will be and ain't nothing nobody can do about that. Is her blood pressure up?

Sky high.

Well you make sure she stay on her medicine. Make sure she don't stop. When she gets real down she tell herself medicine don't don't do no good. She stop taking it you don't stay on her. That boy's gon feel worse than he do now if something happen to his mama.

Sometimes I get close to hating him. Everything inside me gets cold and I don't care what happens to him. I think about all he's done, all the people he's hurt. The way Mom is now. And that man who got killed in the robbery. I know it's not all Tommy's fault. I know he's a victim in a way too. But on the other hand he's hurt people and done wrong and he can't expect to just walk away. But he does think he can walk away. Like he walked away from his wife and son. He's still like a child. He always wanted every day to be a party. A party from morning till night. He'd wake up looking for the party. It's that attitude I hate, not him. I want Tommy to live, to have a chance. I want him to be a thousand miles away too, but I want him to see what he's done. I want him to take responsibility.

Wish I knew something to tell you. Wish I could say something to make it better.

I ought to go soon. I'll be staying at my mother's for the next few days. Or until something breaks.

Well I'ma come over later and sit with Lizabeth. She'll listen to me sometimes.

Quarters clink in the jukebox. They are heavy and don't fall straight. Whole machine shakes when a quarter falls, you can hear it hit the dead ends and bang over the edges like somebody made out of metal tripping down steps. Colored lights dance across the top of the jukebox and do funny things to Violet's face. She studying the numbers and letters you push to get your record. Her shoulders shake when the music come on. She's shivering beside the jukebox like somebody just opened the front door and let the Hawk fly in. She wrap her arms around herself and squeeze her own titties. Then the Hawk gone and she ain't shaking she's smiling that big-mouthed, gappy Violet smile and playing the row of buttons like they was a piano. Long green nails tapping the buttons and the wheels inside the jukebox turning and spinning out colored lights in her face.

Play B-12, babe.

This ain't no Bingo Game.

274

Go on, play it. You know that's my tune, babe. Push it three or four times and bring your fine self back here and lay one of those Rocks on me. (Four?)

Colored people is a shame. Minute ago you begging me to play the jukebox for you and your nice nephew. No sooner I start to doing that you crying for me behind the bar.

B-12, sweets.

You know I played it, man. You know I ain't hardly not played it with you sitting here. Wonder B-12 ain't wore out.

Good ones don't never wear out. Good ones might stretch little but you sure can't wear them out.

Go on with your nasty self, Carl.

Ain't nothing nasty about it. The truth ain't never nasty. It just be the truth.

Listen to him. Listen to this man trying to sound heavy. You trying to show off for your nephew. He's an educated man. I can tell that just by looking at him. Now I bet he could get real heavy if he wanted to. Shy as he is I bet he could talk that talk if he wanted to.

Violet is behind the bar again. Talking loud to somebody else down the other end. Music makes it harder to hear what people saying so Clement just leans back in the booth, runs his tongue down in the Seven-up for that last bit of sugar if his thumb ain't pooped it all out. Carl pours the Rolling Rock into his glass. (Four?) He tilts his glass so it won't be all foam. The color is pee. Beer going in and beer coming out look the same. That's why he don't drink it. He just takes a glass of sweet wine when he can get it. If wine come back out you'd be dead because wine coming out would be blood.

Ain't sweet at all so he pulls back his tongue and pokes out his lip and the train starts through the tunnel. Slow and soft at first but then he blows harder and it's haul-assing. Shake the Brass Rail just like a real train.

What you doing, Clement? Don't you be making that noise when B-12 comes on. Didn't even know that boy was still behind me till he start to making all that noise. Young boy like him oughtn't be hanging around in no bar all day.

Where he supposed to be then? Out on the corner shooting dope like the rest of these hoodlums his age. Clement's alright just where he is.

Hey Clement. Stop that foolishness and make yourself some change, boy. Run this figure over to Big Bob's.

Clement watches Carl take a stubby pencil from his shirt pocket and write on a napkin and wrap three quarters in the paper. As Clement takes the wad of wet napkin and coins and the dime Carl drops in his other hand, he looks for Tommy in the tall stranger's face.

My nephew don't be playing no numbers, Clement. He ain't crazy like the rest of us round here.

Clement felt the man's eyes. They were the eyes of the ghost on Bruston Hill. Eyes that could scream across a room, through a wall. Eyes that could name things when they weren't screaming. Ghost eyes that knew his mother's name.

Tommy

BEFORE the dream of his son and the golden, endless beach he had dreamed of Sarah. The kind of dream they say you have when you're drowning, or on a scaffold waiting to be hanged, or blindfolded with your hands tied behind you and your back against a wall. The kind of dream which lets your whole life run like a movie before your eyes, a crowded, sad movie which seems to take forever but starts and ends while the bullets are in the air, while the rope snaps tight, while you fight for one more breath and can't make it and stop fighting the black waves. While he slept on Bruston Hill he watched a dream of his life with Sarah flashing past so it took no time from start to finish, but each image, each memory like a city he could enter and live in forever:

Where have you been? Sarah is sitting on the couch beside the suitcase she had packed a month before. The bag is baby blue, for luck she said when they bought it at Woolworth's, for luck and a healthy baby boy she said while he counted out the nine dollars and ninety-eight cents into her hand. A new bag and everything inside it new. Not for me, she said. For the baby, for our baby to have a fresh start. Her belly has tugged the mini-dress to the tops of her thighs. She looks ready to explode, her stomach twice as big as it had been earlier in the day.

Dammit, man. Where have you been?

You know I been at the pool room.

I called an hour ago. Somebody said you weren't there but would be right back and he said he'd give you the message.

Had to make a little run, Sweetheart. You know. Take care of business. But I'm here, Sugar. Got a cab waiting downstairs.

It's been over an hour.

Nobody told me nothing till a minute ago. Been flying ever since. Take it easy, baby. Get yourself together now. Cab's downstairs with the meter running.

They're coming so fast. Put your hand here. Her stomach hiccups beneath his fingers. The contraction feels like a belch sounds, rippling, a rise and fall, an echo dying in the body's caverns. He stretches his fingers over her roundness, palms her belly like a basketball.

Better get you to the Man. You ready to pop.

Damn the waiting. Damn all the waiting in the world. Sitting on that damned couch scared to death. Scared the baby would start coming and I'd be here all alone and God knows where you were you said you'd be right back you said you'd just be gone a minute.

Then she's talking too much, too loud and moving down the steps too fast for somebody with a belly ready to pop. Heat so heavy in the stairwell it bumps your face. You could make heatballs and bounce them off the sweaty walls. Her voice trails over her shoulder. Telling every nigger in the apartment house their business. The back of her paisley dress is wrinkled, a corner of it folded up above the seat of her panty hose. He wants to smoothe the hem. Wants to dry the sweat blot between her shoulders. He should be in front of her but she's moving too fast. He should be in front to catch her when she comes tumbling down. He tries to grip her elbow, tries to steady her and stop her and tell her to slow down, tell her he loves her and will protect her and love and protect the child she is carrying. He nearly trips himself with the baby blue suitcase. He realizes how high he is when he reaches for her and his hand comes loose and dangles and his fingers close on nothing. Sweat in his eyes. Funky and sweating like a pig. A wrong nigger leaving her alone up all these steps. Alone to carry the baby in the summer heat. No money to go nowhere. Trapped up there in that hot box and him in the street.

Baby, baby. And he wants to tell her he's sorry. Tell her things be better from now on. Be good to her from now on but she is out the front door and the suitcase a dead weight at the end of his arm and his feet aren't moving. He's nailed to one step and she can't hear what he's saying. She's outside yelling at him to come on.

I'm sorry, baby. He wanted to say he was sorry but all that came out was a big grin as he settled in the cab beside her and patted her knee. The driver slams the door behind him. A spasm catches Sarah and drains the blood from her face. He would kiss her but the tight, thin line of her lips says no. Says too late. Like kissing a razor he thinks and shoves her new blue 5&10 bag under his knees. He wants to tell her the baby is the most important thing in the world. Baby wasn't real till Bubba gave him her message. Then more real than anything and he hollered and flew out on Frankstown. Almost killed hisself jumping in front of a cab. Told the driver, I'm having a baby, man. Laughing and the baby getting more and more real as the cab raced through the Homewood streets. Wanted to tell her how scared he got and then the calm flashes when he knew everything gon be alright. Laughing at hisself because he was high as a kite. Sitting in that cab he could hear Ruchell tell the story years later. Your old man was something, boy. Your pops was a mess. Somebody else chiming in. Yes indeed. Your daddy flying when you was born, high as John French got on that Dago Red when his babies came. Old big hat John French should be here to see it. John French shoulda lived to see these beautiful grands coming. . . .

Sonny's getting so tall. All that baby fat just melted away. Tall like his daddy. Got those long hands and long feet like you.

Yeah, little nigger's growing, sure enough. Supposed to grow, ain't he? Looked huge first time I seen him after I got home. She used to bring him in to see me at first. Then she stopped.

It was hard on Sarah. Just getting out to that prison when you don't have a car is hard. Hard enough for her, let alone dragging a baby out there too.

I ain't blaming her. Sometimes I wasn't sure I wanted him to see me in jail.

I wish you could stay with him now.

Too late, Mama. Ain't no way.

He needs a daddy.

Got a daddy. Just ain't got no home. Home with a righteous mama and daddy who ain't screaming and fighting all the time. I tried. Swear to God I tried hard. But it's the same old mess since I been back. I ain't hitting on nothing. No money. No job. Nothing. What I'm gon do for him or his mama? No point talking bout it. Easier if I just don't see him no more.

Christ looks down from the chapel wall. Long, soft, blond hair like a woman's, a cutie-pie beard, blue eyes painted in a tricky way to stare at you, to follow you around the room, to climb inside your chest. Red letters underneath. *Life Everlasting* in blood red letters. Ain't no red blood in this jive Christ. Kool-aid or Pepsi Cola or some damn thing. This Dude be scared he see Elder Watt knee-walkin cross the bare floor of Tioga Street Sanctified in the Blood of the Lamb Church of God in Christ. When Elder Watt praying and dancing on his old knees you could see that nigger's prayers. See them rise and shimmy and wobble and jerk people out their seats. You could see his prayers camel-walking down the aisle, see them like ladders twisting up in the air. Elder Watt would shout Real, real, Jesus is real. Yes He is now. Real Real. Oh so Real. Real Father Real. Out puffing reefer in the alley, listening to the Saints carry on you could see the walls shake, hear Elder Watt tearing down that raggedy building and putting it together again with real real real, each real a block of shiny stone rising from the ruins.

He hears those prayers, watches his mama's tears because he doesn't shut his eyes. Sneaks looks at everybody else because he doesn't understand what happens when they pray. When he closes his own eyes all he can think of is being old, of smelling old like the people around him on the wooden benches. Powder and perfume and the sweet stuff the men slap on their cheeks after they shave. And the stiff clothes rustling, creaking, the women specially because there are clothes under clothes under clothes and if you ever got to the skin underneath it would be dead because it couldn't breathe. So when you shut your eyes to pray it's like a lid over your head and you think of being old yourself and the people already old are dying and you're trapped there under the lid with the old smells and sweet smells and the stale smell of skin trying to breathe.

He peeks again under the technicolor, tricknicolor eyes of that Christ on Benson's chapel wall. Someone is dead behind all those flowers. His father's father. From the dark side of the family where he got his kinky hair. The short, dark brown man who was Grandpa, who would arrive in his red pickup every Saturday morning and dig his shaky fingers into his wallet and find *a little something* to help them get through the week. Never stay'd long, just have a cup of coffee if coffee was on and a sweet if they had one in the house.

Don't youall touch that last piece of pie in the icebox. Your grandpa be coming by tomorrow morning. Sometimes the only sweet in the house was the sugar she spooned in his coffee and then they would sit for a few minutes at the kitchen table till whatever made him hurry away each time he visited made him hurry away again.

He was a good man. Don't know what I would have done all those years if he hadn't been there to help out.

Never stayed no time. Always be popping in and popping out.

Mr. Lawson had his ways. He'd never take anything but a cup of coffee and a roll or a piece of cake, something sweet like that if I had it around. On Christmas he'd take a drink. That's why we always kept eggnog. Why I had to fight youall to leave it alone. It was for him. For that eggnog and whiskey he'd take around the holidays. He had his ways and nothing on God's green earth would change him.

Start to fidgeting and you know he's on his way. Stuttering like well . . . well . . . Well I guess I better be movin long.

I asked him to eat with us a thousand times but he was always in a hurry. That's why it seems strange now with him up there so still.

He could deal with them white folks. He was a tough old dude. Taught me how to work when I was little and used to go with him on his truck. Had him a million hustles. Plumbing and roofing and painting and cleaning yards and moving refrigerators. Best job I ever had. Shoot. Only job I ever had where somebody tried to teach me something.

Sarah said she'd be here and bring Sonny.

Better not let her hear you say Sonny. Sarah be bringing Clyde.

Her son got him a name, a proper, Christian name. Sarah don't dig no nicknames. All niggers got nicknames. You know. Bumpy Slick Junior Sonny. She won't be bringing no Sonny nowhere.

In his family *Clyde* never had a chance. Everybody made up their own names for a new baby. Clyde was *Sonny* and *Sonny Boy* and *Son Love.* Sonny talking and Sonny Boy walking and Li'l Son Love got him a toof and Son Son Baby cradled in somebody's arms *Son son sonny son sonny son son* as somebody made a song of his name and sung Son to sleep.

Don't see him much no more. It's hard but I stay away.

Don't give up so easy. Sarah's a good girl. She waited for you. She tries hard. Youall talk it over. Try a little harder. I'll pray for you. Think of Sonny. Think of your boy. I know how much you love him.

What I'ma do for Sarah. Sarah don't want me hanging round. Can't do nothing for myself let alone Sarah and Sonny.

He remembers Sarah getting rounder and thicker each day. When she was carrying Sonny, skinny Sarah was all butt and belly and breast. She stopped walking and started to move like a boat. Not waddle like a duck like he thought she would but roll easy through a room like the room was water and she was one of those sailing ships easing through it. Trying to tell her all the time she was looking good. Tried to play around with her, but she didn't like it said she was a balloon and he had the string in his hand and she didn't like it cause he could just let go if he got tired holding it.

She is at the door of the chapel, her eyes lowered to the visitors' book like she is looking for a secret in there or like she doesn't know what to write. Like she doesn't know if she is Sarah this or Sarah that because the string is broken and there she stands looking at the book with Sonny in her arms. And that little dude's already too big to carry. Looks long as his mother.

Then he is beside them and says Hey and reaches out to touch them but Sarah tightens her grip and the boy buries his face deeper into her cold-stiffened coat.

Say hello to your father, Clyde.

He is his father so he leans his face closer, nuzzling, nibbling till a smile dimples the plump, cold cheeks. He is closer to her also,

closer to the little hovering Sarah cloud and it surrounds him, perfume and cinnamon breath, the bones under her clothes rustling
brittle from the cold.

Shouldn't be smiling. Even the baby shouldn't be smiling. Not
here. Nothing here but long faces and walking like you on eggs.
Got that organ on tape. Precious Lord Take My Hand. But all the
songs the same. Playing long face and creeping round like your
feet might hurt Benson's floor. Like you ain't good enough to be
alive. Like you supposed to be sorry you breathing. Precious Lord
Take My Hand. He wanted to stop it. Tear the speaker from the
wall. Stomp its dusty face. Snatch the little man inside and smash
his brains out against the grinning teeth of the keyboard. The music
had nothing to do with his dead grandfather. Nothing to do with
life but it dogged his steps as he followed Sarah and his son down
an aisle into the chapel.

Sonny slides from Sarah's arms, bounces a moment on Benson's
pearl grey rug then hugs his grandmother's legs before she sweeps
him up and his knees land in her lap. She wraps her arms around
him and pulls him to her chest and rocks him as she rocks herself
side to side on the funeral parlor chair. Not rocking to the organ.
She's down with Elder Watt rocking on the bare boards. Her face
shines over the boy's shoulder. Bright tears, glad tears as she rises
to higher ground. Her face in two places at once. Worry lines, age
lines say his mother's on the bench beside him. But her eyes are
gone, lifted to the higher ground. She wants to take Sonny with
her. Rocks him back and forth. Her shoulders sway, circle, wing
her to the higher ground.

Think of Sonny. Think of your boy.

He has seen his mother's face cry and laugh like that when he
opened his eyes to watch the others pray. Like she has him in her
arms again. Like she's pressing him to her bosom and squeezing
and he can't hardly breathe. Sonny in her arms now, but he's rocking there too. Spying on people's faces while they sing and pray.
When her heart opens you could fall in. Sonny squirms, pulls away,
big-eyed like he's scared. Like he's in a hurry to find Sarah.

Then they playing keep-away. Sonny pulled from one woman's
lap to another. Passed over him like he ain't there. Like he's monkey in the middle.

I didn't know whether to come. But Mr. Lawson loved Clyde. And he did everything he could to help us. I thought we both should be here.

Of course you should be here.

Talking over him now. Like he ain't there. Like he's monkey in the middle and keep away.

I hoped you'd feel that way.

He'd want you both here. He was a proud man. He'd want you to see him this way the last time. Benson did a good job. He knew he better. Mr. Lawson picked out the casket and the room, the suit he's wearing, everything he wanted, and paid Benson a long time ago. Knew if he want it done right, he better do it hisself. He knew his people. Knew they'd be squabbling over that little bit of insurance money and Benson get it all. He knew his people. Knew us all. Me. You. Sonny. Tommy. Knew us all.

Mr. Lawson never called him Sonny.

No. He knew you. Knew how people get a thing about names. That's why he was always Mister Lawson to me. Never thought of calling him anything else. He always called Tommy, Thomas Edgar. Never just Thomas or Tommy but Thomas Edgar. Said the white man used to call us whatever he wanted. Uncle and Cuffy and Boy. Anything came into their heads. But now we got real names, *entitles* he said, and if man got a name nobody had a right to call him out his name. He said he fought all his life for a name.

Well, this one will be Clyde as long as I'm around.

Youall talking a lot of trash. Nothing wrong with Sonny. Things different now. This is a new day now. I mean I can call my son what I want to. I mean Sonny just as *respectable* as Clyde if I'm the one saying Sonny. I mean I'm his daddy and not some jive white man come along calling him out his name.

You don't see Clyde for weeks at a time. He doesn't see you and doesn't get one red cent from you. Don't sit here talking about your rights. Daddy's just a word. This child can't eat it, he can't wear it, he can't run to it when he wakes up crying in the middle of the night.

My Grandpa's up there in that casket so I ain't gon tell you what I'm thinking. Maybe I ain't even got a right to think what

I'm thinking but anyway I sure ain't saying nothing with him up there. This is his show so I'm just gon sit and respect the dead.

I'm sorry.

I'm sorry too. So sorry I wish I knew a word worse than sorry. . . .

Sarah with Sonny sleeping in her lap is framed in the rearview mirror of his brother's car. He is driving and has to ask her for directions. Away less than a year and the streets had changed. Streets dying, streets blocked, streets made into One Ways, streets gouged out in the middle, streets where the trolley tracks were being ripped from their cobbled beds. Streets going in circles and streets where no cars were allowed. In jail he had depended upon a dream of those streets, a dream in which they never changed their shape, the life in them remaining the same till he returned. Kept a picture of the streets in his mind. Tioga Dunfermline Susquehanna Homewood Hamilton Frankstown Finance a picture frozen like before a commercial on TV. And the streets, the life in the streets would wait for him to return and then everything be moving, everything be just as he left it. Moving again, alive again because he was back. Tioga Dunfermline Susquehanna. The shortest way between places not a question of walking but a matter of being in one place and thinking he wanted to be in another and dreaming the flow of the streets unfurling behind him, beside him till he got where he wanted to go. Gliding from the corner of Frankstown and Homewood, from Bubba's pool room to home. Close his eyes and it happened. Three blocks on Homewood, cut down Hamilton where the trolleys used to run and after two blocks cross over the bumpy street, the tracks which used to guide number 76 to the streetcar barn four blocks farther on from where he crosses over Hamilton to Dunfermline. Dunfermline a short narrow street where Willy Meadows lived and you don't have to stop and kick his butt because he's dead of an overdose and Willy don't wait anymore in his front window sticking his tongue out when you pass so you don't have to try and sneak up on him one of those days when he's playing on the sidewalk and kick his butt you just go on past the little, green-roofed, leaning Meadows house till Dunfermline dies

at Tioga which you cross catty-corner to pick up an alley called
Cassina Way and Cassina is the last street you're on till the dirt
alley where you cut left and come to your back door.

That's how you do it. In his cell he'd dream the streets gliding
past perfect in each detail. The music at the record store, the fried
chicken and fried fish smell of Hot Sauce William's Bar-B-Que,
the blinking red and yellow lights you pay no attention to at in-
tersections. Ghosts of trolley cars make the wires sing over your
head. He kept the streets inside him. Even though they were full
of broken glass, and cracks, the garbage stacked at the curbs and
boards over the empty windows and iron cages over the windows
with anything in them, and black stones still smelling of smoke,
still smelling of dead winos and dead firemen in the vacant lot after
they tried to burn down the streets one hot August night. Even
though he left little bloody pieces of himself scattered all over the
streets, he kept the dream. Frozen storefronts and frozen faces and
music frozen in the darkness of his cell.

In the rearview mirror Sarah's face. She looks out the window.
Not a girl anymore. Not a pretty girl face like a flower nobody
ever touched. Soft girl face gone but she was Sarah, the mother
of his son, the wife lost like everything else lost because he was
evil and cold just like they always said. Good for nothing like they
said. A cold evil nigger killing her girl face, burning it up the way
they burnt up Homewood Avenue.

He had stood beside her on burlap at the edge of the fresh grave.
The drivers from Benson's held the coffin on straps over the mouth
of a gaping hole. The earth was freshly turned and loose under
his feet even though everywhere else the ground was frozen. He
had let his eyes run over the faces of the mourners. Like Sunday
in the Homewood A.M.E.Z. Church. His Grandpa had no church
so they buried him out of Homewood, Reverend Harrison presid-
ing. In limousines from Benson's to the church, the pallbearers in
white gloves so thin you could see the black of their hands through
the material. He didn't want to be a pallbearer. Didn't want to
touch the handles of the coffin. Always been afraid of dead things.
No matter how small, how dead, and it was a dead man in the
box. Limousines from the church to the cemetery and since the

286

dead man was his Grandpa, he'd go this once all the way with him. Go with his son and Sarah since he knew they too needed to go. So he stood on the burlap over the freshly turned earth and stole the faces of the mourners while their eyes were closed and they prayed and chanted their last good-byes.

Yea though I walk through the Valley of the Shadow. Yea though I walk. The voices drift up the hillside, lost in the stillness of brown earth and bare trees. Like a mighty trumpet in Homewood A.M.E. Zion but here under an iron January sky their voices a kind of lost whisper gone before it got started. Sarah's lips formed the words of a prayer but she didn't say it. Just her breath twisting like smoke in the cold air. The words unspoken, dying in warm balloons of air as her lips opened and closed in time with the preacher. In his cell he had tried to put together her face. The feathery lashes, her skin taut over high cheekbones, the brown clean sweep of forehead from her dark brows to the dark tangle of her hair. Wanted her to be like the Homewood streets so he could shut his eyes and slip from place to place, so he could hold her safe inside, so she would be there ready to come to life again when he returned. But he couldn't do it, couldn't find her face the way it was when she was sleeping, the way it was when he'd wake up first and look over at her and forget for a moment the empty day on its way. In her sleeping face he could lose himself. Forget who he'd been, what he was, because she was beautiful and peaceful and for a while nothing else counted. He would raise the covers and look down at her naked body and it would take his breath away because each time it would be like seeing her the first time, the darker brown circles on her breasts, the breasts like eyes seeing through him and around him. A stranger's mysterious body nestled warm and soft beside him and he'd need her, want her but wouldn't say a word, wouldn't break the charm because then the day would start, he'd lose the magic in her sleeping body. In jail she kept moving, turning away, pulling the covers tight around her body, hissing at him for breaking her sleep. He saw the bits and pieces of her spinning, out of focus, a breast, a hand, a thigh pulling away, resisting, hiding itself and the ache in his groin would mount to his throat and the bitter *not taste* of her would be dry in his mouth.

And his hands would pull and stroke and tear at his own flesh because he could not bear the raw emptiness they grasped when she would not stay still in his dream.

Sarah still now, praying silently beside the open grave, lost to the son beside her who fidgeted with the folds of her coat. His son who would never know the man Benson's people were lowering into the earth, his son who would never know the man whose cold evil shadow shivered on the burlap behind him.

Sarah sitting in the back seat of his brother's car so Sonny could stretch out and rest. She rides a vacant stare out the back window and he wonders what she sees in the battered streets. In the Homewood streets so changed in a year he had to ask her directions twice just getting from the cemetery to where she lived.

He sleep?

I think so.

He alright?

It's been a long morning for a little boy. He was upset by people crying. He didn't understand.

What you tell him?

I told him Grandpa had gone away and we wouldn't see him anymore. Clyde called him Grandpa like you did.

Yeah.

You know how smart Clyde is. Nothing gets past him. He knows something terrible has happened. He's been very quiet and sticking closer to me than usual.

Shoulda told him Grandpa's dead. Dead and gone.

Don't let's talk about it. He may be listening. He doesn't miss much.

Kelley Street is one-way now, a wasteland for two blocks after Braddock. Like it's been bombed. All the houses knocked down, snow-cluttered piles of plaster, bricks and lathe boards. Rotten beams jutting from basement cavities into which houses were bulldozed. The third block, seventy-four hundred, had been spared. Bright pink and green and blue, the freshly painted rowhouses grinned at him like somebody with new false teeth. Sarah's is a green one, seventy-four-fifteen. He found a space where the broken curbstone would not scrape the car doors when they opened. The bundle of Sonny lifted out and tucked in one arm, the free hand reaching back into the car for Sarah's, which it brushes for a moment, but she is pushing her black dress down over her knees and scooting to the edge of the seat and out on her own two feet, her heels clacking on the pavement, her long legs briskly scissoring to the green door. Sonny should be heavier in his arms, but the boy is losing his lumpy baby weight, his arms and legs are stretching out. His son's bones drape across his chest, a cling, a lean, a dangle to his body, his son beginning to learn to carry his own weight even while he is held in someone's arms.

On the golden beach again and a blood red sun hangs half in the sky, half hidden beneath the sea so the rippling surface of the water, from his eyes to the horizon, is on fire. He looks back at their tracks in the wet sand. They stretch undisturbed, paralleling the curving shoreline as far as he can see. The tracks are puddles and in those closest he can see bubbles and shifting sand, new life being freed where they have stepped. Sonny's hand is cool and warm in his. He laughs and lets go his son and starts to run. Giant, high-kneed strides like Jim Brown and O.J. jitterbugging in and out of the waves, up and back from the breakers to the sand, dodging, shifting, always escaping the rushing sea swells riding up the beach. Sonny is clapping and laughing too. Watching his daddy zigzagging and high stepping and whooping and free as a bird.

Sarah had been his woman and Sonny would always be his son and he wanted to feel good about entering this green-doored cardboard house where they lived. It still smelled of fresh paint. He recognizes a few pieces of furniture, the rug from their old apartment. He wonders if she kept the king-size bed, the bed where the three of them had slept, where he watched Clyde drinking from Sarah's breasts, her milk-swollen breasts as strange and new as the baby.

Clyde learned to crawl on this rug under his feet. Sarah had wanted something soft and warm, a thick pile rug to hide the cracked floorboards of their apartment, a rug to cut the drafts and cushion the baby's falls. So he lied about having a job and got instant credit and signed a note and promised to pay seven times what the carpet was worth so he could get it delivered the same day he scratched his name on the paper. He bought the rug at the jacked-up instant credit price and received the free bonus of a wall clock.

Neither rug nor clock worked. Sarah used to borrow a vacuum cleaner from her mother. He could see her rocking back and forth, her robe flapping open at each stroke because that watermelon starting to grow and nothing on underneath the robe but skin and the dark hair between her legs. Stroking back and forth, combing the nappy rug. He hears the noisy vacuum she had to cart up all those stairs, sees her naked legs as she sways and the robe parts to her waist and her arm pushes up and back, up and back but the rug always looked like a mangy dog needing a bath. Not four years old yet, he could date it by Sonny's age, but the nappy motherfucker looked a hundred. He wondered if Sarah had ever finished the payments. One day he burned all the bills. Crumbled them and threw them in the sink and burned the mothers just like they had burned half of Homewood Avenue one summer night. He parted the beige fibers of the rug with his toe, exposing the network of grey threads anchoring the tufts. He remembered the balding head of the Jew who sold him the rug and kicked deeper into the bare patch.

Sarah had carried Sonny upstairs. A kettle hummed in the kitchen. When he had that janitor's job for a couple of weeks Sarah would wake up with him at 3:00 A.M. and they'd sit half sleep at the kitchen table waiting for the pig-nosed kettle to whistle. The hum was rising to a high-pitched whine when he lifted the kettle, the same red kettle with the black snout, from the burner. There were clean cups and silverware in a plastic rack beside the sink, a jar of instant coffee on the countertop. Easy to find sugar in the bare cupboards and he was dumping a second spoonful into a cup when Sarah came down the steps.

Like old times.

Thanks for catching the pot. I forgot I turned on the stove and that noise would have waked Clyde for sure.

How long you been here?

A month or so.

Mama said something bout you moving but never said where. Been meaning to get your address. You know. In case something comes up. In case I get my hands on a little something to send you.

I still take my mail at my mother's. They steal it here. Junkies go through the boxes. I know they get in the house when I go out.

But there's nothing worth stealing. I used to be afraid to open my own door, afraid I'd catch one in here and he'd get scared and hurt me or hurt the baby. Don't know why they waste their time searching these shacks. The people in them poor as everybody else around here. Still when I come home after dark, if the light's on next door I ask one of the fellas who live there to come with me while I go through the rooms and turn on my lights. They think I'm crazy.

Coulda stayed at your mother's.

I need my privacy. Anyway we're doing alright here. Just have to get used to being on my own.

Sonny sleep?

I think so. He was whimpering when I put him down. Didn't hear anything before I came back downstairs. He should be tired, but he's a little scared.

Shoulda told him I'm here.

Sleep's what he needs. And a little time to get himself together. He doesn't need any more excitement. He doesn't see you for weeks at a time and he just gets confused.

Shoulda told him Grandpa's dead and gone. Shoulda told him his daddy's here.

Daddy's just a word when there's no man around.

That what you tell Sonny?

I tell Clyde the truth.

Like what truth? Like your truth? Like he ain't got no daddy?

Don't get started. And don't raise your voice. He needs sleep. He's too young to deal with all this. I'm his mother, I'm grown and I can't deal with it. Your grandfather was a good man. He helped any way he could and never asked for a thing in return. I hated to see him just shrivel up the way he did. Lying in a hospital bed getting more and more helpless. I had to stop going to see him. Couldn't look him in the face. It was just too pitiful. Half the time he wouldn't even know if anybody was in the room with him. So I stayed away. Then I got ashamed to go back because I had stayed away too long. I knew he'd be mad and fuss at me and I wouldn't have an answer. He did so much. Everything he could. Even when he got too old and sick to work he shared the little bit he had.

Bone and blood in the back of his hand. Bones and bloodlines from his grandfathers. One white as a white man. Grandpa a dark spot in the snapshots in Geraldine's book. John French fairskinned and tall and lanky till he got old and got that belly. Harry Lawson a shortish, dark, thick-chested man till they took him in the hospital and he had them operations and they start chopping chunks of that solid, dark meat off his bones so by the end nothing to him, by the end wasn't nothing under his hospital gown but feathers and bone. Feathers and bone the time he helped the nurse move him so she could straighten his bed. Like not so much a question of getting his Grandpa's weight up in his arms as it was a matter of holding him tight, circling the feathers and bone with his arms so the old man wouldn't fly away.

John French would throw him in the air. He wore a big hat and drank wine and chewed tobacco. He was a gambling man they said. A rogue they say and taught him nasty songs which made the women say, Hush up boy, don't you ever let me hear you say that nastiness again. And say to his grandfather, Why you teach that child something like that? And John French would roll. He'd slap his knees and laugh and choke till he coughed tobacco juice in the brass bowl sat by his armchair. He had grown up in John French's house. His mother and father separated for the first time and his mother had no place to go but back to her father's house on Cassina Way with the children. The best time of his life. Cousins from up on Bruston Hill to play with, the house full of aunts and him the youngest, the spoiled darling. Then it all went to pieces when John French died. When he died in the bathroom and they couldn't get his big body unwedged from the bathtub and the toilet and the women had to get help and Fred Clark came and everybody screaming and finally they got him laid out across the bed but he was gone and it all went to pieces. There were places in that old house he could never touch again. The places where John French had been dead. Places he still didn't go in now.

It's a bitch out here. I mean the world don't make no sense. I got two grandfathers, right? A black one and a white one. And both them die the same day. Same goddamned day seventeen years apart. December 29. And my birthday the 28th. Now what kind of sense does that make?

And what kind of sense it make for me to be sitting here? Loved you and loved that boy more than anything. But I wouldn't do right. Just couldn't do right to save my soul. Love him and love you and here I sit like some goddamn stranger drinking coffee at your table. He had to die to get us in the same room. Now what kind of sense that make?

It's too late. I'm sorry but it's too late. You don't know who Clyde is, and he surely doesn't know you. If you had stayed with him, with us . . . maybe. But you're a stranger now and it'd just confuse him. Dealing with you here today and then dealing with you gone again tomorrow. You're the nice man he calls Daddy and you bring candy when you come and you tickle him and throw him up in the air and catch him and he watches TV with you till way after his bedtime but that's all there is to it.

Go away. Don't be beating around the goddamned bush. For once in your life say something loud and clear. Say *Go away, jive nigger.* Say it loud and clear.

You're already away. You've been away since before he was born.

Don't start no mess.

I'm tired. I don't want to go through it ever again. Not your little business you always had to leave and take care of, not your lies, not Ruchell and those tacky, junkie whores youall ran with. None of it. That's the past. It's over and done. I thought I had a man but I didn't. I know it now when I stand there afraid to open my own front door. I know it when I have to ask strangers to go in my house and scare away the ghosts. I know it when I have to put a coffee pot on the stove so it will whistle and I won't be alone. Forget it. I know where it's at. And so does he.

He always be my son.

You're the one fucked him in me. That's all.

Don't start talking shit. Ain't ready for no shit today.

I'm not ready either. I'm sad and I'm hurt and I'm scared and I don't have room to feel sorry for you. I don't have the words, I don't have the time to deal with you. You always needed somebody to feel sorry for you. You always need somebody to forgive you. Maybe that's why you did so much wrong. So somebody could feel sorry, so somebody could forgive.

Look here. I ain't asking for nothing. You can get up off my case. I ain't come here for no bad mouth from you. Can't be in the same room five minutes without nastiness going back and forth.

It's all there is between us.

Sonny's upstairs, woman. Wasn't for me he wouldn't be here. Ain't much but it's something. Say what you want about me. I'm still his daddy. I was a wrong nigger. Sometimes I knew I was fucking up and sometimes I didn't know. Sometimes I cared about fucking up and sometimes I didn't give a damn. Now that's a wrong nigger. That's me and I'm dealing with that. Got to deal with it. Look back sometimes and I want to cry. But I ain't crying. No time to cry. Don't do no good no way. Then I get mad. The shit comes down heavy on me. Don't care what happens. Don't care about nothing. Nobody gives a shit and neither do I.

I'm sorry. I really am. Sorry for us both. We didn't make it. But now you've gone your way and I'm trying to make a life for Clyde. You can't come back whenever you're in the mood and put us through changes. You had your chance for a son but you didn't want him. You wanted the street, whatever you loved so much in those gutter-rotten streets, and that's what you choose and that's what you got. It's too late now.

Bones and bloodlines. Wonders why the back of his hand don't blow apart. He gripped the hard edge of the plastic countertop. Why don't his veins split and the black-blood and the white blood of his grandfathers spurt up like a fountain. If he sat still any longer he would explode. She had said he loved the streets and he could remember times when he screamed freedom, he needed his freedom, he needed to get out of the house and be free. Was that what he loved? Was that what the pounding in his head and the bulging veins in his hands were saying now? What was there inside him that needed to be free? What was there inside him so strong that it made him turn his back on Sarah and turn his back on his son, so strong it could split open his skin?

He got up and left Sarah alone at the table staring into her coffee. He passed the steps and walked toward the curtained front window. Other men walk through these rooms, other men stop at the stairs and smile and climb to her bedroom. To the king-size bed nobody had ever paid for. But it's her bed now. And her son.

He parted the green drapes and watched Kelley Street. You can get to Homewood A.M.E. Zion by walking down Kelley. Not this end of Kelley where Sarah lived but the other part below Braddock was one way of going from home to church. No one walking now. Only a dog across the street at the end of the pastel rowhouses up on its hind legs worrying a garbage can lid. The sky greyer and greyer. Perhaps it would snow again. What color was a sky when it was fixing to snow? Did the greyness get closer, lower? Was it mixed with white? Had anybody ever watched close enough, long enough to know? Did the sky always look this weary when people died? Was it like this seventeen years ago when they buried John French? Will people stand on burlap to keep their feet clean when they bury him? Will Sonny be peeking, stealing the faces of the mourners?

The pool room a fifteen-minute walk from Sarah's. The Brass Rail ten. Homewood distances measured in foot time because he'd never had a car. He would tell Sonny what the boy needed to know. What everybody needed to know.

Will you look at that sky. Look at that gold fire on the water. You could march cross the ocean if you got feet like those black Indins walk on hot coals.

Daddy, what is dying?

Dying's what we all got to do someday.

When?

You know not the hour. That's what the song says.

Why?

Cause it happens to everything. Trees, birds, people. Everything got to have a beginning. And if it got a beginning, it's got to have a middle and then it's got to end. People start by being born. Like you was, out your beautiful mama, Sarah. People live and that's the middle. Dying is the end. Even mountains have to die.

Will I die?

Don't have to be worrying about dying for a long time. You just got started, little man.

Will you die?

When my time comes.

Will it come before I die?

Nobody knows. But you just beginning. You probably be around long after I'm dead and gone.

I don't understand. I don't like it, Daddy.

Death's a mystery. Life's a mystery. Your cousin Kaleesha only here a few days. Don't seem to make no sense, do it? Don't nobody understand much bout any of it, you get right down to it. Just hold my hand. Look at that sky. Look at that burning water. Ain't it a sight?

But what is death?

Death's like . . . it's like being gone forever.

For a long, long, long, long time.

Long like that, but even longer. Dead people go away and they never come back.

Where do they go?

They go . . . to the sky . . . to the earth. Different people believe different things. A song I like says *To My Father's House*. Old folks say *Over Jordan*. And songs say other things too. One say *One More River To Cross*. One say *There's A Home Far Beyond the Blue*. Another just say *Farther Along*. Used to hear all them old songs on Sunday morning. Your Grammy Lizabeth always had gospel on the radio. Sometimes the songs made her cry. Sometimes she'd shout Amen, or Hallelujah. Scared me sometimes cause she seem far away. Had to touch her and make sure she still standing in the kitchen fixing breakfast or ironing shirts.

I don't want to go away. I don't want you to go away. I'm scared, Daddy.

And he was two people walking along the beach with his son. Two so one could grip the boy's hand tighter and be scared himself but the other him could sing those old songs and dance on the waves and think of something to make the boy laugh. The other person he was could hear the sea gulls chattering like kids playing jumprope in the playground and make up a nasty rhyme to chant to the rhythm of the turning rope. A rhyme funny and nasty so the boy would laugh because he knew he was getting away with something when the women shushed him and wagged their fingers and fussed at whoever taught him such terrible mess.

Two so he could see the man and boy and the footprints and the crimson sea and sky. So the dream could turn happy again and the stories the man told the boy come true again, someplace, somewhere. On the other side of the green curtain.

Hiding Place

The stairwell in this house on Kelley is narrow. It stinks of raw paint and shellac. Wood squeaks no matter how softly he plants his feet. He is following the trail of Sarah's lover up the stairs, following a dude who smells barbershop clean, who's sharp as a tack, a dude with a job and a new ride, a dude who could do something for Sarah and Sonny. A dude whose new shoes squeak, who goes to the left at the head of the stairs, left to the open bedroom and the king-size bed with its fancy spread. But he goes right, toward the peedy smell leaking into the hallway. He takes his first deep breath since he entered the house. What he's been trying to hold in, sighs out. Pee stings his nostrils.

Sonny's breathing is loud, ragged. It sputters inside his stuffy nostrils. Sonny still wetting his bed. Too old for that. And too young to be standing outdoors in raw weather beside a raw grave so the chill and dampness turn to a frozen puddle inside his body. Snuffling and sneezing and a runny nose. Why is Sonny wetting his bed like a baby?

He pushes the cracked door inward. Grey light leans against Sonny's face. He was sleeping on his side, on the bed near the door, only his face uncovered and one arm dangling from beneath the quilt. He holds his breath and steps through the opening. His shadow crosses the shaft of grey light, crosses Sonny's face. When he reaches the bed, the full-size bed on which the boy's body is barely a lump, he stands aside to let the dull glow from the open door fall again on Sonny's features. Sonny's lips hang open, twitch, are purple in the gloom. His daddy's full lips, heavy eyebrows and lashes, Sarah's fair skin, her delicate, curving neck, her high cheekbones. The boy's face helpless as a mirror. Rattling sighs fill the room. Somewhere in the darkness was a pile of wet, pee-soaked clothes. And his son too old for that. Something wrong to make him still do that.

I hope you didn't wake him. He needs his sleep.

He's sleep. Ain't got nothing to say anyway. Just wanted to see him and let him see me. But he's sleep. What I got to say anyway? Just out here in the street is all. That's all I know. Nothing. How to get over on nothing. Just out in the street hustling to stay alive. So what I got to say to him?

When my other grandfather John French died it just about killed me. Sick for days. Couldn't go to the funeral or nothing. Nobody never told me nothing bout dying. A baby like Sonny but I remember saying to myself over and over, Why didn't nobody tell me bout this? Why didn't they tell me? Nobody said Boo, and then him gone and then nothing nobody could tell me make no difference. Keep seeing this big hole in the middle of John French's house, in the middle of everything and he fell in and anybody could fall in and nobody never said a mumbling word about it till too late.

Then his arms are around Sarah, and the grey sky, the grey light of the streets, the grey light spreading across the floor of Sonny's room are in her eyes. Her brown eyes glazed by grey rain, by slants of grey rain like the bars of a cage. And the bars are steel and he reaches through them to cup her face in his hands, her face which fits the heart shape of his empty hands grabbing through the bars. But she won't stay still. The room goes out of focus as he buries his head on her shoulder, in the Sarah cloud of perfume and cinnamon breath and bones rustling. His hands are busy finding her body under the silky black dress, the deep curve of her back, the springy strength under satin skin. He is saying her name. Breathing Sarah into her shoulder. His hands are shaping the word as they slip over the outline of her panties, as they ride the swell of her hips and squeeze the firm flesh. He sees her robe surrender to the bump of her watermelon belly, the blue robe open up to her waist, her belly pouting above her naked legs. He is whispering her name into her ear. Sarah, Sarah. Drawing her closer and tightening the circle of his arms.

Till he hears what she is saying. Till he feels the iron in her shoulders. Her arms bent at the elbow were drawn up like sticks between them. He hears her asking why. Why, Why, Why, as she she pushes him away.

No. Not this way.

Sarah.

No . . .

Sarah.

We're just feeling sorry for ourselves. I needed somebody's shoulder to cry on. I thought that's what you needed. But you want more. You want everything.

Hey, girl.

Why?

It's me, baby. It's me. Don't it feel good? Don't it feel right? It's me, baby. I need you.

That's not enough.

What you talking bout? Don't talk.

There's tomorrow and yesterday. There's all the lies. All the hardness. All the days I've spent getting together the little bit I could to make a new life. All the things I can't understand about you and never will till the day I die.

He rehearses all the pleas he could make. His gift of words. His rap. His jive, the old front porch, vestibule, couch, doorway, backyard, backseat, Westinghouse Park game he always won. He thought of all the times he'd gotten over, all the raps to all the chicks, and the words churned in his guts like food gobbled down too fast. The grey rain had passed. Everything in the room sharply in focus. He was as naked as the bare walls and his hands had no right being anyplace but at the ends of his arms. His hands hung through the bars, limp, dead, raw from grasping nothing.

There was a time he would have sung to her. Tenor lead of the Commodores down on one knee. *Why do you have to go? The night is still young yet.* Fling his cape over his shoulder like the Count of Monte Cristo, the Duke of Earl, Speedo and the rest of those bad motherfuckers and be chirping and be down and coming on so heavy what else she gon do but get up off some trim, Jack. There was a time. But she won't stand still and all the words from all the songs are smoke in his mouth, are bitter in his throat and he can't even say one word, make one sound but the screaming deep inside, the scream of his hands as they shake the iron bars of his cell.

Sarah.

Yes, yes, yes, Son. That's how you began. Inside your beautiful mama, Sarah. Swimming round in there like a little goldfish, jumping round in there like Froggy the Gremlin and I could feel your little frog legs through your mama's skin and see her belly jump when you hopping round in there. That's the beginning, you're just getting started so don't worry none. Don't you know Froggy went a courtin and he did ride Uh huh, uh huh. Right on down to Miss Mousey's house. Uh huh. And don't you know the goose drank Thunderbird wine and the monkey chewed Five Brother's tobacco on number 88 trolley car line. And don't you know there's black Indins don't feel pain in they feet. They could walk on that burning water all the way out to where you see the sun taking a bath. Now ain't that something? Ain't that a good something to know?

Bess

DON'T nobody set foot inside here but that boy, Clement, who runs to the store for me. He gets me what I need from down the hill and he probably be the one find me dead in here one of these mornings he knocks and I don't answer the door. Some of them used to come up here call theyselves keeping an eye on me but I stop em at the door now. Ain't none their business what I'm doing I been on this earth long before most them even thought of so I stop em now they don't get past the porch now I say what you want or say go away and don't even open the door so they don't bother me no more. That boy's the only one I see regular and he's the only one sets his foot inside my door.

It was your sister, Lizabeth's middle child, the one they call Shirl she one of the last I let in here. Favors her mama and her mama's the image of Freeda, my sister's girl. Freeda was the oldest and the prettiest in her quiet way. But don't you let those quiet ways fool you. She run away with John French quiet enough didn't she? So quiet she fooled everybody till she come back four days later and told Bill Campbell, I'm married. I'm married now. And she was married good. You know John French married her good. Quiet as she was she was married good and you could see the brazen in her eyes you never saw before when she come back after four days talking about she's married to that rogue John French.

She's the one. The one they call Shirl. Don't tell me I don't know youall. I know just who you are. Wrapped up like some Indin Chief in my blanket. Snoring like a hog at my table. I thought you saying something to me and I turns around and what is it? It's you snoring like a hog and I got my mouth open like a fool to answer you.

She sat right where you're sitting. Had that baby with her. Carried that baby all the way up Bruston Hill and that's why I let her in. Summertime too so you know she had to have something on her mind to tote that baby on her back all the way up this wicked hill. Well she said, Hi Mother Bess. Said I brought the baby to see you, Mother Bess. I was on the porch in my rocking chair like I usually be and I had to squint the sweat out my eyes before I could see good who was talking at me. Then I saw Gert. Then I saw Freeda. Then I saw Lizabeth. Then I saw the one they call Shirl with this little brown baby in a sack on her back. That's the way they do nowadays. Carry they children like wild Indins. And that's how I heard Sybela Owens brought them babies from slavery. Had a sling crost her back and brought them all the way from slavery to the top of this hill. So I'm rubbing sweat out my eyes and trying to see who I see because I get to rocking in that old chair and mize well be blind as Sybela Owens, mize well have that black cape she always wore draped over my eyes cause I ain't seeing nothing outside, ain't studying nothing but what I keeps inside and that sure ain't nobody's business and I'll tell em in a minute go on away from here go on and leave me alone.

She said Hi and I said Come on up here and bring that baby out the sun, girl. Cause now I could see that's what it was. A baby back there like them Indins call papoose and she been totin it all the way up Bruston Hill on her back in the broiling sun. Poor little thing probably bar-b-qued back there and I'm wondering if this girl got good sense and wondering what she got on her mind, if she got a mind, climbing Bruston Hill like that.

She sat at the table where you're sitting and drank a glass of this nasty nail-tasting water. Tried to cut it for her but she said No thanks and drank it warm as pie and nasty as it is right out the spigot. Fed the baby out a bottle she had tucked back there with it in the sack. Cute, chubby-legged, little chocolate brown baby. She was wearing a cap to keep the sun out her face and the little thing sweating like a horse under that cap. A whole headful of hair. Looked like a wet chicken all sweated up under that cap. That's your daddy's side of the family. Nothing but good hair on your mama's side. All of us Hollingers had that long straight hair. Was a time I could sit on mine. And Freeda too when she married

John French had that good hair all the way down her back. But this dimple brown little thing look like a drowned hen till her mama dried it and combed it out nice and plaited it again and fixed five or six of them teensy barrettes in there. Said she was *Kaleesha* and I said what'd you say and she said that African-sounding name again and I said I thought that's what you said and didn't say Why you go and name a child something like that. Kept my big mouth shut for once and said it Kaleesha out loud cause it wasn't none of my business. Kaleesha. And the little thing smiled up at me out the biggest, prettiest black eyes I ever seen. Yes they was now. The prettiest I've seen and I've seen many an eye in my day but these was the brightest and blackest and prettiest. Didn't matter they rolled around and crossed sometimes. They was the prettiest black-eyed Susan black eyes under that fuzzy head and I can see them today just as plain as I seen them when she was sitting on her mama's lap right where you sitting.

That's why I went down this hill one last time when they told me she died. Don't know which one it was come up here to tell me cause I didn't open the door but I heard alright and it shocked my nerves. All I could think of the rest of the day was them eyes. Brown as she was and fuzzy-headed too and chubby-cheeked like babies supposed to be I could see her mama in her face and if her mama was there in that baby face you know I seen Gert and Lizabeth and Freeda. Whoever it was on my porch knocking then talking through the door then getting huffy cause I wouldn't let him in. Said they'd bury her on Wednesday and somebody be by in the morning to take me down. Didn't pay no mind to all those words. Heard him talking and heard him getting mad cause I didn't answer but I wasn't studying him or studying no funeral or no Wednesday or nothing else because them big black eyes was in this room and I said Jesus and said Good God Almighty because that's what I say when there ain't nothing else to say even though I ain't been a Christian for years, Jesus and Good God Almighty cause what else you gon say when some old woman ninety-nine hundred years old still living and breathing on the top of this hill and that little baby's gone. I ain't got no life no more I'm just puttering around here waiting to die but that child's dead and I got them eyes, them pretty baby black wandering eyes floating round here.

I let them take me. Let them talk that Mother Bess this and Mother Bess that foolishness and kissed the children they pushed in my face. They think that's good luck. They think I'm mean enough and crazy enough and old enough to have some kind of power so they bring the little ones and push em up in my face. That's why she climbed Bruston Hill with her baby on her back. Climbed up here in all that sunshine and sat where you're sitting and cried at my table. Cause the doctors had give up. They named it then they give up. Some terrible name. Couldn't nobody but the doctors say the name of that sickness killing your sister's baby. She told me all about it. About hospitals and ambulances and shots and oxygen and pills and tests and I didn't understand none of it except them doctors settled on a name and then quit. Said it might be weeks or maybe a year but hardly more than that. Said they'd take the baby and hook it up to machines but just a matter of time either way so she kept the baby home. Kept her home and watched her day and night and if somebody asked me I woulda said it's the mama bout to die the way she looked when she come up here with the baby on her back. Anybody be tired after climbing Bruston Hill but there was something past tired in that girl's face. Wasn't nothing to spare. Wasn't one patch of skin or lump of fat or bone or muscle or gut string to spare. They was all drawed out and all stretched thin as they could get and you could see in her eyes, in the way she carried herself like she weighed three hundred pounds when she wasn't nothing but skin and bones, see how close she was to coming clean apart. How easy it'd be for one string to snap and then all the rest break down and she won't be nothing but jelly. And the baby looked fine. Fuzzy little head running sweat under that cap but she was a bouncy, smiley dimple-kneed sweet little brown baby with the prettiest eyes in the world. Eyes that rolled and crossed sometimes but you look at the two of them, look at mother and daughter, and if you didn't know no better you be thinking the poor babygirl gon be a orphan soon if her mama don't start sleeping right or eating right or stop doing whatever it is make her look like a ghost.

They thought I had a power so Shirl brought her baby to see me and told me all about the terrible sickness and how sickness was in those beautiful eyes already. How it would steal those eyes and

steal her ears and one day the lungs just forget all about breathing
and the heart forget about beating and it was just a matter of time
because those doctors named it and give up. She said all that but
never said nothing about me, about that power supposed to be
in somebody old and evil and crazy because if you talk about it
you can jinx it so you talk about everything else, talk around the
power cause you don't want to jinx it. But I knew she ain't climbed
Bruston Hill just to tell me her troubles so I listened and heard
what she said and heard what she didn't say and thought about
all the babies I kissed all the young ones pushed in my face and
set on my lap. Wet ones and ones stink to high heaven and brown
ones and black and white and fuzzy-headed and no hair at all and
good hair like my side the family. Some of those children grown
and down there in Homewood and God knows where else and some
probably dead by now but they still coming with their babies so
I sat there listening to your sister and tried to keep the power out
my mind, tried not to jinx it or pray for it or promise it. Just sat
there and tried to leave it be, tried to see the faces of the young
ones I'd touched and tried to see them happy someplace and lucky
someplace cause if they down there dying in the streets then why
they keep coming to me? I tried to let the power be whatever it
needed to be, tried to see that little girl running and grinning and
rolling those big black eyes down there in Homewood with the
rest of them.

When he come banging on my door I said Jesus I said Good
God Almighty cause it don't matter what you are, don't matter
if you a Christian or African, don't matter what you are as long
as you got more sense than a stump you know there ain't nothing
else to say when babies die and old dried-up just as soon dead as
alive things like me left walking the earth. What kind of world
is that? What kind of world give that baby beautiful eyes and then
put in a drop of poison so they roll round like crazy marbles and
she can't see nothing and can't hear and can't swallow her food?
What kind of world is that? I'ma tell you what kind. It's the very
kind run me up on this hill. It the kind won't leave you be no matter how far you run, no matter how much you hurry. It's the kind
grab you and chew you up and spit you out and grind you into the
dirt then grab you up again and start to chewing again just when

you thought you wasn't nothing but dust and spit and wouldn't nothing touch you no more. That's the kind of world will catch you no matter how fast and how far you run. That's the kind of world always find something else to kill no matter how much you done buried already.

There wasn't nothing else to say. I just shuffled round here the rest of the day and tried to get used to those black eyes following me. And when they come on Wednesday I let them put me in a car and drive me down to Benson's and set me on a chair. That's the last time. Ain't nothing different down there. Never was. Never will be. Anybody got the sense they born with know what kind of world it is down there. But they still down there lying, still down there calling up *down*, and in *out*, and day *night*, and it don't make no difference. White or black or lying or telling the truth ain't nothing down there. Never was. Never will be. And if I had a mouth I'd tell em that when they come to carry me out the door. But you just a baby. You just sitting there because you ain't got no place else to go. You don't know what I'm talking about and no reason you should. You got young legs and young legs are for running, young legs will run cause that's their nature. They'll run till they get wore down to nubs then you still be trying to scoot around on the nubs cause that's the nature of young nubs and then you be in a chair when you ain't got nothing left below your hips to stand on and when you stuck in that chair you'll rock that chair and dream of running because that's the nature of old crippled-up fools. So ain't no need me trying to tell you nothing. And ain't no need of me listening to your troubles. And ain't no power ever gon change what's gon be. And what's gon be ain't never gon make no sense.

Look at you sitting there where she sat. Look at you wrapped in my blanket and your eyes don't even belong to you no more. Your eyes still down in them streets, your eyes still down there looking back over your shoulder to see who's after you. Scared rabbits in your eyes and why you got to be sitting there where she sat with that poor little pretty-eyed thing. I bet there was some of that pretty in your eyes once. I bet you had pretty long-lashed eyes when they still belonged to you.

So you mize well go on back to sleep. You been hit upside the head? Is that part of your troubles? Did somebody take a brick to your head cause I swear you got the sleeping sickness. You ain't done nothing but sleep since you been here. Standing up, lying down, sitting in a chair don't make no difference you sleeping. Outside, inside, hot or cold you sleeping. Who hit you upside your head, boy?

Talking all the time keep my ownself company and sure ain't gon stop now just cause you sitting here, so you can go to sleep or cut your eyes don't make me no nevermind. Do what I do all the time whether you here or not. Yes indeed. Crazy as a bedbug but that don't make no nevermind neither cause I know all about you. Seen them rabbits in your eyes and gravedust on them long feet. Where else you gon be but out there in my shed?

Clement

CLEMENT was trying to count the times. He needed to remember the first time because you cannot begin without one, one was first and he needed it to count the times he'd climbed Bruston Hill for Miss Bess. The first time she wasn't Miss Bess. She was the old woman one of the men said was kin. Old woman lived alone on top of Bruston Hill and the man had dreamed about her, dreamed two nights straight and Damnit I'm gon play that dream I'm going to play it straight and combinade it and box it and play it in all the houses in both races and get out the Dream Book, Big Bob, git it out and read me that number gon break the bank. The man said she was half-crazy, an evil, funny-acting old woman who lived by herself like a hermit up there but old folks in the family said she had power said she had magic and he had dreamed about her two nights and Git it out Big Bob, get out the Book and tell me the numbers and find you a big box so you can put all my money in when I breaks your bank.

Man said he was kin and said everybody in the family had called her Mother Bess as long as he could remember so he played it that way, Mother Bess, and played the dream lots of other ways, bet all the money he could get his hands on but spread it thin because he played the dream so many different ways — Water and Fire and Death and Dreams and old Woman and Kin and Flying — but Mother Bess was how it hit. Straight Mother Bess and he damned the other ways he tried to cover the dream and damned the two nights of dreaming sent to confuse him cause how a man gon to cover all the numbers in two nights' worth of dreaming so he spread his money thin and damned himself for not riding everything on

Mother Bess because that's what it was about and she was magic
and he just should have stacked all the money on her. And damned
his luck quietly to himself but rode his luck like a fish-tailed, white
Eldorado through Big Bob's front door, riding it and shaking Big
Bob's door so it rang like a fire alarm. I told you. I told you get
a box. Didn't I tell that baggy-butt, no-hair-cutting Negro to git
hisself a box. Cause here I come and I want all my money. Ring-a-
ling-ling, I told you so. Now gimme my money. Ring-a-ling-ling.
Get your greasy yellow fingers in that cash register and give it all
to me.

Get away from that door, nigger. You letting in flies and fools.
Stop shaking that door fore you break something.

Already broke something. Broke your bank, Mr. Big Bob.

Shit. You ain't even scratched the behind of my bank. Now get
away from that door and get on over here so I can run my hand
down in my small change pocket and shut you up. Making all that
noise. Shit. Some niggers can't hold their drink. And some can't
hold their luck.

What you mumbling about? Your feelings hurt? Look at him,
you all. You ever seen a big fat yellow grown man so close to crying?

You play, I pay. Ain't nothing to it. Just another day.

Ring-a-ling-ling-ling. Ring the bell for Mother Bess. Yes indeed.
The old folks know what they talking about. Gimme my money
so I can send something up the Hill. I'ma send her a hundred dollar bill. Clement you know how to get up on Bruston Hill. Soon's
this colored gentleman pays me my money I'ma send her a yard.
You take it up and there's ten in it for you cause I'm feeling good.
Gon spread my luck around.

That was the first time. But it wasn't a hundred and it wasn't
ten. The man told him just keep walking and walking. If you go
past the old water tower up there you gone too far and walk back
a little ways you'll see where she lives over on the side. Looks like
there been a fire there or a wrecking ball but her little shack's
still standing in the middle of that mess. Ain't no bigger than a
chicken coop but that's it. Got a little raggedy porch and she be sitting out there sometime. On your left as you come up the hill. Just
keep walking till ain't no more houses. Just about the top of the
hill. Tall trees in the back. Only house that high up the hill. Just

keep on walking till you think ain't no reason to keep walking and ain't nothing on this damn hill but then you'll see it. If you come to the water tower turn around. Come down a little bit you there.

Don't you lose this. This more money than you ever had in your hand. So you better not lose it. And here's ten for you cause I'm feeling good. Gon spread my luck around.

But the bill rolled and slipped in his fist was a ten. And the bill rammed down in his pants pocket was a one. And the man was scooting him out the door and winking because he knew Clement could count. And the men always be lying. Lying early in the morning. Lying till Big Bob shoos them out the door and it rings the last time except once more when Big Bob locks it and slams it behind him and Clement is alone and the lies still crawling cross the floor, sticking in his broom, hiding under the dirt balls and hair balls so he can still hear those lies as he sweeps the floor, hear them plain as he hears the door saying good-bye when it says hello, as he hears it saying Big Bob is gone again and it's night and saying Big Bob is here again and it's morning.

The first time. The *one* he needs to begin, so he counts it, counts the long hike up and up till ain't no more houses and ain't no more sidewalk. Then he finds it and the porch bends like it might try to eat him and he knocks one, two, three times. Hard but not hard enough to cave in the wall ain't none too solid so he is looking back over his shoulder deciding which way he'll run if the skimpy house starts to falling, checking over his shoulder all the way back down the hill to Big Bob's when she says, What you pounding on my door for? Don't you ever pound on my door like that again. What you want, boy?

Her face is made from the boards of the shack. She is browner and they are more grey but you could patch a hole in the weathered wooden walls with her face and never know the difference. Same lines and cracks and if you ran your finger cross it same splinters stick you. He almost asks, Is you a witch, lady? Almost tells her the story of Hansel and Gretel so she'll know he knows about that oven she got inside and the sharp knives and he ain't about to bend over so she can push him in.

You got a mouth?

He sees hers. Sees a moustache like a man's and her bottom lip
got those spidery cracks like the boards.

He sent me give you this.

Sees her little eyes buried in the creases and the more you look
the more you see the green staring back at you and the green is
not the color of her eyes it is something in her eyes, specks of
something in there that came before the eyes got buried in her face.
The green flecks heavy as chips of stone and that's why her eyes
are so heavy, are sinking, that's why they stare through you from
deep back where they are sinking in her head.

Who sent who to gimme what?

He said he played Mother Bess and Big Bob had to pay him so
he stopped messing with the door and told me take this up Bruston
Hill. It's money and he gave me a tip. He lied but they always
be lying. It's ten and I got one.

Half them fools down there be calling me Mother Bess and I
ain't mama to none them. Never been mama to nobody but once
and that's all over, that's so long ago it don't make no nevermind.
If one them fools fool enough give away they money I'll take it.
Serve him right talking that Mother Bess mess and I sure ain't his
mama whoever it is. Who is you, boy?

Clement.

You Clement, is you? Ain't never knowed a Clement. Didn't
know there was a Clement in Homewood but they got all kinds
of funny names down there now. Like those names make a difference. Like they somebody else just cause they got one them funny
names. Changing names and taking names ain't never changed
no niggers in Homewood. Well, you tell him I didn't say thanks.
You tell him, Mr. Clement, I didn't say nothing and I sure ain't
his mama. And glad of it. You tell him that for me, boy. You got
any name side Clement?

No, Mam.

Well somebody taught you a little manners even if they ain't
taught you no name.

Miss Claudine.

What you say?

Supposed to put Good morning fore your Gimmes.

I guess if you had sense enough to get up here from Homewood and hand me this money you got sense enough to get back down again even if you don't make sense while you up here. You take this back to Big Bob. He the one writing numbers ain't he? He still run numbers out his barbership ain't he? No reason for him not to less he's dead. Unless somebody shot him for messing with they money. You said something about Big Bob's so you know what I'm talking about. He been running numbers out there since before I come up on this hill. You know what I'm talking about, don't you?

Yes, Mam.

Well carry this money back down there and you tell him put it all on seven-fifty-three. You hear that? Seven-fifty-three on the first race. The whole ten right on that. And tell him put my money in this bag.

Yes, Mam. Seven-fifty-three.

And you know why it's gon be seven-fifty-three? Course you don't, but I'ma tell you when you bring my money up here tomorrow. Now you hurry and do what I told you. Ain't got all day to get a number in. Not unless they changed it. And ain't no reason to change it. Ain't no reason to change nothing cause it don't make no difference. But you gon and do what I told you. Seven-fifty-three on the first race. You come back tomorrow with my money in that bag and I'll tell you why it got to be seven-fifty-three.

That was *one* so he is beginning to count. Two was what came next, came when Big Bob shooed them out that night and locked the door and turned out all the lights but one and filled the paper sack with money. The bell said what it been saying all day and Big Bob said: I ain't messing with no Hoodoo Woman. I ain't taking no more her numbers. She got this but that's all. Sending a child down here with one number like that and it hit straight on the nose. It ain't natural. It ain't legal. This is Big Bob talking. This is Big Bob and I pays when you plays but I ain't messing with no two-headed witch sends numbers by children and sends paper bags to put her money in.

Big Bob walking cross the floor and getting in his medicine. But it ain't in no cup of warm milk from Miss Claudine or nothing just the long-necked bottle of J&B and he swallows hard and almost chokes hisself. His fingers go behind the barber coat but he can't get it right the first time. They miss. They don't have eyes tonight because they miss the first time and Big Bob walks the floor end to end, from the window to the back and one more time then he finds the string and unwraps his barber coat and looks at hisself in all the mirrors. Back front and sides all at once if you stand the right way and know how to look because that's how you got to do when you cutting hair. You got to see front and back and sides to get it even. He stands beside the chair looking the way he does when somebody's in it and he don't feel like cutting hair. Just looking like he trying to figure something real special to do with that head in the chair, but he just cut one head too many and he's looking cause he's tired, looking cause he's bone tired and he can't think of nothing better to do than look.

That's right. Can't be no other way. Ain't supposed to be no other way. Can't fight no Hoodoo Lady.

Like he didn't know till just that night and just that bagful of money that he been carrying all that Big Bob weight. Like he knows all the sudden he's been carrying all that yellow meat and ain't had time to be tired till just that night and now he got to be tired this one night for all those other days and nights and he carries that Big Bob weight twice up and back the floor from the back to the red sign twice, and can't do it no more, might not do it never no more. Don't even slam the door, just prise it open easy and turns the key and slides it so it hardly rings, so it just says good-bye and nothing else.

Seven-fifty-three. Ain't nothing special about it. It just come to me is all. I seen it plain as I used to see them letters writ up in the sky. Airplane make a sign up there and you could read it all over Homewood. Saw that number plain as day and knew it was the one and that's why I give you that sack and that's why I'm sitting here this early in the morning waiting for my money.

(Two). He can't sleep. He keeps the bag on his mattress under the blanket with him and the bag rattles and squirms and talks to him all night. So he's up before dawn and hauling butt up Bruston Hill and doesn't even see the sun rise over the city and burnish the hills so all of Pittsburgh is a flaming sea of lava sliding down from Bruston Hill into the rivers he couldn't see even if he was paying attention to anything beside the brown paper sack full of money in his fist. She had promised to tell him her secret and that was on his mind but they said curiosity kilt the cat so it wasn't just curiosity caught him by the scruff of his neck and jerked him up the hill before dawn. He was up and setting down one foot after the other in the blue streets because she called him, because her voice was there in Big Bob's backroom and it wasn't a question of saying yes or no to her but seeing how fast he could get up there with her money. But not so much a voice as a whistle. And not so much the money as it was a matter of returning her bag.

(Two). Is hurrying and out of breath and a moment when the porch is like a grey whale stretching its jaws open and just might swallow him if she doesn't answer the tapping of his fingers on the hangnail door.

How somebody supposed to hear you scratching like that? Mize well knock with a feather. Jump up here and just about kick a hole in my porch then you scratching with a feather like nobody ain't heard you just about knock my house down jumping up here.

You set that down on the table. Young boy like you oughtn't have too much cash money. Just get you in trouble. I'ma give you this dollar and give you more a little bit at a time but give it steady so you always got a little something in your pocket but not enough get you in trouble. You take this and they'll always be some more you come round and run to the store for me and do a few little chores need done round here you always gon have a piece of money in your pocket. You understand me? You understand what I'm talking about, boy?

Yes, Mam.

And that seven-fifty-three. Just forget about that seven-fifty-three. Just got lucky is all. Seven-five-three. Ain't nothing special about it. It just come to me is all. Seen it plain as I used to see them wooly white letters writ up in the sky. Airplane make a sign up there and you could read it all over Homewood. I saw that number plain as day and knew it was the one and that's why I give you that sack and that's why I'm sitting here this early in the morning waiting for my money.

That ain't all there is to it. Course not. But you too young to understand the rest. I could tell you but it's too deep. It's the number my man wore on a chain round his neck. Little round piece of metal, the color of a penny and like a penny somebody had stomped down and mashed thin. Wasn't like nothing I seen before. Didn't have nothing on it but that number 753. Don't know where he got it. I asked him and he said it's my luck. A kinda long silvery kind of chain around his neck and he never took it off and that dog tag always dangling at the end. Never said nothing but it's my luck. I called it a dog tag and he grinned when I said that. I liked to play with it. Shut my eyes and feel the number with the tip of my fingers. Swing it and dangle it and finger it where it was warm from laying against his chest. But you don't know nothing about nothing like that. Never thought there'd be a day I could slip it off over his head and he wouldn't say stop or wouldn't grab my hand. Never thought there'd be a day I could just take it and have it if I wanted it. Never thought I'd leave it laying there on his chest and say good-bye to it and not have it to turn in my fingers and slide up and down that silvery chain while I teased him and called it a dog tag to make him grin. But it's long gone and he's long gone so all that don't make no nevermind. All it makes is seven five three floating before my eyes like those smoky white letters Atlantic and Pacific in the sky. And makes a bag of dollars. And makes seven days and seven sins and seven come eleven if you shooting crap. And five got that hook. Five is a fisher. Five is fever. Five is staying alive. You leave out the evens. You give the white folks the evens. They likes things neat. Two-four-six-eight-ten. Two by fours and ten little Indins all in a row. They like things with corners, things you can break in half, things that got a nature you can tame. But what you gon do with the odds? That's why they's the odds. You got your nine at one end and your one on the other. Now what you gon do with that? Seven-five-three. That's the middle, that's the heart of the odds. Three right next to the gate but it got to wait. Can't get over. Can't get under. Can't get around. But three's trying. Circling everywhich way. Got curves and straight and zigzags. Got a hook too like five. But three is at the gate. Three is two faces and two eyes can't see each other but sees everything else. Three got a mirror in its belly. But how you gon know what I'm talking about. You just a baby. Ain't no way you can get as deep as I'm going and I ain't even wet yet. I'm just playing numberology and trickology. Ain't nothing to it anyway. Just got lucky with 753.

So Clement had *one* and had *two* and the rest be easy. He'd hear her whistle stomp through the streets of Homewood. Hear her walking stick tap, tap, tap and she be standing over him crooking her finger and, Come on boy, hurry up boy her face like somebody took one of those boards off the raggedy shack and poked eye holes, poked nose holes and dug out a mouth. A kind of whistle, howl, moaning call nobody could hear but him when it reached down off Bruston Hill and started to lift houses and pull up sidewalks and tear blue shadows apart to find him.

But now he'd have to start his count again because now it wasn't going up the hill to do for her but going up the hill to do for them. That ghost he had only heard the first time it was up there. That ghost who was the one all the men were talking about. He had never heard her say the ghost's name but Clement knew it was him, was that Tommy Lawson they said killed a man and robbed that dago Indovina the fence. Killed Chubby they said. Said it was a miracle Chubby ain't been dead nine or ten times before. Said his luck finally run out. This time somebody blowed that fool's head off sure enough. Chubby been going for bad since he was old enough to spit. Chubby just as soon walk through people as walk around em. Chubby got hands like a gorilla. A crying shame God put such a little bitty brain in all that body. Yeah, he liked to walk around with his shirt off in the summer showing his muscles. Well, he had some muscles to show. He was big alright. And they say he knew all that Hi Karate and Jew jitsu and stuff. Big as he was wasn't nobody gon mess with him don't care what somebody knew or didn't know. Big burly nigger walking round with his shirt off like Tarzan in the grocery store and who gon tell that big sucker to put it back on. Walked the streets like he owned them. Said he killed a man in prison. Beat him to death with his hands. Prison ain't nothing but a jungle. That ain't all he killed. You remember that mess about Valdez in the paper. All them killings on the North side and those massage parlors and that mess. Well Chubby was in that too. They caught Valdez but Chubby was in it too. Makes sense. He was always hanging with Valdez. And both of them mean niggers Tomming for the dagos. It was just a matter of time. Somebody bound to blow his head off sooner or later. Ain't nothing but a cat got nine lives and you look round here you see plenty dead cats. Yeah, don't care how many lives you got one day they run out, one day you dead don't care how lucky you are, don't care how many dagos covering your ass.

Clement listened. Down in the Homewood streets. Up on Bruston Hill. The man staying with Mother Bess wasn't no ghost, he was a natural man who ate beans and chewed apples and drank Henry Bow's moonshine.

Mother Bess said, You don't see nothing. You understand? You don't see nothing, nor hear nothing and you sure ain't gon say nothing, you understand?

Yes, Mam.

This boy gon be here awhile but you don't see nothing. He's sitting at that table big as life but you don't see him do you?

No, Mam.

That's good. That's nice. Clement a good boy. You don't have to worry none bout Clement. And Clement ain't got nothing to worry about cause ain't nothing here for him to worry about.

Yes, Ma . . . No, Mam.

The man she called a boy. The man Clement could see through but who wasn't no ghost, that Tommy Lawson they all talking bout in Big Bob's and Miss Claudine's and the Brass Rail. He the one Carl and that stranger talking about and he ain't caught yet. Him nor his partner Ruchell. Tommy Lawson's the one. Still loose. But he ain't a thousand miles away. Just up on Bruston Hill in her house.

Or in her backyard like he saw him the third day. The first time was inside, was morning and Clement could hear her talking to somebody before he even got to the porch. He remembered the ghost trying to sneak out the back door. The ghost shouting at him through the wooden walls, *I ain't here, Goddamn it. Go away. I ain't here.* How his ears hurt and head hurt and how he froze on the porch and couldn't take a step forward or couldn't take one backward because the ghost voice inside the shack was warning him, was threatening him, was screaming *I ain't here, Goddamn it* in the silence so the silence was thick as weeds and the screaming was a snake in the weeds and if he put his foot down on the noisy boards the snake would strike. But he had called her and knocked anyway, knocked not for her to answer but to let the ghost know he was there and let the ghost know he wasn't sneaking around but getting out of there as fast as his feet could get him down off the porch. She answered the knock and chased him away and he hadn't seen nothing, just felt the whole house shake when the ghost sneaked out the back. He hadn't seen nothing the first time and the second time neither. Because she told him look through the man, past the man who wasn't a ghost but flesh and blood like her, like him. A natural man with a natural name. Tommy Lawson. But she said you ain't seen nothing so that's what he saw when he brought the shopping bag of groceries the afternoon of the second day. Nothing at the table drinking a cup of something.

The third day he saw nothing in the backyard, nothing on its hands and knees digging in the dirt. A narrow-butt nothing with holes in the bottom of its high-heeled shoes. Digging and straightening up sticks and pushing sticks in. A pile of weeds raked off to one side. Tools scattered around the patch of dug-up earth. Clement had followed Mother Bess through the house. If you counted her legs you'd get three most of the time. And when she poked that bowed walking stick out to the front and side of her the way she does she is as wide as she is high, she makes a circle with that stick in her hand. So he follows the grey sweater which is loose and raggedy and droops like a dusty spider web from her shoulders in the middle of the circle, follows it through the house and doesn't look right or left but keeps his eyes on the bullseye, a rubbed bare spot where there's a lump between her shoulder blades. Because it's easier that way to see nothing and nothing might not even see you if you mind your own business so he follows her through the house and out the back door and it's daylight again, the sun slaps him across the face and for a moment till he blinks away the sharp light he sees nothing till he sees nothing's scrawny backside.

You want this boy bring you something?

Got no money.

You want this boy bring you something, I said?

Iron City. A case. Yeah. And each one sweatin cold. Sure, you tell him a case of cold Iron City.

Get a quart long with the other things.

I'm bout to die out here in all this sun. Ain't no goddamn farmer. Ain't used to scrabbling around in the dirt on my hands and knees.

He is standing. He is like the tall trees don't start to filling out with branches and leaves till near the top. Lean and straight till the wild burst of his Afro.

That's enough cutting and digging. I'm sweating like a pig. Hot and thirsty as I am even that castor oil you got running in your pipes gon taste good. All I wanted was to plant me a seed or two. Didn't know about all the rest of this mess.

If you gon sow you got to prepare the ground. And preparing means chopping weeds and turning the soil.

You sure these seeds still good. How long they been sitting here?

What you mean good?

Alive. They still alive? The way they rattle inside here sounds like they long gone.

Course they dead. Supposed to be dead. Why else you think you bury em in the ground? They dead and you put em in the ground so they can die some more, so they can split open and come apart and get mixed up with what's in the soil and go to growing again. You citified children don't know nothing. Growing up where ain't nothing but pavement youall probably think you plant a hambone to grow a pig.

I ain't never planted nothing in my life. Grew up thinking everything came from stores. You right about that. Everything came from the white man on the corner or from the A&P up on Homewood Avenue. I ain't never tried to grow nothing.

If you gon try this time you get them packets of seeds off the table and come on back outside. It's already late in the season. Just might be too late to get some of them seeds to grow but you bring em all. You ain't too old to learn. Get you a cup of water and come on so I can show you what to do. You gon learn to do it right.

Her hair is grey. But grey is not one thing, it's all the colors from white to black, twisted, tangled under the net sits like a bag atop her head. Ain't curly like a nigger's hair. Long fine threads hang out the bottom of the net. The back of her neck is browner than the boards but deep-grained like the boards, creases long and fine as the wisps of hair hanging out the bag.

You still here, boy? What you staring at with your pop-eyed self?

No, Mam.

A quart of beer with the rest.

Can he get a bag of ice someplace?

He ain't no mule.

Where's the jug. Can't drink this nasty water without nothing in it. It'd be better cold than warm. Little ice might help.

Clement hears but he is not listening. The door closes behind him and his feet sink and he's going down the hill for *them*, not for her, so he'll have to start all over again. Start with *one* again.

Tommy

HE says, *Well, that's that, old woman,* not knowing exactly what he means, saying the words because he's heard them before and said them before so they come easy but he doesn't know what he means, hadn't planned to say anything until the words come out just as he said them, almost as if they had found him and used him to say something they needed to say, used him and didn't bother to let him know what they were talking about. *Well, that's that.* And he addressed the words to her because she was in the dark room with him, because she had taught him to plant, because she sent the boy for Iron City, because she was sipping nasty shine in nasty water with him and it had been three days now and he was tired now, and high enough now to need somebody else to speak to, to draw him out of the fog into which he was sinking. The fog of his own thoughts, his own body, his own life which was settling over him again like the darkness draping her shack.

I got to leave here.

Then he knew what the other words were talking about, why they had found him and used his mouth.

Are you listening to me, old woman? How you think you know so much bout people's business and you always talking never give nobody a chance to open his mouth? You still ain't heard me.

When I was your age all I did was listen. When I was your age in a room with the old people I kept my mouth shut cause I believed there might be somebody know'd more than me and if I kept my mouth shut I might learn something.

That ain't what I'm talking about. That ain't got nothing to do with it.

I'm tired, boy. You done disturbed me out my usual ways and I'm wore out and my head feels like it's full of broken glass and I don't want nothing rattling round in there so you speak soft or don't say nothing but don't you raise your voice one iota.

It's been three days now and I think I better go on back down there and do what I have to do.

They be waiting. They got plenty time. You be dead and buried ten times over they still got plenty time. They the patientest things in the world.

I ain't worried bout the cops no more.

That ain't all that's down there means you harm.

Well, I ain't worried bout nothing no more.

Fast work is all I can say. Mighty fast work. It ain't hardly been three days you crawled up here like something the cat drug in and now you fixing to walk out like King Kong ain't afraid of nothing. Mighty fast.

Wouldna been three days. Wouldna been five minutes if I left when you told me to leave. Sleeping in some damn shed. Come damn near freezing to death. You supposed to be kin. You supposed to be my people and you run me off like I was a disease. So don't be talking bout *how long*. According to you just knocking at your door was too long. Had to shove that wood around and crawl inside there and sleep on the ground like some wild animal.

Where else you gon stay? Course you slept out there. If you had someplace else to go you sure would have gone and I'da been happy to see you go. Happy as a tick on a bloody bedbug. I knew you was out there. I came and got you, didn't I?

After I froze my butt off.

Wrapped you in a blanket off my own bed. Fed you. Listened to your nasty mouth.

Don't start on nasty mouths now, old woman. Ain't never heard nobody talk mean and evil till I heard you. And you don't even cuss. Cussing ain't cold enough for you. No wonder you ain't got no refrigerator up here. Hot as it's been you don't miss ice. You got that cold blood, that ice water blood. Talking bout I was born to die. Telling me I got to pay the piper and it ain't none your business some cop blow me away.

Nothing cold bout the truth. It's just the truth. Like they say the truth and nothing but the truth and that's what makes it true.

How come you ain't got nothing up here? No TV or radio or nothing? Like living in a cave. Gets dark outside and it's dark in here. I'm gon send you a radio up here. A nice transistor runs by battery. Least you could have some music up here.

Don't need that mess. Got my oil lamp. Got candles. Got all I need. And where you gon get money for some radio, anyway? You the one crying since you been here cause you ain't got a dime in your pocket.

I know how to get things.

Bet you do. I bet you a real outlaw.

Do what I have to do to get by.

And what's that? Robbing folks and messing with that dope and killing people so people trying to kill you. What kind of life is that?

My life. The only one I've had.

Didn't have to be that way. Everybody down there ain't like that. You got a brother done alright for hisself. He's a snotty, dirty-talking nigger but he made something of hisself. Plenty people down there ain't got squat but they ain't stealing and robbing. They ain't outlaws.

Tell me bout it. Tell me about Mr. Barclay work all his life and got a raggedy truck and a piece of house and they call him Deacon in the church and when he dies ain't gon have the money for a new suit to be buried in. Tell me about the plenty. Old people burning up in shacks. Kids ain't even ten years old and puffing weed and into anything they can get their hands on. Tell me about those fools marching off to Nam and coming back cripples and junkies and strungout worse than these niggers in the street. And coming back dead. Plenty. Yeah you tell me bout plenty and I'll tell you bout jail and tell you bout old home week because that's where everybody at. It's like high school reunion in there, every-body I grew up with's in there or on the way or just getting back. I got your plenty. Shit. Plenty fools just sitting there letting all the shit fall on their heads ain't got the sense to move. I tried. I could tell you something bout trying. Oh yeah. Work and raise a family they say. Then they say sorry ain't no work. Then ain't no family. Then they say you ain't shit. Then you do what you have to do and you really ain't shit. You an outlaw. But that's what you supposed to be in the first place. And that's my life. The only one I've had. And they gon take that if they can.

Damn. I wish you had some music in here, old woman. It's too damn quiet in here.

Ain't no dance hall.

You got that right.

People used to make they own music. Could play and sing and make music all night long.

Bet you did. Banjos and guitars and harps and all that ole time jumping around and down home hollering.

Best music ever was. Kind of music you can't hear on no radio. You got to be there, you got to be making it or dancing to it or singing with the one singing.

Did you dance, old woman? Did you strut your stuff and shimmy wobble shake? Bet you did. Bet you was cold and mean too. Bet you was a fox in your day, Old Bess. Breaking hearts and carrying on.

Watch your mouth.

Why you stay up here, old woman? You scared ain't you? You been just as scared up here as I been down there. And if I'm hiding, you're hiding too. But I'm hiding so I can run. You just hiding. You let them whip all the run out you. I don't want to go that way.

Had a man who could whistle more music than you find in all them radios. You don't know nothing about the blues. Youall missed the blues.

Thought you was cool at first. Evil and mean and half crazy but cool. You know what I mean. Like nothing could touch you. Like you in your own bag, like you had your shit so together you didn't need nothing or nobody and I felt like a damn fool begging to stay in your house. So cool. Cold cool and even though I thought about busting your head and staying here anyway I was digging you. Digging that cool. Cause that's me. I been trying to stay cool all my life. That's the game. That's what you learn. You got to be cool to stay alive. But what the fuck has cool got me? I been cool and look at me. Stuck in some damn slave cabin.

Youall ain't never heard no music. Hmmmmp.

Hey now. If you gon pour, do me too. Mize well get good and

fucked up before I leave here. Mize well go on and get my head real bad before I fight them streets. Because I'm leaving. That's that. I can't stay up here no longer. Got to be more to it than staying cool. Maybe when you get old it's easy. Maybe you got yourself together and nothing don't matter no more. Maybe you'll just keep on hiding up here till one day that boy, Clement, finds you dead. Like you always be telling me, that's your business. But it ain't no life. That ain't no life for me. I got to take a chance. As messed up as I am I got to get down from here and take my chance.

He could whistle a different blues every time. Just make it up as he goes along and that music be steady talking to you. You'd hear its name and it'd be talking to you plain as day. Different every time but the same too. You'd know the name, you'd hear the name plain as day and think, Hello, hello Mister Hair Brushing Blues. What you got to say today?

I been scared all my life. But I ain't scared now. I ain't killed nobody. Didn't even see Ruchell waste Chubby. They can't put that on me. They can kill me but I still ain't killed nobody and I ain't scared. All they can do is kill me cause I ain't going back to nobody's goddamn jail.

I was scared a long time. Ever since my granddaddy John French died and his house fell to pieces and everybody scattered I been scared. Scared of people, scared of myself. Of how I look and how I talk, of the nigger in me. Scared of what people said about me. But I got no time to be scared now. Ain't no reason to be scared now cause ain't nothing they can take from me now. Lost my woman, lost my son, shamed all the family I got down there. So it's just me and I know I ain't killed nobody so fuck em. Motherfuck em I say. Let them find me and kill me if they can but I know who I am and know what I did, and I'm ready to live now. I ain't ready to die. Hell no. I'm ready to live and do the best I can cause I ain't scared.

That's moonshine talking now. Henry Bow got your tongue and turning it every whichway but loose. Talking like you down there in one of them saloons.

Yeah. You Hard Hearted Hannah, alright. You mize well be under this goddamn hill. You mize well be sitting inside it, riding it like a tank. Ain't nothing gon touch you till that Clement breaks in here and puts his hand on your forehead. And that boy think he's touching ice. And that ice gon burn his young fingers.

I ain't the one running down to Homewood putting my brain up against some policeman's pistol. I ain't the one can't wait to get back down there in them streets where people hunting for me. You go back down there and I'll be hearing about you. It'll be Clement alright, but Clement come to tell me you sure nuff ain't scared of nothing no more.

Tell me bout it. Tell me bout hunting wild animals. Tell me bout dogs in alleys waking up the neighborhood. Tell me bout flashlights poking in the shadow where you trying to cop a minute's sleep. Don't you think I know bout that? Don't you think I want it different? Don't you think I tried?

It's your business.

It's my business. It's the only goddamn business I'm gon to get. Tonight.

This very goddamn dreary quiet ain't got no choice night, old woman. Old Mother Bess. Finish this cup of moonshine and put my foot in the path and say good-bye. Say thank you Mother Bess even if you don't want to hear all that mess, even if you cuss me with your fine old cold self.

Bess

IS it a month, a year, a week, is it the very night he left? She can't tell, can't tell if she's dreaming or if he's been long gone or just tripped out the back door five minutes before. First there had been the stomping and pounding loud as thunder, loud enough to raise the dead because that's what she was, dead in a Henry Bow moonshine sleep and it would take thunder or an atom bomb to jerk her back to life. She knows it's too soon to be awake. She knows she was just starting that good deep sleep. Then the pounding and stomping. She groaned out loud and knew sleep was gone, knew the dreaming which hadn't begun yet would never start. She was reaching for the stick at the head of the bed. Her clothes were still on. Tangled, sticking to her like what was left of sleep. She couldn't see the hand she held in front of her face, the hand batting at the net teasing her eyes. Sitting up in bed she coughed and felt the top of her head fly off. The room was spinning or she was spinning or she sat headless, mired in her twisted clothes while the ball that had once rested on her neck whirled round the room like a runaway top. She was an old woman startled awake in the middle of the night. Like somebody was snapping on lights, powerful, piercing lights that smoked and seared and popped and blinded. From a stupor to this sudden hurting light. She let the stick clatter to the floor. Rubbed both fists in her eyepits to restore the darkness.

Somebody had stomped across her porch. Somebody had pounded on her door. It had to be him. Couldn't be nobody but him. Running. He would be in the shed again. His long feet stomping across her porch and now they'd be poked out the end of the wood shed because he was a tall lean thing like those trees and

327

it hurt her to see those feet when they were so still, so long and raggedy because she could see the run in them, the scared rabbit eyes in them as plain as the holes in his high-heeled shoes.

He was Lizabeth's son and Lizabeth was Freeda's girl. The quiet one born too soon in a snowstorm and May grabbed up the blue baby and plunged it in a snowdrift and the open door crashed again and again like a broken wing against the frame. Her man getting drunk on Dago Red with John French and singing all night long after Freeda' s first child was born dead and saved. John French would carry his little girl on his shoulders to Bruston Hill and Lizabeth would ride down on the sled her man made. Her man was good with his hands. He could make anything he wanted to make. She watched her man's brown hand play up and down her naked thigh, she saw it sanding the boards smooth and shiny, saw it paint-flecked as the brush turned the boards of little Lizabeth's sled bright red. His hand patting the head of the child she couldn't give him, his voice, hold on little motorcar driver, hold on little sky flyer, just hold on and steer with your feet and your Daddy John be there at the bottom to catch you. And after all those years of waiting Eugene finally growing inside her belly and her man's hand plays up and down her plump thigh, her swollen belly and he's saying Hold on, hold on little sweet thing and snow is falling around her and she can barely stand up on the slick cobbled street but she makes the trip every day rain shine snow don't make no nevermind because it's not a letter she hopes to find at the bottom of Bruston Hill. No, because letters lie and nobody but a fool believes what letters say nobody but a fool would be outside in all this snow, fighting all this ice just to get a letter. No, it would be her son Eugene she'd find, find him one bright morning rain shine or snow didn't make no nevermind he'd be there and catch her in his young strong arms when she flew the last few steps off the hill.

He was Lizabeth's son and his sister had brought the pretty-eyed baby for Mother Bess to touch, to lay on her crippled hands and blow her stale Henry Bow breath on the brown baby cheeks. Lady bug, Lady bug fly away. To be magic, to sing magic, to touch with the power they believed she had because she was old and evil and crazy up there by herself on top of Bruston Hill. Because she lived with the dead. Because she was dead herself.

It had to be him, but was it yesterday, last week, just a moment ago that he had stomped through her black, dreamless sleep and cracked all the boards of her door and ripped the covers off her bed so she bolted up shivering and afraid and dreaming.

Where had he learned that song? She was outside and he was in the house, still wrapped in the blanket and she thought still sleeping but people didn't whistle while they were asleep so when she had heard the song she knew he was awake or knew her man was inside with him because what she heard was blues like her man whistled. For the first time in thirty some years she had pulled herself up from the rocker and stepped toward the music and it hadn't stopped. Hadn't faded or run from her so she took another step across the noisy boards and the whistled blues still didn't run, still didn't hide till she pushed through the door and stared at the boy wrapped up like an Indin at her table. The blues hadn't stopped till he said, I thought you was sleep out there and she said, I thought you was sleep in here.

But that last night, that night a year ago or hours ago or whenever it was if it ever was, she had said, Youall know nothing bout no blues. Wasn't that what she had told him? Wasn't that the way it had to be? Because once was enough. Once was one time too many to watch people sing the blues and die. Once was enough to listen and then have it all go away and have nothing but silence. Once and then you got to say good-bye say yes I'm hiding, yes I'm scared but what you know about it? How you gon know anything about it? It ain't none your business. Ain't nobody's business.

She hears a car racing up the hill. It is rushing all the way to the top dragging tin cans and garbage cans behind it, losing its wheels, its doors, pounded apart the way Bruston Hill always pounds apart any car tries to climb its steep, broken side too fast. The darkness winks at her. Opens and shuts its eye so the walls flicker like they're on fire. No one drives up Bruston Hill at night. No one runs across her porch and beats on her door. She had said good-bye. She had said no more of that mess. But the darkness winks and she can see cold light buckling the walls, light flashing in the corners, light touching her things.

It had to be him. And it had to be them after him. She scoots

329

her hips faster than she thought she could to the edge of the bed. Her stocking feet tap the bare floor once but the second time they're on target and she wiggles her toes into the mashed back slippers. She stoops for the cane and realizes how fast she's moving when her back says No says I still got the weight of the world on these old shoulders and you better straighten up slow, real slow if you want to straighten up at all.

Old as she is she has good ears. She hears what she wants to hear. The stick picking its way across the room to the front door, the stick tapping the swaybacked boards. It's him. Who else it gon be? And she hears him telling his troubles and hears herself shushing him and hears him snoring and laughing and whistling and telling lies and damning her and something cracking, like ice, like a brittle shell. Almost on the beat. Less a crackling than quick loud pops following one another like fireworks on the Fourth of July. Her fist is wrapped around the knobby head of the stick. She crashes it against the porch boards, almost on the beat, echoing the string of gunshots exploding in the darkness. She squeezes so hard she can feel the stick coming through the back of her hand, feels it cutting and pushing deeper every time she raises it, everytime she digs it into the splitting wood.

Oh Jesus. Oh God.

How you know so much about people you never give them a chance to open they mouth? How you know so much?

She cannot turn it loose. Her crippled fingers are knotted over the top of the stick. Her arm trembles and the crooked stick trembles with it as she tries to steady herself, as she needs all three legs to hold herself up.

Oh Jesus. Oh Good God Almighty.

She damns the weakness that makes her stand there shaking. She damns the crackle of gunfire and damns the sudden stillness that has followed the shots, a stillness broken only by the sweeping light which makes the crest of the hill blink off and on like a red neon sign.

Only two shuffled steps to the rocker. Against the night chill, against the dew wetting her bare skin when it touches the arm of the chair, she pulls the grey sweater tighter round her shoulders. Slumped in the chair she feels the blood returning to her hand;

her fingers unclench, the stick clatters again to the floor of the porch. A circle of pain in the palm of her hand, a hot, stinging trace of the gnarled stick's head away from which her stiff fingers slowly uncurl.

She can hear sirens whining down below in the city. Above her in the darkness she has turned away from, a voice broadcasts over a radio, a voice frying in bursts of static, a voice she damns and tries to drown in the squeak and groan of the rocker.

More sirens climb the hill. People used to tie cans and stuff to the Just Married cars. Cans and the crepe paper so the cars rattled and fluttered through the Homewood streets. You'd hear them most on a Saturday morning. That crash and rattle and some fool always leaning on his horn and the train of three or four fancied-up cars would rule the streets till they went on about their business and you'd wonder who it was, wonder if you knew them after you couldn't hear them no more. So the heavy-footed police cars rumbled up the hill, screaming to the top like something terrible was chasing them. And the crest of the hill ablaze now with spinning red lights. One long finger of light traces the shape of the tower, finds the curving ladder and follows it to the top, pausing, pointing for a moment where the ladder touches the lip of the huge pot atop the steel legs. She gets up from her chair and steps off the porch long enough to see the false red dawn and the pointing white spotlight, long enough to know she is too old and frail to go any farther. Too weak to punish the police swarming over Bruston Hill just beyond her view. She damns them and hobbles back to her porch, an old woman startled from her sleep in the middle of the night, an old woman in a dark house who knows it's too late to help him, who knows he's long gone, who knows her arms are too weak to lift him and carry him back where he belongs.

She damns her weakness. She strikes a match and lights the grocery bags she had balled up and stuffed under the grate of the stove. Her shadow dances across the ceiling and walls. In the far corner of the room she thinks she sees a spark rising, a bluish spark cast off by the fire in the stove. But it doesn't die as it floats towards the ceiling. The blue spark wheels and climbs and soars and then she realizes it is the angel in the blue-eyed gown, the angel who took apart the cobweb strand by strand and moved it and put it back together again so it could catch the colored light streaming through the stained glass window in Benson's. Her patient little blue-gowned angel who wouldn't hurt a soul, who wouldn't hurt anything. The spark was the flame-tipped wand in her tiny angel hand. She flits through the darkness like a lightning bug, touching this and that with her wand. What she kisses bursts into flame. She has beautiful black eyes. She darts and swoops and zigzags and leaves a trail of blossoming flames. The angel in the blue-eyed gown works with her to set the house on fire.

We gon do it, gal. Yes we are. Thank you you little bluegowned, black-eyed thing. Thank you you little fuzzy-headed got the prettiest black-eyed lazy Susan eyes in the whole world thing. Don't matter if they's crossed a little bit, don't matter if they roll round sometime like they ain't got no strings and gon on about they own business. And you. You get up off that bed, man. Cause it's going too, everything in here going so get your whistling self up off that bed and come on.

He still has sleep in his eyes. Her man's still drowsy and she has to push him out the door. The angel is long gone, gone the same way she got in. Angels have power. Angels will always get where they supposed to get and do what they supposed to do and be gone when they's supposed to be gone. That's the nature of angels. Just like not hurting nothing is their nature.

But you got to push a man sometime. Unload him out the door cause he been on that Dago Red and his eyes are full of wine and sleep and the house filling up with smoke. She wishes he would wake up enough to whistle a Burn Down the House Blues. She would like that. Oh yes. She could surely listen to that this morning. A Burn Down the House, Burn Down the Town Blues as they sail off that long hill together.

Because somebody has to go down there and tell the truth. Lizabeth's boy didn't kill nobody. He wasn't scared. All he needed was another chance and somebody needs to go down there and tell them. And she was going to do just that. Burn down that last bit of shack on Bruston Hill and tell them what they needed to know. That he ain't killed nobody. That he needed one more chance. That he staked his life on one more chance. They should know all that down there. She'll tell them. She'll make sure they hear. Yes indeed. On her man's arms now. Four good legs now and she's coming. She's coming to tell them he ain't scared no more and they better listen and they better make sure it don't happen so easy ever again.

SENT FOR YOU
YESTERDAY

TO DANNY, JAKE, JAMILA

Past lives live in us, through us. Each of us harbors the spirits of people who walked the earth before we did, and those spirits depend on us for continuing existence, just as we depend on their presence to live our lives to the fullest.

In Heaven with Brother Tate

HEY Bruh.

Hey man.

What you thinking, man?

I had this dream. This real bad dream.

Nightmare?

Shit man. Worse than that. Night mare. Day mare. Afternoon mare. Every damn time-of-day mare. Whatever you want to call it. That dream had me by the nuts.

Well, what was it?

Wasn't nothing to it really.

What you talking about then?

Wasn't nothing I could put my finger on. No monsters or funny green mens or nothing like that in the dream. Just a dumb jive ass dream. But it scared the shit out me.

You gon tell it or not?

If you get your lips off that bottle *we* spozed to be drinking maybe some wine help me get started.

Hey man. The *you* part of the *we* done already killed half the Johnson.

Why you got to lie like that? Pass the apple.

Better be a good goddamn story.

Nothing good about it. Ain't hardly no story at all. Just a cripple-ass no-kind-of-sense dream I ain't told nobody never.

Go on and tell it if you gon tell it, man.

See, I was on a train. Don't know where I was going. Where I been. Just knows I'm on a train, and it's pitch black night, inside and outside. Couldn't see the hand in front of my face. It was blacker than the rent man's heart when you ain't got a dime. Blacker than tarbaby's mama. And this train just rattlin on, shakin like it's bout to come apart. Sho nuff shake, rattle and rolling train full all these people. Scared people. And I mean scared, Jack. Stomped down, righteous scared. Too scared to say boo to one another. We's all in there rattling round and nary a word. Nary a peep out nobody. People banging up against you. Knocking your shins and shoulders and what not. Arms and legs and pieces of people slamming all up against you and nobody saying s'cuse me or sorry. People just rolling around like marbles on the floor of that boxcar. Quiet as lambs cept every once in a while all the sudden you hear somebody scream. Ain't no doors nor windows but you know they gone. Nothing left after a scream like that.

Yeah. Funny thing was I knew just why they had to scream. Couldn't put it in words then and can't now. Ain't no words for it, but I knew why. See, cause I wanted to scream. I wanted to cut loose and tell somebody how scared I was. What a evil place I was in. Needed to scream worser than I never needed to pee or needed a woman or needed anything I can think of. But I knew if I'da screamed I'd be gone. If I screamed I'd be like them other poor suckers screaming and flying away. That scream would take me with it. My insides. And all my outsides too. So I didn't scream. Couldn't scream. Just lay there holding it in and shaking with all them wet bodies and pieces of body crashing upside me. Laying there and waiting for one of them lost souls to holler.

Train moving on down the track and I got to sit there and listen and hope it ain't me next time I hear one cut loose.

What happened?

Nothing happened. Told you it was a shitty-tailed nothing kind of dream.

Yeah. But you also said it scared the daylights out you.

Till this day. And still does. Will tomorrow if the truth be told. Tomorrow and the next day and the next.

You leaving something out. Something else musta happened.

Didn't nothing else need to happen.

Aw, man. Gwan. Gimme back the jug. I done had plenty worse dreams than that. Shit man. Freaks be chasing me. And little bitty hairy spiders trying to eat me up. There was one time a whole

army of cops be after me and I'm running for days all over Homewood and finally I got away, got home and my heart's pounding
so I takes a deep breath and I'm thinking they ain't never gon catch
me I'm the gingerbread man and this my briarpatch and shoot
I'm opening the back gate of the house on Finance Street and don't
you know there was a elephant in there. A big greasy-assed elephant chewing his cud in the backyard. Now that was a dream.
That big burly motherfucker in your own backyard after you done
outrun the police and marines and FBI. That was a scary motherfucker.

Yeah. That's what I'm talking about. The elephant.

What goddamn elephant?

The one made you stop. Made you hold your breath cause you
know if you make a sound you're gone.

That's my dream, fool. I just told it to you. You spozed to be
talking bout your own dream.

Couldn't scream. Had to hold it in for sixteen years. Fraid to
open my mouth for sixteen years cause I knowed I'd hear that
scream.

1. The Return of Albert Wilkes

BROTHER Tate stopped talking five years after I was born. When he died I was twenty-one and thought myself too grown for the name he had given me in my grandmother's kitchen. Nearly sixteen years altogether of silence, of not saying one word to any human being. By the time I was old enough to notice and care everybody else had gotten used to Brother's silence and paid it no mind. His strange color and silence were part of Homewood, like the names of the streets and the night trains and hills. But it wasn't exactly color and wasn't exactly silence. If you looked closely Brother had no color. He was lighter than anybody else, so white was a word some people used to picture him, but he wasn't white, not white like snow or paper, not even white like the people who called us black. Depending on the time of day, on how much light was in a room, on how you were feeling when you ran into Brother Tate, his color changed. I was always a little afraid of him, afraid I'd see through him, under his skin, because there was no color to stop my eyes, no color which said there's a black man or white man in front of you. I was afraid I'd see through that transparent envelope of skin to the bones and blood and guts of whatever he was. To see Brother I'd have to look away from where he was standing, focus on something safe and solid near him so that Brother would hover like the height of a mountain at the skittish edges of my vision.

And his silence wasn't really silence. Brother made noise all the time. Drumming his fingertips on the edge of the kitchen table till my grandmother yelled at him to stop, cracking his knuckles, patting his feet, boogeying so outrageously in the middle of the

floor you'd hear the silent music making him wiggle his narrow
hips and pop his fingers and wag his head like the sanctified sisters
moaning their way to heaven. If my grandmother wasn't in the
kitchen, he'd sit there at the gimpy table with the checkered cloth
and flip his lower lip like it was the string of a bass fiddle. He'd
hum and grunt and groan, and Brother could scat sing and imi-
tate all the instruments in a band. When Brother was around you
didn't need a radio. As long as my grandmother didn't shush him
or chase him out her house he would play all the good songs you'd
ever heard and make up plenty nobody ever heard before. Brother
would make all that music, all that noise, but he never said a word.
Not one word in all the years I knew him.

The first time I remember seeing Brother Tate he was scratching the back of his cue-ball head, and the creases at the base of
his skull puckered into a kind of mouth that scared me half to death
because what I saw was a face without features, a round, empty,
flesh lollipop licked clean of eyes and nose, a blank skull growing
a blubbery octopus mouth. And the first time I remember hearing
him he was singing scat. Scat singing *Bodey opp opp boddlely doop*
. . . sitting with my Uncle Carl at the table with the red and white
checkered oilcloth, spooning Kellogg's cornflakes straight from the
box between takes. *Opp Dudedly Poop.* And the first time I smelled
him was again in the kitchen of my grandmother's house when
I got too close trying to figure out the strange noises sputtering from
his lips and he reached around and grabbed me and tucked me
into his shoulder grinning and looking half at me and half at my
Uncle Carl, *Doot. Doot* was what he christened me, tickling a riff
with his hard blunt fingers on my ribs. His smell was the wine,
tobacco, limburger cheese of my grandfather's flannel shirts.

It seems from the stories I've heard that Brother Tate had a son,
a son born about the same time I was, just before or just after World
War II began. Brother's son would be my age now. If things had
worked out differently we might have grown up playing together,
being good buddies, getting into trouble and chasing girls and drinking wine and knowing everything worth knowing about each other.
But it didn't happen that way. One of the stories I've heard about
Brother Tate tells how his son, Junebug, died in a fire on the Fourth
of July. Junebug was albino and ugly like his father even though

his mother was a coal-black beautiful woman named Samantha everybody called Sam. The fire occurred a year or so after the war ended, so Junebug was only five or six when he died. They say that's about the time Brother Tate stopped talking for good. He'd never said much before. He'd go for weeks according to my Uncle Carl, without saying word the first. Brother's silence made people think he was feebleminded. That and his strange color, or lack of color, that whiteness which made him less nigger and more nigger at the same time.

Brother's silence can be thought of as a kind of mourning for his lost son. Perhaps the lost son also explains the particular affection and attentiveness Brother always lavished on me. Brother treated me special because he could see Junebug in me. In Brother's eyes I grew up living not only my own life, but the one snatched from Junebug. Brother took on the job of watching me closely even though it must have been hard sometimes for him because I would be a reminder of both the life and death of his son. I couldn't help carrying both seeds. And Brother couldn't help remembering as he stood guard over me what he'd lost.

So I'm linked to Brother Tate by stories, by his memories of a dead son, by my own memories of a silent, scat-singing albino man who was my uncle's best friend.

I am not born yet. My Uncle Carl and Brother Tate hurry along the railroad tracks on the graveled crest of the hillside which parallels Finance Street. It is early in the morning, a summery spring day, and Carl is daydreaming of running away. He feels the sun on the back of his neck, hears the crunch of gravel, but his mind is on the ocean, an ocean he has never seen except in pictures and daydreams. If he closes his eyes he can see an ocean, red and wild as his blood, an ocean surging past the shimmering curtain of heat rising from the steel rails, an ocean rushing to the end of the world. He would run away that far if he could. To the place where the waters roar over the edge and the sky is no thicker than a sheet of paper. He would run or fly or swim to that place where the red sky and red sea meet. If he could.

Brother wants him to play a scare game. One game is cutting across an oncoming train at the last possible instant. First one to start is the loser. You hunker down at the edge of the tracks. You watch the train fill the sky and watch the shoulders of the one next to you for a sign. You juke your own shoulders and scream and snap out of your crouch. You cheat and push the one next to you hoping you'll scare him into flying first across the tracks. Scream as if your voice could drown out the monster engine chewing and spitting rails as it bears down on you. Brother always wins that game, always has one life to spare so he ain't afraid to leave it like a stomped down, bloody overcoat on the tracks. There is always that split second when you're crunched down so low and tight you think you're going to pee your pants if you don't let go, if you don't vault that first rail and hit the ties clean and leap again with both fists grabbing for air, grabbing for gravel as you flatten out and sail over the second rail to the safe place between tracks.

Brother always waits a half second longer, that half second when the train sucks all the air out your chest, when it turns your knees to runny butter, that half second when nothing inside you works because the train has rammed its fist up your hynie. The worst way to lose that game is nailed to the hillside, your heart trying to jump out your mouth, standing there like Okey Doke the damn fool till the train finishes swooshing past and you can see Brother again, not dead like he ought to be, but wagging his bald head and signifying with his whole self in the middle of the right of way.

The other scare game is getting as close as you can to the outside rail and not flinching when the train bears down on you. One player sets the challenge, scuffs a mark as close as possible to the tracks then dares the other to stand in the footprints. The challenger is the judge. Nobody won that one much. Carl waited for Brother to plant himself, then he stood right behind Brother's narrow back, as close as Brother to the track. Carl started yelling before the smoke settled. He tasted ashes and burnt oil and choked getting his words out.

You moved, nigger. You moved.

What you talking about, man?

You moved. You was inched halfway down the hillside by the time the engine hit.

Sheet. Your mama the one moved.

I don't play that.

You just ain't got no heart, that's all.

Listen who's talking. What about the time the man blew the whistle?

Aw, man. He ain't supposed to be doing that, that ain't part of the game.

You set the world record. Ain't never seen nobody jump so high. I thought you was climbing a tree, man. Couldn't see no tree, but I knew you had to be climbing something. Must have been something holding up your big feet cause niggers ain't supposed to be walking on no air.

Whistle ain't part the game.

Scared is scared.

Well, we ain't talking about that now. We talking about *now*, now. And I ain't moved one bit.

You moved. You know you moved.

You're lying, man. You lying and Miss French got a bulldog dick.

Told you I don't play that shit . . .

So nobody won that game much, but they played it when they couldn't think of anything better to do. But this morning as they hustled along the tracks toward Westinghouse Park they weren't playing anything. My Uncle Carl was dreaming of running away and Brother was chucking rocks, but they had a job and were on their way to do it.

Albert Wilkes is back. Albert Wilkes is back and that means trouble. Carl's job was finding his daddy, finding him and bringing him home.

You tell him I said come home. Right away. You understand? Wait for your father, stay with your father till he starts to move and come back here with your father. You hear me? Don't stop to play. Don't stop for nothing. Albert Wilkes is back in town and if you want to have a daddy tomorrow, you better do just what I told you.

I can see my grandmother shooing Carl out the door, the only door in the row house on Cassina Way. I can hear it slam and echo in the emptiness of the cobblestone alley lined with identical wooden row houses from Dunfermline to Richland. The house on Cassina Way was still there when I was a teenager. Two families still occupied each unit so the people in front lived on Tioga Street and the people in back lived on Cassina Way. You could live in the same house with people and not know their names because of the partition dividing the house and the doors at either end opening in different places. You knew the people across the alley but you seldom went around the block to Tioga, to the little green front porches that made living on Tioga a step up from living on Cassina. Even if you lived in the end house, next to the vacant lot, you seldom had business which carried you around to Tioga. The people who lived on Cassina walked down Cassina to get to Homewood Avenue and the stores. What they knew about each other was enough to keep them knee deep in gossip, so keeping up with Cassina left them uncurious about the strangers whose voices leaked through the thin partitions dividing their houses into two slightly unequal chunks.

That's the way it must have been on Cassina Way. Rows of wooden shanties built to hold the flood of black migrants up from the South. Teeming is the word I think of. A narrow, cobbled alley *teeming* with life. Like a wooden-walled ship in the middle of the city, like the ark on which Noah packed two of everything and prayed for land. I think of my grandmother and grandfather and the children they were raising in that house on Cassina and I see islands, arks, life teeming but enclosed or surrounded or exiled to arbitrary boundaries. And the city around them which defined and delimited, which threatened but also buoyed and ferried them to whatever unknown destination, this city which trapped and saved them, for better or worse, never quite breached Cassina's walls.

The life in Cassina Way was a world apart from Homewood and Homewood a world apart from Pittsburgh and Pittsburgh was the North, a world apart from the South, and all those people crowded in Cassina Way carried the seeds of these worlds inside their skins, black, brown and gold and ivory skin which was the first world setting them apart.

I hear the door slam behind Carl and echo up and down Cassina in the morning stillness. My grandmother cringes because she's told him a thousand times not to run outdoors like a wild Indian, not to bust through doors like a hog out its pen, and each time he flies through the frame and the door swings slamming shut behind him one more nail is driven into her heart. Miss Pollard hears it. She is already stationed in the upstairs window, in the single room she rents from Dot Jones. Miss Pollard. Miss although she's buried two husbands, Miss though ten children who call her Mama are scattered in places like Cleveland, Akron, and Scranton, Pennsylvania. Miss Pollard has the job of watching Cassina from her second-story window and she's on duty and registers the French boy, Carl, whose feet hit the cobblestones before the door bangs shut behind him. Then it's two of them, Carl and the albino who was sitting on the steps, the white boy at his post some mornings before she took hers, early, early before anything moving in Cassina. Like a ghost out there before Miss Pollard settles herself for the day in her fanback rocker next to her window. Maybe he stays out there sitting on those steps all night. He's a peculiar one. Looking and acting. The two of them, the French boy never touching the steps where the white one sits, just flying by straight to the cobbles so the other one must have felt the breeze going by his head cause he's up in a second and clomping after the other one, two pairs of feet trying to wear out the stones of Cassina with their rubber-soled shoes.

Miss Pollard wonders what they're all up to so early Saturday morning. John French first, easing the door shut behind him, hefting his tool bag cross his shoulder and creeping up Cassina like he done robbed his own house and got it all stuffed up in that sack on his back. Then Freeda French popping out the door like a bird out a clock. No coffee cup steaming in her hand this morning, no sweet little wave up at Miss Pollard's window, no pat for the ghost boy's bald head, nothing but her eyes running both ways up and down that empty alley after her man. Then them boys flying. Miss Pollard treats herself to a pinch of snuff to pass the time till the ice wagon rattles down Cassina. After the ice wagon and the ice man's song and the horses' hooves clacking against the cobblestones, Cassina will begin to fill up. Be so many doors slamming and children in and out and so and so yelling at so and so across the way, be so much business out there today it keep a body weary rocking to keep up. She'll call down to one of the little rascals go get her some chewing tobacco over to Indovina's. She'll drop a nickel and drop a penny and he better get on back here with my Five Brothers. Five Brothers. You hear me now? Don't led him sell you noth-

ing else. If he ain't got it, tell him to get it. Hear me now? Tell
him I said get it. Much money as I spend in there. Little crippled
up dago ain't got what you need half the time no way. Too busy
cheating these dumb niggers round here to stock like he should.
Five Brothers. And don't be taking all day, child.

A hophead friend of my brother's will kill Indovina. Shoot the
old man three times in the chest with a .357 Magnum because there
was only thirteen dollars in the cash register, thirteen dollars and
change old crippled Indovina dumped on the floor like he was
emptying a slop jar. Miss Pollard will die in a fire in the single
room she rented on Braddock Avenue. Not a bad fire, everyone
else got out of the apartment building. Smoke mostly. Enough
smoke to suffocate her as she slept because nobody remembered
she was up there on the third floor. She had to move to Braddock
Avenue when the city tore down her side of Cassina. I remember
driving past the row houses where John French and Freeda French
raised my mother and kept me a year or so when I was a baby.
You could see that stretch of Cassina from Susquehanna after the
city urban renewed Homewood. Our old house still standing then
next to the vacant lot. A row of wooden shanties anchored in rubble,
so thin and old and exposed they shamed me and I looked away
quickly, the way I averted my eyes from the crotches of ancient
women in head rags and cotton stockings rolled to their knees who
sat gap-legged on their porches.

The train catches Brother and Carl just before Homewood Avenue. My uncle tries to ignore it but shies a few steps down the embankment as the train passes. Hot, monster breath. His body yanked
from the ground and shaken like a rag doll in a giant, black fist.
When the air stops heaving and shuddering in the train's wake
and he can think his own thoughts again he looks back over his
shoulder for Brother. But his shadow is not there.

You're crazy, man. You ain't got good sense, man.

Brother is squatting in the middle of the right of way, soot
stained, grinning, the red sweat rag around his bald head, his chest
heaving like a little bit of the train's still in there trying to get out.

Ain't no time for games, fool. Come on if you're coming.

Brother stands and pulls off his shirt. The sun strips the skin from
his thin chest. Naked bones pulse like wings. Brother catches his

breath and strolls nonchalantly toward my uncle, rolling his skinny shoulders. Brother's hands tell a story. His fist is a train humping down the track and two fingers on the other hand are naked little white legs sprinting then leaping over the fist as it lunges past. He tells it again, but this time the fist smacks into his palm and the pale legs fly up in the air and flutter back to earth dead as snow.

You play that shit by your ownself this morning.

If Carl's knees pumped a little higher he'd be running. He hears Brother's breathing over his shoulder, huffing to keep up. After the narrow bridge over Homewood Avenue the tracks stretch straight and shining through the length of Westinghouse Park till they disappear in a molten curve too far away, too bright for his eyes to follow. His father could be down in the park beneath that dusty roof of green, under those trees that look like broccoli, tightly packed heads of fresh broccoli in crates outside Indovina's grocery store. He could call down there if he dared, call *John French, John French*, wake up the winos who would be sleeping in the Bums' Forest now that spring was turning warm as summer. He knew his father slept down there on gambling, wine-drinking nights when he didn't make it home to Cassina Way. But his father had slept in his own bed last night. He'd heard John French leave early in the morning with his paper-hanging tools. Heard him cross the landing and tip down the stairs.

You try the beer garden first. Said he had a job this morning so you try there first. Ask for his tools. Ask if they're behind the bar or if he took them on a job. Damn that Albert Wilkes. Damn his soul.

His mother's eyes had frightened him. His mother only damned people when she was scared. And scared was in her eyes this morning. Damning people and talking fast like she couldn't hardly catch her breath. Wagging a finger in his face. Do you understand this? Do you remember that? Are you listening, boy? Go here, go there as if he didn't know, as if this was the first time he had searched the Homewood streets for his father.

Sunshine, you are my sunshine. His father sang that to his mother when she was scared. When her long hair hung down loose, uncombed the way it was this morning and her eyes were red from crying or no sleep, witchy hair, almost, the way it hung so long

over her shoulders and hid so much of her face like a veil. John
French sang *You are my sunshine* when she left one twin dead in
the hospital and brought the other home to die on Cassina. Sang
it and hummed it that sad week waiting for the babyboy who was
also John French to die. Sadness in her hair, her eyes this morning, sadness which was being scared as much as it was anything
else, made her damn Albert Wilkes the way she damned God and
all his angels the week his father sang *Sunshine. You are my sunshine.* He was humming it to himself now, his father's song, his
mother's eyes, the baby brother who lived only a week on Cassina
Way, humming it as he stopped along the tracks and Brother drew
up panting beside him.

From where they stood you couldn't see the path cutting up from
Finance Street through the trees, and if you couldn't see the path
no way you'd see anybody sleeping farther back in the woods.

It's that Albert Wilkes. That goddamn no-good Albert Wilkes
got my mama scared. You know who I'm talking about. He used
to stay over youall's place before he went away. Piano-playing
Albert Wilkes, damn his goddamn soul.

Brother nods, runs his fingers up and down a keyboard.

Yeah, they say he could play. They say he was the best but that
don't make no nevermind. He's back from wherever he's been and
my mama's scared and we got to find my daddy before she starts
crying again.

Brother points to the old station at the far end of the park where
the trains used to stop. Carl pictures his daddy on the broken-down
steps, sitting regal and laid back as if he owned them and owned
the whole wooden-stepped passage from the abandoned train station with its busted windows and crocked sign to Mulberry Way's
cobblestones, owned the steps and anything else he chose to claim
if he decided something was worth tilting the wide-brimmed hat
back off his forehead to stake a claim with his green eyes.

And Carl hopes there won't be too many others sitting on the
steps. Because the men were always teasing. Always signifying.
Junk about pimples and young boys and nasty stuff said in whispers and winks so you never heard it all, just enough to know they
were talking at you, not to you. Signifying so you knew part of
what was funny was you. He hated that laughter, felt his face get-

ting hot, already saw Brother acting a fool, making faces to get the men laughing louder. Somebody would poke a wine bottle at Brother and he'd swig it, wipe his chin with the heel of his hand the way the winos did and roll his eyes and cut wobbly-legged monkeyshines till John French snapped his fingers, snapped them once, as loud as breaking a stick.

What you want, boy? And no matter what Carl had to say he'd get choked up. All the men would be listening and he'd stutter and sound simpleminded. The message he'd said a thousand times over and over to himself would sneak off and hide and laugh at him too. He'd wish he was Brother so he could act a fool and cut monkeyshines. Anything be better than opening his mouth and stuttering like he was feebleminded.

He damned Albert Wilkes again and daydreamed the other places his father could be. With Brother like a shadow behind him Carl could enter the dream, get from one place to another in Homewood just by thinking where he wanted to go and then the streets would slip past as he thought them, Dunfermline, Tioga, Albion, Finance, Susquehanna, Alliquippa, Frankstown, Hamilton, and it wouldn't be a matter of a certain number of steps and turning here and crossing there because the streets were inside him. The streets were Homewood but they were not real till he thought them. Till he glided with his shadow, Brother, up and down and over the streets sleeping inside him.

He knew the idea was silly, but he thought it sometimes anyway: if he didn't wake up one morning, would there still be a Homewood? It was a silly idea because he had a father and mother and they had lived in Homewood before he was born. And plenty of Homewood people much older than his father and mother, people in the stories Aunt May told about Grandmother Gert and her Great-grandmother Sybela Owens. So he knew Homewood was as old as Sybela Owens and slavery days, older than his Uncle Bill and Aunt Aida they called Anaydee, as old as the old dead people in May's stories. Homewood was young too, was starting up again in the kids playing on the sidewalks and alleys and vacant lots where he had played. But he thought his silly idea sometimes anyway. If I don't wake up, Homewood will be gone. If I run away, far away, the Homewood streets will disappear. Mornings like this,

this hard, bright spring summer morning when he was sent looking for his father, it would be easier to run away. To lose himself
and lose his shadow, Brother, in a daydream of some other place.
A place where the streets have new names, a place he cannot see
plainly like he sees the Homewood streets unfurling when he shuts
his eyes. He wouldn't have to search for his father there. The trees
wouldn't look like dirty broccoli. No pee smell along the path. His
mother wouldn't be standing in the kitchen of the house on Cassina
wringing her hands in her apron.

A silly idea. Like most of the ideas he thought up. But it's like
a job. Something he must do no matter what. He had been scared
by his mother's eyes. She was a pretty lady. She had skin white
as a white woman's and long soft hair she wore piled on top of
her head. He loved to see her let her hair down and loved to watch
her comb it because she hummed as she combed it down past her
shoulders. This morning she damned Albert Wilkes, and her eyes
were sad. Red like she'd been crying. But it was his job so he had
to make Homewood this morning like he made it every morning
when he woke up. Make the streets because that's where his father
would be and she needed him to find his father. So he listens to
his shadow breathing behind him and stares as far as he can down
the tracks. The tracks could take him somewhere else, he thinks.
Somewhere shimmering like the steel rails just before they curve
out of sight. Sky drops to meet gravel and steel at that shimmering
point. The world is as thin as tissue paper there. You could poke
your finger through it. He can't see streets beyond that flattened
stretched-out place where the tracks are on fire. Those faraway
streets are not inside him; they have no names.

Brother, he thinks, has no name. My man, my buddy, my ace
boon coon running pardner Brother. No name. No color. No nothing if you think about it.

Carl calls over his shoulder, Hey, Brother. Hey man, you ain't
nothing. And then Carl thinks how easy it is to be Brother. To
have no color. No name. No job. No father you got to find.

Man, you got it easy.

Before they get to the platform they can see it's empty. Trains
used to stop, but now it's nothing but a place where the men sit
when they want to get out of the sun. A beat-up, slant-roofed shed,

a brick wall, some gray planks left from the floor where people once stood waiting for trains, wooden steps down the hillside from the platform to the cobblestones of Mulberry Way. Nobody uses the steps anymore. Beside them, cutting up the hillside, a trail is worn through the weeds. A few of the steps near the top still safe for sitting but the rest so rotten you'd crash right through. Nobody is sitting where the men usually sit. No voices echo under the slanted roof. His father is not sprawled there with his long legs dangling over the crushed steps, his big hat pushed back off his forehead so he can stare down Mulberry Way as if he owns it.

Where is he? Where you think he is?

Carl wonders if it really is easy to have no color. No answers. He's always asking Brother questions, questions like he asks himself, questions nobody could answer. He wonders what would happen if one day Brother started answering. Brother could go for days, for weeks, and never say a mumbling word. He wonders if Brother likes having no words, no father, no name. Mr. Tate is little and quiet. A kind of nice, washed-out, stuttering little man. Mr. Tate never drinks wine or shoots crap in the Bums' Forest or hangs on the corner outside the Bucket of Blood loudtalking and singing and making ladies cross to the other side of the street. The Tates take care of Brother and take care of Lucy, but they are not Brother's real father and mother. Carl wonders if that's easy. Wonders where Brother came from. Wonders if there are two ghosts someplace, white like Brother, who are his mother and father. Wonders if Brother sees the Homewood streets like he sees them. Like a job, like a book in his hand and Carl is turning the pages, trying to find his father, trying to decide where to look next as he dreams the streets, and dreams himself and his shadow in another place.

What would happen to Homewood if he ran away? What would happen to his mother and father if one morning, a bright, lazy spring summer morning, he didn't wake up and start the dream of Homewood? Carl is suddenly afraid. More scared than he's ever been in the scare games when a train shakes the earth behind him. So afraid he does not close his eyes against the roaring thing rushing up behind his back, but opens them as wide as he can to take in all of the broad blue sky. He digs into the gravel, stomping it, kicking it onto the tracks. Quickly, he spins around to face the pale, skinny boy.

Brother, you got it easy, man.

He hears how squeaky his voice sounds. But he's so happy to see Brother he doesn't care. Brother answers with his hands. They are saying the names of all the Homewood streets. But his hands change the sound. The street names are blurred like song words when somebody hums or moans them. The white hands dance up and down a keyboard. Play the blues. A fast-chugging keep-up-with-the-train blues. Brother's hands are playing: C'mon. C'mon. You moving too slow this morning, boy. Train gon catch you you don't c'mon.

Brother's hands play all the streets of Homewood. He throws them down like dice and they come up seven.

Instead of saying it, this time Carl thinks, *Brother you ain't nothing*, but he can't think the words without grinning, grinning at the washboard ribs, the watermelon belly, the pink eyes and pink fingernails racing up and down those black and white piano keys.

C'mon, fool.

And both boys break for the room-for-nothing-but-trains bridge back over Homewood Avenue.

My grandmother, Freeda, is standing in the front room of the house on Cassina Way. She stares down at her hands as if she's trying to remember what they're for. She had winced as she always did when the door slammed behind her son, winced once and waited for a yell from upstairs, a startled-awake holler of annoyance from one of the girls, echoing the gunshot slam of the door. It hadn't come but she stood stock-still anyway, waiting, listening, wishing now for something to break the silence. I'm trying to remember the inside of her house, its shape, the furniture, the way things in it would trap the silence and spin a dusty, beaded web around her so if you peeked in from Cassina you'd see a young woman draped by layers of transparent gauze, a young woman standing up asleep, her eyes open, threads stretched from the top of her head to all the walls, the things in the room, the planes of smoky light surrounding her like wash pinned on lines to dry. That's what I see, invisible in the alley, trying to remember. When I lived on Cassina Way I couldn't have been more than four or five, so my image of the inside of the house comes less from what I saw than from what I've been told since. Yet the cobblestones are real under my feet, slippery and cold from last night's rain, cold and damp until the sun gets high enough to light the shadowed stillness behind me. There must have been a curtain at the front window but the glass is bare now as I peer through. This is the window my grandmother smashed with her fist. She watched a man sneaking down Cassina, a man with a gun, a skinny, pigeon-toed somebody whose eyes were fixed on her husband's back, a sneak with a pistol in his hand getting closer and closer to where she sat with Lizabeth on her lap. Lizabeth was smiling. She loved to hear her mother tell the caterpillar story. When the man in the alley raised the gun her mother's fist punched through the glass, her mother screamed, and Lizabeth screamed and John French gone like a turkey through the corn and the gun blasted the emptiness of Cassina Way twice before it clattered to the cobblestones and the scarecrow man took off toward the far end as fast as John French had ducked round the near corner. All of that happened, but now the glass wears rag stuffing in one shattered corner. A scar zigzags like a caterpillar across my grandmother's knuckles. The hands she stares at make no sense, but they are her hands and she doesn't believe either one of them can save John French's life again.

Freeda looks round at the things in the room. They are so familiar, yet they look strange this morning. As though she's waking up in someone else's house. All this rummage sale stuff that's been in the family and the stuff John French won shooting crap and stuff he "found" patrolling the alleys behind the white folks' houses with Strayhorn, all of it strange as the hands at the end of her wrists, hands that made her think she might be waking up in someone else's body.

Once, washing dishes at the kitchen sink, in another house, another world where the sun hit the second-story window over the sink first thing early in the morning and the tiny kitchen was the warmest, brightest room in the house and nobody lived with the butt end of their house pressed up against the nose of yours like two dirty dogs in an alley, once, when she lifted her hand from a sinkful of suds a bubble was trapped between her thumb and first finger. She had been thinking of all the new people arriving in Homewood. Colored people, they said. Ignorant, countrified niggers, they said, from the South. Downhome niggers they said so black and brown sounded nasty and she was thinking about color when she pulled her hand up out of the water. Her hand was brown as it ever got and that no browner than a cup of milk mixed with a tablespoon of coffee. Not even brown enough to hide the pink flush after it had been sloshing all morning in a sinkful of soap and dishes and pots and pans. A bulky mitten of suds had slowly slid down her fingers when she lifted her hand from the sink. She shook her wrist so it slid faster. That's when she saw the bubble webbed between her thumb and first finger, a long, jelly-bellied bubble with see-through skin that held all the colors of the rainbow.

She had raised the rainbow to her lips. The bubble quivered when she breathed on it. She thought of dandelions and wishes, of ladybugs who'd carry your whispered secrets to the Good Fairy when you opened your fist and let them fly away. A little harder, if she gently blew just a little harder, maybe she could loosen the bubble from the arc of her thumb and finger, maybe she could make a wish and set the rainbow free. Tilted in a certain way the colors disappeared and the glistening skin reflected the kitchen, the kitchen made tiny and funny-shaped like a face in a spoon. With one puff she could set the room and the rainbow free.

My grandmother Freeda had been just a girl then. In that other room, that other world, enchanted by a soap bubble. She remembered its exact shape now. A long watermelon blister of soap quivering between her thumb and finger. Something had broken the spell, made her look away and the strange bubble had burst. She'd never been able to recall what had distracted her from the soapsuds' little trick. But something had made her look away, and in that instant the bubble had popped. Gone before she could whisper her wish, set it free. She couldn't remember what had pulled her away, but it continued pulling, drawing her past the edges of herself. Since that day, whenever she looked away from something, she was never sure it would be there when she looked back. Alone in the downstairs of the half a house on Cassina Way listening to dishwater gurgle and burp down the sluggish drain she was afraid they would never return, not the girls sleeping at the top of the steps, not the man nor the boy she sent to search for the man, not even the boy's white shadow or the shadow of herself, that dreamy part of herself just beyond the edge, not afraid to look away.

Perhaps things happened, she thought, perhaps all the moments of her life had occurred not to make her somebody, not because there needed to be a Freeda French, but because living was learning to forget. The next thing happened because you needed to forget what was happening now because what was happening now was nothing but a way of forgetting what had happened before. In church they sang *Farther along we'll know more about Him. Farther along we'll understand why.* What did those words mean? Would there be a bright day, a clear singing day farther along when the dead ones, the lost ones, the ones hurt and suffering beyond tears, the ones who sinned and the ones who prayed would all come crowding back from Glory, a day farther along when you understood once and forever that He forgot no one, nothing, that He never forgot but always forgave, that He took his own sweet time but everything was all right, had to be all right and you understood farther along?

But if her life had a shape, if she was Freeda French, it had nothing to do with memories she could line up, not the babies, the nights with John French, not the golden Christmas turkey basting in the oven not the snow on Bruston Hill, or the gray rain or the enemas and coughing in the night or the prayers or the song. If her life had a shape, the shape was not what she could remember, but what kept tearing her away, the voice which could make her look and look away, the voice beyond the edges of herself making her lose what she had in her hand, making her settle for whatever came next.

Sometimes the songs helped. If you loved God and loved your man and loved your children you were safe. The music would say that to her. Farther Along. Everything could be taken away tomorrow and still the music made her feel how good it would be when He folded her in His arms. The music could soothe her, quiet her, and she'd see her worst fears were nothing more than a child's cry in the darkness. He'd understand, He'd snap on the light and rock her back to sleep. All that in the music. A garden in the music where she could come to Him alone, where the dew was still on the roses. And the voice she'd hear as she tarried there, that voice was in the music too. A place to rest, to lay her head, her burdens, she heard it all in the hymns they sang in Homewood A.M.E. Zion Church. But the same songs that saved her could leave her stranded just short of the promised shore. She wouldn't rise up new and shining on the far bank but slip into icy Jordan waters, waters black and cold and still would close over her head. She'd found in the songs a vast emptiness, a desert of bones, rows and rows of caskets, moaning oceans of tears. The songs taught her to fear death, to fear the sky which could fall on your head like a hammer, to fear the smothering earth, to fear the fire in thunder and lightning, the rotting hands in the black depths of the water waiting to drag you down. Tempest, trial and toil and snare and miring clay. They were all in the songs. You could die alone, suffer alone forever in those vast, empty places where the songs carried you.

But she held on to her God, and held on to her family and swore to herself she would cling as long as there was breath in her body. And the oath was strong, and her arms grew strong but never stronger than the voice tearing her away.

It was Albert Wilkes scratching at the window last night. Scratching and tapping like a cat. She couldn't hear what was said after John French went out into Cassina, but she knew that alleycat tap scratching, hadn't heard it in seven years but knew it when she heard it again. Knew it was Albert Wilkes again and trouble again.

She had lain awake till her man mounted the stairs, till he stepped across the landing and peeked into the children's room, till the landing buckled again and creaked again receiving his full weight again and he snuffed out the wall-climbing flame of the candle and pushed through the door of their bedroom. The last thing she heard was the clang of his belt buckle when he draped his pants over the end of their brass bed.

That was him at the window last night, wasn't it?
Him? Watchyou talkin bout? Him?
You know just who I mean.
If you talking bout Albert Wilkes he sure nuff got a name. And you know it. He ain't no *Him* if you talkin about Albert.

Then he's back.

Yes he is.

And couldn't wait to get hold of you. Had to come here scratching like some alleycat in the middle of the night. Couldn't wait till daytime. Couldn't knock at people's door like a civilized human being.

You know that's his way.

Always sneaking around.

You know how he is.

I told him to keep his Devil self away from here. So he sneaks round like an alleycat in the dark. Why won't he leave you alone? Why won't he just go on about his business? Why'd he have to come back?

He's my friend. Where else he gon go if he in trouble?

Albert Wilkes born to trouble.

Can't help that. Can't do nothing bout none of that. But he's my friend. Ima do what I can, and that's all there is to that. Now you go on back to sleep. No need gettin all in a bother. I got that job over on Thomas Boulevard to go to this morning. I got to go, but you mize well get your rest whiles you can. The children still sleepin. You go on back to sleep and don't be studying no Albert Wilkes.

I hated that whistle of his. And that scratching at night. Because that's all he'd have to do. Stand out there in Cassina and purse his lips and don't care what you doing you're gone. You hear him whistling at you and you're up and gone. It'd make my blood boil. I'd want to run outside and strangle him. And it was worse at night. You'd hear it in your sleep. Jump out of bed to run the streets with that man. Now he's back again and scratching again. Please don't act a fool with Albert Wilkes. Albert Wilkes got nobody to answer to but hisself. If I don't matter nothing to you, think about the children. Don't go getting mixed up in none of Albert Wilkes's mess.

Hush now. You gon wake them babies if you don't hush. I got that job this morning and you needs to go back to sleep. He's my friend. Ain't nothing else to be said on the subject.

Can't find him, Mama. Looked everywhere and he ain't noplace.

Stop, just stop right there. First thing is how many times have

I told you two not to come running in here out the street like a
pair of wild Indians. And the second thing is you left the door open
like I've told you a thousand times not to, and every fly in Homewood be in here and you know better. And the third thing is me
talking myself blue in the face and you paying me no nevermind.
You still talk like some field hand fresh from Georgia every chance
you get. You're going to be the death of me, Carl French. Now
wipe that sweat out your eyes and put your shirt on your back
and shut the door quietly and say what you have to say like a
human being.

She hated the fat, buzzing flies. Flies in Cassina Way had never
been bad till all those people from the deep South started arriving
with their dirty boxes and bags and spitting in the street and throwing garbage where people have to walk. It was like having all those
people in her house when the flies swarmed through the open door,
those careless, dirty people lighting on her things, crawling across
her ceilings and floors.

We can't find Daddy.

You looked . . . everywhere?

Everywhere, Mama.

What's on your feet, boy? That's black soot from the train tracks.

We had to look everywhere, like you said.

I didn't say walk those tracks. I told you never to walk those
tracks. You've been up on that crossing, haven't you? Doesn't matter
how many times I say no, you're still going to be a hardhead. You
still have to do it your way. That's all I need on top of everything
else. A hardhead son. How hard's your head gon be when somebody
comes here, *Mrs. French, Mrs. French. Oh my Goodness, Miz
French, I'm so sorry Miz French but that Carl, that boy of yours
been hit by a train.* That's all I need around here. One more fool
in the house trying to get hisself killed. You get in the bathroom
and clean yourself up. And pull off those shoes before you take
another step. And you better not make a mess in there and those
shoes better be clean and looking better than new next time I see
them. You're through for the day. Brother, you go on now. Carl
through playing for the day.

The albino stood slack-jawed, his eyes on the floor. This is when
he's ugly she thought, ugly as sin. When he stops moving and hum-

ming and has nothing for his hands to do, Brother dies. He is lumpy, colorless pie dough. His skin is raw and wrinkled like a plucked chicken before you wet it and roll it in flour and drop it in the bubbling grease. If she let him, he would stand there, dead in that bag of white skin till Carl returned. She thought of the flamingos in Highland Park Zoo. How they tucked one leg up into the bag of their pink bodies and stood frozen, balanced on the other stick leg for as long as you could watch.

Go on. Find something to do with yourself. You need to take that shirt from round your waist and put it on, too.

She flinched twice in anticipation before the door actually slammed, and when it did slam she flinched again. Carl and Brother like two peas in a pod. They walked and listened alike. Her son handsome and Brother pug ugly but they looked alike. Both of them rolled their narrow shoulders to get the mannish John French weight in their steps. Both had those potbellies and bony arms. Though she'd seen them together a million times, she didn't know who was taller. Neither one looked colored. Carl tanned slightly by the middle of summer, but he was like her and the girls, the sunbrown tint of their skin never deepened, it was a goldish dust, a shadow which disappeared altogether in some kinds of light, a coating thin enough for the wind to erase. Both boys had that deep seam down the middle of their backs, and shoulder blades poking like spatulas under their skin. Those big, restless bones seemed out of place. Maybe both boys supposed to be something else. Maybe both of them missing a set of arms or wings. Maybe something else supposed to be stuck on back there and waiting for it was what made them so alike.

Strange and ugly as he was she had barely noticed Brother when he first started coming around. Now he came and went just about as he pleased. Part of her life, part of what she'd become. It had taken no time to live her life. It had taken forever. Hard now to recall when Brother hadn't been around. She wasn't surprised anymore when she opened the door and found him sitting still as a statue on her steps, part of Cassina's quiet, the peace she needed to taste with her coffee before the rest of the house was awake. She'd pat his bald head. Looked like it should be cold, like his whole body be frozen out there hunched on the bottom step so early some mornings the chilled air set her coffee to steaming, but when she patted him, patted that head smooth and bare as a stone, her fingers found warmth humming in the web of blue veins crisscrossing his skull.

Up and out early with her coffee cup because she wanted to be alone. Funny how Brother could be on his step and Miss Pollard already pulled up to her window but Freeda was alone anyway. Funny how being alone had something to do with knowing those two would be at their posts. They helped her find her peace those mornings she needed to be up before the others, out in Cassina before anybody called her name or called her Mama.

Brother almost like one of her own children. They start out so light you can carry them round the house in one arm. Then before you know it, they're carrying you. Mama do this and Mama do that and Please Mama and if one ain't calling your name or begging you for something or trying to steal that moment's peace you thought you had coming you're lost as a helpless little child. They're carrying you around and you're weak as a baby. You're light as a feather and their silence heavy as stones in your heart.

Brother came and went now as he pleased just like the other strange things in her life. Once in the middle of the night a terrible dream had driven her out of bed groping down those steep, treacherous steps and she'd found him at the oilclothed table eating a bowl of cornflakes and milk. Brother alone in her kitchen, at her table, in the middle of the night, munching cornflakes and glowing in the dark like some moony ghost. Well, it didn't faze her. She said nothing to him and he just kept working on those Kellogg's cornflakes. Sounded like mice playing in the walls.

She had been born and raised in Homewood and if there was a time in her life when Brother hadn't been around, she couldn't remember it. And one day I'll die in Homewood, she thought. One night he'll be at my table nibbling like some big white mouse. One night the terrible dream will come looking for me in my bed and won't be nobody there to scare. She could see herself disappear, see herself gone forever in the emptiness of Brother's pink eyes. Some days she knew she'd rather die than have to touch him. Yet

Brother just a boy, a big-head, potbellied boy like her son Carl and she remembers Lucy Tate pushing the albino in a baby buggy up and down Tioga Street till the buggy rotted and Brother was bigger than Lucy and nothing left of the buggy but springs and frame and Brother clinging like a monkey to the skeleton. She had heard people talk about the Tates and Lucy Bruce who became a Tate after her mother burnt up in the fire on Hamilton Avenue. Brother had been part of Homewood for as long as she cared to remember. He was just a boy but sometimes he seemed older than she was. Sometimes he was older than old Mr. and Mrs. Tate who they say found him and raised him in that big old house of theirs. Old Mr. and Mrs. Tate had raised half the orphans and strays in Homewood in that big house of theirs. No children of their own but always kept a houseful of kids.

If she let herself she could start crying this morning. Get weepy and be good for nothing the rest of the day. She could get her mother Gert on her mind. Her beautiful mama with furs and feathers and beaded necklaces hanging to her waist and silver bracelets and turquoise rings. Real diamonds in her ears she said and lifted the curls off her neck to show anybody who wanted to see. Her Mama Gert who went with white men and died somewhere far away. Her Mama Gert who Isabelle Lewis called no good, whispering *No good* loud enough for everybody in the church vestibule to hear. And little Aunt Aida waiting outside for Isabelle Lewis. Caught Isabelle Lewis soon as she stepped that one step out the church down to the street.

You put my sister's name in that nasty mouth of yours one more time and you gon be spitting teeth with your lies. This child standing right there and you badmouth her mother. In church, too. Lucky it was church too, or you'd be gumming your lies right now. Church or no church I hear something like that again Ima snatch you bald-headed and tongue-tied. Trifling wench like you got the nerve to be talking bout who's good and no good.

Hush now, Baby. Good and no good ain't got nothing to do with it. Gert is Gert. That's who she is and what she is and always will be. Always be your mama too. Onliest one you gon get, onliest one you gon love like a mama. And Gert love you long as she's

Gert. Long's she got breath in her body. Cause she's Gert. And that's her way.

Gert's way was laughing like a bird. Laughing like a bird and flying away like one too. Winter come she's gone. Spring she pops up again. Here one day gone the next. Then she come pecking at your window the very day you thought the sun never shine in your back door again.

Lookit my girl. Lookit how tall and pretty she's getting. Her way was perfumey hugs and lipstick kisses and a soft-gloved hand wrapped round yours for walks in Westinghouse Park. Gert lives in a fashion magazine and because you're her daughter your buck teeth will straighten one day and the freckles peel from your nose and your knees stop knocking and your ankle bones start holding up your socks. Gert's way was chatter and coo and smile back at all the men who smiled at her, a picture-book lady in the Sunday rotogravure the men couldn't keep their eyes off, a fashion ad suddenly appearing on a bench in Westinghouse Park with her little girl beside her, the little girl they'd wink at and smile at too cause they knew someday, some bright spring afternoon, all her dumpy, ugly-duck feathers fall away and she'd shine like her mama shined when she landed in Homewood.

On summer Sunday afternoons they'd watch the other strollers, and Gert, who was her mother, would hold her little girl's hand while the sun went down and the park emptied out. They'd sit till they were alone and dusk falling cool on their shoulders. Sky turning to fire and her mother still as the dancer poised on one toe atop the gold music box when the song stops. Quiet as the wound-down, glittering box at night in its dark corner beside the bed with all the other precious things her mama had brought her. The stories of good times, of fine times, of Homewood's handsomest, richest, nicest men ending suddenly. Her mama quiet and snuggling closer on the slats of the wooden bench and pulling a handkerchief from somewhere in her fabulous clothes and the whole shadowed park lavender like the sweet scent of her perfume and Gert would sniffle and blow her nose and whisper, Excuse me, Darlin. Excuse me, Darlin Baby Girl.

Gert's way could make Freeda shamed of Aunt Aida and Uncle

Bill, of the cramped rooms above the Fox Bar and Grill where they lived and she lived when her mama flew away again into those slick pages of the magazine. But as she grew older, Anaydee's way and Uncle Bill's way made her shamed of Gert. But Anaydee always said: She's Gert. And Gert's Gert. Ain't no good or bad about it.

Freeda had learned the streets of Homewood walking beside Gert's rustling skirts, her hand wrapped in Gert's. She had learned to call Gert her mama on those long walks, those long afternoons in the park. She wouldn't wash her hand when she bathed in the clawfoot tub. She'd keep the perfume alive so she could sniff it again in her bed when her mama was long gone, gone to Louisville or Detroit or Cincinnati where she died one day far from home. Her mama gone for days but Freeda could find her in the hollows back of her wrist. Even now she'd catch the back of her hand sneaking up toward her face, rubbing her cheek, her lips. Even today with John French God knows where and Albert Wilkes back in town, when she didn't need to be crowded by no dead woman's perfume, no dead Mama's laughing eyes. Streets treacherous enough without that distraction. Close to tears anyway, and she didn't need sadeyed ghosts reminding her to call them Mama.

My grandmother cleared the cobwebs of rainbow and bubble and perfume from her mind, tied a scarf around her hair and set out into the Homewood streets to find her husband. Her face hurts this morning when the air hits it. Feels like a toothache, swollen and sore to the touch. She feels the whiteness of her face hanging out this morning, something silly, a big ugly white pumpkin on her shoulders. Even though the streets are empty and quiet, even though you could pretend at this early morning hour they were still the old Homewood streets before the black tide of immigrants from the South changed Homewood forever, even though her footsteps tapped out the silence into precise little icy chunks so she could hear silence and see it, she couldn't forget who the streets belonged to now. Dark faces and bodies crowded three and four into every Homewood spare room. Hordes of burr-head children knock you down if you're not careful. Their mamas outdoors in next to nothing, heads uncombed and uncovered. Summer heat chasing them outdoors. The men in undershirts and no shirts at all. Like roaches when you light the gas stove in the morning, fleeing every which way from the cracks and crevices where they hide at night. Running and oozing into the streets. Their streets now. Brazen now. Loud talk and nasty talk and country ways and halfnaked like children, like people in the jungle.

But the last block of Susquehanna before it ran into Homewood Avenue was a nice street. Neat brick row houses set well back from the sidewalk. Most had porches and three or four steps, so you knew when you mounted them you had left the pavement, which belonged to anybody, and you were entering somebody's home. Brightly painted wooden porches and straight, solid steps and trim flower gardens and here and there a little knee-high white picket fence. No boarders crammed into every nook and closet. No sweaty eyes staring out the windows. No men draped like dirty laundry over every railing and women spraddle-legged on the steps. Nobody's Victrola playing for the whole block as if everybody wanted to listen to nastiness about my man done gone and left and good jelly rolls and if you don't like my peaches don't shake my tree. Bad enough the children and any decent folk walk by the Bucket of Blood can't help hearing that terrible mess they always singing and playing round there. Now it wasn't a question of detouring bad places like the Bucket of Blood because the music was everywhere. If you couldn't hear it you could see it. In those funky undershirts the men rolled down off their chests and let dangle round their hips like raggedy skirts. In the way the young girls switched their narrow fannies and the old big-butt ones stood wide-legged, hands on hips shouting back and forth across the alley, putting their business in the street like it was everybody's and nobody's.

The music was everywhere. Sneaks in like a stray alleycat and hides in your house just waiting for a chance to slink out and take over. Like the wine bottles John French hid in the cupboards and drawers. And worst of all, that low down, down home stuff had crawled inside her. Messed with the way she walked and talked and thought about things. As she searched for John French this morning the nasty music dared her not to listen. But she paid it no mind. Wouldn't give it the satisfaction. She held her head high.

The moon was still up, looking lonesome and out of place, but still hanging on. Not shining like it does sometimes early, early in the morning when she blows steam off her coffee and eases into the quiet of Cassina Way. The moon was a pale, whitish blue now like everything in Anaydee's china cupboard when she forgets to polish the glass doors.

The music in her own house now. One day last month here come John French and Strayhorn pulling Carl's old wagon down Cassina Way. It's rolling and bumping over the cobblestones and they got something big sitting teeter-totter up on the yellow rails of that little wagon and John French in front pulling and Strayhorn stumbling beside it supposed to be steadying the load but he's been in that Dago Red you can tell it before you smell it because he's bobbing and weaving worse than the big box they got sitting up on Carl's old wagon. *Who's holding up who* she had wondered as they bumped along and then she could hear the bottles rattling around in the wagon's bed. As they got closer she could see it was a Victrola. Dials and fancy trim and shiny wood panels without even a smidgen of dust. She had groaned inside and closed her eyes. Prayed she wouldn't hear a policeman's whistle or sirens or a crowd of angry white voices coming to take her man away. Then she could smell sweet wine and groaned out loud because when they were into that dago red they'd do anything. John French try to walk on water if you dared him, lift her and the chair she's sitting on by one leg in one big fist. Get down on his knees and huff and puff till he looked like he'd bust wide open and she's scared he will before he gets her up and scared he will before he gets her down again out of the thin air and she doesn't even breathe till she feels all four legs hit the floor. He'd try anything and die trying before he'd give up. So she searched up and down the block for a policeman or white men red-faced and huffing and puffing like John French when he did that silly chair-lifting trick.

Watch it, boy. Watch what you doing. Ain't come all this way for you to dump my pretty box on these cobblestones. John French grinning like a Chessy cat. The handle of Carl's rusty yellow wagon swallowed in one big paw while he pats the Victrola with the other.

Some fool throwed away this good machine. Strayhorn found it back of some white people's house out in the alley behind Thomas

Boulevard. A shame, ain't it, honey? Some people's got nothing and some can just throw away stuff as fine as this. Shoot. I ain't too proud. No indeed. Take somebody's leavings and fix them up and make do best as I can. Help me lift it off here, Strayhorn, fore these stones tear it up.

She could hear the police coming and hear the shouting and hear her heart in her throat. Because when John French and Strayhorn drinking wine they were capable of anything, even marching into white people's living rooms and loading a Victrola, which probably cost more than John French earned in a year, on that child's yellow wagon and pulling it through the Homewood streets, calm as if it were a watermelon from the A&P they had picked out and paid for.

Why you doing this, man? Nobody throws away machines like this. Not those rich folks on Thomas Boulevard nor nobody else on God's green earth about to throw away something like this.

Yes, Mam. Strayhorn said the same thing. Figured something had to be wrong with it. Yeah. That's why he didn't take it hisself. Probably don't work right. Youall probably right. Probably wasted my good time hauling it all this way in the heat. But it look nice in that corner over by the window even if the damn thing don't play.

But it did. Loud and perfect. Never had to do a thing but turn it on and twist in a steel needle, a box of which, sharp as pins, John French found when he lifted the machine's lid, needles thrown away like somebody had thrown away the Victrola. So the music wasn't only in the streets. It was prowling inside her own house now like something slinked in out Cassina Way. Shaking peaches from trees and moving on down the highway and lonesome train whistles blowing and hollering like a mountain jack and See, see rider, gal, See what you have done. Every time she lifted the lid and peered into the well of the Victrola the stack of records was higher, and one day she'd take a hammer to them all. Smash the shiny discs the way she had crushed the nest of Tokay bottles, snug in their straw bottoms hid up under the steps.

In the streets, in her house, in the church. The music everywhere now, even in her head as she waited a minute outside 725, waited to see her husband's big hat and broad shoulders ease round the block. But nothing turned round the corner or filled up the sky, nothing but a little bit of that music, a sigh of music dark and slow as the shadow of her sauntering man would have been if it was him instead of nothing meeting her eyes.

Anaydee's house was on the corner of Susquehanna where Albion, the last street before Homewood Avenue, crossed. The house was not exactly on Albion and not on Susquehanna either but recessed in the far corner of the vacant lot at the intersection of the two streets. Like an extra tooth sprouting behind the neat smile of row houses on Susquehanna. Uncle Bill Campbell never allowed that the house was anything but 725. Not 725 Albion or 725 Susquehanna. Just 725 because that was the number he had been playing for twenty years when one day a white man, a stranger to the Fox Bar and Grill had gotten drunk and friendly and whispered 725 into Bill Campbell's ear after two or three boilermakers and the one on the house Bill Campbell always served up to his best customers or people who seemed to have plenty of money to spend. Seven twenty-five and don't you know I got to thinking. Got to thinking about working every day of my life and them cigar butts and spittoons, and every kind of filth curled up in that sawdust. Got to thinking about the stink of stale beer every morning and shoveling snow so some drunk Irishman won't slip and crack his noggin coming or going out the Fox. Don't you know I thought about all the money I had made for Mr. O'Reilly and how he give me a bottle of brandy with a fancy label on Christmas and a dollar on my birthday and give Aida a fur piece his wife tired of. I got to thinking, man. All them years working for O'Reilly, and me and Aida in them little bitty rooms over top the bar and me spending most my time slaving down there in the Fox and what we got to show for it. And don't you know all the sudden something said to me Bill Campbell get that little teapot from behind the bar. Run your fingers down in there and get every red cent. Teapot was where I kept my tips. Let them fatten up a month or so and take the few dollars be in there and put it with the rest me and Aida been saving so if I wake up dead one morning she might have a little something to get along. And I says to myself you been a penny, nickel, dime man all your life, Campbell. You been breaking your butt and making the white man rich and what you got to show for it? What you gonna have the day they lay you out in Allegheny County Cemetery besides the suit you got on your back and the suit ain't really yours cause it's bought on time and you and suit both six feet under but Aida still be carrying payments to the man. Man, I said to myself, hear me out now, I said, Damn these pennies and nickels and dimes. I told Clark who tends bar in the afternoon so I can get me a little nap before the night shift, Clark, I says, man you come on back here awhile. I got to go take care of some business. Tipped on up the stairs (Aida be nappin that time of day) with what that white man had whispered still burning in my ear. Funny how wasn't nothing special bout him. A big head like a lot of them and that white fringe around his ears and bald on top. Red-faced like a lot of them get after knocking back a couple boilermakers but nothing special bout him. But when he whispered my number, my 725 I been playing twenty years, I kinda got loose in the knees and my heart beating 4/4 time and thinking all kinds of things to myself so I untied my apron and tipped up the steps and got that money we been saving and took it to the bank and had them count me out brand-new, crisp bills for the pennies, nickels and dimes and wadded up paper notes we had hid in the shoebox under the bed. When I took that money to Joe Westray who was numbers king then, I snapped them bills down one by one, nice and new and stiff. Popped them down like old Clarence Brown pop that rag when he's shining shoes and said to Joe Westray: When I comes to get my hit I want it all just like I'm giving this to you. Pretty new money, Mister Joe. Course, he laughed. And I laughed too. But I laughed again next morning and been laughing since.

Seven-twenty-five was that money Bill Campbell won. 725 was the house he and Aunt Aida bought the day after his big hit. Now, at least Bill Campbell dying between walls he owned, his big body propped up on the bed in the front room of his own house. Freeda's Uncle Bill the only father she ever knew, the man who had raised her in those tiny rooms over the Fox.

Yoo-hoo, yoo-hoo. Aunt Aida had taught Freeda to holler instead of knock at people's doors. Aunt Aida which everybody in the family said so it came out Anaydee said you should let the people inside the house hear your voice so they'd know who they was opening they door to. Wasn't so much the robbers or strangers

or bill collectors you didn't want to open your door to as it was
the Devil who could slip in unseen while you holding the door open
and wondering if you really heard a knock or if it was wind or
kids playing a trick or somebody in such a big hurry already gone
before you could let them in. So at the door of the little house tucked
behind Albion or tucked behind Susquehanna, after she waited
and looked up and down the block one more time for John French,
Freeda yodeled, Yoo-hoo, yoo-hoo, Anaydee.

Zat you, Freeda?

Better be. Don't know who else it might be, if it's not me.

The clapboard house was yellow with shutters, doors, and trim
painted deep green. Uncle Bill had made a walkway of flagstones
through the vacant lot to the front door. The scratchy heads of
Aida's sunflowers had inched past the bottom sill of the big window beside the door. The garden Bill Campbell had staked out
the year before with sticks and string had been reclaimed by weeds.
After Uncle Bill's stroke nobody had fought back the jungle. You
couldn't tell he'd hacked down the weeds and turned the soil. As
hard as he had struggled chopping weeds and digging out rocks,
it was a shame he never had a chance to seed the ground. She'd
get Carl over here. Brother would help. Carl was big enough now
to keep the yard looking decent. Time for him to start helping the
older people who had always loved and supported her.

If it's something in that pretty skin that ain't you, Freeda French,
it's gon get a hot welcome pretty quick. Just sprinkled me some
fresh salt all out there this morning.

Nobody but me, Anaydee.

Yes it is you, you pretty little stranger you.

The door of 725 was cracked only wide enough for Anaydee to
poke her head into the bright sunshine. A blinking, squinting moon-
face the color of the pages in the old Bible Anaydee had given Freeda
when she married John French. The Bible with family names and
birthdays penciled in a faded list on the front pages, split-seamed
and tatter-edged, held together by a thick rubber band. Moon-
face creased and pitted, but not so dry you were half afraid to touch
it, let alone dare to slip off the gumband and turn the leaves. Anaydee had always parted her thick, dark hair in the middle, and the
curls, pressed flat against her forehead, curls accented with silver

threads, were two wings framing her face. High cheekbones like Gert her dead sister. Eyes widely spaced and deep-set behind the flesh, which over the years had drifted against her high Indian cheekbones. A green sparkle in the depths, in the smallish eyes so when she smiled you saw the dance of jade and forgot the creased surface of the moon.

Mr. Bill, guess who's here? Guess who's come to see us, Mr. Bill?

It was black inside. Freeda heard the door slam behind her and Anaydee fidgeting with locks. The interior of 725 was as familiar as her own house, and she knew what she'd see when her eyes became accustomed to the niggling light. Yet some shapes were impatient. They groped toward her through the darkness. Uncle Bill in his bed, the white sheet pulled to his chin. When she thought of him he was always wearing an apron. Tending bar he liked it to ride high under his armpits so it looked like a giant white bib. How many times had she watched Anaydee tie the apron in the morning and loosen it at night? She saw Uncle Bill aproned again now, whiteness draping him and draping the bed in its folds.

Freeda gal. Come on over here and gimme some sugar.

He don't much like light no more.

Ain't no light no more for Bill Campbell is what she's trying to say. And she be telling the God awful truth, too. Can't see the hand in front my face. But that don't make no nevermind. Just come on over and gimme some sugar.

Freeda picked her way across the room to the bed where he lay, sheet to his chin, head propped on a mound of pillows. She leaned over him, into the sour cloud of sickness, pressing her lips against his cheek. He was fair-skinned like John French. Deep shadows made his face a skull. The mask of flesh was gone, his face bone and black emptiness.

That's light. That's sweet light. All I ever need to see.

She was stepping back as he spoke, *fleeing*, a deeply shamed part of her scolded, *fleeing*, and she stopped and hugged his shoulder and rubbed the chilly cotton undershirt. He had been a big man. She'd ridden on his shoulder when it was a mountain halfway to the sky where he balanced her and toted the huge wooden kegs of beer up from the cellar of the Fox.

How do you feel, Uncle Bill?

Like a man just been kissed by a pretty girl.

You're teasing me. And not answering.

Don't he always be teasing. Like some big overgrown boy lay-ing up in that bed, and I can't hardly believe a word he says. Don't talk nothing but teasing and foolishness.

You're something, Uncle Bill.

No gal. Your Uncle Bill ain't nothing special. He's just lucky is all. Lucky.

The last word, the *lucky* was almost a whisper. His voice trembled. Each word was a struggle. He coughed, and the springs of the bed squeaked, the top sheet jerked like dogs fighting under it.

Oh . . . Mr. Bill, take some water.

Cool Jordan water get me to the other side. But Campbell ain't quite ready yet.

Don't try to talk.

Who you trying to hush, little gal?

Let em be, honey, can't tell this hardhead man nothing. He's just like that John French of yours. So much like him that's why he got out his shotgun when he heard youall run off. Just leave him be. No sense in trying to tell Mr. Bill Campbell nothing he don't want to hear.

John French never was no bad man. A dangerous man, but he ain't bad. I'd a shot him dead if he was bad. Just didn't want my little sweet gal here to love the kind of man be here today and gone tomorrow. Dangerous man ain't got no choice day to day.

John French done good by Freeda. Gave her beautiful children. And he works hard.

Never surprised me. Ain't never said he was a bad man. Just a dangerous one. But he been lucky. Lucky like me.

Freeda rubbed the scar on the back of her hand. Saw her man loping down the alley and the phantom behind him raise the pistol and point it at his back. Lizabeth is in her arms. They are in the house on Cassina, staring at the grayness as it settles between the row houses. Their peaceful, end-of-the-afternoon time at the front window, the only window on the bottom floor. Cassina Way filling up with dusk. Her image, if she stared a certain way at the glass, staring back at her. Wondering if the babygirl ever saw herself floating in the emptiness over the cobblestones. John French about to die in the space framed by the window. Freeda's fist slams through the glass to shield him, to shield her child from the black mouth of the gun.

Rubbing the luck of John French, the jagged lightning stroke behind her knuckles, the scar which had saved him once and which, as she traced it with her fingertips in the shadowed room where no one could see what she was doing with her hands, she prayed might save him again. Though the scar was nothing but a furrow plowed by broken glass, nothing but the shape of her fear, the shape of her pain, the pain of the man in the bed who spoke even though each word hurt him. She could walk for miles and miles along the zigzag path scarring the back of her hand.

Anaydee, I need to know where Albert Wilkes is. I know he's back, but I don't know where in Homewood he would try to hide.

Albert Wilkes. Oh, my goodness gracious. Albert Wilkes done come back home.

That Albert Wilkes. Yes, him.

It's God's will. Bring him back home so he can die in peace. Albert Wilkes a doomed man. Once another human being's blood on your hands, ain't nothing you can do but go in circles till you come back where you shed it. What goes round, comes round.

Woman, . . . what you talking about? You don't know nothing bout it.

I know he shot a police, a white police, and they gon hunt him down till they get him.

Wasn't no policeman. Was a white man coming after Wilkes cause Wilkes been messing with the white man's white woman.

Found him dead in his uniform.

Wilkes knew what that white man was after. Uniform didn't make no nevermind.

Lord saith vengeance is mine.

Ain't no vengeance to it. Man come to kill Albert Wilkes. Albert Wilkes got his shot in first. Lord didn't say nothing about standing still and dying just cause some peckerwood decide he needs you dead.

He come back to Homewood to die.

He's a fool to come back. You got that right.

Where would he be? Where would he stay, Anaydee?

Him and John French like the hand in the glove. Wonder he ain't been round to youall's house. John French and Strayhorn and Wilkes. Three the biggest devils ever run these Homewood streets. Don't you be grinning at me, Mr. Bill. I ain't forgot you was out there with em. See one, you see em all. And see em all, you know they's into something. Know they just looking for devilment. But they could sing. Yes, Lawd, those boys could sing. Ain't gon tell no lie. Your Anaydee young once her ownself. Young and foolish and just half listening to the Lord out one ear and the other ear steady listening hard to whatever Devil music going around. They could sing. Hear them boys singing when you pass the corner of Hamilton and Homewood where they all hung out. Every kind of song. Ask Mr. Bill. He know something about it. He'd play that guitar of his. Yes, Mam. Your Uncle Bill had his day out there with them hounds. But he ain't played that thing since you a little girl and we was still over the Fox. Don't believe that guitar made the trip to 725.

She sure was a pretty one. Twelve steel strings and fancy work all inlaid on the neck and body. Called her Corrine, but I ain't never told nobody why. Brought her up here from Virginny. Only thing I had when I got here. Just me and that box and all these hills and mean white folks and smoke and coal mines and boys with nothing just like me arriving every day. I been luckier than most. Real lucky.

I remember you singing to me, Uncle Bill. I remember Corrine.

You's a sweet thing. You got me thinking bout good old times and all my miseries gone. You like medicine, gal. Just what the doctor ordered. Albert Wilkes ain't gon come near youall and them children. John French wouldn't let him. Wilkes probably over to the Tates. Albert Wilkes used to work on old Mr. Tate's truck. Albert work for nothing long as he could get at that piano.

Tate the one give him money to get outta town after all that mess. But not many people know that. They go way back. Yeah, he was always messing on that piano, and I bet that's where Albert Wilkes be hiding now.

Standing beside him, above him, she could feel the man's will, strong as the cloud of sickness hovering around the bed. His voice was weak. My grandmother had to listen closely to pick out the words and between the words were spaces unnaturally long, but he was saying what he had to say, what he wanted to say. Yes, she remembered Corrine. But never heard the instrument strummed so sweetly, softly as it sang in her memory this moment. *Ride a shiny little pony / Ride a shiny lit-til-po-o-ny.* Rumble of the Fox beneath their feet as Uncle Bill hummed and plucked at the strings of the guitar. To her a fox would always be a monster with a huge belly that churned and rattled, a belly where all the people it swallowed argued and fought over how to get out. And a *po-ny* something blue, light blue with wings and a warm, furry place between them to sit. She would soar up into the air, and the tiny clouds bobbing like bubbles in bathwater would smell just like Gert's perfume, and the wings of the pony carrying her past the stars would rustle like her mama's skirts.

Thank you, Uncle Bill.

Nothing to thank me for. How's all them beautiful children?

They're fine . . . fine.

Don't get to see them much.

You know how children are. They stay on the go. But I'm going to catch that Carl and send him to see you and Anaydee. That big-head boy can cut down those weeds in your front yard.

Don't put him to no trouble on account of us.

I'll send him. And the girls too . . . Bye, Uncle Bill . . .

Bye, little gal. Don't you worry none bout Albert Wilkes, John French know what to do.

God bless, darling.

Bye, Anaydee.

Kiss the children for me.

Bye.

Gotta close this quick. Light hurts his eyes these days. Don't know who be lurking around here. Put down some fresh salt this morning . . . but . . .

The door slams. Uncle Bill is coughing again, rattling the wooden walls. A dead bolt rams home. Freeda is dazzled by sunshine. For a moment she is confused. She can't find the stone path Bill Campbell had laid from the street to the front door of 725. So overgrown now you could hardly even call it a path. But her feet keep to it. She brushes back the waist-high weeds and thinks how Anaydee, little as she is, would be lost in this jungle. Carl and his shadow, Brother, better get over here and take care of business. When they finish, 725 be a fairy-tale house again. The frilly white curtains open again and light flooding through the big front window and the window box full of gladiolas and the smell of gingerbread or a blueberry cobbler welcoming you at the threshold when you *Yoo-hoo*.

Meanwhile, Albert Wilkes had sure enough returned. If someone had asked him *from* where, the image of a deck of cards broken in half and riffling back together under a dealer's thumbs would have flickered an instant in Wilkes's mind. The days away had passed that swiftly. Days different as hearts and spades and diamonds and deuces and queens, but they all disappeared the same way in a double-backed blur between the dealer's hands. If someone had asked *to* where, Wilkes would have gone blank inside, his eyes would have picked something, anything, and stared at that piece of Homewood, that crack in the pavement, that tree, that brick, that shadow moving across a windowpane, stare as if it was his job to keep it in place and if he faltered, if he lost concentration for one split second, the thing would disappear and all of Homewood with it. But nobody had asked any questions of the pencil-slim man in the gray duster who had stood like someone who might be lost, oblivious to his surroundings, consulting an invisible scrap of paper scrawled with a name or address which would tell him the direction his next step should take. He carried no bags. A black locomotive belched and snorted and wheezed clouds of steam behind him. Passengers helloing and goodbyeing, the rumble of baggage carts trundling over the cobblestones, the shouts of trainmen and porters were magnified in the cavernous station and trapped under the metal canopy arching over his head. He had stood motionless in the din and steam and coalsmoke till a conductor pulled the courtesy step off the platform, boosted his blue-uniformed self back into a Pullman car and chanted *All aboard*. Nobody had asked any questions as he walked across the city, and now as dusk deepened to the gray of his long duster coat, Albert Wilkes stared at Homewood, making it stay put with the power of his eyes. Now he was no closer to knowing the answer to the questions nobody asked than he was seven years before when he glanced over his shoulder one more time at Homewood then turned away again and hurried into the darkness.

A darkness aglow with snow. Snow beginning in the morning and still falling that night seven years before when he had fled. White piling up in the darkness, the darkness shining. Old Mr. Tate in his stocking cap. Lucy's walleyed teddy bear in the rocking chair. They were his audience when he sat down at the Tates' piano and played those last few licks he had to hit before he left town. One more time. Somebody had named the notes, but nobody had named the silence between the notes. The emptiness, the space waiting for him that night seven years ago. Nobody ever would name it because it was emptiness and silence and the notes they named, the notes he played were just a way of tipping across it, of pretending you knew where you were, where you were going. Like his footprints in the snow that night. Like the trail he tramped that was covered over as quickly as he made it.

Through the deep shadow under the railroad bridge and he knew he was in Homewood again. Sure he had made it back. This was the exact place, this daylight after the dark tunnel, this door you pushed through to get into Homewood, this line you stepped over, danced over if you were the 501 Engineer Corps returning from the war. You stopped marching and started dancing because this was the edge, the very moment you knew you'd made it home one more time. Soon he'd be invisible again. His gray coat and black hat disappearing into the night just the way they'd vanished in the darkness of the tunnel whose topside held the trains passing over Homewood Avenue. If he hadn't pawned the gold pocket watch, now would be the moment he'd tug on its chain and note the hour. Just enough light to read its gold face and he'd announce to himself: On this day, at this precise hour, minute, second and a half, Albert Wilkes returned. He could hear it ticking, feel the knurled winding stem twist between his thumb and first finger. He would name the hour like they named the notes.

Who was the first one to see him? You could get a good argument going in McKinley's about the answer to that one. Which was why people called McKinley's the Bucket of Blood. You could get an argument on just about anything. And occasionally the argument got too deep and they took it to the street. Nobody necessarily won, you could get another argument going on that, and nobody necessarily got bloody, but somebody would shut up or be shut up long enough for the talk to move on to other things. McKinley said the one man who died in the Bucket of Blood and whose spilled blood made the mess some people say gave McKinley's its bad name was a stranger and the man who cut his throat a stranger too, and neither one said a word to the other except a woman's name nobody knew. So it wasn't dangerous in the Bucket of Blood if you opened your mouth and fussed at people. Never was bloodshed except that once, McKinley said, unless you count Fricassee's bloody nose when he went to sleep standing up and his head hit the bar, or count Bump Mallory's piles when he sits on his fat behind all day on one of my stools and don't even order a glass of beer.

You listen to McKinley he'll tell you it's not even about blood. He'll say blood is wine and niggers would drink it in buckets if he served it in buckets and some try to drink a bucketful anyway so mize well go on and call it Buckets of Blood which cause niggers is lazy with *s*'s is Bucket of Blood after a time. Or tell you any fool know niggers is bloods and you come in his place Saturday night look like somebody dumped bucketfuls of bloods in there so it's Buckets of Bloods and you lose the *s*'s again, it's *Bucketablood* either way. Either way ain't really no blood in it. Just baptized with a terrible-sounding name. Just like all these niggers round here got a bark worser than they bite.

You could get a good, loud argument about who was the first to see Albert Wilkes when he came back. Even long after Wilkes was dead and buried, even from people who should have known better, people who couldn't have seen Wilkes first, second or last because they weren't even born that day in 1934 he returned.

Course I seen him first. First thing when he push through that swinging door. I'm sitting on the first stool inside the door. How my gon miss him? In that long black coat and black cowboy hat looking like some Jesse James outlaw train robber. Wilkes wasn't above the average height, but the man thin as spaghetti. Wasn't *no round* to him. Just shot straight up so he looked tall, real tall even though his eyes come to just about here, just about where my eyes is. If he be standing here next to me wouldn't be a inch either way if he took off his goddamn ten-gallon Stetson.

That ain't nothing nowhere near first cause you see I was on my way out. Had my little taste and I was heading home. You know how you get. Feeling good but a little shaky. Just a touch on the high side, so when I goes to push the door and it swings away spooky fore I touch it, I kinda follow my hand a little ways, might even have stumble some, nuff to make old Wilkes smile and back up a little and hold that door for me so how's anybody gon see him fore I did?

Yeah. We seen you falling out the door. You so drunk you didn't even know I was behind Wilkes with my hand on his shoulder. I'm the one guiding him in. I'm the one said let's stop here Albert and lemme buy you a welcome back drink.

All youall lying. Wasn't nobody here but me and Fricassee and Lemuel Smart God rest his soul. And Fricassee sleep like he always is and Lemuel talking to that bottle so who's that leave? Who's the one seen him first?

Gon nigger. You wasn't even bartending yet. McKinley still tending bar then.

Now here he come with his lie. Here he come with that met-him-at-the-station tale.

Wilkes parts the swinging doors enough to see in but not be seen. Neither John French nor Strayhorn at the bar so he lets the doors glide back together. Nobody he wants to see yet. Nobody he wants to see him except John French or maybe Strayhorn. He feels the night ride up under his gray coat. Homewood Avenue nearly deserted. A moon. Narrow doorways and storefronts already deep in shadow. Two blocks away the faint light of the poolroom. He's hungry and his feet hurt. Seven years away but he had believed he remembered everything, every detail of the streets, people's names and faces, the sound of the doorbell in the little restaurant on the corner where Saunders could cook you a porkchop better than you could ever cook it yourself. Hear the pan sizzling while Saunders talks bout Paree, the best days of his life and he's going back, sure nuff going back soon's he saves the passage. Wilkes had believed he held every detail of Homewood exact in his memory, but now he wasn't sure. This street was too small. If he shouted his name, they'd hear him on Hamilton and hear him at the bridge by Finance. No room on this street for what he remembered. He had remembered a song, a song too big to ever play through, to ever finish. For seven years he had recalled phrases, chords, runs, teasing little bits and pieces reminding him of what he was missing. And he had expected the song to dance out and just about knock him down when he returned. He wanted to feel happy, to feel good, to hear the music rushing through him again. Wanted it in his fingers and toes so he could reach up and snatch that pale moon and shake it like a tambourine.

Nobody answered his knocking so he called Tate . . . Mr. Tate. Seven years and old man Tate might be dead now. Dead and gone and somebody else in his house. Seven years ago Tate had shuffled down the steps in his stocking cap and night shirt. Half dead then. Wheezing and shaking on his spindly legs, legs no bigger round than the candle stuck in a bowl he carried to light his way to the front room. Shaky, old Mr. Tate on that night seven years before. The walls bending and buckling cause he couldn't hold the candle still. And his stutter . . . Al . . . Al . . . Al . . . Albert . . . Wi . . . Wi . . . Wi . . . Like he'd never get it all out so you had finished it for him. Albert Wilkes Yes, it's me. Albert Wilkes. Shadows bouncing on the walls and ceiling. Following Mr. Tate's crooked, spidery legs, his mashed-back slippers wide and flat as a duck's feet. What . . . wha . . . wh . . . Whasmatta . . . b . . . b . . . boy? Wilkes remembers the moment when he was ready to scream, to shut his eyes and shut his ears because everything was coming apart, was fallin to pieces in the dance and sputter of the old man's hobble and broken words and that candle had been like a sword chipping away at everything it touched.

Tate. Mr. Tate. If he could, he would have taken back the words. He was talking to a dead man. Mr. Tate nearly dead seven years ago so he's surely dead now. And dead people could answer. Could blow that cold, dead breath in your face, in your ear, tickle the bare skin back of your neck with those icy ghost fingers. Wilkes shivered in the dark vestibule. Peered through the Tates' colored front-door glass to locate the light he'd seen from the street. His hand dropped automatically to the brass knob and turned and pushed. The heavy door squealed then shuddered when it hit the high spot still not shaved after seven years. A job Wilkes had promised Tate he'd do. And Tate dead and still waiting for Wilkes to sand the buckled place in the wooden hallway floor. *Tate . . . Mr. Tate.* This time the words rise up the stairwell and bounce off the high ceiling, chiming fainter and fainter, till they echo inside Wilkes, till he's not sure if he's calling Tate's name aloud or just whispering it to himself.

He liked you, Albert Wilkes. And I did too. With that little monkey cute face of yours.

For some reason Wilkes didn't bolt and run but took three long steps toward the quaking voice, toward the light flooding from the living room. Like the door's squeal, the bump and rattle when it hit the humped floorboard, the voice startled him and reminded him at once. You've been here before, you knew this was going to happen. So rather than haulassing back out the front door he snapped to attention and strode toward the voice, ready for what would come next, listening for what he'd forgotten in seven years away.

Wilkes remembers how old she is. Old Mrs. Tate in her rocker. The bright light hurts his eyes. He fidgets, weight on one foot then the other, like little Lucy when she was too busy to go pee, back and forth like the walleyed teddy bear in the rocker Mr. Tate had pushed up and back in time with the piano that night seven years before.

Mrs. Tate doesn't seem much bigger than a teddy bear. Her wool-stockinged toes dangle above the floor. In the ladderback, cane-bottomed rocker she measures her words by the slow nod of the chair.

All you cute little monkey-faced ones. That's the ones come to our door, that's the ones we took in. Days when this house full of children. Didn't know all they names. But loved all youall. Sorry to see you go when you had to go.

None my own. Nothing down in that dry place he called my pretty Pussy-in-the-well. Mr. Tate always worked hard. A good man. Loved children. Loved youall running round here. Had a little more than most folks so we took in the little cute monkey-

faced ones with no place to go. Now you standing there Albert
Wilkes with that face we took in and it's old as me now and why
you hollering for my dead man?

Never looking at him as she spoke. Talking to the couch or the
tall, fringed, pinch-waisted lampshade on the end table. Speaking at him, but not to him.

Mrs. Tate shrunken to doll-size, rocking in the highbacked chair.
The old woman's voice stopped, but Wilkes could hear it playing
on and on in the squeak of the chair, the slow, steady up-and-back
beat changing her words into things he had seen, places he'd been.
In that story she rocked out phrase by phrase, he was just as she'd
said, older than she was, older than she'd ever be. He listened,
forgetting her like she'd forgotten him. He remembers a dream
about a piano. Big and black and greasy as a train hurtling down
the track. A piano filling the sky. Gleaming just a few feet away
and you catch the beat of the rocker and step in the footprints it
carves in the floor and the piano bench scrapes a discord when
you pull it from beneath the keys but that sound is in another world
you don't hear it any more than you hear yourself settle and sigh,
any more than you hear the snaps of the duster unfasten one by
one or the swish of its skirt when you flip it away and it drapes
the back of the bench and falls slowly to the floor. You push up
your gray sleeves. Then you are stepping right dead in the middle
of her story and you play along awhile, measure for measure awhile
until the song's yours. Then it's just you out there again by yourself
again and you begin playing the seven years away.

The night grows blacker as Wilkes plays. A moody correspon-
dence between what his fingers shape and what happens to the
sky, the stars, the moon. At some point that night of his return
he leaves the Tates' ramshackle brick house, and his feet carry him
where they've been wanting to get all day, all night, all seven years.
He scratches, as my grandmother said, like a cat and whistles in
the stillness of Cassina Way and waits for John French. What he
says to John French has my grandfather rising earlier than usual
and has him creeping down the alley like somebody stole something from his ownself as Miss Pollard thinks watching him dis-

appear down the dark tunnel of Cassina. John French up and gone because Albert Wilkes is back.

John French is first on the corner this morning. The night chill hangs in the air. He can't tell from the sky what kind of day it's going to be. A changing day most likely. A hot gold and reddish band, clouds bumping and losing their shape, what's left of the moon, pale, melting down like a chunk of ice in a glass of tea. Yellow as a cat's eye late last night. A Halloween moon as he stood in the shadows of Cassina Way. Too early, too damp now to be outdoors sitting on a crate. The first man this morning on the corner of Frankstown and Homewood where the white men drive up in their trucks with that little piece of work you might get if you're lucky, if you're early and smile and act like Jesus hisself behind the wheel of them pickups. Grin like the white man gon carry you to Great Glory but you knowing all along he gon take you to some piece of job and pay you half what he pay one his own kind. John French stretches and yawns and rubs the evil knot at the end of his spine, the tight place sore from standing all day and stretching all day too many days. His wallpapering tools in a sack beside his knees. A canvas drawstring sack it takes a good man to heft. From the breast pocket of his flannel shirt he pulls his tobacco pouch and loosens its bright yellow string. The tool bag and tobacco sack look like different-sized twins. He pinches out brown shreds of Five Brothers. Spits to make more room for a fresh chaw. Like blood it splats and sizzles, alive a moment where it lands on the pavement.

If he squats too long on this crate, in this damp, the misery be in his back all day. Sometimes he can hear the little drops of pain pinging into that hollow just above his backside. Nasty-colored drops that harden and ball up so it's like somebody rams in a fist back there and knuckle grinds his spine every time he moves. From hanging wallpaper. The stretching, the bending, the ladders. He walks like a cripple old man, taking those bent-over, short, tippy steps when he gets up out his chair. Needs to walk the length of the house, from the window on Cassina all the way back to the kitchen before he can straighten up. Bent over like he's looking for something on the floor, like he's picking cotton and got a two-hundred-pound sack slung cross his back.

The sky can't make up its mind. He chews and pulls the high crowned hat tighter down on his skull. The snub-toed brogans are a mile away when he stretches out his legs. Only way he can tell they belong to him is that twinge in the small of his back. They used to put people on wheels and pull them apart. Pull the arms and legs out the sockets just like a kid do a bug. Albert told him that. Albert had seen pictures of it. Boiling people in oil and slamming their heads in a helmet full of spikes, and horses tearing men into four pieces and that wheel with ropes and pulleys stretch a man inch by inch to death. The rack, Albert said. Said he didn't know exactly what ailed him till he saw the picture in his white woman's book, and then he understood exactly. They got us on a rack, John French. They gon keep turning till ain't nothing connected where it's supposed to be. Ain't even gon recognize our ownselves in the mirror.

The brogans were spattered with every kind of work John French had ever done. Paste and paint and mud and plaster. They didn't have a color anymore. He wondered if they ever did, because he couldn't remember what it was if it ever was. The sky now. What was the right color of the sky? The first color? Did it start one color before it began going through all those changes? Was it one thing or the other? Blue or white or black or the fire colors of dawn and sunset the first day it was sky? You could use a chisel on his shoes and never get down to the first color. Carl's friend Brother was like somebody had used a chisel on him. A chisel then sandpaper to get down to the whiteness underneath the nigger. Because the little bugger looked chipped clean. Down to the first color or no color at all. Skin like waxed paper you could see through. This early in the morning things seemed to be closer to the way they used to be, to first colors or first shapes, to the quiet before there was a city always snorting and roaring like some animal prowling these hills.

Lots of nights crazy Albert never went to bed. Gambling or play-ing that piano all night long. When Albert finished playing, no matter how tired they thought they were, they'd wake up, even though they hadn't been asleep yet. Wake up and stagger into the red dawn, the quiet time when anybody got good sense is sleeping. A rooster crowing somewhere inside Albert cause he gets wide-awake and shouting happy. C'mon. C'mon, French. You ain't tired, man. It's a new day. We own all this motherfucker. This fine bitch got her legs cocked wide open just waiting, French. Everything you see, man. We own it all. And he'd walk like he did. Jigger-legged, getting out those kinks from sitting all night at the piano. Gleam in his eye. Hat pushed back on his forehead.

French, you a family man. How come you a family man? You like it out here just like I do. Acting a fool. Running wild. Come and go like you please. How come you a family man?

Nothing to do but shake your head. Albert start with those questions you always be asking your ownself, questions that ain't got no answers. Just look at him so he knows you know he's crazy and you ain't paying him no mind.

Go on, boy.

No, French. You gon answer me this morning. You gon testify right here where ain't nothing but sweet light and you and me and the truth if it's in you.

Cause I got a family, fool.

Now wait a minute. That's too easy, ain't it? I mean you trying to say all I need is a family and Albert Wilkes be a family man too? That's too easy, French.

Ain't nothing if it ain't easy.

Then you telling me the truth? So help you Tokay?

So help me Tawny Port and Dago Red and all the wine in all the grapes ain't even wrung out yet.

Being a family man meant one day he caught Lizabeth standing in his work shoes. Tops of the iron brogans come to her knees. She can't lift them off the floor, and kinda shuffles along like a tugboat pushing coal barges down the Allegheny River. Only she can't get the brogans to go straight, the toes bump and skew off catty-corner. Nothing to her skinny little twig legs. She bends down to work the shoes back the way she wants to go. Her little butt pokes over the back of the uppers. She doesn't see him watching. She smacks the crusty toes, jibber jabbers and winds up mad as a wet cat. Standing again as tall as she can, hands on hips, cussing his brogans nastier than he thought she could.

Which meant his boots least as old as Lizabeth. But they were old then, didn't have a color then, when he caught her planted like a flower in his boots, in that polka-dot dress Freeda had made. His boots past old now, down there a mile away at the end of his legs. The seed gets planted. So course you gon water it and watch it grow. You gon see the first color and the first shape and watch the changes, and sitting here on a crate this morning you can't remember what anything looked like at first, but you know you know something about what's under there. Closer to knowing on this kind of quiet morning so what else you gon do but pull on your brogans and go to work and be a family man.

But you never could tell Albert Wilkes nothing. Not about family nor nothing else. You said on one those rooster mornings, Boy, you crazy, boy. White woman's got your nose open and you riding for a fall. Wagged your head and said your piece and rolled your eyes but you knew you mize well be talking to the wall as try to tell Albert something. But you let him hear it anyway. Then shame on him. He's grown. It's his behind. His neck. If he's bold enough to traipse up to Thomas Boulevard in the middle of the day and knock on the front door of that white woman's house and bold enough to stay long as he wants to and march out when he's good and ready like he's been fucking rich white ladies and strutting down rich white folks' streets all his life then more power to him. And shame on him.

John French stings the gray pavement exactly where he was aiming. Wine color, blood color. He shoots the tobacco juice between his teeth again. An arc from the slatted crate, over the curb into the street. That be all that's left of Albert when they catch him up on Thomas Boulevard. Black splat where they squash him on that white street. Wouldn't be so bad if he used the back door and creep around at night like anybody with good sense. No. Not Albert Wilkes. Albert gon play it like he plays that piano. It's him. Couldn't be nobody else but him you hear him play once and nobody else get on them keys sound like Albert.

Gon do it, French. Mize well do it right.

Well, doing it right was not doing it like this. He'd promised he'd meet Albert early. Early, early before anybody else be on the corner. Still early but too late if Albert didn't want to be seen by nobody else. Boys be right along. Still half sleep. Evil and blinking back the light. And Albert ain't coming. And that was Albert.

Have your ass out in the cold. Out before dawn and my back hurting already and he ain't even bothered to show up. And you know where old rooster butt was. Sure as nothing was never gon be like it used to be, Albert back up there on Thomas Boulevard laid up in his white woman's bed.

John French remembers how Lizabeth had jumped when he shouted: Hey, Little Sugar. Where you learn to talk so mean? And where you going in my brogans? Better git your hands off your hips and sit down before you fall down.

Lizabeth had yelled Stoppit and Leave me alone, but then he had snatched her out his boots and whirled her round and round. He jiggled her at the end of his arms till she stopped fussing, till the braids pinned across the top of her head pressed the ceiling, till she giggled and laughed his name.

Daddy.

Daddy.

And there is no color underneath that. He lets her down from the ceiling and they rub noses and she's squealing again as the walls spin round them. He is Daddy. What else he gon be with her strong, tight, little body wiggling in his hands, her big bird eyes popping open wider and wider as the merry-go-round speeds up.

Sunshine. My only sunshine.

He stands and stretches. The crate is bowed from his weight. Easy does it now. Little bit at a time. Locking his knees and tensing his backside and letting that hard ball of pain unravel slowly. His hands are empty reaching into the undecided sky. Reaching for her laughter again. Her cries. In his empty fingers.

Lizabeth had swiped at his hat, tried to steal it off his head. Her big eyes would swallow it. And swallow him. And that's why he's a family man. And he couldn't say more than that. Couldn't talk about what he thought when he shut his eyes and saw pictures of Freeda and pictures of Lizabeth. So he'd just snap hisself out his dream and say: That's why, Albert Wilkes.

And Albert would say: Truth ain't in you, French.

And John French answer: Get your nose out that white woman's behind you might see something true, boy.

Can't think of no place I'd rather be. Nothing I'd rather see. You a dog, boy.

And you a family-man dog.

John French hears Rupert and Clyde. Before they turn the corner he scratches the place badly needs scratching that ain't none of their business. Scratches it good then sits again on the crate.

How you, Brother French?

How de do.

Thought we was up early this morning. But you sure beat us here, didn't you?

You sure up early this morning. You waiting for somebody this morning?

Why don't you mind your business, Rupert?

You my brother, not my keeper. Seem like you might have learned that after thirty-two years.

Damn. It's been that long. I been putting up with you that long? Somebody ought to give me a medal.

Man told me he had three rooms needed papering. Supposed to run me up there to see them this morning. Told me he had the paper and I could start today.

You lucky then. Little work as there is these days.

French is lucky and good. Can't nobody hang paper like French. Even these hunkies know that. They all want French if it's a particular job.

You right about that. French a paperhanging fool.

The corner is crowded in half an hour. Men on the crates. Men in the doorway. McKinley got the Bucket of Blood open and coffee boiling on the potbellied stove in the back.

John French rolls up the sleeves of his flannel shirt and plants his elbow on the bar. Nobody had cleaned the brass spittoons. McKinley was slipping. Place used to shine in the morning. Like ten miles of bad road by closing time but McKinley used to have it clean to start the day. He'd get one wino or another and stick a broom and some rags in his hand and promise him a jug and the place be nice in the morning. All day McKinley have steins and mugs in his towel polishing them clean as a whistle. Or wiping the bar or shining the mirror. Hey man, you gon rub all the niggers off that glass. But now when it's slow, McKinley just hunkers back against his counter. Keeps a towel over his arm but his heart ain't in the swipes he takes every now and then. Glasses don't sparkle like they used to. Spittoons full and nasty round the edges.

Nobody bothered McKinley about it. If McKinley slipping, he wasn't slipping alone. All Homewood coming apart. He'd have to ask Albert. Albert would see how things had changed. Seven years. Couldn't see it with Albert's eyes unless you been gone those seven years. John French loosens the straps of his coveralls. Wouldn't be needing the vest much longer. Let the straps and the bib hang down and pull off his wool vest before he went back outside. Stuff it with his tools in the sack. The white man had said eight sharp. Be on the corner at eight sharp. Like eight sharp the only minute in the day the white man be at Frankstown and Homewood. Like they don't take their own good time. They tells you one thing then come when it suits them. You could wait an hour, wait all day if you fool enough or broke enough to believe they mean what they say. Well, this morning they gon wait for him.

He wonders what Albert will see. Wonders if Homewood's really gone down as bad as he thinks. He could ask the men around him. Start a conversation with McKinley or Strayhorn when Strayhorn pulled in. But they didn't have the seven years. They were trapped like him. If Homewood falling apart they were falling apart too. And the blind can't lead the blind. Albert Wilkes had those seven years. And seven years be like eyes on his chest and his shoulders and behind on his back. He could push through McKinley's door and see what nobody else could. Albert wouldn't have to say a word. Be like a mirror in the middle of the floor and you could walk up to him and see what you been missing. When Albert on that piano it was like a mirror anyway. Not cause he went round with his silk handkerchief and flicked off every spot of dust before he'd sit down to play, not because he polished the keys and the gleaming wood like McKinley used to do his glasses. It wasn't him fussing and worrying the wood and ivory and brass of the piano like he was a janitor or something. It was after he got it just like he wanted it and the music started coming out that you could find yourself, find your face grinning back at you like in a mirror.

But if Homewood slipping, maybe everything slipping, maybe the whole world and Albert Wilkes too, so when you hear him play again won't be no mirror or nothing else. Just you feeling sorry cause he been away too long and his fingers clumsy and you feel sorry for him and sorry for yourself. And shame on Homewood. Damn, boy. Why'd you stay away so long? Why'd you have to go and lose it? Maybe he don't even play no more. Maybe he's back to say he quit. Maybe he forgot the way it used to be. The good old days when Albert be playing and Homewood hanging on every note.

French thinks about silence. Not the silence before things get started, not the stillness underneath things you can hear when you're peaceful and the sky is spread out so you know you're just one little lump, one little wrinkle like everybody else under the blanket of sky. With a mouthful of Tokay in his cheeks he squeezes his eyes shut and rinses the tobacco taste from his mouth. He thinks about the silence after things end.

Albert will have something to say. He could talk to Albert Wilkes like he couldn't talk to nobody else. In the Bucket of Blood with the men waking up around him, with their voices filling the emptiness, he realizes how long the seven years have been, how long he's been waiting to speak to Albert. Not a word in seven years. You could be on one side of Homewood Avenue and your buddy on the other and the earth could split, could open up between you and the two sides of Homewood go blasting away in different directions till there's an ocean between you instead of a little strip of street. You could scream bloody murder but his side the street keep sailing away. That's what happened. Seven years nothing to do with it. That's what happened sometimes when a song was over. When Albert stopped playing you could look down at your toes and see that black pit start to open. See your crusty toes dug in at the edge of nothing. You could snap your fingers once and seven years be over. You could keep snapping till the skin breaks and the bones break and ain't even a raw bloody stump left to wiggle and seven years ain't even started.

He finds Rupert and Clyde. Four years apart but the brothers alike as two peas in a pod. See one you see the other. And Fricassee at his end of the bar and Lemuel already on his stool at the far end where the first thing you see is his narrow back when you come out the bathroom. All the men doing what they do so the Bucket of Blood like it is every morning of the week but Sunday.

Could wake up in China or on the moon you still know what they be doing here. Shut your eyes and see them doing what they do. Nobody looking round like they worried, nobody forgetting what they supposed to do. You could hear them on the moon. If it be morning the men be in the Bucket of Blood and it be sounding like this, looking this way. Albert gone seven years. Never did see him here in the morning unless he had that rooster crowing inside and he's up cause his back never hit bed that night.

Albert's time late afternoon. When he strolls in it's four or five o'clock. It's a different time of day but it's like morning cause you can count on it. It's a picture you can close your eyes and make. You could roll over in Hell and if there's a clock on the wall and it's saying four-thirty in the afternoon you can bet they doing what they always do that hour in the Bucket of Blood. Nobody forgets, nobody worries, nobody gets tired. Look around. Everybody busy, everybody in place. Albert Wilkes gone seven years but if he walks through the door this afternoon he'll know who to speak to, what to say, where to stand and nobody'd hardly notice. Like he never left. Like he got a brother, like Rupert got Clyde, and that brother hangs around in Homewood and saves Albert's place till Albert gets back. Almost see him sometimes. Albert's shadow moving round in the Bucket of Blood like a natural man. Nobody bothers him, nobody gets in his way. Wouldn't be the Bucket of Blood if they did. Wouldn't be Homewood if you couldn't hear Albert's music when you walking down the street.

So it wasn't so much a matter of missing Albert as it was a matter of having him around when he's gone. All those shadows and pieces of Albert moving through the bar but you can't call him over, you can't tap him on his shoulder because it's just that ghost holding his place till Albert gets back. Albert Wilkes around like that fine piano music's around, and it's not a matter of being gone but being here and being gone both. Like a tune you can start and hum some of but you can't get the best part, can't hum it through and finish it like Albert would.

Nobody this morning looks like they miss Albert Wilkes and nobody believes they might be the one missing tomorrow. Nobody sees the grass and trees growing up through the floor. Nobody knows how hot the fire will be sweeping away these boards one Sunday afternoon. John French hears it crackle and sizzle. Hears the timbers pop like matchsticks and the flames screaming like all the mothers ever lost a child. A burnt pit. Ashes and a few black bricks from the basement and maybe the toilet burned white again, clean again in the middle of the pit like a bone poking from a grave. If you counted back, used your toes and fingers a couple times to count the years, these bloods in this bucket all be down home, all be in the cotton patch sweating for Massa. If you counted ahead a short minute, touched your fingers and toes two or three times apiece all these boys be dead. All be lost as Albert's ghost haunting these walls if Albert don't come back.

He can kiss my ass.

What you say, French?

Said I'm leaving here.

What about the man? What about them walls he want papered?

Tell em I'm gone. Tell em I got business. Tell em don't need no corn and lasses. Tell em kiss my ass.

At the very moment John French sidles out of the Bucket of Blood and nobody speaks to him because his jaw is set and his high-crowned hat slanted down over his eyebrows and his tool bag stashed with McKinley behind the bar, at the precise instant John French stalks out with a jug of Dago Red in his fist, evil so high in him the others can smell it and don't say hello, good-bye or nothing else, not to him or to each other till his broad shoulders bump through the swinging doors and disappear, Albert Wilkes rises up on his elbows and remembers he's late. He stares down at miles of satin. Remembers the only words he can recall his daddy saying: Your black head ain't made for no satin pillow. And his daddy's hand upside that black head and stars and shooting comets because he was acting uppity about something, about a bone he didn't want to chew, or greens with cold grease caked on their ribs or wanting a blanket or more room on the dirt floor between him and the next farting pickaninny. Acting spoiled and getting slapped from daylight to stars and red comet tails flashing across his brain. No face. No body. Just a growling kind of angry voice and a hand upside the head. Did he forget the rest of his daddy because it was worse? Was this the good time, the best time with that man his mama said to call Daddy? *Kapow.* Black head ain't made for no satin pillows. But here he was looking down over acres of satin, and satin under his black head sure nuff and his woman getting perfume sweet again in a bathroom bigger than the whole shanty that his daddy shook with his voice. And his fine woman whiter than his daddy's whitest dreams. So white she could be black if she wanted to. Talk like a nigger, act like a nigger. Treat white folks like a nigger'd like to. Be black when they played under these satin sheets. Black so he couldn't see her and she couldn't see him so they had to find each other with toes and tongues and fingers and breath.

Look here, French. You know how it is. Didn't know if she'd open the door. Didn't even know if she was still living there so she could open it. Seven years. Seven years, man. So when she was there and did open it . . . ow whee.

You know how it is. So poke your lip back in. And don't roll your eyes at me. How many times I been waiting high and dry for you and you ain't showed? Yeah. So I ain't hardly gon apologize.

Wilkes can't hear her feet on the soft carpet. Doesn't know how long she's been standing there wrapped knee to shoulder in a baby-blue towel. Water still draining from the tub. The bright shaft of light from the open bathroom door doesn't quite reach the foot of the bed where he lies. She stands so one side of her is silvered and the other soft as velvet in the candlelit room. She hugs herself in the blue bath towel, loosens it and briskly dries her skin with big handfuls. She lets the towel fall to her ankles and steps daintily out of it, bending quickly to gather it from the floor as she steps backward deeper into the shadow.

I know what you're thinking. You're thinking how easy it is to come back.

She's in the glare of the light again. Her arms flash as she unwraps a second matching towel turbaned around her head. Red hair splashes down to her shoulders. Her skin is like snow, like ice in the hard light, her wet hair black against its paleness. Perfect and naked as a statue he thinks as she poses at him an instant before she shakes her head like a soaked dog and attacks the tangled mass of hair with the towel.

She is leaning forward so the towel drops like a hood over the muddle of hair. Her long pale fingers dig through the cloth into her skull.

You're thinking how easy it is. How easy this easy woman is no matter how long you stay away. I know just what you're thinking.

He didn't answer her. Even though he knew she was wrong. She had never heard John French's name let alone knew about his pouting, about his jaws getting tight because he's out there on the corner of Frankstown and Homewood waiting for somebody who ain't showing up.

Seven years ain't put a wrinkle or a ounce of fat on you, woman. Looking good as I left you. Looking better if you want to hear the truth.

Her face jerks from under the towel. She snaps loose ringlets of hair away from her eyes.

So easy you can go away and utter not one word in seven years but she's so easy she'll smile at the first lie you tell her.

If I'm lying, I'm flying. He feels a wet spot on his cheek. Water-drops flung from her hair darken the satin sheet.

Well, maybe you should be flying. Maybe you just ought to get your black ass out of my bed and fly away from here.

You know you don't mean that.

Don't I? Am I so easy you can tell me what I mean and don't mean now?

The towel hangs limp from the hand cocked on her hip.

Am I one of your easy mamas now?

What you talking about, gal?

Gal. So I'm a gal now. I'm one of your gals now. One of your fast, little, red-hot nigger gals.

You always did look good when you got mad.

I ought to break your neck. I ought to whip you back out in the street. Stretching the ends of the towel apart, she twirls it till it's taut and pops it over the foot of the bed.

Whipping's too good for you. Ought to just let you lie there and choke on your lies.

Don't mind choking if you come on back under here and choke with me.

I'd sooner crawl in bed with a black snake.

398

Got one them too under here.

You devil. You damn fool.

Hurry up. Let me grab a handful while it's all wet and smelling like lemon pie.

Damn fool. She snuffs the candle flame between two damp fingers. Shivers as she crawls across the silky darkness to find him.

How long you been waiting?

Lemme see now. Long about seven years seems to me. Seemed like seven hundred years this morning with my ass out in the cold and my back stiffening up. Seems like too long to me with my butt sticking to one them crates on the corner.

Look here, French. You know how it is. You know I had to go see my woman. Didn't know if she'd open the door. Didn't know if she was still living there to open it.

Well, you found my door. And you got me out in that alley to open it. Like some damn alleycat scratching and whistling. Like something chasing you. Meet me in the morning, French. Got to see you first thing in the morning. Early before anybody around. Early so you can sit on a cantaloupe box and get stiff as a board. So I can lay up in that white woman's warm bed and laugh at French propped up like some damn fool Eskimo Kewpie doll out there in the cold.

You exaggerating now. Wasn't cold this morning.

Whose ass was out in it? Guess it wasn't cold where you was.

Seven years. Seven years, man, and I didn't even know if she still alive. So when she was . . . and when she opened the door . . . you know how it is.

Yeah. Ow whee and all that mess. But I don't want to hear nothing about it.

Got here soon as I could. How long you been waiting?

Bout a jug long.

Got anything left in there?

Ain't no more waiting left in there.

Many times as you left me up a tree and hound dogs barking and snapping at my heels. C'mon, man. You know how it is. Gimme a swallow that blood.

You back then? Back to stay?

If they let me lone.

You still wearing a horseshoe round your neck, ain't you? Already been in that white woman's bed. Already drinking my wine. Bet you been over to the Tates' on that piano, too.

Ummmm, that's good. Tastes like heaven. Tastes like three dozen pretty angels singing.

You think the police done forgot you?

Hell no. Motherfuckers never forget. Naw. That's what the man's about. Not forgetting. Not forgiving. Naw, they ain't forgot nothing, but they ain't got no special reason to start remembering today. It's been seven years. Whole lotta people come and gone in Homewood in seven years. And you know one nigger look just like the rest to the man.

Yeah but only one nigger fool enough to go marching back to that white woman's door in broad daylight.

It was dark last night.

Then you ain't going no more? You ain't gon be Albert Wilkes and strut right up Thomas Boulevard when you want to?

French, you on page ninety and I just opened the book. Got time to think about all that. I just want to be here awhile. Get used to the old place again. Thought I remembered it. Thought I could draw a picture if I needed to. Thought I had Homewood in my mind and could say it easy as saying the alphabet. Say the streets and people's names and talk that talk with everybody just like I used to. Like I could just pick it up and start again and never miss a lick.

Albert Wilkes takes the wine bottle again. Wine is black inside the green glass. Three fingers all that's left. As he tilts the bottle, it catches the sun and wine shimmers like wet tar. Wilkes stares into the glistening oval floating inside the bottle. It's blacker than a mirror in a dark room. He swallows a mouthful, then wipes the lips of the bottle with the heel of his hand. In the green glass he can catch a reflection of scraggly treetops silhouetted against the sky. He plays the light and shadow till French rolls across the glass, all head, then all belly, then legs flattened and curling around the glass like fingers. Then his own face. The shape of a spoon. Greener than the trees, the grass, the weeds of the Bums' Forest where he'd known John French would be waiting.

They sit on stones. French sprawled over three or four big ones which form a chairlike backrest and seat. Wilkes on a single rock, gullied in the middle as if all the behinds over the years have managed to rub their shape into the granite. A blackened space, bare except for charred kindling and a ring of small stones lies between the men. A smaller bare patch of earth is hard and flat enough for dice to roll true when you bounce them off the board propped along one end of the square. Shattered glass spits back the sunlight. Wilkes can almost hear the crap game. *Fever in the funk house looking for a five. Pay the boss, the poor hoss lost.* The singsong magic words chanted at the bones, the bones rattling in somebody's cupped hands, the bones talking back as they stare up at the faces staring down on them.

How's all your pretty babies, French?

Four now. One born whiles you gone. Another little girl, Martha. Lizabeth and Carl and Geraldine and Martha. The oldest one's getting grown now. Lizabeth more like her mama everyday.

My man, the family man. Wouldna never believed it.

No way round it. Man find a good woman he better go on and grab her. I got a good one, Albert.

Must be. Must be good and strong to haul you out the streets. You a big, ugly, fighting fish to land.

Still got the fight in me.

You still tipping round to see Antoinette?

She got three babies herself now.

Any them babies yellow and ugly and bald and chew Five Brothers tobacco and wear a big brown country hat?

She got a husband, too.

That ain't what I asked you. Asked you if you tipping, man. Husband ain't never made no nevermind if wife be willing. Cat's away, mama will play.

It's ole Jody niggers like you keep things stirred up.

I ain't the one sneaking over to Antoinette's.

You the reason niggers keep shotguns leaning up in the corner. Wonder as your backside ain't full of buckshot. Just ought to be if it ain't.

Seems to me the last time I remember hearing a shotgun I was on the far side of a fence and it was somebody else's posterior up on top, somebody else's britches caught and yelling for Jesus and thought he was dead when that shotgun blasted. Seems like I remember the alley behind Kelley Street and two sweet little chocolate sisters and their evil yellow daddy taking aim at Mr. J. Q. John French esquire couldn't get down off that fence to save his soul. Seems like I remember taking my own precious life in my hands and ripping some fool down off there and him leaving half his drawers stuck to the fence and walking down Homewood Avenue with his hat held over his bare behind where pants supposed to be.

Didn't know no better then.

And now?

It's a new day.

Things ain't changed that much. Couple babies ain't gon change Antoinette's big, pretty legs.

She's still a fine-looking woman.

And you still tipping, ain't you?

Seven years ain't changed you. Ain't said nothing bout yourself but trying hard as you can get in my business.

Legs like Antoinette's every man's business.

You still a fool.

And still thirsty.

Well, you hiding or what?

Tell the truth, I don't know. Seems like I should walk easy awhile. I mean maybe I ought to lay low. Find a place on the Northside or Downtown or the Hill maybe. Thought I'd do that. Thought I'd ask you what you thought. You know. About being here. About being seen. Thought you might have some idea how safe that'd be. Whole lotta new people. That means things is different. But I missed you this morning and been slipping round till now and nobody ain't said a word. Hello. Good-bye. Welcome back. You're under arrest. Ain't nobody been after me with no shotgun. Nothing. Maybe they have forgot Albert Wilkes. Maybe I can just settle down and mind my business and they'll let me alone. Call myself Tom Smith or Jim Johnson and nobody know the difference. Just one more ole country boy come to the city to slave for white folks.

One more country boy who makes love with rich white ladies

in broad daylight. One more country boy who plays the piano like nobody before or since Albert Wilkes. How long you think this ole country boy gon lay low and mind his business? How long before he marches up to Thomas Boulevard or marches into the Elks after that piano?

Don't know.

Well, I don't know neither. But I know it take more than seven years for a leopard to lose his spots. I know if he's a leopard he got them spots till he lay down and die. And you ain't no ghost, is you? Got all the spots you ever had under that coat. Yeah, you under there all right, Mr. Wilkes. Got to be.

Shit, French. What you saying, man? Damned if I do and damned if I don't.

You sure nobody seen you?

They seen me. But didn't seem like nobody knew me. Got some strange looks. You know. Little warm out here for this kind of coat.

Ain't a whole lot of hats like that, neither. Strange kind of hat for somebody don't want people to see him. Mize well have a billboard on top your head. Mize well have smoke puffing out that stovepipe.

That's the whole idea. Folks see the duster and see the hat. Now nobody trying to hide be wearing nothing like that. Folks see the big hat and see the long coat and don't think about somebody trying to hide. They think well here's one more fool trying to show off so they ignore whoever's in the hat and coat.

Why don't you steal you a elephant from the zoo and hang some bells on his ears and ride up and down Homewood Avenue singing Dixie. Then nobody pay you no mind for sure.

I'm telling you people don't say boo. Like I was invisible. Had to kick a can a couple times to make sure I was still alive. Niggers looking right through me like wasn't nothing under that hat but air.

Less seven years changed your mind about white pussy and piano playing they gon find you soon enough. They gon notice you real good and blow some holes in that coat.

That's what you think then?

I think that horseshoe's working overtime keeping you hid till now. Think you better find you a hiding place till I can check around.

Was at the Tates' last night. Old Mrs. Tate must be there by herself. Didn't see nobody else.

Little Lucy is there and Brother. They must been sleep. Never could quite figure out who's keeping who over there. They take care the old lady and she takes care of them. Since Tate died the three them been together and they gets along. Funny little Lucy and the albino boy and Mrs. Tate, she must be a hundred. Must be older than Homewood. She was old when I come here. My boy, Carl. He's over there much as he's home. Him and Brother like we was Albert in the old days. See one, see the other.

Those were some good days.

Owned Homewood in those days.

Far as we could see.

Damn. We gon figure something out. Got to figure out something. How they gon chase you out your own briarpatch? How we gon let em? No way, my man. You just cool it for a little while till I figures something out. You lay low in your invisibility clothes and keep rubbing that horseshoe for luck and we'll find something to do. Sure as my name's John French. Sure as you Albert Wilkes with all your spots under that blanket.

Who told on Albert Wilkes was another thing you could get an argument about. Except wasn't nobody claiming to be the one who told the police Albert Wilkes was back. Huh uh. Nobody bragged about being the one who told like they all bragged about being the one who saw him first. Nobody wanted to be the one John French had promised to kill with his bare hands. But there were plenty stories going round. People had their favorites and would shout down anybody didn't agree. Gather all the stories, listen to every tale and all of Homewood guilty. John French have to strangle every man, woman and child in Homewood if you believed what the stories said. Strangle every nigger in Homewood and most the white folks up on Thomas Boulevard too. Because lots of the stories blamed white people. Course everybody knew it was white cops who shot Wilkes. But what counted wasn't the murdering puppets in uniforms so much as it was the ones who pulled their strings. The ones who ran Homewood without ever setting foot in Homewood. The ones whose lily-white hands held Homewood like a lemon and squeezed pennies out drop by drop and every drop bitter as tears, sour as sweat when you work all day and ain't got nothing to show for it.

Was that white woman Albert Wilkes had. Course it was her. Give Albert all her loving. Giving him her money too. She was scared he was gon run away again. Scared he'd take all her money and run off with some other woman and there she'd be. Cause she couldn't say no to him. Couldn't hold him and couldn't let him go neither. Nothing worse than a jealous woman. Nothing crazier or meaner. Course she called the cops on him. She can't have Albert Wilkes, nobody else would. I can see her dialing the phone. Them long scarlet fingernails. And a silk handkerchief dabbing at the tears as she tells the police where he's at. Shedding a tear for poor Albert and feeling sorry for herself cause she knows she ain't never gon have that kind of loving man again. I can see her weeping and stirring the ice cubes in her drink real slow with one those bloody nails.

Wasn't nothing to do with white folks. Niggers dirty enough to do their own dirt. That's the way it's always been. We our own worst enemy. Always find one nigger who'll snitch on the others. Always find a Judas. Don't need no pile of silver. Just a dime. Just a extra slice of watermelon. Find one them sneaky-type Negroes sell you to the white folks for a dime. That's the way it always been. In slavery days it was niggers keep watch on niggers. It's your own people tell on you you try to run away. Wasn't for treacherous, back-stabbing niggers no way they keep all those people slaves. It's the same today. You watch. A brother try to make something of hisself, a blood rise up to where he can do something for his people, who it gon be that drag him down. You name the one tried to rise up and lead us and I'll name the nigger dragged him down. Wasn't nothing white about it. Just one these trifling Homewood splibs dropped a dime on Albert Wilkes.

The Lord giveth and the Lord taketh away.

Probably one the children. You know how kids is. Let something slip. Didn't mean no harm but they said it and walls got ears. You know how that is. Little pitchers got big mouths. And walls got ears. Poor little things got blood on they hands and never even know it.

By the time John French returned home that day that everybody was looking for him and he was looking for Albert Wilkes, the early evening sky was salmon pink and streaked with fiery drifts, and still hadn't made up its mind. Steel mills down along the river belched up clouds of smoke so there was something for the sunset to hang on, to paint. If you didn't know the smoke could kill you, if you didn't think of it as an iron cloud pressing the breath out your body, the dirt and soot and gas coloring the sky made a beautiful sight.

When John French walked into the kitchen of the house on Cassina Way he saw my grandmother sitting alone at the table quietly crying. He was full of oranges, golds, purples, the knife-edge keenness of the light shaping the sunset. He wanted to share the sight with his woman. But if they didn't hurry outdoors the sky would change. The lavender boards of the shanties in Cassina turn gray again. The rivers of fire in the sky become ash. He wanted to take his woman by her hand and walk with her out the door and down the narrow corridor of Cassina. Walk far away where rooftops ended, where Homewood and Pittsburgh and anything else with a name or a shadow was long gone. He wanted to go to a place where nothing got in the way and the sunset touched the earth. Instead he stroked her shoulder and ran his thumb up and down the hollows at the back of her neck. Her hair was piled on top of her head. The scarf she'd tied that morning was still knotted in place. Her neck was long and slender, the smooth ivory color of piano keys. He massaged the taut cords beneath the softness. A neck long and delicate as Lizabeth's. So much of this woman, this Freeda his wife, he'd never seen till after Lizabeth was born. His daughter growing more like her mother every day. But it was like Freeda growing younger too. Starting over again from the beginning so he can watch her becoming a woman. Freeda a girl again in her daughter's skin and bones. Sometimes he'd spy on Freeda through the cracked bathroom door. Watch her step out the tub, watch her naked body, so he could remember how beautiful she was under her clothes when she came out dressed. See two Freedas at once, later when she puttered quietly round the kitchen. His woman moving naturally and unaware in nothing but her ivory skin. His sweet woman in a housedress working her magic on the food for everybody's dinner. As Lizabeth grew up in the house on Cassina he could steal secret looks back at the way Freeda must have been. The bony awkwardness. The little girl shadow that the years had dressed as a woman. He saw one in the other. Could see where one body was headed, where the other had been. When he touched one, he touched both.

He wished he could tell my grandmother all the good things he felt. Something to change the way her day had been. Words to take them both back to the morning when he'd awakened beside her and she cuddled closer, warming his side a moment before he eased away and hung his stiff legs over the edge of the bed. What could he say about the long day he'd been away. She'd needed him and he hadn't been there. What could he tell her that would make up for the hours of worrying, the weariness. He stroked her shoulders and neck. Like touching that hot sky. Like running your fingers up and down the razor light, like poking them in the fire. He'd been the one whaling her body with the whip and now the same hands trying to heal, trying to mend the broken places. He saw in his wife's slumped shoulders the certainty that one day even Lizabeth would get old. He remembered the night both of them never went to bed. Remembered Lizabeth's fever and terrible hacking cough, his helplessness and fear as his daughter sat on the side of her bed, shivering, barely able to catch her breath, her little girl's round shoulders huddled under the blanket he'd draped over her. Nothing he could say, nothing he could do would change what was hurting her. He had been with Albert or waiting for Albert all day. And now there wasn't anything he could say to Freeda, no way to give back the day he'd taken.

Albert's in trouble. Can't stay here and he don't want to be nowhere else.

I can't talk now. Don't want to think about anybody else now. All day it's been you on my mind. Wandering the streets and praying nobody'd come running up to tell me you were dead. And seeing you dead. And having to tell the children. Watching their little faces break up when I say Your daddy's dead. How am I supposed to say those words to them? How would I say something like that to my ownself? Worrying myself sick all day about you. Trying to talk away the worst that could happen. Putting the worst in words and saying the words so it wouldn't really happen. Worrying about you. About them. All day long other people on my mind and now it's just me. I need to think about me. I'm sorry for Albert Wilkes and sorry for everybody else but now I just need to sit here awhile and be sorry for me.

He'll stay at the Tates' tonight. He'll be all right over there.

And where will you stay?

Be right here with you.

How long? Till he comes scratching and whistling?

How you gon be a friend you don't help when there's trouble?

There's all kind of trouble, man. Didn't you hear what I said to you? Wasn't I talking about trouble? Ain't I been in the deepest trouble there is today? Just cause you walk in here and squeeze my neck and rub my shoulders you think my trouble's over? You think I care whether Albert Wilkes at the Tates' or burning in Hell? I have these babies to face, these babies to feed. And a man act like he ain't got wife nor child the first. That's real trouble. You-all just playing games. And Albert Wilkes the worst. He looks for trouble. He made all the trouble he ever had. He don't belong nowhere. Don't answer to nobody. He needs trouble. Couldn't find enough wherever he was those seven years so he's back here again. Back to stir up trouble and you just itching to be out there in it with him.

The man needs to come home.

Man like that don't have a home. His home is trouble. He tears up homes. Never heard a good thing about him. Except he could play the piano. And what's he do with that piano but cause more trouble? Playing nasty music and driving a bunch of drunk niggers crazier than they already are.

He's a man just like I am. Breath and britches. Walks on two legs. He ain't got no horns sprouting out his head. Ain't got no tail. He's a man like me, and I been knowing him ever since I been in Homewood. Seems like we go back further than that. Seems like I always been knowing Albert, and if he's in trouble I got to do what I can.

You have to be with him all hours of the night and day so when the police come to kill him they'll kill you too? Is that what you mean? Is that why you've been gone since dawn and why you'll go running again when he comes scratching tonight?

Nobody bother him over to the Tates'. Just old Mrs. Tate there and those two children. Nobody knows Albert's there.

You send him to a house with children? He's at the Tates'? And where do you think your son goes running first thing every morning? Where do you think he spends every day after school's out?

Nobody knows Albert's over there. Nobody's gon bother the children.

How do you know that? Unless the devil granted him wings Albert Wilkes had to walk to the Tates'. How you know nobody didn't see him? How you know the police ain't on their way right now?

Albert got this long coat and a hat. He . . .

He's a fool. He killed a white policeman, and he can stay away a hundred years, they still be waiting to kill him when he come back. You know that. You said that to me. So how you know nobody ain't recognized him? You know the police would burn down the Tates' and everybody in there to get him.

Gotta help him. Have to figure out something and till I do the Tates be all right.

Well, Carl won't set his foot outside the door tomorrow. And if it'd do any good I'd get down on my knees and beg you in God's name not to go either.

Don't talk like that.

Talk's all I can do. Nobody listens but what else can I do? Where the children?

Lizabeth taking them for iceballs. Told her go straight there and straight back and they better be home before dark.

She's a good girl.

And I want her to stay that way.

People look out for Lizabeth. They know she's my girl. Wish I could have seen them marching down Homewood Avenue. They growing up too fast.

Carl better listen to his sister. Warned him he better stay with her and come back with her. Started not to let him go. Bad as my nerves was this morning, him and Brother walking those tracks again. Told him a million times to stay off those tracks, but his head's hard as yours. Chased Brother away from here but I bet they back together now. Brother and that fast little Lucy too. He just better be back here before dark. He better listen to his sister and they all better be home in a few short minutes.

Won't be dark for another hour.

Be black in another hour. Just about dark now.

You should have seen the sky tonight.

Lots of things I should have seen today instead of worrying over you.

So pretty it scared me.

Walking around all day with a ghost, you should be scared.

I know you ain't wanting to hear nothing I got to say but Ima tell you bout the sky anyway. Kind of sky gets you to thinking. Looked up and saw it all streaked up and thought about how it was this morning and how the sky is always up there doing what it has to do just like you doing what you got to do down here. Made me think about things like that. Like everything got its own life but you don't hardly never notice nothing but your own. Too busy with your own business. Then one day you look up and see the sky and can't remember why you so busy doing what you doing.

Please stay here tonight. Please leave Albert Wilkes alone, and if he comes whistling around here in the middle of the night tell him to leave you alone. Say yes. Say you will.

The sky colors are like bits of music. He can remember the oranges, the reds, the purples. They flash back to him, he can see them, but he can't put them together the way Albert puts together the chords, the phrases, the bits and pieces into a whole song. He remembers how good it looked, how it swallowed him and filled him and just about took his breath away but he can't picture the whole thing, the stretch from the earth to the stars, from right to left along the horizon.

I'll stay.

She smiles across the table at him. The kind of smile which begins as anything but a smile and can't make up its mind till the last minute what it's going to be so a little bit of everything's in it. Then she reaches across the checkered oilcloth and lays her soft hand on his hard one, her young fingers on his old fingers, her little-girl, Lizabeth smoothness on his rough paperhanging crusty-as-brogan skin. She takes back her hand and he stretches out his long legs and both listen for the children returning.

2. The Courting of Lucy Tate

THE strange thing was that nobody taught him. The stranger thing was that nobody cared. One day Brother Tate sat down at the piano and began playing. Lucy remembered the hours she had spent with Brother watching Albert Wilkes. In the daytime in the living room, at night hiding in the shadows at the top of the stairs when they were supposed to be sleep. And Carl remembered the funny way Brother would play the air, pecking at an imaginary keyboard with his pale fingers. Brother could always scat sing and he'd drum on the oilcloth tabletop in the kitchen of the house on Cassina Way till his fingers were a blur and my grandmother mad enough to stomp in from another room and think about the butcher knife in the drawer and ten bony little quiet white sausages and peace at last as she shouted at him to stop.

Nobody cared that Brother hadn't ever played a note before Thursday because what they heard Saturday was so fine you just said Thank Jesus a day early and paid every iota of attention you owned to what was dancing from the Elks piano. And it wasn't strange at all that somebody got happy and shouted, *Play, Albert. Play, Albert Wilkes. Albert's home again*, because good piano playing and Albert Wilkes were just about the same word in Homewood. You'd look for one and here come the other. If you shut your eyes that Saturday night like a lot of people did during the down tempo, bluesy parts, slow dragging with your baby or just sitting stirring your drink and thinking your own thoughts, you wouldn't remember who was playing. You wouldn't care. All you'd know is that you'd heard the music before and that was why it

411

sounded so good, so right, right now. And you knew you'd need to hear it again. One more time.

Brother was three times seven the first night he played the piano at the Elks Club. My Uncle Carl said it surprised hell out of him. Scared him too. The three of them, Lucy, Brother and Carl, were out that night. Nineteen forty-one because the war had just begun. The three musketeers drinking and smoking a little reefer and it was round about midnight and the band on a break, circulating in the crowd and the crowd like it gets then, lots of people out their seats, ordering another round at the bar, visiting other tables, jawing with the musicians, hustling to the toilet before a line formed and somebody made a mess in the sink or used up all the paper towels. One minute Brother right there across the table. Next minute he's on the piano stool and the notes are like somebody coughing, clearing his throat and getting your attention at the same time because just about the moment you look up to see who made the noise it's not noise anymore it's somebody taking care of business on the piano and you squint through the cigarette haze and the clink of glasses and the seesaw mutter of talking and laughing and it's Brother up there, your main man you've never seen close to a piano before unless it's that imaginary one, that invisible one he plays in thin air.

Brother wasn't supposed to be up there, Brother wasn't supposed to know how to play. He was my main man, and I knew better than anybody else he wasn't supposed to be doing what he was doing. So not only was I surprised. I was scared. I mean if he could just get up and start playing like that then what else could he do I didn't know nothing about. It's like you been knowing a fella all your life, knowing him and knowing his name is Tom just as well as you know your own name is Carl then one day somebody says that ain't Tom, that's Chuck. And everybody else says, Yeah. That's Chuck all right, and they shout you down and Tom is nodding too and laughing at whatever notion got in your head to call him Tom. So that's that. But where's it leave you? You know better but they say it's Chuck and he says it's Chuck so what you gon do?

Anyway I listened like everybody else and popped my fingers and patted my foot under the table and clapped and shouted like everybody else. Brother stopped three times and three times we hollered and whistled and stomped till he sat down again and played some more. Talk about a joint jumping. Man, Brother turned it out. All by hisself at the piano. The more he played the better it got and I didn't have time to be scared nor surprised. Tell you something though. I couldn't look over there at him. I could listen and groove but I knew better than to look over at the bandstand where he was playing. Didn't know what I'd see. Didn't know what I wanted to see. Cause it wasn't Brother over there. No way it could be him. And if it wasn't him I didn't want to see who it was.

Seemed like hours. Then it seemed like he'd only been gone a minute because there he was all sweaty and grinning at me across the table again. Like he'd only been gone long enough to pee, but there'd been that music for hours, for days. I didn't know what to say. If he was Tom I sure wasn't going to call him Chuck, and if he was Chuck I didn't know him anyway and wasn't about to start speaking, but Lucy understood and said:

Ain't you something. Then she said, I heard you messing on the piano. Heard you since Thursday messing around down there at night. Wondered what you were doing. Wondered what you thought you were doing. Sneaking around like that.

Brother still grinning like the cat swallow the canary.

Must of been Albert Wilkes taught you. And you hiding it all these years. Hiding it all this time then getting up on the bandstand and showing out tonight. Ain't you something, lil brother.

But Lucy knew better. Albert Wilkes dead seven years at least. And Brother wasn't more than six or seven when Wilkes ran away. So what's that make? How's he supposed to learn when he just a baby? How he's supposed to keep it in his head and in his hands all those years? So I was scared again. Lucy just making excuses. And why she gon make excuses less she know something I don't? Unless they got a secret. And if they got a secret then I don't know what's happening. Brother's not even her real brother. Tates raised Lucy who was a Bruce before she was a Tate. Mama got burnt up in a terrible fire but the Tates took Lucy in and she goes by Tate, just like Brother's not really a Tate. They just took him in and he became a Tate like Lucy did. He's not her brother and not younger either. Lucy was with the Tates first and Brother was older than her when he came but because she was there first he was her little brother. Pushed him around in a baby buggy till the wheels wore off. Looked like a big spider in there. Legs and arms dangling and knees poked up in the air. Her little brother Brother twice as big as she was, and she's pushing him up and down Tioga Street till wasn't nothing but wheels and frame left of that buggy and probably still be pushing him around if the wheels hadn't broke.

Seemed strange then and still seems strange now, that nobody bothered about a thing strange as that. I mean, one day Brother was one thing. Hands dumb as mine or anybody else's. Next day he's got all that music in his fingers and nobody asks why. Or asks how he got it. Guess folks didn't care as long as it sounded good as it did. So the three of us at the table and the place still buzzing and Brother's fingers still burning. Half expected that glass of Scotch and ice somebody sent over to start sizzling when he picked it up. But it didn't. He just grinned and downed it and Lucy smiling too and paying the strangeness no mind so I decided then, neither will I. If people gon change overnight, if they're gon be one thing one day and something else the next and it don't bother nobody else why should I let it bother me? Drinks getting lined up on the table. Everybody setting Brother up and setting up his table so why not? Didn't spend one more dime that night and drank till dawn. Shucks. I've heard there was a time when niggers knew how to fly and knew how to tell the truth. And if people could manage all that and forget all that then I'd be a fool not to listen when the listening good and drink when the drinking's good. Nothing but a party anyway. Whole thing ain't nothing but a party so why should I be a fool and sit there and fret?

I was born about six months before that evening in 1941. So already I was inside the weave of voices, a thought, an idea, a way things might be seen and be said. I had heard them talk about Brother that winter and heard about the war and the harshness of the weather which wouldn't be matched till I was twelve years old visiting my grandmother's house and watched the Big Snow begin one morning and bury the garbage cans in the vacant lot by night. Seven feet of snow in two days. And weeks of stories about snow. How Aunt May saved my mother Lizabeth by dunking her in a snowbank. How they had to chip the ice off old Mr. Wilson when they found him in his shanty and how he moaned when he thawed in the undertaker's back room and you can still hear him some nights where his shack used to be, crying and groaning in the wind.

In 1941 it's quite possible I heard Brother play the piano, if there was a day nice enough for my Uncle Carl to steal me from my mother and bundle me up and carry me over to the Tates'. If I missed Brother playing between '41 and '46 then I missed him forever, because after Junebug died Brother stopped playing the piano just as suddenly as he stopped talking. His terrible headaches began and he never played again. One day in one of the stories I'm sure someone will tell me, I did hear Brother play. On such and such a day while the sun was shining and the wind died down and them trenches dug in the street so's you could get around I remember Carl getting you ready and your mama saying No, saying it's too bad outside, saying it while Carl is wrapping you in sweaters and a snowsuit so you looked like a bowling ball and Cold could have run over you with a truck and you wouldna felt a thing. . . One day I'll be in the Tates' living room listening. I'll hear Brother. I'll hear Albert Wilkes.

But it's spring now. Spring one more time in Homewood. I'm not born. Not even thought of, let alone born, as somebody would remind me if I needed to be reminded. Late spring and all the trees I've never learned the names of glow with new life. The big trees you still find on the nicer streets in Homewood grew everywhere then. Canopies and tunnels, arches heavy with leaves drooping over the sidewalks. After a rain you could drench the kids walking behind you by jumping up and shaking a branch and it's like a bucket emptied on the ones trudging home from school behind you. Brother Tate catches my Uncle Carl daydreaming, lagging behind, and jerks down a flood all over Carl's school clothes.

Shit man, why'd you do that dumb shit?

Brother had caught him real good. Soaked him to his skin. Water hit the pavement like a load of bricks. Wet leaves on the branch Brother jerked down still swayed in front of Carl's face. Behind him rain pattered in the tunnel. Brother was so easy to soak it had stopped being fun. Fool even acted like he liked it sometimes so Carl had given up on that trick, forgotten it almost till he stood dripping, wiping water out his eyes, mopping the back of his neck with his wet sleeve. Brother was already too far away to catch now, across the street, jumping up and down and showing all his teeth in a horsey grin. Carl searched along the curb for something to throw.

You got me you cream-of-wheat motherfucker. You got me good.

Brother sidled closer then stopped in the middle of Tioga threw back his head and with a puzzled expression searched the blue sky for rain. He raised his hands over his head and pantomimed a column of wiggly drizzle, avoiding it at the last minute by ducking away from his falling hands. Pointing at Carl now, the look of wonder broke into a grin and the grin to a titter and the titter exploded to snorts and whinnies.

OK. OK. You win this time. You got me and we're even this time.

But when he stepped toward Brother, Brother's gone. Flying back across Tioga and halfway up the next block before he checked behind to see if Carl's chasing him.

Hey man. Peace, man. How my supposed to go home now? Carl curls his little finger and flicks water from inside his ear.

Wait up, fool. I ain't gon home wet like this. My mama kill me.

Brother waits, doing a little skittish toe-dance shuffle on the far, treeless corner. In the time it takes to reach him, Carl figures it's no win. Either arriving home on time with wet school clothes or being late with them dry, he'll catch hell. So he decides to catch it for coming home late *and* being over at the Tates'.

Don't want you playing on those tracks and don't want you hanging around the Tates'. Nobody over there to supervise you children. Don't want you worrying Mrs. Tate. Got enough on her hands dealing with Brother and that fast Lucy.

Yes, she's said it a million times. And yes, he knows better. And yes, Mam. I'm sorry and I know Ima catch hell. Yes, Mama. Your hand upside my head. And straight home every day after school. Yes, I know you'll watch the clock. Count the minutes and tell Daddy if I don't do right and Daddy got that razor strop and I ain't too big for it yet. Never will get too big for it.

Beside Brother now he fakes a punch and Brother dodges not so much to get away as to get a better look at the damage up close. Brother raises both hands and crouches Joe Louis style, bobbing and weaving, circling Carl and popping holes in the air with his jab.

C'mon, fool. Go get dry over your place.

The air smells like the salve his mama rubs on his chest at night when he's got the croup. Rain had rushed in and out again barely giving the sky time to change. Lots of thunder and crackling lightning. Like night suddenly in Miss Petronia's classroom. Dark anyway in the little seventh grade room in the middle of the hall. People jumping and squealing and acting crazy like nobody never heard thunder before. Miss Petronia at the blackboard scratching the answers to long division. She jumped the first time. Everybody did even though you knew it was coming. Dark like when the shades pulled down but she kept doing the problems on the board as if nothing happening. Squeak and scratch and tapping that chalk and it's blacker outside and blacker inside, but she don't turn on the lights, don't look over her shoulder to see how everybody's fidgeting and pointing to the window or staring at the puddles of shadow getting deeper round their feet. When it got us all wrapped up and it was dark as the inside of a drum in that room, somebody hit it, an arm as long as Homewood Avenue took a tree in its fist and slammed it down on top of Homewood School. *Baroom.* She stopped then. Jumped high as the rest of us. Dark in there but I could see the whites of her eyes getting wide while she stood there with the chalk in her hand trying to add up all the little niggers sitting in rows behind her. Told everybody be quiet and act like adults and switched on the light and switched her fine little Italian behind back to the board. Miss Petronia was fourth period and by eighth the sky is blue again, the black clouds fluffy white, the air dead still and smelling like his mother's hands when he's sick.

He follows Brother's narrow back up Tioga. Rain is itchy and chilly under his clothes. His mama kill him if he catch cold. Carl wonders if Lucy is home yet. If she wasn't, she'd be there in a minute. She didn't mess around like they did, doodling like doodlebugs to stretch the time between school and home. Lucy didn't join the packs of girls who had their own female doodling way of taking lots of time to get home from school. Nobody told Lucy what to do so she told herself. She acted so grown-up sometimes. Acted like him and Brother were kids. Lucy cooked and washed clothes and kept her house clean like his mama. She'd nag Brother like his mama nagged him, fussing, wagging a finger in his face. Too grown-up for a little skinny girl Carl thought and wondered if his mother called her fast because Lucy did all the grown-up chores Mrs. Tate couldn't do anymore. *Fast little Lucy Tate with her fast ways.* When his mother said it like that she wasn't talking about chores. She was talking about what was between Lucy's legs. His mother meant *womanish fast* when she kind of shook her head and twisted her lips tight together. Womanish fast. And when his mother said *fast* like she said it about certain girls on certain streets in Homewood or said it to his sisters about a crowd that was too fast for them to run with, he couldn't help but think of the space between Lucy's legs and think of wings or racing car wheels or the flying thunder of a whole posse of sheriffs chasing outlaws across the screen.

He'd dreamed once of Lucy growing in a red crockery flower-pot like his mother had beside the living room window. Lucy grew *fast*. Faster than an onion. Nothing but a little girl string bean but as he watched she sprouted nubs on her chest and apple cheeks on her behind. She was bare and smooth all over and it wasn't like peeking at the woman parts of his sisters because Lucy was planted in that pot and growing faster than a storm just for him.

The Tates' house sat a short cement walkway, five steps and a porch from the sidewalk. A three-storied, gable-roofed, brick building, it dwarfed the adjacent row houses and made old Mr. Tate seem a rich man to his neighbors. Brother squatted on the top step in the shadow of the porch roof. When you played on the Tates' porch it was like being indoors. If you stayed on your knees nobody passing by on the sidewalk could see you through the solid brick porch wall, and the overhang of the roof kept out rain and sunlight. A cave for them where everything they did could be a secret. Inside the Tates' house were high ceilings, bare rooms, unlit hallways and creaking stairs, doors Carl had never opened, an attic and basement he'd never enter even with Brother beside him or Lucy waiting inside. The porch was their secret place, but inside belonged to old, dead Mr. Tate, old, stooped, stuttering Mr. Tate with his giant ring of keys rattling and jingling like chains as he shuffled from room to dark room.

Brother's face was saying, Stop here, sit down here and do nothing awhile. Carl understood the look, understood how it felt to be used by older boys who wanted to get next to his sisters. They said things to him about his sisters they wouldn't dare say to Lizabeth or Geral. Treated him like a rug or a highway. He'd come home beat up then get yelled at because he wouldn't explain the bruises, couldn't repeat the nasty words that made the big boys laugh and made him mad enough to attack them. He understood Brother's look but only stopped long enough to pop his knuckle once on Brother's bald head before he skipped across the porch, through the vestibule and landed in the footprints of Albert Wilkes.

You looking for Brother?

Lucy said the *you* like you'd say *boo* if you were trying to scare somebody. And she got him like she usually did, caught him and sent him jumping six inches out his skin. She was behind him, her back toward the front door. He tried to make his voice cool, but they both knew she'd caught him again.

Brother's out on the stoop.

No, he ain't.

Well, he was.

Well, what you looking for then?

Me and Brother just come from school. My clothes wet.

You too big a child to be peeing your pants.

You know I ain't done that. Fool pulled a treeful of water on me.

Too big a child for that kind of messing, too. You sure not the one takes care of washing and ironing clothes at your house. If you did, you'd know better.

She's got her hands on her hips and nagging and smirking cause she knows she caught him again. Whenever he was alone in the Tates', he couldn't help thinking of dead people. That's what he was thinking in the hallway when he busted in from the street and didn't see anybody. Old dead Mr. Tate and dead Albert Wilkes dressed up in sheets and wagging their clammy ghost hands. Lon Chaney and hunchbacks and werewolves and Dracula and anything else dead and bloody sneaking up to grab him. So when she said *you*, said it like some goddamn moony-eyed owl in the middle of the night in the middle of a cemetery, of course he jumped. Nothing funny about it neither. Just cause her and Brother don't know no better. Just cause they go to sleep every night in a haunted house full of chain-dragging, piano-playing ghosts don't mean he got to be crazy too. Lucy glides past him. Still grinning, still quiet and sneaky as a ghost. Like there wasn't nothing dead on the floor, no spilled brains and vampire feathers and no hands dripping cold gravy come out the floorboards to grab her bare feet.

You got any peanut butter?

Might be some.

Fix me a sandwich.

Boy, you better act like you got good sense and fix what you want your ownself.

Can I have some milk?

Gwan and get what you want. Know as well as I do where everything is. You and Brother messed up my kitchen enough times, you just ought to know, if you don't.

Want one?

One what?

Peanut butter and jelly sandwich.

Oh. You gon get in my jelly too. Guess you gon fry my bacon and scramble up my eggs on this peanut butter sandwich you're fixing. Boys ain't nothing but eating machines. And all that food goes straight to your feet. Seems like some ought to rise to your brains. Ought to get smarter or something, all that food youall be wolfing down.

Carl sits alone at the kitchen table. If he stops chewing, the peanut butter will cement his jaws together. He is not hungry. His stomach floats up to the pit of his throat and just lies there, a flat, gassy little bag, and there's no place for the food he crams in his mouth to go. When he's in the Tates' house he needs to eat, he's never really hungry but he needs to eat. It's work. Packing peanut butter and jelly and bread into the tiny sack, into the lump which makes it hard to breathe right till he leaves the Tates'.

That's half a jar of jelly you got on there.

He had been wishing for Lucy's voice. Wishing and keeping

his eye on the door so she couldn't sneak up again and spook him again. He wanted to reply in a firm, steady, man's voice this time but his mouth is full of peanut butter sandwich.

Lucy is handing him a tall glass of milk. He wonders why he had forgotten to get one himself. He avoids her eyes as he takes the glass and says thank you and thinks of Brother's watery, milky color. The icebox door clicks again. She's after something for herself. She's chewing something crispy. One of her end toes is crooked. It curls up from the floor and hugs the one next to it. Her toenails are painted pale pink, almost the color of Brother's eyes. Painted nails and painted toes. That was fast. And her ankle bones and bare feet looked fast. Fast little wing-boned feet smacking against the linoleum when she brought him the milk. Naked feet slipping quiet as a cat when she wanted to sneak up on him. He could almost hear the fast hum of blood in the veins crisscrossing the hump over her high arches.

You counting my toes, boy? They all there you think?

The top part of her was string bean thin and the bottom half lost in a pair of man-size corduroys rolled at the waist and baggy and rolled again above her ankles. Her school clothes hung up neat on hangers in a closet somewhere upstairs. Out of them fast because she's grown-up and keeps her clothes clean. Growing fast as an onion. If he wanted to see her the way she was in his dream he'd have to pull down the green corduroy like you peeled the green shell of a buckeye. Peel green spiky layers and layers of brown skin and damp white meat and delicate membranes. At the buckeye's core it's green again, a tiny green seed with a tree inside if you knew how to plant it and make it grow.

Mrs. French die if she saw you now. Sitting up there all goggle-eyed and face full of sandwich and you know she don't allow you over here after school.

Lots of things she don't allow. But I ain't no kid no more. Got my own rules now.

My, my. Listen at Mister Man. Bet you wouldn't be talking that trash if your mama was here.

Say what I have to say. And do what I have to do.

Listen at this child. Since when you so grown?

Since I could walk on water and swim on dry land. Since I been

Long John the Conqueroo and crossed seven seas and whooped seven tribes and carried my people to the promised land.

Git out my face, boy.

Too high and heavy for you, ain't it? If I ain't grown, grits ain't groceries and eggs ain't poultries and Mona Lisa was a man.

You been listening to them winos in the Bums' Forest. You been listening, but that don't make you grown. Grown is working if you the man and cleaning and cooking and having babies if you the woman. Jive talking nothing to do with being grown. I could tell you something about being grown. And show you something too.

Show me.

Not what you're thinking, boy. That's one thing you surely is too grown for. No more that doctor, nursey, playing house with you and Brother undressing me on the porch mess.

You the one said you had something to show.

And you better believe I got it.

And the something she shows first is the ladderback chair in the living room with one rocker raw and split down near the bottom.

Knocked it over. Spilled poor Mrs. Tate right out on the floor like a sack of potatoes. She ain't been in it since. Her favorite chair, too. Police carried her upstairs when the shooting was all over, and that's where she been ever since.

The next something Lucy shows him is the holes in the piano, and beneath the piano's rolltop cover Albert Wilkes's blood on the keys. You had to look closely, but it was there, a purplish stain on the ivory like the pigment showing through at the roots of dark people's fingernails.

The last something begins as Carl follows Lucy up the stairs to the room where she sleeps.

Had to go find Brother because I wasn't exactly sure. Albert Wilkes gone a long time. So when this stranger come here in a big hat and a long gray coat there's something makes me look real hard at him when he ain't looking at me, but I ain't sure what it is. I was just a baby when Mr. Albert left. So I found Brother and we ran every step of the way back here and didn't stop till we was looking the stranger in the face. I was sure then. Didn't even need to look at Brother then to be sure. He had on a long dusty-colored coat. Kinda funny looking to be sitting at a piano in a coat but he had the sleeves rolled up and the tail of that coat pushed off his hips so it draped over the back of the piano bench. A big black hat beside him on the floor. Smiling at us like he knew us but didn't have time to say hello or nothing because he was in the middle of something and he'd speak later when he wasn't so busy. Couldn't remember his name but I knew who he was. And Brother knew too. Brother start to fidgeting beside me and moving his fingers like he's playing a piano so I said, *Play*. And Mr. Albert Wilkes did. I couldn't have called his name if you paid me, but I knew he could play that piano so I said as nice as I could, *Play*. And you talk about playing. My oh my. The sweetest song a dead man ever played for his own funeral. Course I didn't know he'd be dead before he finished. Course he didn't know neither, I guess. Not so sure what Albert Wilkes knew and didn't know. Shucks, honey. While the man was playing I didn't care. His name came back to me right in the middle of the music. That sweet, sweet good music. Sometimes I think I'd be willing to die if I could play one time as fine and sweet as Albert Wilkes played that afternoon. Maybe he did know he was gon die. Maybe he didn't care. I sure didn't. Didn't nothing matter but the music. And poor old Mrs. Tate, God rest her soul, rocking all the while. Couldn't tell what she might be hearing or seeing or thinking. Probably didn't even know Albert Wilkes was back, let alone hear what he was playing or know he was going to die and she'd be in jail before he finished.

Lucy's butt is half on, half off the bar stool. One long leg dangles to the floor, the other is drawn up to her chest and she circles it with both arms, stretching it, testing her sleek, dancer's muscles. When she stops her story she rests her chin on her upthrust knee. Carl has seen her in a skirt or dress sit the same way, on the same barstool, talking slowly and exercising absentmindedly so anybody from her stool to the front door of the Velvet Slipper could tell you the color of her underwear, if it was a day she was wearing any. Lucy had a way of letting you look if you wanted to look, but letting you know that looking was your business and she had nothing to hide and what you saw wasn't her business because her business was private and you could stare till your eyeballs froze over and her business still be hers and still be private. Carl thinks back to the time he first knew he loved her. When he'd take pictures of her with his mind and carry them around. Lucy never stood still. Always changeable as the weather so he needed the snapshots in his mind to study, to figure out who she was. Always changing, always a mystery so he'd stop her trap her in those little white-framed pictures like a bee in a bottle he could study without getting stung.

No music like that ever before and none since. Music's spoiled for me. That crazy, lazy brother of mine could have played if he wanted to but don't look like he ever will. Shucks. Listening to Albert Wilkes play the way he did that day spoiled all the rest of music for me.

Rest of us ain't spoiled. Put a quarter in the box, Cat.

Yeah, Cat. Drop some change in that thing. Play something got that old-time swing to it.

Shot poor Albert Wilkes to pieces that day. And I saved me one.

She had opened the skinny top drawer of the dresser in the far corner of her bedroom. She unfolded a handkerchief, emptied it carefully into her hand as she crossed the room again toward the door where Carl stood.

Shut that door and come on over here.

Lucy had closed her fist and stopped abruptly. One backward bounce landed her buttocks-first atop the high four-poster bed. The swayback springs squeak as she squirms to a comfortable position on the green chenille spread.

You deaf, boy? Shut the door and hit that light beside it and c'mon over here before I change my mind.

When Carl is on the edge of the bed beside her, she wiggles away to offset his weight, scooting a little farther from the edge so her legs dangle. She chucks him once under the chin, then uncurls her fist slowly, close to his eyes. Her fingers almost touch his face. Carl can hear her bones unwind. Smell soap.

The bare bulb stuck in a ceiling socket cooks the dust gathered on its surface. Sounds like a moth circling above their heads. The blind over the room's one window is closed, so the bed floats in shadow. All the light in the room is drawn to the object in Lucy's palm. The third something she shows him that afternoon after school is white and hot looking. A pearl. A baby tooth. A chip of ivory. A piece of seashell. A rare, white pebble from the grimy hillside where the trains run.

Don't know what you're looking at, do you, Mister Grown-up? Well, that's a piece of Albert Wilkes.

Lucy grabs his wrist and sets his hand in her lap. *Turn over. Open up.* She dumps the object in his hand. It's light as a pigeon feather. And cold as ice. It burns a hole through the meat of his palm.

What you holding is a piece of his head. Albert Wilkes's skull the police blowed a hole in and scattered all over the living room.

I had to clean up after they was gone. They rolled Albert Wilkes in a blanket and carried him off. One run a rag or something over the real wet place and run it once down the piano keys. Looked like he didn't even want to do that much. Somebody probably told him he had to so he sopped up the wettest spot and wiped a little here and there with a frown on his face. Used Albert Wilkes's coat to mop the floor. They shot it clean off him. It was laying in a heap beside Albert, and the flunky stuck his toe in it and scrubbed it around after they moved Albert Wilkes off the floor. Held it down with his boot and ripped off a sleeve or something and ran it over the keys and made a little tinkle of music. He smiled then like he'd done something special and threw the rag down and followed the rest out the door. That's all the straightening up they done behind the mess they made. Except one dog stomped down Albert Wilkes's black hat. And oh yeah. They picked old Mrs. Tate off the floor and slung her upstairs. Poor thing didn't know what to think with all them police crowded round her. Sometimes I believe she thinks they put her in jail and she ain't allowed to move. Wouldn't move now unless me and Brother move her. Sometimes I think that's what's wrong with her. Poor thing thinks she's locked in jail.

So cleaning up was on me. I had to do it. Get up all that pretty glass from the door they busted in. Purple glass and green glass and yellow and blue. Pretty as a church window. Had to sweep and mop. Started to save a hunk of bullet. Didn't even know what it was at first, mashed up and everything. Thought bullets supposed to be pointy-nosed and long like sharks so I didn't recognize it at first when one slid up in the dustpan. Sent another one rattling out in the hallway when I swiped the broom under the lamp table. But I didn't keep none of it. No bullets, no little diamonds of colored glass. Just this piece of Albert Wilkes's headbone they shot away.

Carl knows it's just a seashell sliver, and she's trying to scare him. Like she does when she creeps up and hollers boo. Testing his manhood. The heat he feels is not in his palm but on the back of his hand resting against her thigh. Fast womanish heat from between her legs and he can feel it throbbing, follow its path, red and pushy like an army of ants crossing the sidewalk, follow it up through his hand and arm till it's burning in his chest with the smoke thick as peanut butter cementing his mouth shut.

This the biggest piece I found. Clean just like you see. No blood. No hair. White and clean.

Well, it is something. I do admit you showed me something.

Carl stares down at the seashell. He would taste it if he had the nerve. Run his tongue over it and taste the salt. He knew better than to believe what she said. Albert Wilkes a black man like him. Bones had skin. You'd see the brown of Albert Wilkes if it was really him laying there. Both Carl's hands resting on Lucy's thigh now. He had ventured his finger closer to the white object, closer so if it was chalk the white dust would come off when he rubbed it. But he couldn't touch it and his hand had dropped short beside the other in her lap. Double heat, double-time marching in his chest. He uses both hands, one cupped beneath the other as though he needed the strength of two arms to lift the something and return it to Lucy.

She has turned away. At first he thinks she's laughing at him. Her narrow shoulders are shaking. Then she faces him again, and he sees the tears.

He was playing so beautiful, and they just busted in and killed him.

Carl half tosses, half drops the skull of Albert Wilkes as he leans too far and gets twisted up with the soft bed sinking under his shifting weight. One hand brushes her lap again trying to catch the speck of bone and the other reaches for her shoulders, and wet-eyed Lucy collapses toward him. He loses his balance, and all that matters is catching her some way so they don't bump heads or tumble off the bed.

He remembers thinking something was wrong. Like now, of all the damnedest times, he had to pee. So much happening at once. Coming out his wet clothes and peeling Lucy out hers. Skin and hair and teeth and bones and smell and blood boiling and rushing. Little Lucy so smooth, so much naked Lucy skin he doesn't know where to begin, where to stop. She's not bare like his dream. Curly hairs down there like his big sister in the bathtub. And he pats it and she lets him. Then that locomotive heating up in his gut. Like needing to pee. But pushing harder and hotter than the fullest bladder ever did. Pushing hard and hot and loud like it means to blow out his eyes and ears. If that engine keeps coming, he's going to explode and Lucy feel the egg running down her leg. Beans and cornbread having a fight. Beans and cornbread fighting to get out and he doesn't know whether to holler or fart but knows he better not pee on Lucy, knows she'll jump up and never let him touch her again if he's not grown enough to hold his water. But it's good, it's scaring the breath out his body but it's so good. Shaking his eardrums and asshole and the ends of his toes. He hears her saying so too. That coffee grinder and those jelly eggs running down her legs. He thinks of his wet school clothes on the floor. Of those big, old baggy pants and the little skimpy ones Lucy wore underneath. You peel them down with your thumbs. And she wiggles. And you squeeze both buns and hold on and it's the scare game. It's that train flying like a giant black bullet at his back. And you can't run and you can't hide and you can't stand still. And he damns Brother for grinning, for laughing as the train smashes into him and shrinks to the size of a BB and roars out again full size through the end of his joint spewing black smoke onto Lucy's belly.

But it's not black and not smoking. A little sticky whitish puddle and scattered driplets, cool to the touch as he finally tests one with the tip of a finger. Not black, not smoking and thank God, not pee.

In the Velvet Slipper at the end of a Friday afternoon, listening to the jukebox take over the room, watching Lucy return from wherever her Albert Wilkes story had carried her, Carl wonders about love and if it's always so confusing. If anybody besides him was ever so sure something was wrong before realizing how right everything really was.

Hey, Bruh.

He knows his albino pardner is behind him. Doesn't know why he knows but would bet his life Brother hovers just behind his right shoulder.

Cat. Give this cream-of-wheat motherfucker an Iron City.

The music sucking up people's quarters could kick down a door. Loud enough to drown the noise of trains crossing Homewood Avenue. Like they fighting a war to see which instrument could kill all the others. And if your horn ain't tooting loud enough you scream and holler or blow a police whistle in your microphone. Mize well snap your fingers and tap your toes. Try to ignore it and it'd tear your head off.

You don't remember that piece of paper, do you, Bruh? No reason for you to remember. It was way back. We was just kids. Raining like a dog that day but you brought it over anyway. Member you sitting at the kitchen table soaking wet. My mama was up and mad cause she found you out on the stoop all wet and had to let you come in to get dry. I was scared she knew something. Scared maybe Lucy told you and you got mad and told my mama. Didn't know what to think finding you all wet at the table first thing in the morning. Had me a real bad case of guilty conscience anyway. Seemed like everything tattling on me. Wanted to burn my clothes. Wanted to be invisible so nobody could see what I'd done. Felt like I was striped or spotted and anybody look at me know I been doing something I ain't supposed to.

Can't even hear me, can you? I'm shouting but that goddamn music's too loud. No reason for you to remember anyhow. Was between me and Lucy but she did send you with the note so you're part of it even if you don't remember. Your jacket on the back of one of those kitchen chairs and a puddle on the floor where it been dripping. And you looking like a drowned rat. And my mama mad anyway cause I got home so late from school the day before and she had already laid down the law. A whole week of nothing but straight home and doing the dishes every night and talking about the strop next time I mess up. Sure didn't expect to see you or nobody else that morning. Didn't want to see nobody neither. I remember thinking how did this fool get so wet and keep this piece of paper dry. Do you remember how you slipped it on the table soon as Mama went upstairs? Grinning and laying it down and I just knew you had to be counting the stripes and counting the spots. Still don't know just how much you knew. I carried that paper around so long it shredded up in my wallet.

Just because I showed you that bone don't make you grown-up. Don't you forget it.

ME

The note was on Big Chief tablet paper, blue lined, speckled if you looked close. Lucy used a whole sheet and printed her message in the middle. Brother was soaked, the note was dry. On the drainboard beside the sink a bowl and spoon. The waxed inner bag of the Kellogg's cornflakes hadn't been rolled down into the box. Carl'd heard his mama fussing at Brother first thing in the morning, and he'd almost turned around and tipped back up the stairs to bed. Guilt like gobs of red paint sticking to his face. Like when he forgot to go potty and tottered round bowlegged like his mama wouldn't see the mess in his pants. But he's grown now. His business, his business now.

Don't you think I don't know where you were, either.

Called that over her shoulder as she left him alone with Brother in the kitchen. Then Brother slid the note across the oilcloth.

Carl leaned against the icebox and read the note standing up, paper in one hand, his other hand on his hip. *Just like John French*, people in the family would say if they had been there to see him. *His Daddy to a T.* A big spoon in one hand, the other hand on his hip. Like John French leaning up against the icebox taking his good time eating whatever he finds, with that big wooden-handled spoon. More like a shovel than a spoon. Shoveling food out the icebox. Carl's like a picture of John French as he reads Lucy's message the morning after they made love the first time, because he needs his daddy's footprints to stand in, needs to set his jaw and suck his teeth and thrust out his hip like he's claiming space beside the icebox, and if you got good sense you'll mind your own business and leave him alone.

Brother sat hunched over the table shivering. His tan jacket hanging on a chairback was seven shades darker than usual. Puddles glistened around each of the chair's back legs. The kitchen was bright. One of Carl's jobs was to keep three bulbs burning in the fixture over the table. Brother nearly as wet as the dripping jacket but somehow he kept the note dry. Why had he grinned when he slid it cross the table?

Just because I showed you that bone don't make you grown-up. Don't you forget it.

ME

Carl slowly refolded the note, carefully letting it close along the creases already in the paper, the creases which were the first places to rip later as the paper aged in his wallet. What did Brother know? Why'd his mama throw those words back over her shoulder? He needed to read the words again. He'd forgotten them because he wasn't paying attention the first time. He'd been saying words to himself and seeing Lucy and now he couldn't get straight which words had been his, which hers. He'd been thinking of Brother's grin and telling himself his mother couldn't know a thing and thinking of how his daddy saunters into the kitchen and pokes his spoon into the icebox and then he's there, solid as a rock slouched up against the icebox but gone too, in another place. The words of the note flashed by as Carl was dreaming, and now he could recall the dream but he'd missed the words. Lucy's words were in his pocket and he couldn't take the paper out again, not with Brother sitting there ready to grin.

Were the last words of the letter, *Don't forget me?* Didn't you say that to somebody when you were leaving? When you were going away? Did she say she wanted to *give* him something or had she said *show*? A million words in the letter. Why'd he only take a minute when he needed days to read them all?

He wanted Brother gone. Rain or no rain. Just put on that jacket and go catch pneumonia if you have to. Just go. Split. Nobody told you to sit like a dummy in the rain. So get up, turkey, and . . .

But Brother was part of it now. He had splashed five blocks through the rain to deliver the note. That's why Brother was smiling. That's why the paper was dry. Brother was part of it. Would always be. The three of them together in it now. Whatever *it* was.

Carl flips Brother's jacket to an empty chair. He plops down without noticing the wet spot spreading against his backside. He leans over the note as he smooths it open on the oilcloth.

Brother. She didn't say *me*. She said *it*.

Brother nods and smiles and begins drumming the table edge. And scat sings *Oppy Doop Doop Opp*. Softly. Background music as Carl deciphers the million words. It was all right. It was the three of them now. No secrets.

In the Velvet Slipper at the end of a Friday afternoon. Listening to the jukebox filling the room, watching Lucy return from her story, wondering about love and if it's always so confusing the first time. And if there's ever more than a first time. Because it's the three of them still. Brother part of it, always part of it.

Brother beside him sipping an Iron City. Nodding, yes. Slipping his hand in his jacket pocket and fondling something out of sight. And bringing the empty hand from his pocket to his lips, grinning, kissing it. Yes.

Brother at the table that first morning after to tell Carl that Lucy could take back what she'd given. That she hadn't *given*. She had *showed* him something. She showed it to him, but it was still hers, like that piece of Albert Wilkes in the handkerchief in her drawer.

Lucy could still scare him and amaze him. Even today she could do it. Pounce from the shadows of the Tates' house and yell *Boo*. Today climbing those stairs he'd still worry about ghosts creeping up behind him. And when he came down and shut the heavy door behind him and stepped down off the Tates' porch he'd wonder if she was writing another note, if she was taking something back, if she was writing good-bye.

Another Rock, Cat. Can't you turn that mess down some?

Turn it down and in a minute I got three asking me turn it up again.

Well, who's the boss?

The ones putting in the nickels.

Used to be a nice quiet place in here.

You getting old, honey. People like it noisy now. You getting old and set in your ways.

Just might be right, Cat. Be thirty soon and wasn't worth a good god damn at twenty. You just might be right.

Carl bolts the shot glass of Seagrams Seven and wets his lips with the last of his Rolling Rock.

Scored then, Bruh? Yeah, I can see it in your eyes. Got a scoreboard in your eyes, nigger.

He'll clear his throat with a fresh Rock and then get Lucy off her stool and it'll be the three of them, the three musketeers again and they'll walk back to the room where Albert Wilkes died and shoot up and dream.

Lucy and my Uncle Carl both thirteen the first time they made love. The next time was three years later and the next seven years after that. The second time was early summer. Brother and Carl had been sent to clear the weeds from Anaydee's yard. Every year they'd cut the weeds and 725 would sprout up again. Anaydee and Uncle Bill hanging on till they're rescued again from the jungle surrounding their little house. Lucy tagged along to watch and wound up raking the stone path and weeding the patch of sunflowers whose pointy-haloed black faces nodded in front of the windowbox. Carl had taken the long-handled rusty scythe Anaydee handed through the cracked door. The sickle, which meant squatting in the sticky weeds, he passed to Brother. From his bed Uncle Bill Campbell had grunted something Carl couldn't understand, but Anaydee chirped. Your Uncle Bill says they need sharpened. Three swipes through the waist-high weeds and Carl knew the tools needed to be pitched in the garbage because he mize well beat the weeds with a club as swat them with the blunt scythe. He whipped the rusty halfmoon around again in a tree-toppling arc, his weight back on his heels, his arms taut in a Babe Ruth home run swing. The weeds leaned away, some even bent, but not one throat cut. Mize well lay down and roll over them because that's all his tool could do. Mash the weeds down a minute or two till that sticky green juice inside sprung them up again. Brother looked like he was cutting hair. Down on all fours, just about invisible except you could see the racket be was making where the tops of the weeds danced as he crawled around below. Snipping one or two or three at a time. Pulling them straight then sawing at the roots he'd slice them a hair at a time. Brother would get every weed if he stayed down there five or six years.

Carl chose a flattish, gray stone from the pile beside the house. He sat on the pile so he could sharpen the blade without the handle being in the way. He scraped up and back with the gray stone. The blade did look like the moon. Streaked, pitted. Its beveled edge chipped so it had as many teeth as a saw. How's somebody supposed to work with something like this. He stood up and pitched the scythe against the stones. Its clatter brought Lucy around the side of the house.

Mize well stomp on these weeds as try to cut them with this goddamn rusty banana.

She said sharpen it.

Ain't no sharpen in it.

Got to try. Lay it down on one of those big flat stones and then you can press hard down on it.

She must have been spying. She must have been waiting for a chance to bust in and mind his business. It's too hot to argue so he tries it her way, grinds the metal between two stones. One curved tip is crumbly and breaks off, but he scrapes enough of a cutting edge to try again and this time his first home run cut with Lucy watching topples a handful of weeds. He hacks at the rest while they're down and can't help grinning at the little cleared space and grinning at Lucy even though his back's to her.

He can't tell if she's still watching him or not. Doesn't matter because he's got her fixed, caught with the eyes in the back of his head so he can stare, can study without getting stung. Her bare arms and legs. The honey-colored skin sun-darkened now except where her shorts and sleeves begin. The skin lighter and softer in those places under her clothes she had let him see, let him touch once. The first time with Lucy crying and Albert Wilkes's skull grinning up from the bed seemed like a dream. Then the note taking everything back, then three years of remembering, of trying to tell himself it had happened, convince himself their lovemaking hadn't been a dream. How many times had he reached for Lucy, wanting to touch her the way he did on the mushy bed, wanting her hand on his, guiding him, helping him to all those places he was afraid to start after himself. He'd scheme ways to catch her alone in the big house, times when Brother was gone, when Mrs. Tate asleep like she always was. Lucy didn't seem to notice. The rocking chair became her favorite place. For rocking, for ignoring him. Once he started up the stairs by himself, nearly reached the first landing before he called down to her. Called again straddling two steps, poised, frozen, listening to the steady creaking of the rocker till his back leg got fuzzy and his jaw so tight he had to run down the steps and out the door to keep from snatching her out the chair and stomping it to pieces. He hated that chair anyway. Especially the pop of the cracked rocker, exploding like a gunshot in the silence. He'd always jump. Jump like somebody jagged him with a pin. Jump every time like some goddamn jack-in-the-box fool so Lucy'd have one more reason to laugh. One more reason to take back what she had shown him.

Crazy for six months after the first time. Was it him? Was each new pimple on his face, each spot in the crotch of his underwear driving her away? Did she know about *Doctor's Office*, spread-eagled under his mattress? Had she spied on him with his thumb in his mouth and his hand under the covers and his eyeballs sniffing the photos of the bare-tittied white ladies in *Pix?* Did she know he tried to peek under every woman's clothes? Young, old, sister, mother. No shame. Nothing but a spyglass or binoculars, looking anyplace, anytime he could. Trying to remember, to learn. Or was it her being a bitch, teasing him with this pussy business like she teased him about anything else? She was cold. She was Hard-Hearted-Hannah, pour water on a drowning man. Only she'd pee on him. Those baggy corduroy drawers pulled down and then the skimpy, silky ones and her perfect little buns, honey-colored, bright and creamier than the sun-toasted rest would hang there, bare and perfect and fringed with curly hairs and he'd reach out like he did before but they'd disappear, his dream wasn't strong enough to keep them still, they'd be hanging out bare to the world and he'd grab for them but they'd wiggle away and it'd be just like she was squatting to do something nasty on him.

When the scythe banged against one of the rocks Bill Campbell had missed in the yard of 725, the blade flew off the handle and buried itself in the ground. Carl had been chopping weeds an hour, hypnotized by the motion, by the hot sun on his naked back. Lucy was somewhere watching he was sure. He didn't want to see her sitting cross-legged in the weeds. Little Miss Muffet on that warm, soft tuffet, her long legs bare in the itchy grass. Sweat on her honey skin sweet as lemonade. Not like the sewer water rolling down his gritty back. Not like the boogery rolls inside his elbows where the sweat collected. After a while he'd forced himself to stop remembering the first time. That or go crazy. But the heat, the sweat, the singsong sway of his arms mowing weeds, the dream of Lucy naked on the bed, her quiet presence in the background, sitting cross-legged, plucking weeds from between the stepping-stones, digging in the flowerbox at the window, weeding the patch of lolly-headed sunflowers brought the first time back. As he hacked the iron-necked weeds it was *she loves me, she loves me not,* one then the other carved by the blade swinging back and forth through its arc. His arms swung faster and the words got closer together. She loves me, she loves me not. If his arms whipped a little faster he could be in both places at once, lovemelovenot one ripple of sound, always yes and always no. Loving me and not loving me all one word. The Lucy he kills on a downstroke made whole again as the pendulum rises. Faster and faster till he hears his mother's warning *Youall be careful over there,* hears it drowned by the clang of the blade on an unseen rock. He hears his mother's voice at the same instant he realizes it's not sweat running down his ankle.

They go to the Tates' not because it's closer but because Lucy hovers beside him and inspects the gash and takes his hand and leads him to Tioga Street, then up the steps, across the porch, up to the second floor, past the bedroom where Mrs. Tate has only a few more years of her sentence to serve, the room where Mr. Tate used to talk into the mirror while he undressed, speaking to the picture of his wife curled under the covers, saying things like, How's my p . . . p . . . p . . . Pretty little pu . . . pu . . . pu . . . Pussy-in-the-Well while he unbuttons his shirt, tipping past the silence and darkness which seeps from under the Tates' closed door to Lucy's bedroom where they had made love the first time three years before. Carl wonders if he's left a trail of blood spotting the floor, wonders why she is loosening his belt and pulling down his pants to get at the cut she could easily reach by rolling up his trouser leg.

Oh, didn't he ramble. Before they make love the third time, Carl will travel round the world. On Okinawa he'll push stacks of dead Japanese marines over the edge of a cliff into the sea with the blade of his bulldozer. He'll carry dead GI's back across the beaches into the ships which had sailed them across the sea to die on that bloody island. He gains thirty pounds, broadens in the shoulders, and his skin gets as tanned as any of the red-bone Frenches ever get. His hunger for Lucy grows stronger, deeper as he learns the bodies of other women. All the sizes, shapes, and colors he'd been trying to imagine so many years led him right back to where he started. In the same space of years I'm born. Carl's sister Lizabeth's first child. John French's first grandson. John French my first daddy because Lizabeth's husband away in the war. By the time Carl and my father returned from the Pacific, I was big enough to empty the spittoon which sat beside Daddy John French's chair. Grown enough for that chore and for opening the yellow string of his pouch of Five Brothers tobacco when I sat on his knee.

Soon after Carl returned home Brother Tate caught me by my arm and tucked me into his chest and named me *Doot*, one of the scat sounds Brother talked with instead of using words. After the war Lucy spent lots of time in my grandmother's house on Cassina Way. Not as much as Brother who seemed to be around always, but I remember her from those days. Her eyes mostly. The teasing, sparkly eyes no one warned me away from but which I knew instinctively were more dangerous than steep basement steps and sharp knives and hot ovens and matches.

I remember. Partly because I was there in my grandmother's house, partly because I've heard the stories of Cassina Way a hundred times.

My grandfather's brown hat rests in the top of my cupboard. A sweat-blackened ring separates the high crown from the brim. The edging of the brim has worn away, leaving the cloth tattered in places. A mud-colored hat, soft as felt where dried sweat hasn't turned it brittle. A souvenir of John French. Like his razor strop my Aunt Geral keeps, hanging in her bathroom. Geral saved the hat and gave it to me. I don't know what to do with it. Clean it up? Get a fancy, feathered band to hide the stains at the base of the crown? Could the hat be cleaned, could somebody mend it without destroying it? Should I consider wearing it? Would John French like the idea of his hat reborn, his grandson wearing his swagger, his country-boy, city-boy lid? Damned if I know what to do with it. And leaving it sitting in the top of a closet is no answer. I can't decide what to do with the hat because it's not mine. John French dead twenty-five years now but his claim on the hat so strong I still can't touch it without looking over my shoulder and asking him if it's all right.

The stories of Cassina Way sit like that. Timeless, intimidating, fragile.

My Uncle Carl turns on his barstool. Doot. Doodledoot Doot. Sitting up here grown as I am. You ain't supposed to be grown yet. And got the nerve to have children calling me Uncle Carl just like you was doing yesterday. Yesterday. My, my. That's all it seems sometimes. Just yesterday you was a baby and we was all over there on Cassina Way. Brother named you Doot while we was still on Cassina.

At the kitchen table. With the checkered oilcloth.

Yessiree. He sure did. At that very table. Seems like yesterday.

Shut up about yesterday, man. You starting to sound like Methuselah's granddaddy. Whole lotta yesterdays since this nephew of yours been a baby. How old you now, Doot? I know you got to be pushing thirty.

Thirty next June.

Shoot. You ain't even started the prime of life yet. You still a baby.

Who's talking old now?

I know just exactly how old I am, Mr. French. To the minute.

Bet you do. To the second, probably. Cause you was there directing traffic, wasn't you? Looked at your watch and told them Miss Lucy Tate's ready to be born.

Know how old I am and know I ain't old enough to be sitting around sighing about yesterday this and yesterday that. That's old people talk. Sighing and going on about the good old yesterdays.

Brains turning to cream of wheat when you start talking like that.

Wasn't talking to you in the first place. I was addressing my nephew here before you butted in. In the second place you got what you half heard all twisted around. What I said didn't have nothing to do with old.

What's it got to do with then?

Just the opposite.

Opposite of what?

Yesterday.

You talking in circles.

That's right. Cause that's the way the world turns. Circles and circles and circles inside circles. Don't you understand nothing, woman? Doot don't make me feel old. Don't make me feel young neither, sitting there with children when I remember him in diapers. Point is I can see him back then just as plain as I see him now and it don't make no difference. Just a circle going round and round so you getting closer while you getting further away and further while you getting closer.

You understand that, Doot? Doot's a college man and I bet he don't understand that mess you're talking any better than I do.

Well, if people minded they own business they might give other people a chance to mind theirs.

He's always talking about yesterday this and yesterday that. If that ain't getting old, I don't know what is.

Told you once and I'll tell you again. Yesterday ain't got nothing to do with it. Boy, don't ever try and talk sense with a hardheaded woman. And they all of em got hard heads, Doot.

Go on with that mess. Only sense you got is the sense good women knocked into your thick skull and your nephew don't want to see me going upside your head, so just hush and tell him some more about Brother like he asked you in the first place. Your Uncle Carl getting senile. Poor thing begins a sentence then gets way off, you got to remind him to finish what he started.

I'm getting to Brother. Like I was saying it was in the house on Cassina Way before we moved to Finance and Lucy was teaching you to dance. You was a cute puppy then. Lucy saw you patting your foot to the Victrola and leaned over and took you by the hands. She pulled you on your feet and started swaying you to the music, side to side, but you jerked away. Wanted to do your own thing. She got you moving but she had to turn you loose. I cracked up. Everybody did. Hardly big as a minute and out there dancing by yourself. Count Basie playing. Basie with Jimmy Rushing on vocal. Think that's what it was. A new record Lucy brought to play on the Victrola Daddy and Strayhorn found. I remember that Victrola from when I was little, and it was still sounding good the night you got up to dance.

Daddy in his big chair with his big feet stretched out to the fireplace. Couldn't get out the room without tripping over his feet. Like a gate snoring in his chair. He wasn't really asleep. Just heavy on that wine, so he looked like he was sleep but he was just nodding. Didn't miss a thing. He slapped his knee and got to laughing when he saw you cut your little steps. Just about fell out that chair laughing, and the next minute he's nodding again. Brother scatting with the music like he always did. Everybody feeling good. Good music. Good times. Homewood was jumping. Lots of war work, so people had a little change in they pockets. Homewood different then. Hadn't turned ugly the way it is now. I mean now you take your life in your hands just walking down the street after dark. It was different in those days. No dope. No hoodlums prowling around looking for a throat to cut.

Yeah . . . I believe it was Basie with Jimmy Rushing. Lucy loved Jimmy Rushing. She loved you too. On your fat little bowlegs trying to get down. We were tight in those days. Me and Brother and Lucy. Called us the three musketeers. We did everything together, everything we were big and bad enough to do. Homewood was something then. Almost married Lucy. But didn't seem no point to it. Couldna been no closer.

Brother would have been your brother-in-law.

Brother-in-law Brother. Does sound kinda funny. That'd make him something to you too. Some kind of uncle-in-law or cousin or something.

Carl pats the empty stool beside him. The red vinyl cover is puckered by the shadow of Lucy's weight. Carl nods his head toward the ladies room door.

Make her your aunt.

Did Lucy really push Brother around in a baby carriage?

439

Rolled him around till wasn't nothing left but wheels and wire. That's what they say. She used to get mad when anybody'd tease her about it. Said it was serious business. Kept the top down so the sun wouldn't hurt his white skin. Just little doses at a time. That girl always had strange notions. Still does. Don't know why I didn't marry her. Still might. Cept now with Brother gone . . . with him out the picture, the picture ain't quite right. I mean living married together without Brother make us both think more about him. Like we had a baby once and lost it and see it every time we look at each other. We'd always be remembering what we once had. You know what I mean?

Carl. Why do you think he killed himself?

They kill everything.

But didn't Brother kill himself?

Found Brother dead on the tracks. Wasn't no blood so he was dead before the train hit him. It was something else or somebody else killed him, killed him just like they killing everything worth a good goddamn in Homewood.

They hear Lucy fussing all the way back to her stool: Bathroom's a pigpen. Just wait till I see that Conkoline head L. T. Riding his fat behind round in a Coup De Ville but can't pay nobody a quarter to keep the ladies room clean.

Lucy plops into the shadow she'd left. She makes herself mad at L. T. like she made herself mad at her hair in the cloudy bathroom mirror. A plucked chicken. Woody the Woodpecker. She thought she'd combed an upsweep, a neat pile leaning away from her face, soft waves brushed so they climb the topside of the pyramid. But a wild woman staring back at her from the mirror. Hair shooting every whichway. Mad anyway at the dirty bathroom, so she let herself get madder and didn't have to think about Brother. Who was everywhere. In the mirror. The music. In her hands smoothing the skin of her face while she stood in the tiny bathroom wondering where the time had gone. She didn't want to hear Carl's stories. Yet as soon as he began one she needed to get her two cents in. Help him say what she didn't want to hear. Brother was gone. Long gone. Past tears. Past the silly pause when her fingers wrap around the front doorknob and she thinks she feels warmth in the metal, the print of his hand so when she turns it and opens the door he'll be there in the wingback chair grinning at her.

Are you saying Brother could talk if he wanted to? How could he just stop speaking? I always thought he had some kind of handicap or deficiency.

He was ugly. That's for damn sure. And he loved sweet wine. But if drinking wine or being ugly's a crime half of Homewood be behind bars.

Did he talk to you?

Now you know better than to ask that. You know how tight we were.

I mean actual talk. Not scat sounds or gestures. Actual words.

He named you Doot.

That's a noise.

It's your name. Stuck all these years, ain't it?

But sixteen years. Not a word in sixteen years?

You listening but you ain't hearing, Doot. You keep asking the same question and getting the same answer. That what they teach you in college? Brother said what he needed to say in his own way. Be messing round in what everybody called the Bums' Forest, you know, over there beside the tracks before you get to the park. Course you know. Brother'd cut a fool for the winos and they'd hee haw and egg him on. Think he was feebleminded and whatnot him being albino. Give him wine even though he was a kid like me. Brother loved sweet wine, and all the time they laughing at his monkey-shines he's sucking up that wine and laughing at them. I could tell you a hundred ways Brother got over. Didn't need words. People thought he didn't have good sense cause he was white and didn't talk much. Well, Brother had more sense than any five these Negroes sitting around here in the Velvet Slipper put together.

How old was he when he stopped?

Like I said he never did talk much. Week go by and then he'd say something to me and I'd think *Damn*, been a week since the nigger's opened his mouth. Bout twenty-six when he stopped altogether. Just after the war. Right around in there people started to notice and say Brother don't talk. Twenty-six cause it was right after what we used to call his birthday. Didn't know his real birthday. Brother never had one till Lucy said let's say January first.

New Year's Day. Everybody needs a birthday so let's say Brother's is the first day of the new year. Brother least a couple years older than us even though Lucy called him her little brother. She had her own way of counting, but I know Brother had a few years on me. Brother about twenty-one that first time he played at the Elks. Make him round twenty-six when he stopped talking. Started playing like he been playing pianos all his life. Scared me, too. Like the music just moved in. Like Brother just reached out his hand and the music was there. Ain't heard nothing like it before or since. Then he stopped. Sudden as he started, he stopped. Stopped playing and talking both, right after the war.

Same year Junebug burnt up.

Lucy says the helping words. Can't stop herself even though she knows where they lead. She bites her tongue, but it's too late. Carl's heard and Junebug's story begins to open. Like a fan, she thinks. One of those tissue-paper and stick fans from Murphy's Five and Dime all folded so you can't see what's inside, but you roll off the gumband and spread the sticks and it's sunsets and rainbows and peacock tails. A fan she thinks listening to Carl lean on the helping words and begin to tell his nephew about Junebug. She knows already what the fan will look like, what's painted inside when the creases open and the picture hangs like a broken wing, before the dust-colored tissue rips and the bones snap one by one in the wind.

Poor little thing. You must of heard of Junebug. One of Samantha's children. Sam who lived back of Albion on Cassina Way. You heard of Crazy Sam. The one with all the children. They had to take her to Mayview. Little Junebug got burnt up on the Fourth of July. People say that's what pushed Sam over the line. She had a whole bunch of kids in that shack on Cassina. Must of been ten children and Samantha no more than twenty-five, twenty-six years old. A good-looking woman too. Long dark hair and coal black. Kind of girl with that velvety smooth skin. When I hear of beautiful African queens, Samantha comes to mind. She's the image. Black and comely. You know what I mean. Ninety-nine and forty-four one hundredths percent black. Yes indeed. Ivory snow black. You could set a glass of Chivas on top her head and go on about your business and come back a hour later not a drop be spilled.

Long-legged, straightbacked, tall-walking woman. All them babies and she still looked like a sixteen-year-old girl. Walk by her yard and see them all in there you couldn't tell mama from the kids. All them kids black and beautiful like Sam. Except Junebug.

Carl's voice gets busy telling the story his way. A big man. Pale like all the Frenches. More like his daddy every day, she's heard Lizabeth or Geral or Martha say a million times. His belly pouts. She used to sit with Carl in Westinghouse Park and watch the young girls and boys courting. In spring when the leaves were coming back and the brown grass turning green again. They liked to spend those first few fine days together, days when you knew you could go outside without a jacket or sweater and toast on a bench in the park even though the ground still mushy from the last snowfall. Spring getting warmer and better till the park lit up like a garden, and Lucy would sit with Carl watching the squirrels and the kids acting like squirrels, giggly and teasing or suddenly quiet and checking out everything around them before pairing off arm in arm for a stroll around the path circling the park. Carl'd say, Be a watermelon up under that one's dress by summer. Lucy would shush him and think of squirrels and say they're just kids, just playing around. In October when the leaves turning and starting to pile up on the grass and the paths, he'd say I told you so when one the little spindle-legged, pigtailed girls shuffles by in an old lady's dress with the belly poked out. A watermelon under there is how Carl looked now. His middle a tub for all that Rolling Rock and Iron City he can't do without. She thinks of her man's smile and soft, pale hands. They say his daddy, John French, was a gentle man. A loving, generous man in his big hat and grizzly bear shuffle down Homewood Avenue. Under the edge of the bar, in the shadows, her man's heavy thighs flapping like wings. When he gets excited some part of his body always shows it. Not his eyes or his voice. A part hidden like his long thighs under the edge of the bar. Or a part you don't pay attention to unless you're looking for the telltale sign of something riling him, exciting him. Fingers drumming on the table. One hand worrying the other. Her big man with the pillow under his Hawaiian shirt. They may be kids he'd say and they may be playing but you watch, wagging his head and batting his curly French eyes at me, you watch and see if that

443

little thing don't turn up wearing a housedress and slippers and watermelon by fall.

He's settled back now. Into Junebug's story now. She knows without hearing what he must be saying. The parts unfolding like a fan. Sharp creases and inside them, the sad gray story. Couldn't hear if she wanted to. Doot between them, the music booming, rocking the Velvet Slipper. She sees enough on Doot's face. Reads the words plain as day. He's browner than his uncle but French is there in his bones, in his eyes. Brother named him Doot. Now he wants to name Brother. She'll leave Carl's story alone. He doesn't need her helping words, her amens, her reminders of dates, of names. She's telling it to herself. Her way:

For some reason Junebug's story must begin with water. With getting clean in the Tates' giant, clawfoot tub.

Albert Wilkes is hot and mad. He's on his knees and the floor is wet, but he'd rather get wet on his knees than bend over to reach into the soapy tub. Funny how those piano-playing hands, those long smooth fingers begin her story not where they should be, not on the keys playing the blues or like she heard them that last time in the living room, playing sweet sweet before the cops blew him away. No. Albert's in an undershirt. Albert Wilkes wearing suds up to his elbows and got a washrag in his hands scrubbing her back. Standing in the tub she's as tall as him. He's too wide to be so short. Must have little midget legs or no legs at all like the bearded man she saw that time who lives on a board with wheels and scoots himself with long arms pushing on the pavement scooting faster than she can run because in her dream she knows he's going to catch her. Those growling skate wheels rolling up behind her and his long arms punching the street and his nasty breath each time he rows his arms *uhhh uhhh* closer and closer she can feel it explode hot and puky in her ear. Albert Wilkes's bare arms and sweaty face and mad eyes because bathing Brother like trying to wash a cat. Catching Brother and scrubbing him like trying to hold a bar of slithery soap. Brother looks like soap. The good kind they have sometimes. White and lean and sweet smelling. But Brother's a skunk. Won't hold still and nobody likes the job so he can go a week before Mrs. Tate gets tired of smelling him and goes to the

living room and catches Albert Wilkes at the piano and hands him
a washrag and a bar of soap.

Lucy stands so her butt and everything above it hits the air,
and she shivers even though Albert Wilkes is sweating. Then he
rubs her with his piano-playing hands and wrings hot washrags
full of water down her back to rinse the soap and does it again
and pats her drier with the balled-up washrag and picks her up
and sets her down wrapped in a big towel. She shivers again, a
warm, cuddly shiver this time because all the heat of the bath water
is under the towel with her. Behind her, Albert Wilkes goddamns
Brother again and it's a fight again like the time Mr. Tate bought
live chickens and tried to kill one himself Sunday morning behind
the locked bathroom door. Tried to slit its throat with his straight
razor for Sunday dinner and a storm of squawking and flapping
and cussing and then not a sound. Quiet as a grave and we thought
the chicken had won and me and Brother scared to open the door.
Old Mr. Tate was just catching his breath and the chicken getting
hisself together too because they started up fighting again. I swear
you could hear that razor slashing and feathers and blood flying
all over the place. We ate that bird but he sure didn't die easy,
and Mr. Tate sold the rest of the live chickens. Sounded like that
behind her, and she was scared to look till she heard the stopper
come out and the water start to gurgle down. Saw blood for a
minute all over the front of Albert Wilkes's undershirt and soaking his knees. Dark like blood for a minute like Mr. Tate when
he came through the bathroom door and you still didn't know if
him or the chicken had won, if him or the chicken doing the bleeding. Just water though on Albert Wilkes and Brother wrapped in
a towel matching hers.

Her story started like that. When she thought of Junebug she
thought of Brother when Brother was little. Albert Wilkes bathing them because Mrs. Tate too feeble and tired of smelling skunk
so she trapped Wilkes at the piano and how's he gon say no sitting
up there in the Tates' house like he owned it and owned the piano
he was playing. Mrs. Tate probably said *Please*. Cause that's the
way she was. Nice to everybody. Wouldn't step on a roach unless
she caught it in the act. Didn't blame nothing on nobody just let

anybody come and go as they please so she'd probably ask him with her eyes and hold out the soap and rag and say, Sorry to interrupt your playing Mr. Albert but could you please do something with that stinky boy? She thought of Junebug then thought of Brother then Albert Wilkes kneeling over the tub and his piano hands scrubbing her and then she'd see Samantha. To tell Junebug's story you had to be Samantha and it's wintertime and you shiver at the thought of being naked. In a bathtub or anyplace else. Even the thought of your bare skin under the piles of clothes you wrap around yourself is enough to make your teeth chatter. Wind twists up the winding driveway to the gray building on top of the hill. Always a Sunday when she visited Samantha. The bus left you off at the bottom of the hill. Many a time she almost begged, Please Mister Driver, get me a little closer. Just halfway up the hill if you can't make it to the top. On cold, windy days she just about opened her mouth and said what she was crying inside. A little head start up the steep hill, cobblestoned just like Cassina Way. She could imagine the tires sliding and popping up the broken road. The snarl of the engine finding a gear to pull it to the top. And pretend she was inside, warm, watching out her window as Mayview loomed closer. Not so much a feeling of riding up as it was the sensation of watching the building sink, the whole gray mess settling slowly in the ocean or a river and her standing on the banks a witness. As she set down one foot after the other up the steep hill and the wind scratched at her face and tore at her clothes, she'd dream of riding, of arriving at the gate warm, her cheeks flushed from the one gust of wind she didn't mind smacking her as she scurried down from the bus to the curb and through the gate.

You had to be Samantha to understand. Sometimes Lucy thought that's what the visits were about. Being Samantha. That's why they had Mayview for crazy people like they had Highland Park Zoo for wild animals. You go to remind yourself you're not one of them. You go to see the bars that keep them in and you out. You need to make sure the bars are still there so you get as close as you can. You like the cages which are nearly invisible but you also like the low stone walls and the iron bars spaced almost wide enough for you to wiggle through because you can tease yourself, think about what would happen if you jumped over or squeezed in.

If you are Samantha you're waiting for Lucy. You know Lucy is on her way. Staring through the screened window which chops the world into little steel-framed cells you can see Lucy struggling up the hill. A scarecrow leaning into the wind. Shuffling one foot after the other on the frozen pavement like she just might not make it, like she doesn't want to make it to the crest of the hill and the heavy doors and the barred gate inside. If you are Samantha every day is the same and you pace back and forth in the emptiness of your room wondering where they are taking you, why the journey's so long. Nothing changes outside your window, just night to day and day to night and the seasons giving way one to the other just as monotonously, as grayly as dawn to dusk. There are days longer than seasons, days the color of the sky before snow, a blind white heaviness weighing on her skin, a prolonged stare she can't escape unless she smashes something the way she smashes the prying eyes of clocks. But she can't make a fist, let alone gather strength to drive it against the spying light. Days like that longer than seasons, and seasons flash by quicker than days. The pills they feed her could steal a whole summer or spring. Now I lay me down . . . and black dreamless oblivion till she awakens to find the wind howling and the snow driven in slants across the bars and then she catches movement, an ant crawling along the snow-packed sill or an intruder farther away, down the steep hill, inching its way raggedy and black against the swirling whiteness of gusting sheets of snow.

Lucy Tate trudging up the hill like she's bearing her cross and toting one for everybody else in Homewood on her scarecrow shoulders.

What you doing out there in all that mess?

Samantha watches for days, pacing, waiting for a sign of land, some humpbacked silhouette of island and trees to crop out of the mist, to break the monotonous ripple of gray sea.

Once, when she was blue-eyed and fair as once-upon-a-time and a golden braid wound like the tiers of a wedding cake atop her head she dreamed of a sailor calling to her, his voice bobbing clear as a bell: *Come Down. Come Down.* His voice curling through the iron bars of her tower's one round window. Let down your golden hair. Unfurling it in rippling bands, a golden snake thicker than her waist she fed it through the bars hand over hand, its silky weight plummeting through the emptiness to meet his song.

Lucy Tate bringing news and buttermints. What's she got to say I don't know already with her busy self stumbling like a roach got that Kills-em-Dead powder sticking to his legs? Carry that dust home on all eight feet and kill the rest his family he so busy bringing home the news of the day.

Lucy. Lucy Tate. You hear me, girl? Don't be coming up here bothering me, girl. I know he's dead. Knew before you and anybody else. Course he's dead. Been a ghost since I been knowing him. Ain't never been nothing but a ghost. So you crazy to love him and crazy if you think you lost him cause he ain't never been nothing but a ghost. Never been live in the first place so don't be coming up here bothering me and trying to make me feel bad. Ain't crying for no ghost. No tears left for nothing. Just go on back where you come from.

Once she had seen a tree outside her window, a tree with leaves flashing bright as mirrors. It was taller than Mayview. Samantha couldn't see the top and she was on the top floor, so the tree must be higher than the roof. You couldn't look long at it. All those mirrors turning and flashing burn out your eyes if you didn't squint and didn't turn away real quick. And the mirrors kind of banged a little bit into each other so they tinkled like the wind chimes Carl French brought back from the war. The chimes used to be on the French front porch and once she went as far as the steps with Brother but didn't go inside, didn't want to be away from her children too long so she said They're pretty and said Let's go back now, and Brother nodded and smiled and she could hear the chimes as they walked back to her house and the chimes made her think of faraway places like Okinawa where Brother's friend had been a soldier and paper houses and warm, sea breezes and giant flowers and tiny birds. The rectangles of cloudy glass were etched with black markings. Japanese writing, she thought, a message if I could read the designs, a message dangling from strings so the glass squares bumped and sang and she remembered Brother's skin that day.

How you could almost see through it like you could almost see through the chiming glass squares. You see nothing for so long, for days and years longer than you ever thought you'd live, just the gray, nodding sea, but then for no reason you'll ever understand or try to understand, one day a tree grows up like Jack's beanstalk outside your window and dazzles you with its leaves flashing like mirrors. And next day it's gone.

Samantha. Brother's dead. He won't be coming to see you anymore. He's gone, Samantha. Do you understand?

Samantha, Samantha, let down your golden hair.

And she presses her head against the window and lets her braid fall through the bars. But it's not golden. Not syrupy sunshine. It's her black nappy wool plaited into a hundred pigtails and the bars dig into her skull and she hears the scrape of a match against the stone and her hair twisting like a vine around the walls of the tower begins to burn. Black worms dancing and howling. Then the fire is inside. Raging, consuming the bones. She is hollow as moonlight. *Please. Please.* A voice calling again. Pleading again. Fire climbs hand over hand and the skin of her face is peeled by flames. Her lover moans. He cannot touch the burning twigs of hair. Ashes in her mouth. Fire licks between the bars.

Do you understand, Samantha?

Silly Lucy Tate reaches out to touch her. Same fingers she uses to pick her nose and wipe her ass. Naked. Her fat mittens buried under the heap in the chair. You could kiss the hand or bite it while it hangs there naked, dripping snow from bloody fingertips. Sam shrinks away. Lucy's touch would be like ice. Bringing the cold, the news to her warm room.

Pipes gurgle and clank. Something hisses through them. Rushing like seawater against the sides of the ship. Metal sighs and hiccups again, and Samantha can't help laughing out loud. She points at the radiator and giggles. Somebody's guts frozen and painted pea green like the walls. Maybe hers, maybe anybody's insides stolen, standing in the corner belching and farting. Somebody's loop de loop pig gut. Somebody's dark cave filled with air. Sometimes she couldn't help farting when she fucked. Nobody but Brother ever thought her farts were funny.

Sam.

Lucy don't think it's funny. Lucy stares down at her own silly feet in silly rubber baby booties. Wet. Lucy studies the bars. The mountain peaks of ocean splashing the top of the tower.

No one comes to see me. No one asks me to dance.

Lucy stares at the gray sea. Hardly in the room five minutes and she's forgetting Samantha already. Already scheming ways to slip through the iron bars. If Samantha could, she'd help you escape. But ain't no way out. Years on this same slow, gray trip. Nothing changes. Brother dies again and again. And you keep coming up that hill to make Sam cry. They gave me pennies for my eyes. Doctor raised his Klu Klux hood so I could see his pink face when he talked. You take these, the dirty peckerwood said. Once a day. Every day. You lay them on your eyes and count pigeons till you fall asleep. Pennies heavy as this building. He had yellow ga-ga on his crooked teeth and had the nerve to be smiling, called hisself smiling when he handed them pennies to me. For your eyes. For your eyes. Like I couldn't hear the first time so he said it twice. For your eyes and dropped them in my hand but Sam ain't all kinds of fool. She crazy as a bedbug but she ain't everybody's fool. So soon's he turned his back I popped them nasties down the toilet. Ain't about to lay up here with them pennies on my eyes. No indeed. Can't tell where they been. People suck on money. Don't know what they hands been doing just before they touch it and give it to you. You should be shamed treating Sam like a child. Saying the same simple thing over and over when she already knows. Knew before any youall.

Knew he was a ghost first time he come to my door.

He stands in the doorway. A white blackman. He watches her dance. Kids out in the yard playing so she's dancing alone, humming a song her feet follow. She'd never seen a ghost before. Brother Tate had passed her a hundred times on the street and he was part of Homewood like the storefronts and trees, but in her doorway the albino was different. She knew his name and knew he didn't talk much. She'd heard people say he was feebleminded and crazy. Nothing she'd heard or seen accounted for him standing silent as the moon grinning in her doorway. If she looked away he'd be gone so she smiled back at him and beckoned him into her dance.

I'm dancing. I like to dance.

She stopped humming. The music only in her feet now, in her head, but she knew he could hear it.

When the kids outside playing I dance a lot. Dance with them too. Got a little raggedy Victrola. They wear out my records. Some of them fast rascals already dancing better than me. Put me to shame.

She stares at him. He was white, a color she hated, yet nigger, the blackest, purest kind stamped his features. The thick lips, the broad flaring wings of his nose. Hooded eyes with lashes clinging like blond ash.

Hey, white man. You come to stay awhile or you just going to stand there peeking.

He steps past her into the shanty. Cinnamon and bananas. A hint of sour wine. Then he takes his time sniffing around, the way a dog checks out a bush, little mincing, wary steps, poking his nose up and under and around, skittish and taking-over at the same time. She watches his narrow back. He'll disappear if she blinks. He turns, grinning at her again. She wonders why the kids aren't lined up at the door, why they don't swarm and buzz and follow him like they always do when a stranger crosses the yard.

You like my place? Don't allow just anybody in. Smells nice in here don't it? Baby stink and talcum powder and sweet milk. We're crowded in here. Eight bodies in this kennel. Barely room for all us to lay down at the same time. Spoon fashion. That's how we sleep. Have you heard of loose packers and tight packers, white man? Don't matter. But you mize well know before you get any closer. I'm a tight packer. Yes, Lawd. Going to build shelves round the wall after there ain't no more room on the floor. Build me some sleeping shelves around the wall and make a perfect black body for each one. Might lose some. No way round that. Some have to die. Ain't never enough food to go round here, but the strong will survive. When this old Ark docks be whole lotta strong niggers clamber out on the Promised Land.

What you think of that, Mr. White Blackman.

He takes her by the wrist. His grip is not cold, not clammy; the shudder she expected does not shake her body.

He leads her to little Becky who sits in the dirt sniffling, holding her big toe. The white man scoops up the child and carries her inside. Becky didn't fight him and Becky was evil to strangers. Her daughter didn't like anybody touching her. A snappy, mean little thing sometimes but she let the white man take her. She even snuggled into his shoulder and stopped whimpering. He sat her down on the drainboard. Becky the most private of her children, the one who shied from strangers, who'd treat her brothers and sisters like strangers, who'd rather suffer than say what's ailing her, little Becky sat wide-eyed and still while the albino seared the tip of his switchblade in the gas flame of the stove. War when she combed out that child's hair in the morning. Couldn't get her to hold still for the world, couldn't bribe her or scare her or sweet talk Rebecca. Her little iron-willed baby she almost strangled one time getting her to swallow a spoonful of castor oil, that wild child raised her ashy, black twig of a leg and let the albino slice the pink underflesh of her big toe and suck out a splinter.

He spits out the splinter and it sticks to his finger. He snarls at it and flicks it to the floor and stomps it twice. Becky's eyes never leave him. She's smiling. Tear stains like scars on her dimpled, dusty cheeks. He helps her down. Two limping steps toward the door and she bolts from the room.

You ain't no natural man come to Samantha's door, is you? You some kind of hoodoo or trickster, ain't you? Bet you'd jump right out that white skin I sprinkle some salt on you. But I ain't scared. Samantha's an educated Negro. Don't believe in youall. Buried you ghosts under tons of reading, riting and rithmetic. I'se free, ghost. I'se a free, educated disbelieving-in-ghosts enlightened colored citizen. Wouldna believed what I just saw if I hadn't seen it with my own eyes. My Becky says thank you even if you didn't hear her.

Do you know how to dance, ghost? I'm going to put on a record. Dance with my babies all the time but it's nice every once in a while dancing with a body high enough so I can rest my head on a shoulder.

He was the one kicked the door shut. She was the one locked it. Watching Lucy Tate stare out the barred window Samantha can hear both sounds. Hear the scratchy drag of the needle hiss like a match against stone before the music begins. Her door never slammed. It was too shabby. More like a wing flapping with light around the edges and light shining through the feathers. Lock was a hook and eye. You had to pull hard to make the hook reach the eye. Lift and pull and get your finger out the way quick. A tight fit. She remembered her children playing outside. Barnyard noise like geese and chickens after he kicked it shut and she hooked it tight.

Samantha slept only with the blackest men. Men black as she was because in her Ark she wanted pure African children. Then Brother at her door and in her bed that afternoon. Sure enough nigger nose and nigger lips, even nigger silence when he was finished and rolled his bones off her belly, but always that unsettling lack of color, like snow in July, and even though it felt good, part of her held back, part of her was aware it wasn't supposed to be this way. She could see through his skin. No organs inside, just a reddish kind of mist, a fog instead of heart and liver and lungs. She was afraid his white sweat would stain her body. On his knees, thrusting, he had begun to shudder and lose his seed. As he caved in on her breasts she grabbed his skinny backside. Gripping with both hands, gripping with her thighs, her shudders had spiraled into his and she thought of rivers of cool milk, of ice and snow and Ivory Flakes. But were the spasms shaking her body sent to welcome or kill what he spilled in her womb.

As soon as he left she inspected every square inch of her glossy, black skin in the piece of mirror hung on the bathroom door. Next morning with the three youngest children in tow she tramped out Hamilton Avenue to the Homewood branch of Carnegie Public Library. After setting her babies on a blanket in a corner and cutting her eyes at everyone who didn't have enough sense to mind their own business, she found the science books and pulled down the volume she needed. She moved the blanket so she could sit with one eye on her babies and one on the text and learned that:

Melanin is the brown to black pigment that colors the skin, hair and eyes. It is formed in the cytoplasm of the melanocytes by the oxidation of tyrosine catalyzed by tyrosinase, a copper containing enzyme . . . Melanocytes are derived embryologically from the neural crest. Before the third month of fetal life these cells migrate to their resting places in the skin at the

453

epidermal-dermal junction, in the eyes along the uveal tract, and in the central nervous system in the leptomeninges.

She had read to herself in the tone of voice she thought she had forgotten, the tone she would have heard if she had asked the spectacled, lemon-colored lady behind desk for help, the tone of three years at Fisk when she had believed crossing *t*'s and dotting *i*'s had something to do with becoming a human being and blackness was the chaos you had to learn to whip into shape in order to be a person who counted. In that tone of voice the words meant next to nothing, because she'd buried Biology I along with all the other trappings college had prescribed to cure blackness. Why did that voice return. She knew what it had to say about color, about her children. She looked from the text down at her black babies playing on the blanket and felt ashamed. She read the words again, this time listening to their sound and dance and understood that melanocytes, the bearers of blackness, descended from royalty, from kings whose neural crest contained ostrich plumes, a lion's roar, the bright colors of jungle flowers. Even before birth, before the fetus was three months old, the wanderlust of blackness sent melanocytes migrating through the mysterious terrain of the body. Blackness seeking a resting place, a home in the transparent baby. Blackness journeying to exotic places with strange-sounding names. Settling beside railroad tracks, at crossroads, the epidermal-dermal junction. She could see boxcars rolling by. Black boys would awaken in the middle of the night to the shriek of train whistles, learn to love the trains' shuddering rhythm. Learn to hop the long freights. Blackness would come to rest in the eyes; blackness a way of seeing and being seen. Blackness crouched in the shadow of the uveal tract would be a way of being unseen. And of course blackness would keep on keeping on to the farthest frontiers. Cross mountains and prairies and seas. Boogey to the stars, to Leptomeninges, that striped, tiger-colored planet broadcasting jazz into the vast silence of the Milky Way. Blackness something to do with long journeys, and eyes, and being at the vibrating edge of things. Something royal and restless in the melanocytes. What she had known all along before she pulled down the bulky reference book and peeled back her skin.

C'mon, babies. Found what I was looking for.

Samantha lost her fear of Brother's whiteness because she also read under "Disorders of Melanin Pigmentation" what a bad case of albinism could do to people and Brother showed none of the signs, no wrinkled skin, no photophobia or astigmatism or severe defects of visual acuity. No. He was the healthy type. And anyway none of it contagious. Enough blackness in his body to counteract the runaway evil affecting his skin. Nothing in Brother to rub off on her, to transform her into one of those pinto-pony/-looking people with white patches on their faces and arms, the vitiligo and phenylketonuria which were sicknesses, wars in the body between the forces of light and darkness. She had been surprised to learn certain kinds of albinos got darker as they grew older. And that a condition the opposite of albinism turned white people black. So when the ghostly white fog crept over her body again and wrapped its arms around her again, she had no fear. She enjoyed the strangeness, the snow in July, the warmth where she had believed only coldness dwelled, her ghost-white-black man, royal and restless as the best nigger.

Then she was two again, carrying the seed her ghost lover had planted. Lucy Tate. Lucy. Hey, gal. Let me tell you how it was. How good it was getting all big tittied and big behinded and knowing one day you'll pop open like a nut and another beautiful one come rolling out. You ain't never had no babies, have you, Miss Lucy. Well, you missed something. You missed the best. Ain't nothing like it in the world. Afterwhile you get so big you feel like a boat. You stop walking and start sailing. Hips roll and steer your belly. Ain't no stepping to it. Just be floating along and things seem to get out your way. Forget about all that morning sickness and sore ankles and pains in the back. That mess comes and goes, sure it does, but gal you the best thing there is for them nine months you carrying. You the Ark. You the shuttlebus and ferryboat over Jordan.

Lucy Tate sat on the corner of the bed, and Samantha took her place by the window. A gust of wind blasted up the hill, shearing snow from car roofs and hedges and trees and drifts, then extinguishing itself against Mayview's gray flanks, against the bars outside the steel-screened window. A crack like sheets snapping on

455

a clothesline. The building seemed to stagger, to slip on the icy concrete. A roar. A groan in the concrete bowels. Snow swirl blinded the window. Samantha could see the words, could say them to herself after all these years — *tyrosinase, melanocytes.* Remember how they marched across the pages of the medical textbook but she couldn't recall the names of her babies playing on the Kinte cloth she'd spread over the library floor.

A secret to remembering what you wanted to remember and forgetting what you needed to forget. She had begun to learn the secret, and that's when they stuck her in Mayview. When they pitched her in the tower and locked it and threw away the key.

They stole her children when she began to understand the secret. They killed Junebug because he was born with the secret and was teaching it to her.

Little monkey came here in a shopping bag.

Samantha teased Brother about the caul, the gauzy web clinging to Junebug's see-through skin. Old Miss Julia Strothers, Old Mother Strothers, nurse and midwife and baby-sitter and fortune-teller, had gathered every scrap of web and wrapped them in a handkerchief and stuck them deep into her bosom.

Got to be mighty careful. This some powerful stuff, child, Ima take this veil home wit me and do what have to be done. Don't you pay no mind to what I'm doing, you just keep your eye on this little one. He got the sign. Child born with the sign. Sign writ all over this child plain as day. Watch him. Watch him real good.

They came to see the newborn. All her nameless children lining up beside the bed after Mother Strothers put away the bloody rags and combed Samantha's hair and opened the curtain separating the bed from the rest of the one-room house. Samantha watched the older ones who had seen it all many times before, tugging and nudging till each black face could see their mama and the new baby. They stared like she stared when the ghost first appeared at her door.

This your new baby brother. Come and give him a kiss. C'mere and give little Junebug some sugar.

Nobody stepped toward the bed. She watched them clasp hands. Slow motion, the oldest two first, then on down the line, around the ring, like a secret whispered into each ear, her children silently joined hands till none stood outside the circle.

It's just kids. It's just children scared by something they ain't never seen. Junebug is a warm lump against her shoulder. A part of herself drained of color, strangely aglow. Her children don't understand yet. Perhaps they can't see him. Perhaps they look through his transparent skin and see only the pillow on which she's propped his head. She lowers her gaze to his pale, wrinkled skin, his pink eyes, then stares across him to their dark faces.

C'mon youall.

But as if a secret voice has whispered another command, they all step back.

They're scared, she thinks. They're just kids and scared. Like I got a ghost in bed with me, or a little white kitten laying here.

It's your babybrother. It's little Junebug.

When they burst from the room she can't tell whether they're laughing or crying, whether the door when it flaps closed behind them is shutting them out or shutting her in.

Oh, Lucy Tate. It hurt so bad. Learned I could hate my children. Learned I could hate the white one cause the black ones hated him. I blamed him, Lucy Tate. Blamed little Junebug and cursed his white skin and his ghost daddy cause I had to make a choice. If I loved Junebug I had to hate the others when they did those terrible things to him. I had to choose, and I hated him cause he made me build a fence around myself. I had to stop loving and stop hating altogether because it was tearing me apart. One day I just backed off. Put that fence up ten feet tall around me and just watched, watched it happening. Didn't take no sides. Just cried and tended wounds and let whatever had to happen, happen. Couldn't let my feeling for Junebug spoil what I felt for all the others. Couldn't forgive them when I'd see him off in a corner by hisself, crying and them blue bruises showing through so plain on his skin.

For years, Lucy Tate. Dying inside for years. In the place meant for carrying life. Gave my black children another sister and brother. Thought that might even things. Thought they might forget. But the new ones sucked the evil at my titty. Soon's they could, they lined up against Junebug too. I talked to Brother but wasn't nothing neither of us could do. Brother come around and that make it worse. The other children got scared. They'd whip on June unmerciful soon as Brother left. And what was I supposed to do. Couldn't watch them all. Couldn't see what each one doing all the time. If I tried to keep June close by me, sooner or later he'd stray away or another one would need me all the sudden and that'd be the worst time, the times I thought they really tried to kill the child. So I just let it be. Stopped loving and hating. Junebug learned to stay off by hisself. Find a corner and play and hum that singsong way to hisself. Only sound he ever made. That singsong hum I still hear in my sleep. Play by hisself and forget the others and hope maybe the others forget him and give him a few minutes peace.

Told myself it would all be better one day. One sweet bye-and-bye day they was all gon be sorry and go to Junebug on their knees and he'd forgive them, and sweet bye and bye, things be like they used to be in Sam's Ark. Loving again. Brothers and sisters again. Some mornings I'd wake up and swear I could hear them talking to that boy and little Junebug answering and nobody studying war no more and I'd start to fling out my arms and kick off the covers and go running out in the yard and tell the world. Shout it loud as I could. Trouble don't last always. It don't last always. And all the children be laughing and dancing round me and I'd be light as a feather. That be the day I could fly if I wanted to. Me and all my children grow wings and go swooping round the world spreading the news. But then I'd hear somebody crying. And get the awful sinking hole in my heart and know I couldn't love and couldn't hate. Just crawl off my bed and watch and wait another day.

Before she told Brother Tate her dream Samantha had to tell him the facts. The facts were one thing and her dream another and she needed to tell him both but the facts first so he'd understand, so he wouldn't mix up her dream with what really happened. Because the facts were that Junebug got into the kerosene and fell into the fire and Becky screamed when she saw him burning. She told Brother Tate the facts first. His face turned to stone while he listened. Like a giant chalky stone and somebody had chipped eyes and nose and mouth in it and give it a name but it still ain't alive. Brother, she said, are you listening? Do you hear me, man? It was an accident. A terrible accident. June got in the kerosene and fell in the fire and I come running when I heard Becky scream but it was too late. Throwed myself at him. Look at my hands. My arms. I tried to beat out the fire with my bare hands but he was like a torch, a human torch and the fire like wind. I got close enough to beat it with my hands but then it blew me back. Knocked me off my feet. Poor thing gone anyway by the time I got to him. Wasn't Junebug no more when I grabbed the fire. So much going on, Brother. Kids all over the yard and I was trying to keep an eye on them and on the fire and the ribs I had soaking in a tub. I wanted it nice. It was Fourth of July and I wanted it special. Like I remembered old-time picnics when I was a kid. Plenty to eat. Everybody having a good time. So I was going all out. Had my sauce all made the night before, and stacks and stacks of neckbones and ribs. People was coming by later. Grown-ups and anybody else on Cassina smell those ribs and want to come in the yard. A real party and I was jumping to keep everything going, to make everything right for my babies. Then he got in the kerosene when I had my back turned and he fell in the fire and first thing I know Becky's screaming and Oh my God I'm tearing through the yard but it's too late. June's gone before I get to him.

That's what happened, Brother. It happened that way, but I got to tell you the dream too. Not what happened but the way I dream it. Cause if I don't tell somebody it's gon drive me crazy. Cause in the dream I'm him. I'm little Junebug. And that's what makes it so hard, Brother. I know I'm him because I'm making one of those sad little *hmm, hmmm* songs like he used to hum. That's how I know the dream is starting. Everything quiet then I'm inside his song. I'm making the song. It's burning my lips and that's how I know the dream's beginning. Same way every time. Night after night, Brother. Can't get it out my mind. Like he's telling me his side of the story so I have to listen and I'm inside. I get caught and I'm him while he sings it.

It begins and it's the Fourth of July. I'm him. I know I'm him because nobody is talking to me and I can't talk. I'm off by myself watching things happen. I smell the tub of meat. Neckbones soaking in vinegar and pepper and salt. Stones around the fire to keep it in. Big pot of beans in the fire. I get up close cause it smells good and bubbles. Up close it's hot but I like it. A hot day too. Sun way up in a clear blue sky. I got that funny color so I can't keep my shirt off very long. Got to stay covered while the others run around black and shining in their skins. Off by myself. Nobody picking at me or bothering me. Mama Sam inside. The grill leaned against the stones so the fire can lick it clean.

I see it all. Every detail of the day. Like living it all over again each time. A dream but everything seems so clear, so real I feel like it's happening all over again. But it's happening to him. To Junebug. And I'm him. When I think *Mama Sam's inside,* she is inside. She's not me. In the dream there's no Samantha unless Junebug sees her or thinks about her. Then she's not me cause I'm inside June's white skin.

You got to help me, Brother. I know you're hurt too, I know I hurt you when I sent you away. When I had to try and even things. When I gave them a sister and a brother to make up for Junebug. I had to try everything, even hurting you if I could pull things back together. If I could make this Ark ride steady again. So I did what I had to do and hurt you and lost you, and now I've lost June and I'm losing my mind. A person can only take so much. The dream begins and I'm humming his pitiful music, his lonely little song and I know I have to be him because it's the dream again, the day again, it's the Fourth of July and he wanders around, seeing this and touching that and smelling things and liking the day and nobody speaks to him, nobody pays him no mind, but he sees things happening and the singsong humming is about everything he's feeling. He ain't mad at the others. Just sad when they're ugly doing ugly things to him. I watch the others playing. I smell the barbecue sauce simmering on the stones. I feel the heat when I get close to the pot of beans. I'm warm when I think of Mama Sam. A place on top my head waits for her to pat it. The others don't listen to me, but I like that. Cause when they let me alone I can like them. I can watch them playing and be part of their games. It's noisy when the kids running all over the yard and the Victrola in the doorway up loud as it goes, but what I hear is Junebug's song because that's what's inside his head and that's where I am, where I got to be till it's all over.

Something icy splashes my back. Like being high and dizzy all the sudden. I can't breathe nothing but kerosene. I'm tasting it, it's rushing up my nose. I see it shining on my bare feet. Then hands pushing. Becky screams and I fight the hands. I wonder why anybody wants to hurt Becky. She stops the others sometimes when they're hurting me, and now she's screaming *No no no* so I fight the hands and try to turn around and help Becky cause she's in trouble. I'm twisting to find her. The stones are wet and slipping under my feet . . . I'm fighting . . .

He never made a sound. Not a mumbling word. Not a peep from that poor child's lips. So when the scream comes I know it's me. I know I'm not Junebug anymore. Junebug's gone. That's how it ends. Me screaming and him burning up.

I know better, Brother. I know it couldn't have happened that way. I know the facts. None my babies could have pushed him in the fire. None them could have splashed kerosene on Junebug. Becky screamed afterwards. Started yelling when she saw her little brother burning. I know all that. I know the facts. But when the dream begins . . . when I'm him . . .

Out the barred window the sky is blue. Same bright blue as July. Snow sparkles now where it's crusted on drifts. The wind is still. Lucy Tate's track runs up the slope, crooked like a beetle's. Lucy bringing the news of Brother's death. Puddles where her silly rubber baby booties touch the floor. What you doing on my bed? What you doing on my chair? What you doing with your mouth full my porridge? Your mouth full of old news? Stale news? Old stinky fish wrapped up in *The Black Dispatch*.

Never told Brother the other dream. Cause it was worse. It was the same but it was different because I'm not Junebug in it, I'm me. I'm nothing. I'm in the Ark and it's pitch black night and I can't sleep. I'm worrying and worrying that day it happened. It's like a bone stuck in my throat, a sickness in my belly and I turn and toss but can't get right. It's the middle of the night and ain't no clocks in the Ark just my inside time telling me I should be sleeping but I can't. I toss and turn and ain't no use pretending I'm ever gon get to sleep, so I pull on my dress over my head and pull the curtain and slip out where my kids sleeping. Don't know what I'm doing or why I'm doing it but I know I got to. I ask each one the question. I whisper real quiet so nobody hears me till it's their turn. Spoon fashion sleeping on their mats all over the floor. I tip from one to the other in the dark and whisper. Have to bend down each time and each time I stir one I get that sweet child's breath blowed up in my face. All them got long feathery lashes and all them wake up easy and go back to sleep easy after they answer. *Did you, baby? Did you, baby?* And each perfect little face answers. *Yes, Mama. Yes, Mama Sam.*

Then I know it got to be a dream cause I'm naked as a jaybird and tearing down Cassina Way, and every star in the sky is giggling and slobbering and saying *Yes Mama. Yes Mama.*

Hello Samantha.

Hello Lucy Tate.

How you feel today?

Brother's dead, ain't he? You come to tell me he's dead.

You know he's dead, Samantha. Dead seven years now.

Sky's falling.

You feel all right?

If the kids out in all this snow they better be wrapped up good. Last winter the Ark smelt like a Vicks factory. Smearing a different one's chest with Vicks Vapor Rub every night. Sometimes three or four barking at once. Sore throats and noses caked in the morning no matter what I did. Didn't get no sleep and when I did nod off a minute be smelling Vicks Vapor Rub in my dream.

Sam, I got some cards and things for you from the children. From Detroit and Chicago and Atlanta and even one from California. They sure love their Mama Sam. They don't forget you.

Niggers ought to stayed on board. Nothing out there in that Babylon. Just a howling wilderness out there. Ought to stayed on board till we got to the other side. Tried to tell em but mize well be talking to these walls. They said she's crazy. Said she ain't fit to steer no ship in a calm, let alone a storm. Fool can't even comb her nappy head or change her drawers no more. He walks around in his Klu Klux sheet talking about you got to eat if you want to get well. He say don't care how crazy you are you do that again I'll knock you down and make you lick it off the floor.

You want me to read you what the children say?

Dick and Jane went up the hill. See Spot run. See Dick run. See Jane run. See all the niggers run. Run. Run. Run. Run dog. Run cat. I got it all in this nappy head. All the books. Read more books than Carters got pills. Dick and Jane stone insane. I'm a scholar. I got the knowledge and you talking about some goddamn dog and goddamn cat. Like I don't know how dead he is. Like he didn't tell me first thing. Course he told me. Like I ain't got nothing better to do than stand here listening to you tell me what I already know. Go on off from here. Get off my boat, Lucy Tate. I'm tired. Tired of you and me and people minding my business. If they ain't got the sense to stay on board, it ain't none my fault. Ain't my problem no more. I'm tired. I'm crazy. Let me lone.

Two and a half hours getting to Mayview and back. And Samantha gone in fifteen minutes. Lucy remembered leaving the cards and two brown paper, string-tied packages at the desk on her way out. Not even a chance to read them before Sam went to pieces. Worse every time. Samantha losing the little grip she had.

Cat dumped too much water in her gin. Tastes like perfume when it's watery. No point in drinking gin it don't have that sting, those needles when you sniff it. Lucy in the Velvet Slipper now. Junebug's story over now. Yet she still felt it sticking to her. Like the bag Junebug came in. Like a thin, thin skin nobody but you could see. Like you could be one place and another at the same time, traveling in a bag of skin, like a Christmas ball hung up by a string and people see you shining and glittering but you ain't inside cause inside is somewhere else, is summer or spring, a whole world inside there with you and you can't get out and nobody gets in cause they don't even know it's there. She swallows the gin and shakes her shoulders. Should get up on her feet and wag her whole body, shake like a dog to get that skin off, those pieces of Mayview and Samantha still sticking to her. If you tell Junebug's story you have to be Samantha and you have to make that long trip. Buses and hills and barred doors and barred windows. Lucy was

463

always scared in Mayview. Afraid one of the guards would grab her and sling her in a straitjacket and lock her in a room. What would she say? How could she prove she wasn't crazy? All the crazies claimed they were sane. She'd just be one more poor fool yelling what all the rest did. If she yelled long enough and loud enough they'd put her to sleep. If she fought them they'd strap her down. No way to get out. Once they had you things only got worse. If you weren't crazy to begin with you soon would be cause that's what you were supposed to be. Wouldn't be in Mayview if you weren't.

Like ice cracking. She hears the shell coming apart. Noise of the Velvet Slipper. Carl's voice, her own words scratching at the shell, then breaking through. It's down around her ankles. It's like stepping out her drawers and into the bathtub. A shiver as she stands there naked. A split second being two places at once. She could be standing in the tub. She could be waiting for Albert Wilkes to squeeze the warm water down her back. But she's not. Her buns are shivering and they're grown-up buns and she steps out of her underwear and it crunches like eggshell when she hears herself talking.

Cat. Don't you drown my gin this time.

And Cat smiles.

Sorry, Baby. Niggers got me hopping this afternoon. Ima do you right this time.

Lucy pats Carl's shoulder, and she sees the age on him as he turns from his nephew who's grown too and how time flies. How it flies. Yes it does.

He talked your ear off yet, Doot?

Uh uh. Just sitting here taking it all in. I could listen for days. Wish I'd paid attention before. When May and the rest were telling stories.

Well, this here child's had enough of the Velvet Slipper and Bucket of Blood and all these noisy niggers this afternoon. My behind turning to sawdust on this stool. Ima go home and put my feet up soon as I finish this poison Cat poured. Youall come on over when you're finished. Don't matter how late. I'll be there. Got some pork chops you can fix up.

You ain't all bad, sugar.

Know what you can do with your *sugar*, sugar.

Told you she was mean.

Doot, you come on over when you ready. Leave this old man on his throne. Pork chops ain't good for old folks' stomachs anyhow.

Lucy drains her stubby glass and slides down from the stool. A dancer's grace. A quick poke at my uncle's ribs then her hand rests on the watermelon bulge and her fingers spread to its shape. She pats him and winks at me and starts a smile which ends as a frown when he begins to grin back.

That woman's something, ain't she. Always will be. Look at how she walks. Still like a young girl, like her head's in a cloud and she's kinda lost and don't know the way out. Look how she uses her hands. Touching folks and stopping so they can touch her. Like she's blind and got to feel her way out here. Like Bubba Smith's a piece of Braille or something and she got to run her hand up and down him to see him. Both us old now, but to me she ain't never changed. I'm still trying to figure out why she did the things she did way back when we was kids. Old as I am, she's keeping me guessing.

Been looking at Lucy nearly fifty years now and still can't even finish her picture. Started one once. Don't know where in hell the rest of my paintings got to, but I keep the one of her I started when you was little. It's at the Tates' now. In the top of a cupboard with some of Mrs. Tate's old shoe boxes. Only thing right about the picture is one cheek and one eye. Got those right but a chicken scratching in dirt coulda done better with the rest. One eye, one cheek. Should have thought to do her from the side instead of straight on.

Drew her another time too. Don't you know that crazy woman showed up in my life-drawing class when I was in art school. There I sat with my sketch pad and charcoals. Doing charcoals that day, yeah charcoals, and the model was holding poses five minutes and we supposed to sketch fast. Catch what counted and not worry about getting everything down. Well, there I was daydreaming and playing with my sticks of charcoal and thinking if bones was as easy to break as these sticks we'd be in trouble and who strolls

465

in the studio but Lucy Tate and struts up on the platform and shrugs
off her robe like she's been standing naked in front of rooms full
of white folks all her life. I didn't know whether to stand still or
run. Whether to snatch her behind off that platform or go round
slitting everybody's throat looking up there at my woman. Man,
I didn't know what to do. Same old Lucy Tate kind of brazen trick
I been dealing with all my life. Then I thought if she's got the nerve
to pose butt-naked up there, then I got the nerve to sit here and
draw her. So I did. Mashed up a couple sticks of charcoal, then
wrapped myself round one and did just what the others doing.

You know what she said when I asked her why? She said it's
good money and I wanted you to draw me and you never asked.
That's Lucy Tate for you. So I started the painting. Put up my
easel in the Tates' living room. She sat in old Mrs. Tate's creaky
rocker. That was years ago, after the war, and I ain't finished yet.
Just a eye and a cheek. People ain't easy to see. Can't see them
cause half the time they ain't all there. I mean if you look, and
look closer the way you have to do if you're trying to paint a picture, and you keep looking closer and closer, a person subject to
go all to pieces and won't be nothing there to see. That's what they
do with those microscopes. Get closer and closer and things come
apart and the tiniest bit of anything is big as the world. I mean
your skin under one them microscopes got mountains and valleys
and trees like elephant trunks growing in it. And if there's all that,
there's sure enough little-bitty people and animals living in those
mountains and valleys. Like all of Homewood ain't nothing but
a pimple on a pimple if you get far enough away and look real
close. Looking down on the city with God's eye you can't see people
in these streets, just bumpy hills and a little green here and there
for a park and maybe a drool of spit which is the rivers coming
together downtown they call the Golden Triangle.

Don't make no nevermind. I'm rambling like Lucy said. You
want to know about Brother and the dope thing. Well, it was all
us. The three musketeers. Me and Brother and Lucy. I came back
from the war a mess. Couldn't settle down. Couldn't make sense
of nothing. Like the Book says. A stranger in a strange land. That's
how I felt. Nothing seemed right. Beginning with me. I tried a
little of this and a little of that to keep myself going. Hung out

with Brother a lot and me and Lucy started getting real serious, but I couldn't shit and couldn't get off the pot neither, you know what I mean. Betwixt and between.

I'd sit myself down and try to get myself together. You know. Say this is your life, Carl French, the only one you gon git. Now what you gon do with it? What you gon be? Seemed like I could always hear somebody laughing and giggling in the background when I tried to talk to myself serious like that. But I tried anyway till I had to laugh too. I mean, what was out there? What could I do? What was I supposed to do? Finally I started remembering. Yeah. I started listening a little closer to the giggly voice. Wasn't giggling all the time. It was saying you a nigger. You a blackass splib. I started remembering and laughing too and things started getting easier.

At certain moments Carl pauses. His eyes turn inward and he's listening rather than telling his story. The words stop. Nothing moves but his vacant eyes searching somewhere for something that will help him continue his tale, complete the frozen gesture. He's telling his own story, he knows his story better than anybody else, but in the long pauses between words as he sits motionless on a barstool in the Velvet Slipper, he's waiting for a witness. A voice to say amen. Waiting for one of the long gone old folks to catch his eye and nod at him and say *Yes. Yes. You got that right, boy.*

Yeah, Doot. I started remembering what I was. But I'm not telling you nothing you don't know. Just needed to be out here in these streets awhile. Just had to look around me and remember what being a nigger meant. Didn't take too long. They got us coming and going, and it don't take too long to remember. You feel them strings pulling and get them rope burns and you remember fast. I had the GI Bill, and like I was telling you I tried some art classes at Tech. They let a few of us in school. Veterans still supposed to be heroes then, so a few of us got in college and what not, but I only know of one or two who made it through. Times just weren't right. You know what I mean.

But I could draw. I could really draw. Ever since I was in grade school I could draw things, and they look just like real. I knew I had a talent and drawing was something I always liked to do, so I said hell. Go on and try. And I was good. No doubt about

467

it. Teachers at Tech always using my work to show the others how a thing could be done. One the instructors, a white dude, shit they was all white dudes, probably still are, but this one kinda tall and skinny with a moustache bigger than he was, he said, *French, what do you think you're doing?* Jerked my head up from my work. Thought he was talking bout my sketch, and I sort of hid it with my hands then peeked down underneath my fingers to see what was the matter. Always sat in the back of the studio. Far away from the models as I could. White chicks, of course, so I sat in the back so maybe they'd think I was a Turk or a Arab or some damned thing. So when this dude says, French, what do you think you're doing? I got uptight. He wasn't even looking at my pad. Wasn't even looking at me. He was standing there stiff and straight as the Statue of Liberty. Eyes front. Hissing out the corner of his mouth like that moustache too heavy for his upper lip. He said, Come to my office after class, French. So I do. And he sits behind his desk smoking the longest cigarette I ever saw: You're good. We all know that. Best student we have but you're wasting your time here. Can't earn a living with what you're learning here. Said he was telling me for my own good. Companies don't hire colored artists. He didn't say nigger artists but that's what he meant. Asked me to name a famous artist of my race. Name one artist or one painting by a black dude. Shit. Course I couldn't name one. Didn't even know the names of white dudes who was making it. When he was done speaking his piece he stood up and patted my shoulder real buddy-buddy like we just robbed Fort Knox and had the gold salted away and nobody but us knew where it was. Smiling and telling me I got talent and Ima decent person and that's why he was hipping me. The rest of the teachers hypocrites, he said. Leading me up a blind alley. Said he was my friend and didn't like saying what he had to say, but somebody had to.

And that was my graduation day. No way to go back to class after that. Shaky enough being the only spook at Tech. Wasn't like he was asking me if I wanted to quit. And nevermind it wasn't none his business. Shaggy-lipped motherfucker made it his business. Quituated me on the spot.

What do you think you're doing? Damn. I really didn't know. Not then, not now. So he made up my mind for me. Let me know

I was making him uncomfortable so it was time to go. Put it to me so I'd be calling him a fool or a damned liar if I stayed. And shaky as I was I just quit. Gave it up. Those quiet bus rides in the morning to the campus. The leather satchel Lucy bought me to carry my supplies in. Cause part of what the dude said was the God's truth. No such thing as a black painter cept the ones on ladders painting somebody's porch. Not even many of those if you thought about it. Wasn't a damn thing a colored man could do when you got right down and thought about it. Every black man I knew trying to support a family had two or three pieces of jobs that never added up to one good one.

Carl is like his sister, Lizabeth. That fair French skin and a calm, dignified, assured manner. His speaking tone, like hers, is casual. He smiles a lot when he talks, breaking into the saddest stories with offhand, ironic remarks or whimsical details of people's peculiarities, and you can't help smiling too. Anaydee turning green under her nostrils when she cries. Aunt Fanny stuck in the funeral parlor vestibule because she can't get her umbrella down. How he said *Thank you, Dr. Weird* to the doctor named Strange who had tended my grandmother, Freeda, during her last days in Allegheny County hospital. And like his sister, Carl's outward calm is always counterpointed by some part of his body shaking fast as a trip-hammer. One raw nerve-end dangling, visibly vibrating a mile a minute, if you knew where to look.

Ain't changed that much, has it? Niggers still out here scuffling and hustling and ain't got a pot to piss in nor a window to throw it out. Daddy was a paperhanging fool. Be high as a kite on Dago Red and still measure out a room perfect. Drink enough Dago Red to drown an ordinary man, but he'd get up on a ladder and lay that paper so you couldn't find a seam. But laying wallpaper only a once-in-a-while thing. He was the best but couldn't do it steady cause none the contractors would hire him regular. He'd have to sit out every morning in front the Bucket a Blood with the rest of the men waiting for jackleg work. I know all about it. Sat there many a morning myself. Hoping a white man will drive up and mad if one does cause you know he'll talk down to you in that nasty cracker way and work you like a mule and pay you half what he'd pay a white boy. But you got no choice. You got to sit and wait for one them ragtag pickups to sidle along the curb. Then *Beep Beep.* The white man sits there looking you up and down like he's God Almighty. When times real bad, niggers scrambling and pushing one another so he can see em good. Man say jump and you jump. Hey you in the overalls. Step out here where I can see you, boy. And you take what the bastards give. Or take nothing. Hang around there the rest of the day with the rest of the trifling niggers cause you ain't got nothing better to do. I know all about it cause I been out there many a morning. Daddy dead and gone and me taking his place on one those boxes outside the Bucket a Blood.

It's a bitch. Niggers still out on the same corner waiting. Was a time couple years ago whiteys afraid to drive anywhere in Homewood. But they back again and niggers waiting again. You know the thought never even come into my mind that maybe I could make it where all the others failed. Carl French the first black artist. Michelangelo French. Your generation can think that way, Doot. Youall can see beyond your situation. You and the young bloods coming up. Not many get a chance, but a few is better than none, and it makes my heart feel good when I hear one these young brothers damn this and damn that and tell the man kiss my ass. We all going to hell, but it makes my heart proud. Sometimes I'd think that way, but when I was coming up wasn't no way I'd curse a white man to his face. Seems like a long time ago but I'm only talking about twenty years ago, the good old fifties in the good old U.S. of A. Your uncle did what the rest the jive niggers did. Let hisself be pushed down. Started sticking myself with needles. Put the world in a jug and held the stopper in my hand.

And we were the three musketeers, right. So all three of us, me and Lucy and Brother in that dope mess. Couldn't say now who was first. Don't remember a first time, or saying to myself, Go ahead. You ain't nothing. Ain't gon hurt you worse than you already hurt. Wasn't a matter of deciding to do it or not do it. One day you look round yourself and see these jive niggers nodding and sprawled out on the floor and you feel good, you grin at all these junkies in the Tates' living room and wonder a second what I got to be feeling good about but that thought's gone before it gets hold to you and nothing can get hold to you except you know you're feeling good, you got the shit whipped for a while and the wolf ain't at your heels and you're feeling good, real good, better than you ever thought you would.

The bar noise rises and falls. Somebody calls somebody else's name down the length of the bar. A woman squeals. A round of drinks is ordered for the fine lady in blue and her friends.

I ain't gon lie now like I'm supposed to and say how it tore me up to be a junkie. Nope. Cause it was better than being nothing. World was a hurting trick and being high was being out the world. Nothing wrong with that. If you find a way out the trick bag, you a fool not to take it. You take it and it makes you feel good and that's that. Why the hell not? I mean it's your body, it's your life. Shit. Who ever said you supposed to just stand still and suffer. No. You take the freedom train running through your veins. You get on board and couldn't care less where it's headed. Don't care nothing about dues, about the conductor coming one day to kick your ass off. All that's farther down the line. And down the line don't matter. It's the minutes that matter, the hour or the day if you can keep feeling good that long.

Always like Christmas at the Tates'. Like the good old days on Cassina Way waking up on Christmas morning and everybody done outdid theyselves buying presents and you're a kid and it's all for you.

Easy as falling out of bed. One day I looked in Lucy's eyes and saw junk. Lucy looked back in mine, and she musta seen the same thing. Junk. Like I said, Hello. Meet my monkey. And her monkey nodded at mine and then Lucy dead and Carl dead cause them monkeys didn't need us nomore. Get along fine without us, Thank you. Every once in a while I'd notice how bad Lucy looked or see her doing something Lucy Tate ain't supposed to. But then I'd see junk. Remember she ain't Lucy Tate no more. No need to yell or snatch her back from something or take her to a mirror so she could see herself, see for herself how low she was falling. Nothing in no glass to see. Just junk. Junk. Long as we could get it, wasn't no problem. Didn't need nothing else. Long as we had it, wasn't nothing else.

That was the good part. Being high was good. Bad part was you couldn't stay high. Bad part you still had to deal with that

471

asskicking world to get high. You had to hurt people. Knew you hurting them just by being what you were. Stealing, turning tricks, lying. Taking from your family, messing over the people think they your friends. You had to go back out in the world so you could turn it off. Shoot it down. On a merry-go-round. Like a sick puppy on a merry-go-round. Chasing in circles after your own tail. Sooner or later you had to get off the floor, get out the Tates'.

Why? To get back again. Coming through the door you'd see yourself going. Coming and going like you got a ghost and you'd bump into yourself going in when you'd be coming out. Meet yourself in the vestibule and be half out your mind trying to figure whether you supposed to be leaving or just getting back.

That's when I caught the bus to Lexington. After I passed my ghost a few times in that doorway I knew I had to go. Tried to get Lucy and Brother to go but Lucy wasn't ready. She told me she wasn't ready after I got back to Homewood the first time. She wasn't ready to stop and I couldn't either. Had to go back to Lexington again. Then Brother quit. Like magic. The man just stopped one day and never touched it again. Brother was different, always was different from other people. Anyway, he quit and after he got hisself together he ran everybody out the Tates' and locked Lucy in her room and stayed with her while she cold-turkeyed. He stopped and made her stop. Just about killed her, and would have she said, if he had to. So by the time I got back from Lexington the second time they was both clean. I been at it again but everybody helped me and I go for my methadone now but I'm all right. And Lucy's all right. And Brother ain't got it to worry bout no more.

Old cream-of-wheat Brother. I know I'm supposed to be telling you his story. But how Ima tell his without telling mine. And Lucy's. Cause yeah. We was the three musketeers, all right. Woulda followed each other to Hell. And just about did. But that's all gone now. Brother's gone and it's just me and Lucy now and it's time to get off this stool cause I'm hungry. You ready, Doot? You come over to the Tates' and it be three of us again just like the old days.

3. Brother

THE week he turned twenty-one the train dream took Brother for the first time. Snatched him from sleep and twisted him inside out and left him sweating in the darkness. Where are my hands, my God-blessed hands is what he shouted that first night bolt upright in bed because he didn't know if the dream still had him or if it had turned him loose. He was alone in the black room, trying to find the parts of his body, but the hands running up and down his legs, hugging his shoulders, pinching the flesh beneath his eyes did not belong to him. They were not Brother Tate's hands. In the pitch and shudder of the train nothing belonged to anybody. The woman who had been hurled into his lap did not own the soft breasts which dragged over his thighs as she scrambled away. They weren't her fingers which mauled and grasped as she tried to find him and push him away all at once. A stew of bodies sloshed helter-skelter over the wet floor of the boxcar. Brother couldn't stand. He couldn't disentangle what belonged to him from the mass of bodies struggling in the black pit.

Brother Tate sat bolt upright, naked and scared on the mattress in the house of his dead father, trembling because he knew the dream could kill him, knew it could take him again and again until its work was finished.

His legs were wet under the storytelling quilt. His sister, Lucy, had patched and sewed the quilt, and Brother drew it over him every night, winter and summer. Some nights he'd hear the quilt talking story, chattering at him when sleep wasn't sleep, when he swam till dawn in a churning sea of Dago Red. Now it felt like all the people sewn into the bright mosaic of cloth had peed on him. Funky, blood-warm pee. He rubbed his eyes and fingered the parts of his body buried under the quilt. Everything was covered by sticky darkness. Everything was melting and running away.

No way he'd peed on his ownself. He was grown. He'd be twenty-one in two days. His birthday in two days and they'd party at the Velvet Slipper and the Elks. Carl be there and Lucy on her high stool and Cat behind the bar. He was a twenty-one-year-old man in his dead father's house, alone in the house of the old man he'd always called Father because nobody never told him not to. What he look like peeing the bed. His legs were drenched in sweat or blood from those bodies rolling haywire like marbles across the floor of the rattling freight car. Those bodies stink like horse shit or cow shit, and that's what was backed up under the covers with him.

Slowly the dream was turning into nothing as he remembered what it was about. In the dream he had been Albert Wilkes, long dead Albert Wilkes coming back to Homewood again. Brother remembered how real the dream had been, how clearly he'd seen the countryside flowing past the windows of the train. Because that's how it started. A train ride. Albert Wilkes on a train. And stayed that way until the lights went out and the doors slammed and the bodies began crashing into him and the screaming began . . .

He had seen Albert Wilkes's face in the window of the train. He is inside the train and the face running along on the outside. He can see through the face to the trees like broccoli heads lining the tracks. Can see through it to shanties and fields and red earth. The face is there always but parts of it come and go so maybe all he sees is eyes or a mouth or the cheekbone's shadow or maybe sees nothing but a stomped down shack and chickens scratching in a yard and a backside broad and round as two watermelons where a woman is on her knees in a vegetable patch. But the face is dimly there even then, and he's waiting for a time, maybe night-time, when he'll be able to see it all and clearly.

He's going home. He knows that. Knows it because the land and trees and air are changing. Even the sound of the tracks getting more familiar the closer he gets to home. The train is hunkering down, its wheels grabbing tighter. What sings and dances in the hurry of the train starts to get to him. He has been sitting a long time, watching through the face a long time, hearing nothing but the wheels saying I'm tired and still got a long way to go. He wouldn't listen because there was no play in the sound, nothing but a flat, lonely, almost moan like somebody telling the same sad story over and over again in the same tired voice and the wheels couldn't do nothing but keep on telling the tale. Now he hears a beat, a gallop. The steel wheels rising and set down one at a time so it's boogity, bop, boogity boopin a little different each measure.

More trees and rolling low hills. Everything in shades of green. So green the face looks back at him shiny-eyed and black. And for no reason he gets sad again. Gets more unhappy than he was when the land was flat and bare and the wheels moaning because they were standing still. Perhaps it's because home is just around the next bend. He knows there will be tunnels and bridges and a river deep in a valley he must fly over on a thread. Then he will be home again and the sadness comes because now he's sure he's gon make it.

Not just a tune now but words now between the mouthfuls of steel the wheels are chewing. They sing *seven years seven years* and he's Brother again. Ain't got no ticket then and plumb off the train and standing in the Tates' living room beside Lucy and she says play and the playing is *seven years, seven years* and the face out the window ain't even pretending no more it just goes on about its business and when he steps into the station he feels it slap him across the bare bones of his skull and it's Albert Wilkes in the soot and dirt and niggers in red caps and engines smoking and all aboard and steam hissing and people hurrying and people looking through him like he thought they never would. No fingers pointing, no sirens, no nothing but people getting down and people climbing up and niggers pushing boatloads of suitcases and trunks. Then he looks into the playing, looks past the seven years the way he looked past the face outside the window to find the countryside he was speeding by. He is Albert Wilkes all right, and he's caught somewhere in the middle. Maybe he is the window glass. Hot on one side. Cold on the other. Because he is Brother, too. Shuffling

475

his feet and listening to Wilkes playing because Lucy said he's back.

Albert Wilkes steady humping on his piano. Playing honky-tonk and gut bucket and low-down dirty blues. He's playing righteous and deep in his song, but he is staring at Brother too. Trying to see something. Brother feels himself rushing like a river. Like the face on the other side of the glass. Albert Wilkes can see pieces of him. An eye. A mouth. The shadow of a cheekbone. But he also sees the gray sky, the gray water, the shaggy trees. Sees through Brother to all of that so his face is like a flag changing shape in the wind.

Play. And then he goes on about his business. He plays his piano song sad as train wheels when they standing still. He is beside Lucy and he is across the room, seated at the piano Strayhorn brought in Mr. Tate's truck. Mrs. Tate rocks up and back in slow time to something in the music nobody else can hear. Her song in his song. Like Brother hears his. Like Lucy beside him rocks on one foot then the other hearing what she needs to hear.

Like Albert Wilkes when he gets off the train and thinks *seven years*. Been gone seven years. The busy station paying him no mind when he had expected it to be all sirens and searchlights and dogs howling and pistols exploding. After so long on the train he can't stop moving. Part of him continues gliding down the track, sealed in a box so the world rushes past like scenery through a window. But the part of him which won't stop moving is hooked to the end of a rubber band and the rubber stretches as far as it can, then flies back like a boomerang upside his face. That wakes him to the beginning of Homewood. To his hands which have been waiting seven years. Piano-playing hands gone for seven years, gone so long, so far, he knew they were dying, knew he must bring them home. Return to Homewood to hear Lucy say. Play.

In his song like a window Brother could see way down the tracks. To now when he is dreaming. To the time when he will speak to a son. To the time he wouldn't speak to anyone anymore. To the lives he would live and the lives he would be inside. Albert Wilkes's song like a hand over the troubled waters, and then the water was still and he could see everything. Everything gone and everything coming not mixed up together anymore but still and calm. Albert Wilkes's life was hanging on him like a skin to be shed, a skin he couldn't shake off, so it was squeezing, choking all his other lives. It would kill him forever if he didn't shrug it off, so he ran from the living room and up Tioga to Homewood and Frankstown and said to a white policeman he'd never seen before that Albert Wilkes was back. That he killed a policeman seven years ago and now he's back in Homewood at the Tates' on Tioga.

And they stomped in and blew away his skin . . . and the lights went out and the boxcar rattling and the blood and the bodies. But then Brother bolts upright, the quilt shivers down his chest. He counts the parts of his body. He is remembering. Some parts of the dream still seem real, then all of it is real, then none as he remembers where he is, who he is. Parts of the dream real, then less real as he remembers.

The boxcar shrinks. Brother can see inside it now. It's smaller and smaller. It's a coffin now, silk lined, heaped with roses. Albert Wilkes in a tuxedo looking good like he always looked good in his clothes. A rose pinned on Albert's lapel. Albert smiling, winking as the box grows smaller, as it starts to rock and sing a lullaby. Then Albert's gone. The box is too small to hold a man. S'a boy. A tiny babyboy in a cradle rocking and a black hand tipping the cradle back and forth and it's a boy, a boy child white as snow and the black woman rocking the cradle is smiling. She's singing and the train's gone, and it's morning and light pours through the windows of the Tates' old house and birds are making a racket as they always did on spring mornings when there were trees in Homewood.

1946

The train dream returns. It's dark again and Brother is trapped again inside the rattling car. He knows he has been riding five years, trapped for five years, and nothing he believed was real is real anymore. There is only the ride, the darkness, the screaming. Everything else is finished, is made up like the music he plays, like the music he will never play again, like words he will never speak again.

This time he can't shake free. He's naked walking the floor. The storytelling quilt's a tangled mess half on, half off the bed like something somebody fought with and killed and left dying in its tracks. Brother hears the flat smack of his bare feet on the boards. He's marching. Like the Elks Band on V.J. Day under the bridge crossing Homewood Avenue. He doesn't know why. He doesn't care. It's a way of getting up and back, up and back, across the black space of the room. For days, for years, his poor feet wearing a path through the wooden floor. He hears the splat, splat rhythmless march steps going nowhere and tastes gritty, hot soot in his mouth.

S'a boy.

He's my son and it can't be no other way. Never be no other way. So I'm in his corner. Got to be. Always.

Sam is his mama and loves him and do the best she can. I know that and know she won't let nothing hurt him too bad. So I stay away except I'm always spying where they can't see me. I pretend they don't see me and they don't. Slip from behind Mother Strothers's shack and cross the alley and inside Sam's yard and sidle next to Junebug and don't none them see me coming. So there I am beside him. I can hear him breathe and hear them little songs he makes but he don't see me. If he sees me the others will too and nobody's ready for that. He is sad sometime and happy sometime. He is mostly like the others. Not really knowing whether they happy or sad because they got something to do and that keeps them busy. Junebug busy with them songs he makes. Don't say words yet but he's busy making things most all the time. I watch him for hours. But it's hard to stay invisible so nobody see me. Headaches. Got to split. Got to make it on back and be with Lucy or be in the Velvet Slipper. Or sit up by the tracks. More trains now. The kind Carl went away to the war on. The kind got stuff covered up on flat cars you know it got to be guns and tanks and jeeps under there. Keep wondering why so many people want so many people dead. Keep thinking you got a son and it's never gon to be no other way.

I see Junebug walking now. Like he got rubber bands inside them bowlegs and sometimes they's pulled tight enough and sometimes they get loose so he ain't walking he's coming apart and falls down and picks hisself up and puts hisself back together again one or two steps closer to where he wanted to be in the first place. Either way. Walking or coming apart Junebug gets off by hisself now.

It's better now. The others forget him when they don't see him. He can help them forget now. He can find a corner and they leave him alone as long as they ain't remembering. Samantha is the mother of all of them. Samantha going to be the mother of more.

She said:

Brother, I can't stop. While I got life I got to give life. They're killing us faster now. And beating down the ones they can't kill. Our boys over there supposed to be dying equal. It's a crying shame how they do us. So I can't stop. When we cross over, I want a million, million black feet to run up the bank and a million, million black voices shout hallelulah in the promised land. So I got to give life while I got it.

If you ain't felt it, don't think you know nothing about it. Watch some nigger start to coming around Sam and know what she done picked him for. I watched it twice and second time no easier than the first. Worse than the first, to tell the truth. Like the first time a thing happens you can think well it's just a accident. Ain't never happened before, won't again. You tell yourself that shit. But the second time is always. Hurts so bad and you be so low you just know it's gon happen and happen and keep happening and ain't no accident to it. Had to work hard to keep myself this side of that curtain. Ain't no windows. You can't get out the bed except through the curtain. I had to make it a box. I'd seal Sam and the nigger in the box and make the curtain just as stiff and dark as the other three wood walls. I'd pack them in and pack the wood in steel and shoot it like a rocket someplace as far away as the moon. Then as long as I kept it there and kept them dark and silent in it, I'd be all right. Wouldn't have to think on it. No reason to think because the curtain is steel and far away and nothing is moving inside.

She told me she was going to do it, told me she had to and told me why and part of me would listen part of me would nod that ugly pumpkin on my shoulders but most of me be cooking steel and hammering and welding and getting that match ready to blow them to the moon.

Like it was when I watched all Samantha's black children playing in the yard. I loved them like she did. But loving them don't make it no easier when they evil to Junebug. Had my favorites like little Becky I carried in the Ark that first time when Sam danc-

ing. Always thought of her mama dancing when I watched Becky playing in the yard. She the hardest one to fool. She the one would see me if I didn't keep thinking hard. Got my favorite but I love all them children. Any children. I can see little kids hanging on Carl. Half naked and dirty and got sores all over and nothing in they stomachs. Little brown kids like Doot. Halfway color between Junebug and the rest of Samantha's kids. They got slanty eyes and they crying. They ain't got mama nor daddy no more and Carl wants to be home. He empties his pockets and dumps the little snacks from his knapsack. But it's like fighting lions with a stick. Them kids gon die. Ain't nothing to do really but just keep on marching and hoping you be home soon. When Junebug got a sister I loved her. Loved his brother when he come. Love them all but that don't make it no easier when I think of them being evil to Junebug or Sam loving their daddies.

She said:

It's a river runs through me. Said it's the kind of river never stops running. Always moving to the sea. She said the water always changing. Said it's different every time. Different water for them. Different water for you. Not even the same water if you step in one minute out the next and in again the next it's different water every time that quick. It's a river and no one will ever touch me where you touched me. Where you touched me is part of the sea now and the sea is always. It's where we been and where we're going and don't be sad, ghost. Don't you be acting like no jealous natural man, ghost. Not yet. Not yet. I need you different till we get through this thing with Junebug. Just think of it in my way. Think that now there's two more who are going to love him that day we teach them all to love.

But Carl came back from the war and ain't been no sign of love. Just less room for Junebug.

I take Carl by one day. I stop beside Sam's yard to tie my tennis shoe which ain't untied. He knows why. He knows my son and knows what I'm saying. Junebug easy to pick out off by hisself digging in the dirt. Now that Carl's back home I stay away a little more from Sam's place. I think she might be ready to pick another man and I might have to kill him. Kill him over Sam for one thing. And kill him because he'll be stealing the little breath Junebug's got left. It ain't me to think like that. It ain't Brother being that way and I almost tell Carl what I'm thinking so I can kill it in me. Stead of talking we just walk. All over Homewood. Gonna walk holes in the sidewalk or holes in our shoes and then start wearing holes in our feet because the walking is instead of talking and as long as the speech I need to say keeps climbing to my throat I got to keep moving and walk it back down again and Carl is beside me and I hear him tromping on the words he don't want to say either. It's Sunday morning and the bells in the white folks church on Penn Avenue is parading all over Homewood. Like somebody turned a hose on and said let's clean up this mess. The bells chase everything but theyselves out the streets. You got to hear them if you outdoors. No way not to hear them.

They chiming when Carl said:

Daddy used to say only difference between Sunday and every other day back in slavery times was they called you out the fields with the church bell instead of the conch horn. He teased Mama all the time about church. She loved the bells. Said they reminded her of the quiet days when Homewood was different. Daddy would say the day God put some black hands at the end of the ropes be the day those bells be beautiful. He said couldn't no white men play See-See Rider on them bells and that's what he wanted to hear.

Why do white folks run from us? Where do they think they're going? I seen enough dead bodies to fill two Homewoods. Brown and Yellow and White and Black. All the same. All stink the same. That was a job niggers got a lot. Cleanup. Just like over here. But in the war wasn't just garbage and spilled drinks and cigarette butts. War mess is dead people. So they brought over our brooms and mops and scrub buckets and put us on the same jobs they give us over here. You talk to fellows who was in the war and sooner or later they'll tell you about having to pick up pieces of white boy and bury them. That's the way it was for most. Except the ones they allowed to die fighting. The ones they let die so the rest of us be free to bring the shovels and brooms back home.

Carl talking and needing me to listen so I put everything out my mind awhile. Put Sam and Junebug to the side awhile so I could listen, so I could breathe, so I could get the razors out my chest.

Then it was summertime. Days got long and green. We'd drink sweet wine and sit on benches in the park. Half the time it be Carl talking and half the time we be sleeping or spying on the people messing round in Westinghouse Park. Kids out of school hanging around the swings and the tracks. Boys waiting for the girls. Girls strolling by in twos or in little packs so they can sass back when the boys say something ignorant. I watched and listened and tried to make up songs about it all. With the sweet wine in my blood and the warm air on my skin I felt like those tinkling chimes Carl brought back from the war and hung on his front porch. Breeze took pieces of me and knocked them together and I could feel it floating through me, hear it playing me when it moved the leaves and pushed the long shadows across the grass.

June was the month he told Sam he was inside her belly. And she told me and sure enough he came nine months after in February but he was Junebug always and I didn't think of snow and wind and standing in the alley freezing and old Mother Strothers skating like a beetle across the frozen middle of Cassina Way. I thought of summer here to stay like it is when it's finally June and you can lay out all day and let the sun melt you to pieces. So he was always there in the back of my mind those early summer days, but I didn't go around except once or twice to peek in Sam's yard. Then it was July and everything growing thick on the hillside. They still had engines that smoked then and black soot clouds would roll down from the tracks and trains would stop at the water tower and drink. That smoke could get in your throat and you'd be all right one minute then coughing and spitting the next. You'd say, Got Damn. You'd pick up a rock and throw it at the tracks even though the locomotive long gone and couldn't reach it any way from where the smoke caught you standing there sneezing and rubbing your eyes and can't do nothing but holler Got Damn.

I remember cause the state store closed on the Fourth and me and Carl had to go to Bows to get a jug of Dago Red. Bows was the house looked like it's made out yellow mud, on the corner of Tioga and Cassina Way. Bows was where you get your throat slit good you cut your eyes at the wrong nigger but if you want something to drink and everyplace else shut like they is Sundays and holidays you got to go on over to Bows, so me and Carl was on our way when the smoke swooped off that hillside and I could taste it all the way to Bow's back door.

Youall see that ambulance come through here. One them little childs got burnt up over to Samantha's. Say the poor little thing ain't nothing but a cinder, time the ambulance got there. It ain't been gone more'n a minute. Come right through here. Thought you boys might of seed it.

And the smoke taste on my lips and the smoke burning my eyes and ash is everywhere inside me. I die then and remember the cold. Only it's colder than it ever was when I was standing in February waiting for Mother Strothers to come back across the alley and say, S'a boy. So cold if anybody touched me I'd crack and be a million broken pieces all over Bow's back step. Carl asking questions and Bow talking to hisself the way he does till maybe he comes to what you asking him. And I'm freezing. Colder than February. Colder than ash.

Nobody needed to tell me nothing. I knew it was Junebug. Knew he was gone and nothing to say, nothing to do. Nothing bring him back. But he was mine. And always would be and no way around that, so I went on home and started to making that box.

Sam said:

I'm sorry . . . I'm so sorry. Sam said, Have mercy. Have mercy on us all.

She took the wood box I made for him. And took the top to cover him. And Mr. Tucker laid him in it and brought it back to the Ark. And Junebug slept one night more in his mama's house and the house was empty except for him and me. They took the other children away when they took Sam to Mayview. She couldn't hold together so they took her to the hospital and the neighbors that could took a child or two into they homes till Sam got better. So it was just me and him in the Ark that night. His last night home.

That's when I sang to Junebug. Sang to him to save his life. Because he was just a baby. Because he didn't know a thing about leaving or coming back again. So I had to tell him what I knew. Where I had been. I was his daddy and always would be. Just like he would always be my son. I sang to him about crossing oceans. About being on one side of the water and the sun sets in the west while it's rising in the east on the other side. And night one place is day in the other. And the sky's not full of stars but one bright star we only see pieces of because the darkness is a raggedy curtain pulled across it till we know better. I told him his Mama Sam would be better in the morning and that she and his brothers and sisters would come to get him at the first light. And they would sing the old songs to him. And take him out in the daylight and drive him through the streets of Homewood and carry him up the hill which is the quietest place they know. And sing over him again. And promise to meet him bye and bye and scatter ashes over his ashes and one long, green day would pass, a day to be alone, but then he would see the curtain pulled away and the great star reveal itself. Its shine a kind of singing. Its shine warm as their bodies when they gather around him in the dawn.

I told him he would feel all that. I told him to rest peacefully because of all that. But then I told him the secret. That there was more. More fire and pain and singing. That I been through it before. That nothing stopped. That I had crossed the ocean in a minute. That I had drowned in rivers and dangled like rotten fruit on trees. That my unmourned bones were ground to dust and the dust salted and plowed. That I had been chained and branded like an animal. That I had watched my children's brains dashed out against a rock. That I had seen my mother whipped and my woman raped and my daddy stretched on a cross. That I had even lost my color and lost my tongue but all of that too was only a minute.

I sang to him. I let him know I didn't understand any more than he did. Except I had been a witness. I had been there so I could tell about it. And that was all my secret. My magic.

Listen, son. Listen, Junebug. It all starts up again in you. It's all there again. You are in me and I am in you so it never stops. As long as I am, there's you. As long as there's you, I am. It never stops. Nothing stops. We just get tired and can't see no further. Our eyes get cloudy. They close and we can't see no further. But it don't stop.

Brother tasted soot. He wondered if that was the taste of a lie. Had he lied to his son? What bright, shining day ever came?

He looked down at the cracked pavement. His feet were there.

Those were his raggedy sneakers sure enough and the pale chips
of his big toenails where they'd chewed through the canvas tops.
He'd thrown his clothes on. Hadn't taken time to dry his sweaty
body or clean his teeth or find a pair of socks. He was running
from the dream. He was one of those screams trying to tear through
the darkness.

He could see one part of Brother Tate anchored to the busted
sidewalk of Finance Street but he could also see the sun-dimpled
bubble of his bald head floating miles up in the sky, so high the
string attaching it to his feet disappeared before it reached the pale
balloon. Brother Tate wondered what it would feel like to cut the
string, to snip the cord and watch the balloon jet away. Would
the sun pop it, would the air rush out and the balloon zigzag, crazy
as a chicken with its head cut off, across the sky? Would he be
able to hear it sputter and hiss and squeal? Would it finally fall
back to earth, land somewhere on Finance Street and some little
kid pick it out of the gutter and stretch it and poke it and maybe
put his mouth on the dirty rubber and blow it up again?

Brother could be in both places at once. A Brother in the sky.
A Brother humping down Finance Street. In one place he had no
color, he could not speak or play. In another place he watches
and waits.

He knows he should tell someone the train dream. The dream
will return again and again if he doesn't. He had tried to tell Junebug the dream but different words came out and the taste of soot
clogged his mouth and it was too late to say anything more now.
His son gone and there would be many years of silence. Nothing
more to say. He knew as he stepped off the fat-lipped curb of
Finance down onto the cobblestones of Dunfermline, knew at that
very instant, poised in the air over the broken intersection of street
and alley, that he had said enough and wouldn't say any more.

1962

Brother Tate sank deeper and deeper into the neck of his tan
jacket. The upturned collar reached as far as the puckered ridges
at the base of his bald head. The seams there were like another
face, another face staring back at the world as he passed by, a face

hiding its eyes in the fleshy folds of skin when Brother tilted his head backward to laugh at something funny enough to get his whole body jumping and twisting and turned inside out. Laughing like a million invisible grinning monkeys tickling him all at once. When his head jumps back like that and his mouth full of laughing the loose skin creases and anything could be hiding in the piecrust folds of neck. When he really got high on laughing you knew sooner or later he'd melt, all his strength laughed away and you'd have to catch him when he turned to rubber.

Get up from there, fool.

Brother collapsed sometimes when nobody around to break his fall and there he'd be, a puddle in the middle of Homewood Avenue, a dead man till you saw his shoulders twitching or his hind end wiggling then you'd know breath was still in his body and he was just lying there like a damn fool cause he couldn't stop laughing and couldn't get up either.

But this particular moonless night, double dark in the shadow cast by Bruston Hill, Brother had no reason to laugh or cry, no reason for doing anything except to try to lose himself in the skin of his tan jacket. For a while he'd watched people moving in the other direction, toward a huge, lighted tent pitched on the vacant lot just before Bruston started its steep rise. In the shadow of an apartment building, in the darkness of his own shadowy form which he felt enclosing him like a black eggshell, from that invisible wedge between brick walls, from that little patch of nowhere stinking of pee and carpeted with broken wine bottles which crunched like cornflakes if his feet made the slightest move, Brother had watched them parading toward the bright tent. Yes Lawd. They'd get it on tonight. Shout Hallelujah and shake dance in the aisles. He could hear rows of folding chairs crashing down as folks leaped to their feet. Yes. Yes. Something's got a hold to me. They'd party all night long. The old folks and children nodding off, dreaming, farting in their sleep till a cymbal snatches them back from wherever they been to sweet glory. Some were singing softly when they passed. The old-time, get-down, sorrowful songs you couldn't hear nowhere but church or in the morning, Lucy ironing his pants and humming like she had heard Mrs. Tate when Mrs. Tate ironing one of Mr. Tate's white shirts for church Sunday morning. Singing or humming softly and it sounded good to him as he listened to the music pass. Almost good enough to make him leave his hiding place and follow them through the darkness to the shining tent where the singing would be loud and clear, where all the voices get caught up in the old songs whether they knew the words or not.

The collar tickles the back of his bald head. He wishes he could draw it up like a hood. Cover the nakedness back there, the bare white hanging out like a streetlamp begging the kids to stone it. If the skimpy mandarin collar was a hood he'd pull it down over his face, close it so wouldn't be nothing showing but a slit for his eyes. Like that slit between brick walls. And him nothing but an eye. Not an eye that buzzed like the streetlamps, not an eye with no business being out there, spying, signifying in the Homewood night. Not an eye somebody wants to stone. He just wanted to watch. Be an eye that watched and listened. An eye nobody would ever see or hear peering from the folds of darkness.

He almost slipped in line with the people moving toward the empty lot where the star burned. Reverend Somebody's somekind of Holiness and everything else you-better-believe-it Revival cause-the-end's-coming tent. He'd seen the posters all over Homewood. Funny cause he hadn't seen anybody tacking them on the telly poles or leaning them in storefront windows or pasting them on walls, but one morning they was there, everywhere, like snow falling all night, and course you don't hear a thing while you sleeping but there they are, blam, covering everything in the morning. That sudden and that surprising, the posters all over Homewood one morning. Then people starting to talk. Sure. I heard of him. My cousin told me bout the man. He's a famous preacher. He's Moses and Jesus and Haile Selassie and Billy Eckstine all in one. He can light a fire, yes he can. Don't care if you got a hole in your soul. He can fill it up. Yes he can now. Put a dip in your hips, a rock in your walk and a glide in your stride. He's a preaching man. Don't care if the Devil got Homewood in his bulldog jaws. This man snatch it back. Had him round in them olden days wouldna been no Babylon, wouldna been no pillars of salt and Sodom and Gommorahs.

Brother thought hard about trekking with the rest of Homewood to that candle flickering in the middle of nowhere. Woulda done it too if there was someplace inside the tent he could hide, something he could pull over him like a hood, an edge of canvas he could wrap up in like Lucy used to curl up in Mrs. Tate's wide skirt, sucking her thumb. All you could see of her in that rocker going back and forth was one big Lucy eye cause she's wrapped in the skirt and the other eye's behind a corner of skirt she's rubbing up against her nose while she sucks her thumb. If he could be an eye watching and listening to the good music he'd make the trip, but they got a wire or something connected up to a pole in the tent and it's bright as daylight inside there. So he waited till everybody passed and gone on about they business. Then he stepped out from between the funky walls and walked in the opposite direction.

Because not everybody in Homewood was going to no salvation tent. They could bring the Sealtest Bigtop and Barnum and Bailey and plant them in the middle of Homewood Avenue and let everybody in free, and half the niggers in the Velvet Slipper wouldn't see it and the other half wouldn't care. So Reverend whatchmacallit and his Everlasting Fire and Grace and whatever-else Revival wouldn't hardly be getting certain brothers and sisters out their set ways, out their set paths which was straight to the Velvet Slipper from the place they lay down they heads at night. Less the Rev serving communion wine by the gallon jug. Less he turning water to sweet Dago Red, these brothers and sisters patronize the Velvet Slipper ain't going noplace else. Not to pray, not to sing, not to get happy on weeping Jesus. Not to see the Rev close the wounds or sweep the floor with the hem of his milkwhite garment and suffer no corruption there. Not to watch him heal the sick or raise the dead or jump longer than Jesse Owens.

Brother had seen God once and that was enough. When Junebug died, Brother had to crawl through the needle's eye and the kinks still worrying his back so he wasn't about to get down that low no mo. So he watched people slipping past. Little groups on their way to hear the word. Brother had cat eyes. He could see in the dark. See a little group a block away gliding silently toward the black rise of Bruston Hill. But not their feet. Not even cat eyes could pick their shuffling feet out the darkness, but he could see round heads bobbing when they cleared the last houses and made a shape flat as paper against the night. Tall ones and little ones and heads in between, just enough darker than the night air so he could pick them out, clusters of folks moving silent, pressed together like they were in little boats, like there was a river beneath them where their feet all came together in blackness not even Brother's eyes could see. Raggedy boatloads of Homewood people sailing for the Promised Land.

Brother hunched deeper, pulling his shoulders up around his eyes, like he'd pull that hood he didn't have. Seemed like Homewood drained. No cars. Nobody out on the streets. All the houses dark. He knew the Slipper'd be the one place jumping if nothing else was. Seemed like he wanted to get there more than he wanted anything else in the world. Seemed like Homewood had dried up and blown away. Seemed like he could feel the hot wind in his face. Hear it. The dry hot stale wind of thousands of trifling souls, old souls stuffed in drawers. The graves in Allegheny Cemetery opening, a wind flood floating them through the streets so the streets are crowded and empty and everywhere he steps, his feet crush somebody's dry bones, somebody's body busted wide open and dry as a broken wine bottle. He's tramping on Kellogg's cornflakes but it doesn't matter because nobody's left to hear but him, and Brother thinks about lying down right there in the middle of the pavement. Not another step forward or backward ever. Just let all the strength run out his body and crumple here on the pavement and listen while the sidewalks die and the bricks tumble down and the sky cracks, and rain dry as talcum powder buries everything.

It is a Saturday night in Homewood. Brother remembers Carl's story of Japanese human-wave attacks against American machine guns on Okinawa. The Homewood night is unseasonably mild, the streets deserted. Through some odd circumstance of atmosphere and temperature, a peculiar alignment of planets and mysterious, incorporeal essences, Brother hears the screams of dying Japanese, hears the thump of bodies piling up against each other, the rip of thirty caliber machine gun bullets burying themselves in the flesh of those who hurdle a moaning barricade of dead and half-dead comrades in khaki suits and tennis shoes. The dead men look very much like cords of wood, like the bodies Carl pushed off a cliff into the sea with the blade of his bulldozer. Brother smells death in the air. Another war coming. But perhaps he is confused, smells one thing and thinks he smells another. Perhaps it's just Homewood dying. Perhaps Homewood's gone already.

His head pops out like a turtle's from its shell. As bald, as wrinkled as a turtle's head from crown to neck. But white. Pale as a baby bird. Naked as birds look before they get feathers. He scans the immediate area. A turtle's cautious, blinking reconnaissance because Brother needs to pee. For a second there is the crashing of waves, wind or human voices roaring, but once free of his collar, once his shoulders have settled again where they belong and he can breathe freely and see three hundred and sixty degrees around himself, a blessed silence descends. At its edge the faintest hint of singing, of voices in a blazing tent blocks away in the shadow cast by Bruston Hill, but that sound becomes part of the silence, its freshness, its cleansing quiet.

Then the gush of himself. Brother thinks of old John French spitting tobacco. How it danced like popping grease. The blood sizzling on the pavement or exploding in the dust. Brother remembers the time on the corner of Finance and Dunfermline when he felt like a balloon, when he held the string in his hand and a balloon with his funny face bobbed closer and closer to the sun. He wondered if it would pop. Wondered as he made a little river along the curb why the air didn't rush out when the water rushed out. You pulled the plug and the water drained, and why didn't the air leak out too?

He feels his body going limp. All the air hissing away so his cheeks sink and his chest caves and his navel is folding into his backbone and his potbelly shrivels and the faucet in his fingers shrinks till it's nothing but a string, a string attached to the flat kite he's become. Then he starts to rise. The dry wind lifts him. Homewood spreads out below, a patchwork of tiny streets and houses. But as he rises, as the string gets thinner and thinner and his shoulders in the tan jacket become skinny and powerful as wings, even his cat eyes can't penetrate the darkness. Homewood is black as coal. Nothing visible but two winking pinpoints of light. One is the tent. The other must be the Velvet Slipper. But as he rises on the wind and feels his bones swallowing the thin air and the thin air swallowing his bones, as the lightness and giddiness of a height he'd

490

never dreamed overtakes him, the last two lights disappear. First one then the other blinks out. He can't tell if that's what happened exactly or if as he rose the lights merged and became one and then died together or if they died in sequence one after the other and it doesn't matter because he has even higher to go and stops looking back, looking for Homewood or anything else in the black sea beneath him.

Brother shakes once, twice, neatly as if someone is watching and remembering his performance. As if someone will talk about it in the Slipper so he does it just right. One, two shakes so it's not dribbling when he tucks his joint back inside his pants and zips up his fly.

He's in an alley behind Dunfermline. And Dunfermline's not much more than an alley its ownself so if somebody got nothing better to do than spy on him peeing, well shame on his soul.

He walks right past the lights of the Velvet Slipper when he finally reaches them. He almost laughs out loud. Almost gets started and knows he won't stop till he's laid flat out on Homewood Avenue and will stay that way laughing deep inside hisself till some-' body comes by to help him up.

Get up from there, fool.

It's the same way he felt when he was peeing. Let it rain. Let it come on down and take me. His laughter poised overhead inside a cloud looked like a balloon with a funny face painted on it. His laughter ready to drown him and drench the dry Homewood streets if he just peeked up at it. If he gave it half a chance, half a nod the cloud would burst and down it'd come. But he didn't laugh then and doesn't laugh now because he had something to do first, someplace to reach, a duty he'd forgotten till he passed the Slipper and crossed Homewood Avenue and started up the path worn through the weeds to the Bums' Forest.

He wanted to play the game one more time. He wanted to teach it to Junebug. The scare game on the tracks. He needed to teach his son to play so Junebug never be afraid of anything again. Because they were all afraid. All of them and him too. And Brother was tired. So tired he knew he better get on with it. He'd teach them tonight.

So he slogs up the path, picks his way along the hard-packed corridor through the broccoli trees. He cuts up the hillside just before the rotten steps, the steps nobody but Brother could see because he has cat eyes and he remembers the steps and remembers the men who used to sit there. Remembers Carl's daddy John French, the king with his hat slung back and his bald head gleaming in the sun.

Just kids. Just kids playing games.

He sees the steps even though the last rotten board has returned to the earth and nobody would ever know that steps once climbed the embankment to the ruined platform unless they happened to sit down in just the right spot and get a rusty nail in the ass.

This is where they sat. John French and the rest of them drinking that sweet wine and gambling and singing and making little boys feel foolish if they was foolish enough to bother the men here, where they sat minding their business cause they didn't like nobody else minding it for them.

Here's where Carl stood about to pee his pants cause Mrs. French told him he better find his daddy and say thus and so.

Here's where I got me a taste of blood, of wine sweeter than sweet Jesus.

Here's where the white men waited for the train. The train that stopped here special cause they owned it.

Mr. George Westinghouse. Mr. John French. Mr. Albert Wilkes.

Here's where Brother needed to get, and he squats down where the platform used to be. In the shadow of the one wall and treacherous overhang that someday's gonna fall on somebody's head. Brother waits in all that's left of the station for all that's left of the trains which used to fly through Homewood every other minute it seemed. Now just a handful a day. And none stopping. Not at the ancient water tower. Not at the ghost of station. Brother peers across the tracks, which even in this darkness retain enough light and heat inside themselves to gleam back at him. Long yellow cat eyes reflecting the shine of his. Brother never could see all the way across to the other side. Something always in the way. The broad rows of tracks themselves. The trees, the factories like a screen cutting him off from what lay beyond Homewood. Carl always lying. Saying he can see far as the track goes. See Ohio and . . . and . . . and everything way over there yonder. But seeing down the tracks was easier than seeing across. Than smashing your eyes against that wall running alongside the steel rails.

But Brother can see past the wall tonight. Through it, around it, over it and under it. He'd been up under that skirt. Seen the drawers and what's under the drawers and what's under what's under the drawers. He'd seen it all. Watched the last two lights go out and wasn't nothing else to see. Just like wasn't nothing else to say. Except one more time. Play the scare game one more time. Teach Junebug wasn't nothing to be afraid of. Teach them all.

Brother strolls closer to the tracks. Scuffs his invisible footprints in the invisible rocks of the track bed. They sound like cornflakes crunching under his feet. He hunkers down. He's almost tired enough to go to sleep. But he has one more thing to do. One more place to go.

He touches the icy metal. Icy even on this warm night. He puts his ear to the steel. Rail glows in the dark like fish in the ocean supposed to be able to do. If lightning bugs can shine in the dark, then probably fish can too, so he thinks of the rails like long fish and leans down and listens for the hum of their cold flesh. A hum always there, Carl said. And Lucy believed him. She swore she could hear it too. A train's always on the way. Just coming or just going so the rails ain't never quiet. Another one of Carl's lies, but Brother paid them no mind. He knew that sometimes you couldn't hear a thing unless you count the blood boiling between your ears which you subject to hear always less you dead. What you hear in them seashells in Mrs. French's bowl. What you hear you bend down and put your ear to a rail and ain't no train coming or going. You hear your own blood boiling between your ears.

But now Brother hears more. First his blood, then the hurry-up, hurry-up push of a train purring like a cat inside the steel rails.

He'd taught Junebug how to get ready to sleep.

He crawled out Samantha's bed in the corner. Long glowing legs first, then his pants pulled on, then quiet as a ghost out through the curtain and into the dark sleeping room where all the babies growing like weeds. Junebug off by hisself. Or as off by hisself as he could get in that crowded place.

Now I lay me down to sleep.
I pray the Lord my soul to keep.

Brother whispered in Junebug's ear so's not to wake anybody.
So quiet he might not even waked Junebug. But he knew Junebug
was listening. Junebug breathing so there's little spaces for the words
to fit and Brother whispering in the spaces.

Now I lay me down to sleep . . .

Four or five times. That was all. The little rhyme Brother liked
and wanted Junebug to know. It was something nice. Something
you could hum to yourself or say outloud if you needed to. Say
it when you closed your eyes and left here. Like good-bye. Or hello.
Same difference. Cause you going either way. Brother liked how
the words sounded. Liked what the words *Lord* and *soul* and *sleep*
and *keep* sounded like. So he whispered them in June's ear that
night and knew June was listening because June was like him.
Junebug didn't miss nothing even though he never said nothing
about it.
    Something purring in the sleep of the tracks. Something whis-
pering like him in Junebug's ear.
    Brother straightens up. He rubs the hard back of the rail. Strokes
it one last time gingerly like it's sharp as the edge of a straight razor.
    Nothing to be fraid of. It all starts up again.
    He hears John French and the rest of the men laughing over
his shoulder. One throws an empty wine bottle and it explodes
on the tracks. They'll probably be singing before the train gets here.
Or arguing or signifying which is the same thing. Only different
tunes.
    Listen here, boy. Listen to me. Watch me. Cause ain't nothing
to be fraid of. Ima win this one for you. Ima be the best for you.
I ain't gon back down.
    Watch me play.

1970

Lucy steps into the vestibule and stomps. She stares down at
her feet and stomps again. No snow on her hush puppies but she

stomps anyway. Stomps for the company of the noise. Stomps because Sam's still clinging, and Junebug and Brother and all the
rest like the snow on her galoshes those winter days she had climbed
to Mayview. She thought she'd gotten rid of that envelope of skin,
shaken it off in the Velvet Slipper, but now as she hangs her jacket
in the hall closet and crosses to the living room she sees Sam's long,
dark fingers slipping from the edge. Samantha losing the last of
the little grip she had. Black fingers letting go one by one like threads
popping when you rip a seam.

   She'd never really known Samantha. Lucy went to Mayview
because Brother couldn't. She took up that duty and many others
because Brother was no longer around. Seemed like the right thing
to do. The only thing to do. Seemed like a way of holding on to
Brother, too. Doing what he'd done, going the places he'd gone.
She'd walk in Brother's footsteps and there he'd be beside her, grinning, as real as his business she was taking care of.

   Carl would be by in a while. Carl like a mirror. She could see
all her years, everything that had made her Lucy Tate, in his face.
Her lover man, Carl. The first time and every time. Her prince
charming with his beer belly and partial plate and bad feet.

   He had courted her. If ever a woman was courted, she'd been
courted. By his hungry eyes, his silliness, his stories, the bloody
hands he brought back from the war, by the deaths of his father
and mother, by the dope, by Brother who was his brother too,
and tea on Sunday and painting and dancing. Courted right off
her feet by the years and years, the years heavy as his big body
stretched atop hers, years as light as balloons, rising, floating, sailing them both away.

   Courted by this big old empty house and Albert Wilkes dying
at the piano. And Mrs. Tate fading behind her closed door. In jail
where the cops had planted her. Lucy climbs the stairs thinking
of their courtship. The bannister slides smooth beneath her palm.
She grips it tighter, a ship's railing and will it hold her, can she
hang on when the storm begins to pitch and buck? She's in the
dark. Padding up the ancient stairs in the dark. Can't see her shoes
behind her where she kicked them off at the foot of the steps. Old
people stumble in the darkness, fall down steps and crack their
brittle bones and nobody finds them till they start to stink. Eyes

go sooner or later, so Lucy is teaching herself to see without seeing. With her ears and hands and nose she mounts the steps or slips from room to room at night with the lights out. The bannister is soft but firm. It ends a little ways, three steps from the top. Solid wall on both sides of the stairway at the top. The bathroom is to the right, follow the curve of the cool plaster.

She snaps on a light and the bathroom shudders, flickers unreal as a star. A cave of light. Bathrooms make her think of John French and the house on Cassina Way where he died wedged between tub and toilet. But all the rooms at the Tates' are big. This bathroom larger than the room where Carl slept on Cassina Way. She twists the brass faucets and water bursts into the clawfoot tub. Time to get clean before Carl arrives with Doot. She unbuttons and unsnaps dreamily, eases out of her clothes so she won't be ready before the water is. She kneels on the fuzzy oval rug and leans over the tub to test the temperature. Her breasts dangle against the chilly porcelain. Her nipples constrict but the tingle of goosebumps rising over her bare skin feels good. She pours bubble soap in the jet of water squirting from the faucet. Rich mounds of foam begin to form and shudder, break away and spread across the water.

She is up to her neck in suds. Her toes find the faucet and shut it off. The bathroom is suddenly quiet, silence thick and quivering like the blanket of foam stretching from her chin to the far end of the tub. Lucy touches her body to make sure it still sits under the suds. She shuts her eyes then slowly opens and closes her legs to make a gentle current, a submerged ebb and flow over her hidden parts.

She daydreams her men, lined up beside the tub, ready to do her bidding. All her men. The real ones and the ones who come only at times like this when she summons them. One will scrub her back. Another will lean down and do her breasts. As he lifts them, they'll be firm again, ride high and pouting on her chest while he kneads them and rinses away the wrinkles. One good at feet will wash hers so it almost tickles but not quite because laughing out loud would break the stillness, disturb the concentration of the others busy at their tasks. She'll roll over in the water and get up on her knees for the backside man. His hands are large. When he's done she turns over again, sits again, opens her thighs so Carl can do her legs. From ankle to groin he rubs, up to his elbows in warm water, a beard of suds on his chin. One hand washes and the other laps water between her thighs. He makes the same slow motion ebb and flow she had made by opening and closing her knees. Carl is the best. He takes longest doing his job. She can watch his face. He smiles above the silly foamy beard. Then he gets serious. She squirms and sighs, a big fish twisting in a warm pool.

No fool like an old fool. Lucy thinks it, then says the words aloud to herself. *No fool like an old fool* as she pads barefoot down the steps. The Tates' house is drafty and full of echoes, but with a towel turbaned around her head and the terry cloth robe belted tight she is snug and soundproofed. In the kitchen she pulls a package of Swiss cheese from the refrigerator. So much paper for these three pitiful little curled up slices, she thinks when the shiny Isaly's paper is undone. Big as a tablecloth spread out beneath the dried out slices. But that's why she shops at Isaly's. They go ahead and wrap your baloney or cheese like it means something even if you only buy fifty cents worth. Put all that nice paper on and jerk a strip of red Isaly's tape from the machine to seal your package. She likes their attitude and their chocolate chip cookies, but they don't keep their meat as fresh as they once did. Always got to tell the girl don't give me the end. Slice off that brown before you start. Then again where you find fresh food anywhere in Homewood these days? Don't mop the floor but once a week in the A&P. Can't find nothing you want on the shelves no more. Trouble is no white people shopping in Homewood. Not even the hippies anymore who moved in all those big old houses up past Thomas Boulevard.

Lucy nibbles at the grainy ends of the swiss cheese, then breaks them off and gobbles the center of each slice. Old fool sitting in the tub playing with herself like some hot blood young gal. And her man be here any minute. But she had that telephone in her bosom and had to use it once in a while. Ring him up on her time, when it suited her. Call Carl and the rest of her men round the tub. Ring them up with that telephone in her bosom the old folks sang about. If she's getting to be an old fool mize well be a happy one. No reason to be lonely in this big, empty house by herself.

Truth was she could never be lonely here. Truth was she's always tripping over ghosts and shoving them out the way so she could have a little peace and quiet.

Grown man that he was, the house still scared Carl. In all these years he never stayed through the night. Even passed out on dope he used to wake up enough to stumble home before morning. Found him and Brother laid out on the porch once. Frozen so blue she was afraid to shake them. As close to staying all night as Carl ever came. Blue as an icicle curled next to Brother asleep on the porch. Closer to dead than sleep and that's the only way he ever stayed at the Tates' all night. Mrs. French long gone but Carl hotfoots it home like she's waiting for him with one eye on the clock and the other on John French's razor strop.

She crumples the waxy paper and tosses it toward one of the brown bags beside the refrigerator. Garbage needed to go out. She'd get Carl to take it when he left. And tomorrow she'd clean the house top to bottom. Even the rooms nobody used anymore. Because old was letting your filth pile up around you. Was living on cat food and wearing the same nasty clothes every day so you stink up the aisles of the A & P, rattling by with your cart full of cans. Old was too many brown paper sacks to count. A wall of your mess higher than your head and one day it crashes down and buries you. She never let the line of bags beside the icebox get longer than three. Old was losing count and not giving a damn. Old was people busting the locks on your door after nobody's seen you for a week and your lights burning all night and a stink worse than garbage seeping out from under your door they got to bust in when nobody answers the pounding. In Homewood people used to watch out for you when you got too old and feeble to take care yourself. Now they ship you to the Senior Citizens High Rise over on Kelley Street or Mayview all the way out Frankstown Road. But plenty old people dying alone in rooms full of garbage. And young ones dying alone in alleys.

She pops the top of one of the Iron Citys she kept in the icebox for Carl. She didn't really like beer but sometimes it was just what she wanted. Its bitterness, the foam blotting her lips, the bubbles up her nose. Had to drink it sometimes for the simple reason it was her man's drink. How you gon understand Carl French unless you know a little bit about Rolling Rock and Iron City? One beer late in the afternoon would make her drowsy. Not going-to-sleep drowsy but she'd start to feel the mellow, beery, soft edges of things. How things swam together in the easy old gold color of beer. The voices in the Velvet Slipper. The music from the jukebox. She'd watch Carl hold his beer glass against his lips, letting it rest there while he peered into the golden funnel. Beer slowed everything. The way Carl smacked foam from his lips. The way he elegantly swallowed a belch, his hand cupped in front of his mouth, pinky pointed at the ceiling, then the slow trip of the flat of his hand down his chest and over his potbelly, guiding the belch on home, taming it as he swallows its sound.

Old was what happened to poor Samantha. She looked like some-body'd blown her up with a bicycle pump. Hard to believe she was the same woman who used to stride through the Homewood streets like a Zulu queen, turning the men's heads even though she always wore those loose, old-lady dresses. Everybody's getting old. Everybody changing but somebody had pumped Samantha full of air. Her skin splotchy and split like it's ready to bust open. The green Mayview dress like the dresses she used to wear, but she's not a racehorse under a blanket now. Sam is lumpy and puffy like a frog. Half the buttons on her green housecoat don't close.

Old was seeing Doot, taller than his uncle now, sitting on a stool in the Velvet Slipper drinking beer with Carl. Little Doot with children of his own listening to Carl tell about Junebug. Lucy walks to the brown bags, drains the Iron City and drops the can. Her knees crack when she stoops for the balled Isaly's paper which had bounced off the lip of one of the rolled-top sacks. Carl will be at the door any minute. And Doot who likes to get them talking about the old days. He likes to hear silly things like how she pushed Brother in a baby buggy. Plenty more Iron City in the fridge. Enough for her to have another if she wants it. She thinks she probably will, thank you.

Lucy closes her eyes from the kitchen to the living room. The bowed arm of the rocker floats out of the darkness to greet her. She feels its color, runs her hand to the round upright where the tall back begins. She gives it a little shove and there's a Lucy in the chair, rocking up and back, a Lucy snug and wise as the little

499

pig in the story Mrs. Tate loved to tell. The Lucy in the chair shrinks to child size and burrows deeper in the old woman's lap as Mrs. Tate rocks and the wind howls at the house and the wolf huffs and puffs, but the little pig is happy. Little piggy laughs and laughs cause him got him brothers in there wit him and that pot of water boiling in the fireplace under the chimney and the big iron bolt's cross the door.

When Lucy sits down and her weight pops the cracked rocker, the sound is like an old pain. It's part of the mellow gliding up and back, up and back, like the swings in Westinghouse Park, like the rope turning and spanking the pavement each time she bounces on her toes to miss it. The sound is familiar, even welcome because it's part of the glide, the turning. She wouldn't be Lucy Tate if it didn't hurt just when it did, just how it did.

Play. She commands Albert Wilkes again. Play. She hums his song. A song so full of Albert Wilkes the pieces of him falling around her, drifting lazy and soft like huge, wet snowflakes and she can see the shape of each one. Falling like snow or rain or the names in the stories Carl tells Doot.

Albert Wilkes's song so familiar because everything she's ever heard is in it, all the songs and voices she's ever heard, but everything is new and fresh because his music joined things, blended them so you follow one note and then it splits and shimmers and spills the thousand things it took to make the note whole, the silences within the note, the voices and songs. Lucy rocks up and back and hums quietly to herself. She wonders how such a gang of folks can keep so quiet, can go about their business and get in other people's business and stay so quiet you'd think she was the only one in the Tates'.

The chair again, like a gunshot in the silence. A trick of the damaged wood, the wounded rocker splitting apart as the chair tilts up and back, the sound of that afternoon they killed Albert Wilkes stored in the rocker. The chair popping like that used to scare Carl. Probably still did, he was such a funny, skittish, little boy grown man. With his peculiar ways and talk and belly hanging over his belt. Carl and Brother both sported those pickaninny watermelon bellies when they were kids. Their ribs like fingers reaching for the bowling balls pushing out their belly buttons. Carl

pale. Blue veins like a spiderweb on his tight bubble belly. Sometimes looked white as Brother. From a distance, looked like two
white boys playing with a bunch of colored kids. Closer you would
notice how Brother's skin was soft cellophane you could see through
and Carl one of those light, bright, pretty Frenches like his fabulous sisters. When Lucy pushed Brother in the buggy she kept the
canopy down. No sun allowed on his delicate skin. He needed a
hat. Only one she could find to keep the sun off his face and neck
was an old one of hers, all frilly-edged with bows and ribbons pink
as his eyes. Brother was a boy and would never live down such
a silly bonnet, but to save his skin she clamped it on his head and
tied it under his chin every time they left the house. Then she kept
the top down so nobody could tease or start stories when she pushed
him up and down Tioga Street. So she wouldn't have to kick butt,
so Brother could come into the world with no sissy rep or tales
people whispered behind his back. Kids almost bad as the sun.
Mean, signifying devils give her brother hell anyway just because
he was white and ugly as a frog's tummy. And he was her brother.
She decided he would be from the beginning. Her baby brother
even though he was a foot taller and twice her weight. He'd be
her baby brother and then they'd all be a family. The Tates. All
of them Tates even though she knew she was a Bruce and knew
Brother was from the moon or wherever people with no color and
no names came from, all be Tates if she was his big sister and old
Mr. and Mrs. Tate loved them both.

Lucy unwraps the turbaned towel, leans forward so her bare
feet rest on the floor and the rocker stops. Her fingers dig and
massage her scalp down to the roots. Mrs. Tate taught her about
hair. How to shampoo and oil and comb and braid. When she could
do her hair herself is when she stopped sharing the tub with Brother.
Washing her own hair took time, took privacy. She needed to be
alone, so she let Brother bathe first then she soaked as long as she
wanted, as long as it took. She never felt any shyness about her
body's being different from his. And nobody ever told her she
shouldn't climb into the tub with him or play with what made
him different or let him scrub her places she couldn't reach, scrub
her with the same light dancing touch she remembered in Albert
Wilkes's piano-playing hands. Nobody told her anything she did

with Brother in the bathtub was wrong, but she learned to wash and oil and braid her own hair and then she needed space, then she had to tell Brother, *Gwan. Go first, boy*. She'd supervise him sometimes but mostly went about her business till he finished, and then she checked the places kids were lazy about and sniffed him when he wasn't looking and made sure he hung up his wet towel. Then her turn. Alone, taking as long as she needed. Funny how Albert Wilkes returned just about the time she started needing to sit and soak by herself. Funny how, shutting the bathroom door behind herself and hearing Brother go off to mind his own business and running the water till suds bobbed at the curled rim of the clawfoot tub and stepping in and splashing the floor, she had thought of Albert Wilkes returning and Albert Wilkes dying while she drained off enough so she could settle into the steamy, fragrant water. Funny too how the first time she bled was in the water and the ghost of Albert Wilkes there again, his bare arms and smooth, strong fingers helping her stand but chilling her also as she rose frightened from water to air. She remembered how he had leaked on the ivory keys when the handfuls of suds she scooped away from the center of the tub revealed a crimson blush twisting and spreading in the water.

Young girls today learning again what Mrs. Tate had taught her about hair. Patterns of light and dark, twists and plaits following designs which spoke if you knew how to listen. Mrs. Tate named some of the designs. A Garden, Darling. This your Garden, child. Humming while she rocks, while her fingers weave and dance the strands of hair. Some designs took many hands to make. Lots of hands and lots of time when women could be alone, together. Quiet time like everybody needed. Time to comb and oil and braid. Time to clean your body.

Lucy loved Carl because he allowed her that time. He had learned she needed it and had learned to give it. After she showed him that piece of Albert Wilkes's skull and pulled him on top of her, inside her, she taught him the space she needed. Taught him with years so he could understand inches. Like she had to teach Brother. At first he pouted and sulked outside the bathroom door with his lip poked out. Finally she had to shout *Shoo, boy* through the closed door and hurt his feelings, but then everything was all right. And she had to clean up after Albert Wilkes and save his white skull bone to teach herself what she had to teach her lovers. Yes, her lovers. Carl. Brother. Albert Wilkes. Her men.

Yes. Like rain. Like rain. She'd heard it sung sometimes that way. Blues falling down like rain. But love rained too. When the rain starts to falling my love comes tumbling down. The songs Albert Wilkes played. And Brother. Her love, her men, her blues in this room, in this chair where she sits in an old woman's lap and listens to a story about pigs and wolves and listens to a dead man play everything she's ever heard, play it so it floats and hangs and she's inside one those little crystal balls you buy at Murphy's Five and Dime, those balls you turn upside down so they fill with snow, lazy floating warm suds of snow. Falling down. Falling down.

So you loved them. And cleaned up behind them. She sees Samantha finding one of Junebug's toys in the yard. Sam has to stoop way down, low down through the needle's eye. She stoops down and picks up a three-wheeled truck. Something broken with most of its paint gone. Just enough yellow or bright blue to catch Sam's eye and make her remember whose toy it was and kneel to dig it out. The other kids have left it alone. Yard dirt's begun to cover it. The toy leaves a little hole after Sam plucks it up. And the hole is a black pit opening at her feet. She wants to bury her face, her weary body in it. The earth rises and spins. She needs to stay on her knees or drop down farther, flatten her belly on the hard-packed belly of the dirt. Let it take her. Fall down and cry like a baby and say You won, you won. You got the best so go on and take the rest. She wants to give up and let the dirt win. Because you can only clean up behind somebody dead so many times. Then it gets you. In your mind, in your bones. Twice in this life enough for me Lucy says to herself or to Sam or to the emptiness of the Tates' living room where the rocker teeters through its arc.

Lucy remembers a broom in her hands. Remembers how she had swept the fragments of colored glass into a pile. All that was left of the pretty front door window after the cops busted in. Old Mrs. Tate upstairs in her room. Albert Wilkes dead somewhere. The white men smiling as they pulled off his bloody clothes. Lucy remembers how hard it had been to clean up after they killed Albert Wilkes and how much harder it had been when she was alone in Brother's room cleaning up again. Another one of her men gone, and there she was again, pulling Brother's sneakers out from under his bed, stuffing Brother's things from the closet into shopping bags. Emptying the pockets of his pants sprawled across the dirty clothes pile. Brother had worn those shoes and shirts and underwear. He had opened those drawers and watched himself move in that mirror. He'd sat on the end of his saggy bed and untied his shoes. He was the one wrapped an old stocking around and round the bedpost to hold the broken footboard. His fingers had wound it round and tied the knot. Ten years and the knot still holding. Some of the dust she was sweeping he had stomped off his feet or shrugged from his shoulders. He had carried Homewood into his room and carried out something from the Tates' into the streets. He'd coughed in his room. Had broken wind and cried and slobbered sweet wine on the mattress and the floor. She had to clean it all up, and then it'd be clean forever. Wouldn't be no Brother ever mess it up again. Ever track in mud or drip rain or bring the stink of the Velvet Slipper home on the seat of his pants.

Cleaning up that afternoon she had found the shopping bag full of pictures. At first she'd thought they were Carl's. They were on the paper he brought home from art school. Long pebbly sheets rolled in the bag so they looked like the wallpaper samples John French used to give them to play with. And they were Carl's in a way. On one side were sketches of naked women from the art school, but on the back side, the smooth side, were Brother's pictures. Had to be Brother's. Who else but Brother would put wings on all the people in his pictures? Little wings sprouting out the top of people's shoulders. Wings like little handles so you could pick his people up or set them down without touching anything but the curly nubs on their shoulders. A few with wings on their feet. Like Brother is saying they're my pictures and I can draw people any way I want to. Wings or tails or color them all green because what's it matter anyway they're his pictures and he can do them the way he likes.

The other surprise was how well Brother could draw. One more thing she never knew about him. Never saw him with a pencil or a crayon in his hand. But Brother could draw. When he made a person you could tell who it was. The faces are like cloudy photographs yet she can recognize the person right away even though they have those wings and funny clothes Brother drew on his people. Homewood people staring back at her when she unrolled the sheets and spread them atop the piano and held down the edges. Some of them she knew by name. Others she'd passed a hundred times in the street, not wearing the old-fashioned clothes Brother dressed them in, or the wings he stuck on their shoulders, but clearly the same Homewood people she'd been greeting and speaking to all her life.

Lucy had carried the bag of pictures to the living room, to the best light in the house, the bright goose-neck lamp on the piano, so she could study what Brother had drawn. She began to understand why some faces she couldn't name looked so familiar. Brother had drawn the old people young again. The old clothes made their faces young again. Mr. and Mrs. Tate. John French. Freeda French. Young again. Owning Homewood again. They smiled back at her under the heavy light. In their long dresses and big hats and coveralls and eight-buttoned suits and high collars like an extra set of tiny wings around the men's necks.

She hurried and took her time. She wanted to see them all but didn't want to pull the last rolled sheet from the shopping bag. Brother could draw. It was like listening to people who can really sing or play an instrument. Doesn't matter what they play or sing, they put you in it and carry you away. Carl's mother and father, Albert Wilkes, the Tates. All the good old people and good old times. She could see Brother's hand, pale as the paper, moving across each sheet. Like the magic hands of the old-time healers. See him laying on his white hands and see through them to the old Homewood streets, the people coming to life at his touch.

Brother's people had wings, had knobs on their shoulders so you could lift them and see through them, see under them and around them. So you could touch their shadows, so you could study the darkness while they hung in the air. They had wings so they could be two places at once. So they could move faster than anyone could follow and live whole lives in the air before you'd even notice they were gone.

Lucy had finally emptied the shopping bag of drawings. The long, rolled sheets of art school paper jostled each other atop the piano. A life of their own as they curled back to the shape they'd held for so many years stuffed in the bag. They belonged in the shopping bag. Pressed together, standing up like the samples of wallpaper John French gave them.

Lucy rocks in the empty house, trying to recall the last time she'd unfurled them, treated herself to the surprises each sheet held. Perhaps she should show them to Carl. And Doot. Perhaps they'd understand why she'd kept them to herself this long. Part of Brother's business she'd decided to mind. Part of Brother belonging to her because she was the one who had to clean up after his death.

Carl calls from the vestibule:

Hey Babe.

She closes her eyes. Sinks Carl and Doot in darkness and guides their steps through the Valley of Shadow they cannot see. The eyes blind sooner or later. She wants to be ready. Wants her men to be ready.

Well, look what the cat drug in. Mr. Carl French, Esquire. And Mr. Doot.

Hi Lucy.

Hi back.

It's a mess out there. Wind blowing to beat the band. If I'da spread my arms and let the wind get up under my coat I believe I'd still be flying.

Must be typhoon and tornado and hurricane all at once out there get that ton of Iron City you're carrying around up in the air.

Told you she was evil, didn't I, Doot? Ain't hardly got my foot in the door and she's signifying already.

Just talking about how much of you there is to love. Especially if a gal loves belly.

Speaking of belly . . .

You know where the Iron City is.

Doot, you want one . . . course you do. And Miss Bad Mouth?

Gwan out my face, man, and get us two cool ones. I been thinking about Brother and Sam and little Junebug. They been heavy on my mind and I'm tired. Feel old and tired now thinking about all that.

Told Doot about Sam and Junebug. Ain't no happy story, that's for sure.

How long. How long. That old blues just creeped up on me. Wasn't thinking about any song in particular. Just sitting here rocking waiting for youall. Trying to empty my head and get ready for youall but don't you know it creeped up on me and before I know it I'm hearing it and then I'm humming it and then this chair is keeping time. Been keeping time all the while. Up and back. The music's got me and it's How long, how long. How's it go? I got the tune and got the how long but how's it go? What's the words, Carl?

Goes:

I can hear the whistle blowing.
Can't see the train.
Deep in my heart
There's a crying pain and How long . . . how long
Tell me how long.

That's it. That's what this chair's been rocking. Now you gwan and get that beer. What you grinning about? You know you can't sing a lick so don't stand there so pleased with yourself.

Is *How long* the name?

Only name I ever heard, *The How Long Blues*. You have to ask Carl, though. He's the one remembers all the old songs. You heard him.

Never heard him sing before.

Well, consider yourself lucky. He knows the words and that's enough. I ain't gon talk about him cause he ain't here, but where I come from we don't hardly call what he was doing *singing*. Yeah. You heard me, didn't you Mr. Big Ears? Just get on back in here with that beer.

One for you and one for Miss Ungrateful Pup. You just ain't used to good singing. Your ears don't know what to do with it.

How long.

Good singing.

How long things got to stay the hurtin way they is? It makes me tired. Makes me feel old and tired. Like I just want to curl up in this chair and let it rock and let the world go on by.

Least Sam got a roof over her head. At least she's not freezing to death or starving to death like plenty old people still out in the street ain't even got social security. You look in the paper you read about one every day. Starved or frozen. Or burnt up in some tinderbox. Cold don't get em, fire will. It's a shame. A crying shame how they do these old people.

Who you talking about, *they?* Ain't no *they* doing nothing, Carl French, and you know it. We're the ones. We're the ones standing by letting it happen. Those old folks *our* people. *They* ain't never gave a good goddamn. *They* never have and *they* never will. You know that. So don't be blaming no *they*.

I know what you mean, but shit. What am I supposed to do? I'm just Carl French. Never had nothing. Never will. Won't be long I'll be selling pencils and rattling my tin cup. Then one day I'll get my name in *The Black Dispatch* when somebody finds my ashes. Nothing I can do about any of it. How my supposed to change what's been happening all these years? Mize well try and feed the starving babies in Africa and China as change the way things always been in Homewood.

Homewood ain't always been the way it is today. That's just why I never married you, Carl French. That's just why.

Whooo, Babe. What you talking bout?

Maybe you never had a chance. Maybe it's not your fault. But you gave up too easy. Maybe you were suppose to give up easy. Maybe it's not your fault. But even so I still couldn't marry you. I'll grow old and silly with you. Might even be the one light the match and send us both up in smoke, but I can't marry you. Couldn't be faithful. That's the sticker. And I'm not talking about body faithful. That's hard enough, but that ain't no real problem. It's my mind. My mind would be unfaithful. I love you more than any man, but the old Homewood people taught me you don't have to give up. I mean John French, your daddy. And Mrs. French and Albert Wilkes and Strayhorn and the rest of them. The old

508

folks. The ones dead now. And Brother. He's one of them now. Always was one.

Doot. Did you come to hear this song? I think somebody pushed the wrong button.

I'm gon shut up in a minute. Don't mind me, Doot. I stopped making sense long before you were born. Couldn't do nothing but stare all moony-eyed at you and wonder if you'd be different. Looked for something different in your eyes. Looked for the old folks in there. And you just listen another minute, Carl French. Tell me if you could ever look through your daddy and the rest of them. Tell me if you could see through them or if they were solid. Brother didn't even have skin, but he stopped people's eyes. He was solid, real, like all a them. They made Homewood. Walking around, doing the things they had to do. Homewood wasn't bricks and boards. Homewood was them singing and loving and getting where they needed to get. They made these streets. That's why Homewood was real once. Cause they were real. And we gave it all up. Us middle people. You and me, Carl. We got scared and gave up too easy and now it's gone. Just sad songs left. And whimpering. Nothing left to give the ones we supposed to be saving Homewood for. Nothing but empty hands and sad stories.

So that's why you never married me. Hmmmmmmm. Always thought it had something to do with the fact I never asked you.

Believe that lie if you want to, man. Been over here with your tongue hanging out ever since you grown enough to know you had a tongue. And know it was hanging.

Like the song says: *Got two minds to leave here, only one telling me stay.*

You can whistle and waggle and try to sing if you want to, but you know I'm speaking true.

Doot don't want to hear all this mess.

He wants to hear about Brother, don't he? Well, that's what I'm talking about. About Brother and the rest of them. They were special people. Real people. Took up space and didn't change just because white folks wanted them different. Down sometimes but they didn't get dirty. Brother picked the way he wanted to live. And how he wanted to die. Now how many people have you heard

509

of like that? Jesus maybe. And one, two others like the Africans flying and walking cross water and turning sticks to snakes. Believe what you need to believe, but Brother was special like that. Not some spook or hoodoo, but a man who could be whatever he wanted to be.

Lighten up, child. Whooa, girl. Already got the blues three different ways.

Warned you, didn't I? Nothing but empty hands and crazy stories. Cept I got six or seven pork chops in the icebox and a bag of flour already salted and peppered with a little garlic and some talking cayenne too. Waiting for the fine, eye-talian hand of my loverman and sweetheart, Mr. Carl French, who can fry up some chops when his lip ain't poked out. Smile now cause I got chops and some frozen spinach we can boil and pretend it's fresh greens. Gwan Sweetcakes and get you another one those Irons and the grease is in a Crisco can on the shelf under the chops. You know you love to fry meat.

The first floured chop is eased into hot grease and makes the sound of ice cracking, the spatter and sizzle of great ice floes colliding and breaking apart. Lucy hears the skillet as she rocks in Mrs. Tate's ladderback chair. The sound reminds her she is sitting, saying nothing to her lover's nephew across the room. He's sunk in the wingback chair. Brother's chair when he sat still long enough to need a chair. The second Iron City is cold, half-gone in her hand. Doot's face is shadowed. Only one light, the gooseneck lamp atop the piano, spilling its glow so the polished wood looks wet. The piano, spotlighted on an empty stage, waits for someone to materialize from the dark corners of the room and play.

Doot quiet in the chair. Like maybe he's feeling his beer too. His face a pattern of light and darkness. More brown in his skin than the Frenches. His mama Lizabeth married below her color. But still in the dim room his face is mottled, the brown a kind of light against black shadow. If her eyes were better she knows she could pick out the places in his face which were French. He is tall like his granddaddy and his uncle. She tries to recall which record was playing when she got him up to dance how many years ago in the Frenches' front room. John French was sprawled sleeping in his overstuffed chair. The Victrola gleamed in its corner. Not Sarah or Dinah or Ella or Billie singing but a man, uptempo, growling, belting out the tune. They had been listening to a fight. But not for long. The Brown Bomber had duked out his man before they even got the station tuned in good. Static crackling like chicken in a skillet as the announcer counted down. John French whooping and clapping, kicking his long legs in the air. *Get em, Joe. Whup all them crackers, Boy.* He was snoring by the time Carl had switched from radio to phono and played two records.

On the same gleaming RCA console combination she had heard the news of Pearl Harbor. She thinks she remembers snow. John French had slammed his fist into his meaty palm and spat a long nasty string of curses almost as bad as what she'd heard those few times the Brown Bomber had hit the canvas. Little as she understood world politics then, she knew the white voice from the radio, the voice usually full of fancy words about England and France and parliaments and prime ministers and wars overseas, the voice which had nothing to do with colored people, this time the voice was speaking to Homewood. Everybody in Homewood gathered round their radios was going to war. She knew that and the walls of the house on Cassina started tumbling down. John French, hopping mad as he was about the low blow the sneaky Japs had landed, was too old to go overseas. Brother in his cellophane skin was too strange. She was a girl and Doot a baby. But the walls tumbled down, and Carl rolled out on the cobblestones. Soft and naked and full of young blood, sooner or later he'd have to go.

Lucy understood in an instant. Heard the rumble and knew. The voice gone but its message hung in the air strong as the smell of tobacco, wine and stale socks from the corner where John French and his indignation percolated. More bulletins then and crackling silence. Then the *Hut-Sut Song:*

Now the Rawlson is a Swedish town,
The rillerah is a stream . . .
The brawla is the boy and girl
The Hut Sut is their dream

Somebody playing the song just after the news of Pearl Harbor. Lucy hated the silly song. John French said it ain't nothing but an old riverboat song, "Hot Shot Dawson," he'd heard many a time in the Bucket of Blood. Boys sing it on the waterfront when they be loading boats. Nothing but that old nigger paddleboat ditty the white folks got hold to and messed up like they did everything black they got their hands on. The silly Hut-Sut song grinning in the middle of the war news. And the news screamed plain as day her man had to go. Had to go fight the white folks' war and save their silly music.

Hut Sut Rawlson on the rillerah and a brawla, brawla, soo-it.

Played so much it got inside you. You sung it and hummed it even though you hated it. Lucy hadn't thought of the Hut Sut Rawlson song in thirty years but it was still there, still lurking back there like a sneaky belch gets up in your throat before you know it. Across the room in the depths of the wingback chair the young man's face is hidden. Is it his face? A French face? Is it young?

You're awful quiet.

I'm waiting for the story you promised.

She wonders what he really wants. He raises his beer and she remembers hers, half gone, wet in her fist. She sets it down. Rubs her hands together. She can touch and smell the memory of the Frenches' front room, the room looking out on Cassina. But something is wrong. She is collapsing one time into another. The news of Pearl Harbor came in the afternoon and Doot danced his first steps after dark. Dark through the window, the image of the front room doubled, glowing on the far side of the glass. It was the same window in the story about somebody trying to shoot John French. Mrs. French punched a hole with her bare fist. The scar runs like a caterpillar across her pale hand, the light-skinned French hand like Carl's. That quiet lady punching through a window to save her man. But Lucy is confusing times. She sees John French whooping it up after a Joe Louis knockout. Kicking his feet in the air like a baby on its back. But she had been alone when she heard the war news. Alone and frightened and wanting to be close to Carl. The songs on the radio were "God Bless America" and "America the Beautiful." Then one sounded like a funeral, and she was scared. She expected any minute the drone of war planes, bombs bursting, glass shattering, sirens, machine guns. She gripped the whorled ends of the rocker's arms. Had she jumped up and turned the dial? Had she found the Hut Sut song or did they get tired of drums and trumpets and choirs and play it themselves?

Sent for you yesterday, and here you come today.

Not Dinah or Billie or Ella or Sarah. Had to be, who else could it be, Jimmy Rushing. Mr. Four by Four backed up by Count Basie. Jimmy Rushing out front. And fine as wine the Prez and Sweets and Jo Jo and Dicky, the whole shiny band, fine as fine wine and sharp as tacks, pressed clean in tuxedos and white-on-white wedges splitting the elegant black. No wonder little Doot got up and tried his wings.

No Brother stories tonight, Doot. Need to tell something happy tonight. Too much thinking on the others starting to get me down.

Whatever.

There was the time I got you up to dance. But you've heard that before.

Never from you.

Sometimes I have trouble getting it all straight. Carl going to the war and you being born and Junebug and all that other mess going on about the same time. Just a baby myself at the beginning of the war. Not even twenty years old yet. But I grew up fast. Had to. So much happening. Everybody grew up fast. Carl went in the army. Your grandmother cried for a month after he left, and Brother fussed cause they wouldn't take him too. Somewhere in there you come along and brightened up Cassina. Somewhere in there was when it got to be all right for me to visit the Frenches' house. I guess Mrs. French figured at least she'd know where we were and what we were doing if she could hear us in her front room. So it was the three of us, Carl and me and Brother, in the Frenches' or over here till Carl left. We'd listen to your grand-daddy's blues records. That's where Carl learned all the words. Boy, I bet some them old records worth a fortune now. Stacks and stacks down in the bottom of the record player. You talk about blues. John French had it all. Big thick records but the kind break if you look at them cross-eyed. You know what I mean. You're old enough to remember those old seventy-eights. He used to buy them from a man come through Homewood selling Watkins products. The man got them down South somewheres. All kind of funny labels. Like Black Swan and stuff like that. Black people making their own records then. You'd go hear a group, and they hustling their records after the show. Black people making money too, till the big companies saw what was happening and started letting niggers sing for them. John French had tons of blues, and then me and Carl started buying the Big Bands. Duke and Count Basie and the rest. Wonder where all that good music went. Got to ask Carl about those records. You know what I'm talking about, don't you? You must of heard them. Know you heard them once. I was sitting right there in the room with you when that good music playing. Your Granddaddy John French's music and the sides we bought when we heard something good on the radio. We'd listen for hours. And the bands would come through here too. Play at the Masons' picnic and all of Homewood be dancing in the woods in South Park. At the clubs you could hear the bands live. The Hurricane and Ann Mulvehill's and Crawford's on the Hill and Taylors right here in Homewood on Frankstown Avenue.

Went to those places first time during the war. People had a little extra change in their pockets. War work. Hell. I was nineteen years old and had the best paying job I've ever had in my life. Wasn't Black git back, then. Was Arsenal of Democracy and overtime and time-and-a-half. If you could drive a nail or turn a wrench you had a job. Good work and good money. Women and girls making more than their men ever did. Ever would. Good jobs and good times. Thought I'd found heaven when I started hanging out in the clubs listening to that good time music. Boy, thought this child had died and woke up in heaven.

Jam sessions in the after hours joints. The Vets and the Elks. They'd go all night after everything else closed. Mrs. French wouldna never let me put my foot through her door if she'd seen me in my glory all silk-stockinged and a frilly red shimmy dress barely come down to my knees and blinking my six-inch false eyelashes at some stoned piano player just rolled in from Kansas City on the night train still going strong on Jeep's Blues at five o'clock in the morning.

Brother's always there to keep me out of trouble. I could flirt and tease and lollygag around. Have me a natural ball and know

Brother'd keep me out of trouble. A young girl needs a chance to try her stuff. Just like youall. I know I must have made more than one gentleman want to wring my scrawny neck with my bodacious carrying on and then backing off from serious business. But I didn't mean no harm. A girl got a right to try her wings just like you men. Except we're supposed to get caught. I mean it's youall's game. We ain't supposed to be playing, we just out there to get caught. And once we get caught we're out. We're third prize forever once we're caught, but youall keep playing long as somebody will have you. Well, I say bunk to that. Had my chance to play. Had my chance to be a butterfly and poke my nose into a little this and a little that and I took it.

Wonder what happened to those records.

They're someplace. Got to be.

Lots of stuff in my grandmother's basement. Cartons and stuff wrapped in newspapers. No telling what's down there.

Hey, Carl. Where's all those records your daddy used to have?

Can't hear you . . . these chops is talking.

Go ask him, Doot. Bet he knows.

Lucy rocks, humming to herself the old tunes. How long. How long. And if I could holler like a mountain jack. Go to the mountain top and call my Baby back. One of the brittle black discs sails toward her. She is amazed by its flight, how it glides without a wobble, like it's on an invisible turntable while it hangs graceful and weightless in thin air. But it's sailing toward her and when it lands it shudders, spinning like a top losing its balance. A swhooshing sound before settling into a hundred black fragments on the floorboards. Then another disc knifes past her, aimed at her because she had to duck to avoid its dangerous slicing edge. Rodney Jones is crouched beside the phonograph. Price tags still dangle from the record player's knobs.

All these jive-ass, old timey motherfuckers got to go.

Rodney Jones talking in his dope sleep and digging into the stack of seventy-eights and sailing them to every corner of the Tates' living room. Over prone junkies and sitting junkies and junkies on all fours and the ones who are leaving and the ones flying out the way and the ones who couldn't care less groaning in their dreams as the records smash and scatter.

Lucy thinks about crying and thinks about screaming and thinks she will kill Rodney Jones and thinks why not, why not get all the black discs up in the air at once. All spinning at once like she saw a juggler on the Sealtest Big Top get twelve plates dancing on the end of twelve sticks. They are lazy blackbirds. Crows resting their wings, laid back on currents of air. Swimming, she thinks. Like she is floating effortlessly in some medium which supports her. Stoppit you goddamn fool, she is thinking. And running as fast as she can because here comes John French through the door and he is twirling that razor strop over his head. Somebody's going to pay for breaking his records. Somebody's going to pay she knows as she flees. Big Brown Bear John French growling Who ate my porridge and who slept in my bed and who broke my Baby's chair, and she's flying down the street as she hears the pop of his strop and the squeals of the niggers he's whaling. Somebody has to pay and she is thinking *Stop*. Stop as Rodney Jones snatches another one and curls his wrist backward and sends the record careening to its death.

She wants to cry. Or kill him. Or just keep floating wherever she is. Or go for help. None of the others in the room seem to mind. Aren't bothered by the huge black snowflakes twisting around their heads. Maybe if she listens hard enough she will hear the tunes. Maybe Rodney found a new way to play John French's records. As they rotate, they magically unravel music into the air. The room crisscrossed with music, with flying songs like a net. She thinks she can hear them, the songs rushing past like the clickedy-clack steel wheels of a locomotive, all the music stored in the records exploding like a train does when it's dropped on the tracks and swallows you and then is gone. She thinks of broken pieces. Of the mess Rodney Jones is making. She knows someone will have to clean it up. Albert Wilkes sat on the wall and Albert Wilkes had a great fall. And she will have to find every piece. Dig them out of the dirt. Every splinter of shattered egg. The white pieces and black pieces and she can feel the broom in her hands and grasps it so tight it wobbles. A witch's wand. Another shaky leg to stand on. Because she needs another leg. She passes the broom over the floor like the preacher passed his hand above the open hole as the pitiful little box Brother made was lowered. She needs three or four feet to stand steady on the canvas laid round Junebug's grave. The coffin Brother sawed and nailed and sanded in Mr. Tate's basement is lowered by straps, and the apron of canvas is to keep your shoes clean and the preacher's black hand waves, scattering dust and she is the one who has to clean, who must sweep it all away, even while the gunshots boom and echo in the room.

Just told Doot what happened to those records. Don't you remember what happened to those records . . . hey, Babe . . . hey . . .

Look at you with that apron on. A sight, ain't he? Ain't he a sight? Chef Boy-Ar-Dee. The Cream-of-Wheat Cook. Get back on out there . . . finish those pork chops, man. I'm tired and hungry. I'm just weary and tired. And you go with him, Doot. Just git on out there with him. Just go on now, go on. Can't you see . . .

What's wrong, Babe?

Just go on and cook the greens and don't you dare burn the chops and open me a can of beer out there which I'll get to soon as I can.

I am in the kitchen of the Tates' big brick house on Tioga Street with my Uncle Carl. He turns out the fire under the skillet and puts a lid on the pot of bubbling spinach. He opens an Iron City and sits it on the table for Lucy. He says: Only the second time in life I've seen that woman's tears. He faces away from me as he says this, and after he speaks the kitchen is quiet for a long time. The burp of the spinach getting tender is a pulse measuring, accenting the silence. The pot lid rises slightly as the spinach simmers over low heat. A dribble seeps down the side of the pot into the flame which flares yellow, sputters and hisses. He turns then and says:

Shame about those records. Got destroyed just like a lot of innocent bystanders got destroyed by junk. Shame about Daddy's records and shame on us all.

Lucy joined us that evening in the kitchen, and we ate what Carl fixed and drank beer and finished the pint of Seagrams Seven Carl pulled from his coat pocket.

Then we are back in the Tates' living room and Lucy finishes the story and says, The song you danced to was "Sent for you yesterday, and here you come today." Then she turns on the FM.

Not jazz and not blues and not rock and roll but it's Black music. Not fast and not slow, a little of both. The off-speed of Smokey Robinson on "Tracks of my Tears." Brother Tate appears in the doorway. He's grinning his colorless grin and pointing at the piano and Albert Wilkes starts unsnapping the duster and aiming his behind for the piano bench. I know how good it's going to sound so I start moving to the music coming from the radio. I know Albert Wilkes will blow me away so I start loosening up, getting ready. I'm on my feet and Lucy says, *Go boy* and Carl says, *Get it on, Doot*. Everybody joining in now. All the voices. I'm reaching for them and letting them go. Lucy waves. I'm on my own feet. Learning to stand, to walk, learning to dance.

ABOUT THE AUTHOR

JOHN WIDEMAN was born in Washington, D.C., in 1941, and grew up in the Homewood section of Pittsburgh, Pennsylvania. He graduated from the University of Pennsylvania with a B.A. in English in 1963. Wideman played basketball at Penn and earned All-Ivy honors as well as a place in the Philadelphia Big Five Basketball Hall of Fame. In 1963 he was one of two black Americans to receive a Rhodes scholarship.

As a Rhodes scholar, Wideman spent three years in England studying eighteenth-century literature and received a B.Phil. degree from Oxford in 1966. He subsequently spent a year at the University of Iowa Writers Workshop as a Kent Fellow and became an instructor at the University of Pennsylvania, where he advanced to professor of English and chaired the university's African-American studies program. In 1975 Wideman became professor of English at the University of Wyoming, and his works began to gather extensive praise, establishing his reputation, according to the *New York Times Book Review*, as "one of America's premier writers of fiction."

Wideman's widely acclaimed books include the novels *A Glance Away* (1967), *Hurry Home* (1969), *The Lynchers* (1973), *Hiding Place* (1981), *Sent for You Yesterday* (1983), *Reuben* (1987), and *Philadelphia Fire* (1990); his collections of short stories, *Damballah* (1981) and *Fever* (1989); and the nonfiction *Brothers and Keepers* (1984). *Damballah*, *Hiding Place*, and *Sent for You Yesterday* were subsequently reissued together as *The Homewood Trilogy* (1984).

Wideman's short fiction, reviews, and critical articles, often on the work of black writers, have appeared in a number of publications.

About the Author

A *Washington Post* review of *Reuben* referred to Wideman as "one of the half-dozen leading black novelists alive today." Recognition of his work has also come in the form of prizes and awards. *Sent for You Yesterday* was listed as one of the fifteen best books of 1983 by the *New York Times Book Review* and won the PEN/Faulkner Award for fiction in 1984. *Brothers and Keepers* received a National Book Critics Circle nomination in 1985 and the Du Sable Museum Prize for nonfiction. *Philadelphia Fire* won the 1990 American Book Award and the PEN/Faulkner Prize for fiction, the first time a writer has won the prize twice.

Wideman is currently Professor of English at the University of Massachusetts at Amherst. He is married to Judy Wideman and has three children, Daniel, Jake, and Jamila.